Praise for *Irish Ab*

"Prepare to be transported through 1920s–
epic story of love, loss, and the strength of o
—Martha Hall Kelly, author of *New York Times* bestseller *Lilac Girls*

"Mary Pat Kelly's masterful saga of Irish-American life and history comes to a thrilling conclusion with *Irish Above All*. . . . A great read."
—Patricia Harty, cofounder and editor-in-chief of *Irish America*

"Ahead of her times, Nora Kelly is a fascinating woman of vision and an inspiration to today's generation of women photographers."
—Barbara Kasten, internationally recognized artist

"*Irish Above All* combines the myths and magic of Ireland with the grit and energy of Irish-American Chicago in the first half of the twentieth century."
—Roma Downey, *New York Times* bestselling author of *Box of Butterflies*

"Nobody knows the Irish like Mary Pat Kelly."
—William Martin, *New York Times* bestselling author of *Bound for Gold*

"We all have our favorite novelists. Mary Pat Kelly is mine."
—Peter Quinn, American Book Award–winning author of *Banished Children of Eve*

Praise for *Of Irish Blood*

"Kelly captures the drama, the turmoil, the excitement of the complex history of Irish and Irish Americans in the early twentieth century."
—Mary Gordon, award-winning author of *The Company of Women*

"A rare reading experience."
—Thomas Fleming, *New York Times* bestselling author of *The Secret Trial of Robert E. Lee*

Praise for *Galway Bay*

"So rousingly epic that it can't help but reach readers' hearts." —*People*

"A book that should be in every Irish-American household library."
—*Irish America*

ALSO BY MARY PAT KELLY

FICTION

Special Intentions

Galway Bay

Of Irish Blood

NONFICTION

Martin Scorsese: The First Decade

Martin Scorsese: A Journey

Home Away from Home: The Yanks in Ireland

Proudly We Served: The Men of the USS Mason

Good to Go: The Rescue of Scott O'Grady from Bosnia

IRISH ABOVE ALL

MARY PAT KELLY

A TOM DOHERTY ASSOCIATES BOOK

NEW YORK

This is a work of fiction. All of the characters, organizations, and events portrayed in this novel are either products of the author's imagination or are used fictitiously.

IRISH ABOVE ALL

A Forge Book
Published by Tom Doherty Associates
120 Broadway
New York, NY 10271

www.tor-forge.com

Forge® is a registered trademark of Macmillan Publishing Group, LLC.

The Library of Congress has cataloged the hardcover edition as follows:

Names: Kelly, Mary Pat, author.
Title: Irish above all / Mary Pat Kelly.
Description: First Edition. | New York : Forge, 2019. | "A Tom Doherty Associates Book."
Identifiers: LCCN 2018045877| ISBN 9780765380883 (hardcover) | ISBN 9781466875876 (ebook)
Subjects: LCSH: Ireland—History—20th century—Fiction. | GSAFD: Historical fiction.
Classification: LCC PS3561.E39463 I75 2019 | DDC 813/.54—dc23
LC record available at https://lccn.loc.gov/2018045877

ISBN 978-0-7653-8089-0 (trade paperback)

Our books may be purchased in bulk for promotional, educational, or business use. Please contact your local bookseller or the Macmillan Corporate and Premium Sales Department at 1-800-221-7945, extension 5442, or by email at MacmillanSpecialMarkets@macmillan.com.

First Edition: February 2019
First Trade Paperback Edition: February 2020

Printed in the United States of America

0 9 8 7 6 5 4 3 2 1

For

Barbara Leahy Sutton,

friend of a lifetime

I'm glad we belong to the people we belong to—the Clan O'Kelly—and I thank all of them. I ask God to give them eternal rest and happiness in heaven. "Eye has not seen nor ear heard the things God has prepared for those who love Him." Granny Honora believed we would all see Ireland after we died. We are Americans, yes; Chicagoans, of course; but Irish Above All.

–Sister Mary Erigina Kelly, B.V.M.
(Agnella) 1889–1996

PROLOGUE

BAYFRONT PARK—MIAMI, FLORIDA

FEBRUARY 15, 1933

I saved Franklin Roosevelt's life and killed the mayor of Chicago with two words—"Move closer."

I was in Bayfront Park that night to take the photograph Mayor Cermak said would save our city. "Get me and the president-elect shaking hands. Pals. I'll put that shot on the front page of every newspaper in Chicago with a big story about how FDR's promised me millions in federal funds," Cermak had said the night he'd hired me. "Enough to pay the cops and the teachers. Save us from declaring bankruptcy. Force those bastards who are withholding their taxes to pay up. Can you do it, Nora?"

"You want her to ambush Roosevelt?" my cousin Ed Kelly had asked him.

Ed was Chicago's chief engineer and president of the South Park Board, where I was the staff photographer. Though never elected to office himself, he was a power in the Democratic Party and knew that our city was not a priority with the new administration. Cermak had supported Al Smith—not Roosevelt—for the nomination, and those around the president-elect were freezing him out.

Cermak had said that Roosevelt would go along, if it was a woman taking the pictures. Even one my age.

I was fifty-four—five years younger than Cermak—but still presentable enough. I'd never been a beauty. Too tall, too thin. But my mother always said I was fine-featured and my red hair was distinctive. Though the color had faded a bit now.

Ed and I had met Cermak in his suite in the Morrison Hotel, where he was hiding out. Nitti and the Outfit had threatened to kill him, and twenty thousand teachers had marched on city hall because they hadn't been paid for three months.

Cermak had offered me a hundred dollars. A fortune.

"I want to do it, Ed," I'd said. He'd shrugged and, just like that, I stepped into the flow of history.

If Roosevelt had died that night, we'd be living in a different world. There would have been no New Deal from a President John Nance Garner, who took his orders from Texas oilmen. The America Firsters probably would have kept us out of World War II, while the Nazis and the Japanese conquered Europe and Asia, and then invaded us.

Plenty of other people have claimed credit for thwarting the assassin. One woman said she'd jiggled the chair he'd stood on, and a man claimed he'd knocked the gunman's arm away. Just as well. I didn't like to think about how I had framed Roosevelt and Cermak in my lens seconds before Zangara fired. Cermak had climbed on the running board of Roosevelt's car. "Move closer," I'd told him.

The bullet hit Cermak. Four others in the crowd were wounded but had survived. Not Mayor Anton J. Cermak. If he had recovered, Ed would never have become mayor of Chicago. My cousin would not have swung the Democratic National Convention into nominating Roosevelt for a third term in 1940. We would have lost him as president right in the middle of the war. Nor would Harry Truman have been vice president, and then president. And, as for John Fitzgerald Kennedy . . .

Of course, neither Ed nor I had any idea what awaited us when he met me at Union Station that summer morning in 1923. I was back in Chicago after ten years in Paris.

PART I

THE FAMILY

CHICAGO
1923–1933

1

MARCH 21, 1923

"Come on, come on." After rushing from New York to Chicago in twenty hours thirty-four minutes, a record the conductor told me, the 20th Century Limited seemed to be panting its way along the last yards of track into LaSalle Street Station. I was desperate to get off the train. I'd left Paris two weeks ago in response to Rose's telegram, "Mame dying." Mame McCabe Kelly—Rose's sister, my brother Michael's wife, and my pal since we were girls. She was still alive, but weak, Rose had told me on the phone last night when I called from New York as soon as the *Normandie* had docked.

Mame's doctor had told Rose there'd been some complications after "the operation for female problems." He'd been vague, Rose said. A hysterectomy, probably an infection. Mame was not recovering. The prognosis was not good.

"What can you expect," I'd said to Rose. "Mame had five children in seven years and she was thirty-one years old when she gave birth to the first. I mean, dear God. . . ."

"Nonie, please," Rose had said. "She and Michael wanted a family and . . ." Rose had stopped. She and her husband John had tried so hard for a baby. Three miscarriages before I'd left and probably more since.

"Your sister Henrietta won't let me see Mame," Rose had said.

"I'll handle Henrietta," I'd said.

"I just think if the three of us were together again it might give Mame strength," Rose said.

Finally the train stopped. The doors opened. I was down the stairs and onto the platform and there was my cousin Ed waiting, wearing a bowler hat and spats. Always dapper was Ed.

"Welcome home, Nonie," he said. After ten years of being Nora, I was Nonie again. My nickname in the family. Ed was bringing me back into the fold.

He tipped his hat. Not much gray in his red hair. Three years older than me, so forty-seven. No bulge of fat under the double-breasted jacket of his pinstripe suit. Does he still run along the lake in the morning? He'd picked up the habit when he was boxing champion of the Brighton Park Athletic Association. His start in politics. I opened my arms but he stepped back. No hug. Not in public with a uniformed railway official next to him.

"Any word?" I said.

"No change as far as I know. We'll pick up Rose and John Larney and go straight out to Argo." Ed's mother and Rose's mother-in-law, Kate Larney, were sisters. One more strand in the web that bound us all together. "Let's go," Ed said to the official who led us off the platform.

A Red Cap followed behind with my Gladstone bag. "No other luggage?" Ed asked me as we walked through the station.

"No," I said, "just this and my camera bag." I planned to return to Paris as soon as . . .

Ed took the bag from me and gave the Red Cap a dollar. "Thank you very much," the Negro man said.

"You a South Sider?" Ed asked.

"Yes, sir," he said. "Bronzeville."

Ed nodded. We walked toward the LaSalle Street exit.

"He probably voted for Thompson. The colored people in Chicago will support any Republican running because it's the party of Lincoln. But we finally beat Big Bill Thompson. We've elected a good man, Nonie. Our first Irish Catholic mayor. Bill Dever. Decent Dever."

"Well, that's good," I said.

We were out on Canal Street now. "More people and cars in the streets than I remember, Ed."

"Chicago is growing," Ed said. "The population has doubled since you left. The city limits are expanding. That's why we have to get a respectable government. Change our reputation."

"I know, Ed. Even in Paris when I said I was from Chicago someone would do this . . ." I made a tommy gun with my hands and pointed. "Ack, ack, ack."

Ed shook his head. "Thompson took millions from Capone. Gave him the run of the city. Dever has already forced the Outfit's headquarters out of Chicago into Cicero. It's a start. With Dever in office, we're moving ahead," he said.

Ed walked up to a long expensive-looking black automobile. Took keys from his pocket and unlocked the door.

"Nice," I said to him. Ed had been doing alright for himself when I'd left—a good city job as an engineer—but this was a rich man's car. Not the time to ask questions, but I wondered.

"I started buying Packards because Mary liked to take drives out to the country on Sundays," Ed said.

Mary. Ed's wife. Poor girl. Only twenty-five when she died in the 1918 flu epidemic. Pregnant. Terrible that women who were expecting were the most susceptible. Both she and the little one gone.

"I'm so sorry about Mary, Ed," I said. "I should have mentioned her right away."

"Nothing to say really. Everyone tells me time will help. But it's been five years and I miss her every day."

"So sad," I said.

"I wonder would the baby have been a girl," Ed said. "Mary wanted a daughter and Ed Junior was looking forward to a little sister."

I reached out and squeezed his forearm. "Oh, Ed," I said.

"She's buried in Calvary. A Celtic cross in Connemara marble. She'd be pleased."

"I want to visit her grave," I said. Some comfort to know the one you loved was tucked into a lovely grave, I thought.

Ed held the passenger door open for me. I got in. He put the bag in the back seat. Sat in the driver's seat. I pulled the skirt of my suit down over my knees.

"That's pretty short, Nonie," he said. "And is that a man's jacket you're wearing?"

"It's the fashion, Ed," I said. "Haven't Chicago women turned up their hems?"

"Not ones your age," he said.

"In Paris, forty-four is not old," I said.

"But you're not in Paris now," he said.

I'd spent ten years as Mademoiselle Photographie, a woman with a profession who earned her own living and was friendly with artists and writers. I'd been part of a group of Irish rebels clustered around the Collège des Irlandais near the Pantheon.

Honora Bridget Kelly was my baptismal name. I'd been called after my grandmother, Honora Keeley Kelly, but I preferred the more modern Nora. Granny's name connected her to Ireland and a history I'd only recently discovered. Now I would be Nora, Nonie in the family, on my way to my brother's house to look after his sick wife. Doing my duty. I was a Kelly of Chicago. A meat-and-potatoes town where grown men did not paint strange pictures or write obscure books and women lived for their husbands and children, of which I had neither. I had to wonder would the Biblical father have slaughtered a calf for a prodigal daughter? Probably would have told her to get into the kitchen and start the dinner.

Ed turned west on Jackson Boulevard. Though the Kellys and Larneys were South Siders, he told me Rose and John had broken with tradition and were living in a bungalow on the West Side.

"It's closer to police headquarters, at Twenty-Sixth and California," Ed said. "John's working out of that station now." Excusing the defection.

I'll see Rose in a few minutes, I thought. Rose, Mame, and I. My brother Michael called us "The Trio." Three young women marking the century's turn with a vow to live our own lives and support each other. We would not marry at sixteen as our mothers had. We would have jobs that used our intelligence and skills. We would march and demonstrate until women could vote. Until our rights were recognized.

And we had won. The three of us had started at Montgomery Ward's as telephone operators, taking orders from all over the country. We were required to sound like proper American ladies. Another trap. But we'd burst through the restraints that the anti-Irish Miss Allen had put on us and moved up. Mame became the private secretary of the vice president of Montgomery Ward, mastering that new machine, the typewriter. Rose and I set up our own Ladies Fashion Department. Twenty-five-year-old successes. The new women. Confident and unafraid and then, well . . . Rose fell in love with John Larney, married him. Not proper for a married woman to continue working. Not when she wants a family. And Mame was secretly in love with my brother Michael, the forty-five-year-old bachelor who didn't dare declare his love for her openly for fear of our sister Henrietta. Henrietta, nearly seven years older than I am . . . she was just fifteen when she married a cousin of ours called Bill Kelly and moved with him sixty miles south of the city to a small Illinois farm town. I remembered visiting her in the little house surrounded by fields. Bill worked long hours farming and in a local food processing factory. Henrietta had three little ones in six years and then suddenly she and the children were back home with us. Bill Kelly dead in an accident at the factory and Henrietta a widow at twenty-two. Granny Honora had tried to explain to me that Henrietta was cranky all the time because she was mourning her husband. But I don't think Henrietta gave Bill Kelly much thought. She'd only known him such a little time.

No, Henrietta was mad because she didn't have her own house. Never occurred to her to get a job and work for the money to go out on her own. Henrietta had been a maid in one of the Prairie Avenue mansions when she was fourteen.

"I'm never taking orders from some prune-faced woman again. I married Bill Kelly so the only floors I'd have to scrub were my own," she'd told me when, after a year of living with us, I repeated what my friend's mother, Mary Sweeney, had said, that Henrietta could get a good job as a housekeeper.

We pulled up in front of John and Rose's bungalow. Rose came running out. I hurried up the steps to meet her. We stood on the porch hugging, and I started crying. I'd missed her, missed Chicago, missed myself, really, the Nora that should have been. I loved my life in Paris and would be back there soon, but . . .

John walked out. "Good to see you, Nora. Hello, Ed."

"And Mame, Rose?" I asked.

"Very sick, Nonie. That's what Stella Lambert, their neighbor in Argo, says. She calls me. I haven't seen Mame in a month. Your sister Henrietta is like a woman possessed. She won't let me in when I go there. Poor Michael is in such a fog, spends hours just sitting next to Mame's bed. The kids are terrified. And Henrietta's, well, she's hard on the little ones."

"Don't tell me," I said. "Spare the rod, spoil the child. Her favorite saying. I'm home now, Rose, and I'm well able for Henrietta."

An hour later we arrived at Michael and Mame's big corner house, surrounded by trees and grass. A very small town and very pleasant-looking Summit was, even if the huge corn starch factory made everyone call Summit "Argo."

Henrietta's dream come true.

Toots, her youngest son, opened the door. In his thirties now, a bit spindly with a belly that slopped over his belt, but grinning with the same smile he'd turned on all of us when he was a child, making us laugh with his dancing and singing ("A regular George M.!" Mam had said). But it wasn't so funny when they expelled him from St. Bridget's school. Hard place to get kicked out of, if you were a Kelly.

We'd all been baptized there. Granny Honora had worked in the parish office in the year dot, and Michael, my brother, always had put wads of bills into the collection basket. But Toots had stolen the other kids' pennies and lied to beat the band. Deliberate badness too. He was only five when I'd seen him take Granny Honora's clay pipe and drop it with great concentration on the slate floor in front of the hearth. Crying, of course, and saying it was an accident. Then he'd begged a dime from Michael to go buy another pipe for Granny, though pipes were a nickel. He kept the change. A chancer.

"My little fatherless boy," Henrietta would croon to him, and I'd think, Ah, well.

But then I was fatherless myself, and hadn't my da and aunt and uncles lost their father young and suffered in Ireland as no children should? Yet they were decent. Each and every one of them. I mean, dead fathers were two for a penny in Bridgeport.

"I'm afraid Toots has a wee quirk, Henrietta. You're not helping the boy by indulging him," Mam had said to her when he was ten and had been expelled from a Bridgeport public school.

But Henrietta had let him lay in bed until noon and then he'd run errands for her, often coming home with half the groceries and some story about giving them away to a woman with two children who needed food. Mam, who had a horror of people going hungry, would only nod, just in case he wasn't giving out his usual line of rubbish and someone had really been in need. I talked to Michael once, but he'd only shrugged. Peace at any price, our Michael.

In those days, Michael was hardly home anyway, going off on jobs or out to boxing matches or Democratic politics. A big man for banquets, Michael was, master of ceremonies at the Knights of Columbus and a dozen others. Of course, in those years, he was secretly courting Mame and I had been besotted with Tim McShane, so no one had taken a hand with Toots. Henrietta, so stern with her other children, made a fool of herself over her baby. Not that I'm one to talk about blind love.

"So, the prodigal returns," Toots said.

"Show some respect for your aunt," Ed said to him.

"Oh, I have great respect for anyone who gets out of this town," he said.

And then there was Henrietta. The same gray hair pulled back into a bun, and could that be the same purple housedress she wore ten years ago?

"You," she said to me. And, "You," turning to Rose and John. "You are not needed here."

Ed spoke up. "Now, Henrietta, isn't it grand to have Nonie home? Your own sister."

"No sister of mine. She gave up that right," she said.

"And what about my sister?" Rose said. "I'm here to see Mame."

"Which she will do, Henrietta," Ed said. "And no scenes."

"Please, Henrietta," I began.

But she stuck her finger in my face. "You brought evil into this family! Your hoodlum boyfriend attacked me!" Screaming the words.

"Stop it, Henrietta," I said. "For God's sake, do you want the children to hear?"

But it was too late. Two young girls stood in the parlor doorway, one holding a baby in her arms. Next to them, a young boy held the hand of a small girl—all looking up at us. Michael and Mame's children—ten, eight, six, four, and two years old.

The boy and littlest girl rushed into Rose's arms, and the older two moved close. Rose took the baby.

"Aunt Rose, I'm sorry," the oldest girl said.

Rose embraced them. "Sorry? For what?"

It was the little fellow spoke up. "Aunt Henrietta said we were so bad that Aunt Rose and Uncle John wouldn't visit us anymore." He walked over to John. "She said you would put me in jail and that I may even die in the electric chair."

John picked him up. "Your aunt Henrietta says some very foolish things, Mike. You're a good sturdy lad and a comfort to your mother. Why would I put you in jail?"

Henrietta screamed, "I never said any such thing!"

"She did," said the oldest girl.

Then Rose said to her, "Come on, Rosemary. And Ann, bring Frances. We'll go back in the kitchen. John, bring Mike and Marguerite. You'll finish your breakfast and then meet your aunt Nonie. She's come all the way from Paris to see you."

That's when Mame called down from her bedroom, "Who's there?" Such a weak voice.

"Go up to her, Nonie," Rose said to me.

I ran up the stairs. Wood-carved banisters with stained glass windows set along the wall so the sun threw patterns onto the dark green carpet. A lovely house. All Henrietta had ever wanted, but it wasn't hers. Demented with jealousy. Dear God, were we better off when we were all poor together?

"Mame, it's me. It's Nora," I said. Very dark in the room, only a little lamp, like a vigil light.

"Nonie! Nonie! Home at last!" Mame said.

"And Rose is here too," I said.

"Rose? But Henrietta said Rose was too sick to come," Mame said.

"Rose is fine and she's here, and John too. And Ed."

"But Henrietta . . ." Mame half sat up.

"Forget about Henrietta, Mame."

"But she's been very good, coming in to help with the children. She said no housekeeper would take on five children and a woman as sick as I am. And it wasn't fair to expect Rose to . . ."

I settled her back on her pillows. "For God's sake, Mame, don't you know better than to listen to Henrietta? Rose is here, and I'm here. The Trio together and you're going to be fine, Mame, and up with those gorgeous kids of yours soon."

She smiled. "They are gorgeous. The oldest, Rosemary, named for Rose and my mother, and then Ann for your sister—she was great with the children when they were little, but she's her own life now. Henrietta tells me a policewoman must be on call. And our son was born on Christmas Eve, 1916. We were going to give him Victor as a middle name, a kind of prayer that the war would end. But then Michael said that Michael Joseph Kelly was your grandfather, who died in Ireland, and his own name which he wanted his son to carry on. Marguerite was named for you, Nonie."

"Me?"

"So many Margarets and Maggies and Peggys and Marguerite is French, and with you in Paris . . ."

"Thank you, Mame."

"And little Frances is in honor of St. Francis Assisi. I was praying to him because the doctor thought we wouldn't have any more children. But look at her. Beautiful. And I was just fine until I started bleeding and . . ."

Then Rose was there. "Mame," she said, and walked over to the bed and pulled the spread straight. "You could use another pillow."

"Oh, Rose," Mame said. Rose leaned over and the two of them held on to each other until Mame said, "You're very good to come, but I didn't want you to be upset."

"Upset? Me? Not a bother on me and you're going to get well, Mame." She walked over and pulled open the curtains. "Let some sun in here. Henrietta's been a help but I think it's time for me to lend a hand. I'll stay in the room on the third floor. Isn't it grand to have Nonie home and looking so glamorous? Might even get me to bob my hair. Mame did."

And I saw that, yes, though her hair was matted, Mame did indeed have a shingle.

"And your dress, Nonie. Puts me in mind of our uniforms at St. Xav's," said Mame.

"The designer was raised in a convent school, an orphan, or kind of an orphan." I started to tell them about how I had become a friend of Coco Chanel and all about Paris, until I noticed that Mame was closing her eyes. I looked at Rose.

She waved me away and I left the two McCabe girls together. I'd come home ready to make peace with Henrietta. But now . . . how could she keep these sisters apart?

I could hear Henrietta's high-pitched yowling and Ed's low tones as I walked by the closed parlor door. Leave them to it, I thought, and found the kitchen where the children huddled together around a table. A young colored woman stirred a large pot at the modern stove. Electric.

"Hello," I said. "I'm Nora Kelly. Their aunt Nonie."

"About time," she said. "I'd walk out of here if Mrs. Michael wasn't such a kind woman. My name's Jesse Howard."

So Henrietta had help with the house and the cooking and was still complaining. Jesse ladled what looked like oatmeal into a bowl and sat down at the table.

"Me and Rosemary and Ann will finish eating, then clean up. You take the three little ones out until the war to end all wars is finished in the parlor," Jesse said.

"But maybe I should—"

"You're Nonie? Well, she's been shouting your name. Better hightail it."

I brought the three youngest—Mike, Marguerite, and Frances—out into the backyard. So flat, Chicago and Summit/Argo had no tall buildings to hold back the prairie. It came lapping at our ankles despite the green slatted fence Michael and Mame built to enclose a bit of the wild. They'd stuck in peony bushes and hollyhocks and called it a garden. But weeds and tall grass were scattered throughout the yard. I thought of the Jardins Luxembourg and Parc Monceau, with their obedient flowers and shrubs.

I carried Frances and followed Mike, who led Marguerite and me to the far corner of the yard and a gap in the fence. Just beyond, in the open space bricks were stacked one on another in a square about as high was my waist.

"Our fort."

"With Bobby," Marguerite said. "His friend. They fight Indians."

"They do? Well, did you know that the Kelly family ate their first Christmas dinner in America at the home of an Indian family?"

They shook their heads no.

"Well," I said, balancing on one surprisingly sturdy wall of the fort, holding Frances while Marguerite and Michael sat in the dirt. *"Fadó,"* I started.

"What?" Michael said.

"Once upon a time," I said, but I'd hardly begun when a very elegant woman holding the hand of a young boy came walking toward us.

"Bobby!" Mike said and ran toward them.

"I'm Stella Lambert," the woman said. "I see the children are getting dirty."

"Well, I—"

"Good," she said and then echoed Jesse. "About time."

My brother Michael arrived just after noon. I saw him from the window as he slowly got out of his car then took one look at Ed's Packard and started running up the walk, taking the porch steps two at a time.

Henrietta got to the door first but Ed, Rose, John, the children, and I were right behind her.

"Ed, is it Mame? Is she . . . ?" He was halfway up the staircase to the bedroom before Ed's voice stopped him.

"She's fine, Michael. She's sleeping."

Michael looked down at us gathered below him. "Then why are you all here? Rose, John and . . ." He saw me.

"It's me, Michael," I said. "It's Nonie."

"Nonie?" He walked slowly down to me, squinting through his black-rimmed glasses. "Nonie, you're here."

"I am that, Michael. Just off the boat and the train. I arrived this morning."

"Oh she's back alright." Henrietta stood with her arms folded, Toots next to her.

I paid her no mind, stepped right up to Michael and hugged him hard. "The prodigal has returned," I said.

Now Mike, Ann, and Rosemary swarmed around Michael, holding his legs.

"Everybody came, Dad," Mike said.

Michael put his hand on his son's head. "You want a drink, Ed? John? Tea or something, Rose? Nonie?"

He turned to Henrietta, but Rosemary spoke up. "I'll tell Jesse to bring some food, Daddy. Come on, Ann."

Henrietta didn't move. She's feathered herself quite a nest, I thought, and what was she doing? Only scaring the kids half to death, practically telling them, "If you're not good, your mother will die." Ridiculous. And yet she'd said the same to me when Mam passed away, telling me, "She cried about your life, Nonie. You helped put her in an early grave. I only thank God she was dead before she found out about your final degradation."

And somewhere inside me, I'd believed her. If I'd married at nineteen, Mam would be alive today. Nonsense, but Henrietta could be so convincing. My big sister who brought home those lovely babies for me to play with. And Agnella, what better little sister than Agnella, holding tight to my hand and smiling up at me as we walked the streets of Bridgeport. ("An aunt's better than a sister," she told me once, and then whispered, "and nicer than a mama.") Agnella had entered the convent . . . and it would break her heart to know her mother was *une connasse*, as the French would say.

Jesse came in with the girls, carrying sandwiches and a big pot of tea, and set them on the parlor table. "I thought you'd have to stop talking long enough to eat. There's ham and roast beef," she said. And then to Henrietta, "I know you said to save this meat for you and Mr. Toot's lunch, Mrs. Kelly, but . . ." She stopped.

"Fine, fine, Jesse," Henrietta said.

Ann put a pile of plates and napkins next to the tray, and as we helped ourselves, I remembered all the parties at the flat on Hillock—aunts and uncles and cousins laughing. Mam, Granny Honora, dishing out plate after plate of colcannon, potatoes mashed with onions and cabbage running with butter, thick slices of beef and ham straight from the meatpacking houses.

Even after the boys moved on to better jobs, there was always someone we knew working in the stockyards to bring home the best cuts of meat. But Mam and Jim dying so close together changed everything, took the heart out of our house. Family parties were held at Uncle Steve's—Ed's father's place—and we were the guests.

Did the other Kellys draw away from our family just a wee bit? Da dead so young and then Mam and Jim; Granny Honora, Aunt Máire and Uncle Patrick gone too, but they were long-lived. Was our family the hard luck Kellys? A widow, two spinsters, two bachelors. One brother had married and moved away. I had my work and Tim McShane. While Michael, Ann, Mart, and I had neither chick nor child, the other cousins had loads of children. Then the great burst of joy of Michael and Mame's wedding and that wonderful party, until Tim McShane ruined the night and I . . . I closed my eyes and leaned against the back of the armchair.

Then suddenly, Rose was shaking me.

"I must've fallen asleep."

"You must be exhausted," she said.

I nodded. "Hard to sleep on the train."

"Take a nap in our room, Aunt Nonie," Ann said.

But Ed was standing up. "My mother has a room waiting for Nonie at our place," he said. Aunt Nelly had been looking after Ed and his young son since Mary had died.

Rose walked over to John.

"Don't leave, Aunt Rose. Don't leave!" Mike said and the girls joined in, holding on to Rose's hands, her dress, any part of her they could clutch.

"Stop that," Henrietta said. "You'll wake your mother. Quiet. No wonder she's sick, with such ruffians running around this house."

"That's enough, Henrietta," Michael said.

"I'm staying," Rose said. "If that's alright, Michael?"

"It's not alright," Henrietta broke in. "I'm not staying under the same roof as you, Rose McCabe. All of you scheming against me."

And Michael woke up. Like that. In the snap of a finger. He stood up. "Then go, Henrietta. You and Toots. Go back to Hillock with Mart and Ann. Now. Today."

Then ructions!

Stella Lambert put down her mug of tea and got her Bobby, Mike, and the girls moving and out the door. "I'll give them dinner," she said.

We all just stared at Henrietta as she roared and raged until finally Toots took her by the arm. "Come on, Mother. We won't stay where we're not wanted."

Never saw Michael so strong-faced and determined. "Get ready and I'll drive you," he said. Then to Rose, "You'll explain to Mame? Tell her I'll be back."

"I'm sorry we dragged you home for this, Nonie," John said as I got into Ed's car. "But Rose said she just couldn't face Henrietta alone and didn't want to bring Ed into it on her own. Rose is not afraid of anybody, but Henrietta seems to have the kibosh on her."

"On me too," I said, "and believe me, the battle's not over. Henrietta's lost round one but she'll come out fighting. I'm glad you'll be staying here with Rose," I said.

"Are you too tired for a quick stop on the way to my house, Nonie?" Ed asked me, as we turned off Archer Avenue onto a highway that was new to me. A very grand stretch of road going along the lake.

"I'm fine, Ed. What's this avenue?"

"South Shore Drive," Ed said.

"Your dream come true."

Ed had been talking about building just such a highway since he was fourteen. "This is only the beginning," he said to me. "Close your eyes, Nonie," he said.

In a few minutes he stopped the car. "Look up," he said. There above us on a rise, twenty or thirty white columns marched against the sky.

"Dear God," I said. "It looks like a Roman temple."

"Not Roman," Ed said. "Greek. Those are Doric columns."

"So tall," I said.

"Each one's a hundred and fifty feet high," Ed said. "That's fifteen stories. And there's another colonnade just like it on the east entrance and this is just the façade. There's ten acres down below that are being made into the best stadium in the country. The field will be a half a mile long with three tracks going around. There'll be seating for one hundred thousand. We've already had inquiries from people who want to hold events here. Things like championship fights. The cardinal called me about having the Eucharistic Congress here. It's going to be a gathering place for the entire city of Chicago. It's not coming cheap. Probably going to cost ten million dollars, but there's fifteen thousand jobs in the project and can you imagine the money that's going to come into the city from all the events. It'll be like the Columbian Exposition all over again."

He pointed toward Lake Michigan. "I want to create an island and build museums and parks."

"Wonderful, Ed."

"With Thompson gone anything is possible. Private money is available and tourists are coming back to the city."

There was honking behind us. A line of trucks trying to get to the construction site. Ed pulled out of their way back onto the drive. I tried to listen as we drove south but my eyes got heavy. I woke to find we were parked in front of a mansion.

"Jesus, Mary, and Joseph! Where are we?" I asked.

"Mary and I bought this house right before she got sick. We wanted room for our children."

"But it must have cost a fortune," I said. "How . . ."

"I've worked hard," Ed said, "and been lucky in my investments. Got some good stock tips."

"But," I began. Ed was getting out of the car. He came around, opened my door. Subject closed.

Yes, I thought, as we walked into the three-story redbrick house, set back from Ellis in the nicest part of Hyde Park. There should be loads of kids running in and out of the place, bringing their friends. Instead I found room after room sparsely furnished—no carpets, no curtains—and Aunt Nelly, Ed's mother, in the kitchen serving liver and dumplings to a six-year-old boy. Ed's son . . . Ed Junior.

She hugged me, this woman who'd known them all—Granny Honora, Aunt Máire, Uncle Patrick, my da and mam, all of home in her embrace, and that's what she said to me.

"Welcome home, Nonie."

"I'm too tired to eat," I told her, and she took me upstairs and gave me one of her own nightgowns. A soft white tent of cotton. Comforting. "Thank you, Aunt Nelly."

"Ed will bring your bag in from the car. You can unpack tomorrow." No questions. No chat. But then Aunt Nelly's half German. Nice that, sometimes.

I turned on my side, feather pillows under my head. Closed my eyes and then, as I did every night, I visited that part of my mind where Peter Keeley waited. The man I'd fallen in love with in Paris. Sometimes we were in the library of the Irish College, near the Pantheon, and he was translating the skirl of letters in an old Irish manuscript. So intense, as he opened my heritage to me. Or we were sharing our bed in my room overlooking the Place des Vosges. Tonight I found him in Connemara, on the shores of Lough Inagh, coming toward me. But then. Stop. Stay there. I couldn't let my mind rush ahead to that freezing night just before Christmas when Cyril Peterson arrived with news from Ireland. The worst. Peter was dead. Killed in the civil war that had broken out just as Ireland had finally gotten Britain to withdraw. Former comrades shooting each other. No. Go back, go back. Imagine Peter smiling. Run to him.

I fell asleep with Aunt Nelly's nightgown wrapping me. Chicago. Welcome home.

2

"Do you remember," I said to Ed, as we drove out to Argo the next day, "when we lined up to get on the Ferris wheel at the World's Fair? Me fourteen, and you seventeen, Ed. So excited, you were, telling me about pistons and horsepower and such until all of us Kellys, fifty-strong, piled into the gondola as big as a Pullman car for our ride to the top. The whole family together, Granny Honora holding Agnella. Such a happy moment, just dusk, when the colored lights outlining every building flashed on! Every one of us, child and adult, sighed, 'Ahhh!' then 'Ohhh! Ohhh!' as the darkness was suddenly bright."

"I remember," Ed said. "That's what I want for Chicago, a skyline shining against the night sky, buildings gathered along a great highway: Lake Shore Drive. Nonie, I want to have a grand fountain, all lit up, shooting spumes of red, yellow, blue, and green water up toward the heavens. Chicago can do it. I'm on the South Park Commission now. The land we need is under our jurisdiction. We've the plans Daniel Burnham made. And we can get the money, private as well as public, to fill in the lakefront. Rich people want roads for their new automobiles, so they'll let the poor have parks. And I can do it. I know how to get crews of men to work. Pat Nash's company is ready to go. He'll lay all the sewers we need.

"But there's this fellow Wilcox, who calls himself reverend, though of what church I don't know, who's sure I'm the Devil incarnate and out to steal the taxpayers' money. Calls our projects boondoggles. He started his own newspaper just to attack me and the other fellows working for the city. Accuses us of giving bribes and taking bribes. But Wilcox doesn't know what it takes to actually construct something. And if the wheels have to be greased a bit, so what?"

Ed certainly wasn't hurting. He told me his salary as chief engineer was fifteen thousand dollars a year. Amazing! Twenty times as much as either of our fathers could ever dream of making, and yet his car had to cost five thousand, and that house . . . Mary Roche came from money herself, and I suppose she'd left some of that to Ed. Not that his house could compare to the real mansions on Prairie and Michigan Avenues where the Armours, McCormicks, and Potter Palmers lived. Okay to make big wads of money, as they had, from buying cheap and selling dear, from paying your workers buttons, but wrong to get a bit of the commission on a job well done? Why shouldn't Ed give the contracts to Pat Nash when his company did the job best?

Ed explained to me that as well as attacking him for his lack of qualifications ("Didn't I learn more working with the Army surveying team than some Eastern university can teach?"), Wilcox was after him for featherbedding—putting too many men on a crew and overpaying suppliers.

"Let him try to pave a road or get concrete delivered on time. Does he want mobs of fellows without jobs wandering the streets, getting into trouble? No telling what a man desperate to feed his family will do. Jobs, that's what makes Chicago great. We know how to put our people to work. And all this folderol about sealed bids and such? Technicalities. I want the contract to go to a company we can rely on. I've no patience with these Reformers. . . . They could never push one big project through from beginning to end. We're building the greatest stadium in the country. If I could shake off these gadflies and get to work, who knows what we could accomplish."

He said that the just-elected Democratic mayor, Bill Dever, was with him, but the Republicans were determined to get Big Bill Thompson, the biggest crook the city had ever known, back in office.

"They can't bear to see the Irish getting real power," I said.

"Good to have you home, Nonie," Ed said as we pulled up to Michael's house. "I always could talk to you."

"Cousins," I said. "Closer than friends, less complicated than brother and sister."

Ed jerked his head toward the back seat where Ed Junior was trailing his hand out of the window and probably listening to every word. Ed turned to him. "That's how it'll be for you and Mike." And Ed Junior smiled.

Aunt Nelly had washed and ironed my blouse for me. "Lovely stuff," she'd said. "But what do you have for everyday?" Taken aback when I'd pulled out the trouser suit. "Dear God, Nonie. Please. Enough talk already about . . . ," she'd said. And she'd stopped. What has Henrietta been telling people about me? I wondered as I followed Ed up the front walk.

Rosemary and Ann were out with their friends. After school they moved from the front porch of one to the backyard of another, with occasional trips to Stone's Drugstore. But Marguerite was staying close to Rose, next to her while she cared for baby Frances. Marguerite seemed afraid her aunt would disappear. Ed Junior joined Mike, Bobby Lambert, and the gang of small boys who roamed the prairie from early morning.

"A peaceful house without that *other* Mrs. Kelly," Jesse said as the two of us went through the kitchen cupboards, making a shopping list. "Your sister and that son of hers went to other stores on their own," Jesse said. "Not great quality considering the amount of money they claimed to spend. But poor Mr. Kelly never questioned her, and it wasn't my place . . ."

Toots up to his old tricks, and Henrietta going along with him. Ed had driven over to Michael's plumbing office, and Mame was sleeping. Quiet.

But late that afternoon the children came into Mame's room. She sat up in bed with a framed photograph on her lap—a portrait of the family I'd noticed on her dressing table. The girls snuggled up. Mike stood at the side of the bed. Ed had picked up his son, and they'd left. I planned to spend the night. Rose sat at the foot of the bed holding baby Frances, with me next to her.

Ann traced her mother's face in the photograph. "Tell us the story again," she said.

"Alright." Mame smiled up at us.

"Once upon a time," Mame said, "there was a very happy family that lived together on a lovely, leafy street in a place called . . ."

"Argo," the children shouted together.

"There were four sisters," Mame said.

"Rosemary," the children said together, "Ann, Marguerite, and Frances." As they went on, they pointed to themselves in the photograph.

"And one strong brother," Mame said.

"Named Michael," the girls said in unison, and Mike put his finger on his own face.

"And a wonderful mother and father," Ann added.

"Yes," I said.

"But one day a very sad thing happened," Mame said. "The mama got sick, and she was very sorry that her body became so weak and tired that she had to go to bed."

"And then the wicked old aunt came," Rosemary said.

"Stop, Rosemary," Ann said, "that's not part of the story."

"It should be," Rosemary said.

"Go on, Mama," Marguerite said.

Mame continued. "Now these children had two very lovely fairy godmothers. One lived far away . . ."

"That's you, Aunt Nonie," Ann said.

". . . and the other didn't know the family needed her."

"Like you, Aunt Rose," Rosemary said.

"But the mother knew those women loved her and her children very much. And so she prayed to Our Lady to send them to Argo to help their godchildren."

"And you came!" Ann said.

"Be quiet," Rosemary said. "Let Mama finish."

"And when the mother saw her two friends, she felt ever so much better, and everyone lived happily ever after."

Little Marguerite clapped her hands. Rosemary and Ann each kissed one of their mother's cheeks, and Mike stroked her hair.

"Please God," said Rose, as she rocked baby Frances.

"And now that your two godmothers are here, we're not going anywhere," I said, and picked up the photograph. "This is a wonderful piece of work, beautifully lit, you all look so natural."

"Mabel Sykes is the best portrait photographer in Chicago," Mame said.

"You know your aunt Nonie takes pictures, girls," Rose said.

"I do," I said. "Soon I'll bring my camera and take a picture of you all, but not as posed as this—outside in the yard, say."

"Or we could go on a picnic like we used to," Ann said. "Remember, Mama, when you drove the car all the way out to the woods and we had sandwiches and lemonade and cake? Nobody else's mother could even drive a car, and you brought us on an adventure."

"Mama's word for fun," Rosemary said.

"I remember," Mike said.

"I do too," Marguerite said.

"You don't. You were too little," Rosemary said.

"But I do, I do, Mama."

"I know, Marguerite," Mame said. Then she closed her eyes and went into a half sleep, where she spent the rest of the day.

"She gets so tired," Rose explained after we had sent the children downstairs to the kitchen and Jesse for an early dinner, had put the baby down, and were sitting on the front porch. Michael wasn't home so we had a chance to really talk about Mame's condition.

"The doctor said she can't throw off the infection. I wish she'd never had the operation. That's when Michael let Henrietta move in to help with baby Frances and the others. But she didn't get better. Henrietta kept saying it was TB, but we've never had TB in our family," said Rose.

Still shameful to contract TB, a disease of the poor, crowded into basements, drinking dirty water. . . . "But the doctor said she needed the operation because of 'female problems.'"

"That's what I told Henrietta," Rose said. "But she told me Michael had probably bribed him to lie. That's what led to our big fight. It was terrible, Nonie. I actually took Henrietta by the shoulders and shook her to make her stop. Mame was upstairs. If she had heard . . ."

"What does Mame think is wrong?"

"She blames herself for not getting better."

"Poor Mame," I said. "That doctor . . ."

"I know," Rose said. "Too late to do anything about him." She took my hand. "We have to help her children, Nonie. If Mame . . . well, we have to make them ours."

"I'm sure you and John—" I started.

"We need you, Nonie. You have a way with Michael and Ed, can talk politics with them, make them laugh. You'll stay, won't you, Nonie?"

"Alright, Rose. But we're being too gloomy. Mame may rally."

"Yes," Rose said. "Too awful though to think of these children losing their mother so young. I was twenty-five when Mam died, and a blow then. Who else loves you no matter what, except your mother?"

And Mame did seem to hold her own. All through April and May she was stable. Sleeping a lot, but able to get up for an hour or two—even sit in the yard. Dr. Gillespie came once a week. "The will to live can be powerful," he said.

I settled into a routine. I had a nice room at Ed's. Aunt Nelly, Ed Junior, and I spent the evenings playing cards together and listening to a fellow called Uncle Bob read stories on their big radio when Ed was out at political meetings. Most days I took the Archer Avenue streetcar out to Argo to be with Rose, Mame, and the Kelly kids.

But one night in May, Ed said he was spending the next day out at the stadium building site. “Let me go with you,” I’d said, “and take some photographs.” I’d come down to breakfast dressed in my trouser suit, Seneca in hand.

Aunt Nelly looked at Ed. “Do you have an account at Field’s?” She turned to me. “We’ll buy a few skirts and sweaters for you as a welcome home gift. Until then, come upstairs with me—I think I can find you something to wear today.”

What could I say? I put on what probably had been a dress of Mary’s and went with Ed to the stadium site. I took the usual-type shots of Ed with the workers and the foremen. But then I posed him between two of the Corinthian columns, the light slanting in behind him creating a kind of halo effect.

Ed had my photographs developed and printed, and a few days later laid them out on the dining room table after dinner.

“Excellent, Nonie!” Aunt Nelly said.

“You look so big, Dad,” Ed Junior told his father.

“Well done, Nonie,” Ed told me. “I want to frame these and put them in my office.” He handed me a ten-dollar bill.

I shook my head. “You’re supporting me,” I said. Room and board and a Chicago wardrobe. I started to imagine Mame cured and me returning to Paris.

There might be a letter waiting for me now, at the Irish College. Cyril, Peter’s comrade-in-arms, had promised to write and tell me where Peter was buried and when I could safely visit his grave. “Best to stay away during all this tit for tatting,” he’d said when he brought me the terrible news. “We’ll wear ourselves out sooner or later.”

Then, in June, Mame relapsed. In bed all the time. I took Mike, Ed Junior, and Bobby Lambert to the Fourth of July parade to see the Civil War veterans from the Irish Legion and the Irish Brigade march down Archer Avenue. A good few of them still alive, since they had all been so young when they enlisted. My dad at twenty-one had been one of the oldest to join. Granny Honora and Aunt Máire never stopped arguing about whether or not the boys should have fought.

Michael had let me take his car after I’d proved to him that I could drive by going around the block five times. I started to tell him how I’d been at the wheel of plenty of ambulances, taking patients from the battlefield to the American hospital in Paris, but he’d said to me, “Not now, Nonie.”

I’d dropped Ed Junior back at his house.

I wondered if Ed Junior understood how sick Mame was, and was he remembering when his own mother was struck? What age had he been . . . about six—Mike's age. Old enough to remember.

My brother was with Mame in her room when we returned. He still slept beside her every night. Mame liked to have him close, Rose had said to me, because she was afraid she'd die in the night and no one would know.

So hot in the room, drenched in the afternoon sun that day. Michael patted Mame's forehead with a damp towel while Mike told his father about the soldiers and the flags, and how I'd said that his grandfather had fought in the war along with all his uncles and cousins. Michael only nodded his head, though I thought Mame started to say something to him and then stopped.

That night, I stayed over, sharing the guest room with Rose. I got up after midnight to go to the bathroom, and there was Mike standing in front of his parents' bedroom, holding a stick on his shoulder.

"I'm guarding Mama," he said. "Something's trying to kill her, but I'm going to get it first." After a pause, he asked, "Will my mama get better?"

"Your mother wants to stay with you more than anything else in the world. She's fighting very hard," I said.

"I wish I had a whole lot of soldiers to fight with me, like those men with rifles in the parade. I'd stand with them and never go out or play or sleep or anything."

I heard soft voices coming from Michael and Mame's room. I brought Mike in to them. He stood next to the bed at attention as his mother smoothed his hair, and his father lay with his eyes closed, though I knew he was awake.

That next morning, Mame's breathing got very labored. Michael told Rose and me to bring the children to her room. They stood together, each one finding some bit of Mame to touch. Ann and Rosemary each held one of her hands, Mike and Marguerite the other. Rose cradled Frances while Michael sat on the bed and stroked her cheek.

Mame opened her eyes. She looked at Rose. "Take care of them, Rose. You and Nonie. Help Michael." And then she smiled. "Ah, Michael," she said.

"Oh, Mame," he said, "Mame, don't go. I love you so."

"I love you," she answered, "all of you, so much."

Rose knew the moment had come when, with the softest of sighs, Mame left us. Rose looked at me and shook her head. Michael saw the exchange.

"No," he said. "No, Mame. Wake up, please! Mamie, don't go. Not yet."

Then Rosemary started crying, sobbing.

Ann said, "What? Is Mama . . . ?"

Mike and Marguerite pulled on Mame's hand.

"Mama. Mama. It's warm out, Mama. We could go to the lake," Mike said. "Take a picnic."

Marguerite dropped Mame's hand and ran to Rose, who picked her up, holding Frances on one hip and Marguerite on the other. Rose moved slightly from side to side, rocking the little girls and murmuring, "It's alright. It's alright."

But it wouldn't be alright for the Kelly kids, not ever again. They would recover from the most awful parts of grief and would go on, I hoped, to find happiness with families of their own. But always, always, this scene would wait in their memory. Mame's death. And the terrible, sad days that followed.

3

"But, Aunt Nonie, they're laughing!" Ann was crying as she pointed to the crowd gathered in the biggest viewing room of the Kelly–Doran Funeral Home. Viewing Room—that's what was written on the card in the doorway. Viewing Room, and poor Mame on display in the same silk dress and pearls she had worn in the family portrait taken by Mabel Sykes. In fact, Ed had given the photograph to his chief embalmer so that he could see what Mame had looked like before the last months when she got so thin.

"She looks wonderful, Mr. Kelly," I heard a woman I don't know say to my stunned big brother, who stood next to the coffin with Ed.

Ann and I sat on a couch a few feet away, hidden by a line of tall floral pieces, set like a wall around the coffin. A far cry, this whole shebang, from the home wakes common in Bridgeport before I had left for Paris.

Leave it to Ed to know the coming thing and take advantage of it.

"I own the building," he'd told me, "and rent out the ground floor to Lallys, who put in a grocery store. Jim Quinn took the basement for a tavern, but no one wanted the upper floors. Then Jim Doran came to me and said he'd gotten his undertaker's license, and would I like to go into business with him. I thought people might like to say goodbye to their loved ones in a place they know, without the trials of a home wake."

"Loved ones"—another term, like Viewing Room, that seemed part of funeral home vocabulary, I thought.

"Also, a way for the mourners to duck downstairs for a quick shot and a beer," I'd said.

"Of course Jim Quinn had to close the tavern when Prohibition became law," Ed said.

"Of course," I'd said, though both of us knew full well that, while the Quinn's Tavern sign was gone, anyone wanting a drink only had to walk around to the back basement entrance and knock on the door. Either Jim Quinn or his partner, George Keefe, would be behind the bar, drawing beers and pouring shots.

And I'd say quite a few of the men standing talking to each other now at Mame's funeral had made such a visit—because Ann was right, they were laughing and chatting to beat the band.

Though this woman, who was now pressing Michael's hand, looked suitably solemn. I kept my arm around Ann and didn't greet the woman, but she came over to us.

"I'm Mrs. O'Donnell," she said. "Jim's wife."

I nodded. Ed's sister, Ella, married an O'Donnell, so I assumed this woman was part of that clan.

"I'm sorry," I said. "Ella's not here right now. She'll be back soon. Should I tell her her sister-in-law was here?"

"Ella?"

"Ella O'Donnell," I said. "Ed Kelly's sister. His mother's sister is a Larney, and her son married Rose, Mame's sister. So . . ." Surely enough people to make a connection from.

"Oh, we're not those O'Donnells," she said. "My husband's family are from St. Rose of Lima. And I grew up in St. Elizabeth's."

"Oh, so you must know the Garveys," I said.

"St. Elizabeth of Bohemia," she said. "I'm not Irish."

"Oh," I said. And now Ann stopped crying to listen. Even at nine, she understood the Chicago two-step of "what parish?"—which told everything about someone's background. But I didn't know how to decode a Bohemian parish, and so there was silence.

"I didn't understand Irish wakes, either," the woman said to Ann, patting her shoulder, looking into her red eyes, and glancing at the handkerchief Ann clutched in her fist.

"When Jim's mother died, I was horrified. Ten in his family, and with all the wives and children and friends piled into the house, it was like a big party. A hooley, as you Irish say. 'What's going on?' I'd asked Jim. 'This is terrible.' 'Ma deserves a great sendoff,' he'd told me. 'And didn't she have a grand life?

And not one of her sons dead before her. A great accomplishment, considering our business.'"

Our business? Maybe the O'Donnells are all firemen or lumberjacks.

"But today," Mrs. O'Donnell went on, "a mother with small children. So sad. I thought things would be more subdued. But . . ."

I moved over on the couch, where Mrs. O'Donnell sat on the other side of Ann. It was as if the three of us were huddled together in a small boat, afloat on an ocean of laughter and chat. Rose had taken Rosemary and the three younger children home, after they had said a prayer at Mame's coffin. I'd been against them even coming to the wake. But Michael was in a daze, and somehow Henrietta got to him and convinced him that it would be good for the children to say goodbye to their mother, and to see how many people came to pay their respects.

Henrietta had shown up at Michael's house only hours after Mame had died, making a great fuss over "these poor motherless children." Why he put up with her, I don't know. He was eight years older than she, so I wondered if it wasn't some childhood habit, taking care of his little sister. It was beyond me. But at least he hadn't let Henrietta move back in, though I wondered how much longer Rose could live apart from John. Impossible for John to move in with her, because Chicago policemen had to live within the city limits.

Ed had told me there were a lot of politics in the police department, and some begrudger could very well turn John in if he moved into Michael's house in Argo. Lots of knives out for John anyway since his brother, Tom, had been assigned to work with Elliot Ness and his Feds. Not popular with the Chicago police force, that Mr. Ness.

I'd insisted to Henrietta that the children leave with Stella Lambert after an hour. But Ann had wanted to stay with her father. Early evening now, the air thick with smoke and the smell of beer. Time to get her away.

"I think I'll ask John Larney to take us home," I said to Mrs. O'Donnell.

"He's the police detective. Right?" she asked. "A decent enough fellow according to my husband, though he doesn't play ball."

"No. John's not an athlete. Maybe you're thinking of our cousin, who played for the White Sox, but he was called Michael Kelly, and . . ."

A fellow, her husband, I supposed, joined us now.

"This is my husband, Jim," she said. "And this is . . ."

"Nora Kelly," I supplied.

"Pleased to meet you," he said. "Sorry for your troubles. And is this Michael's little girl? Your father did a grand job putting in the plumbing in my house." Ann nodded.

"Thanks for coming. I think Ann and I will be going," I said. He reached out his hand. Helped me up. And then Ann. And then his wife.

"We could drive her home. Couldn't we Jim?" Mrs. O'Donnell asked.

"Sure. Sure," her husband said.

"That would be kind of you, but we're out west, Argo."

"Okey dokey," her husband said.

We'll just slip out, I thought to myself. Get Ann out of there without a lot of goodbyes. And I was just at the door when who stopped me . . . only Henrietta.

"So you're leaving," she said. "It's just like you to think only of yourself, and leave me here to support poor Michael on my own." She was talking loud enough so that two or three men turned around, and Ann started sniffling again.

"Mr. and Mrs. O'Donnell have offered me a ride, and I think Ann's had enough." Henrietta looked behind me at the couple. She lowered her voice and clenched her teeth. "So now you've taken up with another gangster," she said, looking at Jim O'Donnell. "Spike O'Donnell, how dare you come here!"

"Henrietta," I started, but Spike only shrugged as she stomped away from us.

"A man pays his respects," he said to me.

"He does indeed," and it was the voice I'd heard in my nightmares for ten years. Please God, no. Please. But there he was, my own personal demon, Tim McShane. Or, at least, Tim McShane was somewhere inside that fat old man, shrouded in smoke from his own cigar, who blocked the door.

"Hello folks," he said. "Welcome home, Nora," and I couldn't say a word.

Ann grabbed my hand. Spike O'Donnell's wife looked at me. "Hello, McShane," Spike O'Donnell said. "Didn't know you were a friend of Michael Kelly."

"Not his friend," Tim said. "Hers," and he took my arm. And now, I did start to talk.

"Not here, Tim, please. Not here. Come outside. Please." Henrietta had seen him. She was on her way back toward us. "Go to your aunt," I instructed Ann and pushed her toward Henrietta, then slipped my arm through Tim's. "Please," I said to him, and he let me turn him, lead him out the door and down the stairs.

I held the dark wood railing with one hand, pushed Tim with the other. Please let me get him out of here. Please. No one was coming up the stairs, thank God, and we were out and onto the front stoop. Tim had stopped resisting, and smiled at me now. A flicker of the fellow who had lifted me onto Johnny Murphy's old horse tram all those years ago.

"Take it easy now, Nora," he said. "No reason why two old pals shouldn't have a chat. Only trying to do the decent thing and pay my respects to Mame. Here," he said, pointing to the gangway that ran between the two buildings. "A private word after all these years."

He pulled me into the brick passageway between the Kelly–Doran Funeral Home and the three-flat next door. So narrow. Only the width of my outstretched arms. Almost like a tunnel. Hard to see the alley at the end of it in the gathering dusk.

I stopped and turned. But Tim pushed me hard. I put my hand against the uneven brick, trying to get a hold in the crumbling mortar. No pretense at manners now from Tim. No soft talk. Shoved me further down the gangway.

He blocked the entrance to the street with his bulk. Grabbed my wrist. "You bitch. You jumped-up, full-of-yourself bitch. Who do you think you are, anyway? Standing up there at the casket. Still holier than thou. Fooling that lot upstairs, when I know you're nothing but a slut. A double-crossing, two-timing slut."

He pushed me up against the brick wall, holding me by the neck, and slapped me. His thick hand covered my face from forehead to chin. He's going to break my cheekbones, my nose . . . I thought. I got my free hand up to deflect the next swing, but he only laughed.

"Go on. Fight back. More fun for me." He took my arm, bent it behind my back.

All my horrors came alive. The fear I'd fought off in Paris, when my mind was telling me Tim was far away and couldn't get me. But still, I'd wake up with my mouth dry. The blood pounding in my temples. That clutch in my stomach. And, now . . . this was real.

Say something to him, I thought. Say something. Don't scream . . . he wants that. Talk to him. You escaped him once with words. Come on, Nonie.

"Geeze Louise, Tim," I managed. "You've certainly stayed fit. You almost took my head off, and now you're going to snap my wrist in two. More bones in the wrist than in any other part of the body. I learned that when I was nursing in France. Soldiers. French, American, and even Irish fellows. Who knows—I might have taken care of some relative of yours, Tim. Where are the McShanes from again, in Ireland?"

"God how I hated all your palaver," Tim said. "Forgot how annoying you are with all that gabbing."

But he'd loosened his grip on my throat the slightest bit. "Throwing around big words, and pretending to know something about everything."

"True enough, Tim. That's me. Why, you should have heard me in French. Rattling on, and half the time not sure of what the words coming out of my mouth meant. I once said to a woman, *'Comprendez vous?'* and she said *'Oui. Je comprends. Mais vous parlez en Français bizarre.'* Wasn't that funny, Tim? My French was bizarre."

"You are nuts."

"That's me. Bizarre."

He leaned forward. Close enough so I could bring my knee up. "If they catch you, go for the bollocks," Cyril Peterson had told me when we were running from the Black and Tans in Ireland. I'm not afraid of him, I thought . . . Jesus, it's true. I'm furious. So mad that if I had a knife, I'd push it right through his heart and not think a thing about it.

How dare he put his hands on me? Using the strength he has, only because he's a man. Muscles giving him the last word in every argument. No risk to him, and me going along, letting Tim trap me because I was worried about what the neighbors would think.

Where are you Queen Maeve? Come on Grace O'Malley, pirate queen of Connacht.

And I roared. Not the high-pitched scream Tim was hoping for, but a war cry rising up from somewhere deep inside me as I brought my knee up with all the anger I felt at Tim, the Black and Tans, and all the idiots who bullied us into the Great War then watched from the sidelines as young men died and women and children starved. Starved as my own family had done in Ireland.

I remembered the story of the battle rage of Cúchulainn; even his hair became a weapon, standing out around his head, every strand razor sharp. A jolt went through my whole body, and my knee connected with something soft and fleshy between Tim's legs. He yelped, let go of my neck, and cupped his hands over his balls.

"Go for the bollocks and run," Cyril had said. So I headed toward the street but I stumbled, and Tim managed to grab the hem of my skirt. I went down facefirst into a patch of dirt on the side of the gangway.

Fool. Fool, a voice inside me said. You've lost all chance to sweet-talk him. He's an animal now. And I knew that Tim would strangle me as he had Dolly and her maid Carrie, and leave my body right here in this dark gangway. Another death for Michael's children to absorb. The final proof that the world was a brutal place.

No. No. He pulled me back toward him, but I found the buttons at my waist. Undid them, until it was only my skirt he had in his hand. Then, I was up and running, almost to the street, when again Tim grabbed me from behind, wrapping his arm around my middle, and lifting me up.

"Let me go. Let me go!" I said. But he shook me up and down—the way a bear must do before he crushes the life out of a baby fawn.

"Put her down." A fellow stood on the sidewalk in front of the gangway—a command. Too dark to see his face. "Do it, Tim," he said.

"Get out of here, Spike," Tim said.

Spike O'Donnell, and his wife behind him. "Help me! Please," I tried to yell, but Tim squeezed me so hard the words came out as grunts.

Spike's wife stepped toward me, but Spike stretched out his arm, stopping her.

Is Spike O'Donnell going to leave Tim to it? Some man–woman Donnybrook going on, and he's not going to involve his wife in something ugly. . . . Plenty of Bridgeport couples tussle back and forth, and a fellow raised to use his fists sometimes forgets himself . . . though not in public and not when both are well into middle age.

I heard Spike tell his wife to go back to the wake. "Bring the Larney brothers down." Tim heard that, too.

"Calling in the coppers, are you Spike?" Tim said. "A good joke to tell the fellas. Big, bad Spike O'Donnell crying for the cops. Ha. Ha. Ha."

And now, Tim laughed, a horrible sound. Spike came forward. "You've gone nuts, Tim. Let her go. I'll take you for a beer downstairs."

But Tim was backing up, all the time braying in my ear and squeezing the breath out of me.

"That's enough, McShane." John Larney's voice. He and his brother, Tom, were there with Spike. Thank God. They'll stop him. But I mustn't pass out. I mustn't. "Nothing lower than a man who beats a woman," John Larney said.

"Feck off, Larney. This bitch has had it coming to her for years. No broad makes a chump of Tim McShane. Dolly McGee tried, and where is she now? Burning in Hell with all the other mouthy dames who tormented their husbands. Got away with it, didn't I? Fooled all of you."

The two Larney brothers stepped into the gangway, and Tim eased his grip for a minute. I managed a breath. Twisted my shoulders, but then I felt something cold pressed against the back of my neck. Dear God. A gun. And I knew Tim was going to shoot me. Right there with the Larneys looking on, he'd kill me. Beyond any calculation.

"A gun," I managed to get out. "He's got a gun."

"Move, and you're dead," Tim said to me. "My car's parked in the alley, and the two of us are going for a spin, Nonie dear. I remember how much you liked riding with me."

We backed away from the Larneys. Getting further from the street, and any hope. He will get away with it. Dump my body somewhere and take off.

"It's over, Tim." The voice came from behind us. "Drop her, and get out of here."

Tim turned, still holding me, and there was Spike O'Donnell only a few feet from us, holding a pistol with two hands. "Go on, Spike, fire, and you'll kill her, and I'll kill you," Tim said.

Spike lowered the pistol and stepped to the side of the gangway. "Leave her and go."

Tim laughed again, pushed me forward. I managed to get my feet down, and we were parallel with Spike when I saw the barrel of Spike's gun come up a few inches. I swung my legs toward the wall, and pushed hard. Tim staggered. A gunshot. "My knee," Tim yelled. "You bastard." I dropped to the ground.

Tim fired at Spike O'Donnell. But the bullet hit the wall. Spike fired again, not aiming at Tim's knees anymore, but trying to kill him. He did. Four more shots into Tim's chest, and now I was screaming.

The Larney brothers ran in from the street. Tim was a heap, wedged between each side of the walkway. John knelt down, put his fingers on Tim's neck, and shook his head.

"Self-defense," Spike O'Donnell said. "You both saw."

I crawled away from Tim's body and stood up. All I felt was relief. I'm alive. Thank you, God. I'm alive. And Tim McShane was dead. I'm alive. I looked up at Spike O'Donnell, who was talking to John and Tom Larney now. "Self-defense," John Larney said, nodding his head.

"Three witnesses," Spike added.

"You saved my life," I said to Spike. "I'll tell . . ." I stopped. Witnesses. I'll be in court on the stand, telling the whole world about my relationship with Tim McShane.

"And he confessed to killing Dolly McGee," John Larney said.

"Poor old Dolly," Spike said. "My mother took me to hear her sing at McVickers. Lovely woman. Beautiful voice."

He put a foot on Tim's shoulder. "A bully. No jury in Chicago will convict me. Probably congratulate me for avenging Dolly McGee."

"True enough, Spike," Tom Larney said. "A waste of time and money to bring you to trial. I think John and I heard shots, and found McShane dead in the gangway. Not a surprise these days."

"Not a surprise at all," Spike said. "Might find my body like this one of these days."

"No," I said.

"No?" John Larney said. "You want a trial?"

"I mean, no, Spike's not going to be killed. You'll die in bed, Spike. I promise. What you've done for me will bless you. You'll die an old man in bed."

Which he did. Twelve attempts on his life, but Spike survived them all. Became an actor, if you can believe it. Usually played the bad guy.

4

"I'm perfectly capable of managing the house with Jesse's help," I said to Rose. "Go home to John."

"He was willing to move in here—plenty of room. But police have to live within Chicago city limits, and even if John chanced ignoring the rule, some begrudger would report him, and—"

"Don't worry. I spoke to Michael this morning."

A month after Mame's funeral. Mid-August. School starting soon. Rose and I were back on the porch. The little ones napping, the big kids out playing. Jesse on her afternoon off. I had the logistics all figured out. "Michael can drive Rosemary, Ann, and Mike to St. Blaise School in the morning on his way to his office, while I dress Marguerite and Baby Frances and give them breakfast. Jesse arrives at nine and stays until six, so I'll walk over and pick up the older kids, help Jesse get dinner, and—"

"I thought you planned to return to Paris," Rose said.

"I do eventually. But I can't leave these kids now. Michael seems undone by grief, and well . . ." I stopped. "They're lovely children. Ann has Mame's smile, and sometimes Rosemary lifts her head in a way that's my aunt Máire to a tee."

"And I see my mother's eyes in those big blue ones of Marguerite," Rose said.

The McCabe girls' home place was in County Cavan, near Mountain Lodge. Though only Rose had ever seen the family farm. Their father had died before Mame was even born. Rose and their mother, pregnant with Mame, were sent back to live with the Lynches, her mother's people in Bailieborough, until Mame was born and was old enough to be left with the grandmother so Rose and her mother could set out across the sea. No place for them. It would be ten years before their mother earned enough money to send for Mame. A neighbor brought her on the ship, and sent her by train to Chicago.

A little girl with a note pinned to the front of her coat.

Mame told the story in the essay that won her the medal in the *Sun-Times* when she was in eighth grade. She'd written that she'd thought the Statue of Liberty was a very big Blessed Mother, welcoming her to America, and promising her that she would soon see her own mother. Which she did.

But the distance separating these little ones from their mother could never be crossed. Oh Mame, so much sadness in your life. She and Rose had never taken to the man their mother married to survive in Chicago. He'd lived on after their mother died too young. Which was why they moved into Aunt Kate Larney's boarding house, and finally had a bit of luck.

Rose married John, Aunt Kate's son, and she'd connected them both to all of us Kellys, because her sister was married to my uncle Steve, and Ed was their son. For a time it seemed Mame and Ed would marry, but it was my forty-five-year-old confirmed bachelor brother, Michael, with whom she fell in love and walked down the aisle of St. Elizabeth's Church in Brighton Park.

"I keep thinking she'll come down from the bedroom, ready to take the kids for a run in the car," Rose said.

"I'll take them on adventures, as she did. And, Rose, I have a bit of a secret plan. I mean, Argo's nice enough. A feel of the prairie out here, even though we're only five miles from Bridgeport."

"A good place to raise children," Rose said. "Lots of families are leaving the city for Riverside, and Beverly and Evanston."

"Exactly. Families," I said. "But how will Michael's kids feel with all their friends cocooned with a father, and a mother, and a dog? I think he should move back into Chicago, where they won't be slapped in the face with happiness every day."

"I don't know," Rose said.

"Look at our block, Hillock, in Bridgeport. My unmarried brother and sister living together. Below us, the Widow Hannigan, with her three grown children, and one downstate in prison for armed robbery. And across the way, the Rooneys, whose youngest will, always as his mother says, 'have the mind of a three-year-old.' She worries about what will happen to him when she goes. Which may be soon, she says, because there are bad hearts on both sides of my family."

"Poor woman," Rose said. "There's hardship everywhere. My mother used to say if everyone stood in a circle and put their troubles in the center, you'd pick up your own."

"True enough," I said. "But in Bridgeport, you'd know everyone else's trouble. Here, sadness is hidden by lawns and porches. Easier for Michael to meet a nice woman if he were going to Mass at St. Bridget's, attending the Corned Beef and Cabbage Dinner on St. Patrick's Day, and maybe calling the numbers at Bingo."

Rose said nothing. Me and my big mouth. As if Michael would replace Mame.

"Of course, Michael will be in mourning for a long time," I said. "I just meant that eventually . . ."

"And will eventually come for you, Nonie?" she asked me.

That's Rose. A saint, even now thinking about me.

"I know you had a . . . a . . . ," she said.

"Husband, Rose. I had a husband."

"Oh, Nonie, will you never stop lying? It's like you have a disease."

"What?"

Rose and I turned at the same moment to see Henrietta stand in the kitchen doorway.

I stood up so fast, I knocked over the wicker rocker I was sitting on.

"What are you doing here?" I said.

"My brother asked me to come," she answered. "He very kindly picked me up, along with my son who has offered to sacrifice himself to live here and help out. And none too soon. Next, you'll be telling the girls stories about your so-called husband. Show me a marriage certificate if you can."

"Jesus, Mary, and Joseph," I said.

"Watch your language, Nonie. It's behavior like that makes you such a bad influence."

I didn't bother to answer her but walked into the house and shouted, "Michael! Michael!"

He was coming in the front door, carrying what had to be Henrietta's suitcases.

"What is going on?" I asked.

He set down the suitcases and stayed bent over for a moment, as if he couldn't summon the effort to stand up straight.

"Nonie," he said. "Let me be honest. I know you mean well, but taking care of a house and children just doesn't suit you."

How I hate when somebody says "let me be honest." It always means "let me point out your faults . . . the ones you refuse to see."

"That's not fair. After all, I've fed and clothed myself for forty years, and I'd say I could do the same for you and your children." Not the time to go on about how I'd nursed soldiers during the war, I supposed. Though I was ready to launch into some defense.

"Here's the thing, Nonie. The girls are so young and impressionable. Easily influenced. And you . . ." He stopped.

"Are you getting ready to repeat some speech you learned from Henrietta?" I asked.

"She did mention a few things to me. I didn't realize how people, especially women, judge a family. I mean, Nonie, you haven't lived a conventional life. I would hate for the girls to find out about Tim McShane. Murdered at their own mother's wake."

"That's not fair, Michael. And, besides, the Larneys hushed that up."

"That's only one thing, Nonie. I wouldn't want your living with us to affect my girls' chances to make the right kinds of friends."

"You mean if you have a fallen woman living with you, your girls would be tarred with my brush. I'd be the rotten apple spoiling the barrel. The wolf decked out in sheep's clothing. . . ." I was trying to make him laugh by imitating Henrietta, and the cliché-ridden arguments she must have made to him.

I hoped he'd say, "Why the hell did I listen to her? We need you, Nonie. Stay."

But now, Henrietta was in the hallway.

"You are a slut and always have been," she said.

"For God's sake, Henrietta, I'm forty years old."

"You're forty-four, and still don't know how a decent woman behaves. And as for your so-called marriage—where's the proof? As I said, show me your marriage certificate."

"Now, Henrietta . . . ," Michael started.

"Michael, you can't put this madwoman in charge of your children," I shouted.

"Stop it. Both of you. Stop it," said Rose in a louder voice than I'd ever heard her use.

"But, Rose. It's not me. It's Henrietta," I said.

Then I heard crying from the nursery. We'd wakened Marguerite and Frances. Rose was shaking her head as she walked up the stairs.

If Rose turned on me, then I was done. "The children are in the backyard with Bobby and Stella Lambert listening to this—this unfair attack on me." I was still ready to fight my corner, but if Henrietta had convinced Michael that I was a fallen woman, and a bad influence on his children, imagine what she'd gotten the neighbors to believe. No smoke without fire is one of Henrietta's sayings, and I'm sure she has fanned every possible flame.

Dear God, I can hear her. Disappeared for ten years. Reported dead. Does Nora Kelly really think she can pick up where she left off? Become a member in good standing of this parish or any other, after doing things a respectable woman can't even put words on over there in Paris, France?

Now I could try to circulate another story. I was the widow of a fighter for Irish freedom, a hero. And why shouldn't I? It was true. I suppose I hesitated because Peter Keeley belonged to me alone, and I didn't want to trade information about him for a good reputation. I didn't have a marriage certificate. No civil ceremony, only that three-minute ritual in the chapel of the Irish College.

Worse for her to then spread the news that her poor sister, Nora, had stooped to lying about her past, which, of course, would confirm me in a shame I did not feel.

Get out, I told myself. Ed will lend you the money. You'll never fit in again. Stop pretending. It's not working anyway. Go back to Paris.

But then Mike and the two older girls swarmed around me. Ann and Rosemary each took a hand, and Mike wrapped his arms around my legs.

"Don't leave, Aunt Nonie," Ann said.

"Please, Henrietta, Nonie. Please." Rose had come down the stairs carrying Frances and holding Marguerite's hand.

I took a breath.

"Your aunt Henrietta and I both love you," I told the children. "And if she and I . . . Well, you know sisters, even grown-up ones, sometimes argue."

"Rosemary and I fight like cats and dogs," Ann said.

So. When John came to pick up Rose, I went with them. I'd go back to Ed's, for the time being anyway. I wasn't going to leave the Kelly kids, at least not now.

Stella Lambert told me I could call her anytime. "And when you come to Argo, knock on my door," she'd said.

Jesse had agreed to stay on, and I knew she was well able for Henrietta. Even she had said that with school starting, the children needed a regular schedule and Henrietta was a good organizer, if nothing else.

Mike was mad at me for leaving. He disappeared when it was time to say goodbye to me. I knew where he was. I'd found him before, in his mother's closet on the floor, her dresses a curtain to hide behind.

I took his hand, brought him out. "I'll visit you all the time," I promised. "Take you for treats and grand adventures. Your aunt Henrietta needs a place to live, and you wouldn't want her wandering the streets without a home. Imagine her and Toots sleeping on a bench somewhere," I said. "Not a pretty sight, Mike. Because you know she snores and snorts something awful. A public nuisance." And I pretended to be Henrietta—dropping my mouth open, and sending odd sounds through my nose.

He giggled. And then laughed. "You don't want the neighbors talking about that crazy Kelly woman. No, Mike, I'm afraid you have to be good to Henrietta. And I swear if she's not good to you, I'll, I'll . . ."

"Beat her up?" he asked.

"Yes, I will. Until her nose bleeds. I'll knock out her front teeth."

"And twist her wrist like she twists mine?"

"Absolutely," I said—and then I knew. I would guard these children no matter what. Henrietta was not going to destroy their spirits.

I'll stay in Chicago until I know they are safe, I thought. Please, God, sooner rather than later.

I couldn't go on hating Henrietta like this. Only one thing to do, go see Agnella.

I shouldn't have been shocked. After all, nuns had always been a part of my life and I had seen plenty of different habits with their pinched and pleated white head gear. But it was hard to believe that this was Agnella's face squeezed into this birdcage. But then she smiled and there she was; the little girl that Henrietta had brought to live with us all those years ago; those same blue eyes. Yes, this tall nun, Sister Mary Erigina, BVM was still Ag. I hadn't seen her in nearly fifteen years. How old is she now? Ten years younger than I was. So thirty-three—thirty-four, but ageless in the habit. We were in the parlor of Holy Family School in Mason City, Iowa, where she taught first grade.

"I would have come sooner, Ag, err, Sister. But your mother told me only immediate family was allowed to visit. And aunts didn't count."

Ag said, "I'd say you were immediate enough, Nonie." She smiled.

"You really are in there," I said.

"I am," she said, "and ready to listen."

"How did you know I . . ."

"No letter, no telephone call. Sister Portress came up to me during vespers just now. Touched my shoulder. Told me it was an emergency."

"I didn't mean to get you out of chapel. I can wait or come back tomorrow." I stood up.

"No, no, Nonie, sit down, tell me."

Oh dear God what do I say? How can I tell her that I hate her mother with every cell in my body? That she is making my life miserable. Tearing the family apart.

Agnella was so calm. I couldn't believe it. But I could see traces of Henrietta in her face. She must have known I needed some time to think because she started talking.

"I'm sorry I couldn't come for Mame's funeral," Agnella said. "But my mother is right. There are rules. It was hard for me to explain to Mother Superior how close an aunt by marriage can be. Two years ago Uncle Michael brought my mother and Toots along with his two oldest girls, Rosemary and Ann, down to visit me. I am so grateful to him for being so kind to my mother."

"Yes," I said.

He hadn't much choice, I thought to myself.

"And you, Nonie. What a wonderful surprise to have you alive. A real Easter miracle. I am so sorry you were so angry with the family that you pretended to be dead."

"That's not exactly what happened," I said.

"My mother wrote me and said that you didn't want to bother with us. But that she was very happy that you were alive."

I couldn't let that pass.

"Oh dear God, Ag. Your mother engineered the whole plan. She wanted me to pretend to be dead so Tim McShane would stop bothering her. I admit I went along. I was terrified of him. But she knew I was alive all along and didn't tell anyone."

Agnella paused and said, "I suppose she thought she was helping you in some way. My mother said McShane was murdered, found in an alley."

"She keeps you informed doesn't she? But believe me, Ag, I never wanted to be separated from you. All the time I was in Paris, I thought of you and the family."

"Paris," Agnella said, "was it very beautiful?"

"It was."

I found myself telling her things I hadn't mentioned to anyone else. Afraid they'd think I was bragging, having notions.

But Ag asked me question after question. "What was Notre Dame like? Did you walk along the Seine?"

I told her about my life there and the people I had met. "So many women, Ag, living lives that didn't depend on men." I described Madame Simone and Coco Chanel, who had created their own very successful fashion businesses. Gertrude Stein and Alice B. Toklas, who'd nurtured artists and writers. Natalie Barney, who'd constructed her own world and, of course, Maud Gonne, who had mixed revolution and poetry. "I suppose it's hard to imagine so much female power."

Agnella started laughing. She threw her head back. Her veil whipped behind her. The starched linen of her headdress seemed to stretch. "For heaven's sakes, Nonie. What do you think we sisters are? Thousands of us joined together, running schools and hospitals. Hundreds of orders of women throughout the world. . . . That's power!"

"Well yes," I said. "But nuns, Ag? They're bossed by bishops and priests and . . ."

More habit-shaking laughter from Agnella. "We bob and weave, Nonie. The men can be annoying, no question. You know our foundress, Mary Frances Clarke, never intended our community to be under the jurisdiction of the Church."

"She didn't?"

"She and four friends in Dublin simply wanted to get together and open a school for girls. A most unusual notion in the 1830s when women were not educated, especially poor women. But this action threatened the powers that be. Had to draw lines around them, call them religious women. Make them conform. Mary Frances had no choice, really, but to go along. There was so much need in Ireland and among the Irish over here! Sometimes I think Mary Frances and her friends decided to come to the American frontier to get away from the Irish hierarchy. The Presentation Sisters down the road have the same story, and so do the Sisters of Mercy. All founded by extraordinary Irish women who had to figure out a way to placate the hierarchy so they could follow their vocations. Oh yes, we wash and iron Father's surplice and serve him bacon at his after-Mass breakfast, but we do it so we can have the Order's bank account in our name and own our own property. We open schools and hospitals where there are none and give a leg up to the poor."

"Revolutionaries!" I said. "Like Maud Gonne and her Daughters of Erin."

"Oh, nothing as spectacular as that, Nonie. We fool them with our humility. Take my name, for example. The priest chaplain, a very educated man, gave me Sister Mary Erigina as a kind of joke, I think. What would a seventeen-year-old girl from Bridgeport make of a ninth-century philosopher monk who traveled from Ireland to the courts of the French kings and debated all the scholars of Europe? What kind of patron would that be for a first-grade teacher? But I read up on him in the novitiate. He was a great fellow, Nonie. He signed himself Johannes Erigina—John the Irishman—and got his theology from St. John. God is love. No divisions. He wrote that we were all one in Nature." Ag lowered her voice. "He didn't believe in Hell. God was all good, beyond small-minded judgment."

"Oh, Ag," I said. "If only you had known Peter Keeley, my professor at the Irish College. He probably had manuscripts written by your fellow Erigina." And so I told her about how I had loved Peter, and that brief ceremony in the chapel. "We were united in the eyes of God, and still are, Ag. Death didn't change that."

"Of course not," she said.

"A part of me doesn't believe he's really gone. It was hard enough for me to accept Mam's death. For a year, I woke up expecting to see her in the kitchen, putting on the kettle. And I was at her wake and funeral. I never saw Peter's body, or visited his grave. Part of me hopes . . ."

"But he *is* still with you, Nonie. Erigina wrote that the souls of the dead and the living share one reality, beyond time and space," she said.

"I guess I meant something more material."

"Denying pain won't make it go away. That was the mistake my mother made. It leads to bitterness and . . . I really wish my mother had found a husband. Only twenty-two when she was widowed. Now I realize how young that was, and with three children."

"Who would ever want . . . ?" I started.

"Oh, Nonie. I wish you could see beyond my mother's bluster. She's a lonely woman who feels hard done by."

"Let's be honest, Ag, your mother is sick."

I thought I'd gone too far. But Ag nodded. "Sick and suffering. I pray for her every day. And I thank God she has Michael's children to love."

"Love?" I said.

Ag said, "She does care for them. Give her a chance, Nonie."

"But Ag, I feel like she just can't stand me."

"I blame myself for that. Think of it, Nonie. She was only fifteen when I was born. My mother thinks I preferred you to her. It was just that we were having such a hard time out in the country after my father died. And Granny Honora was so welcoming to us. You were so much fun, Nonie. You inspire me even now."

"I do?" I asked.

"I try to make every day in the classroom joyful for my dolls and buttons. I am so lucky to be teaching them. It's the delight of my heart. Only five or six years old when they come to me, those little faces shining. Every one is so different with the beauty of God in each. I thank Him for the joy that teaching them gives me."

She's really happy, I thought. How can I tell her that her mother makes me miserable? Must be some good in Henrietta to produce a daughter like this.

Dammit, maybe I always have assumed the worst about Henrietta. Maybe I have to try harder to see my part in our feud. A mother at fifteen. No wonder she resents me.

"You will try, Nonie," Agnella said to me as I was leaving, "and be good to Ed. He gives so much to everybody. He needs some support. And you and he have special bonds as 'the redheads.'"

At least after talking to Ag I was able to be civil to Henrietta.

"Sister Mary Erigina wrote to me about your visit. She said she'll be praying for you," Henrietta said to me at the next Sunday dinner.

"For us both," I corrected her.

5

CHRISTMAS 1923

I'd hoped Ed would help my brother to look beyond his suffering, but I actually heard Ed tell Michael, "It's not true that time heals. It only pushes the hurt further down, and it can flame up at any time. Like now at Christmas."

Only a few months after Mame had died. Rose and John, Michael and his children, Henrietta and Toots joined my sister Ann and brother Mart, who still lived together in the flat on Hillock where we'd all grown up, at Ed's. Our aunt Nelly, Ed's mother, had decorated a big Christmas tree with the ornaments her German father had used during our childhood when the whole Kelly clan gathered to dance and to tell stories at the Lang house.

I remember Mam telling me Aunt Nelly and her sister Kate looked like their Irish mother, whose brother had worked digging the I & M Canal with my great-uncle Patrick. The family had lived in Lockport before they came to Chicago. Both sisters married Irish men—Nelly to Uncle Steve, Ed's father, and Kate to James Larney. Both sons wed Irish girls—Ed to Mary Roche and John Larney to Rose. Funny how the Irish find each other, down through the generations.

A sad occasion, that Christmas. The girls were very quiet. Even Mike and Ed Junior barely spoke to each other as they sent the Lionel Train, a present from Ed Junior's father, circling around the track in the living room.

I had to borrow money from Ed to buy the book I gave each child, and for the film I loaded into my Seneca to take photographs, acting the fool to get a smile from the children.

I had been visiting the kids in Argo almost every Sunday and taking them out for a spin. Rose and John joined us for dinner most weeks, and sometimes Ed and Ed Junior came. Henrietta had won, and whatever Ag had written to her, she was at least pleasant. Though, last Sunday, she asked me how did I feel being waited on hand and foot in a big mansion, with poor Aunt Kate run ragged and Ed doling out pocket money to me as if I were a child.

Believe me, many a time I had wanted to ask him for the price of a boat ticket back to France. But Ed seemed to enjoy talking about the projects he was working on, and I'd been back to the stadium site a few times to photograph the progress of the construction.

Rose told me over and over I brought some enjoyment to all the kids. Forty-four years old and in charge of fun. My trouser suit hung in the cedar closet as a kind of challenge. A few more months, and I'd put my true self on again, I thought at the end of that Christmas night.

I needed a job. I had to earn my own money.

Ann came up and touched my camera. "It was a lady took our picture, too."

"That's right, it was." Mabel Sykes. Maybe she could use a helper.

"I keep copies of all my photographs," Mabel Sykes said, as she went through a file drawer looking for the portrait she did of Michael and Mame and the kids. I'd mentioned it when I introduced myself, and Mabel wanted to see it.

"Never know when somebody wants another print. Of course, it's the movie stars that really sell. I make about five thousand dollars a year with my Rudolph Valentino collection. He told a newspaper I was his favorite photographer, and that's what stirred up the market. I wish that Gloria Swanson would do the same. Talk about difficult. She'd like everyone to forget that she was just another Chicago kid, working as an extra at Essanay, when I took those pictures of her that got Hollywood interested. In town just last month. She was promoting a movie she did with Valentino, and he managed to get her into my studio. But Geez Louise, what an ordeal. Gloria's only five foot nothing, and she wanted me to make her look tall and regal. In her movies, they shoot her stretched out on pillows, dressed like a hoochie-coochie girl in the desert, but I wanted something classier. Finally did that close-up."

She pointed to an enlarged portrait over her head.

"Look into those eyes. There's the woman who fought her first husband, Wallace Beery, to a standstill. I just heard she's divorcing number two. Why do we smart dames clutter our lives up with jerks?"

She stopped and looked at me. Does she know about Tim McShane? Keep your mouth shut, Nonie, I told myself.

"My first, Melvin Sykes, was a disaster," Mabel said. "I was only nineteen when I married him, and he was close to forty. Sold me a bill of goods. Said that I was so beautiful that I owed it to the world to be photographed."

She stopped going through her files. "I found out soon enough that that was the line he used on every woman he fancied. Girls, really. Went for the young ones. A month after I divorced him, he got himself engaged to a seventeen-year-old—and he was forty-eight. Can you believe it? Then he had the nerve to send me a bill from a beauty shop, where he'd gone for the full 'Restorative Treatment.' Hair dyed. Facials. Manicures. And injections with some kind of youth serum. And I had to pay. At least the girl's mother stopped the marriage, but Melvin just went on and found another dumb young woman. Number four. Living in California now, though. Far away, thank God."

Again she looked at me. I wondered, Does she just assume I have some rat in my past?

"And then, don't I go out and marry again. Barsanti thinks he's a duke or something. At least Melvin taught me photography. Men. Can't live with them, can't live without them. I hope you're not entangled."

"I'm not," I said.

"Oh, here it is," Mabel said. "The Michael J. Kelly family." She held up the photograph to me. "I remember them. A nice family. How are they doing?"

"Ah, well, Mabel, it's a sad story." I pointed to Mame in the portrait. "She's dead."

"Did her husband kill her?"

"What? Of course not. How can you say such a thing?"

"Sorry. Sorry. I've got murder on the brain. Maurine Watkins, you know the gal who reports for the *Trib*, wants me to go to Cook County Jail and photograph two accused murderesses. They're going on trial one after another. But how the hell could I get my lights and equipment into the jail? Plus, the *Tribune* doesn't pay much, and I can't see there being a market for pictures of women who murdered their husbands."

"I could do it. I could take the photographs."

"You?"

"Yes, look." I held up my Seneca. "I don't need lots of equipment. Only this and a light pack. I could get candid shots."

"Candids?" She spit the word back at me. "A fancy name for snapshots taken with a Brownie camera. Do you know how much money my lights, my backdrops cost?"

She shut the file cabinet and led me to the main section of the studio, where four lights were mounted on tall stands, aimed at a kind of stage.

"I pose my subjects against carefully chosen scenes," she said, and took me to a section behind the stage where dozens of painted theatrical flats leaned against a wall. She pulled one out. "See? This is an English garden."

Pushed it back and took out a painted forest and, then—would you believe it?—Paris. With the Eiffel Tower front and center. I laughed.

"I used to take pictures of people standing in front of the real thing," I said.

"Mmmm."

"Sometimes I'd print the photos at odd angles, or play around with the light. . . ."

"Oh no. You're not an *artist* are you?" she asked, as if repeating a bad word.

And I said, "No. No." All the time apologizing in my mind to Eddie Steichen, who had given me the Seneca that afternoon in Paris, and who definitely believed that photographers should be artists.

"Anyone who comes here looking for a job, telling me they're an artist, gets thrown out. They can't focus the damn camera, and call fuzziness art."

"Terrible," I said.

"Okay, Nora, it's nearly noon. I'm supposed to meet Maurine for lunch. Come with me, and see if you can convince her to hire you. All I want is ten percent of the fee and the photographs."

"But, Mabel, I thought you said you couldn't resell pictures of women who kill their husbands."

"Well, you never know. Come on."

Maurine Dallas Watkins wore a rope of pearls, looped three times around her neck and a knee-length skirt with a tailored jacket that hung just so from her narrow shoulders. Mabel Sykes and I watched as she made her way through Henrici's.

The head waiter had bowed to us when he led us to a table in the corner, facing the door. Reserved for Maurine every lunchtime.

I recognized three aldermen, the chief of police, and Spike O'Donnell with two of his fellows in the restaurant. Spike winked at me, but said nothing.

Maurine had been a half hour late, and was in no hurry to reach us. She stopped at every table. Saying something that made the men laugh. Though, after she'd passed, I saw them look at each other. They're afraid of her, I thought.

"Sorry," she said, sitting in the seat facing the room the waiter had told us to save for her.

"In court all morning."

"The murder case?" Mabel asked.

She nodded.

"Beulah Annan killed her lover, but the fellow was a louse. She's guilty as sin, I'd say. But William Scott's putting on quite a show. Self-defense, he says, though Annan's lover was unarmed. I think the fix might be in. The judge accepts all Billy's evidence and sustains every objection he makes to the prosecution."

"Did Billy bribe the judge?" Mabel asked.

"I don't know," Maurine said. "Billy Scott's mother is a daily communicant at Our Lady of Sorrows, and the head usher at the church is the judge's brother. The judge will probably instruct the jury to issue Beulah a medal. Justice, Chicago style." She shrugged and turned to Mabel.

"I can get you into the jail to get a picture of Beulah, and her cellmate, another dame who rubbed out her lover. Two in one. I think it makes a better story. The revenge of the flappers."

"Here's the problem, Maurine," Mabel said. "I'm booked solid for the next month. Wedding photos, big shows at the McVickers and the Schubert, and—"

"What's wrong with you, Mabel? Don't you want to help free our suffering sisters?"

"Are you going to add something to the *Trib*'s chintzy payment?"

"Don't be ridiculous."

"Well then, I offer you Nora Kelly." She pointed at me. "Trained in Paris. She'll do it. She'll work cheap."

Maurine didn't say anything.

"And she's connected. Ed Kelly's cousin."

"Ed Kelly," Maurine said. "The fellow who became the city's chief engineer because he can land a punch. Interesting. Did you know that's the story Colonel McCormick tells at dinner parties?" Maurine asked me. "McCormick goes on about how, when he was president of the Sanitary District, Ed came before him, thinking he'd be fired for socking the evil foreman who favored Republicans. Instead McCormick gave him a raise. The grand gesture. That's my boss's way. Of course, when I asked for more money, he told me I was being ungrateful, and should be satisfied at what I was being given, and how many women were reporters on a big city daily? I suppose your cousin was a boxer."

"As a matter of fact, he was."

"Figures. The *Tribune*'s about to sponsor a program for young men. 'What is it?' you may ask. A course to teach them how to be auto mechanics, carpenters, or even how to play the fiddle? Oh no. We're going to be putting on the Golden Gloves—a citywide contest with boxing matches in every division, from feather to heavyweight. Young lads will be rewarded for beating each other to a pulp. Caesar and his gladiators, I guess."

I tried to explain to Maurine that clubs, like the Brighton Park Athletic Association, really provided a place for young men to gather, and that boxing was only part of it.

"Oh, I know that," she said. "Politics is the main bout. That's where the aldermen organize the army that gets out the vote, and guards the ballots. Democracy's young warriors."

The waiter arrived to take our order. "The usual," Maurine told him. "Try it," she said to Mabel and me. "Smothered pork chops with mashed potatoes and gravy." She held up three fingers.

"Whatever about Colonel McCormick, you can't deny that Ed worked hard to learn engineering. And he has wonderful plans for Chicago," I said.

"Good luck to him. Nothing's going to happen until Thompson gets back in. The powers that be in this city, in this country, still see you people as the alien invaders. Oh, you're entertaining. We like to watch you Irish box, play baseball, sing and dance, and, no question, you've got a flair for politics. But you're not us, and us are the ones in charge."

The waiter set our plates down, and I must say, the pork chops were good. No talking while we ate. When Maurine finished, she put down her fork and said to me, "Now about those murder cases I'm covering. I'm calling Beulah Annan the beauty of the cell block, and Belva Gaertner, who was a cabaret singer, the most stylish babe on Murderess Row. You wouldn't believe these two. They give each other permanents and manicures. Treat the trial like some kind of fashion show, and Annan's husband is footing the bill. I need your pictures for my big article in the Sunday edition. But I'm also writing a play about the cases. Beulah's going to be Roxie Hart, and Belva, Velma Kelly."

"But you're making them both Irish, and they aren't. Are they?"

"No, Beulah is a Bible belter from Kentucky, and Belva was born in some little Protestant town downstate. But Broadway audiences expect immoral babes to be Irish. They like to be confirmed in their prejudices. Besides, it gives them a chance to laugh at what they fear—a Mick with a gun."

"But, Maurine, that's not really fair," I said.

"I'm not asking your opinion. I just want to know if you can take the photographs."

"I can," I said.

"When?"

"How about right now?"

Maurine laughed. "Thank you, Mabel," she said. "You brought me my kind of dame. Come on, Nora. You and I are going to Cook County Jail."

"Ten newspapers competing and all determined to give the people what they wanted, which was murder and mayhem, with a good-looking dame in the middle of it," Maurine explained to me in the cab on the way to Cook County Jail. "Hire women to get the sob sister stuff."

Beulah and Belva weren't the only women being tried for murder that year, but Maurine made them the embodiment of the whole kit and caboodle. Flappers and jazz babies, the modern woman asserting herself.

In most cases, it was more like some wife who was sick of being beaten up by her husband. But Beulah and Belva were different. After all, they'd shot their lovers. "Not good to mix gin and guns," Belva told me that day when I took her picture.

The Seneca let me shoot in low light, so I was able to photograph Beulah stretched out on her bunk, reading a magazine framed by the bars of her cell.

I caught Belva with her head in her hands.

Maurine did go on to write her play, and made her heroines Irish. She called it *Chicago*, and it did okay on Broadway. Then Cecil B. DeMille made a movie of it. Only, in his version, Roxie suffers—whereas, in real life, Beulah got off.

Maurine liked the photographs I did. "Good," she said. "They look forlorn and remorseful," and told me she'd be willing to work with me again on a story. "See if you can get some tips from Ed Kelly. Some contractor who's getting paid three times what the job's worth, and spending all his money on a floozy. You know what I mean."

And I'd said to her, "What about a feature on how Ed's trying to save the Palace of Fine Arts?" The other members of the South Park Board were determined to tear down the only building left of the White City so proudly built for our 1893 World's Fair. But Ed was fighting back, though he was losing.

"The demolition's contract has been awarded," I told Maurine.

"Somebody's getting a kickback from the wreckers," she said.

"Ed asked them would Paris tear down the Eiffel Tower? But he was outvoted."

"You might have something," Maurine said. "The Chicago women's clubs are trying to save the building, and getting nowhere. Not one politician is willing to put an ounce of clout behind them. Do you think Ed would join the ladies?"

"Oh yes. As a kid, Ed spent every spare minute watching them build the Fair. That's why he's an engineer. He'll get involved—no problem."

"The wife of Potter Palmer II and Ed Kelly. The beauty and the beast. Let's try."

"Jesus, Nonie, I couldn't meet Maurine Watkins in Henrici's," Ed said to me that night at home.

"Why not?"

"The word would go around that I was leaking a story to her."

"Why not at the building itself?"

The next evening we were waiting on the steps of the Palace of Fine Arts. The only structure left of the 1893 Fair. It had lived on a bit as the Field Museum of Natural History, exhibiting artifacts from the Fair. But then, Marshall Field had built a brand-spanking-new building for his collection closer to downtown. And now the poor Palace was crumbling.

"Think about it, Nonie," Ed said. "Chicago beat out every other city, even New York, to host the celebration of the four hundredth anniversary of Columbus's landing. And then we were a year late. Opened in 1893, not 1892. A lesson there, Nonie. If you make something happen, people forget how you got it done."

I walked over to one of the tall white columns. "Chicagoans do have nerve," I said. "Imagine creating a whole world in, what, three years?"

"Yes," he said. "Remember how I haunted this place during construction? Mostly Irishmen on the crews, and ready enough to explain what they were doing to an interested kid. I remember this fellow called Disney, from King's County in the middle of Ireland, said the place would be Tír na nÓg, a real fairyland. That people would visit over and over. And he was right."

"Hard workers, the Irish," I said. "No matter how people slander us."

"We built America," Ed said. "Canals, railroads, skyscrapers, highways. It was the Irish above all who did the work." He waved his hand at the empty park. "These sixty acres were covered with the grandest buildings. Exhibitions from every state, and most countries."

"And the Ferris wheel. Don't forget the Ferris wheel," I said.

"Such a feat of engineering. Ten stories high. 'Make no small plans.' I heard Daniel Burnham himself say that."

"Sad that it's come to this," I said. I pointed to the vines growing around the columns. Weeds were breaking through the cement steps. The whole building was gray and dingy. Paint peeling and half the roof gone.

We climbed the broken stairs as a small roadster came bumping over the grass and stopped right below us.

"What a dump," Maurine said as she came up to us on the steps. "This place is not worth saving."

"It is," Ed said.

"How you doing, Ed?" Maurine asked.

"Very well, Miss Watkins," Ed replied. "I think it would be wrong to give up and destroy the building. But it'll cost some money to restore it."

"Millions. But then you fellows are good at getting bond issues through," Maurine said.

"There's private investment, too. Julius Rosenwald's interested."

"Oh, for God's sake. I heard he's got some nutty idea about a science museum. Why would a city interested in women murderers want to learn about science?" she asked.

"You might be surprised," Ed said.

"What did P. T. Barnum say? No one ever went broke underestimating the American public," she said.

"You're very cynical, Miss Watkins."

"But she's not," I said. "She can do the sob sister stuff as well as anybody."

Maurine laughed. "Alright, get that little peashooter out." I held up the Seneca.

"The light's great," I said. "Do you want Ed standing next to the pillar?"

"Hang on," Maurine said. And just then a chauffeured Daimler pulled up behind Maurine's little car. A woman got out.

"Jesus Christ," Ed said. "It's Mrs. Potter Palmer."

"Always punctual," Maurine said.

She was a tall woman with a pleasant face, dressed in a bright blue suit, her skirt below the knees, and her hair dressed in a kind of semi-bob. No flapper, but not an old fogey either. Ed and Mrs. Palmer stood together looking up at the derelict building. A bit of sunlight washed over the white pillars, settling on the two of them.

Nice.

"I've got the shot," I said to Maurine, but she was looking away. Then I heard a motor. Not an automobile engine, more like the sound of a locomotive.

A bulldozer grunted its way toward us. Big, painted a shiny yellow. Black smoke poured out of the tailpipe.

"The driver is going to crash into the building," Mrs. Palmer shouted. She ran right into the bulldozer's path. Ed moved fast. I thought he would pull her away, but instead he stood next to Mrs. Palmer. Both of them waved their arms, shouting, "Stop! Stop!"

"Get the picture. Shoot that!" Maurine yelled at me. And I did. Ed and Mrs. Palmer confronted the bulldozer.

As the big machine moved ever closer I kept snapping pictures.

Less than two feet between the bulldozer and Ed and Mrs. Palmer when the driver finally stopped. Turned off the motor. He climbed down from the cab. Started shouting at Ed.

"What the hell's wrong with you? You want to get killed?" the man yelled.

"You idiot," Ed yelled back. "What are you doing?"

"My job," the man said, "Adams Demolition. We're pulling this wreck down."

"You have no authority," Ed said.

"My boss told me to bust a wall or two. Get things going. Once a job's started, it's hard to stop."

"I'm Ed Kelly of the South Park Board. We never authorized this."

"Somebody did."

"Get out of here until I figure out what's going on," Ed said.

"Screw you," the fellow said.

Ed moved forward. "Listen, pal. I don't want any unpleasantness in front of these ladies, but . . ."

Ed had the fellow by about fifty pounds and five inches. The guy grumbled and turned around.

"Admirable, Mr. Kelly," Mrs. Potter Palmer said as Ed walked her to the Daimler.

"What luck," I said to Maurine, "that the bulldozer came along just as Mrs. Potter Palmer arrived."

"Luck had nothing to do with it," she said. "Who do you think called Adams Demolition? Now," she said. "Those photographs better be good."

And they were, thank God. Mabel Sykes let me use her darkroom, and I worked on the prints, turning each photograph into a dramatic contest between good (Ed and Mrs. Potter Palmer), framed in light, and evil (the bulldozer), dark and ominous.

Maurine got the story on the front page. "Park Board Member Ed Kelly Joins Women's Clubs in Battle to Save Our Heritage," said the headline, spread out over the three-column photograph.

Maurine wrote, in her usual snappy style, about the society dame and the big redheaded Irishman. She quoted Mrs. Potter Palmer II as saying: "Women are taking our place in public life. This grand building will be bulldozed over our dead bodies." And she told me my picture sold the story.

"Great to portray a millionaire society woman as a damsel in distress. Ed is the big Irish galoot, the corrupt pol, who grows a conscience because of her."

"And she's not Irish? Right?" I said.

"Can't be. Do you think anyone would have paid attention to Jane Addams, if her name was Jane O'Toole, or Jane Lipinski? She'd be just another immigrant woman bellyaching. But Jane's a blue blood. Could have had an easy life. Instead she's working in the slums. Lady Bountiful. A kind of melodrama. People like that."

"So you tell people what they already think they know?"

"Got it in one, Nora. Of course the details matter. And the picture."

Ed loved the story, but still didn't know if he could get the board to vote to save the building. The Republicans on the board had given Adams the demolition contract, and he was screaming bloody murder. Ed's only hope was if George Brennan, the Democratic boss, could rally some opposition.

An interesting man, Brennan. He'd been a coal miner in Braidwood, south of the city, and lost a leg. He got a job teaching the miners' children, moved to Chicago and became a power in the Democratic Party. But, as Ed explained to me, there was no unity in the party.

"So many factions. The Irish fighting among ourselves, and then the Poles, Czechs, Bohemians, and Jews each with a candidate they want to run for alderman, and everyone's looking for a share of the patronage jobs."

"But our campaign is working," I said to him. I pointed to the piles of letters on his desk. We were in his office, three days after the story broke.

Chicago might be rushing forward into the future, but the past held memories we all shared. Almost everyone in the city older than forty had visited the World's Fair, remembered the fun of the midway, where a tribe of Moroccan Bedouins danced next to the wild animal shows, and Buffalo Bill's extravaganza played four times a day.

Every country had an exhibit. Granny Honora brought all of her grandchildren to the Irish village, hoping to awaken in us a love for the language and traditions of Ireland. I remember Granny Honora saying that if we Irish lost our language and the old stories, we'd lose ourselves.

But I must say the corned beef and cabbage in Mrs. Hart's Donegal Castle, complete with entertainment, had been more popular than the display of ancient manuscripts, and it was the Ferris wheel that had captivated us.

How many families such as ours had ridden up the top as night fell and thousands of lights outlined the White City? How could we destroy the last souvenir of that time?

"I'm going to see Brennan this afternoon," Ed said.

"Let me come," I said. "We'll take the letters you got, and the ones the *Tribune* received."

"Well, not many Democrats read the *Tribune*," he said.

"What about the ten thousand signatures Mrs. Potter Palmer and the other women have collected?" I said.

"Not much compared to the five million voters in Chicago, Nora. But come with me if you want."

"The South Park Commissioners should respond to the will of the people, George," Ed concluded, after what I thought was a very good presentation. Ed had shown him the letters, and I brought a blown-up copy of the confrontation-with-the-bulldozer photograph.

We sat in Brennan's office, and he hadn't said one word beyond "Good afternoon." But now he looked up. "Ed, you're wasting your time with those society suffragettes," Brennan said. "None of them will ever vote Democratic. They'll do what their rich Republican husbands tell them to."

Not much of the Braidwood coal miner left in this well-dressed man. Hard to believe that he was from a place where I'd seen men walking bent in the streets, their faces streaked with black. Down in the mines before sunrise, and not home until after sunset.

"You can't assume these women don't have minds of their own," I said. "They're fed up with Thompson and Capone, and if the Democrats really get behind this effort, who knows?"

Brennan looked at me. "So you're a political expert?"

"I'm not, but I am a woman, and I've got common sense. Ed may not be a politician, Mr. Brennan, but he's a builder. This building could inspire Chicago kids today, the way the White City did us. How does destroying a symbol of hope help anybody?" I said.

"Where'd she come from?" Brennan asked Ed.

"Bridgeport," Ed said. "But she's got a point. Why not take the high road?"

"Well, it's a road without a lot of traffic," Brennan said.

"Listen, George," Ed said. "The renovation could be done mostly with private money."

"Ed," Brennan said, "I just don't see what's in it for us. That building is rotting away, but the land is worth a fortune. I've got ten guys lined up with plans for apartment buildings, stores."

"Plenty of other places for that kind of development," Ed said.

"What's Payne's position?" Brennan asked Ed. The president of the board, a fellow named John Barton Payne, was a Democrat. But not exactly one of us. Born someplace in Virginia, he'd lived in Chicago as a young man, become a lawyer and a judge, then left the city for Washington. A member of Wilson's cabinet and later head of the Red Cross, he'd started an art museum in Richmond. No sharp elbows.

A figurehead, I supposed. Seventy years old, in office for twelve years since 1911, and probably happy enough to go along with the majority. I wouldn't have said Mr. Barton Payne was looking for backhanders from demolition companies, but he wasn't about to stand up to the fellows who were.

The South Park Board were all for tearing down the Fine Arts building and dug their heels in even more after the newspaper articles. How dare Ed go behind their back to the press. Not a gentlemanly thing to do, Payne had told him.

"Neither is destroying Chicago's heritage," Ed had responded. But Payne wouldn't budge. George Brennan agreed there was nothing for Ed to do but run against Payne for president, which meant getting some of the Republicans on the board to support him.

"Take care of a Republican and he becomes a Democrat," Ed said. "Or at least he's willing to deal."

And deal they must have, because a few weeks later, Ed was elected president of the South Park Board. The first thing he did was ask the Chicago voters to approve an eight-million-dollar bond issue in order to rescue and restore the Palace of Fine Arts. And it passed. Overwhelmingly.

"All thanks to you, Nora," Ed said to me the day the returns came in.

"Not really, Ed. Maurine and I might have gotten the ball rolling, but, dear God, the maneuvering you fellows have to do to make something happen."

"Well didn't Bismarck say that politics is the art of the possible?" Ed said.

"I don't know how much art's in it, but I suppose that other saying, 'The end justifies the means,' is true," I said.

"Yes," Ed said. "Though I sometimes wonder, Nora. I really do."

No fun in a victory that isn't shared, I thought. I wished Ed had a wife to pat him on the back. Ed and I were close, and I was grateful to be living with him, Aunt Nelly, and Ed Junior in that big Hyde Park house—but Ed needed to marry again and I had just the woman for him. His Mary had died five years ago, and enough time had passed. She would have wanted Ed to find someone.

Get Ed settled. See the Kelly kids through to the summer. Save the money I had started making working with Mabel and Maurine. Then I could think about returning to Paris and, from there, go to Ireland to find Peter Keeley's grave. Confront the pain, accept his death, and find some peace, as Ag had said. But first Ed needed a wife, and I had just the candidate. I wrote to Margaret Noll Kirk, the woman I'd nursed with in France who was living alone in Kansas City now that her mother had died, and invited her to visit me in Chicago.

She arrived in the middle of February. Nearly six years since I had seen her. Though she hadn't changed much. "Contained" is the word I always associated with her. Even her hair behaved. Molded to her head. The waves just so. Not like my flyaway bob.

A woman made to wear elegant clothes, Madame Simone had said, delighted to sell Margaret the copies she made of the great couturiers. Though Margaret herself went around the corner to Rue St. Honoré to buy from Coco Chanel. And it was a Chanel suit she wore now. The skirt well below her knees. Nothing of the flapper about Margaret.

Aunt Nelly took to her right away. After all, Margaret had an Irish mother and a German father, just as Aunt Nelly did. And Ed—well, not smitten, exactly. No boyish leap of the heart, but I could tell that he saw in Margaret what I had. A good woman who'd faced her own hardships—her mother dead, her brother killed in the war—and had come through. Of course, the fact that she was attractive helped. But I really think they connected on a deeper level. After a week in Chicago, during which Ed drove Margaret to every one of his construction projects, a match seemed obvious. But then, Margaret insisted on telling Ed about her two marriages. She'd asked me to come to Ed's study. Moral support, she explained. He sat at his desk as she explained how she'd been wed at age fifteen to a man who had a house that could accommodate her mother and brother, at a time when her family had no place to live. The union had not lasted. "He had our marriage annulled because I couldn't . . . well . . ."

Ed raised his hand, as if to say no need for details.

"I was old enough the second time, but I chose badly. He deserted me. In order to go to France, I had to divorce him, Ed."

There it was. Divorce. Not tolerated by our tribe.

"But, Margaret," I said. "He's dead. Tell Ed that. That husband is dead."

Margaret nodded.

"So there's no impediment to another marriage. Margaret's a widow, Ed," I said. "Tell him, Margaret."

But Margaret was silent, watching Ed. Now Aunt Nelly had told me that Ed had taken no interest at all in any of the young women she and her sister, Rose's mother-in-law, Aunt Kate Larney, had introduced to him. I of all people understood Ed's reluctance. No way I could replace Peter Keeley. But Ed needed a companion, and Ed Junior a mother. Aunt Nelly had told me she was feeling her age, and longed to turn over the running of the house to a capable woman. And here was Margaret. But, divorced. I waited.

Ed got up, walked over to Margaret, took her hand and turned to me. "Give us a few minutes, would you, Nonie?"

Please, God, I prayed, led Ed be open-minded. I thought of Agnella's fellow Erigina—God is love, not rules. Come on, Ed. Take a risk. Follow your heart.

And he did.

6

Margaret and Ed married in April of 1924 in a little church outside of Kansas City. They set themselves up in Chicago where she transformed that empty barn of a house in Hyde Park into what the *Tribune* called "a gracious home with a well-appointed ballroom." A ballroom . . . can you imagine?

"Mrs. Kelly entertains the crème de la crème of Chicago society."

Done and dusted, I'd thought. Ed happy and taken care of, and now if only my brother Michael could find a kind woman who would be a mother to Mame's children, then I could ease my way out of the web of Chicago, go back to Europe, and find Peter's grave in Ireland.

"Please don't go, Nonie," Rose said, when I told her I was thinking of leaving. "I don't get over to Argo as much as I want. John has been suffering recurring bouts of croup. Stay at least a few more months."

But where was I going to live? Ed and Margaret needed their privacy. But I couldn't spend the rest of my life on Hillock with my brother Mart and Ann, the three of us aging together. Ann was a policewoman and valued in the department, an undercover officer. She'd get a job in a factory to make sure the bosses paid the workers properly and obeyed safety regulations. She'd insisted that there be a safe exit in the Jackson lingerie factory. And when some idiot tossed a lit cigarette butt into a pile of scrap cotton, setting the whole place on fire, it was Ann led thirty women out of the place. She and Mart, who owned a small candy store, had developed their own way of living together.

No. I had to make enough money to rent the Chicago equivalent of my flat in the Place de Vosges, which wasn't as grand as it sounds. The servants' quarters under the eaves really. With a tiny bathroom, where a bidet took up most of the space. Amazing how chic Frenchwomen can be with such limited options for washing themselves. Though I suppose the bidet makes up for a lot.

"I don't understand why you can't stay here with us," Ann said to me, when I explained my plan to her. "Why would you want to leave Bridgeport?"

Why, indeed. I tried to tell Ann that walking those streets I knew so well, while comforting, was also disturbing. If Henrietta had convinced Michael that I was a fallen woman, and a bad influence on his children, imagine what she'd gotten the neighbors to believe. No smoke without fire, Henrietta often said, and I'm sure she'd set the meetings of the Altar and Rosary Society of St. Bridget's aflame.

But if I were to be able to rent a place, I needed a real salary, not just the bits and pieces I got from Ed. So I went looking for a job. Hadn't my pictures been on the front page of the *Tribune*? I would be a newspaper photographer.

"Who are you?" the fellow asked me. A small man with a big camera. A speed graphic, I'd say, with a built-in flash. "I'm Nora Kelly," I said.

"Waiting for the boss?"

I sat on a straight chair, ten feet from the wooden door with a glass panel that said "Dan Lewis, Photo Editor." His office was stuck away in the basement of Tribune Tower. Maurine had told me Lewis hated the chaos of the newsroom. Claimed he couldn't work on visuals with all that noise. She'd arranged this interview.

I'd been so nice to Henrietta since Ed and Margaret got married that my jaw hurt from clenching my teeth. Didn't want her asking too many questions about Margaret's past. To be fair, Henrietta didn't beat Michael's children or anything. She made sure Mike and the older girls were up, dressed, and got off to school on time. As for the little ones, well . . . thank God Marguerite was a good little mother to Frances.

Stella Lambert looked in every day and called me with any news she got from Jesse. Henrietta flat-out told Rose and me not to visit the children during the week, as it disrupted their schedule and interfered with their schoolwork. But she couldn't keep us away on Sundays, and we were there for dinner, though sometimes John Larney could not join us. Ed and Ed Junior no longer came . . . Ed and Margaret always seemed to be busy. They had taken a subscription to the opera and their pictures were often on the society page. "Who does Margaret Kelly think she is anyway? Swanning around in fur coats and diamonds," Henrietta had said. "Making a show of herself in the newspapers, like no decent woman should."

As president of the South Park Commissioners, chief engineer of the city, and the driving force behind the new stadium, Ed was in a good position to get rich people to underwrite construction projects by offering to put their names on public buildings. Julius Rosenwald of Sears had promised to help Ed turn the Palace of Fine Arts into a science museum, though God only knows what would happen if Big Bill Thompson got in after the next election. He was threatening to run, but for now Ed was a hero. He was news. Though I worried a bit. Too much flash and the reporters would turn on him.

"It's Ed wants us to be out and about," Margaret had told me. "He wants to stay friendly with the people who helped save the Fine Arts building."

"I suppose Mrs. Potter Palmer and the society women do have influence," I'd said.

"And the Club of One Hundred," she'd said.

This group of businessmen also wanted to make ours a beautiful city. Bankers, business owners, the top men in Chicago. Fellows who would have seen Ed as just another Mick on the take were now inviting him to lunch at their clubs. Introducing them to his elegant wife in the lobby of the Lyric Opera made it easier for Ed to do business with them, I supposed.

I understood that Ed and Margaret needed to have a life of their own. But I missed them at the Sunday dinners. Though I didn't blame Margaret for not wanting to put up with Henrietta. And, of course, forever contrary, Henrietta took offense that they no longer came.

"Of course, she's a barren woman," Henrietta had said on one of those Sundays. "So what can you expect?"

I was leaving after dinner. "Oh, Henrietta, that's so mean. Margaret might have children yet. I know Ed would love a houseful."

"Then he should have married a girl from Bridgeport. I had my three children in six years."

"But you were young," I said. Hard to hear Henrietta going on about being a mother when I'd never seen her embrace the Kelly kids.

"Oh, you always take Margaret's side. I suppose it's because you're two of a kind," she said.

"Barren women?" My teeth grinding together.

"You and that Rose Larney. Are you glad now you gave up having children for that stupid little job at Montgomery Ward?"

I sucked in my breath. Don't say anything, Nonie, don't, I told myself. She wants a screaming row in front of Michael so that she can convince him that I'm too unstable to be around the children. I was used to her attacking me. But to hear her slag poor Rose, who'd suffered all those miscarriages—and now her husband John was ill. So far, though, I'd outsmarted Henrietta and kept the peace. The thought of Agnella kept me from out-and-out war, which would have disturbed Michael and the kids. I had to get my own apartment.

So here I was applying to be a *Tribune* photographer.

"I'm Manny Mandel," the fellow finally said to me after he'd looked me up and down. "We'll be seeing a lot of each other if you get hired."

"I hope we do," I said. See how jumping to conclusions can be wrong? Just because he's wearing that plaid suit, I thought, and slicks the last of his hair back with tonic I can smell, doesn't mean he's not a decent fellow.

"I take most of the front page pictures. So you have to be sure my credit gets typed on the prints when they're sent to the composing room. The boss's last secretary was a ditzy blonde who couldn't spell, but I suppose a woman of your age should be able to get things right."

"Oh," I said. "You think I'm applying for a secretarial position?"

"High-class, too, aren't you?" he said. And mimicked me, saying in a high voice "secretarial position."

"I'm a photographer, Mr. Mandel," I said. "Perhaps you recall the three-column shot on the front page last year? Ed Kelly, Mrs. Potter Palmer, and the bulldozer?"

"Oh, right. You're the cousin—Ed Kelly's flack. I told Maurine it was disgraceful for her to let him dictate to us like that. She should have called me. Next thing you know, we'll be running his press releases as news stories."

"Now, Mr. Mandel," I said, and stood up. "How dare you," I started.

"Button it, sister," he said. "Maurine's not a real reporter. She's lucky that crazy dames are trigger happy. She could never write a real news story." And Mandel walked away, leaving all the things I should have said spinning in my head.

Just then a voice called out through the door, "If you're out there, come in." Dan Lewis was no Manny Mandel. Tall and gangly, older than me, his desk piled with prints and photographs.

"I told Maurine I could give you five minutes, so talk," he said.

And I did. Told him about my time in Paris. Eddie Steichen's encouragement. The camera he gave me. My work with Floyd Gibbons, the war correspondent. He nodded at that.

"I knew Floyd," he said. "Went over to radio. Deserted newspapers."

I said nothing, but spread a selection of photographs on the desk.

"All very nice, Miss Kelly. But the *Tribune* doesn't hire women photographers. This is a dangerous job. Our people cover gang rubouts, and have to catch public officials unaware. Thank you very much."

"I took the photograph that saved the Fine Arts building," I said. But Dan Lewis wasn't listening, shuffling through prints on his desk. Didn't look up as I left his office.

"I'm trying to move out, Ed, but my job hunting has not gone well," I said to him that night. I told him about my encounter with Manny Mandel.

"He's a snake," Ed said. "Always trying to catch someone in a place he shouldn't be. He tips off Wilcox."

"Anything for a story, I guess."

"Listen," Ed said. "There's enough happening between my building projects and the events we're holding at the park fieldhouses. How about becoming the official South Park photographer at twenty-five dollars a week?" He reached in his pocket and handed me a twenty-dollar bill and a five. You don't often see such big denominations. "Your first week's salary."

So now, I was a cousin with a city job. Our numbers were legion.

But where would I live? Girls lived at home until they married, and then they lived with their husbands. Even widows set up their oldest son as "the man of the family"—a handy façade. Unmarried women attached themselves to a married brother's or sister's family; or lived with a bachelor brother, as my sister Ann did; or found positions as maids or housekeepers. I had to figure out how to have a place of my own without shaming the family. Concierge, I thought. A respectable profession in Paris. Why not in Chicago?

7

"And you say Ed Kelly wants you to rent a flat here?" the construction foreman asked me, as he led me down a hallway, still full of cement dust, toward a big oak door.

What a place! Smack dab on Lake Michigan on a little curve of a street coming out from the Drake Hotel. Michael was putting in all the plumbing in this new building and had talked about it at Sunday dinner. Four bathrooms in each flat. Imagine! I'd introduced myself to this man as Michael's sister, Ed's cousin, and told him that I was working for the South Park District office and was interested in an apartment. The foreman had laughed.

"Only the likes of the Potter Palmers or the McCormicks can afford to live here," he said. "No place for you unless you're married to a rich old man."

A palace. Faced with stone that was almost too white. I could only imagine what the façade looked like when the sun rose out of the lake and flooded it with color. And to be only steps from the beach. I remembered how Granny Honora would take us for picnics on the only bit of the lakeshore that wasn't used as a rubbish heap in those days.

"This is as close as I can get you to Galway Bay," she'd told us. "Now, half close your eyes and pretend you're seeing water bluer than this, turning scarlet and gold as the sun goes down. The most beautiful sight in the world."

And how right she was, because I myself had waded in Galway Bay and seen the setting sun lay down a shining path leading toward the west—to the enchanted isles, and Amerikay. The road my ancestors had followed.

But here in Chicago we faced the sunrise. Our lake came alive at first light. To see that spectacle right from my window every morning. Amazing. And me living here would kill Henrietta. I mean literally. She'd have a heart attack and die. Just to register her displeasure.

But, of course, I didn't really want her dead. Too much sorrow in our family—but, oh, how I wanted to live here. Surely there must be some way.

The man was laughing. Really hee-hawing, his head thrown back. "You? Live here? Not unless you get a job as one of the tenant's maids."

"Oh, so you do have servants' quarters," I said.

"Nah," he said. "We were going to put the help up in the attic, but the tenants who rented the apartments prefer to have the maid and the cook live behind the kitchen. Handier, I guess. Many of them doing away with live-ins altogether. Our tenants have big houses up North," he said. "Only want these for when they're in the city."

"Mmmm," I said. "And I suppose they'd appreciate the services of a good concierge."

"A what?"

"Concierge. When I lived in Paris, no building could survive without one."

"Paris, huh? Well I know Mr. Marshall wants these places to be Frenchy. Called the rooms by all sorts of foreign names. We got a janitor going to live in the basement. Is that what you mean?"

"No. No. A concierge is not a janitor. She—and it's usually a woman—takes personal care of the tenants. Sorts their mail. Screens their visitors . . ."

"Oh, we have doormen for that."

"And are your doormen available to keep someone's cat, or take care of their children in a pinch? Find a good seamstress? Or hairdresser? Get the tenants the best reservations at restaurants, or theater tickets?"

"The people who will be living here can do all that themselves."

"Can they?" I asked. "Should they be expected to? In France the concierge is paid a salary, but I'd be willing to trade my services for a place in your attic at a reduced rate."

"I don't know," he said.

"Well, at least get me an appointment with Mr. Marshall," I said.

Again, that hee-hawing laugh. "They're too busy to give the time of day to some dame with a screwy idea," he said. "Besides, what will people think?—a single woman living on her own. Not respectable!"

"Oh, that's too bad," I said. "My cousin, Ed Kelly, is president of the South Park Board. Didn't Marshall and Fox design that building across from Jackson Park? The Windermere? I remember Ed saying something about helping them get the land, and their permits, and—"

"Alright, alright," he said. "I'll see what I can do."

Three days later, I walked right past the receptionist at Marshall & Fox, Architects, into Mr. Marshall's office. He was the born-and-bred Chicago fellow of the two. So we began with the who-do-you-know game. And, although he was a Protestant and not woven into the web of parishes, he'd hired construction crews and bought steel girders and cement, and so we could bat a few Irish names back and forth.

And, of course, he knew all about Parisian concierges.

"I'm a frequent visitor to the City of Light," he said. And so we went down that road of favorite restaurants and sights, with a few detours for the war, and my service at the American hospital.

"Well," he said. "It might not be bad to have a trained nurse on hand for our tenants." And I nodded, God help me. After all, I had nursed, and even though "trained" might be stretching the truth a bit, I could handle any first aid emergency and call an ambulance. And I could see that by having some kind of position, I became less suspect. Not a fallen woman—a concierge.

"We planned to leave the attics unfinished," he said. "Servants' quarters are old-fashioned."

"I'll finish it. Put three rooms up there."

"There's no plumbing," he said. "That could be an expensive proposition."

"Mr. Marshall," I said, "my brother is Michael Kelly. Give me a week and I'll have it ready." He agreed to charge me only $50 a month.

I needed to live there. I had to be close to the lake, and Michigan Avenue was as close to Paris as I could get in Chicago. The Magnificent Mile—shops and hotels, and . . . Well, I wanted to bring the Kelly kids and Ed Junior into a world different from their own.

Oh, Mame, wouldn't that be swell? Your kids and Ed Junior, staying the night with me in a playhouse in the sky. Take them right away from the sadness for a bit. Malts at the Drake Soda Fountain. Summer swims in the lake. Shopping with the girls at Saks. Watching Ed Junior and your Mike throw a football around the park.

"Let's go visit Aunt Nonie," they'd say. "We're always happy there."

"Please, Mr. Marshall," I said. "It's very important that I live in your building. Please."

"Bring me a letter from Ed Kelly, and we'll see," Marshall said.

So now I was "please, please, pleasing" Ed in his office on LaSalle Street. "I don't know, Nonie," he said. "I thought our family had gone beyond being servants."

"Come on, Ed. In Paris, a concierge never considers herself a servant."

"Margaret thinks it's still not quite respectable for a woman to live on her own, even in 1924," Ed said. "But I suppose widows do become housekeepers, and maybe you are, technically, a widow, and—"

"Write the letter, Ed," I said.

"Alright. Alright. But you realize if Marshall gives you this position, he'll expect something back from me."

"I suppose," I said.

Ed opened his desk drawer. Took out a sheet of paper. Unscrewed the fountain pen on his desk—one of the new ones where the ink is on the inside. "I think this should be a handwritten note from me. Not typed up on official paper."

"Fine," I said, as he began writing.

Only a few lines. He looked up at me. "Marshall and Fox might want to know about my plans for the parks. Building apartments near them would be a good idea. There are acres and acres belonging to the board that are still empty."

"I thought that land was unstable. Half submerged in the lake," I said.

"It could be shored up," he said. "We could take the garbage that's still being dumped on the beaches. Compact it, and turn it into landfill. It would be a start."

He got up from his desk. Walked over to a cabinet. Took out big sheets of paper with drawings on them, and spread one on the top of his desk. "This would be an aquarium—the biggest one in North America. Showing marine life in its natural habitat is a popular attraction in Europe."

And here it was. The moment that Ed let me in on his plans, when I saw for the first time that he intended to remake Chicago. No longer just the "City of the Big Shoulders—Freight Handler to the Nation," but a gracious city with attractions that would both entertain and educate its citizens, and bring in tourists. I mean, they'd come for the White City, why not offer a permanent world's fair? And he was confiding his dreams to me.

He went on, "John Shedd's very interested in the sea, and he'd give money to build an aquarium here on the lakefront." He laid another sheet down. "Max Adler is interested in astronomy. He wants Chicago to have a planetarium, and he'll pay for it. See? Here's a design of the roof. It'll open up to see the stars. We'd have the very latest telescopes."

"With Adler footing the bill?"

"Rich people want to have their names on things. Monuments to themselves. So why not the Shedd Aquarium? The Adler Planetarium? The Clarence F. Buckingham Fountain?" He showed me a complete drawing. "This fountain looks like the one in Versailles. But better, because ours will shoot up colored water—and Kate Buckingham will pay for the whole thing in memory of her brother, plus set up a fund for maintenance."

"So what's stopping you, Ed?"

"The other Parks board members. They're all Republicans and don't want to do anything while a Democrat like Dever is mayor. They're Big Bill Thomson's boys, and think they can drag their feet until Thomson gets reelected. Then he'd get all the credit."

"So your projects will get built then?" I asked.

"Maybe, but not by me. If Thomson is elected, he'll kick me off the board. Put his own man in. Thomson's a clown. He shouldn't even get the Republican nomination. But politics is a funny business."

"But you'd still be chief engineer of the Sanitary District?" I asked.

He shrugged.

"You've got to get yourself into the newspapers again, Ed," I said. "Those articles saved the Fine Arts building. Why not let the people know about your ideas? You . . ." And I stopped.

"Are you crazy, Nonie? All the papers care about are scandals."

True enough. The *Tribune* called them the "Whoopee Boys"—the men who worked, or rather didn't work, for the Sanitary District. They'd been indicted for fraud, taking bribes, giving out no-show jobs, the usual, by the state's attorney, who was a Republican. Most of the Whoopees were Democrats and Irish, and could be relied on to say nutty things that made good copy, so the headlines persisted.

Now the worst of the offenses happened before Ed took over as chief engineer, so he'd escaped the spotlight—so far. But that Protestant minister, Wilcox, was convinced that Ed was allowing the same kind of wild and wooly behavior, just being more devious. "The unsanitary engineer," Wilcox called Ed. The other reporters in town often ran quotes from Wilcox, because he said things that even their newspapers would have been afraid to print as their own opinion.

Wilcox always made sure his readers knew a fellow's religion. He called Alderman Jake Arvey of the Twenty-Fourth Ward "The Israelite" and Ed a "follower of the pope of Rome." He'd documented all the overages on Soldier Field.

Ed folded up the plans for the aquarium.

And that could have been that—no lakefront, no biggest-in-the-world attractions for Chicago. I wish I could have leaned across the desk and whispered, "You'll do it all, Ed." I mean, now it seems as if that cluster of monumental buildings was always there—but without Ed Kelly they wouldn't exist.

I began to photograph events like the Silver Skater races, the monthly Polish Polka Party at the fieldhouse on Cicero, the track meets in Jackson Park and place the pictures in neighborhood newspapers. I made sure every caption included "Sponsored by South Park Board, Edward J. Kelly, President."

Another year in Chicago . . . but now I'd have a place of my own.

So. A somewhat bemused Michael had a crew run pipes up to the attic of 209 East Lake Shore Drive, and Ed sent the carpenters, who usually worked building fieldhouses for the Parks, to make three rooms in the space Mr. Marshall allotted me in the attic.

"You Kellys know how to get what you want," the building manager said to me. And I only nodded. Our family has had more than its share of sorrows, so why not use what clout we did have?

"Oh, Aunt Nonie, it's like a fairyland," Ann said to me. The whole bunch of them—Kelly kids and Ed Junior were lined up to watch the headlights of the cars sweep past us on the drive below. Delighted with my new flat, which, they said, was like a tree house.

"That's my dad's road," Ed Junior said.

"It is indeed," I said.

"Now watch," he said to the other children, "all the cars will slow down." And we did see a long line of red taillights, as the cars were braking to cross the narrow bridge that connected the North Drive to the South.

"My dad's building a new bridge, isn't he, Aunt Nonie?"

"He is, Ed. He is," I said.

I should know. Haven't I spent the last week tromping through snow up to my knees to take pictures of the site of this new bridge? I then moved on to what Ed was calling Grant Park—not as grandiose as his other projects, but one he'd managed to get the board to agree to. Just a big empty space now, but Nash Brothers were busy putting in a sewer system, blasting through the frozen ground. But how do you make a sewer system visual?

Pat Nash instructed his workers to dangle sewer pipes from cranes, and I shot them just when the sun was rising. I did wonder what Eddie Steichen and Matisse would think of my work, but I was earning money, and snug up here in my attic, warm and cozy, entertaining the children I had grown to love so much.

I peeled the kids away from the window and tucked the girls up in the twin beds I'd bought at Smyths with a good discount, because Smyth was a member of the Irish Fellowship Club. I'd sleep on the couch I'd also purchased.

The boys had made themselves a fort with pillows and my two armchairs. Also from Smyths.

"One last battle before we go to bed?" Ed Junior asked me. I nodded and watched as he and Mike moved the lines of toy soldiers back and forth, yelling at each other, and then making terrible groans as one of Ed's soldiers knocked down Mike's.

I had to look away. Images from Belleau Wood came into my mind. Those young Marines marching straight into machine gun fire. And still tit-for-tat violence going on in Ireland. De Valera and his fellows were ambushing Free State soldiers whenever they had the chance, and the government reacted to these attacks by rounding up rebels and sticking them in jail. Men who'd stood together fighting the British were killing each other. I'd finally received a letter from Cyril Peterson, forwarded on by the Irish College in Paris. "Don't come over here. Not a time for sentimental journeys. Say your prayers for Peter Keeley from that side of the Atlantic," he'd told me. Yes, take care of my responsibilities here, and then . . .

I'd framed the one photograph I'd managed to take of Peter, and kept it on a small table near my bed. Always a nod good night to him. Soon, Peter—soon.

"Come on guys. Bed."

"Aunt Nonie," Mike said to me as he burrowed down next to his cousin in their pillow fort, "next year I'm going to soldier school with Ed."

"Nothing's decided," I said. "Ed might not even be going."

"Oh, but I am," Ed said. "My dad told me."

"But won't you be homesick?" I asked.

"I will miss Dad, Nana, and Lou," he said.

"And your, errr . . . Margaret?" I asked.

"She's nice enough. But she hates noise, and I forget, and run up and down the stairs 'louder than a freight train,' she says."

"Me too, Aunt Nonie," Mike said. "Aunt Henrietta calls me the fire engine. She says children should be seen and not heard. But that's very hard, Aunt Nonie."

"Now that Mike doesn't have a mother either, like me," Ed said, "we're going to be blood brothers and join the Marines when we grow up, and fight in wars, and—"

"There's not going to be any more fighting," I said. "And how do you know about the Marines anyway?"

"I saw them in a movie," he said. "Everybody knows about the Marines."

"I really think he's too young," I told Margaret when I dropped Ed Junior to Hyde Park, after I'd delivered the Kelly kids back to Argo. Henrietta hadn't even offered me a cup of tea, and Michael was out fixing someone's frozen pipe. The two boys had actually saluted each other when they said goodbye.

"But Ed Junior wants to go, Nora," Margaret said. Now I had to be very careful. Margaret was my friend, and she was good for Ed, no question. Look at this house, lovely altogether and hospitable. The two of us having tea and home-baked scones right now. None of Henrietta's begrudgery here.

The newspaper on the table before us was open to a double-column photograph that headlined "Edward J. Kelly, President of the South Park Commission, Chief Engineer of the Sanitary District, and His Wife, at the Opera." Margaret wore a full-length white ermine coat, and Ed was in white tie and tails as he smiled down at her.

"Quite an outfit," I said, pointing to the picture. Wilcox will love this, I thought. He'll start doing sums with Ed's salary.

"Ed likes me to dress well," she said. "Now as far as Ed Junior goes . . ."

She was sitting up very straight with her back away from the chair. "Ed thinks it will be good for him to be around boys his own age. Boys from good families." Those good families, again. "The fellows from St. Ignatius high school are from good families," I said.

"But not much variety there," she said.

"You mean no Protestants?" I asked.

"Culver Military Academy will give Ed Junior a chance to meet and make friends with boys who will become men of influence," she said.

"Margaret, he's eleven years old," I said.

"Mrs. Armstrong, who was in the box next to us at the opera, told me that her husband and his business partners all went to the same boarding school, and they're millionaires, every one of them."

"Ed's not doing too badly," I said, "and he left school at twelve."

"And regrets it every day, Nora. He wouldn't have the newspapers questioning his competence as an engineer if he had a degree."

"But Ed learned from experience, from hard work," I said.

"Which is why he doesn't want that for Ed Junior. Four years at Culver and then Notre Dame, or even Harvard or Yale."

"Oh, please, Margaret, you can't send him east, or we'll lose him entirely. And I suppose he is a bit of a handful, loud and all." I stopped.

"Has he been complaining to you?"

"No. No. It's just—well, little boys. And I suppose if you get into a delicate condition and need a rest or do start considering, um, adoption . . ."

"So Nelly's been talking to you?"

"I don't know what you mean."

"Well I suppose we wouldn't be able to keep an adoption secret. You see, Nora, the doctor says it's very unlikely that I'll be able to have children of my own."

Barren women, I hear Henrietta shouting, barren women!

"So I have inquired with the sisters at St. Vincent de Paul. Early days though. Ed thinks we should wait a bit. Doctors have been wrong, he says. After all, his mother had her youngest at age forty-two."

"And my mother was thirty-nine when I was born," I said.

"Funny, isn't it? I always felt sorry for those women who had a child a year," Margaret said, "and now I envy them. You know Ed's first wife, Mary, was pregnant when she died."

"I know," I said. And me far away in Paris.

"If she'd lived, I'm sure they would have had a large family. Another reason Ed still mourns her."

"Oh, Margaret, Ed loves you. I know he does."

"I want to be a mother, Nonie. I want Ed and me to be parents together."

"But you are. And then Ed Junior is—"

"Mary's son. He looks like her, doesn't he, Nonie? As he gets older, I see the resemblance to the portrait of her."

She pointed to the oil painting on the wall of the dining room.

"Well, he does have her eyes, and that smile. A grin really. So full of fun, so warm . . ." My voice trailed off. "Sorry," I said.

"No, Nonie, I'm not jealous of her. The poor woman died so young."

We both looked up at the portrait.

"It's just that I wonder sometimes if Ed and his son aren't too close. Culver will teach Ed Junior to stand on his own two feet. Be his own man. And the parents of his classmates won't be bothering Ed for jobs, which is sure to happen at St. Ignatius. I think Culver will be good for him, and I'd appreciate it if you didn't interfere, Nora."

"Well he'll have the summer, and I suppose by next fall he'll be older and . . ."

Margaret took a sip of tea. She drank it black, no sugar or milk. Careful of her figure. "He's starting after Christmas," she said.

"Of course," I said. What else could I do?

"I suppose I have to remember that Ed's boy and Michael's kids are not my children," I said to Rose.

John just couldn't seem to get better. That vital man relapsing over and over again. The fever wouldn't leave his system—Rose was housebound with him. People were afraid to visit, though I knew John was not contagious. We met at her house the day after my tea with Margaret.

"Alright for me to take them for treats, even have them for a night over now and then, but I'm on the sidelines of their lives," I said.

"We're the aunts, Nonie. We have to keep our love for these children contained."

"Build a breakwater, I suppose," I said. "Not easy."

"Not easy at all," Rose agreed.

Mike insisted on seeing his cousin off on the train. He was with Margaret, Ed, and me on that early January morning. "I'll be with you next year, Ed," I heard Mike tell him. Already in uniform, our little soldier off to the wars. At least he's not in danger, I reassured myself. Safe. Except he wasn't. An ear infection. He'd been away three months when the school called Ed. His son was sick. Ed immediately drove down himself, to take him to a hospital in Chicago. Too late. How can a strong young boy die from an ear infection? Dear God, how could you? Dead.

8

MARCH 1926

It was the guard of honor made me cry. I'd held myself together during the last terrible days, trying to be strong for Ed. But now, Ed Junior's entire class from Culver, all in their dress uniforms, marched up the main aisle of Holy Name Cathedral and stopped at his casket, draped in black, waiting in front of the high altar. Their uniforms were modeled on those at West Point. Gray jacket and trousers with a stripe down the side of the pants. Their hats had a strap under chins that have never known a razor. Babies, I thought, these little boys, eleven, twelve years old. Dear God, marching no less. What did that Marine Martin Berndt, an officer at Belleau Wood, tell me?

"We parade," he'd said. "Walk in time and in step because in combat every instinct says 'Run.' We press our uniforms. Spit polish our boots. Pretend that in combat they won't be covered in blood and mud. Military rituals are designed to disguise the reality of war."

And are these boys being trained for war? I thought. But hasn't "the war to end all wars" been fought already? Yet this school was getting these boys ready for something. Is that why they let Ed Junior lie in bed with that horrible pain in his ear? Toughening him up.

Now the shortest of the toy soldiers moved into the pew in front of me. I heard the jerk in his breath. I lifted my hand to pat his arm, but stopped myself. He'd hate being comforted. Blinking now, and with a quick swipe of his gloved hand at his eyes, he sat down.

Let yourself sob, I wanted to say to him. I wondered—I asked Martin

Berndt in my head, because Martin was dead now too—if boys cried more, would there be less fighting?

I remembered Carl Sandburg's poem, "Sometime they'll give a war and nobody will come." I thought of Mother Ireland's sons killing each other. Couldn't men just stop showing up for the battles. Won't someone say, "Enough is enough"?

But Mass had begun. I translated the Latin words in my head. *"Introibo ad altare Dei."* I will go to the altar of God.

Another corps of young boys, dressed in white surplices with red capes, answered—*"Ad Deum qui laetificat juventutem meam."* To God who gives joy to my youth.

Dear God, why did you take him? Isn't it enough that Ed's first wife and the baby she carried died? How could you claim another child? Are you a monster, God? Is all this folderol of flowers, costumes, incense, and churches with stained glass windows, like the dress uniforms, shiny boots, and the military parade, a way to disguise that truth? That you are a monster, a heartless tyrant who enjoys watching us suffer?

The music almost saved the ceremony for me. I knew the singer, Catherine O'Connell. Her voice had elevated many a dull wedding Mass or perfunctory funeral.

"Ave Maria," she sang. *"Gratia plena."* Full of grace. And for the duration of the song, the image of Mary, Our Mother, comforted me. I remembered the statue of Our Lady of Paris in Notre Dame Cathedral. That young princess in stone who held her child on her hip. The Blessed Mother, at least, had compassion. Cared about us. Wonder what she'd say about a boy of twelve dead because some idiot doctor in Indiana did not treat him properly? A crime.

Had that little boy in front of me heard an older boy tell Ed Junior to be tough? Said to him that it was only an earache. And what about the headmaster? There he was, the plump fellow in a version of a cadet's uniform, sitting on the left. Had he said, "Kelly, you're a malingerer?"

A word I'd heard over and over at the American hospital in Paris. I wish more of my patients had malingered. Most were only too ready to go back to the front lines to their pals. Probably the same at this school, worried about the pals. Well, damn the pals, I thought. Take care of yourself.

All those boys, but only one of you, Edward Joseph Kelly Junior. One.

"Nunc et in hora mortis, In hora mortis nostrae"—Now and at the hour of our death, Catherine sang, repeating the phrase over and over, *"In hora mortis, mortis nostrae, in hora mortis nostrae."* Her voice filled the Cathedral. I've prayed, "now and at the hour of our death" a hundred thousand times, sure

that the hour of my death was far away. I'd be an old woman sleeping her way into Heaven. But for an earache to bring a young boy to the hour of his death . . . Horrible.

Ed wouldn't hear anything against the school or let Pat Nash send a police detective down to question the staff.

"What good, Nonie?" he'd asked. "Nothing will bring him back."

The cardinal was talking, saying something about God's will. Accepting God's will. Is the Almighty a potentate on a throne, dictating rewards and punishment? His will. Never heard a priest say "Accept God's will," when good things came.

Did Ed believe all this? He sat staring straight at the cardinal. Margaret beside him. She took Ed's hand. I'm not sure what Margaret believed. Catholic, of course. But she never understood when I tried to explain that guilt kept me from even going into a church in Paris during my first six months there, until Father Kevin absolved me.

That strange confession in the courtyard of the Irish College, when he told me loving the wrong man wasn't the worst sin.

"Not loving is the crime, Nora." And his matchmaking with Peter Keeley. Father Kevin helped Margaret too, I remembered. Got both of us back into the tribe of good women. Forgiven. But by whom? You up there who lets children die and dresses up their going in all this pomp and circumstance?

The boy soldiers were moving out. And the little one who sat in front of me held his head up, standing straight now. Learning not to feel.

I understood why families invited people for a meal after the funeral. The rituals are over, and it's time to visit and talk. Nothing wrong with that, and surely Ed and Margaret's big house in Hyde Park had plenty of room so all the people who were pushing their way in could give their condolences.

But usually there are lots of tried-and-true phrases—"He had a good long life," or "His children and grandchildren will always remember him." Phrases like that. But no one in this crowd could find anything to say to Ed.

Pat Nash only shook his head as he took Ed's hand and hugged Margaret. I heard "heartbreaking, just heartbreaking" as Margaret pointed at the big dining room where waiters stood ready, waiting to carve a whole turkey, a huge standing roast, and a baked ham.

How did Margaret manage to assemble all this food? I wondered. A pile of Parker House rolls, bowls of potatoes, and a heaping dish of peas and carrots were piled up on the table.

Margaret had even gotten flower arrangements, as well as a whole array of pies and cakes. A full bar, of course—Prohibition or no.

Ed nodded his head toward the bar behind me. I knew he wanted a Jameson and water. I went behind the bar, poured two myself, which the bartender didn't like, then carried the crystal glass over to Ed. I offered the second one to Pat. He shook his head and watched Ed drain the glass and reach out for the second.

"Ed," Pat started, but then stopped and touched Ed's shoulder. A clutch of aldermen and their wives arrived and headed for Ed, but Pat stood with him so no one had a chance to say more than "Sorry for your troubles."

Margaret directed guests to the buffet. The voices in the dining room were getting louder and there was some laughter.

Johnny Gilhooley lit up a cigar. Margaret didn't allow smoking in the house, but she said nothing. Ed handed his glass to me. I took it back to the bar.

"Two Jamesons straight," I said, when the bartender finally turned toward me from the crush of men. All the whiskey was the real thing. In bonded bottles.

Three wooden cases of illegally obtained liquor had been left on the front porch that morning. No fear of a raid, I thought, as a sergeant in full uniform handed a glass to the chief of police in his dress blues.

I gave Ed his Jameson, and then drank mine.

Pat was still running interference for Ed. Even the cardinal only got a few minutes. Pat sent him toward the dining room.

I saw a young priest ignore the line at the bar and get His Eminence a drink.

I heard my name and turned around to see Rose with my brother Michael and Ed's mother, Aunt Nelly. I set my glass down on the windowsill behind me and moved through the crowd to them.

"How is he doing?" Michael asked me.

"Dazed," I said. "Barbaric to put him through this."

"People want to pay their respects," Michael said.

"They had two nights of a wake and a funeral," I said.

"But the meal after is something special for the close friends," Michael said.

"That's who this mob is? Looks more like a meeting of the South Park Board or a smoker at the Brighton Park Athletic Association," I said.

I reached back for my drink and took a sip.

"Nonie," Rose started.

"Don't worry. It's not hooch. The real thing. Smuggled in for the occasion from the Emerald Isle itself I'd say. Three crates on the doorstep this morning and one of Harveys Bristol Cream sherry."

"Spike O'Donnell probably," Michael said. "Can I get you ladies a sherry?" he asked. Rose and Aunt Nelly nodded, but I said "Jameson straight," and handed Michael my glass. He went toward the bar. Aunt Nelly headed for the dining room. Looking for Margaret.

"Don't drink too much of that whiskey, Nonie," Rose said.

"Ed has the right idea. Dull the pain for a while," I said.

"And then what?" Rose asked.

"A hangover, I suppose. But today will be over. How is John?" I asked.

"The same," she said. "Mrs. Devlin from next door is sitting with him," she said.

"I hope . . . ," I started, but what was there to say? Hope didn't stop death.

"Did you see the cadets?" I asked.

"I did," Rose said.

"Pitiful. Why they ever sent Ed Junior to that boarding school . . . ," I said.

"Nonie, please. People can hear you, and now's not the time," Rose said.

"Look at the poor kid," I said.

I guided Rose over to the piano and pointed to a framed picture of Ed Junior with his platoon.

Platoon. I ask you. Little boys dressed up and told they are a platoon. I'd taken the photograph when I had visited him on parents' weekend. Margaret had one of her headaches, so I went with Ed. Brought my Seneca. Gorgeous day. That southern Indiana woodland touched with the gold of early spring. I wanted to pose Ed Junior alone under a redbud tree, but he'd asked that the whole platoon be in the shot.

"Look at him," I said to Rose. "Doesn't even put himself in the first row. Hidden almost. Told me afterward that his father had said he shouldn't brag about his dad. 'I think he wants me to be humble,' Ed Junior had said to me. 'A lot of Republicans in this school,' he told me."

"True enough," Rose said.

"He said that one fellow had asked him how did it feel to have a father who was a crooked Mick," I told her, "I asked him what he said to the fellow. 'I didn't say anything,' he told me. 'I put my fists up, and he ran away. Didn't even have to hit him. You have to stand up to bullies like my dad did when he punched the foreman who was trying to cheat him out of his job on the canal.'"

"Ed's famous punch," Rose said.

"Ed Junior told me that his dad thought he'd be fired. But the Big Boss said he respected a man who stood up for himself."

The Big Boss. Colonel Robert J. McCormick, head of the Sanitary District then. Publisher of the *Tribune* now. A member of what I supposed was the wealthiest family in Chicago—although the Potter Palmers could have given them a run for their money.

"I wonder will McCormick come to the house?" I asked Rose.

"I saw him in church. Very nice of him to attend Mass. Him being a Protestant and all," Rose said.

Then she pointed. "My goodness, Nonie. Look at that fellow. Going right to the head of the line and now he's pulling Ed away from Judge Normyle. So rude. Who is he?"

"I don't know." Whoever he was, he'd certainly shut up the crowd. All Ed's consolers were staring at this blob of a man, whose suit jacket hung open. He had dirty blond hair and a many-layered chin.

"Wilcox! How does he dare?" Pat Nash was standing next to me, and grunted out the words.

"So that's the crazy reverend who writes all those terrible things about Ed!" I said. "Stop him. Throw him out!"

But Pat shook his head. "Best not to rile him."

"Why not?"

Pat said nothing. Dear God, I thought, he's afraid of Wilcox. Doesn't want to be attacked in that paper of his. Fearless Pat Nash was cowed.

Well, I wasn't. I crossed the room. "Excuse me," I started, but Wilcox was holding Ed's arm.

"I have come to offer my condolences," Wilcox said. "The Lord works in mysterious ways. He knows that only a blow such as this would make you examine your ways and beg his forgiveness. He took your boy as a way to save your eternal soul." Ed said nothing—only stared at him, and pulled away.

I'd moved next to them, so I saw that Ed wasn't taking in what Wilcox was saying. Didn't understand Wilcox was telling him that God had killed the son as a way of getting back at the father. Then, suddenly Ed realized what Wilcox meant.

"You're saying it's my fault that my boy died?" Ed said.

"I am. A lesson from the Almighty for which you should be grateful," Wilcox said.

"Stop it!" I said. "This is a private reception. Get out."

"Paid for from the public purse I suppose," Wilcox said. "All of you are the spawn of the Devil. God smote the firstborn of the Egyptians, and he will do the same to you. Papist idolaters. Blasphemers."

Ed brought up his fist, but Pat Nash stepped in front of him. "That's what he wants Ed," he said. "A Donnybrook. An Irish wake turned into a ruckus. Let him go."

I turned to Wilcox. "Have you no decency? Leave us alone," I said.

"I know who you are," Wilcox said. "Another parasite."

The chief of police and two policemen were headed our way. Wilcox saw them.

"Take off, buddy," the chief said. The patrolmen drew their nightsticks.

Wilcox turned away, walked through the silent crowd and stood at the front door. "The Lord will smite thee! My pen is His sword."

Then he was gone.

"Send that man to Bughouse Square!" someone shouted, and the crowd laughed.

I made my way to the bar. "Two more Jamesons," I said to the bartender.

The Irish phrase *"Uisce beatha"*—which means water of life, became, in English, "whiskey," but as often as not, the bottle can bring death, or at least oblivion. And it seemed as if Ed would succumb in the days after Ed Junior's funeral. He was drinking alone, locked in his study, which frightened Margaret and brought me to the Hyde Park house at midnight.

I found Ed, collapsed in his big leather chair next to a sputtering fire. He didn't seem surprised to see me.

"Do you think Wilcox is right? Did I kill Ed Junior? Did Mary and our little one die because of me? Is God punishing me? Is He, Nonie . . . ?"

"Oh, for God's sake, Ed. Wilcox is a bigoted bastard. What would he know about God except using His name to fatten his collection?"

Ed picked up a big photo album from the floor. Opened it up. Passed it to me. A page of Ed Junior's baby pictures. In his mother's arms.

"Such a sweet boy. After Mary died, he said, 'Don't worry, Dad. I'll be good. The way Mom would want me to be.' Were they too good for me? Is God teaching me a lesson, Nonie? Is He?"

"Oh, Ed," I said. "Ed."

Margaret was at the door of the study with a tray, a silver coffeepot, and china cups.

"Ed, please," Margaret said. "Pull yourself together." She looked at me. "Such good news. The sister from St. Vincent de Paul called. A young girl is having twins. She can't keep them. She asked Sister to find them a good home. Ed, they could be our babies."

But Ed didn't seem to hear her. He took the album from me, pointed to a picture. "Here's my baby. My little son. He's dead. Nothing can bring him back. Nothing."

"Give me the tray, Margaret," I said.

"You have to stop this, Ed," Margaret said. "If Sister thinks you're a drunk, she'll never let us adopt the twins."

I put the tray down on the desk, poured Ed some coffee.

"You have to get him away," Margaret said to me.

I noticed papers spread out on top of the desk. Blueprints. "What are these?" I asked.

Ed stood up from the chair and came over. "The plans for the house in the Northwoods that Ed Junior was helping me design. He was going to be an engineer like me."

He crumbled up the plans. "I'm going to burn them. Throw them in the fire."

"No. No. Don't do that. This is Ed Junior's legacy. You have to build the house in his memory, Ed," I said. "This is your most important project." I took the blueprints and smoothed them out on the desk in front of him. "Tell me, Ed. Tell me what you and Ed Junior planned. Shall we drive up to Eagle River and see the site?"

Ed was running his finger along the front of the blueprints. "It was Ed Junior's idea to have a wall of windows facing Catfish Lake. 'We can't have that much exposed glass,' I told him. 'Why not try, Dad?' he said. 'Let's try.' Always ready to try, that kid."

"Let's go, Ed. For your son," I said.

He looked down at the blueprints, picked up the plans, and then looked at me and nodded. We gave Ed no time to think. Margaret and I each took an arm and walked him right out to the car.

They rented a small cabin every summer on the grounds of Everett Resort near where the new house would stand. "There are clothes up there," Margaret said as we eased Ed into the passenger seat.

"Can you drive the whole way?" Margaret asked.

"I can," I said.

Twelve hours. I hope I can make it, I thought. Can't imagine stopping anywhere. Thank God Ed was asleep by the time we got on Lake Shore Drive.

9

Now the house in Eagle River would become Ed's Tír na nÓg—a place of rest and renewal where the family could come together, away from Chicago and politics, apart from the world. I was there the time a few years later when a telegram arrived from President Roosevelt, inviting Ed to a meeting at the White House the next day. Ed wired back that he couldn't get there from here—enclosed by the Northwoods—a state of mind as much as a location. But that was still in the future. Now as we pulled up to the cottage at Everett Resort, which Ed rented every summer, I only hoped this bender would end. I'll say this for him—he was a quiet drunk. He sat in his room, downing Jameson after Jameson, for the next few days. Not like some of the fellows in Bridgeport who go on the batter and become a danger to themselves and others.

All I had to do was supply him with grilled cheese sandwiches and soup. The groceries were delivered by the Everett caretaker, who told me his name was Patrick—a member of the local Ojibwe tribe, he said, though I wondered at his gray-blue eyes and what seemed like a touch of red in his graying hair. He kept us supplied with wood and started a fire each evening. Cold up there still. I'd sit in the living room as Ed drank, then dragged himself to bed. The fire comforted me. So did John McCormack, singing to me from Ed's fancy phonograph.

What I wouldn't have given to have my love, Peter, sitting in the easy chair beside me, reading—a companion, as well as a lover. I tortured myself listening to "Believe Me If All Those Endearing Young Charms" over and over.

How the Count's voice soared on those words, "The heart that has truly loved never forgets, but has truly loved on to the end." Yes, that was me, and there was no other man I could imagine in that chair. Better to have my memories and my independence. I thought of Agnella and the nuns, who had to conjure up their bridegroom from the get-go. At least I'd had some time with Peter. Enough, I'd say to myself. Go to bed.

I brought my camera and challenged myself to be up and out on the dock, ready to photograph the sun just as it rose. It was on the fifth morning that I heard footsteps coming down the path.

"Nonie, you out here?"

"Ed," I said. "Be careful. The fog's thick, and the pier is slippery." All I needed was for him to fall into the lake.

But he said, "Sounds like a description of politics."

He must be feeling better, I thought. I pushed one of the deck chairs over to him. "Better wipe it off," I said, handing a towel to him.

"The foggy, foggy dew," he said, and began to sing. *"But the Angelus bell o'er the Liffey swell rang out in the foggy dew,"* and smiled, for the first time since Ed Junior died. "Not quite John McCormack."

A silver disk was floating up, out of the mist that covered the lake. I lifted my camera, pressed the shutter. "Got it!" I said. "Imagine . . . this happens every morning."

"With no help from us," he said.

The sun swept the fog away, and the pine trees began to appear. Black shapes turning green, and reflected in the water.

I raised my cup in a salute and took a sip. A blue, blue Northwoods sky emerged. "Enough blue to make a Dutchman a pair of pants, as Rose says," I said to Ed. I could hear crows now and a loon's dominating cry. I closed my eyes and felt a splash of warm sun on my face.

Poor Ed. He didn't complain, but he must have had a terrible headache. "Beautiful spot," I offered.

"Do you want to see the site Ed Junior and I picked for the house?" Ed asked.

"Very much," I said.

He got up from the chair and started walking up the pier. "Did you ever notice that Ed Junior had his mother's profile? The spit of Mary," he said.

Oh no, I thought. That's it. He's going to head right back up to the cottage and the Jameson. But he kept walking. The fog burned off, and the mystery lifted. Just Catfish Lake now, Everett's Resort, a lodge and a collection of cabins along the lake.

I followed Ed past the boathouse up the path into the dense woods and along a narrow peninsula that ran into the lake. We came to a giant tree. Pine of some kind.

"Most of the Northwoods was cut down in the last century," Ed said. "Very few stretches of virgin forest. This is one."

"Don't you remember Uncle Patrick's stories?" I asked him. "He talked about the logging camps up here and how he'd traveled from one to the other, enlisting the Irish fellows into the Fenian Brotherhood."

"Vaguely," Ed said.

"Of course, we were the ones Uncle Patrick and Granny Honora lived with," I said. "I talked to him more than you did."

"I do remember his stories about the Ojibwe tribe in this area," Ed said.

"You should," I said. "His Ojibwe ointment saved your father's life as a child. You wouldn't be here except for that." Uncle Pat said that the Irish and the Indian should be allies, since both had their land stolen.

"My father talked about that often. One reason why I wanted a place up north. Of course, half of Chicago is here every summer. My land adjoins Mont Tennes's place," he said.

"Wilcox will love that. I can just see the headline, 'City Official Vacations with Notorious Gambler.'"

Why had I mentioned Wilcox? That would start him drinking again, I thought. But Ed was staring up at the tree.

"A clever fellow, Mont. And really, by setting up wires to the race tracks, he gives the bettors a fair shake."

"Mmmm," is all I said.

"I just can't get excited about gambling," Ed said. "I'd like to see it made legal so the city could collect taxes. Though Mont claims he does pay a kind of unofficial tax by supplementing the pay of the cops."

"Mmm," I said again.

"They should raise policemen's salaries. After all a man has to feed his family," Ed said.

I sometimes wondered if the reason that Irish politicians didn't worry too much about bribes was because we all had a bone-deep fear of starvation. We'd inherited it from our grandparents, who'd barely escaped death in Ireland when a million died after the potatoes failed.

Not a lot of talk about those days from Granny Honora and the old ones. But enough that we got the message. The English landlords tried to wipe us out once and for all, sending the healthy crops away to feed their own people, and leaving us with nothing but barnacles, unmilled corn meal, and nettles to eat.

If my kids were crying from hunger, and a fellow offered me a sawbuck to ignore a betting parlor, I'd take it too.

"The architect Ed Junior and I consulted wanted me to cut down this tree. It blocks the sun on the porch in the afternoon. I told him no. Something this majestic deserves to live."

"Good morning," we heard. Ed and I turned. Patrick from Everett's stood right behind us. A very quiet walker that fellow.

"Do you know what this land is called?" Patrick asked.

"Indian Point," Ed said.

"Yes," Patrick said. "This tree holds the spirit of our ancestors. There's an eagle's nest up there. So few eagles left," Patrick said. "The paper mills have poisoned the air and the water, and many farmers shoot them. Indian Point has always been their refuge. And now they have returned. Eagles are the totem of my clan. Tonight the full moon will rise at eight o'clock. I will come for you at seven."

"Pardon me?" I asked. But Patrick had walked away.

And at seven, there he was. I'd been expecting Ed to start on the Jameson at five, as usual. He made it a point of honor to wait until cocktail time before he began to get skittered. But tonight he sat at the dining room table, studying the blueprints for the house, making notes and eating a ham and cheese sandwich as he worked.

Patrick came right in, followed by an older woman. He stopped, stepped back, and said very formally, "May I present my mother."

Hard to guess her age. Not many wrinkles, but white hair in two long braids, and those same blue-gray eyes.

She smiled. "My name is," she began, and paused.

I expected a difficult Ojibwe name, but she said "Bridget."

"Bridget?" I repeated.

"Yes," she nodded. "My father was your kinsman, Patrick Kelly." Setting the words out one by one. "I am his daughter."

"What the hell?" Ed said.

"You must have known that Patrick Kelly lived with the Ojibwe," Bridget said.

"Yes," I said. How many times had Granny Honora told us how the whole lot of them would have frozen to death if Uncle Patrick had not shown up with a load of furs he'd trapped in the Northwoods and saved them all, their first Christmas in Bridgeport. None of us Kellys, including Ed and me, would be alive today if Uncle Patrick hadn't rescued our fathers. But had he left this woman behind as a baby in order to save us?

“He never told us he had a child,” I said to Bridget.

“My father didn’t know about me,” she said. “My mother told me that soon after I was conceived she had a dream. Little children crying, two women lost. All calling, ‘Patrick, Patrick.’ The next morning, she told my father that his own family needed him. He argued with her. His family was far across the sea, but my mother insisted. She said they were where the river emptied into a lake near many buildings.”

“Chicago,” Ed said.

“Yes,” Bridget said.

“And that was it? He left?” I asked.

“The dream came to my mother after she’d taken the sacred medicine. We honor such messages,” she said. “So even though she suspected she might be pregnant, she sent my father away.”

“So she sacrificed herself and you?”

“My mother didn’t think like that. She followed the old ways. Even her time with my father came because she saw him in a vision—a man wounded within and without, who must be healed. He was very sick when he came to the tribe,” she said.

“We didn’t know that,” Ed said.

“Lost and alone in these woods during a blizzard. Two of our men found him. One was my grandfather. He brought him into his lodge, and my mother cared for him. She saved him and loved him. But . . .” Bridget stopped. “He was with the Ojibwe for a year. He wanted to marry my mother, but she would not. That caused my father pain.”

“But why did she refuse?” I asked. I thought of that strange short ceremony in the Irish College Chapel. My wedding—a few minutes while some fellow waited to take Peter into revolution and death.

“My mother said she always knew my father must return to his own people one day. And, indeed, he told her there was another woman he cared for but that she was married to his own brother and so they could never be together. My mother did not want to be bound to a man who could never give her his whole heart,” Bridget said.

“She didn’t want to be bound,” I repeated. “Usually it’s the man who wants no strings.”

I thought of Tim McShane, who’d convinced me I was a different kind of woman, who could take my pleasure like a man. No sniveling—his word—about marriage. No whining. Except when I did try to leave, he was the one refused to let me go. I could still feel his hands on my throat. Again I thanked God and Spike O’Donnell that Tim was dead.

"You see," Bridget went on, "there was another man from the Two Rivers Band on Lake Superior who had come to Lac du Flambeau and met my mother years before. He was a holy man, a shaman, and had told my grandfather my mother was the woman meant to join him on his sacred journey. But my mother was only fifteen and was afraid of the path this man called her to. Three years later Patrick came. After he left, she sent a message to the shaman. She was ready."

"But did she love this other man like she loved Uncle Patrick?" I asked.

"She respected him and understood the great honor it would be to serve our people at his side."

"An impressive woman, your mother," Ed said.

"Yes," Bridget said. "And a very happy one."

"But didn't she ever wonder about Patrick?" I asked. And then, I remembered. "But wait. Patrick came back to the Northwoods years later with my granny Honora. Surely he tried to find your family."

"My mother lived far away in Two Rivers. My grandparents died soon after she left. Her brothers scattered. I don't think my father could have found my mother. And, besides, I had a new father. A kind and good man who taught me the secrets of healing, and how to become one with the sacred plants and animals."

Bridget reached over for Ed's hand and mine. "We are cousins, and now you will come with me. They are waiting for you, Ed," she said.

Bridget made me promise never to reveal the details of the ceremony she performed at Indian Point that night, as the big orange moon rose out of the lake and shone on the water. I'm not sure I could. I remember the beginning. The fire of cedar logs, burning within a circle of stones. Bridget offered us what she called "the medicine." First, special tobacco in a pipe we shared, and then sweetgrass, which she wound around our wrists. Then, sage—a big clump of it lit in the fire, making clouds of smoke that enveloped the four of us. Finally, a paste we chewed.

Then Bridget and Patrick began drumming, exchanging rhythms, and chanting. I looked over at Ed. I could only see a bit of his face, illuminated by the firelight and the moon coming through the trees. He lifted his hands and closed his eyes as his body began to sway.

"Mary," I heard him say. "Mary," and then "Ahh. Ed." He smiled.

The fire seemed to dance, colors changing. Orange and red. Blue, green, purple. The drumming got louder and louder. I closed my eyes and saw the kitchen on Hillock. Mam and Granny Honora laughing. Surely Peter Keeley would appear to me. I waited. And then . . . I must have fallen asleep, because suddenly the drumming got louder. Bright bursts of sound that seemed to call forth the sun. And there it was—a red tip, pushing up from behind the pine trees.

"Look," Patrick said and pointed. A pair of eagles was heading right toward us. They rode the air, then swooped down. The drummers went wild. Then the eagles wheeled in the air, shot straight up, and disappeared above the clouds.

"Some men are born to be eagles," I heard Patrick say to Ed.

And that night changed Ed. I'm not saying he never drank another drop, but he was never drunk again.

"I want to start on the house so we can have it finished up by the end of the summer," he said to us over dinner, Patrick and Bridget joining us for a real meal.

"You're building it then?" I asked.

"Of course," he said. "Ed Junior wants me to. And Patrick told me anytime I sat under the tall pine tree, I would feel his presence."

"Great," I said. I didn't understand what had happened to Ed, but he seemed full of purpose.

Bridget took a leather pouch out and gave it to Ed. "It's to be your medicine pouch," she said.

Ed opened it. I expected to see a bear claw, or eagle feather, or a muskie tooth. Instead, Ed pulled out a medal, an actual religious medal, bigger than usual, a dull copper color, and the size of a silver dollar, an image on each side. Mary as the sorrowful Mother on one and Jesus crowned with thorns on the other. Both faces seemed worn away a bit.

"My father, Patrick, your great-uncle," Bridget explained, "left this with my mother as a sign of his gratitude and love. He told her his own mother had given it to him. My mother didn't want to take the medal. 'This should be kept in his family,' she'd said. But he insisted, and gave it to her, along with many beaver pelts. But my mother told me that she resolved that if any of Patrick's family ever came back to the Northwoods, she would return the medal to them."

"But Patrick had no other children except you," I said.

"I am the daughter of the Ojibwe," she said. "And my son Patrick is a shaman. No, this medal is for you."

I picked up the medal. "So this belonged to Patrick and Michael Kelly's mother," I said to Ed. "Our what? Great-grandmother?"

"Yes," he said. "I didn't think they brought anything from Ireland with them."

"Grellan's crozier," I said, and Bridget laughed.

"Ah yes, Grellan's crozier. Patrick caused much confusion among our people with that golden staff. You know its power?" she asked me.

"That it grows hot in the hand of someone who is lying?" I said.

"Dangerous in a small tribe of people to know too much truth," she said.

"So it worked?" I asked.

"After the first experiment, Patrick took the staff back and never used it again here. Where is it?"

"Old St. Pat's Church in Chicago." I turned to Ed. "Might come in handy for you."

"But," Ed said. "This medal belongs to you too, Nonie, and all the cousins really."

"You must take it," Bridget said and pushed the medal across to Ed. "Yours is the most difficult path."

"An eagle," Patrick said to him.

10

Before we went back to Chicago, Ed asked Patrick to hire a construction crew. He wanted to start on the house immediately so it would be ready for August 1, always a day Granny Honora celebrated, though I can't remember why.

On May 1, 1926, the twins arrived. Margaret was over the moon. She named them Patricia and Joseph. Maybe her own father was Joseph. It did have a kind of German ring, and they were gorgeous. Irish heritage there, I'd say. I wondered about their mother—the girl who'd asked the sisters from St. Vincent de Paul to find a home for her children. Was she anguished or relieved? And the father . . . had he refused to take responsibility? Judge not, Nonie, I thought to myself. Remember Agnella and Erigina. God is love. Providence. That's the way Ed saw the twins.

"God's gift, Nonie." Ed was very serious. The two of us were in his office at the South Park headquarters, the old in-charge Ed back. Hard to believe that this was the same wreck of a man I'd driven up to Eagle River just weeks before. He reached into his pocket, took out the medal that Patrick had given him, and rubbed it.

"Margaret longed to be a mother her whole life, and now she is. I don't want anything to distract her from the care of her babies. I want this summer to be the happiest she's ever known. Can't you imagine the little ones with their feet kicking in the lake? The clear air, those blue skies, no Big Bill Thompson or Reverend Wilcox. A place for all the family to come to for my mother and Aunt Kate."

"Michael and his kids," I said. "Rose and John."

"We Kellys are country people after all," Ed said. "Wasn't our grandfather a farmer? And Granny Honora's people fishermen? We need to connect to a simpler life."

"You're not exactly building a cabin in the woods, Ed," I said. I pointed to the blueprints on his desk. "Eight bedrooms. Two thirty-square-foot rooms on the main floor."

"A place to gather," he said and pulled a sheet from the bottom of the pile. "Look at this. We're going to have our own movie theater. With the projector in the loft and speakers in every corner."

"Impressive, Ed," I said. I didn't think there was a private house in Chicago with its own movie theater. Can't ever forget that Ed is an engineer. Leave it to him to make the simple complicated.

"We need this house," he said. "And I've got to have someplace where I'm not always looking over my shoulder. Lots of people I respect are building homes up there."

"Our own Tír na nÓg," I said.

In June, Ed called me into his office. "Patrick is ready to start on the interior. I want you to go and supervise the decoration."

"Me? Surely, Margaret wants to fix up her house . . ."

"She's busy with the twins, and besides, this place is for all of us," he said.

"House of O'Ceallaigh," I said.

"What?"

"That's our name in the Irish language."

"Good," he said. "I like that. We'll carve the words into the stone gates."

So. I was on the train the next day.

The exterior was impressive. A two-storied house with a wide center section flanked by two arched roofs. Windows galore. Dozens of panes of glass outlined in white fitted together. Walls of windows, just as Ed Junior had wanted.

I vaguely remembered Granny Honora's story about how her husband, our grandfather Michael Kelly, built her a cottage with a glass window so that she could look out and see Galway Bay and the fisherman's cottage where she'd been born. Very proud of that window Granny had been. I'd heard her tell Mam that before she left Ireland she'd smashed that window so that the thief who'd stolen their cottage would not get pleasure from her husband's gift.

Wish you could see your grandson's cottage, Granny, I thought, because that's what the workmen called it. The Indian Point cottage. And your nephew Patrick is building it, Granny, son of your husband's brother. The man who was your second husband. Nothing straightforward in our family. I heard Granny Honora in my head. Her laugh, and then her voice saying, "So now the Kellys are *flaithulach* with windows."

I stayed at Ed's Everett cottage and was up at dawn every day. The workmen started at 7:00 a.m. and sometimes worked well into the night. Patrick was determined to finish, and Ed authorized double pay for overtime.

The men were paneling the first floor in wood but weren't using local pine or balsam. Ed wanted his floors made from redwood—stronger—so these planks came on their own freight car from California. Two German woodworkers directed this part of the project. A pleasure to see the way they stroked the fragrant woods as they fit one next to the other.

After the floor was laid, they used the remaining wood for the stairs and the banisters. When it was time to panel the walls, one of the men had an idea.

"Plaster," Gunther Himmelsbach said to me when Patrick brought him over to the desk I'd set up in what would be Ed's study.

"Plaster," Himmelsbach repeated.

"What?" I said.

"In Germany, I worked on many churches," he said. "I covered the walls with pictures." He brought out a sheet of paper where he'd drawn pine trees, boats, deer. A fish jumped out of the lake, a beaver pounded the ground. "I can make these from plaster."

"Wonderful," I said. "Go ahead."

Himmelsbach would start his work when the crew left. He worked by the light of lanterns to create the amazing scenes in the great room.

When Patrick's mother, Bridget, came to inspect our progress, she was not impressed with the bare floors. "Little children will fall, hit their heads. You need carpets."

Bridget organized a team of Ojibwe women to weave squares that could be sewn together. She drew the designs using woodland flowers—daisies, buttercups, orange Indian pipes, black-eyed Susans, and a load of others that had Indian names she couldn't translate. I paid three dollars a square, and soon the women were doing eight, nine, ten a day, making more money than the men. Gorgeous, each one of them. Every one just a bit different.

As I got to know Bridget I found her knowledge and spirituality fascinating. How this Ojibwe lore would have intrigued Peter. The tribe had the same connection with nature that the early Irish monks had. Very Celtic altogether.

"It's a full moon," I told Bridget, "and the summer solstice. I wonder? I mean, is there . . . ?"

"A ceremony?" she offered. "Yes. At Lac du Flambeau, the reservation. Hundreds will be there."

"Oh," I said. I was still disappointed that Peter Keeley had not appeared to me in that first ceremony. Maybe . . .

Bridget seemed to know what I was thinking. "You wish to contact someone."

Not a question. "I do," I said, and went on a bit about Peter. Tried to explain how her philosophy and Peter's would intersect and why, I was sure, his spirit would manifest if the circumstances were right.

So once again, Bridget and Peter drummed and chanted, while the fire danced and the full moon lit the lake. And I was visited—by a whole array of figures from my past, including Michael Collins. But not a trace of Peter.

I was silent the next morning as Bridget and I sat, drinking coffee in the cottage. Patrick had gone off to work. Finally I asked, "Why didn't Peter come to me? I've been so faithful to him."

"Maybe he wants you to go on with your life. Marry again."

"What about you—where's your husband?"

"Dead for many years."

"And . . . what did you do?"

"I too have been faithful," Bridget said. "Also . . . I don't want to risk being bossed around by a man."

I laughed. "But do you see your husband during the ceremonies?"

"Of course," Bridget replied.

"Then why don't I?"

Bridget set her coffee cup down. She closed her eyes and sat still and silent for what seemed a long time. Then she began talking. Praying, I suppose, in her own language. Finally she opened her eyes and looked at me. "Your Peter is not in the spirit world," she said. "He's still alive."

"That's impossible," I said. "I wish it was true, but he was killed. Fell in battle. Maybe warriors go to a different place and you're just not seeing him?"

Bridget didn't answer. What could I say? Cyril Peterson had seen Peter die. I had to accept his death. No point in pretending. As Agnella said, I must go through the pain. And yet . . .

There was a knock at the door. Our women weavers were ready to go to work. Bridget stood up. "You have to believe in order to see," she said.

Whatever that meant.

By mid-July, we had a thousand squares. One night we laid the squares out on the floors of the Great Room and sun porch, then knelt down to stitch them all together. It was Bridget who started the singing. Not an Ojibwe chant, but old songs—"A Bicycle Built for Two" and "Has Anybody Here Seen Kelly." By dawn, both rooms were covered. The flowers of the forest bloomed all around us. Light poured through the windows as the sun came up, and we looked up to see the workmen staring at the entrance.

One by one, the men entered the room, took off his work boots and stepped on the carpet. The two fellows from the Micmac tribe crouched down, rubbing their hands along the surface. The Ojibwe men on the crew crawled along the carpet on their hands and knees shouting out words to each other.

"What's going on?" I said to Patrick.

"My mother has drawn flowers and plants that are medicine for us, and the women have made them grow right here. See this?" He pointed to a spread of leaves with a few white blossoms. "In English this is sheep sorrel, and that"—he pointed to the next square—"is burdock root. There is rhubarb. Combined, they make a tea called Essiac. A very strong medicine."

An apothecary had sprung up under our feet.

"As you can see," Patrick said, "the gifts of the Creator are endless. Giving not only beauty, but health."

During all this hubbub, the women stood silent—looking at each other and then to Bridget. "I had no idea," I said to her, "I just thought they were pretty flowers."

"This is the herb"—she pointed with the toe of her moccasin—"that cures fevers."

Was the medicine Uncle Patrick had given to Stephen made from this herb?

"Wonderful," I said. "This will mean so much to Ed and to Margaret. They'll be so grateful. I am, too. Thank you, thank you," I said to Bridget.

"We are all grateful to the boy," she said.

"A boy? Where is he? Bring him here."

Now Patrick spoke, "He's been with us from that first day. Every morning he stood at the lakeshore smiling at us through the mist. A little soldier in a gray coat," Patrick said.

"Shiny buttons," Bridget went on, "round glasses."

"Dear God," I said, "Ed Junior. You saw Ed Junior." I started weeping. Bridget took me with her to sit on the bench under the tree with the eagles' nest.

"But I don't believe in ghosts," I said. "I don't."

"And, until today, you didn't believe that the flowers of the forest can cure sickness. Your believing or not believing doesn't matter. The boy was here. Those who can't believe can't see. Tell Ed Kelly the house is ready," she said. "My mother is pleased. Our two peoples united. Blessed."

And so we were that summer. Blessed. Margaret and the twins, Ed's mother, her sister Aunt Kate, and Rose and John came along with Michael and his kids. We all spent those last weeks of August together.

I remember the sun shining every day. Magnificent sunsets and a dark sky full of the brightest stars, with a week of meteor showers that thrilled the children and me. Every morning, Patrick would take Ed, Michael, and Mike out fishing, while Rose, John and I, Aunt Kate, and Aunt Nelly would sit with Margaret on the screened-in porch. Meanwhile, Rosemary and Ann, thirteen and eleven now, spread a blanket on the lawn, set the twins in the middle, and invited Frances, six, and Marguerite, eight, to their picnic.

"Henrietta would not allow that," I said to Rose.

"No," said Rose. "She'd worry about grass stains. Was she always such a tyrant?"

"Yes," I said. "Just be glad she decided to visit Agnella and left the children to us."

"Nice to hear the girls laughing," she said.

"That's what this house is going to be for. Laughter," I said.

Aunt Nelly and Aunt Kate had both fallen asleep in their big wicker chairs, and Margaret had gone in to see about dinner. John was napping upstairs.

"Ed was talking to me about buying a house in Chicago for his mother and Aunt Kate," Rose said, "if John and I would agree to live with them and take care of things. He'd pay for everything and even give us a kind of stipend but . . ."

"But what?" John could not work. Money was tight. This would be a great chance for her. To live in comfort while helping the family.

"Ed's looking at places in Beverley," she said.

"But it's lovely out there and you could sell your house and have some money."

"Right," Rose said, "but Beverley's very far from Argo. I want to be close if the kids need me. There are hardly any trains, and the buses take forever."

"Ask Ed for a car and driver."

"Nonie! Such an extravagance."

"He'll do it, believe me. Ed has decided to spend his money to make us all happy. He built the house for good times and family. That's what he and Ed Junior planned. This will be a space apart for all of us."

"Kind of him. So strange. I know we're up here in the Northwoods, but when I look out at the water, it's the little lakes of Cavan that I see," Rose said.

"And for me, it's Galway Bay." I wanted to tell Rose about my efforts to contact Peter Keeley, but I didn't. She was so very Catholic.

"We make a good team, Nonie," Ed said to me the last weekend of that summer at the lake, when we sat fishing at the pier watching red and yellow leaves drop from bare boughs onto the water. "Lots of projects to complete and document."

"I can't promise I'll be in Chicago forever," I said. "I've unfinished business in Ireland, Ed. You see . . ." And I launched into the whole story of my love for Peter Keeley, his death, and what Bridget had said. "I have to be sure, I have to find his grave, kneel and say an Ave there, so he can sleep in peace until I come to join him."

Ed's rod hit the wooden slats. He was fast asleep. He hadn't heard a word I'd said. I shook him.

"Dreaming," he said.

"They came to you?"

He didn't answer . . . only nodded.

"I'll never be the same man I would have been if Ed Junior, Mary, and the baby had lived. But they want me to go on with Margaret and the twins now. A family. I need to get back to work and I need your photographs to make the progress real."

"Good," I said. *Help Ed,* Agnella had said. *He needs your support.* Alright then. Peter would have to wait a little longer.

11

OCTOBER 1926

Back in town, I got a nun pal of Agnella's to write out these words in calligraphy on a piece of parchment: "Make no small plans. They have no magic to stir men's blood. Make big plans. Aim high in hope and work." Ed's favorite quotation from Daniel Burnham, the fellow whose 1909 Plan of Chicago included a magnificent lakefront with parks and museums. Very aspirational at a time when the people of Chicago used our beaches, or any bit of open ground for that matter, as garbage dumps.

I'd put it in a nice oak frame, brought it to Ed's office, pounded in a nail and hung it on the wall. He had already built the stadium now named Soldier Field, created six miles of new shoreline using landfill, and turned piles of refuse into Grant Park.

Ed's determination to finance new projects with private funds was paying off.

Which was why I was in Ed's office, to photograph him with Kate Buckingham. She had donated $250,000 to construct a monument to her brother Clarence on the plot of land Ed and the South Park Board had given her at the entrance to Grant Park. The Buckinghams were a well-known family in Chicago, originally from Ohio, I think. The father, Ebenezer, had made his fortune in grain elevators, as had so many of the early Chicago pioneers, and like a number of them, he'd started collecting art, as a tribute to his success. His son, Clarence, had made more money and expanded his father's collection. And here was Kate. She had inherited the whole shebang when her unmarried brother had died suddenly ten years before, at age fifty-four, and their sister had followed a few years later.

Something of a recluse, Miss Buckingham, but here she was in Ed's office. About seventy, heavyset with strong features and lovely white, white hair. She wore black. In constant mourning, I'd say. The dress wasn't fashionable. The hem touched her shoes, but it was well cut, custom-made from expensive material. She and Ed stood next to his drafting table under the double windows, with the afternoon sun lighting the papers spread out there.

"Miss Buckingham and I are discussing the progress of her fountain."

"My brother's fountain," she said. "A monument to him."

"She's concerned. The groundbreaking was last year, and there's not much to see. But I've assured her that now the preliminary excavation's been done, the real construction can begin," Ed said.

"I hope you're correct, Mr. Kelly. I'm not confident . . ."

"Oh, you can count on Ed to get things moving," I said. "Look at Soldier Field. How many were there for the Tunney-Dempsey fight last week? A hundred thousand?"

"More," Ed said.

"And millions of dollars coming into the city . . . ," I said.

Ed interrupted me. Kate Buckingham had swayed just a bit, and was holding on to the drafting table. Not a fan of prizefights, I guess.

"Buckingham Fountain will bring a touch of the sublime to Chicago," Ed said.

Kate stood a little straighter.

"Miss Buckingham, I'd like to introduce my cousin Nora, my photographer. I'd very much like to have a picture with you."

Miss Buckingham nodded. "Nora's spent some time in France," he said. Ed didn't usually mention my career in Paris.

Now Kate Buckingham smiled at me. "Then perhaps you know the Latona Fountain in Versailles that inspired me."

"Latona?" I repeated.

"It features the goddess who was the mother of Diana and Apollo, though she wasn't married to Jupiter, their father, which annoyed his wife."

Miss Buckingham looked at Ed, and could it be? Was that a giggle?

"Instead of mythological figures, we are going to have four giant bronze sea horses," Ed said, "each representing one of the states that border the lake—Indiana, Illinois, Wisconsin, and Michigan."

"All based on Indian words," I said.

Since our time with the Ojibwe, I'd become more aware of all the native words that we've claimed and distorted.

"The English did the same in Ireland," I went on. "Twisted place names from the original Irish language into their own labels because they could. Those early settlers that we are so proud of were imperialists and—"

"Very interesting, Nora," Ed said in a tone that meant that's enough. "As Miss Buckingham and I were saying, the statues are being designed and cast in Paris. Buckingham Fountain will be twice as big as the one in Versailles, over ten stories high with water that shoots a hundred and fifty feet into the air."

"Colored water," Kate Buckingham said to me. "Rainbows."

I posed the two together, first looking down at the plans then smiling at each other, and snapped a few good pictures.

"I promised Miss Buckingham that the fountain will be open in August," Ed said. "Imagine what it will be like on a summer's night with families strolling along the plaza taking in the spectacle."

"And listening to the music," Buckingham added.

"Mayor Dever has authorized double shifts for the crews," Ed said. "Get as much done before the real winter sets in."

"A good man, your Mayor Dever," Kate Buckingham said. "I would not have begun this project while William Thompson was mayor. He was dreadful."

"And yet your people elected Big Bill twice. Gave him not one but two terms," I said.

Kate Buckingham shrugged. "We were Republicans and while he seemed to be one of us . . ."

"Rich?" I said

"Please Nora," Ed said.

Miss Buckingham said, "Let her speak. She has a point. We were fooled. His father, the colonel, was a friend of my parents. And though William was a bit of a harum-scarum growing up . . ." She paused.

I couldn't let that pass.

"He was a spoiled brat," I said. "And a menace. He and his friends would gallop their horses through the city streets . . ."

"But he was only a boy," Kate Buckingham said. "Thirteen."

"Ed and my brother were both working at twelve. Thompson caused real damage. Growing up in Bridgeport I heard stories about how he and his gang would come riding hell for leather over the bridge at Bubbly Creek. They knocked down a little girl called Janie Donohue. When she tried to jump out of their way, they laughed at her, Miss Buckingham. That part was always told—those boys from so-called good families thought she was comical. My grandmother said it reminded her of the landlord's coach rushing through an Irish village running over children. Remember her saying that, Ed?"

"I do," Ed said. "But Thompson didn't have the nerve to run against Dever. He's finished."

"I hope so," I said.

Kate Buckingham couldn't help but defend the Thompsons. "His family did try. They sent him out to the West to their ranch," she said.

"And he's played at being a cowboy ever since," I said.

Tim McShane had been a pal of the fellow who referred to himself as "Big Bill." One thing to be given a nickname but to hang one on yourself? Maybe he was afraid he'd be called "Fats" Thompson because he was. Tall too. But still wore boots and a ten-gallon hat to make himself more massive. Tim told me he met him in gambling houses that I now realize were brothels in the Levee, that strip of wickedness on the near South Side where Carl Sandburg had seen the "painted women under the gas lamps luring the farm boys." Although there were plenty of local city slickers patronizing any number of fancy mansions there too. Thompson was one of them.

When he'd returned to Chicago at age twenty-three, Thompson took over his dead father's real estate company just as the World's Fair of 1893 started Chicago booming and the Levee exploded with customers from all over the country, the world, really. Thompson left the running of the company to the woman who had been his father's assistant. She made him a fortune. Big Bill married her, but according to Tim, never changed his ways. For a laugh, Bathhouse John Coughlin and Hinky Dink Kenna, the "Lords of the Levee," who were the aldermen of the First Ward, glommed on this rich *amadan* and ran him as alderman for the Second Ward. They managed to squeak him through. But once Thompson got on the city council, he was taken over by the slightly more respectable Fred Lundin, who discovered that Big Bill had a natural ability to rant and rave in front of an audience.

"We're the real Americans," he'd tell a crowd of white Protestant males and go on about how they had to fend off the scum invading Chicago. He described immigrants using the slurs that we were taught never to say, which delighted his supporters. He was well known in the city, a character no one took too seriously when I left in 1911, so I was shocked when the *Chicago Tribune*'s Paris edition reported in 1915 that Big Bill Thompson had been elected mayor. Ed must be tearing his hair out, I'd thought. The *Paris Tribune* called Big Bill "the Clown Prince" and enjoyed making fun of his antics. Not so humorous, though, when Al Capone and a pack of New York gangsters came to town after Prohibition. Big Bill overcame his disdain for "grease balls" and gave the key to the city to the Italian outfit. Levee-style vice flooded all of Chicago with gang violence. The *Paris Tribune* wrote a big article about how much money Capone contributed to Thompson's campaign for a second term as mayor, which he won thanks in part to the support of respectable people like Kate Buckingham.

"How any church-going citizen could have voted Republican is beyond me," I said to her. "He's immoral and stupid and greedy."

Kate Buckingham held up her hand.

"I agree with everything you're saying, Miss Kelly. Let me assure you that Thompson will never represent the Republican Party again. And I may even vote for a Democrat."

Ed and I smiled at her.

"I will have these photos ready in a few days," I said. "We're all grateful to you for this fountain, Miss Buckingham. I know it will cost a great deal of money."

"I have a great deal of money, and I loved my brother, Miss Kelly," she said.

"A memorial," I said, "because the dead still are with us."

And she smiled at me, a real smile. We have more in common than you know, Kate, I thought. I heard those words again. I loved my brother. Does Henrietta love Michael? Never considered that before. I knew she wanted him to support her and her children, but love? Once again I heard Agnella's voice: "You don't understand my mother. She's sick and suffering." *Mmm.*

After Kate Buckingham left, Ed said to me, "Remember how the stink of the stockyards held down the air in Bridgeport until we could hardly breathe in the summer? Now relief will be only a bus ride away. Next week Julius Rosenwald is bringing his brother-in-law Max Adler to talk to me. Julius says Max is fascinated with tracking the stars and planets and might be willing to fund a planetarium in Chicago. It would be the first one in the United States."

"So they're Julius and Max to you now?"

"They're nice fellows, Nora," Ed said.

"Well, be sure to tell them the Irish practiced astronomy thousands of years ago. Before the pyramids were built, the ancient inhabitants of Ireland created passage graves that face east. On the day of the winter solstice, the sun comes through an opening and illuminates the interior of the grave at Newgrange."

"Oh," Ed said, but he was rooting around on his desk. He held up a letter.

"This is from John Shedd, the retired president of Marshall Fields. He's interested in marine life and wants to build the biggest aquarium in North America. This letter is full of compliments for Mayor William Dever. He even said a few nice things about me. Shedd wrote that he had started as a stock clerk, and admired me as another man who began at the bottom. Listen to how he described me," Ed said. "'You acquired not only the skills necessary for success but the manners and deportment of a gentleman.'" Ed smiled at me. "See?" he said. "They had written us Irish off as greedy roughnecks, like Hinky Dink and Bathhouse, but now . . ."

"Margaret dresses up in an ermine coat, and you put on a top hat and tails and go to the opera. Ed, why don't you tell them that the Irish monks were translating Greek myths when the English were painting themselves blue?"

But Ed wasn't listening. He rolled up the plans he'd shown Kate Buckingham.

"I want you to photograph every phase of the fountain's construction."

"No small plans," I said.

FEBRUARY 1927

But Chicago winters have a way of disrupting plans, no matter how large, and the construction of the fountain proceeded in stops and starts. It wasn't until February that the sea horses could be installed in the basin. The crew had gotten used to me showing up at dawn, dressed in the version of Coco Chanel's trouser suit I'd had Rose copy for me in a nice heavy, worsted wool.

At first she'd protested, "Oh, Nonie, what will people say?"

"Come on, Rose. You weren't afraid to try new things when we had our studio at Montgomery Ward. You loved to whip up new designs," I'd said.

"Nonie, you work for Ed," John had told me a few weeks before Christmas. "He's given you a lot of responsibility. If you start running around in pants, it'll give the opposition another stick to hit Ed with."

"Rose, we marched for women's right to vote. Surely I can choose to be warm," I'd said. "Are you afraid of what Aunt Kate and Aunt Nelly will think?" She and John were living with them now. I'd given in once to Ed's mother but I wouldn't again, so I went to her and said, "Aunt Nelly, I need Rose to make me a kind of uniform for work."

"Fine, dear," she'd said. "Go ahead."

"We three have been through too much together," Rose said. That Christmas she handed me a box with beautiful pants and a jacket, warm and comfortable and perfect for an early morning's photo assignment.

What had Ed said about the fountain—sublime? The very word, I thought, as the rising sun splashed onto the pink marble basin. Still cold on this February morning, but I'd noticed a few crocuses pushing their way up through the strip of grass that edged Michigan Avenue in front of the Art Institute. Here's a masterpiece no one would have to pay to see or even dress up to brave the Institute's Protestant-built halls and galleries. Like the crocuses, I thought as I smiled to myself and tipped my camera up to catch that stream of luminescence.

Then I heard someone arguing behind me. I recognized the foreman Chris Garvey's voice but the other fellow was shouting in French, *"Les chevaux marins,"* repeated over and over. I turned to see a man holding Chris by the shoulders.

Now Chris was a Bridgeport fellow, a decent guy and fairly open-minded. "She's from the neighborhood, boys," he'd said to the crew the first morning, stopping the catcalls I might have expected when I arrived wearing my woolen trouser suit. His grandmother and my mother had been friends and like most of the men from Bridgeport, he had a strong sense of his own dignity. He did not like this Frenchman grabbing him. He'll sock the guy, I thought. I'd better step in.

"Pardon, monsieur," I said. And to my surprise the language I'd used in Paris for ten years came creaking out and the fellow understood me.

He explained that he was Marcel Loyau, the sculptor of the *chevaux*. The sea horses. He was trying to make sure that these "idiots," a word that unfortunately sounded the same in French as in English, placed them properly.

I saw Chris start to react. "Hey, Chris," I said, "how about a picture with you and monsieur here? The South Park Commission is putting out a special pamphlet on the construction of the fountain. I'd like to photograph you and the artist."

"Beauty and the Beast," Chris said. I forgot that Bridgeport fellows also have a sense of humor.

I translated for Loyau as he and Chris went over the plans, a meeting of the minds, and finally I lined up the whole crew with Loyau in the center. "Not a bad guy, Chris," I said. He told me he did the monument for the American Cemetery of the Somme.

Chris nodded. "A lot of our crew fought in France."

By now my French was flowing and I began telling Loyau that I had lived in Paris. He made that noise with his lips that meant "so what?" in French. So I started batting names at him—Henri Matisse, Gertrude Stein, Coco Chanel—until Loyau told me that he was having lunch with his patroness, Mademoiselle Buckingham, and gave me the Gallic equivalent of a bum's rush. Chris Garvey observed the whole exchange.

"He's an artist, Chris," I said as we watched Loyau walk toward Michigan Avenue. "And you have to admit that those sea horses are amazing."

"But why get a Frenchman? Surely there is someone in Chicago who could have made these statues. Big Bill says that Dever and Ed Kelly are letting themselves get bushwhacked by the rich who pretend to be Europeans, as if America isn't good enough for them."

"Big Bill Thompson," I said. "I can't believe you would listen to that loudmouth. Remember whatever he says, he's a Republican underneath it all with no use for the working man."

"I just happened to catch one of his rallies," Chris said. "He does put on a good show."

Today was the primary election. Thompson was running for the Republican nomination for mayor. The party had tried to ignore him, so he had staged a debate where two rats in cages stood in for his opponents. Got big coverage in all the newspapers.

I'd asked Ed about Thompson's chances. "None," he'd said, "though I wouldn't mind if he were the nominee. Dever would clean his clock."

So, I should have been prepared when I went to Ed's office that afternoon—prints from that morning's photography session in hand. I had my darkroom in the basement of the South Park Commission offices where I also kept a change in clothes. Ed had asked me not to wear pants in the office.

Pat Nash was on the phone, holding the receiver so Ed could hear what was being said. "The Republicans have nominated Thompson," Ed said to me.

Pat put down the phone. "Thompson got a better turnout than anyone expected, but that's among Republicans. The general election will be different. No Democrat or any rational person for that matter will vote for the man," he said.

"I don't know," I said. "One of the crew this morning was talking about the Thompson rally he went to, sounded like he was getting a kick out of him."

"One of *our* fellows?" Ed said. "Working on a job *we* got him? What's his name?"

"I'd rather not say," I said. Both men stared at me for what seemed like a long time.

"Alright, alright," said Ed. "We can't pretend that Big Bill's not entertaining. It's only six weeks until the election. Somebody's got to go to one of his rallies and find out what he's telling people so Dever can expose him." And they were staring at me.

Which was why two weeks later I headed for the Medinah Temple, my Seneca in my bag. I followed a circus parade made up of Thompson's supporters—a big crowd of four to five thousand. We were led by a camel with a sign on its back that read "I can go days without a drink, but who wants to be a camel?" Thompson was running on his opposition to Prohibition. The Democrats were against the Volsted Act too. After all, it had failed to reform drinkers and only opened the door for gangsters. But Decent Dever had said as long as Prohibition was the law of the land, he'd enforce it in Chicago which only meant Capone moved his headquarters a few miles outside the city limits to Cicero.

Now we were at the entrance to the Medinah Temple. A barker stood near the main door shouting, "Come in for the best vaudeville show ever seen. Singing. Dancing. Girls." We filed in very orderly because the ushers who stood at the head of each aisle were gangsters. Capone's men no question.

Once everyone was in their seats, a boy dressed in rags led a donkey down the middle aisle—a pitiful animal, skinny and mangy. The sign he wore said "Democrats." Just as the donkey made it to the stage, out from the wings came a black horse with Bill in the saddle. He was dressed in cowboy gear, complete with a ten-gallon hat. He rode straight at the donkey. The poor animal pulled away from the boy and took off. Everybody around me was laughing. Finally, Big Bill dismounted and, still holding the horse's reins, started bellowing at us.

"Real American men should be able to drink a beer without the police breaking into their homes." The crowd cheered that.

"Let's run Dever out of town. Stop all those Micks and Dagos and Bohunks and kikes who support him from feeding at the public trough," Thompson hollered.

Not as many cheers. I noticed that there weren't many women. Too sensible, I thought, for this nonsense. So I was impressed when an older lady stood up and called out, "What happened to the thousands of dollars you raised for flood victims? None of them got a cent. You kept the money for yourself."

"Who do you think you are?" Bill called down to her. "Jane Addams?"

Another roar from the crowd. The woman who worked with immigrants wasn't popular with this group either. Two ushers came down the aisle. Took the woman by the arms and started walking her toward the exit.

This is a photograph I should get, I thought. Show these goons manhandling her. I took the Seneca out of my large handbag, raised the camera as the woman and two men came toward me. Perfect. I had the frightened woman's face, the two bruisers in my viewfinder. But just as I was about to press the shutter, somebody pushed me from behind. I went forward into the row ahead of me and was just able to hold on to my camera. "No pictures." It was the fellow next to me who'd hit me. A perfectly ordinary looking man. "No pictures," he said again. "Leave Big Bill alone."

Dear God, what was going on?

I was not surprised when Big Bill won. A third candidate had run and taken away some of Dever's votes. Still Thompson carried not only the typically Republican precincts including Bronzeville, the colored neighborhood, but he got a sizable share of usually Democratic wards.

Even my Gold Coast neighbors voted for him. Of course, our poll watchers had looked very much like the ushers at Thompson's rally. A young dark-haired man who'd been standing in front of our polling place followed me right up to the desk, and looked over my shoulder as I signed the register. "Vote for Thompson, Miss Kelly," he'd told me. "That's a nice building you live in." The election official had said nothing.

A week after Thompson's inauguration, the mayor came to Ed's office at the South Park Commission. I was there showing him the shots I'd taken of the fountain. All the sea horses were in place and the jets were being installed.

"You'll meet the August deadline," I was saying to Ed as Big Bill came through the door followed by Bessie O'Neill, Ed's secretary

"Just a minute," she said. "Mr. Kelly is not expecting you."

"I don't care what he is expecting," Thompson said, and lowered himself into the big leather chair in front of Ed's desk.

Even seated, Thompson was massive. More flab than muscle though, in spite of the way he always bragged about his time as a water polo player. What kind of a sport was that anyway? Played in country club pools. Ed was still the trim boxer of his youth. He stood up, walked around his desk, towered over Big Bill. If only Thompson's nickname had been Fats, we wouldn't be stuck with him now.

"Heard you had your own bailiwick over here, Kelly. Set yourself up like a little king."

Now Ed's office was nice enough. Two big windows looked out on the drive. He had an antique walnut desk Margaret found for him, two green leather chairs, and a matching sofa. Nothing outrageous. The big draftsman's table in the corner, piled with blueprints and plans, took up most of the space. A working office.

"Nice to see you, Mr. Mayor," Ed said. "If I knew you were coming I'd have arranged for some refreshments."

"Refreshments? I don't waste time on tea and cookies. I heard you can't hold your liquor anymore. Have become a teetotaler," Thompson said.

Ed said nothing.

"Look, Kelly, I don't have much time. I know you hate me so let's not pretend."

"Hate's a very strong word, Mr. Mayor," Ed said. "You're a political opponent. You won. We lost. But I work for the people of the city of Chicago, so whoever's mayor, I'll do my job."

"Hogwash, Kelly. Hogwash."

Ed laughed. "You've got quite a vocabulary, Mr. Mayor. I do want to cooperate with you. In fact, I'd like to have a photograph with you for my wall. This is my photographer."

"I heard about her. Some relative and screwy to boot. I didn't come here to play nice. Here's how it's going to be. I'll let you do your projects, Kelly, because they're good for Chicago and, therefore, for me. But I want you to tell Pat Nash and those ward heelers in the Democratic Party that all the jobs and patronage will stop if they try to double-cross me. If I find out, and I will find out, that you're putting together a 'Stop Thompson' group, there won't be another foot of concrete laid in this city by any Mick contractor. And stay away from that Bohunk Cermak if you know what's good for you. I can do business with you Micks, but not those Bohunks. And don't try to blarney me or play me for a fool. I'm smarter than you are. A genius."

Doesn't Thompson know, I thought, that we Micks had eight hundred years of practice in pulling the wool over the eyes of people like him?

"But here's the thing, Kelly," Thompson said. "I need my first year as mayor to be spectacular."

Thompson stood.

"I'm going to be president, Kelly," he said.

"President of what?" Ed asked.

"Of the United States, you moron. I've got the Republican convention next summer all lined up. Already have a bunch of delegates committed to me. But I want to get a lot of good press. I'll give you whatever you need to get your projects up and running by the summer so I can go to the convention in Kansas City with a reputation as a fellow who gets things done. I'm going to beat that sissy Hoover on the first ballot. President Thompson. It has a ring."

Ed said nothing.

Big Bill Thompson as president. It didn't bear thinking about.

It wasn't even an hour later that Pat Nash was in Ed's office and me there too.

"President? Thompson is going for president? Hard to believe," Pat said.

"Nora heard him too," Ed said.

"I did, Pat, and he was serious. But the Republican Party would never nominate a buffoon like Thompson would they?" I said.

"They might," Pat said. "I didn't expect him to be elected mayor. Thompson knows how to get attention and he'll promise to put his own money into the campaign. Probably buy off a good few delegates and intimidate the rest in the same way he scared the voters here. He's got a bully's self-confidence and that can be dangerous."

"We have to stop him," Ed said.

"Why?" Pat said. "He'll be a terrible candidate for the general election. If we can convince the Democrats to nominate Al Smith, opposing Thompson might be the only way a Catholic like him will get elected."

"But isn't that taking a chance?" I said. "What if Thompson won?"

"Nora's right," Ed said. "Strange things happen in elections and Capone will give him all the money he needs. We have to tip off somebody in the Republican Party."

"They won't appreciate advice from us, Ed," Pat said. "They'll think it's some kind of a trick and be more determined than ever to back Thompson."

"Couldn't you call Colonel McCormick, Ed?" I said. "An article in the *Tribune* about Thompson's plans might—"

"No," said Pat. Just like that, a flat no. "Thompson will find out where the information came from. We have to work with the bastard for the next four years. Can't rile him up now."

After Pat left, Ed said there was nothing to do but keep our heads down and concentrate on the work. Over that summer, Buckingham Fountain was finished and ground was broken for both the planetarium and the aquarium.

On August 26, 1927, Ed, Margaret, and I walked through the fading twilight toward the dark shape that was Buckingham Fountain. In an hour, Kate Buckingham would say the word and the memorial to her brother would be turned on for the first time. A humid Chicago night with the lake just managing to send a breeze across the gathering crowd.

"No stench from the stockyards here," I said to Ed as we approached the entrance to the raised outdoor stage where I could see Big Bill and the woman I thought of as his poor wife although she was rich enough. As we got closer, I noticed that Kate Buckingham was sitting right next to the mayor. Ed had told me that the final cost of the fountain was $750,000 and Kate had paid the whole kit and caboodle plus added another $300,000 as a maintenance fund and gave the money happily.

"A kind of immortality," she'd told Ed.

A line of aldermen on the stage. It made me angry to see how even Democratic politicians had fallen in line behind Thompson.

"Waiting in the tall grass," Ed reassured me, but I wasn't so sure. Capone kept Thompson supplied with unlimited cash that he spread around. A squad of uniformed policemen and a few of the ushers stood at the entrance to the stage.

"Hi, boys," Ed said to the cops. No answer. Then one of the ushers said, "Only special guests of the mayor allowed in this section. No more room."

I expected Ed to ream the guy out, but he said nothing. So I spoke up. "This is Edward J. Kelly, head of the South Park Commission. This fountain wouldn't exist without him. You go tell the mayor . . ." But the fellow was pointing to the stage where Thompson stood looking in our direction. The mayor very obviously put his thumb down.

I raised my arms ready to wave back at Thompson and shout, but Ed stopped me. "Don't give him the satisfaction."

And so the three of us stood near the back of the crowd during the ceremony. I couldn't believe Ed could be so still and stoic as Thompson went on and on about how Buckingham Fountain was only the beginning of what Big Bill the Builder was going to do for the City of Chicago. He talked about the aquarium and the planetarium and the lakefront beaches and parks that he was bringing to Chicago. I couldn't take my eyes off Kate Buckingham who was nodding and smiling at Thompson's boasts and bluster. And then one by one each of the aldermen stepped up to the microphone to praise the mayor. Democrats kissing the ring of this buffoon.

"All that's missing is Al Capone," I whispered to Ed.

"Look who's in the back row," he said. "Frank Nitti." Capone's cousin and second in command.

The ceremony ended with a quartet of uniformed policemen singing a song whose refrain was *"Big Bill the Builder, Big Bill the Builder, Big Bill the Builder. He's Number One."*

"Let's go," I said to Ed and Margaret. She hadn't said a word during the whole fiasco but now she spoke up.

"It's Ed's fountain. Let's watch the lights come on."

"One, two, three," Thompson bellowed.

And then magic. From every corner of the plaza, floodlights illuminated the pink marble basin, and kazam—water shot up from dozens of jets, frothing out of the mouths of the sea horses and then as a geyser rushing toward the dark sky. Colored lights turned the water red and blue and green. There was music. A recorded orchestra played from hidden speakers.

Margaret looked up at Ed. "You did this. You. What do you care about . . ."

and she pointed to the stage. But he did care and so did I. Maybe Ed would be safer if he did his work and let Thompson take the credit. But Big Bill the Builder was using these projects as a springboard to the White House. He had to be stopped.

12

"Miss Buckingham! Miss Buckingham!" I called out. Finally. I had been lurking for an hour in the lobby of her building at 2450 North Lakeview, which was quite a bit north of the Gold Coast but had a great view of the lake and Lincoln Park. Here she came. Two weeks after the dedication of Buckingham Fountain.

Dave Murphy, the doorman, another Bridgeport fellow, had assured me that Miss Buckingham took a walk through the park every afternoon at two o'clock. I'd come at one o'clock, and he'd let me wait in the mailroom of this grand building. Even the rich were living in apartments now.

I had written to her asking for a meeting and had gotten no response. She was ashamed of herself, I thought. She knows she should have insisted that Ed be on the stage at the dedication ceremony for her fountain, but then I wondered if rich Protestant women surrounded by servants who tell them they're wonderful ever did feel guilt. Isolated. The way she was right now with a woman in a white nurse's uniform holding one of her arms and a young blond man in a gray business suit holding the other. He was the one who answered me. "Please. Miss Buckingham doesn't wish to be disturbed by strangers," he said.

"But I'm a friend of hers. Well, an acquaintance anyway and I have an important message for her." Kate Buckingham and the nurse had stopped at the front door when the young man turned and spoke to me. Now I stepped forward.

"You remember me, Miss Buckingham, don't you? I'm Ed Kelly's cousin, the photographer."

"Now look here," the young man said, "if you don't leave right now, I'll have the doorman eject you."

"She's not dangerous, sir," Dave Murphy said and then turned to Kate Buckingham. "I can vouch for Nora Kelly."

"Oh, yes, now I recall," Miss Buckingham said. She turned to the young man. "She's the woman who took those quite extraordinary photographs of the fountain under construction, Stanley." She smiled and told me, "I have framed the series. Your work hangs on my walls right next to Cézanne and Renoir. Those are very important French painters."

"Yes," I said. "Well, if you recall when we met in Ed's office, he told you that I lived in Paris. In fact, Henri Matisse and I—"

But Stanley interrupted me. "Miss Buckingham has an appointment."

"Oh, yes. It's very exciting," Miss Buckingham said. "I'm planning to erect a statue of Alexander Hamilton in the park just down the block from this building."

"Alexander Hamilton," I said. "Why?"

"He's the forgotten man," she said. "He was a great favorite of my brother Clarence. After all, Hamilton invented our banking system. And he had such a fascinating background. Much more interesting than George Washington who was after all just another Virginian."

"I don't recall much about Hamilton," I started.

Stanley couldn't resist explaining to me that Hamilton had been born in the West Indies and though his father had been some kind of a Scottish lord, he had not married Hamilton's mother. He looked over at Miss Buckingham, who nodded. "Hamilton's mother was French," he went on, "with some African heritage possibly."

"He had quite a time breaking into the inner circle of the Founding Fathers," she said.

"Because he was an immigrant?" I said. "Hamilton's lucky there was no President Big Bill Thompson at that time or he would have been shut out entirely."

That got her attention. "President Thompson? What do you mean?"

"Big Bill thinks he's got the Republican nomination sewn up. He's lined up lots of delegates. Now, it's one thing to tolerate a few years of him as mayor, but dear God, president of the United States? Washington and the others won't just be turning over in their graves, they'll be rising up, running amuck. They'll—"

"Easy, Nora, easy," Dave Murphy said.

I'd moved very close to Kate Buckingham. I didn't want to spray her with my earnest spittle. "I know Ruth McCormick is a power in the Republican Party but I have no way to get to her. But you do."

"Ruth is a friend of mine," she said.

"Could you arrange a meeting with her? I can invite Mrs. Potter Palmer," I said. "She worked with Ed to save the Palace of Fine Arts and she has influence. The convention is next month. We have to do something quickly. Please, look I'll leave my phone number with Dave here. Call me and tell me when it's convenient."

"I am Miss Buckingham's secretary," Stanley said, very offended. "I arrange her schedule."

And now the nurse spoke up. "And she has to conserve her energy."

"For heaven's sake, Kate, you're seventy, not dead. You owe Ed and me, and the country for that matter, at least two hours of your time," I said.

Which is why a week later, Kate Buckingham, Mrs. Potter Palmer, and I sat in the lobby of the Palmer House enjoying their high tea of scones, strawberry jam, and whipped cream while we waited for Ruth McCormick. Pauline and her husband, Potter Palmer II, were spending more and more time in Florida, but they were in Chicago for the spring season, she told me.

"At least we don't have to travel to Europe as much. My husband's mother Berthé loved to spend time in the great houses of England. She was a special friend of the Prince of Wales."

"Who Thompson wants to punch in the nose," I said.

"I try not to think about Mayor Thompson," Mrs. Palmer said. "After all, the beautification of Chicago is going forward."

"Because of Ed Kelly," I said. "Maybe Chicago could survive a term with Thompson as mayor, but the country cannot. The harm he could do as president will affect generations."

"President?" she said and half stood up.

"Sit down, Pauline," Kate Buckingham said, and turned to me. "When I asked Pauline to meet us I didn't tell her why. I thought you could be more emphatic about the risk of Thompson getting the Republican nomination."

And emphatic I was.

Thompson and Capone were partners, I told them. Big Bill had no morals. He cheated on his wife. Spent time in the Levee. It was one thing for men like Hinky Dink Kenna and Bathhouse John Coughlin to run that place. They had come from nothing, but Thompson had opportunities and still he wallows . . . but Mrs. Palmer stopped me.

"You've convinced me and I'll certainly make the case to Ruth McCormick."

Ruth Hanna McCormick, the colonel's sister-in-law. Daughter of a

Republican senator and wife of another, she had been married to the oldest McCormick son, Joseph. He was the fellow meant to run the *Tribune* but word was that his nerves couldn't take the pressure, so he'd gone into politics. Which didn't make a lot of sense to me except, to the McCormick family, the Republican Party was an extension of the family business.

Joseph had been a congressman and then senator. But two years ago the party had withdrawn its support and nominated someone else. He died in Washington. Now Ruth was running for his seat in Congress

"Ruth is a very brave woman," Mrs. Potter Palmer said. "Her husband's death was a terrible blow."

"What was it?" I say. "A heart attack?"

Mrs. Palmer lifted her teacup and took a sip. "Well I don't know all the details but his body was found in a hotel room in Washington and, well . . . the circumstances were never revealed." She stopped, split open a scone, covered it with strawberry jam and whipped cream and took a bite.

"Oh," I said. "Did he take his own life?"

"Don't say anything to Ruth," Mrs. Potter Palmer said.

"I wouldn't," I said.

Ruth McCormick had one of those austere faces that upper-class women seemed to be issued with. I panicked a bit as she sat down. She waved away the scones. Poured herself a cup of tea and looked at the two of us.

Mrs. Palmer launched into the story of how she and Ed and I had teamed up to save the Fine Arts building, which proved that Ed Kelly was able to take a broader view than most of Chicago's politicians. And Kate Buckingham added her bit. No Buckingham Fountain without Ed.

"Yes," I said. "Ed cares about getting things done and is willing to look beyond party labels. In that same spirit the women in the Democratic Party want to help you get elected, Ruth."

Ruth nodded. "I'd appreciate that."

"We can pass the word that having a woman in Congress is important, even if she is a Republican. Though I was surprised to find out that Thompson is going to be your candidate for president."

"What!" she said. "That's ridiculous."

"Please keep this information confidential, but I heard him myself. He's making a run for it, Ruth." All Ruth McCormick's self-possession dissolved.

"Never," she said. "Not while I have breath in my body. I'll stop him."

And stop him she did. She organized the delegates at the convention and Thompson wasn't even considered. Thompson never forgave her. Ruth was elected to Congress that year, but when it came time for her to run for the Senate, Thompson put the kibosh on it. It would have been great to have a woman senator from Illinois. Or even a president. How did a deplorable man such as Thompson stop such a capable woman? Inexplicable.

AUGUST 1928

Thompson stayed away from Chicago for the rest of the summer after the convention in Kansas City. He was humiliated. We had a big celebration in Eagle River. Pat Nash and his family came up from his place on Paw Paw Lake in Michigan, where he had built his bit of Ireland, as Ed had in Eagle River. Idyllic really. Every morning Margaret and I would take the two-year-old twins down to the lake. We'd each hold one up and let them kick their feet in the water. "This is what's really important," I said to Margaret. "The kids growing up, healthy and happy."

"That's what I try to tell Ed," Margaret said, "but." She shrugged, and pointed up toward the house.

I knew Ed and Pat were up there plotting and planning. Thompson had been wounded. There was blood in the water. The aldermen that had been supporting him were looking for another leader.

That night at dinner I was surprised to hear Pat explaining how city politics were really an ancient Irish invention.

"While European countries were allowing themselves to be ruled by a king, the clans in Ireland were governing themselves. Each chieftain had to depend on the loyalty of the men under him. They weren't like the English or the French or those other kings who inherited their positions, and told the people that God had set them up for the job."

"The divine right of kings," I said.

"Right. Those fellows said all the land belonged to them and people paid them taxes for the privilege of living in their kingdom. And they had to serve the king. Slaves really. But it was different with the Irish. The clan owned the land in common, and the chieftain was elected. When one chieftain died all the male members of his family gathered, and that was quite a few, because everyone was related to everyone else, and no one was concerned if some of the fellows had been born outside of his official marriage, or marriages.

"I'd say there was a bit of politicking during the process, and jobs were promised. When the chieftain got into office, he had to take care of those who put him there, so he passed out what we call patronage, and every family got their share because somebody belonging to them was on the inside. I'm not saying the chieftain didn't skim off a bit for himself, but," Pat said, "the ancient Irish weren't that bothered about material possessions. In fact, some monk that came over with the Normans condemned the whole place because he couldn't understand why the Irish wasted time on parties, when they could be making money."

"Some things don't change," I said.

The next morning, Ed told me that he and Pat had decided on the chieftain they were going to support. The best way to get the Irish to work together was to unite behind someone who hadn't been involved in previous battles. Anton Cermak was a tough, smart politician who'd managed to get the support of the Poles, Lithuanians, Germans. He had a ready-made coalition for the Irish to step into.

"There will be an Irish mayor of Chicago one day. Just not right now," Ed said.

Good, I thought that next morning. Ed and Pat have stopped trying to manage Thompson. They're ready to take him on. I was on the pier taking the mail from the driver of the Chris-Craft who delivered the mail on this great chain of lakes by boat. A thick packet for Ed. I found him sitting under the pine tree sipping his coffee.

He opened the envelope, took out some papers. "Oh hell," he said. "Wilcox again. The two latest editions."

The reverend himself had sent them to Ed at the lake, letting us know he was aware of the location of Ed's summer retreat.

Ed handed one copy to me. I wondered what it cost Wilcox to publish *Thunderin Every Little While*. At least a dozen pages with plenty of pictures. Expensive to print the thousands and thousands of copies he distributed to downtown newsstands where a regular parade of office boys from city hall bought the latest issue.

This one seemed to be about the rise of Moe Annenberg from a quick-with-his-fists newsie to a head of circulation for both the *Trib* and the Hearst papers. According to Wilcox, Moe was a gun-toting gangster who strong-armed the newspapers onto the streets and made enough first to buy papers himself, then start both the *Racing Form* and a wire service that sent results from tracks all over the country to illegal horse parlors.

A gambler pure and simple, Wilcox said. He referred to Annenberg as the "Israelite" in the same way he called Ed and the other Irish fellows "Papists."

Now I heard Ed laugh. "Listen to this, Nonie," Ed said and started reading from the paper. "Jack O'Brien, head of the janitors' union, has stopped giving positions to his cousins. Did he run out of jobs? No, he ran out of cousins."

I smiled but then I saw Ed turn the page, read for a minute, then slap the paper down.

"What? What?" I asked.

"Wilcox is quoting," Ed said, and began reading. "The great writer Victor Hugo said 'The history of men is reflected in the history of the sewer. The sewer is the conscience of the city. The social observer must enter these shadows for they form part of his laboratory.'"

"So what?" I said. "Did I ever tell you I lived next door to Victor Hugo's house on the Place de Vosges? It's a museum now and . . ." But Ed wasn't listening to me.

"This next bit is all about me," he said. "Supposedly I've used the sewers to betray the people of Chicago. I conspired with Pat Nash to gouge the taxpayers for every foot of sewer pipe laid. He said that I was appointed chief engineer of the Sanitary District by a corrupt system so my cronies and I could rob the taxpayers. Jesus, Nonie, he's got a list of every business we've ever given a contract to. This is awful," he said.

Ed set the paper down.

I picked it up. "Dear God," I said. "Look what he's advertising for the next issue. 'Ed Kelly's Incompetent Cousin and Her Immoral Past.' What are we going to do, Ed?"

"I can't do anything. Pat says we just have to ignore him. Can't give his ravings any attention."

Both of them afraid. Geeze Louise! "Maybe you can't do anything, but I will."

The next morning I was on the train back to Chicago.

"Because you are evil, Miss Kelly." Wilcox's voice was flat and even, with a little bit of downstate Illinois in his accent. "An abomination and so is your cousin. Why is it that you people have so many relations? The higher races seem to be declining, while you foreigners multiply like rabbits. Sad really." He shook his head. A man bearing his burden with patience and understanding.

I sat in the dining room of his bungalow on the Northwest Side, a neighborhood of neat brick houses lined up together on a grid of streets with a small town feel. The large round table was covered with papers piled up in leaning towers, while the seats of the eight chairs held stacks of newspapers. The floor was a maze made up of walls of fat manila folders.

Wilcox had been startled when I arrived at his door. "How dare you come here?" he said. "How did you find me?"

"Your address is on *Thunderin*," I said. Was he wearing the same suit he'd had on at the funeral? Couldn't close one jacket over that stomach. A blob, alright.

He waved me in through a normal-enough-looking living room into his hive of accusation and innuendo. He cleared a chair and, after I sat down, began to explain in that oddly expressionless voice why Ed was the Devil's tool and I was one of Satan's helpers. "Your photographs distort the truth, Miss Kelly," Wilcox said, in that eerily earnest way.

"What? I take pictures of new construction but also track meets and basketball games and folk dancers . . ."

"Yes. Propaganda that lures the unsuspecting masses into these dens of iniquity, where they are brainwashed into supporting corrupt politicians."

"For heaven's sake, Mr. Wilcox, people play checkers, put on plays in the fieldhouses, and have cooking classes."

"All the while being told that Ed Kelly and his Democratic cronies have given them this opportunity. But the Lord has intervened. He has sent William Hale Thompson to stamp out the vintage where the grapes of wrath were stored."

And now Wilcox laughed. A high-pitched kind of cackle.

"Then why don't you leave us alone? Give Ed a break. After all, Buckingham Fountain, the aquarium, the planetarium . . . Big Bill Thompson takes credit for them all now. It's just crazy to keep going after Ed and me. I'm not important."

"Oh, you're not the first to impugn my sanity. All crusaders are considered unbalanced. But I'm being led, Miss Kelly. Led by a light beyond my understanding. Sometimes even I, myself, don't know where my inspiration comes from." He gestured at the newspapers. "A hint. A few words on a page can open a Pandora's Box of vile corruption. I will show how Mayor Thompson was able to rescue these projects from the clutches of corrupt men, who intended them to be simply get-rich-quick schemes for Kelly and his cronies."

"Well, maybe the companies that did the building made some money, but what's wrong with that? I don't see you going after George Pullman for his profits."

"Pullman produces something tangible. You people don't. It's your fanciful nature. Never contributing anything solid to the world. Song and dance men the whole lot of you."

"You mean the Irish?"

"Of course. You're the most dangerous of all the mongrel groups invading our country because you can learn to walk and talk like your betters. At least the other inferior races can be identified."

And now Wilcox leaned over the table toward me.

"Darkness, Miss Kelly. They are marked with darkness. The black skin of the Negro is the most evident. But look into the eyes of the Jew, the Italian, the Mexican, the Eastern European; nature gives us markers. But you Irish managed to inbreed with your Nordic masters, and so deceive the observer."

What was this man going on about? And go on he did.

"Science, Miss Kelly, science. All explained by Madison Grant. Here."

He handed me a brown book with a title in gold letters, *The Passing of the Great Race*. I turned the pages as he talked. Maps with arrows, and page-long paragraphs.

"My family, Wilcox, is Nordic, as were the colonial settlers of America. We carry the genes of the race that produced the knights of chivalry, those designed by the Lord God to rule the lesser races. But that mandate has broken down because you people, the Alpines and the Mediterraneans, have come together producing the Capones, the Nittis, the Torrios."

"Come on, Mr. Wilcox, don't you think it was Prohibition that produced the bootleggers? Everybody went for a piece of the pie."

"If Prohibition had been applied correctly we would not be facing the disaster we are. The Nordic races have been committing race suicide. We must make ourselves pure. Stop letting the mongrels poison us with their liquor and music. Young people of fine families are lured into speakeasies, where jungle music and alcohol addles their brains, leading to," he lowered his voice, "race mixing, Miss Kelly. Race mixing. But thanks to Madison Grant, steps have been taken. Those of our rulers who still have clear Nordic reasoning have outlawed immigration from the inferior countries. Perhaps," he said, "Providence will take a hand, as it did in Ireland. If only God's work had been allowed to go forward, my task would have been so much easier, because you, and your kind, would not exist. The Lord God smote the land and punished the idolaters, but in those days America was too naive to understand the consequences of opening her doors. If only, if only . . ."

"Wait a minute," I said. "Are you talking about the potato blight? The Great Starvation?"

"I'm referring to how the laws of nature right the balance when an inferior race outbreeds its master. Read this," and he pushed a pamphlet toward me. "The addendum to *The Passing of the Great Race* explains that famine is a tool of science."

"Famine," I said. "Famine's not even the right word. There was plenty of food in Ireland, raised by the people who were starving, but it was taken by the landlords for rent and . . ." but Wilcox was holding up his hand.

"Nature finds ways to cull the herd, Miss Kelly. The mistake was that man interfered with Her work."

"Interfere? The British government allowed a million people to starve to death."

"Exactly. Only a million. Not nearly enough. And then poor America, with our misguided sentimentality, stopped Nature's work by offering refuge to those who should have died where they were."

And he smiled at me. Oh God, I thought, where do I start?

"The Irish built this city. This country. Fought for America in every war, and these new immigrants will do the same." And now he actually patted my arm.

"We will stop you." He pushed a chart over to me. There were four drawings. The first showed an ape. In the second the ape features became those of an Irish man, with a clay pipe and a *caipín*.

"Oh please," I said. "This is ridiculous."

"This illustration was done by a prominent professor of eugenics, Miss Kelly. So dress yourselves up as you will, I will expose you. 'By their fruits you will know them.' The wolves in sheep's clothing, be they top hats or fur coats, will be stripped bare."

He pounded a fist on the table.

"I plan an entire issue of *Thunderin* around this." He tossed a photo of Tim McShane himself onto the table. And then a shot of me in my trouser suit, taking a photograph.

"It will be quite an issue, Miss Kelly. *Thunderin* indeed. I wouldn't ordinarily be concerned with someone like you, though you are being paid to do a ridiculous job. In fact I told the young man that. But he persuaded me that your past needed to be exposed."

I stood up, looked down at Wilcox, close enough to smell the starch in his shirt. This fellow comes to work in his dining room, I thought, but still dresses every morning in the same suit and tie, with a boiled collar that cut into his flabby neck. A nut, Ed had said, but a dangerous nut.

"What young man?" I asked him.

"One of my many citizen reporters. I always put a few lines in *Thunderin* inviting anyone with information to get in touch with me, and offer to reward their diligence."

"You pay people for tips? But anyone could say anything."

"Oh, I check my sources carefully, and confirm their reports with records and documents. I'm aware that disgruntled relatives may have vindictive motives, but that doesn't mean that what they say isn't true." He took a paper from the open file. "For example, I have your name on a passenger list on a boat docking at Le Havre in January, 1912."

"So what?"

"Well, that tallies with this young man's story that you fled Chicago because of an illicit relationship with Mr. McShane."

"You can't know that," I said.

"*I* can't, but your nephew Mr. Kelly can. He brought me a letter from his mother, who was an eyewitness to your disgrace."

Oh no, Henrietta! And the young man must be . . . "Toots," I said. "Toots Kelly informing on me, but Mr. Wilcox, my nephew is unbalanced. He'd say anything for money."

Wilcox scrabbled through more papers. "Do you deny that you took up residence in Paris and supported yourself by dubious means for nearly ten years?"

"Dubious? Nothing dubious about it, Mr. Wilcox. I worked with a great couturier. . . ."

"Oh, yes, I have a note on that. Here it is—Madame Simone, who illegally copied designer fashions for the tourist market. A crime that's taken very seriously in France. And you were her accomplice."

"But Toots couldn't know that."

"According to this letter his mother does."

I thought of the times Henrietta had quizzed me about my fancy clothes, accused me of spending fortunes, and how I'd told her about Madame Simone's business, and my job scouting new designs for her by going to fashion shows in the great houses. Damn.

"But your readers couldn't possibly care about such frivolous things," I said. I started pacing now, weaving around the paper towers.

"They care about the men who served our country in the Great War, and then were subjected to inferior medical treatment at the hands of untrained women like you and Margaret Kelly who probably did more harm than good," he said.

I stopped pacing. "Now that is crazy. I worked as a nurse's aide and did a good job. Our hospital served thousands of soldiers."

"Oh, please, Miss Kelly, the low morals of the so-called nurses in France are well known. What respectable woman would volunteer to handle the lower extremities of strange men?"

"These were soldiers wounded in battle. Mrs. Vanderbilt ran the hospital, for heaven's sake."

"A divorced and remarried woman, rejected by society." As Wilcox went on about the loose morals of nurses in general, and those in France particularly, I remembered all those awful songs implying that we "Red Cross Girls" were no better than we should be. Why is it that whenever women step up they get slapped down?

I remembered Henrietta's questions, her curiosity and disgust. What had I said to her? Probably something smart about how I'd been a regular Mademoiselle from Armentières. Why is it that I'm compelled to shock Henrietta?

And, of course, Margaret had worked beside me in the hospital, so anything Wilcox said about me could be applied to her. I thought of those brutal days and nights. The lack of sleep, the heartbreak when a soldier would die, or, even worse, we'd heal a fellow only to see him sent back to the front to be killed.

My mind started throwing up jagged bits of memory—young Johnny who'd left our ward for Gallipoli, and those Canadian soldiers being led from ambulances, their eyes bandaged because they had been blinded by mustard gas. And Margaret in the midst of the chaos, cool, competent, and caring. And now this bastard dares to turn our service against us? He held up another sheet of paper. "And on your return you took up again with the same gangster who was suspected in the murder of his own wife."

"I did not."

"Even inviting him to a family wake."

"That's not true."

"Really? And isn't it a fact that this criminal, this McShane, was murdered only yards from the funeral home, with you yourself present."

"I-I . . ." What could I say?

He smiled now. "I plan to devote an entire issue of *Thunderin* to you."

"But why? I'm not news."

"As you point out, this kind of gossip isn't my usual fare and I am a bit reluctant to go forward unless . . ." He paused.

"Unless? Unless what?"

"It would be very useful to me to have a real insider. Someone privy to private conversations in Ed Kelly's office. There's always been rumors of bid rigging, outrageous overages, but Kelly himself has been able to dodge any indictment. I will bring that jumped-up Mick down!"

"You want me to betray Ed?" Oh my God, he was trying to enlist me against Ed.

"Betray is a strong word. Truth is what I want. Only the truth, Miss Kelly."

13

"You've got to get something on him," Maurine Watkins said to me. Two thousand miles away in Hollywood, her voice was clear, as if we were sitting together at Henrici's. Except this call was costing me more than five lunches, but I couldn't think of who else to turn to. I'd walked out of Wilcox's house sick to my stomach.

I'll kill Toots and Henrietta, I thought, but, of course, I'd end up arrested and in Cook County Jail with my story on the front page, and Ed and Margaret dragged in to the "Killer Cousin" case.

The sensible part of me said go right to Ed. But how could I tell him my, well, indiscretions were threatening his job and, worse, his wife's sanity? Margaret would not be able to bear this kind of exposure. Maybe I could just find some harmless information in the office and pass it to Wilcox.

Oh, for God's sake, Nora, I told myself. You're making up a plot for some movie with you playing Evelyn Nesbit's role in *I Want to Forget*; and that's when I called Maurine. After her play had been made into a successful movie starring Phyllis Haver, she'd moved to Hollywood. Maurine had written telling me Cecil B. DeMille, who had directed the movie, had offered to help her find work as a screenwriter. He'd said that pretty soon all the movies would be talkies, and they would need somebody who could come up with snappy dialogue. Here was a woman who'd attended four colleges ready to put words in the mouths of working-class girls who all seemed to start out as heroines but end up as victims. *Mmm.*

I'd written back asking whether she was still going to make all her characters Irish when she had no earthly idea of what we were really like. Her answering letter said she gave the audience what they wanted and that ended our correspondence. But Maurine was a sharp cookie no question, and had had her own run-ins with Wilcox. Plus she'd sent me her phone number in the last letter. "My office at the Fox Studio," she'd written. A bit of bragging there, but now she answered the phone on the first ring.

"Hope I'm not interfering with your writing," I said, and that got her going on the tussles she was having with this fellow named John Ford, who was going to direct the movie she was writing, called *Up the River*, about escaped convicts.

"Ford's a real Mick," she said, "and is teamed up with this chowder-head actor named Spencer Tracy, and they're not crazy about the other star, a guy named Humphrey Bogart, who's a bit of a stiff. I tried to get the part for young Clark Gable, the actor who played Amos Hart in *Chicago* on Broadway. But Ford and he didn't click and—"

I stopped her.

"Listen, Maurine, this is costing me a fortune and I've never heard of any of these people. I'm really in trouble—I need your advice." So I told her about Wilcox and his threats. "And the worst part is that he thinks he's doing God's work—saving the white Anglo Saxon race." I repeated as best I could Wilcox's wacky scientific theories trying to get Nordic, Alpine, and Mediterranean straight.

"Of course he's right," Maurine said, "but that doesn't mean he can torture you."

"What do you mean right? Wilcox is a bigot, dressing up his prejudice in fancy phrases and maps and charts."

"You should read the book, Nora. We studied it at Radcliffe. The Nordic race is superior, but there's also a place for you and the others. My play, *Chicago*, would never have been as popular if Roxie and Velma were Protestants."

"But they were, Maurine. I mean in real life they were two farm girls whose families came from that old colonial stock that makes up your so-called great race."

"Which is why I had to change their names. Audiences just wouldn't believe that women from their backgrounds would become murderers."

"Maurine, would you ever listen to yourself? You're making no sense at all." Oh my God, did she secretly agree with all of Wilcox's nonsense?

"Nora," she said, "I have a script meeting to go to. You want my help with Wilcox? Here's what you should do." And then she made her suggestion that I get something on him. "Fight fire with fire."

"But, Maurine, his whole life is that damn newspaper. You should see how he lives, or doesn't live," I said.

"Does he eat? Have a roof over his head?" she asked.

"Yes. So what?"

"So he's not supporting himself and paying rent on twenty-five cents a copy."

"He lives in a bungalow off Nelson. I think he owns it."

"Even more reason to find out how he affords the mortgage."

"Maybe it's a family home that he inherited."

"Easiest thing in the world to find out. Go down to the county clerk's office. Look up the deed. Check the tax rolls."

"Maurine, I don't want anyone to know I'm interested in Wilcox."

"You think the girls in the office care? Ask for Alice. Bring her a strudel from Dinkel's Bakery."

"But—"

"No buts. Start with the money. Remember people in glass houses shouldn't throw stones, and Wilcox has been launching boulders for a long time."

"Thanks, Maurine. Thanks. If there's ever anything I can do for you."

"Well, maybe there is. They've got Claire Luce to be in this picture and . . ."

Claire Luce? I certainly knew who she was. Came to Chicago in the cast of every big Broadway hit. A beautiful dancer. Very elegant.

"She's really not right for the character of Julie Field, who's supposed to be a tough Irish moll in a woman's prison who falls in love with a convict from the men's prison, and—"

"So make her a society lady or something."

"No. Not what the audience wants."

"Why are your characters always incarcerated, Maurine?"

"Women behind bars sell."

"So maybe I should murder Wilcox," I said, "and then Henrietta and Toots. . . ."

Silence.

"I'm joking, Maurine."

"Well if you do kill them I can sell the film rights for you."

Tell them. Tell Ed and Margaret, the sensible part of myself kept repeating. Let Ed figure this out. But I can't, I just can't. Instead I called Wilcox from the payphone in the drugstore at the Drake Hotel, and now I was quoting Maurine-like dialogue.

"I'm onto something big," I said. "Give me a few more days."

I bought two strudels and went to the county clerk's office in the basement of city hall.

"Thanks," Alice Murphy said to me as she took the wrapped packages. "All the girls like something sweet with our coffee. Now what is that you want?"

Half an hour later Alice brought me Wilcox's deed and the tax rolls from 4400 North St. Louis Avenue. In fifteen minutes I found out Wilcox owned his bungalow free and clear. Just bought it last year. Alice came in and looked over my shoulder.

"Unusual that he has no mortgage. Must have paid cash. Want me to check out his bank account?"

"You can do that?"

"Sure. My cousin works at the Harris Bank. When we get somebody who's not paying their taxes I give her a call and she finds out whether they're really broke, or just reluctant. Let's look at Wilcox's property taxes."

She turned a few pages in the file. "Well, this is interesting. He bought it at a tax sale, after the guy who built it for his family got behind in his taxes. But look at this note. Wilcox wrote to us fingering Anderson, the original owner of the property, for non-payment. Not a nice person your Mr. Wilcox."

"Reverend Wilcox," I said.

"Reverend?" she said. "Wait a minute." She was back in twenty minutes. "I looked him up in our tax exempt rolls. Wilcox lists his address as a house of worship, so he doesn't have to pay taxes."

"It didn't seem like a church to me," I said.

"Tax fraud is a crime," Alice said. "Here." She gave me her cousin's name and number.

"Laura's partial to Dinkel's cinnamon rolls."

"He's loaded," Laura told me. "Has almost thirty thousand in a savings account. And deposits a thousand dollars in cash on the first of every month."

So, somebody was bankrolling Wilcox. But who? And would knowing that help me? I mean, it wasn't against the law to get money and maybe he was operating some kind of a small church. But the whole thing was odd, no question.

I waited for Wilcox at the Buffalo Ice Cream Parlor on the corner of Irving and Pulaski, only blocks from his house. I had been very mysterious on the telephone to him. Said I had information and the confirming paperwork. I was surprised when he suggested this place. Most ice cream parlors were fronts for speakeasies, but the Buffalo was the real thing. Wooden booths, a marble soda fountain, and, to underline its innocence, little angels decorated the walls.

"Could I have a hot fudge sundae with peppermint ice cream please?" I asked the waiter. On our last outing I'd taken the Kelly kids to a place called Petersen's and had the most delicious ice cream, full of chips of peppermint candy, covered with a dense chocolate sauce, and, well, I honestly felt I needed the courage this total indulgence would give me.

"No," the waiter said to me. "We have chocolate, vanilla, and strawberry. Best in Chicago, all you need." He looked as if he indulged a bit himself. His stomach was a prosperous mound under the white shirt, and his moustache had a few white specks in it. He carried a linen napkin over his arm.

"This a Greek place. We Greeks invented ice cream. We know what's good."

"I'm sure you do," I said, "but . . ."

"What is it with you? You a troublemaker?"

"No. But what's wrong with being a little bit creative?"

"You *are* a troublemaker. John, John," he called out, and another man, who must have been his brother because they had the same shape and facial hair, came over.

"What's the matter, George?" he said.

"Peppermint. She asked me for peppermint. Only need stuff like that when the ice cream itself is no good."

"Look," I said, "I didn't mean to start anything, but, it's just that, do you know Petersen's in Oak Park? They . . ." and George took the napkin, hit his own arm, and then the table. I pulled back as he thwacked along with each word.

"Oak Park. What do they know in Oak Park. Couldn't last in Chicago. We're the best in Chicago. Make the best. Three flavors. All made here. Great toppings, all from our kitchen," and then he pointed to a row of silver mixers, "malted milk the best."

"Easy, George, easy," the other brother, John, said to him. "Is her first time. She doesn't know. We show her."

Well, within minutes a mélange, one of Madame Simone's words, appeared before me. Three tulip-shaped glass bowls, one with a scoop of chocolate, the next with vanilla and the third with strawberry. A hard shell of caramel topped the chocolate ice cream, a large dollop of fudge covered the vanilla, and butterscotch sauce swirled over the strawberry. Peaks of whipped cream swirled over each sundae with cherries stuck on the summit.

"I couldn't possibly eat all this," I started, and then stopped, because who was standing above the booth? Only Wilcox himself.

"Disgusting," he said right out loud. "Can't you people control any of your appetites?"

"But I didn't . . . ," I tried again.

"Ah sit down, take a load off," George said to Wilcox, who did.

"Your usual?" George asked him. He nodded, and George said to me, "Always orders the same thing. A chocolate malt, with extra syrup, extra malt, and"—he pursed his lips—"chocolate ice cream. Not a good idea. You need vanilla to balance the flavors." He shrugged and walked away.

Now I wasn't about to dig into my sundaes with Wilcox staring at me. But then John, the brother, was back, saying to me, "Taste, taste."

I started with the caramel chocolate. "Yikes," I said. "This is delicious."

He watched me as I moved to the hot fudge, spooning up some whipped cream with the vanilla and fudge mixture. Excellent. I smiled at John and forgot all about Wilcox as I moved on to the strawberry butterscotch sundae.

"So you still going to talk about Oak Park and peppermint?" John asked me.

"What? Where?" I said, thinking I'd make it up to Petersen's next time.

George brought a tall glass filled with the darkest malted milk I'd ever seen. Again, there was whipped cream on top and a cherry. He set it down in front of Wilcox and then put a frosted silver container from the mixer that held the rest of the malted milk on the table. Wilcox pushed a straw into the middle of the whipped cream and I watched him suck the malted milk up through the straw. A continuous stream. He breathed through his nose so he could keep swallowing, and a good half of the malted was gone before he looked up at me.

"You'll get a freeze headache," I said, but Wilcox didn't hear me. His eyes were half closed and he was off again, drawing the malt up. There was something too intimate about watching him drink. I looked away and took another mouthful of the caramel chocolate sundae.

I was surprised to see George come back with another malted glass and silver container, which he placed down in front of Wilcox.

I can't just sit there and watch him suck this one up, I thought, I had to say something.

"I didn't realize that the ancient Greeks invented ice cream," I said to Wilcox. "Pretty good for a Mediterranean people."

"The Nordic people interbred with them thousands of years ago," Wilcox said. George heard this and laughed.

"He tells us this crapola all the time. Crazy stuff about the Vikings coming to Greece. Greek is Greek. You have no democracy or poems or ice cream or nothing without us."

I expected Wilcox to answer, but he was halfway through his second malted.

"Mr.—err—Reverend Wilcox," I began. He vacuumed the last bit of liquid through the straw, his eyes closed and he didn't seem to hear me.

"Leave him alone for a minute," George, the waiter, said. "Poor man—he has no wife, no children." George took up the silver containers. "Doesn't even try a sundae every once in a while." George shook Wilcox's shoulder. "Talk to this lady while I make you another."

Wilcox opened his eyes. The crusader was back. He took out a pad and pencil from his briefcase. "Alright. What do you have? It had better be good, Miss Kelly. I've also discovered that you were arrested by the British authorities for murder, and should have been hanged as a spy."

Now he's overplayed his hand, I thought. Publicize my part in the fight against the Black and Tans, and my escape from the very British Army officer who executed the rebels of 1916, and I could run for mayor of Chicago. Publish away, but I did wonder how he found out these things.

"Alright, alright, Wilcox, get ready to take notes because I've been doing a little research myself." I took one last spoonful of the hot fudge sundae then spread my papers across the table. Though one stuck to a patch of goo on the wooden table.

"Now," I said, sitting up straight. "You purchased your house three years ago with eight thousand dollars in cash. Before that you were living in a rooming house paying six dollars a week, at the same time you started publishing *Thunderin*. It cost you two hundred and fifty dollars to print five thousand copies. And you put out four editions that year, which equals a thousand dollars."

"And I sold them, Miss Kelly. Sold all of them at twenty-five cents apiece."

"Except you didn't, really. You gave them to the newsstand operators and let them sell them. Usually for only a few cents, which they kept. So you were losing money on *Thunderin*. Why the sudden change in fortune? No family inheritance, not even the take from your Sunday congregation, because you have no Sunday congregation, Reverend Wilcox, despite the fact that you list your house as a house of worship and pay no taxes on it.

"So, what happened in 1927 to change your luck? Why, that was the year Big Bill Thompson ran for mayor against the very man he'd been afraid to take on in the last election. A man so good his nickname was Decent Dever. And here comes *Thunderin,* full of stories about corruption, but, strangely, all the perpetrators are Democrats. One of your first issues had a big picture of George Brennan, Democratic candidate for the US Senate, and the headline 'Brennan, Beer and Bunk.'

"And it's Democrats you've continued to go after. Not a word in *Thunderin* about the two hundred and fifty thousand dollars Thompson took from Capone, and how his gunmen acted as poll watchers during the election. Even the *Tribune* wrote about the Thompson-Capone connection, but you didn't. Why?"

Wilcox leaned across the table toward me.

"Mr. Thompson needed the money to get rid of those Irish thieves. Sometimes you have to fight fire with fire."

Dear God, I thought, this fellow believes that Thompson can use Capone for good, deluding himself the same way he addles his brain with triple chocolate malteds.

"Come on, Wilcox, Thompson uses dirty money to pay you off to attack his enemies. He started an organization called the Protestant Legion. Isn't that the group that sends you a check every month?" I said.

"My patrons are upstanding members of the Protestant community who understand the threat you people represent. You're enriching yourselves through politics, and using that money to finance your war on our values, our way of life, our very existence. Mr. Thompson explained how important the association is and why he must sometimes lure the gangsters into quiescence by seeming to look the other way, but, really, it's because he wishes to ensnare them. My job is to keep the pressure on the mongrels who have infiltrated legitimate society through their positions as aldermen and committee members, as workers in city agencies."

"So, then you don't mind if my friend at the *Tribune* writes a series of articles on the way your crusade is funded. How Big Bill bought you a house that pretends to be a church, and how you're on the take for a thousand dollars a month?" I said.

"You can't print that information. It's a secret."

"I'll bet it is."

"Mr. Thompson told me no one was to know about our arrangement. That if I told anyone he would have to stop all funds. He's going to think I told you."

"Well I guess your sugar daddy will be cutting you off, but, I think, worse than losing the money, will be the disdain any readers you do have will feel towards you when they find out you're a shill for Thompson."

"But I'm not. I'm not. I have a God-given mission."

"One that's about to end."

Wilcox started waving his hand toward the marble soda fountain, where George was chatting with a customer.

"Another," Wilcox shouted, "another."

Pathetic. "Look," I said, "I don't have to expose you, Wilcox, if . . ."

I paused, and finally he said, "If?"

"You promise to stay away from the personal life of public officials. Leave their wives and kids out of the stories, and forget about my past. I'm not going to ask you to stop publishing," I said, because I knew the fellow was a fanatic and would continue no matter what I threatened. In fact, he would write about how he was being intimidated.

"But, for God's sake, have the sense to go after Thompson too, and start holding Sunday services at that house of yours. Who knows, you might attract a following and big enough collections to support yourself."

"Alright," he said, "alright."

"Remember, one word about Margaret or me, or anyone else's wives or children, and there will be headlines about you in the *Tribune*."

As John set Wilcox's fourth malted down, I stood up. "This is on me," I said, and handed him a five-dollar bill. "Keep the change," I said. Wilcox was hunched over, his face in the whipped cream.

14

"So that's it, Ed," I said, proud of myself. "I've handled Wilcox." We were in his office at the Park Commission, six o'clock but still some light in the sky to the west. The day after Labor Day. Ed back at work. Margaret and the children home.

His secretary and everyone else had left for the day, but I'd asked Ed for a late meeting to explain why I visited Wilcox and describe our strange meeting at the Buffalo.

I waited for his compliments. Instead, he shook his head. "For Christ's sake, Nonie, why did you go near that nut? Better to ignore him."

"But," I started, "I found out that Thompson's funding him."

"So what? Did you think he was some kind of neutral crusader?"

"I suppose I did. He's a pathetic man and full of the worst kind of prejudices, but he does work hard and seems to know things. I've been reading back issues of *Thunderin*, and, well, is it true, Ed? Even if you get rid of Thompson, will Chicago be as corrupt as Wilcox said?"

"Do you mean will there be gambling joints and speakeasies on every block? Will bootleggers break the law in plain sight? Will city jobs get passed around among friends and relatives? Will judges let criminals walk while the cops take regular payoffs? Has the chief engineer of the city of Chicago, and the president of the South Park District, made money over the years from the people he gives his contracts to? Are those your questions, Nonie? Are you accusing me too?"

"I guess so, Ed," I said.

"Well then, the answer's yes," he said. He stood up from his desk and walked over to a window that faced east toward the downtown skyline. Dusk now and the lights in the buildings coming on, headlights moving along Lakeshore Drive, the lake itself stretching out into the darkness. "How many people live in Chicago, Nonie?"

"I don't know. Two million?"

"Five million, four hundred and thirty thousand, six hundred and fifty," he said.

"Oh," I said.

"How many of them would have placed a bet or two, would you say?"

"I don't know."

"At least half," he said, "and then another half take a drink now and then. Say that's four million people. Should they all be arrested?"

"Of course not. But what about the fellows that run the gambling? Sell the liquor? They're the crooks. Surely they should be behind bars."

"You mean men like Spike O'Donnell?"

"Emmm." No quick answer to that. "But what about Capone and Torrio, the real bad guys?"

"They'll end up dead or in prison, Nonie. I'm sure of that. But it's the feds who made the laws against drinking and gambling. Let them enforce them. I have to think of all five million, four hundred and thirty thousand, six hundred and fifty people in Chicago. My job is to give them a beautiful, healthy city to live in. Do you know how many people died from drinking the water in Chicago before Pat Nash upgraded our sewers?"

"I don't."

"About a hundred times as many as will ever take a bullet in the street from the Outfit. Gangsters kill one another, Nonie. I can't worry about them. Don't you remember Uncle Patrick telling us a million of our people starved to death in Ireland because they had no power, couldn't vote? Well, we can now and we're going to live decent lives," he said, "and beat Thompson."

Whew. "Okay, Ed, okay."

"Two years until the election. Best thing we can do is concentrate on building the planetarium and aquarium, putting thousands of men to work. Your job is to photograph the progress and get the pictures in the papers."

"With quotes from you," I said.

He nodded.

And so I did. I worked as I had with the crew on Buckingham Fountain.

Up at dawn, documenting every stage of construction. No time for thoughts of Peter or to plot a return to Europe.

The newspapers were glad to take the photographs, along with the copy I wrote. Great quotes from Ed, talking about how millions of gallons of sea water had been brought up from Florida by special rail cars, along with thousands of species of fish for the aquarium, and describing the planetarium's map of the heavens in the observatory dome.

Then on September 29, 1929, the stock market crashed. At first only the rich seemed affected. My brother Michael spent one whole Sunday's dinner explaining that he was safe because he'd invested his money in Samuel Insull's utility companies, and those bonds were solid. He couldn't have been more wrong. Insull went bust and Michael lost everything.

The only bright spots were the opening, in May 1930, of the Shedd Aquarium and Adler Planetarium. "Thank you, Edward J. Kelly," Max Adler said during the opening ceremony, which infuriated Big Bill.

By February 1931, when the mayoral campaign was in full swing, the Depression had hit and even Republicans wanted someone steady in office.

Still, the *Tribune* said Thompson's race against Cermak was the dirtiest, most violent election in Chicago history. Thompson called Cermak "Pushcart Tony" and got crowds at his rallies to chant, "Where's your pushcart, Bohunk?" And, "Mongrels out."

Cermak's election headquarters were bombed—only luck that no one was killed.

But Chicago had finally had enough. Capone was in jail. Let's get rid of Thompson, too.

When Cermak won, the *Tribune* ran a front-page editorial that Ed cut out and framed.

"For Chicago, Thompson had meant filth, corruption, obscenity, idiocy, and bankruptcy. He has given the city an international reputation for moronic buffoonery. Barbaric crime, triumphant hoodlumism, unchecked graft, and a dejected citizenship. He nearly ruined the property and completely destroyed the pride of the city. He made Chicago a by-word for the collapse of American civilization. In his attempt to continue this he excelled himself as a liar and defamer of character."

Though Anton Cermak didn't fit the image of a latter-day Celtic hero, he had managed to lead the clan in beating Thompson. But what if, as he gave his victory speech on election night, the crowd cheering and Ed and Pat Nash clapping along with the rest . . . what if he'd realized that winning the office of mayor meant he'd be losing his own life? Would he have walked off the stage? Said, "Forget it, boys?" Hard to know.

The Depression spread like an epidemic, and by June 1932, with the Democratic convention scheduled in Chicago next month, Ed's beautiful Grant Park had become a shantytown and our city's treasury was empty. I wondered if Big Bill was having the last laugh after all. It was bad enough that factories had closed, and mortgages were in default, but those Chicagoans with money were refusing to pay their taxes. No income for the city. The cops weren't being paid in cash anymore, but with scrip meant to be redeemed at some imprecise time. At least the gamblers were still paying off the cops, but the teachers had been working without salaries for four months—nobody thought teachers were worth bribing.

Mayor Cermak was talking to lawyers about how the city could declare bankruptcy, Ed told me. We were in his study at the Ellis Avenue house, and Margaret was packing for the trip to Eagle River. He said that Washington was no help at all. President Hoover and the Republicans claimed that "the invisible hand of the market" was at work, and this downturn was necessary. Mustn't do anything that would interfere with the laws of economics, and that included any offering of relief to the unemployed.

"That sounds like the British government's philosophy, during the Great Starvation. They let one million Irish people starve to death rather than intervene," I said. "Some idiot Protestant clergymen called the blight that killed the potatoes 'an instrument of Providence, a way to cull the herd.'" Our great-uncle Patrick gave speeches at Ancient Order of Hibernian picnics denouncing the theories the rich used to justify cruelty to the poor. And here we were again. Wilcox must be pleased.

The city had stopped my salary, too. I knew Ed would have paid me from his own pocket, but I hated asking him for money. He'd lost a bundle in the stock market crash too, and there was no point in trying to collect rent from the properties he owned. People were *skint*—Granny's word, and it sounded like I felt: stripped down. I had depleted my trip-to-Ireland fund and had just enough to pay my rent.

I was glad to spend the summer at the lake where I wouldn't have to worry about expenses and could give Margaret a hand with the kids. She and Ed had added a third child to the family: a little boy they'd named Stephen, after Ed's own father. Not easy to keep up with six-year-old twins and a two-year-old when you're forty-two.

I wouldn't be able to attend the Democratic convention in July, but maybe that was just as well. Ed was not happy about the choices. Al Smith was running for the nomination again, and was expected to be chosen. Ed was afraid he'd lose in the general election, as he had four years before when his Catholicism had sunk him. Ed was impressed with Franklin Roosevelt, the governor of New York, but Cermak was a strong Smith supporter, and disdainful of Roosevelt.

"Cermak thinks that Roosevelt's been so wrapped up in privilege all his life that he can never really understand regular people," Ed said to me, "like Thompson."

"Surely he's not comparing Roosevelt to Thompson!"

"Cermak thinks Roosevelt wants power. Power does strange things to people. I wonder why fellows want it so badly."

"Maybe Roosevelt thinks he's the only one who can save us."

"We'll see what happens," Ed said. "We can't let Hoover back in, that's for sure. This convention is going to be a knockdown, drag-out. I'm glad you'll be up in Eagle River with Margaret and the kids. I'll get out of town as soon as we nominate a candidate, God help us."

In Eagle River it was easy to forget everything, even the Depression, with the wind whispering in the pines, and the sunlight sparkling on the lake. Ed's mother, Aunt Nelly, and her sister, Auntie Kate, Rose's mother-in-law, were with us, and Rose, too. John Larney had died that winter. After all the years Rose had worried about some gunman cutting him down in the street, it was the cancer did him in. Rose accepted his death with the stoic faith that seemed to sustain her. She lived with Aunt Nelly and Aunt Kate, caring for them and grateful to Ed, who supported the household. The city had defaulted on John's pension.

Margaret had decided that while we were in Eagle River we weren't going to read the newspapers, or even listen to the convention on the radio. She was tired of politics. Cermak had been elected mayor. He respected Ed and left him alone. Kate Buckingham, Adler, Shedd, and Rosenwald had all established funds for the maintenance of what were now Chicago institutions. Ed made both the planetarium and aquarium free, and they had become places where the unemployed, homeless, and families could find some refuge. Ed should concentrate on her and his children now.

But when Ed came to us in mid-July after the convention, I could see that he was not about to step out of the political arena. In fact, he was on fire.

"We've found him, Nonie," he said to me, only the two of us up, drinking our coffee on the pier, waiting for the sunrise, "our chieftain—strange that this Dutch-English Episcopalian could be the one to lead us. But Pat Nash agrees. Must be Irish in there somewhere, he thinks."

Ed drank some coffee.

"Cermak never did go along. He forced the Illinois delegation to vote for Smith on all four ballots, even when it was clear Roosevelt was going to win. Jim Farley, the fellow running Roosevelt's campaign, won't forget that, but, dear God, Nonie, you should have heard Roosevelt's speech. The first time that a nominee from either party ever showed up to the convention in the flesh. But Roosevelt was right to come. I've never heard any politician speak the way he did. He's just so confident, so relaxed. I was right near the stage, and I could see he was holding on to the podium to keep himself upright. He has these heavy braces on his legs. I knew he'd had polio years ago but didn't realize how the disease affected him. But you would never know it. Amazing how he connected with the audience. And it was a detailed speech. Point by point, he laid out what has gone wrong, and how we could fix it. Get us back on the march toward prosperity. And you'll like this, Nonie. He said that the Republicans pretend that economic laws are sacred and prate on—a great word, 'prate'—while people are starving. He told us that men make laws and can change them. He ended with promising a New Deal for the American people. That's what we're going to fight for, Nonie, a New Deal."

Then he began singing what had become the anthem of the Democratic party, "Happy Days Are Here Again," and got us to sing along. Only Margaret was silent.

So. What a campaign! Big crowds turned out for Roosevelt all over the country. People dared to hope. In Chicago, Cermak was determined to make up for dragging his feet at the convention by delivering the city for Roosevelt with the biggest vote any presidential candidate had ever received. Democratic Party workers knocked on every door in Chicago. I was getting paid again, hired to photograph the canvass operations and the rallies Cermak led, and try to get the pictures in the papers. Which I'd managed, over the objections of the regular photographers—especially Manny Mandel, the *Trib*'s expert at catching politicians unaware.

Roosevelt won in a landslide. "Happy Days" really were here, and soon Chicago's cares and troubles would be gone, because didn't our city deserve a big, fat aid package?

On January 1, 1933 Mayor Cermak went on the radio and assured the citizens of the city of Chicago that the worst was over. Except I knew, from Ed, that the incoming administration was ignoring our problems. None of Roosevelt's people would even talk to Cermak, though he was desperate to be able to announce some influx of federal funds before Inauguration Day on March 4.

On February 10, Ed called me into his office. "The mayor wants to see both of us at the Morrison Hotel tonight."

I'd first met Anton Cermak during his campaign for mayor. I thought he resembled a high school math teacher rather than "Pushcart Tony," Thompson's insulting nickname for him. Little trace remained of the coal miner he'd been in his youth, after his family emigrated from Czechoslovakia to Braidwood and the mines. As a teenager, he fled to Chicago, worked his way through night school, then made it big in real estate and got himself elected—first as an alderman, then as president of the Cook County Board, and now he was mayor.

He never paid much attention to me until I joined the crusade for Roosevelt and took a photograph of him pinning "Vote for FDR" buttons on smudge-faced miners. It was a dramatic picture if I do say so myself, and it filled the front page of the *Braidwood News*. He had his secretary send me a thank-you note and that was that.

"Why does he want to see me?" I asked Ed.

"I don't know. We'll find out."

Freezing cold in Chicago. There were ice floes in the lake and Michigan Avenue was white, the color our streets turn at temperatures below zero. As we drove south to the Morrison Hotel, Ed explained that the mayor had moved out of his house and into the penthouse suite there as a precaution. Frank Nitti had threatened to kill him. Nitti, Capone's cousin, was running the Outfit while Big Al was in prison. There for tax evasion, of all things . . . the only way the feds could finally get him.

"And Cermak's stopped going into his office after the teachers marched on city hall last week."

I'd photographed the demonstrators—twenty thousand strong, shouting and waving grammatically correct placards. One read "I am teaching your children, but cannot feed my own." They closed down the whole downtown for hours.

"Lots of angry Irish Catholic women in that crowd," I told Ed. "Cermak would have a better chance against Nitti."

"Not funny, Nonie," he said, "Cermak's terrified. It was not very smart of him to order his personal bodyguard to raid Nitti's office." There had been a gunfight at the Outfit's headquarters in which both Nitti and one of the cops had been wounded.

"Nitti could accept the raid, but why the shooting?" Ed said.

I nodded. By now I'd learned the dance between the good guys and the bad guys. Every day a few of the seven thousand–plus gambling joints around the city would be shut down, the operators arrested, then a week later tried and found not guilty. Prohibition was on its last legs, so the cops weren't even bothering with bootleggers anymore. Non-gangland murderers were prosecuted and convicted but "the boys" were mostly left to sort themselves out.

"The Italians think Cermak wants to push them out so his pals in the West Side Mob can take over," Ed told me.

"But that's not true, is it?" I asked.

Ed shrugged.

We pulled up in front of the hotel and got out. Ed handed his keys to the doorman and nodded at the uniformed policemen stationed at the entrance. We walked into the lobby. A plainclothes detective came up to us and said, "He's waiting for you, Ed." We followed him to a private elevator that took us up to the penthouse suite, where two more detectives stood on guard in the hallway. One opened the door. Cermak was waiting for us inside.

"Farley has frozen me out," he said to us after we'd settled down in the living room of the suite, which had been turned into a kind of office. Cermak sat behind a large desk, Ed and I on a couch, facing him.

"But I know if I could get to Roosevelt himself, I'm sure he'd approve an emergency federal grant to pay the teachers. All he has to do is give me his word and I can announce it. We can do the paperwork after the inauguration in March. But how do I get near him? Then I started thinking about that swell picture you took of me and the miners, Nora."

Cermak stopped and looked around as if someone could be hiding in the room. He leaned forward on the desk, then lowered his voice. "You know he's on the Astor yacht now."

"Yes," Ed said, "fishing. After that campaign he needed a vacation."

"On the yacht of one of the richest plutocrats in the country?" Cermak said. "Man of the people, I ask you?"

No one has, I thought.

"Anyway," Cermak went on, "there's an American Legion convention in Miami. I've heard Roosevelt is going to get off the yacht near this park. The Legion guys are staging a rally for him there. Roosevelt will surely give a speech. Afterwards I'll go up to him. You'll be right there, Nora, with your camera. Get me and the president-elect shaking hands. Pals. Take a nice close-up. I'll put that shot on the front page of every newspaper in Chicago with a big story about how FDR's promised me millions in federal funds," Cermak said. "Enough to pay the cops and the teachers. Save us from declaring bankruptcy. Force those bastards who are withholding their taxes to pay up. Can you do it, Nora?"

"You want her to ambush Roosevelt?" Ed asked. "I don't know, he could take offense."

"That's why I want Nora to take the photograph. Roosevelt likes women even when they're not so young. How old are you, Nora?"

"What age are you?" I said to him.

"Fifty-nine," he said. "In my prime."

"Well I'm five years younger than you are, so I'm even prime-ier."

"Alright, alright," Cermak said. "Here's the deal. I'll pay you a hundred dollars plus expenses."

A fortune. Here was my chance to buy that boat ticket to Ireland. A good time to go. All the Kellys were doing well enough. Mike at St. Rita High School, the two youngest girls at Aquinas High School, and the older girls were studying to be teachers at the college in Normal, Illinois. Margaret was happy with her kids. Thompson had been vanquished. Wilcox was quiet. The great Franklin Delano Roosevelt would save the country. I would be able to see him close up, to take an important photograph that could have an impact. Plus I'd earn enough money to travel to Ireland and find Peter's grave.

"I'd like to do it, Ed."

"I don't know."

I looked at him and raised my eyebrows just a bit. I was telling him, not asking him.

Ed shrugged his shoulders. "Whatever you want to do, Nora."

"Why don't you come along, Ed," Cermak said.

"I'm going to Havana with Pat Nash. He has a horse running on the main track there. We're taking some of the boys that worked especially hard getting out the vote. It's a way to say thank you."

"Up to you," Cermak said and turned to me. "Call my secretary. She'll get you a ticket on the Florida Special. Probably good to get down there a day or two ahead of time. Let's see, today's the tenth. Can you leave tomorrow?"

"Yes," I said. Ed and I stood up.

"I'm heading out myself. I'll go down with you," Cermak said. He left the living room and walked into the bedroom. One of the detectives followed him. Through the open door I could see Cermak being buckled into a bulletproof vest.

Geeze Louise.

PART II

MAYOR

1933–1941

1

BAYFRONT PARK—MIAMI, FLORIDA

FEBRUARY 15, 1933

"Better get that thingamajig of yours ready—the motorcade just turned into the park," the newsteel cameraman said to me.

He was very superior, stuck up there on a platform with his big Mitchell NC mounted on a heavy tripod. Totally immobile. I was happy to be right where I was, standing on the paved area where Roosevelt's car would pull in, just below the bandshell in the amphitheater on the south side of Bayfront Park. This stretch of green moss grass palm trees was between the Bay of Biscayne, where the Astor yacht had docked a few hours ago, and downtown Miami. Redmond Gautier, mayor of Miami, had told Cermak and me that the president-elect was going to speak from the back seat of the big Buick convertible the city had lent him, so I was in a perfect position.

"He probably can't get up on the stage," Cermak had said to me, "you know Roosevelt's legs are completely paralyzed. Wears these heavy braces."

I nodded. "Ed told me how brave Roosevelt was at the convention, holding on to the podium for dear life but not letting on, speaking so easily and . . ."

"He's something alright," Cermak said, interrupting me. "I am going to shake his hand if I have to climb in next to him. You'd better get the picture."

I showed him my Seneca. "This camera is light so I can move quickly and get in close," I said. "But as soon as Roosevelt finishes speaking you're going to have to come down those stairs fast." I pointed at the one flight that went up to the stage where Mayor Cermak would be sitting with the American Legion delegation and all of Miami's muckety-mucks.

"Don't worry, I'll clear a path for the mayor," Jim Bowler said.

He was the Chicago alderman who had traveled down with Cermak and was acting as a kind of bodyguard. The Outfit probably wouldn't try anything down here, but . . . "Just make sure there's film in that thing."

"You do your job and I'll do mine," I said to Jim, and walked over to the spot I'd scoped out.

Great energy in this crowd. Gautier said the police estimated it at twenty-five thousand—the largest gathering ever in Miami, and I believed it. The rows of permanent seats in front of the stage—seven thousand we had been told—were all filled. People were jammed together throughout the park. It was a lovely warm evening. Families sat on the ground. Kids ran around. The American Legion drum and bugle corps had marched the colors in, and we'd all stood and belted out a spirited "Star-Spangled Banner." Could we really begin to hope? Could this man truly lead us out of the Depression?

Nine o'clock now. The rally was supposed to start at eight but nobody was complaining or leaving. Dark everywhere but in the floodlit area where I was. Enough light for a good exposure. I'd have to get the shutter speed just right and keep the aperture wide open, but if the newsreel cameraman could get an image, so could I.

Sirens now. And Roosevelt's car was driving right toward me with two Secret Service men riding on the running board. Now I could see him. I could see the president. I was cheering along with everybody else.

A chant began: "FDR, FDR, FDR!" Someone started singing "Happy Days Are Here Again," and we all joined in.

Roosevelt's car stopped. Only about ten feet from me. I could've touched the fender. Great.

Then Mayor Gautier was on the stage. He explained that President Roosevelt was behind schedule. A ten o'clock train was waiting to take him to New York where he'd prepare for his inauguration next month, but he had insisted on coming to speak to all of them. "We welcome him to Miami. We wish him success and are promising him cooperation and support. We bid him Godspeed. Ladies and gentlemen, the president-elect of the United States of America."

More cheers. I looked up the newsreel cameraman. All business now.

A fellow in a white suit came running up to the car and handed Roosevelt a microphone. And now who was standing right there across from me?

Mayor Cermak! Not waiting for Roosevelt to speak, getting near the car. Good. We wouldn't interrupt the president, but as soon as he finished . . .

A husky, strong-looking fellow helped Roosevelt onto the top of the convertible.

Roosevelt's words weren't that memorable, but something about the sound of that voice piercing the darkness. So cheerful, so confident. He didn't orate. He was talking to his friends—to us. Roosevelt said that he was glad to be in Miami, though he'd visited before and would come again. He'd had a great time fishing but had gained ten pounds. Something he'd have to take care of. He was laughing. We were laughing. That was it. That was the speech. He handed back the microphone. Sat down in the back.

A wall of people surrounded the car. I felt myself being pushed from my spot and Cermak had disappeared. Wait . . . there he was. I should've known that a man who'd elbowed his way to the top of the Democratic Party in Chicago could get through a crowd. Cermak stepped onto the running board. Grabbed Roosevelt's hand and turned to me. Both men were smiling. I looked through the lens.

"Move closer," I said, "move closer." Cermak leaned into the car, his shoulder touching Roosevelt. Perfect. Hold the camera steady and now . . . Then that sound. Sharp. Pop.

The assassin fired at the same time I pressed the shutter because one second, I was looking at an image in my viewfinder of the two men smiling and shaking hands, and the next a woman was yelling, "He's killed Roosevelt! He's killed Roosevelt!"

Four more shots. Screams. The crowd running for the exits surrounded the president's car, blocking it. The driver laid on the horn.

"Get out of the way," I shouted at the people around me.

Gunshots don't have to kill. I nursed enough wounded soldiers during the Great War to know that it's shock that's fatal. The husky man I'd noticed before was lying on top of Roosevelt.

"Get him to the hospital," I yelled.

The car started moving. Thank God. Cermak was leaning against Jim Bowler. I ran up to them.

"Oh dear God," I said, "the president."

Cermak asked me, "Did they get him away?"

I nodded.

"And the picture? Did you get it?"

"I did, but the president . . . ," I started and then I looked at Cermak. His hand was at his waist. Blood was leaking through his fingers.

"Plugged," Bowler said.

Without thinking, I lifted my camera and photographed Cermak. I looked past him and saw that Roosevelt's car had stopped. "What are they doing?" I asked. "They've got to get him to the hospital."

"Might be dead already," Bowler said.

"Roosevelt can't be dead," I said.

Then the husky man got out of the back seat of the convertible and ran over to us.

"The president said to put the mayor in with him," he said, as Roosevelt's car backed up toward us.

The man practically carried the mayor as Jim Bowler and I guided them to the car. Roosevelt himself opened the door and we settled Cermak next to him.

"I'm glad it was me instead of you," Cermak said.

Roosevelt put his arm around the mayor's shoulders and I heard him reply, "Take it easy."

"Call Ed," Cermak said to me, "and my daughters."

More sirens. Uniformed cops cleared a path in front of the car. It took off. Behind me I heard a commotion. I turned and saw that two or three of the Legionnaires in helmets had someone on the ground. The gunman. Then two cops dragged him toward the car that had been following Roosevelt, and jammed him into the open trunk.

"Hey paisan. Como sta?" The gunman turned and looked. A flash went off in his face. "Get out of here, you vulture!" a cop yelled.

"Hiya, Nora," said Manny Mandel.

Manny snapped pictures of the four other victims as they were carried into ambulances. Then he came over to me.

"Let's team up, Nora," he said. "You go to the hospital. I'll head for the police station." He started walking toward Biscayne Boulevard.

"For God's sake, Manny. The president was almost killed. Cermak might be dying."

"Why it's such a big story, Nora, and it fell in our laps. All the big-shot reporters are at the train station." He smiled, balancing his Speed Graphic camera on his hip. Manny, who jumped out of the bushes to catch aldermen coming out of speakeasies at 2:00 a.m. and photographed the dead bodies at every Outfit rubout, was looking at a national story.

"The picture is Roosevelt at Cermak's bedside," Manny said. "Here's your chance to be a real news photographer, Nora, not Ed Kelly's flack," he said. "That is if that peashooter of yours can take decent pictures." He waggled his big camera at me.

"Shut up, Manny. I'm not interested," I said and started walking toward the lights of the avenue. There must be a drugstore with a phone booth, then a cab to the hospital, and then . . . But Manny grabbed my arm. "Look, they'd never let me near Cermak, but you can be in the room when Roosevelt comes. Ask Cermak if he thinks Nitti set up the hit—probably on orders from Big Al."

I remembered the mayor buckling himself into that bulletproof vest at the Morrison Hotel. He didn't bother with it tonight. Should have.

"But then again Roosevelt probably was the target. All those oilmen in Texas would love to have John Nance Garner as president. They'd be riding high," Manny said.

"I can't listen to any more of this, Manny," I said. "Cermak's daughters have probably heard the news of the shooting. They'll be beside themselves. I have to get in touch with them."

"Here," Manny said, "gimme the roll of film you shot. I got a lab waiting."

I hesitated.

"C'mon, c'mon," he said, "the coppers might take it off you. Evidence."

I popped the film out of the camera. Handed it to Manny. He took off.

Most of the park was dark now. Only a few people standing in front of the amphitheater, lit by the newsreel crew's klieg lights. Their cameraman had been forced to stay above the action. Wonder if he got anything. Come on Nonie, move. Hard to put one foot in front of the other. Biscayne Boulevard seemed very far away.

Finally, a drugstore. A phone booth. It only took five minutes for the operator to connect me with the front desk of the Havana Hilton. "Mr. Ed Kelly," I said to the fellow who answered, desk clerk, I guessed.

"Part of the Chicago group?" He had an American voice.

"Yes," I said.

"I believe they're still in the bar. Celebrating a victory I understand," the clerk said.

So Pat Nash's horse had won. Shannon Farms, he called his stables. Raced under green and gold colors.

"What is it with you Micks and horses?" Cermak had said to me just a few hours earlier, annoyed that Ed had gone to the Havana track with Pat Nash, instead of accompanying him to Miami.

What if Ed had been here, I thought, as I waited for him to come to the phone. He might have stopped Cermak from pushing his way to the car, or maybe it would have been Ed standing next to Roosevelt. The bullet might have hit him.

"What's so important?" Ed said.

"Ed, it's bad news. There's been a shooting."

"Jesus Christ, not Roosevelt?"

I tried to answer but suddenly my teeth were chattering, and no words came.

"Is Roosevelt dead? Answer me Nonie . . . is Roosevelt dead?"

"No, no, but Cermak's been hit. He was walking and talking but you'd better come. Do boats sail at night?"

I heard Ed talking to someone. Pat Nash, I supposed, and then he was back on the phone.

"We'll fly at first light," he said.

"Fly? But you hate flying. You've never even been on an airplane."

"Get out of there. Get out." Some nut was pounding on the door of the phone booth, yelling so loudly that Ed heard him in Havana.

"You'd better hang up, Nonie. Get to the hospital."

"Right," I said. "Take it easy," I said to the man. He was short and skinny and looked familiar. He was dressed in a white suit and wore a panama hat.

"I'm Walter Winchell," he said. "I'm trying to get a call through to my editor. Move your ass."

I held up my Seneca as a kind of shield and stepped forward.

"Give me that camera," he said.

"No," I said. "Are you crazy?"

"I got a cop getting me in to see the Dago, the gunman. I need a picture. Don't move."

He stepped into the phone booth but grabbed my arm and held it while he put a nickel into the phone. I shook him loose but he stepped out of the booth holding the receiver, pulling the cord in front of me.

"Oh, please," I said.

He shouted into the mouthpiece.

"Save me three columns on the front page and leave room for a picture." He dropped the receiver.

"You're not taking my camera," I said.

"Then you'll have to come with me. Can you really use that thing?"

"So long, Mr. Winchell," I said and took a step toward the door. He ran ahead of me, turned and grabbed my arm again.

"Ten bucks," he said, "and a good word about Ed Kelly in my column."

I stopped.

"Surprised you didn't I?" he said. "I know who you are. Ed Kelly's flack. I remember you from the Dempsey-Tunney fight. I never forget a face. Especially somebody who could give me some information."

"Well, that's not me," I said. "I'm going to the hospital."

"As you should, but if you come with me you'll arrive with the latest dope on the gunman. I'll get him to tell me all about who hired him. I'm betting on Nitti and the Chicago Outfit."

"That's what Manny Mandel said."

"Manny's around? Now there's a real photog. Tell me how to find him and you're off the hook."

"I'm perfectly capable of taking the picture," I said.

"Well come on then. I've got a cab waiting," he said.

A crowd of reporters stood in front of the police station but Winchell ignored them and went into the county courthouse across the street. He ran up the marble steps. Hard to keep up with him. Winchell had been a song and dance man in vaudeville and he could move. He headed through a side door and down a flight of stairs to the basement. A cop stood in front of an open freight elevator.

"Come on, come on," the cop said. We got on. The cop closed the grill and when he opened it we were in the jail. Except two uniformed policemen and a fellow in a suit stood in the hallway.

"What the hell," the fellow in the suit said.

"It's me, Chief. Walter Winchell. And you're about to become famous. You're the man who arrested the most notorious assassin in history."

"Assassin?" I said. "But Roosevelt's alright, isn't he? And the mayor—"

"Four people shot but it looks like they'll all recover," said the police chief.

"Looks like?" Winchell asked. "Is that a medical term, Chief? I got a tip that they're operating on one dame and it's touch and go. And as for Cermak, listen, Chief, the mayor was the real target. The Chicago Outfit hired the zip you've got here to rub him out. And you're the man that will get the headlines. Give me ten minutes with the guy and he'll confess on the front page of the *Mirror* with a picture of you right beside him."

"Ten minutes," the police chief said. He wasn't much taller than Winchell, though broader and much more rumpled. One of the other cops opened a door. As we stepped through it the police chief turned to me. "No dames," he said.

"She's not a dame," Winchell said. "She's my photographer. Doesn't the chief have the right look, Miss Kelly? That firm chin, his forehead."

"Very photogenic," I said.

"Okay," the police chief said.

I expected we'd be walking through a cellblock but instead the cop took us to a single iron door with a square opening. We looked in. There he was, the gunman. Sitting on a thin mattress on top of a slab of concrete. His hands were on his knees, his head down. He looked up at us, not a bit bothered. Dark eyes, olive skin.

"I want my picture taken," the gunman said. "Everybody should know me, Giuseppe Zangara, killed the president of America. Me."

"Roosevelt's not dead," the police chief said.

"But you don't care, do you, Giusep?" Winchell asked. "Because Cermak was the target, right? And you plugged him good."

"Who's this Cermak?" the gunman asked.

"See?" Winchell said to the others. "He's lying. Look at him, he's laughing at us. Open the door. Let's get in there. Come on, Chief, we'll take your photo with him and then watch, he'll tell me everything. I know how to get secrets out of people. Even this guy."

The cop opened the door and we stepped into the small room. The fellow started to mumble and pointed to his stomach.

"What's he saying?" Winchell asked. "Where's an Italian interpreter?"

"I don't think that's Italian," I said. "Probably a dialect." I'd taken enough pictures of the citizenship classes at Park District fieldhouses to know that often immigrants from Italy spoke a language particular to certain regions. Sicilians didn't understand people from Naples. They all knew a kind of serviceable Italian, but it wasn't their mother tongue. Zangara kept speaking.

"So, Miss Smarty Pants, you think you know how to talk to this fellow?" Winchell said.

"Not really, but . . ."

Zangara stood up.

"Whoa there," the chief said. "Sit down." The two uniformed cops pulled their pistols out and aimed at him.

"No shoot me," he said in English, and then a stream of his dialect.

"Siciliano?" I asked him. He shook his head.

"Calabrese," he said.

"He's from Calabria," I told the others.

"Where the hell is that?" the police chief asked.

"The toe of the boot," I said.

"What?" the police chief asked.

"The most southern part of Italy," I said.

"Seems like you know a lot. What are you? Some sort of an anarchist? Communist?" the chief said to me.

"Take it easy, Chief," Winchell said. "She's okay."

"Yeah? Well, this punk must have had accomplices," the police chief said.

"He did," Winchell said. "The Chicago Outfit. He hit the guy he was aiming for, Anton Cermak. Enemy number one of the Capone gang."

"I hate all kings and presidents," Zangara said, his English accented but clear.

"See? He's an anarchist for sure," the chief said.

Zangara was just so small. I was taller than he was and certainly outweighed him. Still, put a gun in his hand and he was more deadly than a six-foot-tall wrestler. He'd shot five people and might have killed Roosevelt if not for . . . Oh God. . . . "Move closer." Could life and death be that random? Was Zangara just some loner, a nut with a gun? I wanted to believe someone smarter and bigger was behind this. Thompson, the Outfit, Garner, somebody, otherwise it just made no sense.

"Hey, you with the camera." Zangara was talking to me. "You take picture now and get out of here. I want to sleep. Take good picture so everybody in Ferruzzano knows what I do. Tell them Giuseppe Zangara is important now. They'll hang my picture in the church. Nobody in all of Calabria is as big as me."

There was just enough light, so I raised my camera. And he posed. Turned his head slightly and smiled.

"Give this to the newspapers in Rome. The captain will see it, that general who treated me like dirt. I am biggest man in Italy, in the world."

Oh dear God, I thought, did this fellow want to kill Roosevelt just to be famous? To get in the newspapers, to astound his neighbors? He was right, the whole world would know his name. That wouldn't have been possible even twenty years ago, but now here was Winchell, the man who could make Zangara known. Horrible. But I took more pictures.

"Okay, fella," Winchell said, "but I need a story to go with these photos. Tell me when you met Nitti. How much did he pay you? Where did you get the money to travel over the last two years?"

"It was from the anarchists, right?" the police chief said.

"Why not ask him about Garner?" I said. "Or even Thompson." But Zangara had gone back to speaking his own language.

"That's it, Winchell. Your ten minutes are up," the police chief said and turned to me, asking, "Where should I stand?" I wasn't sure what he was talking about, but Winchell stepped in.

"Come on fellows," he said to the two cops, "each one of you grab one of the Dago's arms and, Chief, you stand just to the side of them. Remember this guy's bad, a killer. He fought you all the way but you got him." The cops followed Winchell's directions. Pulled Zangara off the cot. Each of them was a foot taller than Zangara, so the gunman looked more like some boy they'd caught shoplifting rather than a would-be murderer or international terrorist.

"Don't smile," Winchell said to Zangara. "You've just shot five people. You might have killed the president of the United States."

But Zangara started laughing. "Me," he said. "Little Giuseppe. Wait 'til my father sees this. I'm not the boy he kicked in the stomach. I am the greatest man ever born in Ferruzzano. I am famous."

And I took the picture.

"Give me your film," Winchell said when we left the jail. "I've got a fellow at AP will wire the photographs. We'll make the first edition. You'll be on the front page of the *New York Mirror*."

It was two in the morning. Ed was flying at first light, so he would arrive in Miami by nine o'clock or so.

"If Cermak dies," Winchell said, "they'll have to have a special election for mayor and this time Thompson and the Republicans will win. Cermak herded all the Irish together but now they'll turn on each other."

"But Thompson almost destroyed the city. He's a disaster."

"Maybe, but he was great copy. He gave the people what they wanted, bread and circuses."

"But even Thompson wouldn't have hired Capone's cousin, Nitti, to get rid of Cermak," I said.

"Why not?" Winchell said. "Assassination has been part of politics for all of history. Look at the kings of England. Henry Tudor murdered his way to the throne, and as for his son, Henry VIII, well at least the men in the Outfit don't kill their own wives. And then there's your Borgias the poisoning popes, Catholics every one. I might use some of this in my column. People like a little history. Makes them feel smart and after all when I was a boy the old people were still talking about where they had been when they heard Lincoln had been shot. And then there's McKinley and Teddy Roosevelt who managed to live."

And Mick Collins, I thought, killed by a former comrade. And Peter Keeley.

"Could FDR have almost died because Zangara wanted to be famous?" I asked. "Incredible."

"Don't underestimate the drive to be famous," Winchell said. "You wouldn't believe what people do to get a mention in my column. The calls I get every day from flacks trying to get their clients a little bit of ink." He stopped. "But then of course you know all about that. You're a flack yourself."

"Good night, Mr. Winchell," I said. The street in front of the jail was clear. The chief of police probably was holding a press conference inside for the reporters, taking his chance at fame. There was traffic moving on the avenue beyond and some taxis at the cabstand. I've got to get out of here. Why did I let this jerk distract me. Insult me. I started to walk away. "Don't you want your ten bucks?" Winchell called after me.

"I don't want your money."

"It's not mine. It's William Randolph Hearst's. Take it. Your cousin Ed will get a laugh, scoring off the enemy. Here, here." He waved the bill at me. "Come on. You can be press now," Winchell said, "paid by Hearst himself."

But I kept walking.

2

No, I wasn't press. Not one of this crowd of reporters trying to get into Jackson Memorial Hospital. It was a huge place, faintly Spanish, with a grand middle building and two side wings. Some of the men were waving cameras at the line of cops blocking the main entrance.

"The president's got to talk to us," one man yelled.

"Hey Jim! Jim! Over here," another called. I saw Jim Farley, Roosevelt's aide, standing in front of the door with two uniformed policemen next to him.

A fellow with a big brain—Ed, who'd gotten to know him at the convention, said.

Farley raised his hand, and the shouting stopped.

"The president-elect has left the hospital," he said. "He'll spend the night on the yacht and come back here tomorrow morning. He's visited each of the four victims, except for Mrs. Gill, who's in surgery. All are doing well and are expected to recover completely."

"What about Cermak?" one shouted.

"Resting comfortably," Farley replied.

"Not what I heard," the man said. "A nurse told me it's touch and go."

"If you fellows had any decency you'd stop bothering the hospital staff and get out of here." He turned away from the reporters and started back into the hospital. "Jim, Jim," they shouted after him.

I'd managed to move down the line and get close to the door.

"Mr. Farley, Mr. Farley," I yelled. "I'm Ed Kelly's cousin. Wait . . . wait, I just spoke to Ed." He stopped. "I came down to do a job for Mayor Cermak," I said. "How is he? Can I see him?"

"Who's the dame?" one of the reporters called out. "No fair talking to her and not us."

Farley let me walk into the hospital with him, then down the hall past the elevator. We stopped at a small waiting room. Tables and chairs piled with magazines. Nearly two o'clock in the morning, so no visitors in the hospital.

"Ed and Pat Nash are flying down first thing in the morning," I said. "I know Mayor Cermak will want to see them but maybe I should go up now. It might reassure him to see someone from home."

"What's that you're carrying?" Farley said. I lifted up the Seneca.

"My camera," I said.

"Are you using your connections to take a picture? A vulture like all those other newshounds!"

"I'm not, I'm not," I said. "The mayor hired me to take the photograph that would save Chicago, but it was me who told him to move closer to the president and that's why he got shot. But then maybe Roosevelt . . ."

I was babbling. But suddenly I very much wanted to convince this dignified man that I wasn't part of that pack outside.

"You people have no decency," Farley said.

"I'm not 'you people.' And I've seen Zangara, the gunman. There could be a plot. Roosevelt may not be safe."

But Farley wasn't listening. He walked out of the room.

I expected a cop to show up and throw me out, but no one came. I sat on a hard wooden chair. My teeth start chattering. My whole body was shivering. I saw it again. Blood coming through Cermak's white shirt at the belt.

"Who are you?"

A nurse stood in the doorway.

"I'm . . . I'm . . . ," I started, but the words wouldn't get past my chattering teeth.

"I'm about to make myself a cup of tea," she said. "You look like you could use one."

A woman about my age. Very starched for the middle of the night. Blondish hair and a bit of a tan, even in February. She opened a closet door. I saw a small table holding an electric kettle, cups, and, like a sign from Heaven, a box of Barry's Tea.

"You're Irish," I said to her.

"Kathleen Quinn, both parents from Galway."

"That's where my grandmother was born," I said, "though her family were originally from Connemara, and . . ." I stopped.

She lifted the kettle, gave it a shake, and then plugged it in. "We keep it filled with water," she said. She looked at me. "You may need yours doctored."

She reached up to the closet shelf and brought down a bottle of Jameson. "Sent over to my da at Christmas. Our relations in Ireland just can't believe that the US government would outlaw drink."

Five minutes later I was sipping strong, sweet tea, full of the wonderful smoky taste of whiskey. The real thing. I'd almost forgotten.

"Father Kevin's cure for everything," I said, which confused Kathleen Quinn, and then I started explaining about the Irish priest I knew in Paris, and my life there, until she touched my arm and said, "Drink your tea. I'd say you're in shock. Were you at the shooting?"

I couldn't stop myself from telling her everything. Why I came down to Miami. How the only reason that Cermak got so close to Roosevelt was so I could photograph him.

"I almost feel like it was my fault that Cermak got shot. Except if he hadn't been there, Roosevelt might have been killed. Oh why did I get involved at all?" I took a breath. "Except that I need the hundred dollars to find my dead husband's grave in Ireland," I told her.

Kathleen Quinn asked no questions. Just patted my arm until the flow stopped.

"Your mayor's sleeping, which is the best thing for him," she said. "The doctors have decided not to operate and take the bullet out. It's lodged in a funny place. But I don't know." She shook her head. "I think they should remove it."

"Always the danger of infection," I said. "Internal septicemia."

"Are you a nurse?" she asked me.

"Not a nurse, but I did take care of soldiers in France."

"Me too." She smiled.

"So I can't understand why I'm falling apart like this. I've seen worse."

"Yes," she said.

"But we were only a bunch of people in a park. Music. Kids. Out for a good night. No one was expecting it . . ."

"No," she said. "A very strange battlefield."

"And I was on a real battlefield," I said. "Belleau Wood. I saw young Marines walk into machine gun fire. Drop down into a wheat field full of blood and poppies. I took on the Black and Tans for God's sake . . ."

Again the pressure on my arm. I cannot stop talking. It was as if I was trying to put a hedge of words around what happened.

"You should go home," Kathleen Quinn said.

"I know I should. I really should get on a train to Chicago right now, but Ed's coming, and Pat Nash, and Mayor Cermak's family will be heading down here and they'll expect me to help and—"

"Whisht," Kathleen Quinn said. "I mean go to your hotel. Where are you staying?"

"Some place on Biscayne Boulevard. Not far from the park." The park. I can't go by that park, but I do need to sleep. "I suppose I can call a taxi," I said, and stood up.

"That might not be so easy," Kathleen Quinn said. "Those reporters have set up in the lobby now. Only way we could control them. Keep them off the other hospital wards. And they seem to have commandeered every cab in Miami. Hard enough to get one at three o'clock in the morning any time, but now most of the taxis are parked in front of the hospital, hired by the reporters. There are some rooms set aside for staff," Kathleen said. "You can stay here if you wish."

"Oh, I would. Thank you. Thank you so much. But that wouldn't get you into any bother would it?"

"This is a big place. Lots of nooks and crannies," she said. "This is the only hospital for the whole area. The East Wing is for whites, and the West for colored people. Some people object to having Negroes and white people in the same hospital." She was looking at me.

"Not me!" I said. "How could you think . . ."

"Well, I'm never sure who I'm talking to down here. I've lived in Florida for twenty-five years, and I'm still a Yankee to them. I couldn't take those Minnesota winters anymore. Come on. A wash and a few hours' sleep are what you need. A medical necessity."

Kathleen found me a room, and I took off the navy blue linen suit and the Chanel blouse I'd put on that morning. A lifetime ago. I washed out my underwear and stockings and got into a hospital gown. My sister Henrietta always said wear clean underwear in case you were ever taken to the hospital. The thought made me giggle, and then I was sobbing, and I fell asleep crying, not only for Mayor Cermak and those wounded in the attack, but for all the senseless violence I'd seen in my life.

"Here you go," Kathleen said, carrying two cups of coffee. She handed me one. Still dark in the room. "It's nearly seven," she said. "My shift is over."

I sipped the coffee. "You really are an angel of mercy."

"You should get something to eat in the cafeteria," she said. "It's open. It'll make you feel better." And I was better. Last night was already becoming part of the story I'd tell Ed and Pat. I nodded at Kathleen. "How is Mayor Cermak?"

"He got through the night. I still think that bullet should come out, but these doctors don't listen to nurses. Mrs. Gill survived her surgery . . . so it looks like everyone survived."

She sat down in a chair at the side of the bed and sipped her own coffee.

"Do you know what time the president is coming?" I asked.

"He's supposed to be here early," Kathleen said. "More and more reporters have showed up. The lobby looks like a newsroom."

"Are you going to wait for him?" I asked her.

"I am," Kathleen Quinn said. "I voted for him. Amazing that he carried Florida with the way people down here talk about him. Lots of Roosevelt haters. After the election, I heard one of the doctors tell another he hoped that the polio would do him in so John Nance Garner would be president. He's more their style."

"If not for a few inches he'd be president right now," I said.

"Hard to believe that some crazed gunman could change history," Kathleen said.

"I remember Sarajevo," I said.

"So do I," she said.

"Of course that was a plot, but then this could be too," I said.

I told Kathleen how afraid Cermak was of Nitti and of Winchell's interview with Zangara.

"Lots of Chicago mobsters down here in Miami. We had Al Capone himself in the hospital, but it won't be a bullet that does him in," she said.

"Right, he's in jail."

"With syphilis. He'll die raving," she said and stood up. "I'll look for you in room 307."

"Is that Cermak's?" She nodded and left.

The Florida sun had risen and was pouring in the double windows. I saw a palm tree. My underwear was dry. I was clean. All last night's victims were alive. Good.

So. With a breakfast of eggs and grits to sustain me, I stood in front of the hospital, waiting for Ed to arrive at 9:00 a.m. More reporters than ever in the lobby. It looked a bit like one of Mont Tennes's horse parlors with telephones everywhere.

A taxi pulled up. But it wasn't Ed. Manny Mandel jumped out of the cab. "Nice of you to be looking out for me, Nora," he said. He handed me the

Miami newspaper. "Here ya go. Front page. On the *Trib*, and every goddamn newspaper in this country. You did it, Nora. You cracked the big time."

I looked down. There were the photographs I'd taken. Cermak and Roosevelt, hands clasped, big smiles and then in the next one, the mayor being held up by those two fellows. The bloodstain very visible. A dark blob on his white shirt. A headline over both—"Roosevelt Escapes Death. Mayor of Chicago Critical." And then below "Eyewitness Report, and Exclusive Photographs from Manny Mandel, Chicago Tribune."

His name was on the line below each photograph.

"Those are my pictures. How dare you steal them!"

"Well, Nora you can't expect newspapers to print pictures taken by a PR flack. Haven't you ever heard of journalistic integrity?"

"You little snake," I said.

"Jesus Christ, Nora. I didn't think you were such a glory hound. You recorded an important moment in history. What do you care where the credit goes? Especially at a time like this."

And with that Manny Mandel walked into the hospital leaving me holding the newspaper. I looked at the photos again. Cermak will be pleased. Roosevelt's grasping his hand and smiling. He probably won't care that Manny Mandel's taking credit. I've earned my hundred dollars. At that moment I wanted nothing more than to get on a ship and get off in Ireland. Away from reporters and politics.

Another cab pulled up. And this time it was Ed and Pat.

"Nora," Ed said. "Are you alright?"

I nodded.

"How was the flight?" I asked.

"Would've been better if we weren't over water the whole time," he said.

"What about the mayor?" Pat Nash asked me.

"He's holding on. Made it through the night. The doctors aren't going to operate. Though this nurse friend of mine thinks they should."

"You've got somebody on the hospital staff?" Pat Nash said. "Good."

We entered the hospital lobby. Manny Mandel headed right for us.

Pat and Ed stared straight ahead.

"Hiya, Ed," Manny said. "Top o' the morning, Pat."

They didn't turn.

There was a commotion behind us. Sirens.

"Here comes Roosevelt," Ed said.

We stopped.

Two police cars, their sirens and lights going, pulled up in front of the hospital. The Buick followed with the top up this time. Four motorcycle cops on each side of it. Secret Service agents riding on the running board. A black Packard came up behind Roosevelt's car, and more agents got out.

Plenty of protection now. Talk about shutting the barn door. Unless the Secret Service and the cops knew more than we did. Maybe Zangara really did have accomplices. I thought of the stunted little man in the Miami jail. Could he be somebody's patsy? An unlikely conspirator.

The pack of reporters came yip, yip, yipping at Roosevelt's car. The agents and the police formed a box that kept the press away.

Jim Farley got out of the front seat, and the same husky fellow who brought Cermak into the car last night opened the back door.

Ed was taller than any of the mob and shouted over their heads, "Jim, Jim."

Farley saw him. Spoke to a policeman, who waved Ed and Pat through the pack.

The husky fellow reached into the back seat and more or less hauled the President-elect up and onto his feet. Roosevelt lurched sideways. Ed stepped forward. Offered his arm to Roosevelt who clamped onto it with one hand, while holding on to the agent with the other. Steady now, he pushed one leg forward, then the other, until he slowly moved through the screen of cops and agents into the hospital.

Farley was in front of him, and Pat Nash behind.

"Over here, Mr. President," a reporter shouted at FDR as he moved through the lobby.

"Any more information on the gunman?" I recognized Manny's voice.

Roosevelt stopped. "I'm here to see Mayor Cermak. You boys should go down to the railroad station. We'll have a press conference there. Leave the sick in peace."

I walked up behind Ed. Farley saw me, but before he could speak, the elevator doors opened and Kathleen Quinn stood there with a cane-back wheelchair.

We all stepped onto the elevator, but Roosevelt waited for the doors to close before he let Ed and the agent ease him down into the wheelchair.

Roosevelt noticed me and asked, "And are you one of the Fourth Estate, too?" pointing at my camera.

"She's not," Ed said. "Nora's my cousin. Nora Kelly."

"Always good to have a cousin. Do I know you, Nora? Were you there last night?"

"I was, sir. Mayor Cermak hired me to get the photograph that would save Chicago. I photographed you with him."

"Oh yes," he said. "You took your picture just as the gunman fired."

"I . . . I did," I said. Did he remember "move closer"? Please God, I hope not.

Roosevelt looked right at me and nodded, but said nothing. The elevator doors opened. He smiled up at Kathleen Quinn. "Hope I'm not too much of a burden for you," and turned around and patted her hand.

"I'm honored, sir," Kathleen said.

Cermak was propped up on pillows. He didn't look too bad for a man with a bullet inside him. Kathleen wheeled Roosevelt to the head of the bed. He touched the mayor's shoulder. "You'll be out of here in no time. I'm saving a front row seat at the inauguration for you," he said.

"More important that you take care of our teachers," Cermak said.

"They'll be paid," Roosevelt said. He looked at us. "Even as we rode to the hospital, your mayor was thinking about the citizens of Chicago." He turned back to Cermak. "Why don't we take a photograph so all the voters in Chicago can see their brave mayor and a very grateful president-elect. Are you ready, Nora?" he asked me.

"Yes," I said, and lifted the camera.

"Wait. I'll stand," Roosevelt said. "Ed?"

Roosevelt used Ed's arm to lever himself onto his feet. Then he took hold of the railing alongside Cermak's bed with his left hand, while taking the mayor's hand with his right.

The handshake again. The same smiles.

I took four shots. Got to get this right.

"Why don't you get into the picture, Ed," Pat Nash said.

"Good idea," Roosevelt said.

A matched pair, Ed and the president-elect, I thought. Both good-looking, and each wearing similar blue blazers and gray flannel trousers—at ease. Can't imagine Pat Nash or Cermak or Farley wearing anything but dark suits. Even dressed in pajamas and sitting up in bed, the mayor looked like he was ready to preside over meetings.

"Would you like to step in?" Roosevelt asked Kathleen Quinn.

She said, "I think you should sit down."

Ed and Farley helped Roosevelt back into the chair.

"Move up here, Kathleen," Roosevelt said. He had her stand next to the chair and put his arm around her waist. "Take our picture, Nora," he said.

Jim Farley said, "It's time to go, Franklin."

"You won't forget now will you?" Cermak said. "A million dollars right away."

"I don't have my checkbook on me," Roosevelt said, "but the day after the inauguration I'll be asking Congress for emergency disbursement to Chicago."

I took a breath. "And, Mr. President," I said, "when I send the photograph of you and the mayor to the Chicago paper, may I include a press release announcing the money for the teachers?"

"You may," Roosevelt said to me.

Cermak leaned back on his pillows. "That's the best medicine I could have. Thank you, Mr. President."

"I think you can call me Franklin, now," he said.

"Why don't you come to the station and see me off?" Roosevelt said to Ed. "One or two things I wanted to ask you."

"Delighted," Ed said.

"I'm staying here with the mayor," Pat Nash said.

"You'd better come, Nora," Roosevelt said to me. "Who knows what pictures you might want to take. Nice to have a personal photographer," he said to Ed. "One who's so concerned about her city."

3

So. We were behind Franklin Roosevelt on the observation platform of the private rail car he would take to New York, where he'd prepare for his March 4 inauguration in Washington. The husky fellow, whose name I'd learned was Gus Gennerich, had helped him out of his car, up the steps and now Roosevelt stood holding the railing. He was entertaining the reporters . . . dozens of them now, with a radio hookup and multiple newsreel crews, including the fellows from last night. Hope that cameraman notices that I'm with the president-elect.

Roosevelt was appropriately serious—very concerned about those wounded in the attack, but grateful that Mabel Gill, the most seriously hurt, had come through her surgery and was doing well. He also assured them that Mayor Cermak was recovering. But there wasn't a bother on him. From the easy way he went back and forth with the press you would never know he could be dead right now.

"Anton Cermak is an amazing man, fellows," Roosevelt said. "I thought we were going to lose him on the way to the hospital but I kept talking to him until finally, perhaps at an attempt to shut me up, he said, 'I'm glad it was me instead of you.'"

Roosevelt shook his head and smiled.

A voice yelled up at him, "To which you answered the mayor, 'I am too.'"

It was Walter Winchell who had somehow gotten into the front row. The other reporters laughed.

"Well now, Walter," Roosevelt said, "I heard you got scooped."

"Some ignatz on the desk at the paper didn't believe an assassin had tried to pop you," Winchell said.

"Maybe your boss Hearst was disappointed the gunman missed," Roosevelt said.

More laughter.

"It's not so funny, Franklin, there's more to Zangara than meets the eye," Winchell said. "Ask that dame behind you—Nora Kelly."

And now Roosevelt half turned to me and said, "What is he talking about?"

"I photographed Zangara when Winchell interviewed him."

Now Roosevelt faced back to the reporters. "The man was delusional, Walter. Don't let your imagination get the best of you."

Roosevelt had been leaning against the railing, stiff legged, the iron braces holding him up. He had to be tired.

"Well, that's it. See you at the inauguration," he said.

The reporters moved away. Ed started down the steps to the platform with me following, but Roosevelt stopped us.

"Why don't you two ride along with me to Palm Beach. Joseph Kennedy is getting on there. He's coming with me to New York."

I'd followed Kennedy's career because he was Irish and married to the daughter of John Fitzgerald, a mayor of Boston known as Honey Fitz. They had a big good-looking family. Even the *Tribune* had run a picture of the nine Kennedy children. Though the caption read "Wall Street Irish Tycoon and His Brood"—as if to say even the rich Irish have too many children. Never called the five Roosevelt children a brood. Ed hadn't had much to say about Kennedy after he met him at the convention except "Lets you know he went to Harvard right away."

"We'll all have lunch and then you and Nora can catch the next train back," Roosevelt was saying. "You'd like Joseph Kennedy, Nora. Very charming to the ladies, isn't he, Ed?"

I wondered if "charming" meant that Joseph Kennedy was not a faithful husband. Ed respected Margaret and didn't like to see any man cheat on his wife. I wondered if that was why he was refusing Roosevelt's invitation.

"Thank you, but I don't think it's wise for us to leave," Ed replied. "Cermak's not out of the woods."

"Oh, come on. You'll be back in a few hours," Roosevelt said. "My son and the other fellows who were traveling with me left last night. I'd enjoy your company, have some things we could talk over. Nora here could take some photographs of us together."

Roosevelt was famously persuasive, and Ed agreed, so we followed him and Gennerich inside, where Roosevelt immediately sat down in a straight-back chair with wheels attached. This was not the armored railroad car that Pullman would customize for the president in a few years, but it was still very impressive. Mahogany paneling and green plush seats were everywhere.

"My lair," Roosevelt said to Ed and me as he pointed us over to a pair of chairs. We sat facing him, the two of us on one side, Jim Farley on the other.

"Listen, Ed, I want to sound you out about Joe Kennedy," he said.

"Joe's an able man, no question," Ed said. "I watched him during the convention. He knows how to operate."

"That's what concerns me, Ed. He's an operator. You don't make a pile on Wall Street without knowing how to pull the levers. I've got a lot of people telling me Kennedy was one of the fellows manipulated stock. Jim here blames him for the 1929 collapse."

"Now I never said exactly that, Franklin," Farley said.

"But Wall Street did get out of hand," Ed said. "Isn't that why you were elected? To rein in those boys. I'd say Joe knows where the bodies are buried and could help you there."

"Unless he's the one who buried them," Roosevelt said. "What do you think, Nora?"

"About Joseph Kennedy?" I asked. Flattered that he wanted my opinion.

"You Irish understand each other," he said.

You Irish. As if we're some kind of subspecies.

Roosevelt waited for me to say something.

"Well there is that saying, 'Set a thief to catch a thief,'" I said, which made Roosevelt laugh.

"That's what I think," he said. "But Jim said the papers will crucify me."

"If you mean Hearst, he'll be after you no matter what you do. Believe me, I know," Ed said.

"Yes, he was rough. Calling me a Bolshevik commissar and saying I'll merge the US and Russia," Roosevelt said.

"You wonder what effect reading stuff like that had on Zangara," I said.

"Now Nora," Ed said, "no point in speculating."

"Nora's right. I know there are Roosevelt-haters out there. If I worried about them I'd return to Hyde Park and forget politics entirely. It is irritating to be vilified just to sell newspapers as you know, Ed."

"I do," Ed said.

I wondered if the fellows who stirred up the hate realized they were making targets of men like Roosevelt. And maybe Cermak and Ed, too.

"Though nothing Hearst said was any worse than what my own vice president accused me of," Roosevelt said, "when he was running against me for the nomination."

"Are there still fellows in Texas mad enough at you to find Zangara and . . ." I started.

"Nora. That subject is closed." Ed made a chopping gesture with his hand.

Roosevelt said nothing.

"Joe Kennedy's friendly with Hearst. Might be able to keep Hearst in line," Roosevelt said.

The train was moving now. We passed through an orange grove and then a small station. Deerfield Beach, the sign over the platform said.

"Ever been to the Boca Raton hotel?" Roosevelt asked Ed.

"I haven't."

"Marvelous place. Those Mizner brothers thought that someday houses will cover this whole area."

"Make no small plans," Ed said. "That was Daniel Burnham's motto. He's the one imagined Chicago."

"I like that," Roosevelt said. "Make no small plans. Poor Mizner lost his dream in the Great Crash. Coffee, Ed?" Roosevelt asked.

A porter wheeled in a cart. He was an older Negro man, gray-haired, who stood very erect. "It's an honor to serve you Mr. President," he said as he poured the coffee into china mugs and set them on the small end tables.

"President-elect," Roosevelt said, "but thank you. What's your name?"

"It's not George, sir."

"I know that," Roosevelt said.

Passengers had started calling every Pullman porter George—because Pullman's first name was George.

"I'm Melvin Grant, Sr.," the porter said.

"And are you a union man?" Roosevelt asked.

"I am. Brotherhood of Sleeping Car Porters," he said.

"I've met your Mr. Randolph. Bit of a radical."

"Yes, sir." The porter nodded. "They call him a Bolshevik, but then they call you that too, sir."

"They do indeed," Roosevelt said.

"We all voted for you, sir. Lots of hope in our union now," Grant said.

He reminded me of one of the Negro officers I'd met in France, named Lieutenant Dawson. A college graduate when none of the men in our family had even finished high school.

Grant poured coffee into Farley's cup. "Nice to meet you too, Mr. Farley. We appreciated your fairness."

"Thank you." And for the first time I saw Farley smile.

"We'll be pulling into Palm Beach in thirty minutes, Mr. President," Grant said. "Time to set up for lunch. Perhaps you'd like to move outside to the platform."

"In other words, get out of the way," Roosevelt said.

"Yes, sir," he said.

"That was a nice compliment for you, Jim," Ed said as he and Farley maneuvered Roosevelt's chair onto the viewing platform.

"Fellow must be a boxing fan," Farley said.

What are they talking about? I wondered, and looked at Ed.

"Jim was head of the Boxing Commission in New York and insisted that a Negro boxer be allowed to fight the champ in Madison Square Garden. Harry 'The Black Panther' Wills wasn't it, Jim?"

"Yes," Farley said. "The fellow could have been Heavyweight Champion of the World, but never could get a title fight."

Don't let them get started on boxing matches. Ed could talk for an hour about the Tunney-Dempsey fight. I was there in the first row and the sound of those punches landing, the sight of all that blood unnerved me. One Irishman beating the brains out of another. That's sport? I'd said as much to Ed at the time.

"How I got my start," Ed had said. "Boxing and politics. A way to climb the ladder."

Negro men are taking their turn now, I thought.

Two Secret Service agents stood behind us, though I wondered if someone couldn't shoot at Roosevelt from behind the bushes and scrub that we were passing through. We were not moving very fast and slowed down even more as we went around a bend. I was looking into the green dimness, imagining the glint of a rifle barrel and not paying much attention until I heard Roosevelt say, "Enough, Jim!"

"But the head of the union's an avowed communist, Franklin," Farley said. "A. Philip Randolph. Why would a man hide his first name behind an initial?"

"If I were a Negro man in this country, I might well be a communist or at least some kind of revolutionary, too. We must offer an alternative, Jim, within the system or else, my friend, all those good people who voted for us, white and colored, might very well tear the whole building down and then . . ."

"Mussolini," I said.

"Yes, some version of the proverbial strong man on the horse," Roosevelt said, nodding at me. "So you should bless unions, Jim."

"I'm with you, Franklin. But you might make that speech to your vice president," Farley said. "He hates unions."

"Garner's served his purpose," Roosevelt said. "I've been elected. He's an understudy who will never go on stage."

"Except he'd be president right now but for a few inches," I blurted out.

Roosevelt didn't even turn his head. He pretended he hadn't heard me, but Ed had.

He shook his head at me. That subject was closed.

4

We pulled into the Palm Beach station. The Secret Service agents made Roosevelt stay in the railroad car while they walked along the empty platform in pairs, looked behind a parked locomotive, moved a baggage cart, and then formed a line in front of the crowd waiting near a barrier made of three sawhorses.

Only a few hundred or so people here.

"More Republicans than Democrats in Palm Beach," Farley said to Roosevelt.

"Including members of my own family. Most of my Roosevelt cousins prefer the politics of Palm Beach and Newport," he said. "It's my mother's people, the Delanos, who made me a Democrat."

Once again the mother decides allegiance, I thought, remembering Padraig Pearse.

"Ah, here he comes. Your compatriot, Nora. Joseph Patrick Kennedy and a member of his brood I see," Roosevelt said.

Brood.

The man striding out of the crowd did look like one of ours. Tall, well set up, with narrow shoulders though. This fellow had never been a boxer like Ed.

The Secret Service barely slowed him down. Whatever he said to the agents, Kennedy was through the barrier in seconds and moved up to the viewing platform. Looking down, I saw he was also a redhead though his hair had darkened, as had Ed's and mine.

A very thin boy followed Joseph Kennedy. About fifteen, I thought. Light brown hair, a bit of it falling into a face that would be handsome if his cheekbones weren't so prominent and his skin so pale.

"For Christ's sake, Franklin. Can't you even make *this* train run on time? Been waiting an hour," Joseph Kennedy said.

Who speaks to the president-elect of the United States like that? Joseph Patrick Kennedy, I guess.

"Jack hasn't been well," Kennedy said. "And standing out in the damp like this doesn't help."

"Damp? It must be seventy degrees out, Joe," Roosevelt said.

"Direct sun's no good either," Kennedy said.

Joseph Kennedy started to climb up onto the viewing platform.

"Hold it, Joe," Farley said. "We're going into the car. You can come in through the door like a normal person."

"He's not a normal person," Roosevelt said and laughed. "You should know that, Jim."

"Louis Howe better not be with you," Kennedy said, as he climbed up onto the train, "or I'm not riding with you to Washington."

The men moved into the car. The boy, Jack, stood below looking up at me.

"Come on," I said, and stretched out my hand.

He took it and jumped onto the platform.

"Thank you," he said to me.

Inside the car a long table was covered in white linen, with five place settings. Real silver and china.

Only five, I thought, but Roosevelt noticed.

"Could you set another place, please?" Roosevelt asked Melvin Grant. Grant laid out new silverware and china, then placed another chair at the table. Jack sat down.

Grant cleared his throat. "If you don't mind, sir, I've asked an assistant server to work with me."

"Do you really need—" Farley began.

"Well you see, sir, the helper is my son. He's only sixteen, but I'm training him, and meeting you would be something he would remember his whole life."

"I don't know if we want an untrained—" Farley said.

"Sixteen," Jack said. "Same age as me. And learning a trade too. Good for him."

"Speak when you're spoken to, young man," Farley said.

"I encourage my children to say what's on their mind and Jack makes a good point. Here's a boy ready to work, following in his father's footsteps," Joseph Kennedy said. He looked at Roosevelt. "I'm sure you won't object."

"How could I?" Roosevelt said.

Grant waved his hand. A young Negro boy, who looked very like his father, came in. "His name's not George either. This is Melvin Grant, Jr." He wore a starched white jacket and dark pants, not the full uniform of his father.

Roosevelt extended his hand to him. "I'm glad to meet you, young man," he said.

A long pause before young Grant was able to return the president's handshake.

"How about a picture, Nora," Roosevelt said, and I took the Seneca out from under my chair, stood up and snapped three pictures of them.

"What about Jack?" Joseph Kennedy asked. "He'd like a photograph with you too, Franklin."

"Of course," Roosevelt said, and Jack was up and next to the president. No hesitation in this handshake.

"And are *you* following in *your* father's footsteps young man? Increasing the family fortune?" Roosevelt asked him.

"He is not!" Joseph Kennedy said. "I've made enough money so my boys won't have to bother with business. Jack here's going to be an author. Write great books."

"That sounds worthwhile," I said.

"I'll write a tome on how my brother Joe became president of the United States."

Joseph Kennedy nodded.

"Good idea. My oldest son is an extraordinary young man. Smart, great personality, a fine athlete on the Harvard football team. I played baseball myself for the college. Won a championship for the old alma mater, as he will. And Joe Junior applies himself to his studies, which is more than I can say for John Fitzgerald Kennedy here. Almost got expelled from Choate. In fact, a bout of pneumonia saved his bacon. He's taking a semester off to catch up. All he does is read, read, read."

"But if I am to write—" Jack Kennedy started.

His father interrupted, "This boy devours history books and biographies, Franklin, but try to get him to finish his math homework, or get in an assignment on time. Never had these issues with Joe, and my daughters are no trouble. Too early to tell about Bobby though. He's a bit too taken with Jack the rebel, and Teddy's a baby. All good stock though. Longevity is in Rose's family and my mother's still alive."

The Grants were serving us now. Fish.

"Grouper," Grant said. "And hush puppies. With corn bread and fried okra."

"A Southern meal," Roosevelt said. "Alright with you Joe, or would you and Ed have preferred corned beef and cabbage?"

I caught Ed's eye.

"This is fine, Franklin," Joseph Kennedy said, "though I could have brought some lobsters. Get them sent down once a week."

Then Joe Kennedy said that he thought the most important cabinet position was going to be secretary of the Treasury.

"And I suppose you're the best candidate?" Farley said.

"I only want to help," Kennedy said.

"I'm thinking of setting up a commission to regulate the market," Roosevelt said. "Figure out a way to stop 1929 from ever happening again. Ed Kelly here thought you'd be a perfect chairman. What did you say, Ed? Set a thief to catch a thief?"

Roosevelt laughed, but neither Joseph Kennedy or Ed joined in. What is Roosevelt up to? I wondered. It was almost as if he were setting Joe Kennedy and Ed against each other.

As if he knew it was time to interrupt, Melvin Grant said to his son, "Tell the gentlemen why they should save room for some key lime pie."

"My mother baked it specially for you, sir," young Grant said to Roosevelt. "I brought it from home in Deerfield Beach."

I watched Melvin Grant make sure that each piece was absolutely equal as he cut the pie.

Grant's son carried two pieces of pie from the sideboard to the table. He placed the first one before the president-elect. Conversation stopped. Farley, Ed, and Joseph Kennedy stared at the young man.

Who was next in the pecking order? "Serve the lady," Melvin Grant said to his son, who put the plate in front of me. A diplomat.

The others got their pie, and conversation began again.

"What about your being treasurer of the United States, Joseph?" Farley said. "A great thing to sign Joseph Patrick Kennedy onto the currency. Decorate the hundred dollar bills with a flourish or two."

"I'm guessing that's a joke, Jim. I'm offering my skills to the president. I don't need to be pacified with some ceremonial job that means nothing," he said.

"Garner told me the vice presidency wasn't worth a bucket of hot piss when I offered it to him but he took it," Roosevelt said.

"Except that's a job with some chance of advancement," Kennedy said.

"As we just saw," Roosevelt said and laughed.

I looked at Ed. How can they joke about the assassination attempt? But then I remembered the soldiers I nursed in France. Their black humor. Ed was laughing too.

"You looked distressed, Miss Kelly," Jack said, keeping his voice down.

"I was there," I said. Roosevelt, Kennedy, Farley, and Ed were paying no attention to us. They leaned toward each other, making a tent of their talk.

"I was photographing Cermak and Roosevelt. I asked them to move closer together so maybe . . . the gunman was right behind me. It was very close, Jack. Roosevelt's a lucky man."

"I suppose survival does depend on luck," Jack said. "I'd say Dad saved me. A few more days in that school infirmary might have done me in."

I nodded. "Ed's son wasn't so fortunate. Got sick at his school, and, well, I think they could have done more for him."

"The headmaster accused me of malingering." Jack Kennedy rolled the word out. "Students are seen as the enemy in those places. The faculty's always on guard."

"They might have thought Ed Junior was faking. I was against sending him away," I said.

"My father thinks it's classier to go to boarding school. If the WASPs do it, so should we. I missed home. When all us kids get together it's great. I'm counting the days until summer and Hyannis. We all pile into the sailboat though my mother's afraid it could capsize and we might drown, but no life without risk," he said. "I've learned that much."

"I'd say Franklin Delano Roosevelt would agree with you," I said.

"My dad told me not to mention the assassination attempt. A nut—acting on his own—that's the story."

"I'm supposed to be silent but I wonder about Garner," I said.

"Can you imagine the uproar in the country if they thought Roosevelt's own vice president wanted to kill him?"

"I'm not saying the vice president is involved but what if some rogue elements in Texas . . ."

"Hired a Mafia hit man?" Jack said. "Doesn't sound very plausible."

The others were finished. Ed took a pack of cigars from his pocket.

"Cubans. I was in Havana when Nora called me with news of the assassination," Ed said.

"The assassination attempt," Roosevelt said. "Remember that, Ed, it did not succeed."

"Tell that to Mayor Cermak," I said under my breath, but Jack heard me.

"But the mayor's going to be alright, isn't he?" he said to me.

"We hope so,"

"Jack, I don't want you breathing in this smoke," Joseph Kennedy said. "Kick up your asthma. Go with Nora for a walk along the platform."

"*My* lungs are fine, Mr. Kennedy," I said.

"Nora," Ed said, and swept his finger across the table.

Young Grant joined us as we walked down the platform to the head of the train and stood next to the locomotive. A Zephyr, Grant told us. Sleek, with a kind of pointed nose almost touching the tracks. Shiny. Did they polish away the soot?

"How many cars can that thing pull?" Jack asked.

"As many as it has to," young Grant said. He led us up the steps into the back of the locomotive. "No coal needed. The steam is generated by—"

"What the hell?" The engineer stood in the passageway that led to the engine proper. "You niggers aren't allowed up here. You know that, boy. Now get."

"Just a minute there, mister," I said. "Franklin Roosevelt himself asked this young gentleman to show us around."

"Who are you?" the engineer said. "A nigger-loving bitch like that wife of his?"

"Look here, fellow," Jack Kennedy started.

"Can't understand a word you're saying," the engineer said. "When will you Yankees learn to speak proper?"

"My name is John Kennedy," Jack said, "and my father is—"

"Who gives a shit?" the engineer said. "No one comes into my locomotive without permission, see. Now turn around and haul ass."

"Do you want us to have to tell the President-elect how you have insulted his guests?" I said.

"That boy's not a guest of anybody," the engineer said, pushing his finger into young Grant's chest. He turned to us. "Tell that commie bastard Roosevelt whatever you want. He's not my president and plenty of people in the country feel like me. Fast women, smart aleck kids, and niggers. That's about his speed."

Suddenly Ed was standing there. "Come on, Nora. We have to get off."

"This man's just insulted President Roosevelt and he was awful to the three of us," I said.

The engineer said, "Oh, I was awful," in a high-pitched tone. "Now git, all of you."

"You really can't talk to us like that," Ed said.

"Oh can't I? And who are you?"

"My name's Ed Kelly, and—"

"A Mick. Should've known. A nigger, a bitch, a Yankee, and a Mick. Sounds like the beginning of a joke. They walk into a barroom—"

"You're drunk," Ed said.

"I haven't touched a drop."

"Well I say you are, and for the safety of the passengers I'm removing you from this train. I've worked on the railroad. I know there's always a backup engineer handy. Come with me to the station," Ed told him.

"You're nuts," the engineer said, and took a swing at Ed.

And Ed Kelly, the Brighton Park boxing champion for ten years running, brought his fist up and hit the engineer flush on the chin. He went down.

"Come on, Jack, let's get this man into the station. And you," Ed said to young Grant, "tell your father to find the backup engineer."

When I said goodbye to him, Franklin Roosevelt took my hand and held it for a moment. "Don't think too much about last night. Move," he said, and paused. "Move on."

We stood with Jack Kennedy. "*Slán abhaile*, Jack," I said. He and Ed and I had watched the train to New York pull away, and he was headed toward a chauffeur-driven car.

"What?" he said.

"That's the Irish language. It means 'safe home,'" I said.

"Slán," he repeated, drawing the word out. "Sounds like 'so long.'"

"It does. A professor friend of mine said lots of phrases in American English are really bits of Irish that, unmoored from their origins, became slang. Gifts from our ancestors. Ever wonder why something new is the bees' knees?"

Jack smiled. "Honey Fitz, my grandfather, described things that way all the time."

"It comes from the Irish—*béasnuíosach*. Means 'a new style.'"

"Interesting," Kennedy said.

"Hundreds of examples. Mind your own beeswax."

"What?" he said.

"*Beasmhaireacht*, it means 'manners.'"

Jack Kennedy shook his head.

"Our people's language was very expressive," I said.

"I never think of the Irish having a language," he said.

"You should. Our literature was as great as England's, and it's older. My professor said Shakespeare himself was secretly an English Catholic and was influenced by Irish priests."

"I should have known we'd find some way to claim him," Jack said.

"I'm not kidding. And 'kid' is another word that comes from the Irish," I said.

Jack waved his hand at me. "Too much to take in. But hey, I'll do some reading."

"Try the *Táin*, that's Ireland's *Iliad* and *Odyssey*, only the hero's a woman. And there's a poem I've been thinking about since the shooting. 'The Lament for Owen Roe O'Neill,' about the chieftain poisoned by the English. Of course there's great songs."

"Honey Fitz's full of Irish songs and stories. Dad said it's all malarkey."

"Another Irish word," I said.

"Well, thanks for the information. But I can't stand here gabbing all day."

"From 'gab,' which means chat," I said. And Jack Kennedy put up both hands to stop me.

"Enough. But if that professor of yours ever comes to Boston, we'll invite him over," he said.

I wasn't about to tell him my professor, Peter Keeley, was dead. Killed by one of his own students during Ireland's Civil War. Let young Kennedy discover Romantic Ireland first.

"I'll send you some books," I shouted after him.

He didn't turn but started trotting and cut through the knot of people still standing behind the barriers.

"The Kennedys," I said.

Ed smiled. "Joseph Patrick's a piece of work."

"A friend?"

Ed shrugged. "I liked the kid," he said.

"Me, too," I said.

"So now you've met the great man," he said.

"I have. Roosevelt respects you, Ed. And that punch didn't hurt. I'm sure someone told him."

"Mmmm."

I wondered if Ed were thinking of Colonel McCormick. Was Roosevelt another WASP fascinated by an Irish tough guy?

The Miami train pulled in and we headed back to the hospital and Anton Cermak.

5

JACKSON MEMORIAL HOSPITAL, MIAMI

MARCH 4, 1933

Nearly three weeks since the shooting. Ed, Pat Nash, and I were with the mayor in his hospital room listening to the radio broadcast of FDR's inaugural address. Cermak's slow recovery was worrying Kathleen Quinn. "Should have taken that bullet out," she'd said to me.

Ed had asked me to stay down in Florida. No hardship not to return to Chicago in the teeth of winter. I was acting as Cermak's press agent and helping Cermak's secretary, who'd set up an office in the adjoining room to answer his mail. His daughters visited every evening but today, only Pat, Ed, and I were with the mayor.

Roosevelt's voice was almost too big for the small Philco radio, pushing the tubes to their limit.

"So first of all," the president started, "let me assert my firm belief that the only thing we have to fear is fear itself."

"Great line," Ed said to me.

"Says it all," I said. "He can really make the language work for him."

Cermak said, "Shush, listen."

"Nameless, unreasoning, unjustified terror, which paralyzes needed efforts to convert retreat into advance," the president continued.

"By God, he's right," Cermak said. "The whole city's been paralyzed, Pat. When I pay the teachers, that'll send a message. Right, Ed? Show that Chicago's coming back."

"Easy A.J.," Ed said to him.

Cermak had pushed himself up in bed, and was struggling. "Nora, help him," Ed said.

I eased the mayor's shoulders back onto the pillows as Roosevelt went on talking about the dark hours in national life in the past, when the people had supported leadership of "frankness and vigor."

"And I am convinced that you will again give that support to leadership in these critical days," he said.

Cermak's eyes were closed. I nodded over at Pat, and Ed and turned down the radio. Cermak opened his eyes.

"That's what we have to tell the people of Chicago, boys," he said to Ed and Pat. "They have to support me."

"They will, A.J.," Pat said. "The whole town is with you."

"They are," Ed said. "There's a photograph of you on the front page every day, thanks to Nora here."

"Yes," Cermak said. "They've been good. In fact, Nora, why don't you snap one of me listening to Roosevelt on the radio. Push it over to me."

I unplugged the radio and put it on the tray near his bed and lined up the shot in the viewfinder.

"Do you want Pat and Ed to stand on either side of you?" I asked.

"No," the mayor said, "after all, Roosevelt wouldn't be giving a speech if I hadn't stopped the bullet."

He leaned close to the radio, acting as if he were listening with great intensity. He looked up at me. "I'm getting the hang of this," he said. "We make a good team. And, of course, if you hadn't told me to move closer that night in the park . . . So you get a little bit of credit for saving Roosevelt too, Nora."

"Generous of you, A.J.," Ed said. Pat and I laughed. Cermak didn't.

"I suppose that was a joke, Ed. Never sure with you Micks. You're not mocking me, are you?"

"Of course not," Ed said. Silence.

"Though maybe if I hadn't told you to move in, the bullet might have missed both of you," I said.

"I don't know," Cermak said. "The FBI told me Zangara was a sharpshooter in the Italian Army. Jesus Christ, he hit five people with five shots. Some shooting."

Cermak stopped. "Unless, of course, he was aiming for me all the time. Then what you said, or didn't say, Nora, wouldn't have made any difference. The FBI told me the guy was just a nut. But I don't know. Nitti hates me. Said I was a marked man. I may still be."

"You're safe enough here, A.J.," Ed said.

The same two police detectives who had guarded the mayor's suite in the Morrison Hotel were on duty in the hospital corridor.

"Yeah," Cermak said, "I'm okay here, but what about when I go back? What do you think, Ed?" Ed looked over at Pat. "What, you guys heard something?" Cermak asked.

"Nitti's not stupid," Ed said. "He won't try again."

"He's been spoken to, A.J.," Pat said. "You're okay."

"You know, if the city didn't need me so bad, I'd quit the whole thing. Let you find someone to take on the damn job, Pat." He closed his eyes, twisted his face, and grunted.

"What? What?" I asked.

"It's the damn colitis. Dr. Meyer says the pain I'm feeling is from that, not the bullet hole. Though, I'd say, getting shot didn't help any."

"We should go," I said to Pat and Ed. "I'll send Kathleen Quinn in to you," I told Cermak. That was Saturday. By Monday, he was dead.

MARCH 7, 1932
MIAMI TO CHICAGO

"Me become mayor? Thanks, Pat, but it's not for me," Ed said to Pat Nash.

The three of us were in the hotel dining room of the Eden Roc. We were having an early breakfast before the 10:00 a.m. departure of the train that would carry Anton Cermak's body back to Chicago. The waiter didn't even bother to take our orders. Regulars now, after three weeks—bacon and eggs sunny-side up for Ed and me, oatmeal for Pat and his own pot of tea, while Ed and I drank cup after cup of strong black coffee refilled, with our slightest nod, by the waiter, who told us he was from Havana.

"You were Cermak's choice," Pat went on.

Ed only shook his head and speared the egg yolk with a corner of his toast.

"If Nitti wants to kill the mayor of Chicago, why would Ed want to risk his life?" I asked.

"I'm not afraid of the Outfit," Ed said.

"You get along with Roosevelt, Ed. He likes you. You saw that didn't you, Nora?" Pat asked.

"I did, Pat." I had noticed how Roosevelt eyed Ed's navy blazer, his gray flannel trousers, the pocket handkerchief. Ed could have been a guest on the Astor yacht also. I'd watched Roosevelt set Ed against Joseph Kennedy and smile when Ed held his own without being unpleasant. Here was an Irish pol who was well-spoken, but still tough.

Yes, Ed could connect to the president and probably do the city some good. But Margaret would hate being the wife of the mayor. I looked at Ed, pressed my lips together. He knew what I was thinking.

"And my wife is a shy woman," Ed said. "Not really fair to land her in the spotlight."

"You mean Margaret wouldn't support you?" Pat said. "She seems very loyal."

"Well, of course, she'd support me," Ed said, "but . . ."

"I always thought she had a strong personality," Pat said.

"Margaret's strong, Pat, but she has the kids now, and . . . ," Ed said.

"Are you saying being the First Lady of Chicago would be too much for her?" Pat asked. "What do you think, Nora?"

"Margaret's able for anything, but . . ." But what? The woman I knew nursing soldiers in France could handle anything. But if Ed became mayor, Wilcox wouldn't be able to contain himself. All the malted milks in the world wouldn't keep him from attacking our family. And Ed . . . he had been off the drink ever since that time in Wisconsin, but what would he do under this kind of pressure?

Pat Nash would not let up.

"Listen, Ed, you're the only one who could talk all those businessmen who are withholding their taxes into paying up. You could make them see sense."

And that was true. The rich people in Chicago, who had gone on a tax strike, liked Ed for the same reasons Roosevelt did. They were comfortable with the way Ed dressed and spoke. Not that my cousin ever pretended to be anything but an Irishman from Bridgeport proud of his heritage, but he didn't make the businessmen nervous the way old-style pols like Hinky Dink and Bathhouse John did.

After all, he'd raised millions of dollars from the likes of Shedd and Adler, Rosenwald, and Buckingham. He'd remade Chicago, which benefited everybody. Surely he'd earned the right to talk them into paying their taxes.

"But I'm not a politician, Pat," Ed said. "I've never been elected to any office."

"But, that's good," Pat said. "You've a record of real accomplishment, built actual buildings. The people of the city will respect that."

"I don't know, Pat. I've been thinking of starting to retire, spend more time in the Northwoods."

"Ed, the city needs you. Finish out Cermak's term, and then you can do anything you want. The very fact you don't want the job will make the boys support you. You'll be a placeholder, while they fight among themselves to be the next candidate." Pat smiled. "When A.J. and I were going through a list of names of possible mayors, he said, 'Ed Kelly would make a good mayor, but if he gets in, you'll have a hell of a time getting him out.'"

I laughed. Ed didn't.

"If I do accept the job, let the boys know that while I'm in office, I'll be the boss. Understand, Pat?" Ed said.

The boss. Our Ed. I watched him pick up the last piece of bacon on his plate. Two crunches and it was gone. Edward Joseph Kelly, mayor of Chicago. Oh, Granny Honora, when you went running for your life from Galway Bay, could you ever have imagined such a thing?

Some comfort for me when the autopsy report came out that morning, and Cermak's personal physician told the newspapers colitis had killed him, not the bullet. But still I couldn't stop thinking about those two words, "move closer."

"Put it out of your mind," Ed said to me when I told him I was still haunted by that night, as he, Pat Nash, and I rode the special train carrying Anton Cermak's body back to Chicago. Had a five-foot-nothing drifter really almost brought down the president of the United States? What if two words from me had changed history? Ed had no patience with such speculation.

"Did you fire the gun, Nonie?" he asked me.

"Of course not," I said.

"Well then," he said. "Might just as well blame Jim Bowler. He's not torturing himself." He stood up from the seat next to me on the train and walked down the aisle to join Pat Nash and Cermak's son-in-law, Otto Kerner, in the back of the club car. "Zangara was a crazy loner. The end."

They knew that back in Chicago there were ructions. The members of the city council were holding very public secret meetings. John Clark, a West Side alderman from a rich district, who was chairman of the finance committee, had more or less appointed himself mayor. He argued that when Mayor Harrison was assassinated in 1893, the then finance chairman had taken over. He had precedent on his side, Clark claimed. A few of the Irish aldermen, who thought it was time for them to regain power, agreed with him.

MARCH 10, 1933

The combatants paused to bury Anton Cermak in one of the biggest funerals the city had ever seen. Five hundred thousand people stood along the route the hearse followed from the train station to the Convention Center. Ed was one of the pallbearers who accompanied the casket up the aisle to the very stage on which Roosevelt had accepted the nomination seven months ago. Cermak had belonged to no specific church, so a rabbi, priest, and Protestant minister delivered the eulogies.

Then the battle began. The city's lawyer, William Sexton, told the council members they couldn't elect a temporary mayor themselves. There would have to be a citywide election, and the earliest it could be held was June 9.

The council did not like that. A special election would cost five hundred thousand dollars. The city couldn't spend that kind of money. Better to pay the teachers and policemen. And besides, couldn't risk Big Bill Thompson throwing his hat into the ring. They voted down the election but did agree on one thing: according to law, the new mayor had to be selected from the members of the city council, so technically Ed could not be a candidate. They appointed one of their own members, Francis Corr, as acting mayor.

Ed was lying low. What I didn't know was that Pat Nash was at work in the state legislature in Springfield. Pat had sent word to the leader of the Democratic Party there that the Illinois law requiring that the mayor of Chicago be chosen from the city council should be suspended. It was.

A committee of five aldermen was selected to make a recommendation for mayor. And now they could choose any Chicago citizen. Given the importance of this decision, the men decided they could not just discuss it in the Morrison Hotel, nor over lunch at Henrici's. No, the five set out on an all-expense-paid trip to a resort in Hot Springs, Arkansas—on the principle, I suppose, that a race track, mineral baths, and two casinos helped concentrate the mind. It took only three days for them to send a telegram with their recommendation. Pat Nash was the chosen one.

Is that it? I wondered. "All this maneuvering so that Pat could take over?" I asked Ed. It had been almost a month since Cermak had died. But Ed only smiled.

"You're getting a lesson on how to herd cats, Nonie," he said. "Pat knows what he's doing."

The next day in the *Tribune,* Pat Nash said that he was honored by the recommendation but that he felt he was too old to take on the job. "The next mayor should be a Democrat, of course, but a man outside of politics, though wholly familiar with politics. Someone who had accomplished things for the city and is able for the challenges ahead," Pat was quoted as saying.

And he sent word to the council, "I choose Ed Kelly as the next mayor. Spread the word."

Four days later, the city council met in chambers. Jake Arvey, the alderman who was close to Pat, read a statement signed by thirty-seven aldermen proposing Edward J. Kelly for mayor.

One alderman asked if they could vote by secret ballot. "What are you trying to hide?" Arvey asked. And so a voice vote was taken. Forty-seven votes for Ed, all the Democrats and fifteen Republicans, with three abstentions. Herding cats, no question. In a month, Pat Nash had maneuvered the party to break with all precedent and select a long shot who had never held public office. Edward J. Kelly was mayor.

I came home with Ed after I'd photographed the midnight city council session that made him mayor.

"I want you to celebrate with Margaret and me," Ed had said. I wondered if he didn't want me as a kind of buffer. Margaret would dread the attention she would have to endure as First Lady of Chicago. One thing to put on a white ermine coat and get your picture taken going to the opera with the president of the South Park Board. Still another to attend Democratic Party events at union halls and ward offices, where men talked to each other in knots, while women rotated around them chatting together about children and recipes. Margaret was never great at small talk.

The press would attack Ed. Big Bill Thompson would be taking pot shots at Ed, too, no question. Probably raising money for his 1935 election campaign right now.

But Margaret surprised us.

"Mr. Mayor," she'd said, throwing the front door open for Ed and me. "I heard the news on the radio."

One o'clock in the morning, and she was dressed in her forest green suit with perfect makeup, her eyebrows drawn on, and her hair freshly fingerwaved. Ed looked at me and smiled.

"Whew!"

Never underestimate Margaret, I thought. We had a celebration. Tea and chocolate chip cookies made by Lu, the cook. Ed still taking it easy on the drink.

"The children will be so proud," Margaret said. They were old enough now to understand—Pat and Joseph were seven, and Steve three—that their father was an important man.

"That reminds me, Margaret," Ed had said. "The *Tribune* wants to do a feature for their Sunday edition on the family. You and the kids and me. They'll send a photographer over in the next few days."

"Send a photographer, Ed?" Margaret asked. "Why, when we have our own photographer right here? You'll take the photos, won't you, Nora?"

What could I say? Cermak had paid me and I had enough money to leave Chicago and head back to that other life in Paris.

I thought of Ireland and Peter Keeley in his grave, waiting for me so patiently. But Margaret was asking me to help make her new life bearable. To survive and maybe even enjoy Ed's brief time as the mayor of Chicago. Pat had assured the other politicians that Ed would fill out the two years left on Cermak's term, until the party found the right candidate for the 1935 election.

So I said yes, of course, I'd take their pictures for the Sunday edition and for whatever else was required. Manny Mandel had called me Ed Kelly's flack. Well why not? And if it meant that I never saw my name on the credit line under a photograph, so what? I wasn't a glory hound, was I?

"Good idea, Margaret," Ed said. "Nora, you've got a new job. You are the official photographer of the mayor of Chicago."

"With a raise," Margaret said.

"Of course," Ed said, though I wondered if Margaret knew Ed had been giving me bits and pieces himself, not taking my salary from the reduced City Treasury.

"When the money comes from Roosevelt to pay the teachers and cops, and the rich people end their tax strike, then I'll accept a raise."

Now, of course, I was excited at the chance of being on the inside of all the maneuverings. Pat Nash certainly could herd cats, but now could he and Ed save Chicago? Because if they stumbled at all, Big Bill was stalking the sidelines ready to take over from the Micks and Bohunks, the sheeneys and lugans, who had somehow captured the city. He'd be bankrolling Wilcox, no question. And there were plenty of Toots-like characters around ready to sell gossip and rumors, and even a few who had the goods on coworkers and were looking for revenge. No, I wouldn't leave, at least not yet.

The next morning I got up early to find Margaret standing at the front window. "Who are these people?" she asked me. "What do they want?" We were standing in the bay window of the Ellis Avenue house as the sun rose. Twenty people had gathered on the wide sidewalk under the Dutch elms—the trees still meeting in a canopy of green over the street, before a disease would infect these Chicago stalwarts and turn comfortable old neighborhoods like this one as bare as the new housing developments on what was once our prairie.

As I stood next to Margaret, watching more and more people arriving in front of the house, I wondered if any of us had any idea of what we were getting into.

"They were here when I got up at first light," Margaret said.

"I saw them from the bedroom window," Ed said, standing beside us, smelling faintly of lavender water. His red hair was still damp, the curls combed into hills and valleys. He wore a new navy blue suit, white shirt, and a tie with narrow green stripes.

"What the hell is this?" Ed said.

"Daddy's swearing," Pat said. She and her twin brother, Joseph, had followed Ed down the stairs. They were dressed in their school uniforms: plaid skirt and blazer for Pat, and navy pants and blazer for Joseph. First graders at St. Thomas, the local parish school.

"Are all those people coming into our house?" Joseph asked.

"They most certainly are not," Margaret said. But a few of the crowd had seen us standing at the window, and two women were waving. Ed waved back.

"Don't," Margaret said, "don't encourage them." But now the crowd was walking up toward the porch, and a few were on the steps.

"I have to speak to them," Ed said. "Come on, Nonie, bring your camera." And so Ed and I spent the early hours of his first morning as mayor taking photographs and requests. Ed wrote each name in a small spiral notebook, while I took pictures of groups with the mayor.

"I'd invite you in," Ed said to them, "but the kids are getting ready for school, and Margaret's in her dressing gown. Why don't you head down to city hall. We'll talk there."

"City hall?" one said. "That's miles away. We're South Siders. You're our neighbor."

"That I am," Ed said.

It was nine o'clock when a black Packard and two police cars pulled up in front of the house. A plainclothes detective got out of the lead car. "You better not have called the cops on us," one man said. The crowd laughed, and so did the detective. White hair, blue eyes. Could only be Irish.

"We're here to take the mayor to work," he said, and gestured toward the Packard and the police escort.

"Doing alright for yourself in America, Ed," another man shouted.

"Let the mayor get some breakfast," the detective said.

"I've got all your names," Ed said, "and addresses. Nora will send you the photographs, and I'll get the boys in city hall to work on your requests."

"We have to move from here," Margaret said, as she poured coffee for the detective, Ed, and me at the massive table in their big dining room.

"Not a bad idea," the detective said. "Though the people will find you, Ed."

"I don't want to hide," Ed said.

"But maybe a place with some security," I said, "where just anybody can't walk up to the front door or look in the front windows."

And, then, I thought of the perfect solution. "What about my building? Where there's a doorman and a lobby, and—"

"And it's on the North Side," Margaret said. "Harder to get to."

"I don't know," Ed said. "I'm a South Sider. These are my constituents."

"But you're mayor of the whole city," I said, "and what could be better than waking up to see the sun rising over the lakeshore that you created."

"But an apartment," Margaret said, "is so much smaller than a house."

"Are you worried that there's no ballroom?" I asked. "Remember you've got the Morrison Hotel and the Drake now."

"Hmm, that's right. The Drake. Your building's right next door isn't it?" she asked.

"It is, and Saks Fifth Avenue is a three-minute walk away. Sometimes I feel like I'm living in the sixteenth arrondissement of Paris."

The doorbell was ringing. A voice called, "Mr. Mayor, Mr. Mayor, I need a job."

Ed started to get up. Margaret put a hand on his shoulder. She looked at me. "Let's see what's available in your building, Nora. Today."

6

APRIL 1933

Chicago City Hall was a square squat building, opened in 1911, that took up a whole city block and had thick columns holding up every doorway. Plain. There were a few doodads, but nothing like the Hotel de Ville, seat of Paris's city government that I had passed every day on my way from Le Marais to Madame Simone's studio on Rue St. Honoré. Chicago people would not have felt comfortable going into a place like that, with statues stuck all over the façade and soaring towers. Intimidating. While the Hall was the people's house, no question. The lobby was always full of citizens looking for jobs or a stop sign on their block.

And Ed was head of the whole shebang.

I'd been surprised when Margaret had suggested that we stop at City Hall on our way to the North Side. "Let's take a quick peek at Ed's office." Which is what we did—though Ed's secretary, Bessie O'Neill made sure that the First Lady of Chicago would at least have a cup of coffee and a sweet roll.

Ed was in a meeting behind the closed door of the inner office of the suite. Margaret didn't want him disturbed, she said. So we drank our coffee and left.

"It looks like a dentist's waiting room," Margaret said as we walked down the wide stone stairs. "But I can fix that. We wouldn't need all the Ellis Avenue furniture when we move."

"When"—not "if."

We turned right off Michigan Avenue at the Drake and found a parking space as close to my apartment at 209 East Lake Shore as possible.

Margaret smiled as the doorman opened the solid brass door to us.

"Secure," she whispered. She looked around the lobby with its gilded ceiling and marble floor, and then walked over to the desk with its uniformed attendant.

"Hello, Dino," I said to the man, a nice fellow from the Balkans, of all places.

"How are you, Nora?" he replied. Margaret looked a question at me: Is the help this familiar to the tenants? But, of course, I was the help, too.

"This is Mrs. Edward J. Kelly, Dino. The wife of our brand-new mayor."

"An honor to meet you, Mrs. Kelly. I recognized you from your pictures in the paper."

"Listen, Dino. I know there's a vacant apartment on the seventh floor."

"There is indeed. Five bedrooms, four baths, a library, and a completely modern kitchen. Not one refrigerator, but two. And the gas stove is self-lighting."

"Very nice, Dino. Mrs. Kelly would like to take a look."

"Sure thing," Dino said. "I've got a key right here. Do you want to take her up, Nora? You know the place, don't you? You used to babysit old Mrs. Lawrence's cats when she was up in Lake Forest."

"I did," I said, and hoped that the cat smell was gone, or else Margaret would not be interested in the place, no matter how spectacular the view.

But there was not a whiff of cat in the apartment, and Margaret said, "Oh," right out loud when she saw Lake Michigan stretched out under the wall of windows.

"If you stand in the right place, you can't even see Lake Shore Drive. Everything disappears but the lake," I said.

"Gorgeous," she said.

Mrs. Lawrence had had a stroke last month and died after a week in Passavant Hospital. Some cousin who'd inherited money in the will came, cleared out the apartment, and took the cats. Probably dropped them right off at the pound. But now, here was this space, open, full of sunshine and the scent of the lake after I cranked open a window.

"Art deco," Margaret said, as she pointed to the fancy grille work over the door that led to a paneled library. And the kitchen was as Dino at the desk had described it. Gadgets galore, black and white tile everywhere. The stove took up an entire wall. Ten burners and a griddle.

"Lu will love this," I said.

"Lu won't be moving with us," Margaret said.

"Oh," I said.

"She's ready to retire. I'm hiring a French cook. The mayor's dinner parties should have certain elegance," she said.

"Oh," I said again. This was the Margaret who had sent Ed Junior to boarding school. The woman who had survived two disastrous marriages and had never flinched when she cleaned the pus off the wound in an amputee's stub of a leg. My admired friend, but a formidable woman.

"And will you keep Bridie?" I meant to sound sarcastic. After all, hadn't this County Cork girl been nurse then nanny to the children since they came to Ed and Margaret from St. Vincent de Paul? Recommended by the nuns, and loved by the kids.

"She'll have to stay, I suppose. Though an English nanny—"

At this, I interrupted her. "Don't," I said.

"The problem is there's only one maid's room here, and the cook may want it. Too bad the building doesn't have adequate servants' quarters," she said.

Now Margaret knew good and well that I'd taken over the attic for my own flat. She looked at me. Does she expect me to offer to share my place with Bridie? Not a good arrangement for either one of us.

The kitchen had a door that led to a back porch and outside stairs. Now the door opened and a woman and young girl stood there.

"Hello. Hello," the woman said. "I'm your neighbor, Edith Davis. Though everyone calls me Lucky, and this is my daughter Nancy. We've only just moved in ourselves, and when Dino told me someone was looking at the apartment—well, I just had to pop up and urge you to take it. This is a wonderful building, but half the tenants are here only sporadically. Needs some livening up."

I had heard from Dino that Dr. Loyal Davis, who was well known in Chicago, and his relatively new wife were now living at 209.

"She was an actress. Did well for herself," Dino had said. "Acted with George M. Cohan, and Spencer Tracy, she told me." He lowered his voice, "Divorced. Met Dr. Davis on a cruise. He was smitten, and here they are. The daughter's from the first marriage, of course. Cute, but shy. Not like the mother. She's a talker."

I expected Margaret to draw back from this blast of conversation, but no, she was smiling at Lucky. "I certainly hope we'll be living here. I'm Margaret Kelly. Mrs. Edward J. Kelly."

"I know. I know. Dino told me, and your husband was just made mayor. Exciting. And you have family? Playmates for Nancy maybe."

"Mine are a bit younger. Seven-year-old twins and a three-year-old boy."

"Wonderful. Nancy loves little children. She'll be their honorary big sister, while I'm their doting aunt."

Wait a minute, I thought. I'm their doting aunt. Though I had spent less time with the twins and Steve than I had with Michael's children. But, after all, Ed's kids had two parents and Bridie. Still I spoke up.

"They're lovely kids," I said. "I remember last Christmas when—"

Lucky interrupted me. "Wait," she said, "I know you. You're the concierge. Dino pointed you out to me one day."

"I am," I said. Come on, Margaret, I thought, say something. And then, thank God, she did. I really didn't want to fall out with Margaret.

"This is Nora Kelly. My very good friend and my husband's cousin, and also a talented photographer."

Thank you, Margaret.

"Delighted to meet you," Lucky said. "We can be friends together. Loyal's been urging me to have a portrait done of Nancy and me. Perhaps you can do it."

"Very glad to. Thank you."

Nancy still had a child's face. Chubby cheeks, but good eyes under those very straight bangs. The mother's the glamour girl, I thought, not very easy for her daughter. I'd like to see what's behind Nancy's shuttered face.

"Wouldn't that be nice, Nancy?" Lucky asked.

"Yes," the girl answered.

"Now," Lucky said to Margaret, "would you like to see my place? It's the same apartment one floor below. You might want to look at the layout. I used an art deco theme. There's a shop on Michigan that imports French and Italian furniture. The owner advised me on my purchases and even helped me decorate Loyal's office. You might want to talk to him about city hall. I'm sure it could use a bit of élan."

Jesus, better not say "élan" in front of the aldermen, I thought, as Nancy and I followed Lucky and Margaret down the back steps.

"And what grade are you in, Nancy?" I asked her.

"Eighth," she said.

"I have nieces about your age," I said. "I could invite them over one day to meet you."

She didn't answer me. "Would you like that?" I asked.

"I'm quite busy," she said. "I go to the Latin School, and they give lots of homework."

The Davis apartment looked like a movie set. All the furniture, even the grand piano, was white, as was the wall-to-wall carpeting. Odd-shaped lamps with funny shades were stuck all over the floor. Nothing looked comfortable. I couldn't imagine sitting down and reading a book or even having a conversation in this room; but, I must say, everything was spotless.

"Must be hard to keep all of this clean, Mrs. Davis," I said. Probably not the most polite remark, but Margaret made up for my lack of enthusiasm.

"Oh, Lucky. This is so sleek and sophisticated. I've never seen anything like it."

"Thank you. The doctor likes everything very modern. His first wife smothered him in Victoriana, but this," she gestured at the room, "lifts his spirits."

"It reminds him of his operating room," Nancy said. Her mother laughed.

"The doctor does not like mess. That's true. But I say a man's home should reflect him, and the doctor has been wonderful to the both of us, hasn't he, Nancy?" The girl didn't say anything. "Hasn't he?" her mother repeated.

"Yes," Nancy said. "And I do love him very much. I'm only repeating what he said."

I was trying to think of something to say to get the conversation going in another direction, when Margaret said, "I'm sure Ed will be interested in meeting Dr. Davis, though I suspect they already know each other. Most successful men in Chicago seem to move in the same circles."

"I don't know, Margaret. You see, the doctor is a staunch Republican," Lucky said.

"Plenty of decent Republicans," Margaret said.

"Who are appalled at what Big Bill has done to their party. I'd say they dislike him even more than we do," I said.

"The doctor is a friend of Mayor Thompson," Lucky said. "Brings him here to play cards."

"Oh," I said. "Well he's ex-Mayor Thompson now."

Lucky picked up a silver cigarette box from the shiny white coffee table and offered Margaret and me what looked like a Camel. I was surprised to see Margaret take one. I thought she didn't smoke. I only had an occasional cigarette, but figured I might as well join in. I helped myself. Lucky took a heavy, oval silver lighter and flicked the wick, passing the flame first to Margaret, then to me. The three of us puffed together.

"You know how it is, girls. Easier to let your husband decide the family's politics."

"I wouldn't think that an actress who . . ." I stopped.

"Who what?" Lucky said, not laughing now.

"Traveled," I said, "and, you know, met a lot of different kinds of people, getting a broader outlook on life, umm . . ."

"I hope you're not one of those judgmental women who think anyone who's been in show business is an immoral Bolshevik, Miss Kelly."

"Me? No, not at all. It's just . . . I mean, come on Mrs. Davis, Big Bill's a buffoon, and he's dangerous." Lucky inhaled and blew out a trail of smoke that floated up the white walls to the ceiling and said nothing.

"Dino told me you appeared with George M. Cohan. I wonder if you ever heard him speak of Dolly McGee?" I asked.

"Oh Dolly," she said, "before my time really, but a legend. George said she was a marvelous singer and real grand dame," she said, making it sound very French. "Something tragic happened to her, didn't it?"

"It did," I said.

"Some man, I suppose," she said.

"Yes," I said.

She pointed her cigarette toward Margaret.

"It's a very fortunate woman who finds a good man. For once I lived up to my name."

"Mother," Nancy said. "It's five o'clock."

"Oh dear," Lucky said, "I have to say goodbye. The doctor likes his martini right at five thirty when he comes home, and I'm the only one can mix it properly—and I also have to make sure that Cook is on schedule. Dinner is on the table at six sharp. But really, Margaret, we must have lunch at the Cape Cod Room," she said. "You, too, Nora."

"And Nancy," I said. "On a Saturday or school holiday." Something appealing about this little girl.

"I don't like fish," Nancy said. Her mother didn't seem to hear her.

"Don't forget about our portrait, Nora," she said to me.

"I could shoot it right here in the living room," I say. "Plenty of light."

"No, no," she said. "That wouldn't work."

"Well, come up to my atelier," I said—better than saying "the servants' quarters."

"Goodbye, goodbye," Lucky said to us, but it was Nancy who walked us to the door. Lucky was picking up ashes from the carpet with her manicured nails.

"But you don't understand, Lucky. Thompson almost destroyed Chicago," I said to Lucky as I posed her with her daughter on my sofa a week after our first meeting. I had pulled it over to the window so she and Nancy were backlit. The two sat close together, though Nancy leaned just a bit away from her mother. I suppose you learn to protect yourself from the woman who more or less abandoned you for the first nine years of your life. Lucky had told Margaret her marriage to Nancy's father had been very brief, ending just after Nancy was born. Lucky's sister had raised the child. They were the all-American family now, and Lucky certainly played the part of a respectable society matron devoted to her husband and little girl, but Nancy sometimes looked at her mother as if asking, "What is my next line?"

"Thompson's trying to undermine Ed now," I said. "Got that little weasel Wilcox out bribing informers. Looking for dirt. Even Margaret's not . . ." I stopped myself.

Nancy didn't need to hear this, though I was sure Mrs. Loyal Davis wouldn't want to see her past dissected in *Thunderin*. But then again she was a Protestant, so maybe divorce wasn't such a stigma. That did seem to be true because now she said, "Oh, gossip. Can't worry about gossip. Jealousy at the root of it. The doctor's marriage was over when I met him on that cruise, with only some legal technicalities to be ironed out—no matter what some people said. And, of course, Nancy's father and I had been divorced for ages."

I saw Nancy twitch on the couch. Hard for a child, even a Protestant, to hear the breakup of her family dismissed so easily. Now, in a few years, Nancy would tell her father that she had asked Dr. Davis to adopt her. From then on, she would be Nancy Davis. But right now, she was still trying on this new life as the doctor's Latin School–attending daughter—and not a little girl living with her aunt while her actress mother toured the country.

"Nancy, lift your chin," Lucky said. "Makes your face seem thinner. Are we ready, Nora?"

"You are," I said, and spent the next half hour shooting the pair from every angle. I put on a bit of an act. Went down on my knees to shoot up at them; stood on a chair pointing the camera down. As I looked through the viewfinder, I thought that both Lucky and Nancy had an actress's ability to project an image. Both could change expressions like slides in a zoetrope. Four different kinds of smiles each: one, a closed-lipped regal version with guarded eyes; then, a warm I'm-just-like-you half grin; a head back, let's laugh together version; and then the slightest upturn of the corners of their mouths, as if they were recalling a secret memory. In the end, Lucky chose the queen and princess shot, and I went down to Mabel Sykes's darkroom to print three oversized portraits.

"Those are two women who know what they want and how to get it," Mabel said.

"Nancy's only a little girl," I said.

"So . . . Hey, I meant it as a compliment to them," Mabel said.

And I did admire Lucky. She'd rowed herself onto a safe shore, and brought her daughter along with her. Good luck to her. But her politics!

"It's just the doctor could never vote for the Democrats," she'd said to me the day of the sitting. "All that corruption. Thompson comes from a very good family. Four generations in America."

"You mean he's not like the Irish and Italian and German and Jewish riff-raff," I started, but she cut me off.

"Now, Nora, I think it's wonderful that people like you and Margaret have bettered yourself, but you must admit most of these immigrants just don't understand how to behave. I was really afraid of moving to Chicago with the doctor. All those gangsters machine-gunning each other in the street."

I stopped her. "Big Bill took money from every one of them," I said. "Al Capone was Thompson's biggest backer. Why, he beat Dever, who was decent and tried to clean up Chicago."

"Oh, well. Capone's in jail now, and Ed Kelly is going to be our neighbor. I guess we just won't talk politics," Lucky said.

"Lucky, I can tell you're not from Chicago," I said.

What would Ed make of them? But, surprise. Guess what? Ed liked Dr. Davis, and the building, and the apartment. He and Margaret and the children moved in a month later, though Ed did refuse to have white carpets and white furniture. "We've plenty of stuff," he told Margaret.

And I did like the way the mahogany chairs, dark wood cabinets, and the blue velvet sofa and loveseat Mary had bought for the Hyde Park house looked in the new space. Made the apartment look more like a home than a fancy hotel suite. Though Margaret had said to me, "This is alright for now, but Lucky took me to meet this gallery owner who imports furniture and paintings. With the light in this apartment, we need to display some fine art."

Ed joined the doctor's weekly poker game. When I asked him how he enjoyed playing with Republicans, he told me, "Nora, I need these fellows on my side. Besides, Loyal told me in confidence that Big Bill is his patient. Now, you know what the doctor specializes in?"

"Neurology," I said.

"Yes. He's a brain surgeon and very eminent, so I wonder what Big Bill's problem is."

"Are you going to ask the doctor?"

"No. I wouldn't want him to violate his ethics, but . . ."

"You'll find out," I said.

"I might," Ed said.

7

JULY 1933

So. I was glad that the couples were becoming such good friends. Lucky Davis and Margaret were both "women with a past" who had managed to return to the heights of respectability. I wondered if they ever talked about what might have been—Margaret single and living alone on the fringes of Kansas City society, and Lucky an actress playing older and older parts while her daughter grew up and away from her. But now, here they were. Living at the best address in Chicago. Admired matrons.

Funny how I felt not the slightest twinges of envy for them. I'd had my love and could never have married again.

I began to think of Ireland and Peter's grave. July, now, and a lovely month there. I still had a chunk of Cermak's money, and I was collecting a salary. Margaret had the children in Eagle River. Things were quiet in city hall. Maybe Ed would give me a few weeks' vacation.

But then, I got a note from Maurine. There was a new fellow in town. Charles Blake, an editor at the *Chicago Evening American*, which was a Hearst paper. He was an old pal of hers and wanted to talk to someone who knew Chicago. "He's not bad looking either, and the right age—in his mid-fifties, like we are."

"Not interested," I'd told her. I'd seen one story Blake wrote where he described Hinky Dink as "the dean of the thick Micks." But Maurine had always been good to me, and she really wanted me to meet her friend . . .

So that's how I ended up sitting in Greek Nick's speakeasy under Wacker

Drive with Charles Blake a week later. Maurine had set up the appointment with him from LA.

"God, Maurine did it. Didn't she?" Blake said to me. "Got out of there and is making real money in Hollywood. She promised she'd sniff around the studios for me. I could do that kind of snappy dialogue. Certainly there are plenty of characters to draw from in Chicago."

We were drinking Irish whiskey, though I didn't recognize the label. Sheerin's, it was called.

"This stuff is bonded," Blake said to me. "Didn't come from some bathtub in Bridgeport, though I wouldn't trust the gin. Won't be long before Prohibition is gone for good. Can't be soon enough for me. It will be interesting to see what the Outfit does to survive. Now let's talk about why your cousin should be in jail."

"What?" I said.

"Listen, Nora, I won't beat around the bush. I've got a source in the IRS tells me, right after Roosevelt was elected, they settled with Ed Kelly for a hundred thousand dollars as tax on four hundred and fifty thousand dollars of unreported income from 1927, '28, and '29."

I stood up. "What the hell is going on? Maurine said you wanted to talk about Chicago. You, you snake. Did she know this was a setup?"

"Why bother her with details? I heard you're close to His Honor and half a newshound yourself. Don't you want to tell his side of the story? Hey, I personally don't care if your cousin was printing hundred dollar bills, but Mr. Hearst likes connecting Roosevelt with a crooked politician."

Now, I knew Ed had had a tax problem that he'd settled. No charges were ever filed against him. Done and dusted. And really, in the early years of income tax, lots of people were unsure about what to report. If anyone was at fault, it was Ed's lawyer. But Blake wasn't thinking of legalities. He wanted to find graft, corruption, bribes—licking his chops, I thought, as he tilted the shot glass back and grinned at me. Maybe I should find out what he knew. I sat down.

"So what?" I asked. "Ed made money, he paid his taxes. A little late maybe, but he did pay."

"A little late? Try six years past due. Think of it, Miss Kelly. Your cousin settled with the IRS for a hundred thousand dollars. That was the compromise he agreed on. God only knows what he really owed. And though I don't personally converse with God, I've plenty of other sources. I intend to find out where Ed Kelly's money came from. And if Roosevelt was involved in getting the IRS to settle—well, we've got a national story."

"Oh, come on. You can't attack Ed and the president. Look at all the good they're doing. Ed's getting Chicago on its feet again. He's only been in office a month, and already he's collected more taxes, paid more salaries, put more people on relief than Thompson ever did. Come on, Blake, the newspapers were screaming for Ed to cancel the Century of Progress, but he's showed how it could be a moneymaker."

"That's bull. The last thing Chicago needs is another World's Fair. Hubris, Miss Kelly. Pure hubris." He looked at me, sure I didn't understand.

"Hubris," I said, "an interesting word. It's from the Greek, though I suppose you wouldn't expect a thick Mick like me to know much about etymology. Though, from your name, you have some thick Mick blood yourself."

"My people were Scotch-Irish, Miss Kelly. A very different heritage altogether," he said.

Oh, dear God. Here was another one. Scratch one of these cynical newspapermen and you'd find another Wilcox. Next thing, Blake will be going on about the pope being the whore of Babylon. I wonder if Blake had ever bothered to examine the McCormicks' tax returns. "So what do you want, Mr. Blake?"

"An interview with the mayor where he gives me a reasonable account of his income over the last five years."

"And if he gives you an interview and shows you that he made his money honestly through investments, property, sales, and consulting fees, you'll stop the story?"

And he nodded.

"On a dime, Miss Kelly. On a dime."

"No. I'd be nuts to talk to Blake. He'll twist whatever I say."

Ed and I were walking along the lakefront, crossing Oak Street Beach, the morning after my meeting with Blake.

"Okay," I said. "Write out a summary, and I'll meet with Blake and give it to him."

"Nonie, I have no obligation to reveal the source of my income to anyone. Privacy is a fundamental right in this country. It's the law. Even the IRS recognizes it. Look at Section 3167 of the Revenue Act of 1932," he said to me—and then didn't he quote it word for word. "It is unlawful for any collector or officer or employee of the United States to divulge or make known in any manner whatsoever the amount or source of any taxpayer's income."

"Jesus, Ed, you've got it memorized," I said.

"Even a thick Mick like me can learn," he said.

"But what would be so bad about coming clean? None of the regular people in Chicago begrudge you the money you've made. I mean, so what if Pat Nash paid you a consulting fee now and then? Everybody knows Nash Brothers are the best sewer company—that they get the job done. Even the Hearst papers admit that. And so what if you got some advance information, now and then, about new roads going into empty bits of the prairie. Isn't buying cheap and selling dear the American way?"

"Except some of my partners in those land deals are rather shy. They wouldn't like to see their names in the paper," he said.

I stopped. Took him by the arm.

"Oh no, Ed, you didn't . . . Not Capone or Nitti?"

He pushed my hand away. Stepped back.

"Goddamn it, Honora Kelly, I don't take that kind of an accusation from anyone, not even you."

Sometimes I forget just how tall Ed is. How broad were his shoulders. Here was the man who'd flattened his supervisor on the canal, who'd punched the train engineer in Florida. "I'm sorry, Ed. I'm sorry."

He started walking. I caught up.

"The fellow I got involved with isn't like those Italians, but the Hearst newspapers would love to connect us. He's a man who bought acres and acres of vacant land on the far South Side. Worthless, unless the city put in roads and sewers. He came to me and asked me to invest in this land, and to recommend the area for development. I said yes, even though I knew his money came from bootlegging and gambling."

"Mont Tennes? But he's gone respectable. No scandal in having invested with him."

"Not Tennes," Ed said. "This fellow manages to get shot at on a regular basis, but he always survives. Blake of the big words once called him the archetypal Chicago hood." And suddenly, I knew the name and why Ed had agreed to be his partner.

"Spike O'Donnell," I whispered.

Ed nodded. "My chance to fulfill a family obligation, was how Spike put it, and make some money while I was doing it."

"Oh," I said. "Oh."

So. I called Blake and said there would be no interview. The next day, an article appeared headlined, "Tsar Kelly Hides behind 'Photographer' Cousin."

"In the tradition of the Whoopee Boys," Blake had written, "who gave swarms of their relatives no-show jobs, Nora Kelly, who takes endless pictures of events that matter to no one, has approached me in a pathetic attempt to stop the press in the exercise of their duties. William Randolph

Hearst has said that the stories they don't want you to write are the ones you must write. And nothing will deter me—neither attacks nor blandishments, nor threats nor insults shall keep this reporter from telling you, the readers, the truth." And then, he reported on Ed's tax problems and his unexplained income.

I read the piece out loud to Ed. The two of us in his office, long after everyone had gone.

"Jesus," I said, "Ed, he sounds like a mailman. Neither rain nor snow nor dark of night. Maybe now that Jim Farley is postmaster, he can give him a job."

That brought a little smile from Ed. The strange thing was that Blake had missed the real scandal about me—my involvement with Tim McShane and his death at the hands of Spike O'Donnell. Odd about reporters. So focused on the dirt they're digging, they miss a better story. But Blake was from New York and didn't have his own swarm of Chicago relations to keep him in touch with the latest gossip. I was almost glad that Manny Mandel had stolen my picture credit because Blake hadn't learned of my presence that night in Miami.

"Hearst wants me to resign," Ed said. "That's what all this is about. I wonder if I shouldn't. Remember what happened to Carter Harrison? Shot by a fellow who believed the lies the newspapers were telling. And then McKinley. Didn't his assassin say that he'd been influenced by the Hearst publications that had said McKinley was a monster whose death would be a service to mankind?"

"I forgot about that," I said.

"Yes," Ed said. "These fellows don't realize that their words have consequences."

"And the worst of it is I don't think Blake cares one way or another," I said. "He wants to make a name for himself. Get a job as a screenwriter in Hollywood. I'm just grateful that he hasn't sniffed out my connection to Tim McShane and how Spike—well, how he rescued me."

"That's because what they really don't want is for us to be able to spend as we see fit. Trying to stop federal money for my subway project. Destroy the Democratic Party," Ed said.

True enough. Hearst had even gotten a senator to propose a bill taking control of New Deal grants out of local hands because Chicago politicians were corrupt.

"Get rid of me, and the others will be easy pickings," Ed said.

"But you're not going to resign, are you, Ed? You're never going to resign."

"Never," he said. But that was Friday. Very early on Sunday morning, Ed was at my door, still in his robe and pajamas, holding the Sunday edition of the *Chicago American*.

"They've gone too far," he said. He walked in, collapsed onto my couch, and handed me the paper. It was open to a story in the women's section. "Wife of Mayor Kelly Suffers from Remote Mother Syndrome." Some woman I'd never heard of had written a very fancy-sounding analysis of Margaret. Lots of so-called psychological terms, but the gist was that adoptive mothers could not really love their children.

"I'm going to that newspaper office, and punch the first person I see," Ed said.

"I wonder," I said. "I wonder if that's not exactly what they want you to do. I bet they have a cop on hand to handcuff you, with a photographer ready to take the picture."

"This has to stop," Ed said. He opened it to the editorial page—"Kelly Must Resign." I skimmed the piece. Same old idea. Corrupt Democratic city officials could not be trusted with the money from New Deal programs.

"And people believe what they read in the paper," Ed said. "If only I could talk to them man-to-man without this barrier."

He shook the newspaper, then balled it up with his fists and tossed it across the room. He stood up, walked over to the window, and looked down at the streams of cars on the Outer Drive. He reached into his pocket and took something out. I walked over and stood beside him. He was holding Uncle Patrick's medal, rubbing his thumb over the image of the Sorrowful Mother, then turning the medal over and pressing his thumb against Our Lord crowned with thorns.

"Roosevelt did it," I said.

"Did what?"

"Talked to people directly on the radio."

Just the month before, right after he was inaugurated, Roosevelt had broadcast what the newspapers called a "fireside chat." He'd used common language and a conversational tone to lay out his policies. The whole country had listened. Radio offered a way to connect so personally to people right in their living rooms. A first. Lots of letters to the editors saying, until they heard him speak, they had believed that FDR was the crazed dictator the Roosevelt-haters in the press made him out to be.

"You should go on the radio, Ed, the way the president did."

Ed laughed. "Roosevelt has a special talent and I'm . . ."

"A thick Mick? Come on, Ed. You do a great job as master of ceremonies for the Knights of Columbus, you and Michael are the best they have. I don't understand why you won't get out and make speeches."

Because Ed had been appointed as mayor, he hadn't had to campaign. And I thought that really Pat Nash would prefer that Ed just go quietly about his business, while the party found a candidate to run in the next election. But Ed did have an easy way about him. A nice deep voice, and he knew how to tell a joke and sing an Irish song.

"Look, Ed, just pretend you're talking to the Knights of Columbus. Lay out your case to the real people."

"I'll sound like I'm whining."

"No, you'll sound like a man defending his wife and family, a fellow who wants to tell the truth."

Samuel Insull, who owned most everything in Chicago at that time, had the most powerful radio station in the city, WENR, broadcasting from the Civic Opera House. Those were the days when Insull was Chicago's beloved benefactor—before we found out he was a crook who stole the life savings of half the citizens.

"I'm sure Insull will let you use his station." So we sat down that very minute to write his speech.

"You've got to start with something snappy," I said, "to get their attention."

"How about this?" Ed asked. "I'm going to tell you the truth. Then, let the people of Chicago decide whether I should resign or not."

"Great idea," I said. "You can ask the audience to call in to the station, send telegrams. The newspapers say you became mayor without winning a vote. Tell the people, 'We're holding the election right now,'" I said.

"I've got to find a way to make them understand that these fellows want to keep money coming from Chicago. We've been making progress. If everything falls apart, Big Bill Thompson will be back in charge before you know it."

I thought Ed would be nervous when the two of us sat down in the little soundproofed room in the Opera House. But when he leaned toward the microphone, I think he really felt that he was talking to people in their living rooms. He rubbed his holy medal, cleared his throat and began to speak.

"My fellow citizens," he said, "a vicious campaign of abuse, vilification, and slander is being conducted against me by the Hearst publications of Chicago." I nodded. Good delivery. No anger in his tone, but strong words. "So long as it was directed solely against me," Ed said, "I remained silent, making only such replies as I deemed consistent with the dignity of the office I hold. But now, the slanderers have attacked, not only the Democratic Party, the governor, and the duly elected and appointed officers of this county and state, they have also reviled the good name of Chicago, and are now taking aim at my wife and children. I cannot remain silent. I personally need no one to fight my battles. My life has been one long fight against the odds. I've been the target of abuse for personal and political gain on the part of those who attacked me, and I have come to regard such tactics as part of public service. But now, this carpetbagger of a managing editor, who's come to Chicago only recently, is trying to bring me down in order both to prevent the men and women of Chicago from obtaining needed employment in necessary public construction and to impair the credit of our city and thus make it impossible to obtain funds for payrolls. Why does he hate our city so much? Why does Hearst focus on me? I, myself, am of the humblest of origins. My ancestors came from foreign shores seeking happiness and contentment, and we have succeeded beyond our wildest dreams. Chicago is my birthplace and is my home—and it will be until my life has ended. I was married in this community to a Chicago girl—and, by death, I suffered the loss of my wife and my young boy, who God in his wisdom called."

And now Ed stopped speaking. He'd been moving through the text slowly and deliberately, and yet not haranguing the audience. Doing very well, I thought. But in the last sentence his voice changed. He was speaking from the heart. He looked over at me. Don't cry yet, I thought. That'd be a little too much for Chicago. He took a breath.

"I am now blessed with a wife of sweetness and patience, and her desire for motherhood was fulfilled by the adoption of three children. Two husky boys and one sweet girl who bear my name and will be a comfort and solace to me when I am old and decrepit, I hope."

Ed smiled, and I think the audience heard that smile. And now he picked up the pace, laying out his accomplishments. The Lakefront, Soldier Field, Buckingham Fountain, Planetarium, Aquarium, the Museum of Science and Industry, as well as the skyscrapers that had grown up along Michigan Boulevard, next to the parks and beaches. He went on to point out that the Hearst newspapers had attacked Roosevelt, questioning his Americanism. He said that Al Smith had been called the most dangerous man in the United States by Hearst. Teddy Roosevelt, "a loose-tongued demigod and woman killer." And McKinley's murderers had been influenced by the Hearst publications.

"I am proud," Ed said, "to be put in this select circle of men. The suggestion was made by Hearst editors that I resign. I don't come from stock that resigns under fire. I shall never surrender to Hearst tactics—but if I'm to remain in office and administer the affairs of the city, I need your support. I believe the march of prosperity is on, and I wish to have you join me in this march. I'm asking you to telephone this station or my office at city hall, drop me a note, send me a telegram, come down to see me on LaSalle Street. We have to show these vultures from back east what Chicago people are made of. We can rebuild our city. We did it before. Fire couldn't destroy us, and neither will lies. I come from a people who were pushed to the brink of extinction, and we didn't die. Let me know if I have your support. If not, I will leave this office with great sadness, but with my honor intact."

Well, the switchboard of WENR was jammed before we even left the studio. And it wasn't only telegrams and letters that arrived at city hall, but lines and lines of people. "We're with you, Ed," they shouted when he arrived at his office the next morning.

I took a picture of him surrounded by his well-wishers, and didn't Ed get it on the front page of the *Tribune* the next day.

Colonel McCormick might have been a Republican, but he had a soft spot for Ed and hated Hearst and his newspapers because, in those days, the circulation wars were really wars. Gangsters rode on the newspaper delivery trucks ready to shoot their competition. They terrified the newsstand owners. Moe Annenberg and his brother started as newsies, kids who bought papers for pennies and sold them for nickels. As the two got older, they made deals with the management of the papers and took over the whole business. Moe was on the straight and narrow now, but Ed always said he was as tough as any of Capone's button men, but just smarter. It doesn't take a lot of brains to build a business, if you're willing to kill your competition like the Outfit does. So though the *Tribune* had their own bunch of thugs, they were trying to rise above the red and yellow headlines that marked the Hearst papers. Not that the *Tribune* spared Ed and the other Democratic officials, but at least McCormick made families off-limits and did, in his way, love Chicago.

"Well, Ed, you did it," I said to him the next morning when I laid the *Tribune* on his desk. "People Rally for Kelly" said the headline. And there was the photograph, credited to me, of Ed surrounded, hands reaching out to him, a big smile on his face.

"Blake will have to remove those quotes from around photographer," I said.

"Dream on," Ed said. I noticed he was rubbing the medal again, a sure sign something was bothering him.

"I've been thinking, Nonie, and talking to Margaret." He rolled his leather chair closer to the desk, leaned forward, and laid the medal on the desk. "We were lucky that Blake hasn't dug too deeply into your past yet, but . . ."

"Wait a minute. What do you mean 'yet'? I'm not important to his story. Believe me I know these guys. He'll move on to the next topic, find somebody else. We beat him. Just like I silenced Wilcox."

"Maybe," Ed said, "but now he knows you're very closely connected to me."

"So what?"

"I didn't realize how many people know about your, well, relationship with Tim McShane and how it ended."

"You mean my running away to Paris to save my life? Or Spike O'Donnell plugging Tim so he wouldn't strangle me to death?" My voice rose, and I started pacing around the office. "What did you do? Take a survey? Or stand with Henrietta on the steps after ten o'clock Mass at St. Bridget's? Consult Toots?"

I couldn't believe it. Ed had always understood me. We were the redheads. Hadn't I seen him at his worst up there in Wisconsin and never told a soul, not even Margaret? But Ed went on.

"I've never asked you about all the things you were up to in Paris and Ireland, but Margaret says that some of those Irish characters you were involved with were pretty violent and, well—"

"You mean the fellows who fought and died so that Ireland could be free? Who protected me from the Black and Tans? For God's sake, Ed, I was attacked by the grandson of the very man who raped our aunty Máire and . . ."

Ed stood up.

"See, Nonie, you're screaming at me." Which I was, but why not? "Imagine if you were with me at a press conference and a reporter asked a question about your past, and you went off half-cocked. Margaret's right. It's not good."

"Are you saying I can't control myself?" I asked. Banging out each word on his desk with my fist. Ed shook his head.

"We both know you've been through a lot, and I blame myself for sending you down to Miami with Cermak."

"I sent myself, Ed," I said. He was talking to me as if I were a difficult child who had to be humored.

"But you're an artist, Nonie. I'm sure the kind of photography you do for me doesn't call on your talents, so . . ."

"Are you firing me, Ed?"

"Of course not."

"Fire me. Go on. I've been trying to get back to Ireland and those violent characters for ten years. Maybe now is the time."

"Easy, Nonie, easy. I—we—don't want you to leave Chicago. My kids love you, so do Michael's. What would they do without their Aunt Nonie to give them a bit of fun?"

"So now I'm an entertainer?"

"You're purposely misunderstanding me, Nonie. Trying to put me in the wrong, and all I want to do is offer you an opportunity. You know the magazine, the *Chicagoan*?"

"I do," I said. A glossy publication trying very hard to be our version of the *New Yorker.*

"Well, I got a letter from the editor. He wants special access for a reporter and photographer to the Century of Progress and I'm proposing you as the photographer."

The Century of Progress was to be Chicago's second World's Fair. Ed had been involved when the idea first was proposed, five years ago. The land the Fair committee wanted to use belonged to the South Park Board, and Ed was the president. Well, he was thrilled with the idea. I mean it was the 1893 World's Fair that inspired him to become an engineer. As a young boy, he'd hung around the construction asking questions; and when it was up and running, he must have gone twenty or thirty times. And now, here was a chance to be part of building another World's Fair. Well, he was over the moon.

The original plans for the Fair were made in 1928. The stock market was booming, people were making money hand over fist. The bond issue that would finance the Century of Progress passed Congress on October 28, 1929. Sound familiar? The next day the stock market crashed. Big Bill Thompson had just beaten Dever, so he was mayor. No money and a jackass as mayor should have put the kibosh on the whole project. But Ed convinced companies like General Motors to underwrite the buildings, and he sold the Fair to Thompson with one word—jobs. The city was beginning to feel the pinch of what would become the Great Depression, and even Thompson had to admit that no one knew better how to employ the maximum number of men on any construction project than Ed Kelly.

And so Chicago's Century of Progress, which had been meant to celebrate our city's growth from a frontier village in 1833 to the City of the Big Shoulders, became an effort to rescue that city and its citizens. Thompson had kept Ed out of the limelight as much as he could. This was going to be Big Bill's time to shine. I think the bitterest pill he had to swallow when he was defeated as mayor was that Pushcart Tony Cermak would open the World's Fair. But, of course, he didn't. Ed Kelly would do the honors, which he had done on May 27, 1933, four days ahead of schedule, with Jim Farley beside him.

But would people come? Ed, with the help of FDR, was dragging the city into solvency. Still families worried about food and the rent. Could they pay fifty cents to see fancy new gadgets in the "Home of the Century" or to watch how cars were made? But then, of course, Chicago was Chicago, and for all the big important scientific exhibits that were advertised, there was another part of the Fair that had become the real draw. Like the Columbian exhibit before it, with its carnival midway and Ferris wheel, the Century of Progress had nightclubs with exotic names, an animal circus and the Sky Ride. In the same way all of us Kelly kids had longed to ride the Ferris wheel and see the lights come on in the White City, a new generation lined up to rocket straight up into the air and ride through the whole Century of Progress from two hundred feet in the sky. Huge crowds from the day it opened.

I could understand why Ed wanted me to photograph the Century of Progress for the *Chicagoan*. Besides being good publicity, the publisher, Martin Quigley, was a friend of his. One of the fellows who went to daily Mass at St. Peter's. Odd he would bring out a magazine like the *Chicagoan*, which was supposed to be sophisticated and a little bit risqué. But then Quigley had made his money putting out movie magazines, and the *Chicagoan* echoed the art deco sets and snappy dialogue of Hollywood.

The magazine contained reviews of nightclubs and dance bands, pictures of men in tuxedos, women in furs, along with articles that mixed intellectual musings with Chicago moxie. Quigley had gotten a group of writers and artists together and had done well from 1926 to 1929. Then the Depression hit. A glossy advertising cars and jewelry should have failed miserably, but the *Chicagoan*, like the movies, provided an escape, as did the Century of Progress itself. And now the *Chicagoan* was focusing on the Fair, and expected the mayor to help.

"Alright," I said to Ed, and thought, I was put out with Ed for banishing me from city hall, but I must admit I was intrigued by the *Chicagoan*. Their offices were at 20 East Wacker. Hard to be soignée on a floor full of dentists, I thought as I got off the elevator the next morning. I could smell mercury and silver fillings.

Martin Quigley himself looked like a man picked to usher the noon Mass at Holy Name, the top tier, just the fellow to hold the collection basket in front of Chicago's wealthiest Catholics. He had very black hair and blue eyes. Black Irish, I thought. "Quigley," I said, after he'd invited me to sit down in front of his desk, "is that a west of Ireland name?"

"It might be," he said. "But our family has been in Chicago for so many generations, we've lost track of where we came from. Of course, I'm very proud of our heritage. The Irish have championed the faith in this country. Did you know that Chicago is the biggest archdiocese in the United States with the most Catholic schools? We've had incredible leaders, starting with Archbishop Quigley himself."

"A relative of yours?" I asked.

"A connection," he said. This guy seemed more like the head of the Knights of Columbus than the publisher of a racy magazine.

"But," he said, "it's your relative that we should be discussing. I have enormous respect for Ed Kelly and how he is saving this city, and I'd like to do him a favor and take you on. But we already have an excellent and rather temperamental photographer. I'm sure you've heard of George Miller?"

"I have." How couldn't I have? Famous for his artsy work. Though I'd always preferred plain portraits.

"And you understand the high bar he sets for the *Chicagoan*? So . . ."

"What's going on in here?"

The man who stood in the doorway of Quigley's office wasn't old. Thirties I'd say, but he didn't hesitate to interrupt his boss. A skinny fellow, blond, and the only one in the *Chicagoan*'s offices not dressed in a suit. He wore gray flannel slacks and a sweater.

"You hire another photographer, and I quit."

Quigley and I turned in our chairs to look at him. "Oh," he said, "they told me Martin was interviewing a photographer, but you're a woman. Are you applying for the job of sorting the photography archives?"

"I'm not," I said, and I held up my Seneca, "I am a photographer. Though I'm not trying to put you out of a job, Mr. Miller."

He laughed. "You wouldn't have much chance with that thing. Is it an antique? Where'd you get it?"

"From Eddie Steichen," I said. Well that stopped him for a minute, but he came right back at me.

"What? Did you grow up with him in Milwaukee or something?"

"I met Eddie in Paris when we were both doing fashion photography." Alright, that was a slight exaggeration. Steichen's pictures of couturier gowns were published in *Art et Décoration,* and mine were used by Madame Simone to make illegal copies of the designs. "Though Eddie told me my forte was women's faces."

Miller snorted. "The Century of Progress is about innovation in architecture and technology—progress—not portraits of googly-eyed Ma and Pa up from Kewanee to take in the Fair," Miller said.

"But how can you get the feel of the impact of the Fair without looking at the people who are attending, finding out their stories?"

"Oh no, another sob sister," Miller said to Quigley. "A so-called journalist who exploits ordinary decent people for circulation."

I decided not to tell him I was the one who'd exclusively photographed the women who Maurine had turned into the characters Velma Kelly and Roxie Hart in her play, *Chicago*. Exploitation no question, though the women themselves were desperate to be taken advantage of. "Make us famous," they'd said to me when they posed.

"Take it easy, George," Quigley said. To me he said, "Have you ever had anything published?"

"Do you have yesterday's *Tribune*?" I asked Quigley.

He lifted a pile of newspapers from the floor next to his desk and handed them to me. I rifled through them and pulled out the front page with my photograph of Ed being greeted by admirers at city hall. Miller came over, took the paper away from me, and held it up.

"First of all, the composition is bad. Ed Kelly's the story, and you have him almost blocked out by the crowd. Too many faces and hands, too. All of them distracting from the main subject. Though the quality and the lighting is okay. And you shot it with this?"

He reached for my Seneca, but I pulled it away.

"Of course you could never photograph structures with that," he said.

"Oh I don't know. I did some shots of Notre Dame."

"In South Bend?"

"In Paris," I said. "Henri Matisse found the photographs interesting. I concentrated on details, took a Cubist approach."

Now I was babbling a bit but, dear God, this young fellow was so arrogant. No wonder he took no pictures of people. Probably offended them with his attitude. "But, as I said, it was the candid shots I took of women that Eddie and Henri liked best."

"French socialites, I suppose," Miller said. "How boring."

"My subjects were American tourists actually."

"Worse," he said.

"Matisse didn't think so," I said. Though I didn't add that the Master liked my women tourists because I brought them to his studio where they often bought a painting. Miller looked at Quigley.

"So she was friendly with the Hairy Mattress himself," Miller said.

"And, Mr. Miller, I suppose you were one of the Art Institute's students who copied his paintings and burned them."

"Let's just say I danced around the bonfire, and regret it," Miller said.

"I have no idea what you two are talking about," Quigley said. "But Nora here can arrange for you to get on the fairgrounds to take those predawn shots you've been agitating for."

"She can?"

"Through her co—" Miller started. I cut him off.

"My boss, Mayor Edward J. Kelly, has agreed to let me escort you through the gate at five a.m." Now, Ed hadn't said any such thing, but if I was going to show this blowhard that my photographs were just as good as his, I had to get this job. And after all, wasn't that what Ed intended?

So. I was hired. Or at least Quigley agreed to pay me five dollars per photograph, much higher than the going rate. I would be partnered with the magazine's best writer, Marvin Mayer, and we would interview attendees. I would have preferred to just wander round and do candid shots, but Quigley thought Mayer could come up with clever questions that would show how superior the *Chicagoan* was, what an arbiter of taste. I was beginning to think the whole staff were stuck-up pains in the ass. Yet, the magazine was so beautifully produced that I longed to see my photographs printed on its pages. Plus, Ed didn't want me around city hall.

"Fine, fine," is what Ed said to me the next day when I told him I'd committed to a dawn tour of the Fair for George Miller.

8

I was at Twelfth Street and the Drive, the employee gate at 5:00 a.m. Miller got out of his car. He carried a large format Hasselblad in one hand and a tripod in the other.

"No assistant?" I asked, as a Chicago policeman opened the gates to us. Still dark, and the lake a stretch of black water. Only the morning star for light.

"The idiot didn't show up," Miller said. "I hired him for his muscles and because he has no opinion. The Art Institute sent me some students, but all they wanted to do was argue about f-stops."

He looked over at the policeman. "Want to make a few bucks, officer? Lugging my equipment?"

The cop laughed. "I had enough of that kind of labor when I landed from Ireland. My job is to stay on this post. I was told Miss Kelly here could be trusted to escort you, but nobody said anything about heavy lifting."

"I can carry the Hasselblad," I said to him. "After all, my Seneca weighs very little."

"Alright," Miller said. "But no bright ideas."

Now Miller was a jerk no question, but as I watched him work, I saw the man was an artist. He used light and shadow the way a painter would. He'd chosen the GM building for his first shot because the sun rising out of the lake would turn the steel building red. "The color will be saturated," he said.

"But aren't you shooting black and white?" There were a lot of rumors that

Kodak was experimenting with color film that would be easy to use. Now, I'd taken color photographs in Paris using Autochrome Lumière plates myself, but they were very cumbersome. I'd gotten used to my Seneca. Push a button and get a picture. What if taking color could be that easy?

"Man and God," he said to me, "are getting close."

"Okay," I said. "I don't know what you're talking about."

"The fellows at Kodak, the two Leopolds, Mannes and Godowsky, nicknamed 'Man and God.' An odd story. They're both professional musicians from famous orchestral families. I guess they met playing together somewhere and found out they were each experimenting with color film. Quite a coincidence."

"Or Providence," I said. But he didn't hear me. He was stretched out on the blacktop in front of the building looking up. I was beginning to see my life as an unfolding of Providence, both the good things and the bad. I hadn't planned to be in Miami that night, or to become so much a part of Ed's life just when he faced the challenges of being mayor. I mean, what if Margaret hadn't come to visit me? She and Ed wouldn't have married. And wasn't it because I was working at Montgomery Ward that Michael met Mame? And, of course, Paris was one providential encounter after another. All leading to Ireland and Peter Keeley and . . . But Miller was on his feet now and yelling for me to set up the tripod.

"Hurry up, hurry up," he said. "The sun, the sun."

He held up his hand as if to keep the red ball below the horizon.

Good luck, buddy, I thought. But I did manage to anchor the three legs of the tripod in time for him to fasten the Hasselblad to the head just as the sun came up over the lake. Miller held his breath as he depressed the shutter release that hung from a wire on the camera. And me? Well I just lifted up my Seneca and got a shot of Miller squinting at the sunrise, his face absorbing the light.

Next, he set up the camera under the Sky Ride. It took us a half an hour to get exactly the angle he wanted.

"That's it," he said, "the light's gone flat now."

We finished at eight, and the cop pointed us toward a shack where the Fair's ticket takers, attendants, as well as some of the early morning barkers at the midway attractions were having breakfast. The smell of bacon and coffee pulled us in. About twenty people sat on benches at two wooden tables, both men and women, lots of chatter—even this early. Why not? Each of them had a job and a free breakfast.

"Would you mind?" I said to one woman about my age, but with white-blonde hair, a heavily powdered face, and red, red lipstick. I'd like to see

Miller's color film capture her. Still, even in black and white, her face would be dramatic. The woman thought I wanted to sit next to her and moved her plate, but I held up my camera. "May I?"

"You don't want to take my picture," she laughed. "I'm a behind-the-scenes girl. Lola's my name. I do the costumes and makeup for the dancers in the Streets of Paris nightclub."

"Streets of Paris? Then you must . . ." I stopped. That was where Sally Rand, the Fair's most famous attraction, danced.

"Keep Sally Rand's fans in shape, and make sure her bubbles are big and round and transparent." She smiled. "And it's not just Sally, you know. There are twelve other girls in the chorus, too. You should be taking their pictures, not mine. Except, of course, there's no photography allowed."

Now Chicago had plenty of strip shows in theaters downtown. In fact, Sally Rand had been performing at the Paramount for years. But for her to do her act right out in the open, on the midway with families strolling by, made her striptease more sensational. There'd been some pressure on Ed to ban Sally, but he'd taken a turn-a-blind-eye attitude. Told the press he hadn't attended her performances and couldn't say whether Sally was actually nude. "Probably wearing some sort of bathing suit," he'd said.

Rand herself said she never let anyone close enough to see what she was wearing or not wearing. In her publicity shots, the fans were modestly placed, and she allowed no one to take pictures during the show. Nor would she pose afterward.

"I work for the *Chicagoan* magazine," I said. "It's a very classy publication. Do you think Sally and the girls might let me take their portraits? I'm only interested in their faces."

"You must be the only one," she said.

"I'm sure they're lovely girls."

"They are, after I get finished with them. Amazing what mascara can do. Come around sometime before the show. I'll introduce you. Then, it'll be up to the girls."

Miller was eating. I got a bacon and egg sandwich on a roll and paid only ten cents for it. I sat next to him. The woman was gone. Miller finished and left. I'd do my *Chicagoan* assignment, then investigate the Streets of Paris.

I met Mayer an hour later at the main gate and we started on the assignment Quigley had given us, interviewing the "great unwashed" as Mayer put it. I suggested we start at the Irish Village, a cluster of thatched roof cottages set around a village green. Very like the exhibition my granny Honora had brought the whole family to during the World's Columbian Exposition forty years before. A blacksmith hammered away at his anvil, the sparks shooting up. An elderly woman led a couple and three small children up to the threshold of a cottage next to the forge. She touched the horseshoe set over the doorway and turned to them. I lifted my camera and got a shot of her as she spoke to the man, her son I supposed. "Brings back memories," I heard her say to him. She's doing what Granny Honora did for us, I thought, trying to share her past. The man saw me watching them.

"My mother says this is the closest I'll ever get to Ireland. She came to Indianapolis fifty years ago but really I don't think she's ever left Ireland in her heart," he told me.

Then he said to his mother, "This is all very nice, Ma, but the kids want to go on the Sky Ride."

Just like us at the other fair, Granny desperate to make us curious and interested in Ireland and all of us straining for the Ferris wheel. Mayer walked up to the son. "Could you give me a short interview on your impressions?"

"As long as it is short," he said, looking over at his wife, impatient, the two older children were pulling on her hands while the grandmother held up the youngest so she could look in the window of the cottage. She put her cheek against the little girl's face and the two leaned forward. I raised the camera and looked into the viewfinder. I not only had the two of them, but their reflection in the window, and even a bit of the hearth where a turf fire burned. I snapped the picture.

"That fire never goes out," I heard the woman tell the little girl. "When a young couple marries, the bride carries a burning piece of turf to her new home and lights a fire the first thing."

"Did you do that, Granny?" the little girl asked. The woman set her down and bent over, talking quietly, though I could hear every word.

"Ah well," she said, "I was very young when I came to Amerikay and I met your grandfather at a dance at St. Bridget's Hall. I was from Kerry and he was from Tyrone. Different customs up there. Now I could hardly carry fire onto a ship, but I did pack a sod of turf in my bag. A fellow at Ellis Island tried to take it off me. Said it could be infested. That I might be bringing foreign pests into the country. But the other official said let her keep it. The only bit of Irish soil she'll set foot on ever again."

She passed through Ellis Island, I thought, so must have come in the 1890s, later than my granny, who fled the Great Starvation in 1849. Still this woman had been forced out by bad times. She'd come to a more prosperous Chicago than the frontier hardscrabble my family found. She'd then gone down to Indianapolis with her new husband. He must have had work. No chance for her ever to return home.

"Excuse me," I said. "I took a picture of you and the child. I hope you don't mind. I'll send you a copy if you like."

"It would be a fine thing to have a photograph of wee Joanie and me," she said.

"I'm Nora Kelly from Bridgeport," I said.

"I'm Hannah Sullivan from Indianapolis," she said.

"You came a long way," I said.

"It's closer than Ireland," she said.

Mayer had finished interviewing the little girl's father. His wife was speaking to him very urgently while the other two children fidgeted.

"Come on, Ma," the man said.

"Where in Ireland are you from?" I asked.

"Kerry," she said. "The Kingdom. The Magharee Islands and you?"

"I was born here. But we're a Galway family. I did go back and find our home place," I said.

Hannah leaned over, put her arm around the little girl's shoulder and pulled her close to her legs. "This little one likes to hear my stories. My dream would be to show her Ireland. Take her to *my* home place. Although the government is forcing people to leave the island. There'll be no home to go to."

"Granny, Daddy wants us," the little girl said. "Mommy and the other kids are getting mad."

"My son married a lovely girl," Hannah said, "but she's German and all this"—she gestured at the whitewashed cottage—"doesn't mean much to her. We've already visited the German village. Very modern with a big beer hall and polka dancers."

Now her son took his mother's arm and moved her away.

Mayer walked over to me. "You took her picture?"

"I did."

"You're wasting your time," he said to me. "One of the rules of the *Chicagoan*, no unattractive old women."

I spent the rest of the day taking straight-on unimaginative photographs of his interviewees, to be developed and printed by Andy, the darkroom technician. But after he finished with the shots for the magazine, Andy let me work on my own photographs, glad to take a cigarette break. Oh dear God, I thought when the print came swimming out at me, I got it—the longing in Hannah Sullivan's face for Ireland, for the past. Her desire to somehow connect her granddaughter to the life she'd led. Their cheeks pressed together, the two sets of eyes looking through the window and yet seeing each other, the light from the fire. I found myself humming "I'll Take You Home Again, Kathleen" as I hung the five prints up to dry. They never would go home, these crowds of Irish people packing this manufactured Ireland.

"Nice," Andy said when he saw the prints.

But Miller said "trite" and Quigley added "depressing" when I laid the photos out on his desk.

"I told you, Martin," Miller said. "She's a sob sister. This sentimental dreck is not of the magazine's caliber." Miller had followed me into Quigley's office, anxious to see the photos I'd taken on my trial run. Quigley approved the shots of the people Mayer had interviewed but he pushed the candid shots away.

"This woman is trying to share her past with her granddaughter," I said, "somehow make Ireland real for the next generation."

Miller just picked up the photographs and tossed them into Quigley's waste basket.

"Sorry, Nora," Quigley said. "George is not only our chief photographer but the photo editor too. What he says goes. I'll pay you fifty dollars for the ten interview shots but well . . . You just don't seem to understand the *Chicagoan* style."

"Mmmm," I said, "he got his dawn exclusive as agreed. The mayor expects me to have a job here."

"I'll call Ed and explain," he said.

"Too bad that you didn't get a picture of that floozy you were having breakfast with," Miller said. "At least she had a little pizazz."

"A performer?" Quigley asked.

"No," I said. "She does costumes and makeup for Sally Rand and the other fan dancers. I did talk to her about doing portraits of the girls but she said no one is allowed to take photographs. But maybe if I just shot their faces the girls may consider it."

"What?" Quigley said. "You think the crowds are piling into the Streets of Paris nightclub to look at their mugs? Come on, Nora, don't you even have one journalistic bone in your body?"

"Is that how an usher at the noon Mass thinks?" I asked but Quigley ignored me.

"That woman's an important contact. If you could bring me a shot of Sally Rand and the fan dancers, well. . . ."

"She won't do it," Miller said and then spoke to me. "You're too old to change. Another maiden lady afraid of life and the human body."

"Go to hell, Miller," I said. I took the prints from the wastebasket and left.

"Only your faces," I said to the twelve girls Lola had arranged for me to photograph. I'll show you, Mr. Miller, I'd thought. I hated the thought of going back to Ed as a failure.

It was noon and the girls were in their dressing room inside the domed building meant to suggest what? The Pantheon? Sacre Coeur? A central tower anyway. Two sets of buildings enclosed a kind of patio crowded with tables under colorful umbrellas that matched the awnings on the buildings. Chicago's idea of a French café—bigger than any in Paris. There was even a church in the background. I wondered if the patrons glanced up and requested a dispensation as they entered the nightclub.

"Mademoiselles de la Dance starring La Magnifique Sally Rand." The first show was at two o'clock, so I didn't have much time with the girls. They all just stared at me deadpan. I have to make some connection, I thought, so "Where are you from?" I asked. Four of them mentioned small downstate towns, Decatur, Clinton, Alton, and Polo.

"Paris," one of them shouted. "Paris, Illinois," which got a laugh. Two had found their way here from Ohio. They'd been touring in a vaudeville show and landed in Chicago in time to try out for the Fair. Two were from New York. They sat together at the far end of the long dressing table. "This is temporary," one said. "We were in Flo Ziegfeld's last show and are headed west to Hollywood."

"You've been 'headed' for quite a while," said another girl, a redhead. "I'm from Chicago," she went on. "St. Gabriel's parish in Canaryville. And these are my sisters."

Three other girls waved at me.

"We're the McNultys but we call ourselves the Reveille Sisters, our dancing wakes you up."

The others laughed.

"Well, I'll start with you," I said.

"I'm Agnes McNulty," the redhead said, "and these are my sisters Alice, Anna, and Alma."

Lola took us through a doorway onto a small stage at one end of the nightclub. "Light them up, Bill," she shouted and the colored spots came on. Each sister grinned at me as I moved close to take their portraits. Irish faces, upturned noses, wide-set eyes. I finished snapping and stepped back. Each girl wore a pink silk kimono tied around the waist. "Okay," I said.

"Okay?" Agnes asked. "Don't you want a full view?"

"I promised Lola faces only," I said.

"Faces won't sell tickets. Get our fans, Lola," Agnes said.

So. I must say the sisters knew how to hold the three-foot-tall ostrich feather fans in exactly the right place to cover their bodies. Though when they showed me the steps of their dance and whirled themselves and the fans in tight circles, more was revealed.

"You want these photos published?" I asked the girls. "What about your parents? The parishioners at St. Gabriel's? The priests?"

"My father told our pastor that his girls are earning two hundred dollars a week. There's food on the table. The rent is paid and he's looking to buy a two-flat in South Shore. Dad hadn't worked in three years and there are four little ones in our family. We're heroes at St. Gabriel's."

"Hurry up if you want to photograph the rest of the girls," Lola said. I brought in the farm girls next. Much more serious expressions in their close-ups and not so careful to block their breasts and buttocks with the fans.

"When you grow up on a farm, you're used to bodies," one said, as she pulled up her leg while the others kicked. One of the two New Yorkers had her own dance using a fringed shawl, while the other gave me a back view facing the fans.

"And you really want these full body shots published?" I asked the girls when I'd finished.

"Yes," they said.

"Alright." I turned to Lola. "And is Miss Rand ready for me?" Sally didn't appear until after the girls did their dance.

"Bad news I'm afraid," Lola said. "Sally decided not to meet you after all. She's been very strict about banning outside photographers and she can't make an exception. She said you'll just have to be satisfied with the Mademoiselles. That should be enough."

It was—almost. "These are great," Andy the technician said. He insisted on processing the shots himself after he saw a print of the first McNulty girl. George Miller approved too.

"Not much technique in these shots," he said when I brought the prints to him, "but the subjects speak for themselves and we'll be the first publication to show the dancers nude."

"And that's a good thing?" I asked.

"Martin," he called to Quigley who was walking down the hall toward his office. "Look at these." I was half hoping that Quigley would be shocked. I mean he was a devout Catholic and while maybe the McNultys could brazen their way through ten o'clock Mass at St. Gabriel's, I doubted if Quigley's buddy, the cardinal, would approve of these pictures. But Quigley was nodding.

"We'll give them three pages," he said, "following the main feature on Sally Rand. Where are those shots, Nora?" he asked me.

"Well, my, uhm, contact couldn't deliver Sally Rand after all. She just won't allow photographers."

"That's a laugh," Quigley said. "Sally Rand called every newspaper in town to cover her Lady Godiva stunt." Sally had been refused a featured place in the Century of Progress at first. She'd waited until opening day and then, wearing a long blonde wig and nothing else, rode a white horse straight through the Century of Progress crowds onto the Streets of Paris led by a young boy dressed as a page shouting, "Lady Godiva returns." The photograph had made the front pages and Sally got the job. But now she'd pulled back.

"Without Sally Rand these pictures mean nothing," Miller said.

"You're right," Quigley agreed.

"But I promised the girls," I said. "This is the first time anybody's taken an interest in them. They're going to use this piece as a way of getting a raise. I can't disappoint them."

"Then get Sally Rand," Quigley said.

"But I know her," Margaret said.

"You know Sally Rand?" Margaret and I had met coming into the building. Ed's radio speech had not only gotten him support from the voters, but the reporters and photographers who had taken to staking out our building were gone. I wondered if Hearst himself might not have called them off. After all FDR was becoming the most popular president in history. No point in going to war with his friends. Okay for Margaret to be seen with me now, too. I guess. I'd decided not to be annoyed about her role in my exile. Why?

The twins and Steve were out for a walk on the new pathway along the lake with Nancy, who had become an honorary big sister. Margaret asked me up for tea, though I could have used a martini. She didn't keep liquor in the apartment. Ed was still on the straight and narrow but why tempt him? We settled ourselves on the table near the window overlooking the lake, while Lu brought us tea and cookies. The Davises were planning to go away for the summer and Margaret would be leaving for Eagle River next week. I told her about the situation at the *Chicagoan* and how I'd probably lose my job if I couldn't deliver Sally Rand.

"She's from Kansas City," Margaret said. "Helen Beck is her real name. She danced at the Empress Theater, not with fans, but she was good and caught the eye of Goodman Ace when he was the critic for the *Journal-Post*. Gave her a great review. She was young—I'd say fifteen or so. My mother sewed beads on her costumes. I guess Helen figured she could find a good seamstress through Nellie Don, who employed her Irish neighbor in her dress business. Nellie recommended my mother. Helen came to our house for fittings. A nice girl who knew she'd hit it lucky with Goodman Ace."

"Wait a minute. Goodman Ace? Isn't he the fellow on the radio?"

"The same. Helen changed her name to Sally Rand when she went to Hollywood."

"Do you think she'd remember you?" I asked.

"I don't know."

"Would you ever write her a note, mention the Kansas City connection, ask her to meet me?"

Margaret shook her head. "Oh, Nora, I couldn't. Ed's not at all pleased that Sally Rand is getting so much attention when it's the scientific exhibitions that are the important part of the Century of Progress."

Poor Ed. I sympathized. Spending the last few days at the Century of Progress made me realize just how extraordinary the Fair was. I'd watched people walk onto the grounds with the same closed look on their faces that we'd all been wearing for the last three years as the Depression took hold. Fewer people were getting married. How could you risk setting up housekeeping when your job could end at any moment? Turn any corner downtown and there was the reminder of what could happen to you. Bread lines. St. Mary's on Wabash and the Pacific Garden Mission gave out soup. Soup!

Plenty of my granny Honora's generation were still living and remembered the Soup Kitchens in Ireland during the Great Starvation. Some were run by Protestant missionaries who required conversion in exchange for food. At least in Chicago we'd gotten beyond that. This generation of Kellys wasn't actually starving. But what if I couldn't get my job with Ed back? I'd always assumed that he'd rehire me after the press moved on to other targets and I wasn't news. But what if he didn't . . . how long would my savings last? No trip to Ireland. Would I end up as the poor relation living off Ed's generosity? He'd resent me sooner or later, and what respect would I have for myself? No guarantee that I wouldn't join the community of homeless living in shanties down by the Chicago River. Don't be dramatic, I told myself, but really nothing was certain anymore. Ed had finally been able to start relief payments to the most desperate now that Roosevelt was in office, but sweet Mother of Jesus imagine if some reporter got wind of me, Ed Kelly's cousin, applying for relief. Humiliation all around. I understood those closed grim faces. But step through the gates into the Century of Progress and all was changed. We smiled. We laughed. Here was hope. Here was the future. Progress. Technology that would do everything from transporting us through space to saving the lives of premature babies. Actual newborns on display in a machine called an incubator. Living and breathing right before our eyes.

"Where there's life there's hope," Ed had said in his opening address, and the crowds attending the Fair agreed, coming in huge numbers. Except when the people left the grounds what did they talk about? Not innovations but the entertainment, especially Sally Rand. I tried to say all this to Margaret and tell her that I understood why Ed was annoyed that a woman dancing got more attention than science, but he was the one that sent me for this job and I just couldn't bear to tell him I'd been fired. Margaret nodded. Then she said, "Of course if Sally Rand herself talked about how important the scientific exhibits were that would really help Ed wouldn't it?"

"It would," I said. "It would. And I'd make that part of the article."

Margaret gave me a letter addressed to "Helen Beck" that I took to Lola. Two days later I was in Sally Rand's dressing room.

"I remember Mrs. Noll," Sally said.

She'd been making up her face when Lola brought me in, seated in front of what must have been a six-foot-by-three-foot mirror that hung over a marble table. "Of course in those days I needed sparkly costumes. Now I can rely on these." She gestured to a row of at least a dozen ostrich feather fans carefully hung on the dressing room wall.

"Funny enough I got the idea of dancing with them when I realized my costumes were falling apart and I couldn't buy new ones. I was here in Chicago with a musical group, Sweethearts on Parade, in burlesque. I'd torn one costume and lost the bugle beads off another. I was walking by a pawn shop on Wabash and saw these two ostrich feather fans in the window. I thought, hmmm, I could cover the rips in my costumes with these. Had to change my act. I used to do the splits and all kinds of things. Remember I had been an acrobat with Barnum & Bailey," she said. "Can't move around too much with the fans."

"I didn't realize you were a circus performer," I said.

"I left Kansas City with the circus, ended up in Hollywood."

"And you did do well in Hollywood, didn't you?" I said.

I was taking careful notes—I would write the article too. Take that, Miller!

"I did. Worked for Cecil B. DeMille himself. He's the one gave me the name Sally Rand. Got it off a book of maps. Cast me as a slave girl on the *King of Kings*. My mistress was Mary Magdalene." She laughed. "You're Irish aren't you?"

"I am."

"I acted in a film called *Braveheart* with Tyrone Power. It was a cowboy movie. He was the handsomest man I ever saw. He told me all his people were actors in the old country, going back for generations. Poor fellow died young but his son is trying the acting game now. Supposed to stop by and see me this afternoon so we'd better get this show on the road. Now, for these photographs I'm stepping into my second skin." Sally Rand picked up a flesh colored body stocking and stepped behind the screen in the corner of the dressing room.

"Oh, Sally," I said when she reappeared. "So you're not naked?"

"Only in the imagination of the audience."

The waiters were setting up the tables for the next show and didn't even look up as Sally stepped onto the stage for our photo session. She was only about five feet tall and had looked tiny in her dressing room, but now, wearing extra high heels and posing with the fans, I could see why one critic called her "a Greek goddess come to life."

"I use classy music," Sally said to me as she got in position. "The New York Philharmonic recorded 'Clair de Lune' for me. And be sure to write that I was a ballerina. Trained right here in Chicago. Always a lucky town for me."

"So you prefer Chicago to Hollywood?"

"Wouldn't say preferred. But I don't have to talk to make a living in Chicago. Sound ended my movie career. You might not have noticed but my voice is a little high and they tell me I have the trace of an accent."

"Mmmm," I said. Sally put the Ozarks into every vowel.

Now she picked up her fans and did a bit of her routine for me while I snapped away with my Seneca. Something about the way the lights played over her body certainly made her look naked but the fans never really did reveal all. The finale came when she stepped behind the screen and let them fall. But a silhouette is only a silhouette. Here was a woman who'd made her own way since she was thirteen years old. She'd managed to focus the whole Century of Progress onto herself. "Sally Rand, Businesswoman." I doubt if Quigley would use it for the headline but that was really the story. Sally was happy to praise the scientific exhibits at the Century of Progress, so Margaret would be satisfied.

"I appreciate you letting me do this interview," I said.

"Well," she said, "Margaret signed her note Margaret Noll, the name I knew her by. But a little bird told me she's Margaret Kelly now, married to the mayor." Oops. "I want to ask Margaret to do me a favor," she said.

"Listen, Sally, Margaret never interferes with Ed's decisions. He's been getting a lot of pressure to have the police raid your show. So far he's resisted but Margaret can't prevent it."

"But I *want* him to raid my show. I want you to bring the mayor here. Sit him in the front row. I want him to be shocked and appalled at how indecent I am."

"What?"

"Yes. Yes. The crowds have been thinning out. A rumor's going round that we're just another girly show. Nothing special. I want to seem so wicked that Chicago, the Sin City of the United States, will be set back on its heels. I want to be led away in handcuffs in front of newspaper reporters. To stand, or rather dance, in front of a judge with every newspaper in town there, along with wire service reporters and even the *New York Times*."

"You want me to bring Ed here so he'll have you arrested?"

"Yes," she said. "You produce him and I'll do the rest."

There was a knock on her dressing room door. "Come in," she called, and the best looking young man I'd ever seen walked into the room. About twenty I'd say, with black black hair and very blue eyes. Sally jumped up, ran over to him. She took his hands and brought him over to the couch where I was sitting. "I'm so sorry, Ty, I wish I'd been there when your father passed."

"He went very peacefully. Actually in my arms."

During my time in Ireland while I was running from the Black and Tans and doing my bit in the Irish fight for independence, in spite of the fear and outrage I felt, I had noticed that many Irishmen were spectacularly handsome. I'd grown up among nice-looking fellows. My own brother Michael and of course Ed himself were considered fine figures of men. But it was when I got to Connemara, Professor Peter Keeley's home place, that I saw boys and young men with the same black hair and blue eyes that made Sally's visitor so extraordinary.

I'd been told that Ireland's Atlantic shore was home to the descendants of Spanish sailors who'd survived the wreck of the Armada and that's why men like this fellow had skin that turned a bronze color instead of bright red like most of the Irish. This young man, whose hand Sally Rand was still holding, would win the top prize in any male beauty contest.

"Hello," I said to him. Sally looked at me, surprised. She'd forgotten I was even there. This young man had blurred me away immediately.

"I'm Nora Kelly," I said.

"Tyrone Power," he said, escaped from Sally's grip, and sat down beside me.

"It sounds as if you've suffered a loss."

"My father, Tyrone Power Senior."

"A very great actor," Sally said. "My leading man." She took a handkerchief from the pocket of her kimono and brought it up to her eyes.

Sally sat down, wedging herself between Tyrone Power and the arm of the couch. The three of us were crowded together. "You remember, Ty? You were only a little boy when you visited the set of *Braveheart* but even then I saw the family talent."

"Are your people from the west of Ireland, Mr. Power?" I asked. "You have the look of a Galway man."

"No, we're from Wexford."

So much for the Armada, I thought. But Wexford. Isn't that where the Kennedys come from?

"Not New Ross by any chance?"

"No, Kilthomas. My great-grandfather was also called Tyrone Power and acted all over Ireland and England. *The King O'Neill* was his biggest hit."

"Oh, I thought you might be related to the Kennedy family of Boston. They're also Wexford people."

"The only cousins I know are called Guthrie. One of them's named Tyrone also. It's a family name."

"So you must have O'Neill roots. Tyrone is Tír Eoghan. Land of Eoghan, Owen in English. He was the father of Niall of the Nine Hostages and—" I stopped. They were both staring at me. I can go on a bit about Irish history.

Sally asked, "How old are you now, Ty?"

"Nineteen."

She looked over at me. "Imagine being that young," she said. "I feel ancient."

"You seem to be doing alright," he said.

"I'm pulling down two thousand a week," she said.

"My God," he said, "nobody makes that kind of money in the movies."

"But my pay depends on customers in the seats and attendance is dropping. But if my friend here"—she pointed at me—"cooperates, I'll be coining it again."

Tyrone Power stood up. "Well I'd better get out front and claim my seat. The man in the box office said you should have a sellout crowd."

"That's what he tells everybody. But after Nora does her part it might actually be true."

We watched him walk out. "Now that's a handsome man," I said.

"So I can expect you and your guest at the nine o'clock show on Saturday night, right?"

"I'll try," I said.

"Don't try. Do it. Or you won't be using those pictures you took of me. My lawyers will make sure of that."

A businesswoman.

"But I've purposely not seen Sally Rand's act," Ed said to me when I proposed he go to her show with me. "If she and those other girls are really nude I'll have to do something. The Century of Progress can't be sullied by cheap burlesque."

"Nothing cheap about Sally," I said.

"I know her, Ed," Margaret said. "She is from Kansas City. Lived on Mersington. When I came back from France I found out that Helen Beck was now called Sally Rand and was acting in the movies. We went to see *King of Kings* where she played Mary Magdalene's slave."

I was surprised when she spoke, and grateful. I'd explained Sally's plan to her but she'd been reluctant to fool Ed. But then so was I. We were back on good terms so why spoil it?

We were in the library of the apartment. Margaret had paneled the room in oak with built-in shelves full of Ed's engineering books. She preferred popular novels and kept them in one corner. I'd opened a copy once and saw that she'd written Mrs. E. J. Kelly on the flyleaf. I checked the others and, sure enough, there was the same signature on each one. Mrs. E. J. Kelly was her identity now and I was asking her to reach back to Kansas City where she'd returned a misfit and had been a woman with a past, sitting in the side pew at the cathedral. Margaret had transformed herself and here I was linking her to the notorious Sally Rand. But she seemed ready to help me.

Keep talking, Nonie, I told myself. "I met the son of one of her costars today. Tyrone Power. His father was in a movie with her called *Braveheart*," I said.

"A western," Ed said. "I saw it. Took young . . ."

He started and stopped. Took Ed Junior, I thought.

Ed reached into his pocket, took out the medal, and began to rub his thumb across the face of Our Lady of Sorrows. Ed was first and last an Irish Catholic, holding on to the faith he had as a boy. When he'd said in his radio speech that God must have had reasons for taking his wife, unborn baby, and young son, he meant it. He might not understand but he could accept God's will. Then God had sent him three more children, "the husky boys and lovely girl." Even the Ojibwe ceremony on the shores of Medicine Lake had further confirmed his Catholicism. He could turn a blind eye to Sally Rand, just as he looked away from betting parlors and bootleggers. He didn't impose his morals on other people, but if pushed he would shut her down. Which is what he told us.

"But that's what she wants, Ed," I said, and told him his role in Sally Rand's publicity stunt. I thought he'd get mad and that would be that. But I couldn't lie to Ed.

"Helen Beck is not the devil, Ed," Margaret said. "She's just a woman on her own trying to make a living. If I remember correctly she even went to Christian college in Columbia, Missouri, for a year. Probably wanted to be a teacher."

Except no teacher would make two thousand a week for three hours' work a night, I thought. And Sally wasn't slaving for some fellow who was forcing her to expose herself. She was selling the product she could charge the most for, her body. And hadn't Margaret and Lucky Davis done the same thing in a way? Would either one have married well if they hadn't been attractive women? Oh, I knew Margaret loved Ed. And Lucky and the doctor seemed a devoted couple. But I bet both women did what I'd seen Sally do. Look in the mirror and say thank you, God, for this face, this figure. I wish women weren't judged by their appearances but they were.

"Margaret," Ed was saying. "You don't really think I should get involved in this charade, attending Sally Rand's show." Margaret looked at me. Please, please, please, I thought.

"Why not?" she said. "You can stand up for decency and help a woman trying to make her way the best way she can. I may come along. I'd like to say hello to her."

In the end Margaret didn't attend the show with us. Ladies did not patronize burlesque and I was careful to be very professional, a photographer at work.

Ed was duly appalled. Now he wasn't a prude exactly. He told the newspapers the Century of Progress was a serious endeavor. Meant to uplift our city and country at a very difficult time, to highlight new technology, medical advances. Okay, he had to build in some fun—the Sky Ride, the German beer halls. Even the Irish Village held dances with jigs and reels for all. But exposing female flesh for money should not be the most publicized element of the Fair. He ordered her arrested the next day.

The judge set a very low bail, then dismissed all charges after Sally told him that she wore a body stocking and couldn't be blamed if "lascivious eyes," her words, saw bare skin.

Ed had stood up for decency and was willing to let Sally away with her victory in court.

A week later Margaret and I met Sally Rand for a quiet lunch at the Cape

Cod Room. Without her makeup and wearing a tailored suit, she was not recognized. Still Helen Beck after all. She remembered that little Noll girl very well, and they had a good catch up.

"We've missed you, Nonie," Margaret said to me as we walked back to 209. I found myself telling her about photographing Hannah Sullivan, and she insisted that I show her the prints.

"But this is art, Nora," she said to me, then brought the photographs down to their apartment.

The next day Martin Quigley accepted my Sally Rand photographs and article, as well as the pictures I took of the Mademoiselles, and paid me $100. But he said because of his contract with Miller my name could not appear on the photographs.

I wanted to fight him. Make him give me credit. Then I realized I wasn't too chuffed (Granny's word) about taking pictures of supposedly naked women. I quit.

Nothing to stop me from going to Ireland now. The family didn't need me. Neither did Ed, I thought. Dino the doorman said his sister would be glad to take over my apartment "unofficially and ready for you when you come back."

But maybe I wouldn't be coming back. After I visited Peter's grave I might very well go to Paris and see if I could reenter that other Nora Kelly's life.

Full summer now. Margaret and the kids in Eagle River, and Ed was driving up the next day. He'd come up to my apartment to ask if I'd like to ride up with him. An all-is-well gesture.

"Ed," I started. "I have my own plans."

"To take more photographs like the one Margaret showed me? You really should, Nonie. That woman reminded me so much of Granny Honora. Not her looks but the longing." He walked over to my window. "What if we came up with a project called 'Face of the City'? I've been concentrating so much on buildings I forgot the real beauty of the city is its citizens. Our own WPA. The feds are paying photographers and why can't we?"

"Very poetic, Ed. And can someone like me with a past be trusted with such an exalted—"

"Come on, Nonie. I panicked."

"Doesn't matter, Ed. It's time."

"Peter Keeley's grave?" he asked.

"I didn't think you even knew his name."

"I listen, Nonie, I do," he said. "Just don't stay away too long. *Slan abhaile*, Nora," he said.

9

AUGUST 1933

I was almost finished packing, with my trouser suit the last to put in. Wonder will I have the nerve to wear it in Ireland, I thought. I remembered that Countess Markievicz had told me she would have preferred to add pants to the uniform she designed for herself to wear as a soldier in the Irish Citizen Army—but appropriating men's clothes was too revolutionary even for revolutionaries.

Con was dead now but at least the Civil War that had divided so many of my Irish friends, one from the other, was over.

Eamon de Valera had won.

His Fianna Fail party controlled the Irish Parliament. I had written to Maud Gonne MacBride, my closest friend among the rebels that I was coming and had asked for her help in finding Peter's grave. No response, but Maud's life was always crowded with politics, a family, and her art. If I appeared at the door of her St. Stephen's Green house she would take me in. I was sure. And then . . . well . . . at least I was on my way, until I wasn't.

Nearly midnight when Ed came knocking at my door.

"Michael's had a heart attack. He's at the hospital. The doctors don't think he will last the night."

My big brother, named for our grandfather who had died in Ireland. He'd supported us all after our own father's death and now he was going too. Dear God.

Michael was unconscious at Mercy Hospital. There had always been rumors that the nuns kept a few special suites here that had been financed by the Outfit for their members. Michael seemed to be in one of those. There was a living room with a fireplace, which is where Henrietta and Toots were when I arrived. He was on the couch reading the *Sun-Times,* and Henrietta was talking to a nun in the corner. My granny Honora had told us stories about how the Sisters of Mercy had started the first hospital in Chicago when our city was a frontier town. The order had been founded to teach girls, and the nuns had opened a school first; but when a cholera epidemic broke out, they turned the school into a hospital. The nuns became nurses. And now they had the biggest medical center on the South Side.

Our uncle Patrick had been a friend to the Sisters of Mercy, sharing with them a portion of the money he'd made fur trapping up north. The nuns had also nursed my own father, Patrick, during the Civil War when he and Aunt Máire's boy, Johnny Óg, were fighting with Colonel Mulligan's men in Lexington, Missouri. Uncle Patrick had found the two boys on the riverboat the sisters had turned into a first aid center. Johnny Óg had not survived but the nuns saved my father's life. I'd known the Sisters of Mercy at St. Xavier's High School. They were no-nonsense women who wouldn't easily let a patient succumb. I imagined them saying to Michael, "Enough of that foolishness. You're a father with five children. Live."

But when the nun came over to Ed and me, the way she took my hand and patted it told me there was no hope.

I walked into the bedroom. Michael was completely still. His chest just barely rising. I didn't pat his hand, I stroked it. No response, and it had been such a skilled hand. When I was young and he was a master plumber, he'd bring me along on his jobs. I'd marvel at how he'd fit pipes together, judging lengths and angles. In those days few people had running water or proper flush toilets, and any fellow who could provide an inside bathroom seemed a kind of miracle worker. I remember when Michael installed our toilet. The relief of not having to go to the outhouse. I mean it can be twenty degrees below zero in Chicago. Awful to rush into the backyard all bundled up, stepping into that smelly shack. The luxury of an inside toilet. And now those hands lay limp.

Ed stood at the head of the bed staring at Michael's face as if willing him to open his eyes. "Michael," he said. "Michael." First in a whisper but then louder and louder. "Michael. Michael. Wake up. For God's sake wake up."

I thought I felt a slight twitch in the hand I was stroking.

"Michael. It's Ed," he said. "Wake up." And Michael's eyelashes did move very slightly. Now Ed started shaking his shoulders and Michael opened his eyes.

"I'll get the nurse," I said. But as I withdrew my hand, Michael gripped it.

"Nonie," he said.

"Yes," I said. "I'm here, Michael."

"Ed?"

"Right next to you, Michael." I turned toward the door and called out, "Sister, Sister." The nun came in with Henrietta right behind her and they stood at the foot of the bed.

"Nonie," Michael said. "The kids? Where are my kids?"

"Oh, Michael," I started, but Henrietta interrupted me.

"For heaven's sake, Michael," she said. "Would you want your children's last memory of you to be of a corpse laid out in a hospital bed? I decided that they'd be better off at home."

"Shut up, Henrietta," I said. "Please just shut up." I leaned next to Michael and said into his ear, "The kids are fine. They're on their way to see you. And you're going to get better, Michael. You are. You're awake."

"But I'm so tired, Nonie. So tired."

"Rest then, Michael, rest. Take a little nap. We'll wake you when the children come."

He was going to see his children if I had to wrestle Henrietta to the ground. Michael was not going to die. Michael was going to live. But he never regained consciousness. Afterward the sister told us patients often rallied for a few minutes before they died.

So the Kelly kids never got to say goodbye to their father.

Goddamn, Henrietta . . . but I had to be civil to her at least until the funeral was over.

I remembered all Agnella had said.

Henrietta has had a hard life. I kept repeating the words to myself. She'd been widowed with three children at twenty-two. Her daughter had left for the convent at twenty. One son lived far away and the other was useless. She can't help being insensitive and she has looked after Michael's kids for ten years.

Well the kids were almost grown now. The older three steady enough. In shock I'd say, but holding up. But the younger girls were bewildered—Marguerite was fourteen and Frances only twelve. They had no real memory of their mother and now their father was gone too. Weeping, holding on to each other as we waited together in the vestibule of St. Blase's Church in Argo for the coffin to be carried in. Henrietta said to them, "No crying. Don't disgrace your father's memory."

Ed and Mike, along with our cousins George and Evan and Bill Kelly, were the pallbearers. Great Uncle Mike, the only one of Granny Honora's sons still living, shouldered the casket, though the others made sure no real weight rested on him. The men walked in step into the church, moving in a slow cadence. Sad that the Kelly men are so practiced in the funeral march. In the last years Mame, Ed Junior, John Larney, and now Michael had gone.

The Knights of Columbus followed the coffin. Must have been thirty fellows in their plumed hats, capes, and swords—very theatrical all together. Michael held some high rank in the organization and it was good of them to come all the way to Argo, especially since we were burying him from a Polish church. It was his parish after all, Henrietta had said, and the funeral home is nearby. She had argued against the expense of bringing him home to Bridgeport, which is what I think he would have preferred. My brother Mart and sister Ann came after the Knights.

"Now," Henrietta said to the girls, "start walking." Marguerite took Frances's hand but Henrietta reached down and pulled them apart. "Fold your hands in a prayerful position," she said to them. Geeze Louise.

Toots offered Henrietta his arm and they moved behind the girls. Henrietta smiled at people she recognized in the congregation. Rose and I came after them. Some bother about having Rose in the procession. "She's not immediate family," Henrietta had said. "If she walks with us all the cousins will be offended. They'll wonder why they weren't invited." It took Ed to calm her down. Margaret had come back from Eagle River, but had stayed home with their children. No need to upset them.

The young priest saying the funeral Mass had not a notion of who Michael Kelly was but then he was Polish and it was hard to understand him anyway. When he said "He's joining his dear wife in Heaven," all four girls started weeping until Henrietta elbowed Rosemary, who shushed the others.

A long line of cars followed the hearse out to Mount Carmel Cemetery where Mame did wait. My name was on the family tombstone too because of when I'd been reported dead. No point in chipping it off the stone. I'd end up here sooner or later, I supposed.

We had managed to overrule Henrietta and went back to Bridgeport for the funeral repast at the Polo Inn on Morgan Street. Dave Samber, the owner, had hosted many K of C banquets in his Old Eagle function room and he pushed out the boat for Michael. He'd made a big floral display with white Irish bells, orange lilies, and lots of green, the colors of the Irish flag. Dave was serving a full dinner for all comers.

"We don't need all this food," Henrietta had said when we arrived and she saw the loaded buffet table. Three hams, four turkeys, bowls of mashed potatoes. Loaves and loaves of soda bread. "The word will go out and every freeloader in the neighborhood will show up. The estate can't afford . . ."

Thank God Ed took her to the side. "Don't worry, Henrietta, Dave and I discussed the cost. Very reasonable. He's always been good to the Kellys, and Michael deserves a fitting send-off," Ed told her.

Many of our old Bridgeport neighbors came. All the McKennas, who still operated the tavern that had opened when Bridgeport was Hardscrabble, were there. Of course Pat Nash attended with a whole slew of aldermen and precinct captains, including that young fellow Dick Daley who Ed said was a comer. Rick Garvey was there. He'd been our family lawyer since forever, and I saw Henrietta pull him over to the corner. Asking him when she could get her hands on Michael's money, I supposed.

The afternoon turned into a bit of a hooley with plenty of drink taken. Catherine O'Connell, who'd sung "Ave Maria" so beautifully at the funeral, did her "Danny Boy" and I heard sobs throughout the place. But then one of the fellows called out to her "Do 'The Old Maid in the Garret,' Catherine." This was her party piece and a favorite of K of C banquets.

"No, no," she said. "Not appropriate."

"Michael Kelly loved a good laugh," one fellow said.

"Alright," Catherine said, and began the story of a woman who could not find a husband. Except the tune was upbeat—at war with the sentiment, as if the old maid might secretly embrace her single state. By the last verse the whole place was singing along. Except for Michael's kids who sat silent with me. How to explain to them that for our people singing and laughing was a way to face down despair? Often the only weapons we had to fight back, but I was glad when the last of the guests left.

"Rose and I can stay with you tonight," I said to Henrietta.

"That won't be necessary," she said.

"We'll be fine," Toots said. To think of those two swanning around Michael's house in charge of the whole place and all Mame's lovely things. . . .

Rick Garvey seemed to have waited for the crowd to leave, because he was standing talking to Ed, who then said, "Rick thinks that since we're all together he'd like to talk to you about Michael's estate."

"I'm the executrix," Henrietta said. "I've signed that paper."

"You and I both," Ed said. "I think it's best if we all sit down."

Dave, ever helpful, cleared a big round table, brought out cups of tea and slices of his homemade soda bread. The children sat side by side flanked by Toots and Henrietta. I was across from them, between Ed and Rose. Rick stayed standing.

"Now as you know, Michael had amassed a good bit of money from his plumbing business and his salary as president of the First Bank of Argo." Henrietta couldn't stop herself from smiling. "Of course he intended that there would be plenty to provide for his children so they would be well taken care of," he said.

"Which they will be, I can assure you," Henrietta said.

Rick nodded.

"I don't believe Michael told the family that he had invested quite a bit of money in Insull Bonds." Uh-oh, I thought, Insull. Only the boys in the know had been allowed to buy into the fund established by the genius financier Samuel Insull, all congratulating each other on the great returns until Insull ran off to London with all the money.

"But," Henrietta started, "Michael always had plenty of cash. Very generous with the household money for me."

"Yes," Rick said. "He was, but he had borrowed heavily against the house. He has no liquid assets."

"What do you mean?" Toots asked. "Just tell us how much cash."

"There's no actual money in the estate," Rick said. "I'm sorry."

Henrietta stood up.

"That's impossible," she said. "You're lying to us."

"Remember, Henrietta," Rick said, "the Depression—"

"I'm tired of hearing about the old Depression!" she said.

"Sit down, Mother," Toots said. "The house is worth a good bit. We can sell it and—"

"I'm afraid, that's not on," Rick said. "Michael had taken two mortgages on the house. He'd made a special arrangement with the bank but the man in charge now is not sympathetic. No payments have been made for over a year. The bank has notified me they are beginning foreclosure proceedings."

"What," Henrietta said. "They're trying to take the house? They can't do that."

"I'm afraid they can."

Ructions. Only for Ed, Henrietta would have completely disgraced us all. I said to him, "Ed, quick, she'll start bellowing in a minute," and the two of us moved toward her.

We got her out of Old Eagle with Toots coming up behind us.

Ed's official car, the black Packard limousine with the Chicago policeman driver, was waiting in front on Morgan. His bodyguard had been leaning against the car and now he opened the door and we pushed Henrietta into the backseat.

"Take your mother home, Toots," Ed said. And then he turned to the driver. "Make sure Mrs. Kelly is comfortable."

Henrietta shouted at us.

"I'm owed. Michael owed me. How dare he squander . . ." But Toots got in the back seat beside her, shut the door and they were off.

"Dear God," I said to Ed. "I think she's really unbalanced. Isn't there some doctor that can help her? Some place she can go? What about that new hospital, Manteno? A week there and—"

"Maybe," he said.

"I'll take the Kelly kids to my place," I said. "It'll be crowded and they'll have to sleep on the floor, but there will be peace."

"The older girls and Mike can come to us," Ed said. "We can all go home in the car. I'll call Margaret to expect us."

Rose asked to join us. "The more the kids can feel they're part of the family the better," she said.

We were all ready to go and had said goodbye to the last of the neighbors, but Ed's car still hadn't returned.

"What do you think happened?" I asked Ed. "I hope he wasn't in an accident or anything."

"I would have heard."

Finally Ed made a call and two squad cars arrived to take both of us back to 209 East Lake Shore.

"Would you like to spend the night with Steve and Joey?" I asked Mike. He and Ed Junior had been very close but he hadn't really gotten to know the younger boys. He agreed and, of course, they were thrilled to have this grown-up sixteen-year-old cousin staying over. Margaret put Rosemary and Ann in her guestroom, both of them quiet, tired, happy to get in bed. The younger girls came with Rose and me into my apartment.

Some of my clothes were still in the suitcase, and I pulled out two nightgowns for them.

"You can share my bed," I said. Rose would sleep on the couch and I would put cushions on the floor for myself. They followed me like mechanical dolls into my little kitchen where I made them hot chocolate.

"Would you girls like to spend a few days with me?" I asked them.

"Oh, Aunt Henrietta would not allow that," Marguerite said. "She says you're . . ." and then Marguerite stopped herself.

"Said I'm what?"

But Marguerite just shook her head. Rose looked over at me. "Let's get these girls in bed."

We tucked them in and Rose sang softly to them *"Siúil, siúil, siúil a rún."*

"I remember that song," Marguerite said. "Mama sang it to us."

"Yes she did. And our mother sang it to us," Rose said.

"As my mother, your grandmother, did to me," I said.

"Are we orphans now, Aunt Nonie?" Frances asked me. "Aunt Henrietta said that if we weren't good she'd put us in Angel Guardian Orphanage."

"That's ridiculous," I said. "You have family all over the place. More aunts and uncles and cousins than you could ever count. We'll take care of you. I promise. Your aunt Henrietta says some very foolish things, but she does love you."

Hard to even say these words, but Michael had made Henrietta his children's guardian and it would be just like her to cut us off from them if we made trouble. Rose started singing softly again, *"Siúil, siúil,"* and the girls closed their eyes.

Rose and I moved over to the couch and sat in the dark, looking down on the lights on the Outer Drive.

"How dare Henrietta threaten to put those kids into an orphanage," I said.

"I think of the poor little ones in Angel Guardian who never even knew who their parents were," said Rose.

"I wonder if Margaret and Ed's children will ever be curious about their natural parents," I said.

"They won't, Nonie. They have a family."

"Do you mourn the children you didn't have, Rose?" I asked.

Now she and I didn't talk about our own barrenness. I only knew about her miscarriages from Mame, and I had never told her how I'd prayed that I was carrying Peter Keeley's child.

"Ah well, God's will I suppose. He's given us Michael's children to care for and really, Nonie, I always think if everyone stood in a circle and put their troubles in the middle you'd pick up your own."

Frances and Marguerite were asleep now. Not little girls anymore at twelve and fourteen. Rosemary and Ann were grown-up women, nineteen and twenty-one. And Michael, sixteen. But they still needed a family. I shuddered to think of turning them over to Henrietta, but Michael had chosen her as their guardian. Nothing I could do. Though I'd not be heading off to Ireland just yet.

10

The sun was pushing out of Lake Michigan when I woke up. Frances and Marguerite sound asleep and Rose too. Coffee, I thought. Coffee. And I was in my kitchen when the back door opened.

"Come downstairs, Nonie," Ed said.

"As soon as I make my coffee and get dressed." I was standing there in my flannel nightgown.

"No, put on a robe," Ed said. "There's coffee downstairs."

In fact there was a whole breakfast laid out on the kitchen table. Bacon and eggs, with Ed's driver eating away. He looked up at me. I was well covered up in my plaid bathrobe. I tied the sash a little tighter and nodded at him.

"Jerry just arrived with the car a little while ago," Ed said. "He'd been driving all night. Tell her."

The driver took a swallow of coffee, which made me pour myself a cup. What was going on? Why did I have to hear Ed's driver's story?

"As you know," the driver began, "I left with Mrs. Kelly and her son from 3322 South Morgan. The mayor told me to drive them home to Argo, which I did. I took Archer Avenue. There are those that think Garfield Boulevard is faster and object to diagonals, but I always find Archer is a straight shot—"

"Jerry," Ed said, "get to the point."

"Well we got to Argo and Mrs. Kelly told me to wait. She said she had someplace else to go, so I thought that she probably needed milk or bread, or whatever, so I said okay. I figured I could take care of whatever she wanted and still be back in time to pick you up. I know you like to take your time saying goodbye, Mr. Mayor, especially when some of the boys are there and a lot of voters—"

Now it was I who said, "Jerry, please."

He took another slug of coffee. "But it turned out that the young fellow, her son, said that he needed my help inside, so I got out of the car. I thought he wanted me to do something like move a table, or get a box off a high shelf. Instead . . ." And now he stopped, took another drink of coffee, and said, "They were stripping the joint."

"What?" I said.

"You won't believe the rest," Ed said. "Go on, Jerry."

"That woman, Mrs. Kelly, was going from room to room pointing to things. She had me carry out all the silverware, the cutlery, a teapot, a coffeepot, an entire set of dishes, lamps. Even made me roll up the carpets. That guy, Toots, had brought up big boxes from the cellar and he used blankets to wrap everything up. Took tablecloths, nice ones too, linen I'd say. My wife got some like them from her relatives in Ireland for our wedding. See, they're from Donegal and—"

"Mame's wedding presents," I said to Ed. "Her silver and china. All meant to be passed on to her girls. Why would Henrietta do that?"

"I can tell you why," the driver said. "We loaded everything into the car and it's a good thing I'm an experienced packer because there wasn't an inch to spare, even in a car as big as yours, Mr. Mayor."

"But where are they? What did they do?" I asked.

"She had me drive them all the way down to Kewanee to a farmhouse. Didn't get there until three this morning. Took another hour to unload all the stuff and then she said to me, 'That's all. You can go.' She never even offered me a cup of tea."

Margaret gave the kids breakfast in her kitchen, but Ed and I said nothing to them about Henrietta's bizarre behavior. Maybe there was some explanation. Maybe she'd telephone. Maybe . . .

But no word as the day went on. Rose and all four of the Kelly girls were with Ed's daughter, Pat, in her room, while his sons Steve and Joe had gone outside with Mike to play on the stretch of green grass between East Lake Shore and the Drive. Ed and I watched from the window as Mike passed the football to each of the little boys in turn. Joe clutched the ball and begin running toward two trees on the edge of the sidewalk, which served as goalposts. Margaret came over and stood with us.

"Are they safe down there?" asked Margaret. "If Joe ran into the traffic Steve would follow right behind him."

"Mike will take care of them," Ed said. "Don't worry."

"That was a good catch for an eleven-year-old," I said. "He'll be one of the Fighting Irish one day."

Ed smiled. I wondered if he was remembering, as I was, the day he'd received his honorary degree from Notre Dame in 1925. A doctor of law complete with a cap and gown. Not bad for a fellow who left school in fourth grade. We had all driven down for the ceremony—Margaret, Ed Junior and me, Michael and all his kids. Ed and Margaret had not adopted their children yet, but Mike's friend Bobby Lambert had come along so we had a load of kids. After the ceremony we'd walked around the campus and Ed had arranged for the boys to go on the football field. I remember how they'd stood there looking at the stands. The green field. The lines marking off the yards. Then Ed Junior gave a yell and ran toward the goalposts. Michael and Bobby took after him, and for a good fifteen minutes we watched an imaginary game of football. I started singing, *"Cheer, Cheer for Old Notre Dame / Wake up the echoes cheering her on."* Michael and Rose laughed at me but then joined in, and Ed sang along. Margaret shook her head but smiled at us. Only eight years ago and yet so much had changed. Hard to believe we'd all been together on that golden autumn day. I wondered if Ed was watching his two sons and thinking of the one he'd lost. And now Henrietta had gone completely crazy.

The doorbell rang. Ed's driver had gone to fill the car with gas, but now he was back. "Sorry, Mr. Mayor," he said as he came in. "I was cleaning out the car and found this note on the back seat." He handed it to Ed.

Rose and Margaret came out of the kitchen.

"It seems as if Henrietta has moved permanently to Kewanee," I said to Rose. "And has helped herself to anything valuable in the Argo house."

I turned to Ed, who was reading the note. "What does it say, Ed?" I asked.

"A lot of it is just palaver," he said, "but here's the important part. 'My brother Michael intended to compensate me for my caretaking,'" Ed read. "'After all, I gave up my own home to help his children.'"

I couldn't let that go by. "She begged to go live with them. Michael's been supporting her and Toots for years."

"Go on, Ed, read the rest," Rose said.

"She writes, 'Michael seems to have squandered his money so I am taking what he would have wanted me to have. I am not returning. I have kept the house my husband built for me as a refuge for my old age. I did not expect anyone in the family to care for me and, thank God, I have my faithful son with me. Michael's two oldest girls are very able housekeepers. I have trained them. There's no reason for them to continue with all that college nonsense. They can get jobs and keep house for their brother and sisters. Since the Argo property is worthless they probably should rent some place in Chicago, as their own house is another victim of Michael's poor judgment.'" Ed lowered the paper. Rose was crying.

"I just don't understand," Rose said.

"Don't cry, Rose. Get angry," I said to her. "How dare Henrietta steal from the Kelly kids. Michael fed her and that lazy son three meals a day for years. Gave them a roof over their heads and most of what she took belonged to your sister."

"Henrietta is a troubled woman," Margaret said.

"She is," I said. "No question. I still think Manteno is the best place for her."

"Please, Nonie. Keep your voice down," Ed said. "We have to figure this out before the Kelly girls come in here."

"They're too young to be on their own," Rose said. "Frances and Marguerite are just starting high school and Mike's only a junior. Ann and Rosemary must finish. Listen, I know what to do. I'll live with them."

I knew Rose enjoyed her life with Ed's mother, Aunt Nelly, and her sister, Rose's mother-in-law. A pleasant house, and Ed paying their expenses. Rose took good care of the two women but Ed's widowed sister Ella could probably take over for her.

"We can find some place in South Shore," Rose said. "Close to St. Rita's for Michael and Aquinas for Marguerite and Frances."

"I can find you an apartment and help you with the rent," Ed said.

"And I'll get a job," Rose said.

"A job," Ed repeated. "I could find you something at the Board of Education."

Which was how Rose, the kindest, gentlest woman in the world, became a truant officer, though most of the time when she found a child who'd been staying out of school she ended up taking them for a malted milk instead of imposing any kind of punishment.

"And I have my salary," I said. "We'll need help the first year, but after Rose and Ann graduate and get teaching jobs we'll be away in a hack, as Mam used to say." I should have known something was wrong. I expected Rose to hug me, or at least squeeze my hand, but she didn't move, didn't look at me. Ed didn't say anything. It was Margaret who leaned over and patted my arm.

"You don't want to give up your place, Nora. You'd never find anything like it," she said.

"I know, but this is an emergency. These are Michael's kids. My own flesh and blood."

"Michael and Mame's," Rose said.

"Yes of course," I said. Rose still wasn't looking at me.

"It's just, Nonie, well, the most we could afford would be a three-bedroom apartment, and, well, you could of course be a part of the children's lives, but . . ."

"Rose, what are you saying?" I asked.

"Nora," Margaret said, "you do have a certain reputation."

"Oh God here we go again." Tim McShane and the trouser suit.

"You made your own life, Nonie, and we respect you for it," Ed said. "It's just that you're unconventional and the Kelly kids have enough to face without having to explain you."

"You've always been the brave one, Nonie," Rose said. "But children like things normal and, well, Nonie, be honest you've never been suited to the kind of daily tasks of cooking and cleaning. And I don't think the women at the Aquinas Mothers' Club would understand your life and . . ."

"Oh, Mother." We all turned to see Pat walking hand in hand with Marguerite and Frances, each of them carrying a very fancy doll. "They like my Madame Alexanders much more than I do. So I've given the dolls to them."

"We just said that they were gorgeous," Marguerite said. "Not that we wanted them. We're too old for dolls."

"But you told me you'd put them on a shelf in your room," Pat said. "And I hate dolls." She walked over to her mother, and Margaret started winding Pat's thick hair around her fingers. Margaret usually made sure her daughter had a headful of perfect sausage curls, but now Pat's hair was sticking out all over her head, straight as a stick, but thick. So different from Margaret's. Somewhere, I thought, there's a woman with that same hair. I wonder if Margaret knows who Pat's birth mother is. Irish I'd say from those blue eyes and the freckles across her nose.

Rosemary and Ann walked into the living room.

"I want to go home," Rosemary said.

"Me too," Ann said. "I want to sit in Dad's chair."

I remembered Ann at Mame's wake, appalled at the talk and laughter. She'd been sitting next to me when Tim McShane had pulled me away and out into the street. Does she look at me and think Aunt Nonie the harlot? Is Rose right? Do I frighten these young women? Margaret stood up and walked over to them.

"Before you go you could do me a great favor, girls. I have some dresses and coats that I've decided are just too young for me. Would you look at them and see if there's anything you could wear and take them away for me?"

"Do you have any hats?" Rosemary asked. Margaret laughed.

"A good few," she said, and the three walked toward Margaret and Ed's room with its huge closet. I looked at Rose. Would she resent Margaret acting Lady Bountiful? But Marguerite and Frances were standing next to her, showing her the dolls.

"I think you should accept Pat's gift," Rose said. "These dolls would make lovely decorations in your room."

"But Aunt Henrietta doesn't like us to clutter up our room. She took down the poster I got of Lake Michigan from the IC Railroad."

Who's going to tell them? I wondered. Rose or me? But it was Ed who spoke up.

"Your aunt Henrietta has decided to retire and live in the country with Toots."

"Toots? In the country?" Marguerite asked and she and Frances started laughing. But Ed went right on. "So your aunt Rose will be living with you."

"And Aunt Nonie too?" Marguerite said.

Bless her, I thought.

"There's plenty of room in the house," she said.

"We've decided it would be better if you lived in the city where you'd be closer to your schools and nearer to all the family," Ed said.

"But our friends are in Argo," Frances said.

However, Marguerite was nodding. "We can make new friends, Fran," she said. "And if we didn't have to travel so far we could sign up to be in the chorus or the school play."

"That's true," Frances said. "Sister Hilda asked me to join the debate club and I said no because I had to catch the Archer Avenue streetcar. My best friend in school, Sheila McGuire, lives in South Shore. I've been to their apartment. It's lovely. Could we live near there?"

"I don't see why not," Rose said.

"And Aunt Henrietta won't be with us?" Marguerite said.

"She won't," Ed said.

"And we can visit Aunt Nonie here? And play with Pat and Steve and Joe?" Frances asked.

"You can, of course," Ed said.

What could I do? Imitate Henrietta and throw a fit? I did like my privacy and in a few months maybe I could think of Ireland again. Take the high road, Nonie, I told myself.

"Ta dah!" Margaret stood in the arch that connected the back hall with the living room. "May I present Miss Ann Kelly."

Ann stepped into the living room. She wore a gray wool suit that belonged to Margaret. I hadn't realized how tall Ann had grown. The jacket with its padded shoulders and nipped waist emphasized her height. She wore an emerald green blouse with ruffles around the neck. Margaret had tucked a green silk handkerchief into the jacket breast pocket. The skirt was slim and hit just below the knee.

Frances clapped her hands. "You look beautiful, Ann."

"And look at those shoes," Marguerite said. The dark green pumps had very high heels. This year's, I'd say and the suit looked new too. Good on you, Margaret, I thought. These weren't discards but new purchases.

"Lovely, Ann," Rose said. "You can wear the suit to Mass on Sunday. With a white blouse of course."

"And on your first day teaching," I said.

"Well," Rose said, "it's a little glamorous for the classroom."

"Who knows," I said. "Ann may change her mind. She might decide to become a career girl. More jobs for young women all the time. In that suit she looks like a woman who could run a company."

Now Marguerite and Frances shouted, "Oh, look!" And here came Rosemary. I'd been a bit worried about her. She was the only one of the girls who could not be called pretty. A nose just that bit too pronounced and very prominent cheekbones. With her white skin and black black hair there was something almost threatening about her. But this woman standing in front of all of us was a knockout.

Rosemary wore a very slinky evening dress covered with black sequins. Much too sophisticated for a twenty-one-year-old girl, but it transformed her. She stood very straight, her shoulders back. She'd been into Margaret's makeup too; her lashes seemed longer. Some kind of shadow on her lids brought out the green in her eyes. Her lips were ruby red and she'd piled her hair on top of her head.

"You look like a movie star, Rosemary," Marguerite said.

"Good," Rosemary replied, "because I've decided that when I graduate in June I'm not going to be teacher after all. I'm going to be an actress."

"Now, Rosemary," Ed said, "there's nothing wrong with dressing up when the occasion calls for it. You look very nice and you're most welcome to join Margaret and me at the opera some evening and that getup would be perfectly acceptable, but as for becoming an actress . . . You know how proud your father was that you were going to be a teacher. He'd already spoken to the principal at the Holden School in Bridgeport who said she'd be delighted to have a Kelly teaching there."

But Rosemary was shaking her head. "Uncle Ed," she said, and her voice seemed pitched lower. "Daddy is dead. Our house is gone and don't movie stars make a lot more money than teachers?"

"Rosemary," Rose said, "don't be rude."

"I'm not," Rosemary said. "I've been in all the college plays and the drama teacher told me I was one of the most talented students he'd ever taught."

Rose turned to Margaret. "It's very kind of you to offer the girls your clothes but I'm afraid it's giving them ideas. I think it would be better if—"

I cut her off. "Don't move, girls. I'm off to get my camera."

"Oh, yes," Margaret said. "Do."

Rose put out her hand as if to stop me but I pretended I didn't see it.

"There," I said when I'd taken the last of a series of photographs. The warm light from the setting sun had created a kind of halo around Rosemary and Ann.

"I have a friend who did all the photos for Essanay Studios when they were based here in Chicago. The company moved to Hollywood but she still has contacts. I'll pass these pictures on to her, Rosemary, and then who knows?" I said.

"Nonie," Rose said, but again I ignored her. If I was going to be the disreputable aunt then I was going to play the role all the way. Encourage the girls and who cares what the Aquinas Mothers' Club thinks.

"You met her, Rosemary. She was the one who took your family picture with your mother," I said.

"Oh yes," Rosemary said. "That strange woman."

"Strange, maybe. A very successful businesswoman and an artist."

"Like you, Aunt Nonie?" Marguerite asked.

"Yes," I said. "Like me."

So. Looking back I think dressing up changed both those girls' lives. Rosemary went to Hollywood after she graduated and did very well for herself. Never a movie star but she found success in radio, acting opposite, of all people, Vincent Price and Boris Karloff in a series of plays that came on every Sunday evening for years. When the series went off the air she came back to Chicago and was a regular with the Drury Lane company. And Ann became the first woman executive at Braniff Airways before she left to marry at forty. It was Marguerite who became the teacher. Frances married young an older fellow who was considered the catch of South Shore. Their future started that day and I decided to take my work more seriously. Why not collect my photographs in a book, as Ed said, even if the City had to publish it?

I'm sorry, Peter, I thought—you'll have to wait a bit longer. But then there's no time when you're dead, is there?

11

SEPTEMBER 1933

Ed and I were in his office the month after Michael's funeral and Henrietta's theft, though I was the only one saying out and out that she'd stolen from the Kelly kids.

"We should go down there and take the stuff back," I'd said to Rose.

"She's gone. Don't rile her," Rose had said and Ed had agreed.

"An ugly incident that we don't want to read about in the newspapers," he'd said.

"So we're just going to let her keep what was Mame's property . . . really?" I'd said. "It's not as if Henrietta is going to be giving dinner parties in Kewanee."

Though it turned out I was wrong about that. She was entertaining to beat the band. Bits of gossip had already floated up the Illinois River to Bridgeport. Henrietta had offered her house as a meeting place for the St. Charles Altar and Rosary Society, according to Rose's friend's sister-in-law who said that the farmers' wives in the parish were very impressed by Henrietta's beautiful things and her exquisite taste. Geeze Louise, Henrietta had been awful to Mame in life, nasty to her children, and now she was swanning around with her things. But Henrietta was gone, thank God, and so I held my tongue.

The bank had wasted no time serving papers on, of all people, young Mike. "The man in the family," the loan officer had said. Ridiculous. Rose told me she'd seen Mike sniffing back tears as he read the documents that took his family's home away. True to his word, Ed had found an apartment for Rose and the kids on Yates Avenue—three bedrooms and a sleeping porch, which young Mike claimed for himself. A cold enough place in the winter but at least he'd have some privacy. Man of the family? Kiss-my-foot-how-are-you. He was only sixteen but then plenty of fellows had come out of Ireland and worked themselves to death at that age or younger. Many families had been kept from starving to death because of the money those boys sent home. Without our uncle Patrick digging the I & M Canal, Granny Honora would not have had the money to escape with her children.

Just enough things left from the Argo house to furnish the apartment, and really when I saw how close the quarters were I was glad I wasn't considered respectable enough to live with my nieces and nephew. I'd gotten used to the luxury of having a place of my own, and yet as I sat in Ed's office at the end of the month I wondered if I'd ever really escape the web of family obligations and get to Ireland.

"Now look, Nonie, I appreciate your talents, I do, after all it was your camera launched me, right?"

"Mmmmmm," I said. "I wondered if you even remembered."

"I do."

"Good," I said.

"I want you to come back, be my personal photographer," Ed said.

"Aren't you afraid Hearst and Wilcox won't approve?" I asked.

"To hell with them! The fair's such a big success they don't dare attack me. Imagine, Noni, over a hundred thousand in attendance every day! People are coming to Chicago from all over the country, all over the world. Spending millions of dollars in the city," he said.

"Happy to escape their troubles for a little while, I guess," I said.

He nodded.

"I've decided to extend the Century of Progress for another year. Instead of ending the Fair this October we'll keep it open until next October," he said. "And I plan to be there on the grounds greeting our famous visitors, and opening the new exhibits. I've started special days of celebration—Polish Day, Irish Day, Negro Day, and so on with free admission offered to members of each group," he said.

"That will be popular," I said.

"I want you there at my side to record these events," he said.

"And take your photograph?" I said.

"Yes," he said.

So instead of a book of the "Faces of Chicago," I'm supposed to concentrate on Ed's face? Not like him to be so concerned about personal publicity. He seemed to know what I was thinking.

"I want voters to realize that I fought for the Fair when everyone else wanted me to cancel it," he said.

"The voters?" I said. "But once you finish Cermak's term aren't you done with the voters?"

And not a moment too soon for Margaret.

"We'll see about that," he said. "The election for mayor is in April '35 so just a few months after the Fair will close."

"Wait a minute. Are you thinking of running?" I said.

I had been there when Pat Nash explained to Ed that he was going to be a "place holder" acting as mayor until the party found a better candidate for the 1935 election. What was Ed thinking?

"Does Pat know?" I asked.

"Ná habair tada," Ed said.

Granny's phrase—*Whatever you say, say nothing.*

So. The grand finale of the Century of Progress had been meant to be the visit to Chicago by the *Graf Zeppelin* on October 26, 1933. But extending the fair would take some of the Germans' thunder away, which probably was just as well.

Ed had done a lot of maneuvering in order to get the *Graf Zeppelin* to agree to come to Chicago on its record-breaking circumnavigation of the globe. Zeppelins were the future, Ed told me. The Germans had been working on dirigibles for years and now had created this huge airship. It was longer than two football fields and four stories high. The *Graf Zeppelin* could cross oceans, travel at a speed of 80 miles per hour. Ed had financed the visit by getting Jim Farley, the now postmaster general, to issue a special stamp showing the airship flying over Lake Michigan toward the Century of Progress buildings. Most of the revenue from the stamps would go to the Germans. Anyone who purchased a stamp could put it on a letter, bring it to the *Zeppelin* and it would go around the world with the ship.

"But the *Zeppelin* is a tool of Nazi propaganda," Milton Goldman had told Ed the month before the dirigible was to land. An older man who taught at the University of Chicago, he was a short, intense fellow who had been one of the leaders of the Jewish community's protest march demanding that Ed cancel the *Zeppelin*'s flight to Chicago. He said that it was bad enough to have a German pavilion at the Fair, but to take part in this charade was playing into Hitler's hands. "Look at all the good press Balbo got for Mussolini," Goldman said.

Jake Arvey had brought Goldman to Ed's office. I'd come to take his photograph with the mayor, but stayed because what Goldman was saying rang very true. A few months before July 15, 1933 twenty-four Italian seaplanes had arrived in Chicago, after their trans-Atlantic flight. One of the newspapers captioned a photograph of the planes this way: "Italy's roaring armada of goodwill sweeps over the Century of Progress." The article went on to praise General Italo Balbo who was one of Mussolini's top lieutenants. He had led the flight that had included a stop in Derry, Ireland.

Ed had invited every Italian civic leader in the city and even some members of the Outfit in to welcome the great aviator at a grand banquet. Balbo went on about all the good Mussolini was doing and how he was restoring the ancient Roman virtues. After I photographed Balbo and Ed, the whole group wanted their picture taken with him. Balbo grandly announced that Il Duce was sending an ancient column to us in order to commemorate the occasion. Chicago wasn't alone in falling for him. Balbo was given a US military escort to New York where millions came out for the parade honoring him and the Italian pilots. But since then, reports were coming out of Mussolini's attacks on Italians who disagreed with him.

Goldman said that as bad as Mussolini was, Hitler was ten times worse. He told us that Hitler's speeches were full of ravings against the Jews, who Hitler called a parasitical people whose aim was to destroy all other Folk, especially the Germans. According to Hitler, the Jews were mongrels who had to be annihilated so Germany could be cleansed.

"Hitler dresses up his hate with poppycock conspiracy theories about how we Jews caused the Great War and are plotting to take over the world," Goldman said.

As chancellor of Germany, Hitler had started confiscating Jewish businesses. Not just shouting out his hate for the Jews in his mesmerizing rants but acting on them, Goldman told us.

"But isn't Hitler a nut?" Ed said. "Surely the German people will wake up and get rid of him. The zeppelins were developed long before he showed up and if *Graf Zeppelin* doesn't land in Chicago it will only go on to St. Louis and Cincinnati and those cities will get the national attention."

Jake then said that the captain of the *Graf Zeppelin*, Hugo Eckener, was known to be anti-Hitler. Maybe we could use the occasion for good. Ed could invite him to make a statement denouncing the Nazis.

"He'd never do it," Goldman said. "Too afraid. Even decent people in Germany have become infected."

But Jake and Ed thought it was worth a try. The *Graf Zeppelin* had to come to Chicago. There was no way around it. I'd say a million people watched the *Graf Zeppelin* circle the Fair on October 26, 1933, and then head north to Glenview air station where Ed and I waited along with a large group of reporters.

"Dear God, Ed," I said. "Look!" Painted on the tail of the ship was a swastika that had to be twenty feet high. All too soon this image would symbolize unimaginable horror.

Eckener was an older man, gray hair cut very short, wrinkled and tired looking. I took a photograph of Ed handing him a mailbag full of letters with the special stamp. The press conference was very short. Goldman asked the first question. Why was Eckener allowing himself and his extraordinary machine to be used for Nazi propaganda?

"I am not here to discuss politics," Eckener said and marched back to the huge ship branded by the Nazis.

I remember thinking of the Yeats quote: "The best lack all conviction while the worst are full of passionate intensity."

But for most people, walking around the Century of Progress was like being transported into the future at a time when even having a future seemed in doubt. If the 1893 Columbian Exposition gave us "The White City," then the Fair was "Rainbow Country," full of color, sleek buildings, and bold murals. I would pose Ed and visiting actresses in the Women's building against the wall painting of suffragists marching forward. We used celebrities to attract the press to the Fair's more nuts-and-bolts attractions. When the movie star Don Ameche came, we took him to the railroad building to photograph him and Ed with the new Zephyr locomotive. On the day the comedian George Jessel brought the girl singers who were on the bill with him at the Oriental Theatre, I set up the photo at the Atomic Energy Building. The girls were called the Gumm Sisters. Though Jessel told Ed he had suggested they change their name to "Garland."

Name any movie star, Broadway actor or actress, or sports figure prominent in the 1930s and I'll bet they came to the Century of Progress and were photographed by me with Ed Kelly. I would write up a press release and send the package to the newspapers. Nine times out of ten they used both. One in the eye for Manny Mandel to see my credit under the photographs. Ed was very pleased with the attention he was getting.

But in October 1934 when the Fair ended, I was more concerned about whether Ed would get the nomination that he wanted. It wasn't looking good.

12

DECEMBER 1934

"You've done a grand job, Ed, no question," Pat Nash said. "But you've had your turn. The other fellows won't stand for you running. They'll say you weren't elected, and have never campaigned for office—which is true, after all—and that you can't get votes. Thompson's going for mayor again. The boys say he'd beat you, hands down."

"They are wrong," Ed said.

Pat had come to Ed's city hall office unannounced and unexpected. I knew Ed thought Pat was down in Kentucky where he was spending more and more time breeding thoroughbreds at his Shannon Farms. Ed said it was because Pat realized reasoning with horses was easier than convincing aldermen. "And horses are more loyal," he'd added.

I was there in the office because even after the Century of Progress had closed, celebrities continued to come to the mayor's office. They often stopped in during their time between trains, since it was still necessary to change in Chicago from East Coast to West Coast lines. They knew a picture with the mayor would be printed in the papers. Good publicity.

I'd just taken a picture of Ed with the Negro film star Bill "Bojangles" Robinson, the one who had danced up and down the stairs with Shirley Temple in the movie that had made all that money, in spite of theaters in the South refusing to show it. I had an arrangement with the *Chicago Defender*, the Chicago-based newspaper that has been read by Negroes across the nation since its founding in 1905. Whenever someone they were interested in visited Ed, I'd send them a photograph. They'd run the shot I took of Ed and Joe Louis on the front page, just after the boxer became World Champion. The editor and founder, Mr. Robert Sengstacke Abbott, told me they had printed twice as many copies as usual, and sold them all.

"I had to bring big bundles down to Union Station," he'd said.

It was the Pullman porters who had brought the *Defender* to towns and whistle stops below the Mason-Dixon Line. I wondered if Melvin Grant and his son were part of the network.

"Some of our people down there would have a hard time believing your cousin made a colored man mayor for the day, less they read it with their own eyes," Mr. Abbott said. He also told me that more and more Southern Negroes were getting on those trains and heading north for Chicago. I almost sang a bit of "How Ya Gonna Keep 'Em Down on the Farm After They've Seen Paree?"—Nora Bayes's hit from 1919. But Mr. Abbott was a very dignified and slightly remote man, and I never presumed.

Though, of course, I would have loved to tell him that I had met William Dawson, a Negro civic leader in Paris, right after the First World War. Dawson was a lieutenant in a Negro unit there. He was in a café with two other Negro soldiers, when a fellow with him sang that very song, and Dawson predicted that the lyrics would turn out to be true for colored farmers as well as whites. I often wondered if Dawson would remember me, but I didn't have the nerve to seek him out. He was a Republican, after all, like most of the Negroes in Chicago. Though how they could have voted for Big Bill Thompson just because he belonged to the party of Abraham Lincoln, I could not fathom. Because, though Roosevelt had overwhelmingly won the Negro vote in 1932, locally that community supported Republicans.

So I knew the *Defender* would take the Bojangles picture and pay me two dollars. Give me credit, too. I had picked up my camera and started to leave the office as soon as Pat came in the door. He hardly looked at me, which wasn't like him. Always the gentleman, Pat. Agitated, another state unusual for him. He'd sat down in front of Ed's desk, and launched right in before I could leave. Now, if I left, it would look as if I were running away from his raised voice. So I stood for a minute at the side of the room. Then, I said, "So long Ed, Pat."

"But," Ed said, "wait a minute, Nora. You tell Pat."

Now I didn't say, "Tell Pat what?" because I knew Ed wanted me to describe the crowds who had gathered during our photo sessions at the Fair. Spontaneous rallies where Ed had joshed with the people. Maybe Ed wasn't a natural showman like Thompson, but I thought that was all to the good.

Big Bill was ready to do anything to take back the office of mayor. Putting up somebody who would try to out-antic the Master of Antics would be a mistake. But I didn't say all that to Pat. I simply reported.

"Pat, Ed makes people feel better. He's steady, and they like that. I've been with him at Communion breakfasts and wakes. He's one of them, and yet there's something of the chieftain about Ed. He can deliver. Look at the Century of Progress. Even you thought it was a mistake to continue it for another year when families were still suffering," I said. "But Ed said there'd be no admission charge for children so fathers and mothers could give their kids a day away from want and worry. And attendance went through the roof. Look how popular the free concerts in Grant Park are. Ed did that. Voters won't forget."

"Oh, Nora," Pat said, "all these years, and you still don't understand politics. It's the aldermen tell their people who to vote for—and if they're against Ed, and they are, well . . ." He shrugged his shoulders.

"But really, Pat, who cares about the aldermen when Ed has the president of the United States in his corner? I bet Roosevelt would even come and campaign."

Ed had visited the White House dozens of times. The connection he and Roosevelt made in Florida had deepened. After all, Chicago was a New Deal success story—public works had cut unemployment in half. The banks had gotten in line. Ed had even found a way to use the Civilian Conservation Corps, the program designed to create jobs in rural areas by planting trees, clearing streams, and building dams. Right now, there were two CCC camps in our Forest Preserves.

Ed and Margaret had attended two White House dinners with the Roosevelts, and Margaret said Eleanor Roosevelt could not have been nicer to her. Not much for small talk—but then, neither was Margaret. Two shy women pushed into public life. Lots in common. Mrs. Roosevelt had mentioned to Ed that she had a number of protégés in Chicago who needed jobs, and I knew for a fact that the First Lady had recommended four Negro women who Ed had working in the county clerk's office now.

"Maybe Mrs. Roosevelt would attend a rally for Ed. That would put the tin hat on it," I said.

But Pat sighed.

"I was hoping I didn't have to tell you this, Ed. That you would just bow out. But I got the word from Jim Farley. Roosevelt told him—and I'm repeating what Farley said—'Take the necessary steps to stop Kelly's nomination.'"

Well, I'd never seen Ed so silent. He just stared at Pat.

"That's terrible!" I said. "What a betrayal! I thought Roosevelt was a more honorable man than that. I—"

Ed raised his hand. "Easy, Nonie," and looked at Pat. "Who?" he asked. "Who do they want? I can't see Roosevelt going for Clark or any council member."

"Merriam is their choice," Pat said.

"Merriam?" I said. "But he's not even a Democrat!"

Charles Merriam was a professor of political science at the University of Chicago who had been involved in local politics for years. He'd twice been elected as an alderman, and had run for mayor three times. Once, on the Republican ticket in 1911, he'd lost to Carter Harrison. Then, he was defeated by Big Bill in the 1915 Republican primary, and again in 1919. Merriam started the Illinois Progressive Party with Harold Ickes. Both of them had big jobs in Washington now. Roosevelt had been careful to bring Republicans into his administration, especially those who had taught at universities and had written books. I wouldn't say either Merriam or Ickes had much good to say about Ed Kelly, or Irish pols in general. Both of them descended from Scottish Presbyterians—bred in the bone for them to see us as Papist idolaters—born to be corrupt.

"Merriam's willing to become a Democrat," Pat said.

"Well, that's big of him," I said.

"That guy treats the city like a laboratory for his theories," Ed said. "He runs for office just to annoy the other professors."

"Thompson will roll over him," I said.

"Not if the Roosevelts support him," Pat said.

"You know," Ed said, "at that last dinner, Eleanor Roosevelt asked me what my opinion of Charles Merriam was. I said I respected him. Didn't know I was measuring myself for the drop. Or that my best friend would deliver the sentence."

He really cares, I thought. Usually Ed was so even—in control. What to say? Find something positive.

"I suppose Margaret will be glad," I said. "And you can spend more time in Eagle River and—"

"No!" Just that—one word. Then Ed brought his fist down on his desk. Once. Twice. Three times.

"Anyone wants to take this job will have to fight me for it," Ed said.

"Dear God, Ed," I said, "you're too old to get into the ring."

"He doesn't mean a physical battle, Nora," Pat said, "although I'd like to see if the professor could take a punch."

He leaned across the desk toward Ed. "Though in Gaelic Ireland, when the clan gathered to select a chieftain and a candidate contested the decision, he could challenge the chosen one to single combat. And, you know which one won?" Pat was looking dead into Ed's eyes.

"The one who wanted it more," Ed said.

"That's right," said Pat. "Campaigning can be a grinding, humiliating experience. Asking for money, for favors, for votes. You're a proud man, Ed. You have the skills to be mayor—but do you have the fire in your belly?"

Now, Ed out of the mayor's office would have been a liberation for me. Rose had the Kelly kids well in hand. Nothing to stop me from heading over to Ireland and finding Peter Keeley's grave. But Ed deserved better than to be tossed to the side.

"Pat," Ed said. "I inherited that fire. None of our family would be alive today if not for the courage and passion of our granny Honora. Am I right, Nonie?" he asked.

"You are, Ed," I said.

"What's fighting an election compared to running for your life from starvation and oppression? We're Irish, Pat. We defeated the greatest empire in the world. I'll get the nomination, then I'll wipe the floor with Big Bill Thompson. I can't wait."

"Good on you, Ed," Pat said. "I'll call Farley and tell him the Cook County Democratic Party is backing Ed Kelly in the primary."

"No. I'll call Farley," Ed said. "And then I'll speak to the president himself."

"Good, Ed," I said. "You tell him off!"

"Not at all, Nonie," he said. "Don't we Kellys also have a talent for blarney? By the time I finish, Franklin Delano Roosevelt will be begging me to run."

And he was.

Edward J. Kelly won the Democratic primary on February 25, 1935—and the next day he took the train to Washington.

Now you'd think Ed would have been angry with the president for trying to supplant him, but really the whole incident only solidified Ed's support for Roosevelt.

"It takes a great man to change his mind," Ed told me after he saw the president. "And really, the president said, it was Mrs. Roosevelt who'd been pushing Merriam because of his commitment to helping the poor, especially Negroes."

Roosevelt, perhaps to make up for stabbing Ed in the back, agreed to approve a twenty-million-dollar plan to build a permanent exposition center on the site of the Century of Progress, which meant thirty thousand jobs. He also promised enough federal money to cover projects that included a subway, which would link downtown to the rest of the city and could put another one hundred thousand people to work.

Ed announced this windfall in the speech that opened his campaign. He explained that he was running for mayor to continue Chicago's economic recovery, which was all due to the New Deal.

"Roosevelt is my religion," he said to the packed city council chamber. Even the Republican aldermen cheered him, and their floor leader told the *Tribune* that there never had been a mayor who presided more impartially over the council than Ed Kelly did.

Thompson got the message and decided not to run for mayor. The only Republican willing to accept his party's nomination was a man called Emil Wetten, a fellow no one knew.

"We're away in a hack," Pat Nash said. A very different atmosphere in the office today. I had just finished taking photographs of Ed for a campaign poster. He had settled on a slogan, "Retain Mayor Kelly." Not snappy but informative, I thought.

Ed had gotten such a big vote in the primary that Pat suggested a very quiet campaign. All the newspapers had promised to endorse Ed, and the unions were with him also. So were the State Street merchants. Better not to spend money on rallies he didn't really need. After all it was still the Depression.

"I'd like to reach out to the Negro community," Ed said. "They voted for Roosevelt. They should support us. I told the president that no one was poorer than we had been and the Irish know what it's like to be discriminated against. We've more in common with colored people than men like Merriam who've never had to worry about where their next meal was coming from."

"Forget it, Ed. Cermak put the kibosh on any chance of winning those votes when he cracked down on the policy wheels," Pat Nash said.

"That was so stupid," Ed said. Cermak wanted to appear to be closing down gambling in the city but he had concentrated on the South and West Side numbers rackets in the Negro community. Hundreds of runners collected nickel-and-dime bets on a combination of numbers that were selected every day. Where once a wheel had been spun to choose the winners, now they were picked from a revolving canister. People hit their numbers with enough frequency to keep them playing and make it profitable for those running the racket. Cermak had the police arrest both the players and the bosses, none of whom were convicted. But this stirred up a great deal of resentment among members of the Negro community for whom playing the numbers was a part of everyday life. The police had not been gentle and people had been hurt. Ed had stopped the raids but the bad feelings continued.

"William Dawson would be the man to talk to," Pat Nash said. "The Second Ward has the biggest Negro population and he was elected alderman there with a big vote. But he's a staunch Republican and I noticed that he did not cheer your speech in the city council."

"But surely we know somebody that could set up a meeting," Ed said.

"What about Mr. Abbott at the *Defender*?" I said.

"The paper publishes Nora's photographs," Ed said. He turned to me. "Great idea."

Of course Ed knew Abbott too. The man had been editing and publishing one of the main Negro newspapers in the country for decades, but still Ed was grateful to me for making the initial phone call. Then he took over.

"Alright," Ed said after he finished his conversation with Abbott. "He'll set up the meeting with Dawson. Interesting man that Abbott. He told me that both his parents had been slaves in the Sea Islands off Georgia. After his father died, his mother married a German sea captain named Sengstacke who took them to live in Germany. Robert Abbot uses Sengstacke as his middle name, and the nephew he's grooming to take over is called John Sengstacke. Quite a story. He told me Dawson's family is also from Georgia."

Now this would have been the time to tell Ed that Margaret and I had met Dawson in Paris. But what if Dawson had completely forgotten about that chance encounter? Still I was glad when Ed invited me to come to his meeting with Dawson.

"If he agrees to support me, you can take a photograph of us and give it to the *Defender*. If they publish it, I'll send a copy to Mrs. Roosevelt," Ed said.

We got into Ed's city car and the driver headed south on the drive toward William Dawson's office. It was rare for me to have a moment alone with Ed, so I had to ask him, "When you're with the president, do you ever talk about Miami and the assassination?" I asked.

"Never. In fact, Roosevelt's secretary, Missy LeHand, specifically told me never to mention that night to him," Ed said.

"LeHand," I said. "Sounds like one of ours."

"Yes," Ed said. "She's Irish and so is her assistant, Grace Tully."

Roosevelt is smart enough to find two Irish Catholic women to devote themselves to him, I thought.

"But, what about the FBI investigation? Are they satisfied that Zangara acted alone?"

"Must be," Ed said.

"It always bothered me," I said, "that Zangara was tried, convicted, and executed within thirty days. I don't think he understood half of what was going on."

"Forget it, Nonie," Ed said. "He was just another misfit who got his hand on a gun like that fellow who killed Mayor Harrison. Easier to believe there was some grand conspiracy at work in these things. Harder to accept that one pathetic lunatic could have destroyed Roosevelt."

Move closer, I thought.

But now we were at William Dawson's law office which was a storefront on Wabash. A waiting room took up the whole front and every one of the twenty or so chairs was filled—men in suits, women with hats and gloves. Going to see a lawyer was serious business.

The receptionist sat at a desk in front of a wooden door with a frosted glass insert. Gold letters spelled out "William Levi Dawson, Esquire, Attorney at Law, Alderman Second Ward, Republican Committeeman, First Congressional District of Illinois."

She recognized Ed and stood up to greet us.

"Mr. Mayor," she said, "we were expecting you but you're early. Mr. Dawson is in with a client."

She was about my age and I'd say her suit came from the special collection at Fields—a mustard color that complemented her skin and hair.

"We're happy to wait," Ed said.

Now the other people waiting realized who was standing at her desk. One woman approached him.

"My name is Mrs. Doyle, Your Honor, and I've been a Republican all my life but I voted for Franklin Roosevelt. The next time you see him please tell him we appreciate all he's doing for people who need help. But there are still WPA projects that discriminate against colored people and I think he'd want to know."

"Of course he would, Mrs. Doyle," Ed answered. He saw that the others were listening.

"Franklin Roosevelt is my religion and I believe in the New Deal with all my heart, but there are many in this country who still harbor deep prejudices. When we Irish came to America we found signs saying 'No Irish Need Apply' on factory gates and printed in the newspapers."

And now some of the other people were listening and nodding.

"We know what that's like," one man said.

"I'll speak to the president and I myself will make sure that any company that applies for WPA funding for projects in the city agrees not to discriminate," Ed said.

"Well said, Mr. Mayor," William Dawson said. He stood as straight as that young lieutenant had all those years ago. Gray in his hair and maybe a few more pounds on his tall frame but he was still a good-looking man. I'd looked up the entry on him in the City Council Directory. He'd been born in 1886, so he was forty-eight, a few years younger than Ed or me. He'd attended Northwestern University Law School, and had been a practicing attorney for all these years.

Ed introduced me as his photographer and told Dawson that he hoped the two of them could pose for a picture together after their meeting.

"We'll see," Dawson said and led Ed into his office.

In less than a half an hour, Ed and Dawson were smiling into my camera. The deal had been done. I'll get the details on the ride home, I thought. But both men looked very satisfied.

"Thanks for coming down, Ed," Dawson said.

"You're welcome, Bill," Ed said.

They were on a first name basis now.

"I'd like to hold a rally for you in the Ward," Dawson said. "Let's fix a date."

"No rallies, Bill," Ed said. "Too many people are still suffering."

"Not sure about that, Ed," Dawson said. "Look at how they flock to the Fair. Sometimes a little diversion helps. One thing about Big Bill, he was entertaining."

And then Dawson sang a few bars of "Big Bill the Builder."

"Oh, no," I blurted out. Just hearing that made my skin crawl.

Dawson laughed and started to sing again only this time it was "How Ya Gonna Keep 'Em Down on the Farm After They've Seen Paree."

"So you do know," I said. "I wasn't sure if you remember meeting us in Paris."

"I do," Dawson said.

"And the other woman who was with me that day is Margaret Kelly, the mayor's wife."

"Quite a coincidence," Dawson said. "It makes me think, Ed, that you and I were fated to work together. Anything I can do, let me know, but you do need a theme song. What would Roosevelt have done without 'Happy Days Are Here Again'?"

I had to speak up.

"Well, Nora Bayes had another big hit that might work really well," I said.

"It was about a girl looking for her boyfriend but we could change the context into the people of Chicago looking for a champion."

I cleared my throat and began:

> Has anybody here seen Kelly?
> K-E-double-L-Y.
> Has anybody here seen Kelly?
> Have you seen him smile?
> Oh, his hair is red and his eyes are blue
> And he's Irish through and through.
> Has anybody here seen Kelly?
> Kelly from the Emerald Isle

All of Dawson's clients and staff applauded. They made me sing it again and this time they joined in.

"That's it, Ed. You're a sure thing," Dawson said as we left.

"Quite an afternoon," Ed said to me as we rode home. "An alliance and a campaign song. Dawson said he can't change his party affiliation officially until his term as alderman is up but then he'll announce that he's joined the Democratic Party and I will nominate him as a candidate for Congress. He'll be the most qualified man we've ever run and he'll win."

"And so will you," I said.

Ed smiled but didn't reply. A few minutes later, I saw that he'd taken his medal out and was rubbing it.

Praying, I thought. Good idea. And I said Hail Marys all the way back to the apartment.

"Be sure to tell Margaret that Dawson remembers us. That's a good omen," I said.

But signs, wonders, and even the Blessed Mother herself could not have prepared Ed for the dimensions of his victory. Edward J. Kelly was elected mayor by the largest majority in the history of the city. He got 799,060 votes, a number I remember because he put it on the license plate of his car. He carried all fifty Wards with 80 percent of the total vote. The Democratic Party increased its share in the Negro Wards by 60 percent.

"God bless Abraham Lincoln," Dawson said at Ed's victory celebration. "May he rest in peace, but I'd say we're Democrats now."

Depression or no Depression, we had what Ed called a helluva party. And believe me, everybody was singing, *"Has anybody here seen Kelly?"*

"I'm right here," Ed said in his speech, "and I am Irish through and through. I dedicate this victory to all our ancestors. We're alive because of them. Thank you, Honora Keeley Kelly."

So. What Pat Nash called "Ed's plurality" changed his relationship with FDR. Made him somehow equal. Chicago delivered the goods again during FDR's campaign in 1936. The President won a second term in a landslide with a big increase in the Negro vote, and Dawson formally became a Democrat. Ed's trips to Washington became more frequent.

"Hard to believe it, Nonie, but the president actually values my advice," Ed told me when he returned from one of these trips in September 1937.

"I'd say he needs all the help he can get," I said.

The world was falling apart. Ireland seemed very far away. No thought of traveling there now.

13

OCTOBER 1937

"You must tell the president Hitler is the Devil, Ed," Milton Goldman said. "First he'll murder all the Jews and then destroy the world."

Goldman had come to the mayor's office with his brother who'd recently arrived from Germany thanks to the visa Ed had arranged for him and his family. I was there to photograph the three of them, but Milton had lost the run of himself. He kept shouting at Ed, "Hitler must be stopped. America must act now." The brother was nodding. His whole body moving back and forth.

"Easy, Milton. Easy. You have to understand the president's position. Hitler was democratically elected," Ed said. "Most of the country thinks we've got no business getting involved with Europe. Congress has passed two neutrality acts. By law Roosevelt cannot intervene. Nobody wants a repeat of the Great War."

"But Ed," Goldman said, "my brother says the German Army has been tripled. Hitler has bought off the people with jobs and a promise to make Germany great again. It's like Mussolini getting the trains to run on time. Ignorant people are blinding themselves to the real threat."

"Some smart people, too," Ed said. "Colonel McCormick brought Charles Lindbergh into my office the other day. They're starting this America First Committee to keep us out of war. They wanted me to join."

"No, Ed," Goldman said, "you can't."

"I told them I'd think about it, but I think you're right, Milton. Bullies like Hitler and Mussolini don't ever have enough. Roosevelt knows that. It's just that his hands are tied."

"But the president must speak up," Goldman said.

"He will," Ed answered.

"When?" Goldman asked.

"Soon," Ed said. "Right here in Chicago. You and your brother will have front row seats."

The Outer Drive had finally been completed. A bridge connected South Shore Drive to the northern portion of the highway. One unbroken Lake Shore Drive. A great achievement because Chicago was a divided city. The North and South Sides didn't even support the same baseball team. If you'd been born south of State Street, you rooted for the White Sox; if you came from the North Side, you were a Cubs fan. Only an accident of birth but a mark of difference nonetheless. But now the bridge would be tangible proof that the city could become one.

When Ed pointed out to Roosevelt that the bridge had been built with money from the New Deal, the president agreed to come for the opening ceremonies. I don't think even Ed knew that FDR would deliver what would come to be called his "Quarantine Speech."

A gorgeous fall day. Ed stood in the center on the stage, surrounded by every important person in the city. The Goldmans were in the front row as promised.

Ed's introduction was full of praise for the president. He concluded by saying, "He is your hero and mine. The man who taught us not to fear, who led us from darkness into light, President Franklin Delano Roosevelt."

President Roosevelt moved haltingly to the podium on the arm of a Secret Service agent. He took Ed's hand. I got a great photograph of the two men together. Ed stepped back and the president began to speak.

He started in the most conventional fashion.

"I am glad to come once again to Chicago. And especially to have the opportunity of taking part in this important project of civic government. On my trip across our country I have been shown many evidences of the results of common sense cooperation between municipalities and the federal government. And I have been greeted by tens of thousands of Americans who have told me in every look and word that their material and spiritual well-being has made great strides forward in the past few years."

Ed led the applause, and the cheers that came from twenty thousand people bounced off the Wrigley Building and Tribune Tower itself where Colonel McCormick was probably looking down at the gathering in disgust. But the crowd agreed with Roosevelt. The worst was over.

The president continued, speaking about the prosperity he'd been seeing across the country. But then his pace slowed. His words were very deliberate. He said that he had chosen "this great inland city and this gala occasion to speak on a subject of definite national importance."

The political situation in the world was a cause of grave concern and anxiety. FDR said that although fifteen years ago sixty nations had signed a peace pact agreeing not to "resort to arms to further their national aims," a reign of terror and international lawlessness had now begun. He said that the very foundations of civilization were being threatened.

"Without a declaration of war and without warning or justification of any kind, civilians, including vast numbers of women and children, are being ruthlessly murdered with bombs from the air. In times of so-called peace, ships are being attacked and sunk by submarines without cause or notice."

The crowd went silent. "Innocent people," Roosevelt said, "innocent nations, are being cruelly sacrificed to greed for power and supremacy, which are devoid of all sense of justice and humane considerations." He warned "every treasure garnered through two millennia will be lost or wrecked or utterly destroyed."

Roosevelt clutched the podium supported by those iron leg braces, but really held up by his own will. He thundered the next words.

"If those things come to pass in other parts of the world let no one imagine that America will escape, that America may expect mercy, that this western hemisphere will not be attacked and that it will continue tranquilly and peacefully to carry on the ethics and arts of civilization. If those days come there will be no safety by arms. The storm will rage 'til every flower of culture is trampled and all human beings are leveled in vast chaos."

Something must be done, Roosevelt told us.

"It seems to be unfortunately true that the epidemic of world lawlessness is spreading. When an epidemic of physical disease starts to spread, the community approves and joins in a quarantine of the patients in order to protect the health of the community against the spread of disease . . . War is a contagion whether it is declared or undeclared . . . We are determined to keep out of war yet we cannot insure ourselves against the disastrous effects of war and the dangers of involvement. If civilization is to survive, the principles of the Prince of Peace must be restored. Most important of all, the will for peace must express itself to the end that nations that may be tempted to violate their agreements and the rights of others will desist from such a course . . . America hates war. America hopes for peace, therefore America actively engages in the search for peace."

When Roosevelt concluded his speech, once again Ed led the applause. He shook Roosevelt's hand, smiled for the newsreel cameras, directed the president toward me. Ed gestured at Milton Goldman who stepped up along with his brother. I heard him say to the president, "Thank you."

Then all hell broke loose. The *Tribune* called Roosevelt a warmonger. But Ed stood firm. Every time he gave a speech, whether he was opening a new Park District field office or the guest of honor at a Knights of Columbus dinner, Ed talked about Hitler and Mussolini. He didn't pussyfoot around like Roosevelt had—railing against the forces of terror and lawlessness but not naming names—Ed was blunt. "We Irish," he'd say, "know what it is like to have a tyrant's boot on our necks. One million of us starved to death because we were too weak to fight back, while the rest of the world turned a blind eye. But we're strong now. America gave us our chance. We stood up for the people of Ireland and helped them win their independence. And now other forces are threatening to destroy people who cannot defend themselves. We must not sit on the sideline. We have to prepare ourselves—not only militarily but in our minds and spirits."

Word of these speeches got to the president. Ed had scared Roosevelt. The mayor was being too blunt. The isolationists who were shouting "America First" were very powerful.

I was there in Ed's office when the call from the president came through. "You want to get me impeached?" he asked Ed, shouting over the telephone. I heard Ed say, "You have to be straight with the people. Let them know that it won't just be the working people, the little guy, who will make the sacrifices when war comes. Tell them that the whole country will act together. The rich as well as everyone else. The voters aren't stupid. They know things are bad. They just want to be sure that someone they believe in will lead them and tell them the truth. That has to be you."

Ed listened, shaking his head. When he hung up he said to me, "Roosevelt said that with only two years left in his term there was only so much he could do. Most of the Republicans aren't getting involved in a European war. So if they win the next election . . ."

Dear God, I thought, I couldn't imagine the country without Roosevelt as our leader.

In April 1939, Ed was reelected with 55 percent of the vote, a landslide in any normal election, but a red flag in Chicago. His vote had gone down.

"You see?" Ed said. "Voters don't always think that deeply. They like variety. They were loyal to Roosevelt but will they support another Democrat for president? I'm scared," he said to me.

We were in his office, a week after his inauguration. Roosevelt's second term would end in a year, and that would be that. How could the party find any kind of comparable candidate to run in 1940?

"James Farley thinks the nomination is his by right. And there's a few other guys that are going to try for it. Why don't they just back off. If there were no other candidates the president would have to run again," Ed said. "Nothing in the constitution says that FDR couldn't serve a third term. We need him."

And did we ever. In September, Hitler invaded Czechoslovakia and the world tipped into war, except for the United States. Most Republicans were against getting American involved in a European war. Public opinion supported them. What if a Republican became president and we turned our backs on the world? Let Hitler rule Europe? It didn't bear thinking about. Only Roosevelt could mobilize the nation, but he was getting ready to retire to Hyde Park.

Ed had a plan to change the president's mind. First, he would convince the Democratic National Committee to have the convention in Chicago that summer. He did, winning approval by one vote, in February. He had until July to convince Roosevelt to run again. But Roosevelt himself was Ed's biggest obstacle.

In June, Ed came back from Washington in despair. I was having coffee with him in his kitchen. Margaret and the kids were in Eagle River.

"The president is worried about how history will judge him. I told him we don't have time for history. If he doesn't lead this country, history will be over. But sitting in the Oval Office does something to a man. Roosevelt kept telling me that George Washington walked away after two terms when the country would have made him king. I guess Washington gave some speech about how no president should serve more than two terms."

"Well," I said, "that puts it in perspective. A hundred and fifty years of tradition and George Washington is the father of our country."

"Yeah," Ed said. "Well he's dead and buried and if he were alive I wouldn't trust him to turn out the vote in the Eleventh Ward." I laughed at the image of George Washington going door to door in Bridgeport. Ed was sure that Roosevelt really wanted a third term but he was being coy. He had to appear to be forced by the convention to accept the nomination.

Ed asked me to stay in the city. He wanted me to photograph him with various delegates—a good way to disguise his politicking. "And I'm going to need some moral support to pull this off, Nonie."

"Of course," I said. "Glad to be asked, and excited to be part of this crusade. The redheads to the rescue!" He managed a smile.

July 15, 1940, was the first night of the Democratic convention. Ed welcomed the delegates with a speech that praised Roosevelt. They had to nominate the president. That was the only way to save the country.

But the next day Roosevelt himself put the kibosh on Ed's efforts. It was early evening when the chairman of the convention, Alben Barkley, stepped up and read a statement from the president:

"Tonight at the specific request and authorization of the president, I am making this simple fact clear to the convention: the president has never had, and has not today, any desire or purpose to continue in the office of president, to be a candidate for that office, or to be nominated by the convention for that office. He wishes in all earnestness and sincerity that all delegates to this convention are free to vote for any candidate. This is the message I bear to you from the president of the United States."

"Oh my God," I said to Ed. I was standing next to him on the convention floor. I must have taken his picture with twenty different delegates, as he went from state to state, talking up Roosevelt's nomination. "So that's it. It's over."

"Oh no, it's not," Ed said.

Now what happened next has been turned into a tall tale. The newspapers joked about "The Voice from the Sewer" who stampeded the convention for Roosevelt, but believe me, what Ed accomplished was significant. In fact, if I saved Roosevelt's life by telling Cermak to move closer, Ed may have saved the world by ensuring FDR's nomination. I mean can you imagine if Jim Farley had been president when the Japs attacked Pearl Harbor?

That night, July 16, 1940, there must have been eighteen thousand people with us in the stadium—a big barn of a place, in a literal sense, the venue for rodeos and horse shows as well as prize fights and every kind of sporting event. The state delegations were set up on the floor of the stadium where cowboys had ridden bulls and lassoed calves. The delegates were packed together and though there were folding chairs, most of them stood chatting to each other and moving across state lines. Each group had a chairman whose job was to keep them in order and round up votes. After Barkley read Roosevelt's statement everything stopped.

I stood with Ed behind the Illinois delegation. I'd photographed him with various members, but now the whole back row turned to look at Ed. What now? He smiled, pointed up toward the balconies. The seats up there were filled with city workers. The Streets and Sanitation Department had sent every garbage truck driver, every maintenance worker, and all their paper pushers over to the stadium. Off-duty cops and firemen had joined them as well as building inspectors and the staff of every single one of the fifty ward offices. Five thousand people at least.

Now from every loudspeaker in the stadium a voice boomed out filling the entire place: "We want Roosevelt. We want Roosevelt."

Ed raised his hands as if he were a band leader and drew an arc in the air. The fellows in the gallery above turned to their people. "We want Roosevelt. We want Roosevelt," they began to chant. Then they marched out of the balconies, down the ramps and onto the floor of the stadium, stamping their feet while they bellowed, "We want Roosevelt. We want Roosevelt."

"What happened," I yelled to Ed. "Who was that voice?"

"Tom Garry is in the basement," he shouted.

"The guy who's head of Streets and Sanitation?"

Ed nodded.

All around me the chants of "We want Roosevelt. We want Roosevelt" got louder. Then the organ started to play "Happy Days Are Here Again" in counterpoint to the shouting. This was no ordinary organ. Over one thousand pipes up there and the organist could mimic any instrument. Now we heard trumpets, bass drums, tubas. All those men in dark suits and the white shirts their wives had so carefully ironed began to dance. Yes, dance.

Conga lines broke out all over the floor. Jackets were thrown off. Ties were loosened. "We want Roosevelt. We want Roosevelt. Happy days are here again."

Yes, we knew that France had surrendered the month before and that the Nazis were probably going to invade England. The world was going to hell in a handbasket. But here in the Chicago Stadium there was hope, defiance. "We want Roosevelt. We want Roosevelt." Screw George Washington. Forget 150 years of tradition. Ignore all objections to a third term. Roosevelt was our religion and we were like some sect of ecstatic worshippers, whirling and singing and pounding our fears away. Hadn't the Holy Spirit on Pentecost transformed a band of terrified men into the fellows who would change the world? Not many saints among the delegates but they were on fire. The demonstration lasted an hour and I found myself hanging on to Ed's waistband as we joined a line that snaked in and out of the delegations. And there was William Dawson, three people ahead of us. "FDR, FDR." Roosevelt was going to be nominated, like it or not.

And of course Ed knew that the president really wanted the nomination.

He was determined to serve another term, but only some kind of spectacular event could allow him to accept.

"You did it, Ed. You did it," I said as we stopped to take a breath. But there are just some men that don't understand what's happening before their very eyes. Jim Farley got up to the podium, pounded the gavel, and tried to call the convention to order. Pounding and pounding until finally the singing and the chanting subsided.

"We are a democratic institution," he said. "We have a very serious task. We must nominate a candidate and it cannot be Franklin Delano Roosevelt."

"Convention adjourned," Ed shouted out. And voices from all the delegations joined in. "Convention adjourned." What could Farley do? He adjourned the convention. The organ started up again and we all filed out singing "Happy Days Are Here Again."

It was after midnight. Later I heard that the taverns and bars surrounding the stadium did more business that night than they had since Prohibition ended six years before. Happy days indeed.

The next day Franklin Delano Roosevelt was nominated by acclamation. It was Eleanor Roosevelt who addressed the convention. Softer looking in person than her photographs, but her voice had a high-pitched and listen-to-me-dear quality that would become so familiar on the radio. Mrs. Roosevelt delivered the president's message. These were no ordinary times, she told the assembly. Eighteen months later our sense of the ordinary collapsed completely. The Japanese attacked Pearl Harbor and we joined the rest of the world—at war.

PART III

THE WAR

1

APRIL 1942

"She's not a hundred percent Irish, but she has two brothers who are priests," Rose said when she introduced me to Mariann Williams, Mike's fiancée, that Easter Sunday at the apartment on Yates. Fiancée! And they would marry in June. Impossible to believe that the little boy who guarded his mother's door against death was now a soldier in this endless war. Not a soldier exactly, thank God, not one of those poor Army fellows chasing Rommel through the deserts of North Africa, or, even worse, among the Marines getting slaughtered on South Pacific islands. Mike was in the Navy. Not on a ship but as a pilot, a naval aviator.

"Princes of the sky," one woman had told Rose and me when we'd gone to Naval Air Station Pensacola in Florida for his graduation from flight school last month. Rose had pinned wings of gold onto Mike's navy blue uniform. Both she and I sniffed back tears, thinking of Mame, her sister, my pal, his mother. Mike told me he remembered her. Rose had always kept that family portrait Mabel Sykes had taken front and center in the apartment on Yates Avenue.

Now young Mike was an officer and a gentleman by order of the president of the United States and the Navy. Handsome and fit in his uniform with the brass buttons shining and a gold stripe on his sleeve, he was a lieutenant, JG. Mike told me that meant "junior grade," but he would soon become a second lieutenant. He was assigned to Floyd Bennett Field in Brooklyn where he'd be escorting the ships carrying men and supplies across the

Atlantic. The sea was full of Nazi U-boats, he said, and they'd been sinking American merchant ships a mile outside of New York Harbor.

"They were using the lights of the Coney Island roller coaster as a beacon," Mike told me when he came home on leave that Easter of 1942. But now the Navy was taking on the U-boats. He said the ships were traveling in convoys protected by special Navy vessels, with Mike flying above watching out for the submarines.

"I have special equipment that lets me see the U-boats. I notify one of the escort vessels and they drop depth charges, and then I let go with a bomb. One less member of Hitler's wolf pack," he said. "My job is to make sure the convoy gets safely to Derry."

"Derry?" I'd said. "What do you mean?"

"Naval Operating Base, Londonderry. That's the homeport of the destroyer escorts that shepherd the convoys across the ocean. It's the largest naval base in the European theater. I hear they have a state-of-the-art ship repair yard and a very modern hospital."

"Derry, Ireland?" I'd said.

"Well Northern Ireland," he'd said. "Part of Britain."

"Don't say that, Mike."

"Say what?"

"Part of Britain. Derry is in the north of Ireland. It's only a political accident that it's not united with the rest of the island and it will be one day."

"Funny, Aunt Nonie, that's what the fellows stationed there call the place. North Ireland. It's the brass who insist on 'Northern Ireland.'"

"I've never heard of this base. I would have noticed if there was something in the newspapers," I said.

"Oh the whole operation was top secret. The Seabees started building it six months before Pearl Harbor, but they wore civilian clothes. President Roosevelt didn't want the isolationists here to know what he was up to, but we were bound to get into the war and the Navy convinced him that it took time to get a base up and running. We aren't the Army where you can throw up a few tents and call it a camp, or the Marines who just sleep on the ground," Mike said.

Derry, the town that had welcomed me and my committee of Quakers when we were investigating Black and Tan atrocities in Ireland. This was before the treaty of 1922 when Britain accepted Irish independence on the condition that the more Protestant parts of the island would remain united with the crown. Then Derry had been firmly part of Ireland. The market town of Donegal, Father Kevin's county.

"Of course my plane doesn't have the range to go all the way across, so I turn over escort duty to a fellow who flies out of an airport near the base. It's called Ballykelly. How's that for a coincidence, Aunt Nonie? Though," he'd said and stopped.

"Though what?" I asked.

"Well there's talk that we'll be refueling in Gander and sent on to Ireland. Wouldn't that be something, Aunt Nonie? Me in Ireland. But I'm not supposed to talk about operational matters."

Better to concentrate on introducing us to his girl. All of us in the Yates apartment. Rose had cooked Mike's favorite meal—roast beef, browned potatoes, green beans with devil's food cake for dessert.

A lovely girl, Mariann. She was twenty-two to Mike's twenty-six. Reminded me a bit of Gene Tierney but with unusual eyes, a kind of golden-brown color that matched her hair. Smallish, nearly a foot shorter than Mike, and slim. Mike had told me she was a fine tennis player. Beat him regularly.

After dinner as we sat at the table, talking, I watched how Mariann listened to Rose, then got up to refill Rose's empty coffee cup. Mike's sisters were chatting to each other but aware of Mariann too.

"Mariann has lovely manners," I said to Mike, who was next to me. "I look forward to meeting her parents."

"Her father," Mike said. "Mare's mother died when she was ten." We looked at each other.

"Very sad," I said. "You both . . ."

"Yes, we have that bond," he said. Mothers loved and lost. A bond indeed.

They'd met at DePaul University before the war when it still seemed life would follow some kind of known pattern. Before the war—the phrase that divided everything. Mike had been on his way to becoming a lawyer like so many of the next-generation Chicago-Irish. Their grandfathers had been laborers like our great-uncle Patrick, digging the canals, laying the railroad tracks, piling brick upon brick, building Chicago not once but twice, bringing it back after it burned to the ground. Their sons were fellows like Ed Kelly and my brother Michael. They'd scratched their way up with no education to speak of. Politics was one possible path. Now their sons and daughters too were going to college, learning professions. They would be doctors, lawyers with degrees and credentials.

I knew Mike himself wanted nothing so much as to take the family business one step further. Senator Michael J. Kelly, and then, well, advisor to the president? He was always interested in stories of Joseph Kennedy and his boys.

And Mariann? Not a hundred percent Irish. Her mother was German and gone out of her life so young Mariann probably had to raise herself. She had eight brothers and one much older sister married and living out of town. Mike had told me Mariann was the baby of the family. Not easy among all those men to become such a fashionable girl. She seemed unaware of the nets of expectation that still held down so many young women. Not worried about what the ladies of the parish thought. Not trapped in our world. She'd gone off to DePaul University with no Henrietta-type warnings about vanity and getting above yourself. An innocent in regard to jealousy and begrudgery, to judge from the way she ignored the digs Rosemary, who had imbibed bits of Henrietta, threw out.

"You and Mike have known each other for years," Rosemary said. "Why did it take you so long to say yes to him? But then I suppose you dated a lot of men in the meantime."

"Sure," Mariann said. "Very nice fellows too, but Mike and I always . . ." She smiled up at Mike and he grinned back at her, which seemed to infuriate Rosemary.

"Always what? You know Mike has had girlfriends too. One a daughter of a judge who was a very close friend of our uncle, Mayor Edward J. Kelly."

"Not uncle, Rosemary," I said. "Cousin." I turned to Mariann. "Ed's father, Stephen, and my father, Patrick, were brothers brought here from Ireland by our granny Honora. She and her sister Máire saved their children from starving to death when—" and Rosemary interrupted me.

"Oh, Aunt Nonie, don't start with those old stories. Mariann isn't interested."

"But I am," Marian said turning to me.

"Another time," I said because I could see Rosemary was picking up a head of steam and there was no point in trying to divert her.

"I work in the mayor's office," Rosemary said, "and I've always called him Uncle Ed. After all we're his blood relatives." She looked over at Mariann. "His own children are adopted."

"Rosemary, please," I said.

"It's no secret," she said. "Though I suppose Aunt Margaret would have preferred to have her own kids. Still she treats the three of them like some kind of a royal family. The clothes she bought for Pat only to have her turn her back on everything and enter the convent. What a pity to leave that wardrobe, but then Pat has always been different. Not one bit interested in clothes even when her mother took her shopping in New York. Where did you buy your dress, Mariann?"

"Fields," she said.

"Mmmm," Rosemary said. "Very fancy. Mike said you work as a secretary in a bank. Don't imagine your salary would cover an outfit like that. Did all those boys you dated give you presents?"

Well that was too much for me. "Rosemary, don't be rude," I said.

"I'm just trying to get to know Mike's fiancée," she said, drawing out the syllables. But it was Frances, the youngest and quietest of the girls who spoke up.

"Rosemary doesn't like it that you're prettier and younger than she is, Mariann." She stood up, walked over and patted Mariann's arm. "You mustn't mind Rosemary, she's trying to be an actress and is always putting on little plays with us in supporting roles."

Mike laughed.

"That's telling her, Fran." He turned to Rosemary. "Mariann grew up with eight brothers. You won't be able to get under her skin."

Rose had gone into the kitchen. I was glad she hadn't heard Rosemary attack Mariann. For her the girls could do no wrong and Mike was the prince.

"Another helping of dessert, Mike?" She had a plate with a slice of devil's food cake with buttercream icing.

Rosemary tried one last jab. "Better go easy, Mike," and then she said to Mariann, "Of course you knew that he had to lose forty pounds to qualify for flight training school." She turned back to Mike. "If you get fat again and they throw you out of the Navy you might lose your fiancée. Come on, Miss Williams, confess, wasn't it the uniform and gold wings that finally made you say yes?"

And Mariann smiled. "No, it was when Mike told me how much he loved his aunts and his sisters. What strong women they were and how grateful he was to them. I always promised myself I'd only marry a man who appreciated women," she said. "Who saw us for what we were."

"Point, set, and match, Rosemary," Mike said. I started laughing. The girls joined in. Rose touched Rosemary's shoulder. "Okay, okay," Rosemary said. "Welcome to our family and good luck. You're going to need it."

As I left, Mike asked me if Ed would have time to meet Mariann and would I arrange it.

"Her brother Jim produces shows at the Auditorium Theater and is a big supporter of the Democratic Party. Two of her brothers are sailors, one in Alaska and the other with the fleet in Pearl Harbor. Then there are the two priests, Jim and the other three are too old to serve. They're all businessmen," Mike said.

"Oh," I said. "What kind of business?"

"Well that's the thing. They own liquor stores and bars."

"Oh," I said. I lowered my voice. "I don't care, but have you told Rose? She still wears her husband John's Pioneer pin and has never had a drink herself."

"I haven't, but Uncle Ed should know in case he doesn't—"

"For heaven's sake, Mike, Ed's not a prude. After all, liquor's legal and it's our bars that have made Chicago the most popular liberty town in the country."

"Yes, well, I think Mariann's brothers got into the liquor business pretty early."

"Ah," I said. "During Prohibition?"

He nodded.

"But of course you've got those aces in the hole," I said.

"The two brothers who are priests?"

"Yes," I said. "And Mariann herself."

We waited for Ed outside the radio studio set up in a room at the top of city hall. Every day the mayor broadcast at noon for five minutes, and all the radio stations in the city carried the program. Ed was head of Civil Defense for the entire Midwest region and so he could talk about any topic that contributed to the war effort at home. Ten seconds of the song "Keep the Home Fires Burning" introduced each program, though once Ed had used almost the entire time to play Kate Smith singing "Johnny Doughboy Found a Rose in Ireland," the number one song on the hit parade in March 1942. The first US expeditionary force headed to Europe to push out the Nazis had landed in Belfast and would undergo training in the north of Ireland. Tens of thousands of American soldiers wore the soup bowl helmets of World War I and were still called doughboys.

They'd been plopped down in the middle of a population of one million spread out through every village. Quite a ratio especially considering that so many of the fellows were Irish-American. The song described how they heard their mothers' brogue in the voices of the girls they met. And didn't distinguish the north of Ireland from the south. Johnny fell in love and "Wanted to make an American beauty of his Irish Rose." Ed had gotten a great kick out of "Johnny Doughboy Found a Rose in Ireland" and so had his listeners, who sent thousands of packages to the troops, encouraged by Ed.

"And be sure to include Milky Ways and Baby Ruths," he'd said. "Those people of North Ireland have been feeling the effects of the war for four years. With sugar rationed, many Irish kids have never even tasted a candy bar." That show had gotten the biggest response of any and the city hall switchboard couldn't handle all the requests. How could people send candy directly to the children, the callers had wondered. Ed had turned to me, "You're the expert on Ireland," he'd said. "What do we do?"

"Go to the cardinal," I'd said. And sure enough Cardinal Stritch had called Cardinal John D'Alton, Primate of All Ireland, who was still located in Armagh, St. Patrick's city, and he sent us a list of Catholic schools so Ed could broadcast the addresses.

"And, of course, the children will invite their little Protestant friends to share the sweets," Ed assured the listeners. Johnny Doughboy was busy alright, and now Mike had told me the Navy was in Ireland too.

Now we heard Ed conclude the program with an announcement of a free concert in Grant Park. The Chicago Symphony would be playing popular songs from Broadway musicals. All visiting servicemen were welcome, he said. "And your mayor expects the citizens of the city of Chicago to show them every kindness."

Ed had turned a twenty-story office building on Madison into a USO with free food and lodging for any service member on leave. All transportation in the city was free too. He'd made Margaret and Lucky Davis co-chairwomen of the USO in Chicago, charging them with providing entertainment for the soldiers. There was another center on the South Side that was just as nice, he'd assured me, that was for Negro soldiers and sailors.

"Segregation?" I'd asked Ed. "That's terrible."

"The Department of Defense insisted on separate facilities. They're afraid of offending Southern servicemen who are not accustomed to mixing with Negroes," he'd said.

"And Congressman Dawson went along with that?"

"What could he do? I explained the situation. Told him their center would have a big budget and that he would recommend the companies that would supply furniture and beds and linen. All the food would come from South Side restaurants." The city would also contribute $10,000 to the Bud Billiken Parade, in which the Negro soldiers and sailors would march.

"Mmmmm," I'd said.

Now the door of the studio opened and Ed stepped out, still talking over his shoulder to the technician. "WGN wants to rebroadcast the program at eleven p.m. so be sure to send a tape over to them," he said.

Very technological now, our Ed. He stopped when he saw me with Mike and Mariann. I'd told him to expect us and he reached out and took Mariann's hand in both of his.

"Well," Ed said, "you're a lucky man, Mike."

Mariann smiled at him. She was used to having her good looks acknowledged, I thought, but I'd hoped Ed would see her strength and character. Ed had always been supportive of me and now he was in charge of defense plants where girls as young as eighteen worked on the assembly line making aircraft parts by pounding rivets into B-52s.

Mariann did look lovely in her gray wool suit with a fitted jacket and slim skirt. Very self-possessed as she shook Ed's hand. She didn't gush but said, "You're a hero in my house, Mr. Mayor. My father said you saved the city from bankruptcy and my brother Jim thinks no one but you could have corralled all the transit companies and gotten the money to finally build a subway in Chicago."

Mike spoke up. "Mariann's family is from the West Side. Austin. Isn't that Tom Casey's district?"

"Oh, we know the Williams brothers," Ed said.

Yikes! Was he going to go straight to the bootlegging stories? Make some joke? I hadn't told him much about Mariann's family but five minutes with any West Side alderman and he'd know everything. I saw Mariann stiffen.

Ed still held her hand. "Such a blessing to have two brothers priests," he said. "Viatorian fathers, aren't they?" Sometimes I really do love my cousin Ed.

He took us to lunch at Henrici's and invited Mariann's oldest brother, Jim, a regular there, to join our table.

Jim and Ed started to reminisce about the old days of Prohibition, and Jim told us how two of his younger brothers would deliver three bottles of bonded whiskey every Saturday night to a certain rectory. They wouldn't go to the door but would leave their car in the driveway with the trunk unlocked while they made a visit to the church. They'd return to find the trunk empty.

"A donation?" Ed asked.

"Well, a healthy discount."

They laughed. Chicago men full of tall tales about how tough they had been.

But Mariann and I held our own. She said Mike had shown her my photographs from the Century of Progress in an old edition of the *Chicagoan* and asked how I'd started my career. Nice to hear the word "career." The whole table listened as I told a few stories of my time in Paris, taking pictures of American tourists and the gowns created by the great women couturiers. But then I stopped. "Poor, poor Paris," I said. By unspoken agreement we'd avoided talking about the war. But there it was. We'd all seen the newsreels of Hitler posing in front of the Arc de Triomphe, bringing darkness to the City of Light. He'd made the French sign surrender papers in the same railroad car where the Germans had agreed to the armistice in 1919 after the "war to end all wars." Still unbelievable that only twenty years later here were the same horrors, only much worse.

"Sorry," I said. "I didn't want to spoil our lunch with . . ."

"We'll drive the Nazis out, Aunt Nonie," Mike said. "You'll have your Paris back again. You will."

"And I hope you'll come with Mike and me. He's promised we'll go to Paris one day. Wouldn't it be wonderful if you were our guide?"

"Yes," I said. "As the Irish say, 'God willing.'"

"We're getting married in New York," Mariann said. She and Rose and I were having lunch in the Walnut Room at Fields. May now, 1942. The Nazis held Europe in their iron fist while the Japanese were winning battle after battle on the Pacific islands whose exotic names hid devastating US casualties. Bataan, Corregidor, and the whole of the Philippines.

Mike was still stationed at Floyd Bennett Field in Brooklyn, New York, flying escort duty for the convoys crossing the Atlantic in ever-greater numbers. U-boats were still out there torpedoing ships and then surfacing to shoot at US planes with ever more sophisticated antiaircraft guns.

Mariann told us that two fellows in Mike's group had simply disappeared. No real explanation, Mike had told her. It happens, he'd said. Some kind of malfunction and they just drop into the ocean.

Mariann was pushing the mandarin orange sections in her Ambrosia salad around on her plate as she talked. She touched the engagement ring on her finger. Not a big diamond but nicely cut so the facets picked up the light, making rainbows on the starched white Fields tablecloth.

"Mike won't talk much but he said there are rumors that his squadron might go to the Pacific, be assigned to aircraft carriers. My brother Jim told me that there were lots of casualties even during training on aircraft carriers," Mariann said.

"That wasn't very helpful," I said.

"No," she said. "I think Jim wants me to wait to get married in case . . ." She stopped.

"Yes, well," I said. I looked at Rose. Widows both of us and yet did either one of us regret the time we'd been married? Would we have spared ourselves the sorrow of losing our young husbands? I tried to find something to say to Mariann but it was Rose who spoke up.

"Mariann, with so much sorrow in the world it seems to me we have to hold on to joy whenever it comes. And we do have our faith to lean on. I was at the novena at Our Lady of Sorrows last night. Full to the rafters with mothers, wives, sisters of servicemen."

The novena had become so popular that Ed set aside twenty city buses to pick up people at churches all over the city to take them to the big basilica on Jackson Boulevard each Tuesday. The Servite priests there put on especially good services.

I remembered how Aunt Máire used to tease Granny Honora about her pilgrimages to every church in the city during the Civil War. Granny would light candles in each one, traveling miles and miles. Walking. No city buses to take you in those days. She'd begin in St. Bridget's, then on to St. James, Holy Family, Immaculate Conception, downtown for Holy Name, St. Barbara's Lithuanian Church, St. Jerome where the Croatians went, St. Joseph's with an Italian congregation, St. Agnes in Brighton Park, praying that her sons would come home and safe. "Didn't save my Johnny Óg," Aunt Máire had said to me.

Best not to think about that. Can't ask Rose, What will these women do if their prayers fail? Gold star mothers, the women who'd lost their sons were called. They were given a banner to hang in their front windows. More and more of these appearing in the city. Little comfort, I thought. But I said none of this as I ate my chicken salad. It was here in the Walnut Room that I'd taken Margaret to convince her to consider marrying my cousin Ed. Nearly twenty years ago now. Neither of us with any idea of what was in store for her. No sense that she'd be the First Lady of Chicago in charge of every variety of women's war relief committee with her own son serving in the Navy and a husband running back and forth to the White House.

"I think you and Mike are right to get married now," I said. "Mike's a smart fellow. He's brave, but not reckless. He'll be okay."

"Mike said there are old pilots and bold pilots, but no old bold pilots," Mariann said.

We laughed but I thought about what it must be to land on an aircraft carrier. Imagine trying to touch down on a platform rocking in the ocean. Mariann was explaining that Mike had told her the planes had hooks and they had to catch a steel line stretched across the deck, or else they'd go over into the ocean.

"The worst part is when they have to land at dusk," she said. "It's hard to see the difference between the sea and the sky."

"Does Mike think he can learn to do this?"

"Yes, he does. He told me he has no intention of dying and that I was really going to enjoy living in Brooklyn and that New York City was an incredible place. I did have a good time there when I went to visit him last month, though Mike wanted to go to some cowboy play on my very first night in town. He'd met a fellow whose wife had a part in the show and gave Mike tickets for opening night. I told him I wasn't going to waste my first night watching cowboys. The musical was *Oklahoma!*." She shook her head. "If only I'd known."

We laughed—please God, Mike would stay in Brooklyn. The next Tuesday I started going to the novena at Our Lady of Sorrows.

"What is so rare as a day in June?" Sister Ruth Eileen would quote that to us when the sun finally came back to Chicago. We would smother our classroom May altar with the lilacs that had just managed to bloom during the month dedicated to Our Lady. Sister told us May festivals represented Irish monks' effort to Christianize the Celtic Feast of Bealtaine, which marked the beginning of summer.

"An optimistic people, our ancestors," she'd said, "as the good weather often didn't arrive until July."

But I'd learned from Peter Keeley that temperature didn't matter. What was being celebrated was the Earth's flowering. The great goddess asserting her power. The seed potatoes planted in March were now tall green plants with purple flowers. Life returning. Except for the years when the green turned black and the great goddess had seemed to desert her people.

But that was another story. Because today we had our victory. Today Michael Joseph Kelly, who carried the name of the great-grandfather who died struggling to keep his family alive, was standing at the altar of the Lady Chapel in St. Patrick's Cathedral in his white naval officer's uniform, waiting for his bride, with another flyer standing next to him and three more in the side pew—each one so young-looking. Mariann's brother Father Frank Williams stood at the altar under the statue of Our Lady of New York. He was staying at the cathedral rectory along with her other priest, brother Father Charles. The Viatorians were teachers, and both were training to become college professors. I'd been surprised when I heard Mariann call Father Frank, who was quite distinguished looking, "Snooky." This was his family nickname. She told me that he'd been involved in show business working for NBC Radio before he entered the order. While he was a student at St. Patrick High School he'd sung in the choir and appeared in all the school plays. When Rose and I had gone to dinner at Mariann's father's apartment in Austin, where she and two brothers lived, Father Frank came to help with the cooking and entertained us with songs from *Show Boat.*

"Only make believe," he'd sung and I'd thought, oh yes let's make believe for a while. Let's pretend Mike and Mariann are simply a couple in love planning a wedding, a home, a life in the usual way. Not surrounded by war and darkness and . . . But I'd stopped myself as we all sang along with Father Frank.

"Might as well make believe I love you for to tell the truth I do."

And then I'd sung what had become my party piece, "Has Anybody Here Seen Kelly?"

Now, as I looked at Mike waiting at the altar of the chapel, I thought of all the girls marrying soldiers and sailors and marines. I understood Mariann's brother Jim's concern. Why didn't all these young women wait until the war was over? Why take the chance that they'd be widowed?

Mike's best man, Jerry Boucher, up there grinning, had just gotten married himself. Mike had stood up for him. A most impressive wedding, Mike had told me, in the big Jesuit church on Park Avenue, St. Ignatius Loyola. Jerry's wife came from one of the most prominent and richest Irish-American families in the country. Her grandfather Murray had been Thomas Edison's partner, and her mother's father, James Farrell, had been president of US Steel. Many bridesmaids and gorgeous music, Mike had said. Mariann told me the bride's dress was covered in handmade lace with a six-foot-long train. Beautiful, she said and Joan, the bride, was a very nice girl for all her family's millions, and was making the same leap of faith as Mariann. Joan's family's money and position couldn't ensure that Jerry would survive. Mike told me they'd lost another member of their squadron just the week before. Gone off on patrol looking for submarines and had never come back. They didn't know what had happened. He could have run out of gas. His instruments might have failed. Or he could have merely gotten lost on the huge ocean. Sometimes your sense of direction deserts you, a kind of vertigo sets in, Mike had said.

There were still rumors that the squadron was going to be transferred to the Pacific. They probably would have been gone by now except the Japanese had sunk so many of our big aircraft carriers there were no places for them.

At the party we all attended the night before, I talked to a young fellow named Denis Barnes, who'd graduated with Mike from Pensacola, then served in the Pacific. We were standing in the cardinal's parlor, which Cardinal Spellman had offered to Father Frank. The cardinal was the military vicar for the US and had a soft spot for servicemen. No wonder cardinals are called princes of the church—the rectory looked like a castle, with thick carpets and scarlet damask upholstery on the overstuffed chairs and couches. There was plenty of food. I'd noticed the young flyer standing by himself and walked over. He told me he'd just come from the Pacific where he'd met survivors of Guadalcanal and Corregidor. He did not have a good word to say for General Douglas MacArthur or the US Congress and went on about how ill-equipped and outnumbered the troops were who were expected to defend the Philippines. This was the first really negative word I'd heard from any of these young fellows. But this boy was angry. Thousands of soldiers had been told to surrender to the Japanese. MacArthur had got away to Australia leaving his troops there to die under brutal conditions in Japanese prisoner of war camps.

"Roosevelt wants the country to concentrate on the war in Europe," he said. "But the Japanese Navy is beating us in the Pacific. We were able to do some damage at Midway but then the Navy got sold a bill of goods with this new plane SBD2. We call it the Beast. Just try to get up and off in that thing with bombs stuck under your wings. You see you have to dive low over a Jap ship to drop your payload while you're dodging ack-ack or fighting off their planes, the Zeros. Most times our bombs never hit the target. Six of us will take off and maybe four will return. Finally the captain of the carrier threw all those planes off the ship. So what do you think of that?" he said. He didn't wait for me to answer but walked away. Poor kid, I'd thought.

"War," a voice said behind me. "You'd think we would have learned." An elderly priest handed me a glass of champagne and we'd walked to a corner dominated by a gigantic oil painting of the Sacred Heart. He lifted his glass as if to salute the image. "The Lord tried to take all suffering onto Himself but mankind seems bent on reclaiming it. Doing in each other."

I lifted my glass and took a sip.

"I was in France during the last war," he said.

"I was too," I said.

"I was a chaplain."

"I was a nurse. Well, kind of a nurse and a photographer. There for the battles."

"So you know," he said.

"I do," I said.

"They don't," he said, gesturing at the young flyers and their girls.

"That fellow does," I said, pointing at Denis Barnes.

"I volunteered to be a chaplain again," the priest went on. "But they rejected me. You're too old they told me. But I said that I was the same age as the commander-in-chief."

I laughed.

"I've appointed myself assistant to the cardinal in the military vicarate. I write to the chaplains. Try to get them extra supplies. Even cash to give to the boys for emergency leaves. Things like that."

"Good," I said.

"It's something," he said, and pointed over at Mike and Mariann. "And I like to make the cathedral available to them."

"So it was you. I suppose my cousin Ed called you."

"Ed? Ed who?"

"Ed Kelly, the mayor of Chicago."

"No. No. Mike and Mariann just rang the rectory bell. The housekeeper got me. I met with them and found them a slot. Nine o'clock in the morning is a little early but that's really when the Lady Chapel is at its most beautiful. Morning light pours through the stained glass windows. And when Mike told me his last name was Kelly, well . . . I knew I had to find him a place. You see it was Eugene Kelly gave the money to build the Lady Chapel at the end of the last century. What a man he was. A self-made millionaire and very generous. Born in County Tyrone not too far from the home place of Archbishop Hughes, whose vision built this cathedral. Can you imagine all those Irish ragamuffins who'd run for their lives from starvation and oppression telling the muckety-mucks in this city they were going to build a gothic cathedral right smack on Fifth Avenue?

"Of course Fifth Avenue then wasn't what it is now, north of the real city in acres of mud. But we Irish did it. We were the lowest of the low and yet we managed to erect one of the most magnificent churches in the world. Of course everybody wasn't poor. We had our successes like Eugene Kelly.

"Be sure to notice the middle window in the Lady Chapel. You'll see the Kelly coat of arms," he said.

"The tower?"

"Yes," he said, and patted my hand as if he'd given me a great gift. "Your crest up there in blue and gold. Unfortunately there wasn't room for the motto."

"Turris Fortis Mihi Deus," I said.

He nodded.

"And do you think it's true?"

"True?"

"Will God give Mike strength? Will my nephew survive?"

He didn't say anything for a minute.

"Ah well, as to that our ancestors did," he said. "And here we are." He drank the rest of his champagne.

Yes, I thought, here we are.

He was right. The morning sun did make the colors of the stained glass brighter. I found the Kelly crest stuck right in the middle of the last panel on the left, and kept my eye on the tower until the music began. Then I turned to watch Mariann come up the short aisle. Only about a dozen pews on each side, but an impressive setting for her as she walked slowly up, her hand on her brother's arm—a sailor. His uniform wasn't as fancy as Mike's. Just the standard navy blue. Here comes the bride.

Oh Mare, good for you. No long white wedding dress for her. She was dressed in a kelly green suit. A fitted jacket flared at the waist, a straight skirt. She wore a big round, white pinwheel hat with a green band. Showing our colors. No ordinary time. No need for bridal gowns and fuss or the pageant of a virgin being given away by her father to her husband. Women as chattel. Bound in long skirts. A costume of subservience. Better this radiant girl walking shoulder to shoulder with her brother. Meeting her husband on equal terms. In a suit she could wear to work on Monday. Not quite the dungarees and bandana of Rosie the Riveter but making a similar statement. She was ready for whatever would come.

I thought of my own marriage ceremony. A few minutes in another small chapel that had been tucked into the back of the Irish College in Paris where Father Kevin had blessed Peter and me. Another young man who'd gone off to battle. A war the Irish had won. They'd beaten the Black and Tans. Wrenched their freedom from the English but then they had turned on each other. Peter killed. Not by the enemy but by one of his own. Ah Peter, I thought, how I wish I could turn to you right here and now in this chapel. Hold your hand as Mike and Mariann make the same pledge to each other that we promised. Love, faithfulness, for richer or poorer, in sickness or in health, 'til death does us part. But not for you the easeful death of old age, the happy death prayed for on the nine First Fridays. St. Joseph, patron of a happy death, dying in comfort with Mary and Jesus looking on. Yours was death by rifle shot, and Mike could fall out of the sky or be cut down by antiaircraft fire.

What had Denis said? Inferior planes, loaded with bombs, diving toward Japanese warships, was that what was waiting for Mike? Stop it, Nonie, I told myself. Stop it. Rose had her handkerchief out, longing for John Larney, I supposed, in the same way I was mourning Peter Keeley. I smiled at her. Sat up a little straighter. We had a job to do here.

"Mame," I whispered to her. She nodded. We were standing in for Mame. Mary McCabe Kelly, Mike's mother, Rose's sister. Maybe for Mariann's mother too, another Mary. I looked up at the statue of Our Lady. You should have taken better care of your namesakes, I said silently. You should have . . . But just at that moment I heard the opening notes of the Ave Maria. The singer was somewhere in the cathedral, her voice amplified by the stone walls, the vaulted ceilings. Alright, alright, I thought, I'll say the prayer. I'll hail you, Mary full of grace. But you'd better take care of these two or you'll have Rose and me to contend with.

After Jerry Boucher, Denis Barnes, and two other members of Mike's squadron held up their swords to make an archway for the newly wed couple. The bride and groom walked down the steps of St. Patrick's Cathedral under this canopy of steel, bright in the sun. We stood at the bottom watching and I couldn't resist tossing a small handful of rice at the couple. Wars and weddings bound together at least since the Greeks fought the Trojans. I remembered the story Father Kevin had told me about a Roman emperor who had forbidden his soldiers to marry on the principle that a man with a wife held back on the battlefield. A young priest named Valentine had defied the emperor, performed the ceremonies, and was murdered himself for his disobedience. Mike and Mariann stood on the bottom step. She looked up at him from under her hat. Such love. So young. Twenty-two and twenty-six. Dear God, let him be careful, please.

Father Chuck, the scientist priest-brother, lined us up behind the couple and began taking pictures using color film, he'd told me. I was happy to turn the photography over to him. I stood next to Rose directly behind Father Frank, still in his vestments. We all faced the office buildings that were called Rockefeller Center. I could almost touch the statue of Atlas holding up the sky in the center of the buildings. Sister Ruth Eileen had told us the story of Atlas. She believed that all Western literature was rooted in the ancient myths so I knew that Atlas had been a Titan who'd fought the gods of Olympus and lost. His punishment was to hold up the sky forever though the sphere this fellow balanced on his shoulders looked a lot like the Earth. We haven't learned much as a species. Here were Mike and his pals who could actually climb into the sky. The dream of flight realized and yet their airplanes were weapons of war. Atlas and St. Patrick squaring off. Two sides of humanity.

We walked together east on Fiftieth Street toward the Waldorf Astoria, where the wedding breakfast was to be held. A procession of joy that made the people we passed smile.

"God bless you," one woman called out to Mike and Mariann. "God keep you." Mariann waved her bouquet of white roses at the woman.

Father Frank had invited the elderly priest from St. Patrick's to join us. His name was Tom Leonard and I found myself sitting next to him. He was an easy man to talk to. When he was a chaplain during the last war, he'd visited Paris and gone to the Irish College but he didn't remember Father Kevin or Peter Keeley. He said that the cardinal had studied in Rome and was familiar with the Irish College there.

"You have to remember," he said, "the popes had intended that the French would control the church in America. All the early bishops came from France. We Irish were Johnny-come-latelys, but doing alright for ourselves now. There are some in Rome who regret that we've taken over, but Cardinal Spellman is a man who understands the ins and outs of the Vatican and is not above reminding fellows in the Curia that the Holy See depends on contributions from the American church. The cardinal set up a special fund to support the scholars working in the Vatican library. A good few came from Ireland. Now that's a life I enjoy. Books and peace," he said.

Yes, I thought, and all Peter Keeley had ever wanted.

Not thinking of his grave so much these days. Too busy praying to keep those I love alive.

2

Mike and Mariann left for their honeymoon in Asbury Park, driven by her two priest brothers in the cardinal's car, lent to them for the weekend. Listening to Father Leonard's discussion of Irish scholars in the Vatican had sharpened the image I carried in my heart of me placing beautiful flowers—fuchsia, maybe—on Peter's lonely grave. But civilians did not travel these days, so I had no chance of going to Ireland until after the war. Besides, should a sixty-three-year-old woman really entertain such a fantasy?

I'd finally lived long enough to be the sensible aunt. Not the family flibbertigibbet of Henrietta's rants. My big sister had died just months ago and now I realized I'd gotten a great deal of fun from shocking her. And settling down into a conventional role didn't seem the defeat it would have if she were still alive.

Henrietta had stayed in Kewanee surrounded by Mame's china and silver, daring anyone to take them away. Once a year Toots drove her to visit Agnella, who'd been teaching throughout Iowa.

I'd stayed in touch with Agnella and made sure to see her at least once a year. We also corresponded. Her letters always included a Sacred Heart badge, a scapular, or a miraculous medal. I'd given one of each to Mike. "Keep these in your pocket when you're flying," I'd told him. And, of course, Ag would be praying away for his safety. In fact, it was interceding for Mike's protection that had been at the heart of Agnella's invitation to me—an invitation that had had such consequences.

She had called me soon after she received my letter telling her that Mike was training to be a Navy pilot. I'd given her my telephone number, but she'd never used it before. Agnella had just begun teaching first grade at Gesu School in Milwaukee—Pat O'Brien's alma mater, she'd written me. She was closer to Chicago than she'd ever been, and I'd intended to get up there to see her. But it was February 1942, and I still hadn't made it.

"Something wrong?" I'd asked, when I'd picked up the phone. No, she was fine, but the pastor had just decided that this Sunday's Mass would be said especially for the members of the parish in the armed forces. It was to be quite a ceremony, with two choirs and a procession of military people.

Gesu Church had been built by the Jesuits, magnificent gothic, she'd said. She was calling because, with Mike and so many other Kelly connections gone off to war, she thought I would want to attend. Even at this short notice. The Mass was tomorrow. "Yes," I'd said, "of course." Easy enough to take the Rock Island Railroad to Milwaukee.

Agnella had asked me to come to the convent beforehand, but I'd missed the early train, and arrived when Mass was well underway. The place was packed. I'd seen black veils concentrated in the four front rows, and found a seat in a pew on the side aisle, not too far from the nuns. I'll give Ag a wave on my way back from Communion, I'd thought—so she knows I'm here.

In fact, I hadn't long to wait because the Consecration was half over. In a few minutes, the priests had begun praying "Pater noster," and I followed along in English. I swear, it was just as I'd said "Forgive us our trespasses as we forgive those who trespass against us," that I heard a spate of coughing I'd recognize anywhere. There, five rows ahead of me—Henrietta and Toots. Now, I would have gotten up and run right out of the place, except . . . I'm not saying my beliefs are so primitive that I feared that God might revenge Himself against Mike if I stomped out of the church. But let's just say I'd stayed put. "*Libera nos a malo. Amen*," the priest concluded. "Deliver us from evil."

I remembered Milton Goldman telling Ed that Hitler was the Devil. Evil incarnate. Deliver us. Deliver us, please God, I prayed. I looked over at Henrietta, her head bowed. All these years, I'd thought of her as evil, but now this bent old woman hardly registered on any scale of wickedness. I wasn't entirely without fault, either. Forgive us our trespasses, as we forgive . . .

So. Agnella caught my eye, as I came back from Communion. Amazing how much entreaty she could project from a face almost entirely wrapped up in linen. I nodded.

Coffee and kringle—a big sweet roll—was served in the basement after Mass. Agnella had snagged me at the church door, and now I was standing with Toots and Henrietta, while Agnella, very much Sister Mary Erigina, introduced us to the parents of her first graders—all of whom had older children in the military.

Toots managed to tell each one about his top-secret employment in the defense plant. Thank God, he was too old to be drafted, I thought. Henrietta could never have borne being separated from her son.

She was very frail and gray. After about twenty minutes, she whispered to me, "Please, could we sit?" I'd seen two empty folding chairs on the side, and led her over there. I'd helped her down and settled myself beside her. "Did Agnella tell you I'd be here?" she had asked me.

"No," I'd said.

"Would you have come?" she'd asked.

"No," I'd said.

"Neither would I, if I'd known you were coming." We'd just looked at each other. So much for "forgive us our trespasses," I'd thought.

And, then, I'd seen Agnella coming toward us. "Sister Mary Erigina," I'd heard someone call. But she hadn't stopped. She'd stood over the two of us, looking down. She'd taken her mother's hand and mine, and joined them together in hers. "Enough," she'd said. "This is what I do with my first graders when they fight with each other. I let them feel the warmth of each other's hands and . . ." Oh, why not? I thought. Forgive us our trespasses as we forgive those who trespass against us. We clasped hands.

"I'm sorry, Nonie," Henrietta had said.

"I am, too," I'd said.

And it was a relief to lay that burden down. Not to feel any guilt at her funeral a few weeks later. Or now, as I climbed the stairs of St. Patrick's Cathedral. I hadn't gotten a chance to really look at it that morning. Midafternoon now, no Masses, but still a good number of people inside. There were pairs clustered in the pews, often a young man in uniform and a girl in a summer dress scattered through the huge expanse of the church. I walked along the side aisle where there were altars to various saints. I nodded at St. Bridget, St. Anthony of Padua, St. Therese the Little Flower. Each had a stand of little vigil lights in front of them so you could light a candle to get the attention of your favorite saint.

Jude had a raging fire of candles at his feet. The saint of hopeless cases. It made sense that he was popular. I was surprised to see an altar dedicated to St. Elizabeth. One of the few women in the cathedral and not a very well-known saint. She wasn't even a martyr, just the Blessed Mother's cousin who had gotten pregnant at an advanced age. But I suppose there were plenty of women who would come to pray at this altar hoping against hope for a child themselves. I wondered whether Elizabeth had still been alive when her son John the Baptist died, beheaded by Herod. And had she consoled Mary after the Crucifixion, sharing their sorrow as they had their joy? So many images from Renaissance painters of Jesus and his cousin John the Baptist as toddlers.

Now I'm not any kind of an art connoisseur, but I did spend a fair amount of time in the Louvre when I lived in Paris. I'd stumbled into the museum to get out of the rain one day and discovered a great gimmick for Madame Simone, my employer who copied couturier dresses to sell at a discount to American tourists. Why not steal from the masters? I'd thought, and had sketched some of the gorgeous clothing on the ladies who had their portraits painted, even lifting a bit of the Mona Lisa's costume. Madame Simone created a very popular Great Masters' collection, and I even stole, very subtly of course, details from the saints. There was a painting of St. Joan of Arc by Ingres that had some fabulous pleats around her armor. I didn't neglect the Madonnas. After all, these painters were dressing Our Lady in the clothes women of their day wore, so why not lift a skirt or a sleeve. And one of my favorite paintings was Raphael's *La Belle Jardinière*, where a very relaxed Mary is playing with a naked Jesus and John the Baptist. Lovely. Two toddlers with not a notion of what lies ahead.

We'd had a print of another Raphael, *Madonna and Child with John the Baptist*, in our classroom at St. Xavier's. *Madonna Della Seggiola,* Sister Ruth Eileen called it. Mary leaned back in a chair, holding Jesus with the slightly older St. John standing next to them. Nothing austere or removed about Mary in this picture or in another print I remembered Sister Ruth Eileen had liked, Ruben's painting of the Holy Family.

"Here's Elizabeth finally," she'd said. "How many of you have an aunt you're close to?" And of course we'd all raised our hands. I was thinking of Aunt Máire and how I could confide in her in a way I couldn't in Mam. "Well Elizabeth was like an aunt to the Blessed Mother. After all Mary went to Elizabeth when she found out she was pregnant. And their children played together. Cousins."

Now I looked up at Elizabeth's statue and thought of how Ed and Michael had grown up together, and of Rose and me, the aunts.

I wondered about the women who lit candles at this altar and never had children. Was there any saint for women who had miscarriages? Who stood outside the mother and child chain of life? Now, Nonie, I told myself, don't start feeling sorry for yourself. You have the Kelly kids, and didn't Mike invite you and Rose to attend his wedding, putting us in his mother's place. He and Mariann will have children and you'll be Aunt Nonie to them too.

A more than life-sized statue of St. Patrick himself was carved just in front of the sanctuary. An old man with a beard, looking as he did in the gigantic stained glass window where he wore red bishop's robes and was lecturing a very attentive group of Irish women. Why was Patrick never portrayed as the young man who'd been taken from Britain to Ireland as a slave? Who'd escaped but then come back to convert the whole place and really become the most famous Irishman of them all? There was an "I shall return" tale that would inspire even Douglas MacArthur. Denis Barnes had shown me one of the matchbooks MacArthur had printed with that slogan and passed out by the tens of thousands. Denis had shaken his head.

I was going to the Lady Chapel to make sure the Blessed Mother understood that she was responsible for Mike's safety. Father Leonard had told me to make sure to visit the altar just to the side of the Lady Chapel. The Archangel Michael—a favorite of all us Kellys since half our fellows were named for him—stood next to a statue of St. Louis, King of France. Father Leonard had told me to be sure to read the plaque to the side that explained that the altar and statues had been built by Tiffany & Co. and were a gift of the Bouvier family. In very ornate letters, Michel Bouvier said that he was dedicating this altar to his grandfather, also Michel (so that was why the Archangel was here) and to his father Jean Vernou Bouvier. His grandfather had been born in Pont St. Esprit, France, and died in Philadelphia where his father was born. In the center of the plaque was a rampant lion. Aristocrats, I would have thought, except Father Leonard had told me that the Bouviers were furniture makers friendly with Louis Napoleon and hadn't made any real money until they came to America. The name, he said, meant herdsman, probably the same root as Bo in Irish, the River Boyne and the cow goddess. Father Leonard was Father Kevin come again, I'd thought. He enjoyed a bit of gossip also.

"The Michel Bouvier who endowed the altar left all his money to his brother's son, John Vernou Bouvier III," he'd told me, "and the fellow turned into a bit of a playboy. A shame really because he married a girl from a good Irish family, Janet Lee. He brought his two daughters by not too long ago, and I took them to see the altar and told them some things about the stained glass windows. He said that he was called 'Black Jack' and his younger daughter was named for him. Jacqueline. Nice girls and very impressed with the beautiful altar that commemorated their family."

Now I moved to the stand of vigil lights at the entrance to the Lady Chapel. Granny Honora had lit a candle every day for each of her sons and nephews who were fighting in the Civil War, and now I took the wooden stick, put it into a flame and started touching it to the wicks. One for Mike, then Ed's son Joe Kelly, Marge's Tom McGuire, our cousin Father Steve O'Donnell who was a chaplain with Patton's army, Mariann's brothers Ralph and Wally, and then a few all-purpose candles for all the friends and neighbors who were in harm's way. There must be acres and acres of flickering candles all over the world, mile after mile after mile, aimed at Heaven. Did I really think God and the saints were up there peering down saying ah there's one burning for Mike Kelly, best keep an eye on him? I don't know but I lit the whole line anyway and settled down for a bit of serious praying. Such silence calmed the noise and bustle of New York City. Then I heard a muted sound, gasps and sobs, coming from a pew farther up front. I looked up and saw Denis Barnes sitting next to a young woman. She was kneeling, crying, her face in her hands. He sat staring at the altar. I got up and slipped into the pew, sat next to him.

"What?" I whispered.

"The orders came. The whole squadron's headed west. A month of training in Hawaii and then to the Pacific," he said.

"Damn," I said.

"Just found out. Jerry Boucher telephoned the squadron from the bar we'd all gone to after the wedding breakfast and got the news," he said.

"So Mike doesn't know," I said.

"We decided to let him enjoy his honeymoon." The girl looked up, turned toward me. "This is my friend, Chrissie. She lives in New Jersey and couldn't get in for the wedding but we agreed to meet afterwards. She dragged me in here from the bar." Chrissie nodded at me. "I'm not even a Catholic," Denis said. "But Chrissie's Italian and . . ." He shrugged. "We've been lighting candles all over this place."

"St. Anthony," Chrissie said.

"Can you ask for something different?" I asked him.

"No," he said. "I'm powerless. I could desert, I suppose," Denis said. "Chrissie said she'd hide me with her family."

"Oh," I said. Desert. If he got caught he'd go to jail, and he would get caught. Every day there were articles in the paper about fellows who'd gone AWOL and were turned in by neighbors or relatives even. Too many brothers and sons and husbands had died while serving, for people to have much sympathy for fellows who ran away. The words of an Irish song went through my head. Mrs. McGrath's son had lost his legs fighting in the British Army: "Have you no sense at all? Why didn't you run from the cannonball?" she'd asked him. Why didn't more men run? Patriotism? Honor? Conditioning? Fear? Denis patted Chrissie's shoulder.

"But I won't desert," he said. "I'll go to the Pacific and fly the Beast off carriers until . . . You'd better keep up the prayers, Chrissie."

"When?" I said.

"At the end of June," he said.

"And could someone, well, intervene?" I was thinking of Ed, of course. "Suggest you boys for another assignment?"

"Just now in the bar Jerry's wife, Joan, said her father knew a lot of people and could call his friends and Jerry went ballistic. He said that we were officers and gentlemen and that we didn't sink to using influence like that."

"Very noble but plenty do."

Eleanor Roosevelt, I thought. Eleanor Roosevelt.

I'd become Ed's unofficial liaison with the First Lady, following up on the requests she sent to him on a weekly basis. Jobs were needed for worthy young women—often Negroes—and I'd been able to place most of them. I had briefly met Eleanor Roosevelt at the convention three years ago, when she had accepted the nomination for her husband. I'd taken her photograph with Ed, and sent it to Missy LeHand for her. Eleanor Roosevelt had written a thank-you note, and recently I'd received another. She was grateful for my help in obtaining jobs for her protégés.

I'd also gotten to know Missy LeHand and Grace Tully, who'd been with the president on his Chicago visits. Two smart Irish Catholic women devoting themselves to a cause and the man who embodied it. And, though Bessie O'Neill was Ed's official secretary, when the president wanted to get in touch with Ed on a weekend or late at night, Missy would often call me at home because she knew Ed and I lived in the same building.

Now I was prepared to go to Washington or Hyde Park or wherever Mrs. Roosevelt was to ask for her help, but I only had to walk a few blocks to Sixty-Seventh Street right off Fifth Avenue.

"She's clearing the place out," Grace Tully told me when I called the White House trying to get in touch with Eleanor Roosevelt. Poor Missy LeHand had worked herself into a stroke. She had suffered from rheumatic fever as a child and I think if it's possible for someone to spend her heart for someone else, she did, giving hers to FDR. Grace told me that Missy had come back to her old room in the White House for a bit when she was recovering from the stroke but she'd started a fire there and had to leave. She was living with her sister in Boston. FDR hadn't seen her. At least he'd been there when Missy received the honorary degree Ed had arranged for Rosary College to confer on her. We'd hoped she'd be able to travel to Chicago, but instead two Dominican nuns from the college came to Washington and gave her the degree. Ed told me that FDR had left Missy half his estate in his will, but it didn't look like she'd outlive him. Grace was in charge now.

"Finally sold those two New York houses," Grace told me. She said that Sara Roosevelt had given the twin town houses to Franklin and Eleanor as a wedding gift in 1908 and they'd lived there since. But the Roosevelts had been trying to sell them since Sara died in 1941. Hunter College finally bought them, she said.

"Eleanor is pleased that a woman's college will have the houses. Take the curse off them," she said. "She's never out and out complained but can you imagine if your mother-in-law gave you a house that was connected on every floor with hers? There are doors leading from one to the other and Sara walked through them whenever she pleased. Anna Roosevelt told me that her grandmother once explained to her that though Eleanor had borne her she, Sara, was Anna's real mother."

"Mmmmm," I said. Sara Roosevelt was dead now and Eleanor Roosevelt in charge. I found the First Lady wearing a coverall as she supervised the movers who were packing boxes in the front room of the town houses at 47-49 East Sixty-Seventh. One front door led into both buildings. Plain enough for such a prominent wealthy family, but then I couldn't imagine the Roosevelts enjoying the kind of fancy decorations I'd just seen at the Bouvier altar. I'd noticed a steep stairway going up five floors. Not easy for a man in a wheelchair.

Grace had called her, so Eleanor Roosevelt greeted me as if we were longtime friends. "Welcome, welcome," she said. "I hope you don't mind if I continue working."

"Must be a lot of memories," I said to Eleanor Roosevelt as we stood together among the boxes, while a maid wrapped china figurines for packing. The First Lady looked at me and shook her head a bit.

"Five of our six children grew up here," she said, "and one died here." She walked across the room, took a clock from the mantel and handed it to the maid.

She walked over to two straight-backed chair with woven bottoms. She gestured for me to sit down and sat facing me.

"Grace said you wanted to see me but didn't tell me why."

"Well, first, I wanted to let you know that we managed to find jobs in the Park District for those last two young women you recommended, and a place in the clerk's office for the third."

"Good," she said. "So many educated young Negro women have difficulty getting positions that they're qualified for, and all three of these women have husbands in the service. I'm grateful for your help with them and the other young women over the years. It's a shame that young Negro men face such blatant discrimination in the armed forces. Why the Navy won't even allow Negro sailors to serve in the jobs that they were trained for. Won't let them on ships. But I'm working on that," she said.

"Good," I said.

"I think at least one ship should have a colored crew, a kind of a test case to show that they can do the job. I'm trying to convince Franklin," she said.

"Good luck," I said. "My nephew is serving in the Navy. In fact—" She interrupted me.

"Please, Miss Kelly, if you are here to ask me to interfere as far as his assignments go, I beg you to please say no more. As you know, my own sons are in the service, one in combat with the Marines and though I would of course like them to be in some safe billet, Franklin and I have made it an iron-clad principle not to use our influence. It wouldn't be honorable."

"Of course not," I said. Now what do I do?

"And now it's teatime. We still have some semblance of a kitchen." She turned to the maid. "Could you please bring us tea?"

Case closed.

"Thank you," I said, though I really wanted to get out of there. Tea was just that. Tea. No cookies, no little sandwiches, no sugar, no milk. I took a sip. It was weak. We sat in silence for a minute and then really just for something to say, I found myself describing Mike and Mariann's wedding. I guess I got a bit carried away telling her about the handsome Navy flyers in their white uniforms making an arc with their swords on the steps of St. Patrick's Cathedral.

"I was married on St. Patrick's Day," Eleanor said.

"You chose that date?"

"Only because my uncle Teddy was in New York to lead the parade and so could be in the wedding. He left the parade at Seventy-Sixth Street and came to my cousin's house. We were married in their parlor."

"Not in church?"

"Better for Uncle Teddy that it be private."

"Oh." Now what? I started to tell her about how I'd gone to Mike's graduation at Pensacola and how Rose had pinned on his golden wings. "Such excellent pilots in the Navy," I said. "Is your air crew from the Navy? Or are they from the Army Air Corps?"

"My air crew?"

"Yes. The fellows that take you around when you visit the troops. I've been reading the articles that talk about how important your visits are to the men's morale."

"I think so. Unfortunately there are some in the military who disagree."

"They think a woman's place is in the home?" I said.

"More or less," she said.

"And you let them restrict you?"

"What can I do? I depend on the military for transport, and every time I mention going overseas there's one general who gets so red in the face I fear for his blood pressure."

"Too bad. It's not just the GIs. Imagine what a visit from you would mean to the people of England, or even Ireland for that matter. I mean Mike has been escorting convoys across the Atlantic and he tells me there's a large Navy base in Derry with a full complement of Marines."

"Really? I've been wanting to visit the Marines in a combat zone because of my son, but I was told they're all in the Pacific and General MacArthur absolutely refuses to give me permission to go there."

"Ireland is a lot closer," I said. "And Mike knows the route very well."

"It is, and I suppose your nephew just happens to be available to fly me over there."

I took a sip of the tea and said nothing. Let her think.

"It's interesting, Franklin has been fretting about the Irish prime minister, that man de Valera. Neutral, but is he leaning toward Germany?"

"Oh no, definitely not," I said. "I've known him for years. He's awkward but you couldn't expect him to commit Ireland to war. The country's barely supporting itself. And you know there are tens of thousands of Irishmen serving in the British Army, not to mention the millions of Irish-Americans serving in our own forces."

"Perhaps if I did go to Ireland I could speak to him. Unofficially of course."

"That's an excellent idea and I could arrange a meeting."

She put her teacup and saucer down on a table. "Yes, you might be an asset on such a trip," she said.

"Think of the good publicity you'd get," I said. "I know that doesn't mean much to you but still, the papers would love it if a young man named Kelly was flying the First Lady over to the Old Sod." I almost said shure and begorrah.

"Something to think about," she said.

Come on, Eleanor, please, please, please. But she didn't say any more, only wrote down the name of Mike's squadron commander.

At the end of June half the squadron was transferred to the Pacific, but

Mike, Jerry, and Denis Barnes stayed at Floyd Bennett Field, and in October Mike called me.

"You won't believe it, Aunt Nonie, I'm flying the First Lady to north Ireland."

And I'll be going with you, Mike, I thought but didn't say. Some things should be a surprise.

3

NOVEMBER 1942

"Good for you, Nonie," Ed said to me when I told him about the trip I was planning with Eleanor Roosevelt and Mike.

The war had taken over Ed and Margaret. More and more responsibility for him as head of the civil defense area covering four states. He was in charge of all war production facilities. Margaret and Lucky Davis now oversaw the care, feeding and entertainment of tens of thousands of servicemen and women—women were enlisting too—passing through Chicago.

Lucky's daughter, Nancy, was a kind of junior chairman with them and took charge of the amateur dramatic shows put on at the USO. She was a good actress herself and had grown into an attractive young woman in a way familiar to the young men watching. Pretty, not beautiful. Dark-haired and small. She wasn't a blonde vamp or an unapproachable movie star, but the girl-back-home all the servicemen hoped was waiting for them. That was the part she played in the skits, always ending with a song. Not a great voice but a lot of personality. I know both Ed's sons had crushes on Nancy.

An intelligent girl, she'd graduated from Smith College. I'd thought she would resist following in her mother's footsteps into acting as a profession. She was Nancy Davis now. Loyal Davis had adopted her when she was fifteen. Lucky Davis told Margaret that Nancy herself initiated the adoption. "She actually met her father for lunch to tell him she was more or less divorcing him." So Nancy became the doctor's very respectable daughter. A student at Girls' Latin School of Chicago and then Smith College. A Chicago

Junior Leaguer. I expected that soon she'd marry some young officer and join Margaret and her mother in that mix of shopping, lunch, and good works that occupied the ladies who lived along Lake Shore Drive. But a few years before, President Roosevelt had sent representatives of the March of Dimes, his favorite charity, to see Ed. They wanted to make a film in Chicago to use as a fund-raiser to dramatize the threat of polio.

Ed suggested Nancy for a part and she got the role and did a good job. Her mother still had a lot of friends in Hollywood. I'd met ZaSu Pitts in their apartment and found out that she knew Maurine Watkins.

"Women used to run the place," she'd told us. "Wrote the scripts, even directed the movies. My friend Frances Marion must have done a hundred scenarios but now, well, it's big business and the men have taken over. But there are still a few of us out there and if Nancy wants to give it a go we can help."

That was before the war. Before all of our lives changed. And yet Nancy was finding a way to act and help in the war effort. Chicago was going to lose one of its young matrons to Hollywood, I'd thought.

Ed told me that only about a quarter of the Army was actually fighting on the front lines. Most were still training. There had been landings in North Africa and terrible battles in the Pacific where the Marines had suffered high casualties, but that was only a small percentage of everyone serving. Sailors were in danger from U-boats but by now the battle of the Atlantic was going our way. Most men were relatively safe except for the airmen. The airmen. Mike and his friends.

We'd gotten more details now about what had happened at Midway and Guadalcanal. The *March of Time* newsreels had shown footage of planes shot down by Japanese antiaircraft guns. A blast of flame and then a plunge into the sea. There were also pictures of planes crashing into the decks of carriers or over-shooting and dropping into the sea.

No safe billets for flyers. I hoped Eleanor Roosevelt's trip would at least buy Mike a little time. How would he react to me riding along? Would he catch on? Think I'd compromised his honor?

Mostly he was confused.

"But surely there are military photographers who could accompany the First Lady?" he said to me when I arrived at his apartment in Brooklyn the night before we were to depart.

"Yes, but I speak the language of the country we'll be visiting."

"Wait a minute, Aunt Nonie, they speak English in Great Britain and Ireland."

"They do but you'll see. Some translation is needed."

We were flying in a bigger plane than the SBDs Mike was used to, and he'd had to undergo extra training. There were three on the crew—Jerry Boucher was his copilot and Denis Barnes the navigator. They were all on board as I climbed the ladder onto the plane the next morning.

"Thanks," Denis Barnes said to me and smiled. I think he understood that I had engineered the assignment. He'd been in combat, had seen friends' planes burst into flames and taken fire himself. No foolishness for him about honor. "Don't tell Mike," I whispered to him as I sat down.

Eleanor Roosevelt was already aboard along with her secretary Malvina "Tommy" Thompson. At fifty, she was the youngest of the three of us. The First Lady was fifty-nine, and I was sixty-three.

We flew for about six hours and then landed at Gander Airport in Newfoundland to refuel. Took off and continued on through the night. Uncomfortable and cold in the plane, but exhaustion put us all to sleep.

Mike called me to the cockpit to see the sun rising out of the sea.

"That's it, Aunt Nonie," Mike said pointing down below, "that's Ireland," a kind of hitch in his voice. He had never known his great-grandmother Honora, or even my mother, his own grandmother or any of the Kellys who had been born here. But still Ireland was the land of his ancestors, and the birthplace of his own mother. We were flying over Ireland, headed for England, but we'd be stopping here on our return.

"It really is green," Mike said, pointing at the fields lit by first light, rolling down into the sea, waves breaking against the rocks.

"Oh, Mike. Mike. That's it. That's Galway Bay. See where the water turns from blue to gray, that's Galway Bay meeting the Atlantic Ocean. Your great-grandmother Honora and her sister rowed a currach full of their children out just at that place and somehow caught a ship and that's why we're alive today."

"Is that true, Aunt Nonie? I thought it was just a made-up story. Aunt Henrietta laughed at Dad when he told it to us."

How dare Henrietta . . . "It's true," I said. "It's true! My father, your grandfather, was one of the little boys."

Jerry Boucher was looking down too. "My family's from somewhere in Ireland but I don't know where."

"Kilkenny, maybe, with a Norman name like Boucher," I said. "What about you, Denis?"

"My family's been in North Carolina forever. My father said we were Scotch-Irish originally."

"There's no such thing," I said. "When your ancestors came from Ulster to America they thought of themselves as Irish. After all it was over three hundred years since they'd come from Scotland and some of Ireland's greatest patriots were Presbyterians from the North—"

"Aunt Nonie," Mike said. "Too early for a history lesson."

Eleanor Roosevelt was standing in the door of the cockpit. "So, land," she said.

Tommy Thompson had come up behind her. "I've never seen Europe before," she said.

"Well, Ireland's not strictly Europe," Eleanor Roosevelt said.

"Excuse me, Mrs. Roosevelt," I said. "There'd be no Europe if Irish monks hadn't traveled over there bringing Christianity and education to people who would have stayed stuck in the Dark Ages."

"Aunt Nonie," Mike said again.

"Sorry. It's just that Ireland is the ancestral ground for tens of millions of Americans. Even some who don't even realize they have such a rich heritage. Charlemagne and his court couldn't even read or write until we showed up and—"

"Maybe you ladies better take your seats. Denis tells me we're going to hit some rough air," Mike said. "We should be landing in England in two hours."

He was right. We got a pretty good bouncing as we flew across Ireland and the Irish Sea. I didn't get up to observe the English countryside and we stayed in our seats as we landed at an RAF base in Bristol.

The First Lady, Tommy, and I would take a train to London where the king and queen would meet us. The royals didn't come to airports.

Our own Army Air Corps had squadrons stationed in England. Mike had told me that B-52s took part in bombing raids over Germany and that soon there'd be more American bases all over England. But it became obvious when we landed that the Brits were in charge.

Two black cars waited for us on the tarmac. Denis opened the door of the plane and jumped down. Jerry handed him a ladder that he attached. Rickety-enough looking and steep. Denis offered a hand to Eleanor Roosevelt but she settled the fur piece she wore around her shoulders and stepped down on her own. Not a bother on her. Tommy followed. But I was glad to reach down and accept Denis's help. Wouldn't do to fall on my face on arrival. A British officer, very correct in his uniform, stood waiting for us. An older fellow. I could see gray hair under his cap. He had a long wrinkled face, though not from smiling, I'd say, because his lips hardly moved as he nodded to Eleanor Roosevelt.

The British officer gestured the First Lady and Tommy toward the car, where a soldier held the door open. They got in. I stepped forward. The boys will probably bunk on the base, I thought. Wonder where we will be staying.

Mike handed me my camera bag and valise. Jerry gave Mrs. Roosevelt's and Tommy's luggage to a British soldier who put it in the trunk of a car. The officer started to get in the front seat of the car.

"Excuse me," I said to him. "I'm with Mrs. Roosevelt."

"Who are you?" he said. Oh that accent. My teeth clamped together. He both swallowed and elongated those words, making them an insult. Listen, buddy, I wanted to say, I've met your type before. One of you tried to hang me as a spy and look where I am now, traveling with the First Lady of the United States on a plane flown by my nephew. So don't you drawl at me.

"I'm Nora Kelly. Mrs. Roosevelt's official photographer."

"Mrs. Roosevelt is spending the next few days with the prime minister and his wife at their country house, Chequers. It's a private visit. Your services will not be required," he said.

"But I think a picture of Eleanor Roosevelt with Winston and Clementine would really be swell," I said. "The American papers will eat it up."

The officer couldn't stop himself from making a face. Only a flicker, but definitely he squinched his forehead and pursed his lips. I'd gotten to him. Good. He sees me as a crass American. Well, I'll be one.

"I regret Miss, what was your name again?"

"Kelly. Nora Kelly."

"Irish?" he said. And the squinch came back. "I'm surprised that . . ." He stopped himself.

"Yes. I'm looking forward to introducing Eleanor Roosevelt to Ireland. Derry is such a beautiful city," I said.

"You'll be going to Northern Ireland which is part of the United Kingdom, and the city is Londonderry," he said.

Mike and the boys had heard the last of this exchange.

"As a matter of fact our whole crew has Irish roots," Mike said. "So we're all looking forward to that part of our trip. But of course we're anxious to see London, too."

"Well as to that there is a train but you'll find hotels very crowded. Accommodation has been arranged for you in the officers' quarters on this base, but I wasn't told there'd be a female civilian," he said.

Eleanor Roosevelt rolled down the window. "Is there a problem, Colonel?" she said.

"Not at all," he said. He got into the front seat, slammed the door and the car began to move away.

"But, Nora," Mrs. Roosevelt called out. I just waved.

The pilots and I looked at each other and started laughing.

"What now, fellows?" I said.

"I suppose we have to walk," Mike said pointing at the hangars that were a good half mile away.

"The English have abandoned us again," I said. But the next thing we knew a young man with the map of Ireland on his face, as the old ones in Bridgeport would say, was running up to us.

"Sorry," he said. "Somebody from the squadron borrowed the company car and it took me a while to find this old banger." He pointed at what looked like a delivery van. "I'm Ray Finucane. Welcome."

"Finucane?" Mike said. "Finucane was the name of the great British ace. Are you?"

"Yes, Brendan was my brother. Still can't believe he's . . . Well."

Brendan Finucane, or Paddy as all the newspapers called him, had been the most decorated pilot in the Royal Air Force with the highest number of enemy planes shot down in aerial combat. Why hadn't I thought to throw his name at old fish face when he said, "Irish?" I should have said, "Just like the greatest hero in the Royal Air Force." The Chicago newspapers reported every one of Paddy's victories. Twenty-eight, and possibly more, enemy planes destroyed. The *Chicago American* had covered an entire front page with a picture of the pilot in his plane decorated with a shamrock. The headline read "Flying Shamrock. Terror of the Nazis."

The *Irish American News* had followed up with a feature about how his father had fought with de Valera in the 1916 Rising. But now the hero was dead. Hit by antiaircraft fire over France. He'd had to ditch his plane into the English Channel. His body was never found. He was twenty-one years old. I remembered the words of "The Foggy Dew." "I'd rather die 'neath an Irish sky." So many Irishmen killed fighting for the English in every one of their wars over the centuries, and now here we were again.

"I volunteered to meet you," Ray said. "We've cousins in Chicago."

"There's a Finucane family in Bridgeport," I said as we got into the van.

"They could belong to us," he said.

"Except they probably would have given interviews to the papers by now," Mike said.

"I don't know. Lot of shy people in our family," Ray said. He turned to me. "And you're Miss . . . ?"

"Kelly," I said, "but call me Nora."

"I've an aunt named Nora but her nickname in the family is Nonie."

Mike laughed. "I'd say we found our man."

Well . . . let me say that I didn't miss being with Eleanor Roosevelt at all. In fact when we finally met up four days later, I'd say we'd seen more of London and of our troops than she had.

Because Ray—Raymond Patrick as his mother called him—took us home to where his parents, a brother, and two sisters lived in a suburb of London called Richmond.

"Now those Finucanes in Chicago," his father, Thomas Andrew—called Andy—explained as his wife, Florence, served cups of tea, "would be second cousins, I'd say. My father's uncle's children."

"I can offer you sugar because Raymond's brought us a good supply," Florence said.

It was still a house in mourning. A picture of their oldest son, big smile, dressed in his RAF uniform with black ribbons attached to the frame hung over the fireplace in the parlor where we sat. A comfortable place. Andy did well as a banker. Florence told us her boys had been educated in good schools taught by the Christian Brothers both here and in Dublin, and the girls were going to the nuns.

I realized that the Irish in London had created their own world just as we had in the States. Very like being in Ireland, chatting and sipping tea with the Finucanes. I stayed there while Ray took the three boys out for a run-around some of his favorite pubs. I told Andy that I'd been in Dublin soon after the Easter Rising and had known both Michael Collins and Éamon de Valera.

"A tragedy that those two fell out," Andy said. "It was why I brought the family over here really. We left during the Civil War. We'd beaten the greatest empire in the world only to turn on each other. When I think how we fought together and then—"

"Now, Andy," Florence said, "no sense in stirring up the past. The present is hard enough." She turned to me. "Would you like a glass of whiskey, Nora? Andy is a Pioneer but I keep a bottle. Brendan liked a drop at night—" She stopped.

"I named my son Brendan Éamon Fergus. Irish heroes all, but the British press erased all that and called him Paddy. We're all Paddies to them," he said.

"They mean no harm," Florence said.

"Don't they? A way to trivialize us," he said.

"Ah, Andy," Florence said, "surely now . . ." She looked over at the picture. "I'm English myself," she said to me. "Born in Leicester. I met Andy in Dublin."

Andy laughed. "Here I was, a rebel taking on the Brits, and I fell for an English lass. Of course I was very young when I got involved. Dev was my teacher at Blackrock College. It was because of him I joined the Volunteers. I was one of the last fighting alongside him at Boland's Mill. And yet my son . . . I opposed his joining the RAF at first. He was only seventeen but he was mad to fly and we still hoped there'd be no war. Sometimes I kick myself for taking the boys to the air show at Baldonnel. That's when he decided to be a pilot. And once Hitler . . . Well, whatever about the government here and the empire, regular English people are decent enough. We've good friends and neighbors here."

"And I'm proud that my son gave his life defending them," Florence said. "Some of the newspapers say the Battle of Britain would have been lost if not for Brendan. A terrible time."

"And yet that's when I saw the English at their best," Andy said. "There's an air raid shelter at the top of our street. It's a Tube station and down there we're like one big family. Cups of tea and sing-songs." He shook his head. "Not sure whether they're just too thick to understand the danger or are just very brave."

"Mrs. Anderson next door lost her father in the Great War and both her husband and son joined up," Florence said.

"Here's a fact for you, Nora," Andy said. "More men from Ireland have enlisted in the British Army than have been conscripted in Ulster. Odd when you think that it was conscription in the last war that led so many to join the Volunteers."

"But, Andy," Florence said, "this war is different. The Nazis are truly evil."

"We wouldn't have this war if not for the last one, and that was imperialists fighting each other to carve up the world," he said.

"I agree with you, Andy," I said. "I nursed soldiers in France and saw the Marines cut down as they walked through a wheat field in Belleau Wood. I consoled myself by thinking, well surely all this will teach every nation a lesson. We won't slaughter each other again."

"And each one who dies leaves a hole in the lives of those who loved them, a wound that will never heal," Florence said.

I heard voices. The front door slammed. Two young girls and a little boy came into the parlor.

"My daughters Margaret and Maureen and our son Eamonn," Florence said. They smiled at me. "Nora's from America. Chicago," and the little boy extended his arms and started making machine gun noises.

"Al Capone," he said.

"Stop it," Andy said to him.

"That's alright," I said. "I suppose if you have to live with being called Paddy, I can accept our gangster reputation."

"Have you ever met a real gangster?" the boy asked me.

I wondered how this family would react if I'd said. "Met one? Why I had a gangster lover who tried to murder me but I was saved by another gangster who killed him and please pass the scones."

Instead I said, "We're not as bad as the movies make us out to be."

Florence sent the kids upstairs to do their homework and explained to me that they got into their beds where it was warmer. Their evening meal was potatoes and bacon, and I knew she was taking less to give me a share.

The boys didn't get in 'til midnight, too late to drive back to the base. Florence somehow found a place for all of us. Her daughters doubled up in one bed and I took the second in their room. Ray, who shared his room with his little brother Eamonn, took the sleeping boy into his parents' room and settled him on pillows on the floor. Jerry and Denis took Ray's room. He and Mike made do in the parlor, Mike on the couch, and Ray in the easy chair.

"This reminds me of the nights all of us kids bunked in your apartment, Aunt Nonie," Mike said to me as I stood in the doorway.

"Yes," I said, "doesn't seem that long ago."

I thought the girls would be asleep, but when I got into bed I heard sobs coming from across the room. Margaret was turned toward me. Maureen faced the wall crying.

"She'll stop soon," Margaret said. "She lets herself think about Brendan before she falls asleep. I told her not to, but . . ."

"And you?"

"Oh I decided I'm just going to believe my mother and Sister Anselm at school. Brendan has a high place in heaven being a hero and all. He's my own special saint and will get me whatever I want. Right now I'm asking him to help me do my maths. He said he would as long as I do my homework."

"So he talks to you."

"I don't hear his voice if that's what you mean. I'm not bonkers like Mary Reagan's mother who said she sees her son Tom who was killed in North Africa last month. It's more like Brendan thinks the words to me."

"Well that's comforting," I said.

"Better than crying myself to sleep. Though Maureen told me I was only fooling myself, that Brendan wasn't up there. Neither was Jesus or Mary or

God even because if they were Brendan would still be alive. What do you say to that, Miss Kelly? Am I silly to pray? Does praying do anything?"

I didn't answer her right away. What could I say? "If it helps the one who's praying then why not?"

The crying had stopped now.

"Good night," Margaret said.

"Good night, girls." I looked up at the ceiling. Okay, Brendan, I thought, if any of this is true, if there is a heaven of some kind and you're up there, I turn Mike over to you. No sounds came from the other bed. I fell asleep. It had been a very long day and many miles traveled.

"I bet you've never seen anything like this," Ray said to us the next day as we drove past blocks of buildings hit by the bombs the Luftwaffe dropped on the city of London night after night. "The Blitz" Ray called it, which had a kind of German sound to it but blitz seemed to describe a quick sharp blow while these attacks kept coming. Such random destruction. One apartment building stood intact next to another whose façade had been sheared off, exposing parlors very like the Finucanes'—a couch, a chair, just visible under the rubble.

"Jesus," Mike said, "this really makes the war real."

I wondered if I should tell them that the streets of Dublin looked very much like these after the British naval guns bombarded the city during the Easter Rising. Had Andy Finucane told his son about the similarity? Probably not. Wouldn't want to equate the British with the Nazis. I shouldn't either so I said nothing.

Ray dropped me back at his parents' house, as Florence had invited me to stay on instead of going to the base and she seemed to enjoy taking me around to meet the neighbor women. I was a novelty. As I took their photographs and listened to their stories I realized I'd always associated the English with the British Army and Ireland's oppressors. With landlords whose allegiance was to the crown and who had watched a million people starve to death while they sold food to England. But these women were very like those I knew in Bridgeport, or in Bearna for that matter, where Granny Honora had been born. I said as much to Andy the last night I stayed with the Finucanes.

"We're all alike really aren't we?" he said. "We want the same things. A decent job. Security. Opportunities for our children. I've always thought that the British government's greatest fear was that ordinary Irish and British people would figure out how much they have in common and band together against all those lords and ladies who want to rule over us and take our money. But even the kindest, most polite English person can't quite see someone Irish as his equal. It's centuries of being told that Paddies are dumb and dangerous, good for a song and a laugh, but not really solid, can't be trusted. We're full of blarney and superstition, Papists after all, very brave sometimes, but inferior really. Without us who would they have to look down on? Rather like the attitude toward colored people in your own country I'd say, Nora. Maybe the war will change all that. Shared danger and shared sorrow."

"I hope so, Andy. I surely do," I said.

The next day I joined Eleanor Roosevelt. Not only had she stayed for the weekend with the Churchills but she had spent two days being entertained by the king and queen at Buckingham Palace.

"They're old friends," Eleanor Roosevelt said. "They visited us at Hyde Park. Franklin made them eat hot dogs. I think they were secretly appalled."

We were at the main Red Cross Club. A four-story building serving the US forces. Mike and the rest of the aircrew were all back at the base waiting for word of our departure. Eleanor Roosevelt, Tommy, and I were helping to serve hot dogs to lines of soldiers and sailors. We were to fly out the next morning, land in Belfast, spend the afternoon meeting the troops, then fly on to Derry and the Navy base where we'd stay.

"We'll spend the rest of the afternoon here," Eleanor Roosevelt said. "Spend the night in the embassy and then we'll leave for Belfast at first light. The colonel is informing our air crew."

I went down to the kitchen for more buns, and as I passed the club entrance I saw a group of Negro soldiers standing at the door.

"Good afternoon, ma'am," said the tallest fellow, who had what I recognized as sergeant stripes on his sleeve. "We heard they've got hot dogs, mustard, and Coca-Cola inside this club. Is that true?"

"It certainly is and you'll never guess who's serving them. Eleanor Roosevelt."

He turned and told the others, "This is our lucky day." Then turned to me. "We love the First Lady. She's done more for our race than even the president has."

The men came through the red-painted door of the club. But when we reached the hallway two MPs who I hadn't noticed before stepped forward.

"What are you doing here, boys?" the first MP asked.

"Going to get some hot dogs," the sergeant said.

"Not here, you're not," the MP said. Both MPs were older than most of the soldiers I'd seen. Army regulars I'd say, big. Southerners from their accents. "Your club is around the corner on Wellington Street," he said.

"Oh, come on," I said. "Stand aside and let these men through. Mrs. Roosevelt expects them."

The Negro sergeant looked at me.

"Isn't that right, Sergeant?" I said to him.

"Yes, ma'am," he said. "And we don't want to be late, so . . ." He waved the other four forward.

"Hold it," the MP said and the two drew their guns. "I don't give a damn what Eleanor Roosevelt wants." He snarled out her name. "This club is for whites only."

"I'm getting Mrs. Roosevelt. We'll see about this," and I started toward the main dining room. But the sergeant took my arm, turned me around, and walked me out of the door. The Negro soldiers followed. "Wait," I said. "You're not going to take that are you?"

"Listen, ma'am, that cracker could have arrested the whole pack of us. Even shoot at us if we back-talked him," the sergeant said.

"He wouldn't dare," I said.

"Oh yes, he would," another man said. "I've lived with boys like that all my life. They're mean as dirt and love to pull the trigger."

"Let's go," the sergeant said. "Find that place around the corner."

"I'm going with you," I said. "It better be as good as this club or Mrs. Roosevelt will hear about it."

"Where are you from, ma'am?" the sergeant asked me as we started walking.

"Chicago," I said.

"There are two clubs in Chicago too, you know," he said. "Jim Crow's a traveling man."

What could I say? It was tough finding this other club. Finally we saw a small sign "US Service Personnel (Colored)." An arrow pointed down the steps into a basement. "Welcome, welcome," a woman said. "I'm Winnie from Jamaica and I'm very glad to have you here."

"Thank you," the sergeant said. "We're really looking forward to hot dogs and mustard."

"Oh," she said. We were the only people in the place. A storage basement I'd say. Two long tables took up the center of the room. Wooden tops, no tablecloths. The Red Cross Club had a complete kitchen but I didn't see any facilities here.

"Sit down. Sit down," Winnie said. "I've some delicious biscuits, cookies as you say. Homemade by our volunteers. All members of my church. And nice cups of tea."

"No hot dogs?" I said. She shook her head.

The men were too polite to complain to her but the sergeant said to me, "I know the Army is segregated but I thought when we got overseas the people might be different."

Winnie had sat down with us and she answered him. "There are a lot of crazy stories told about you fellows. They say tan Yanks have tails."

"That's crazy," I said. "And that's what these men are called? Tan Yanks?"

The sergeant shook his head. "And we were so looking forward to London. This is our only day here. We're shipping out in the morning."

"Where to?" I asked.

"I'm not supposed to say but they gave us these little books." He handed me a small pamphlet. "A Guide to Northern Ireland for US Soldiers, Sailors, and Marines." I laughed.

"Well, gentlemen, I wouldn't be surprised if you meet Mrs. Roosevelt after all," I said.

4

NOVEMBER 9, 1942

Well before first light. We were waiting on the runway while the planes returning from the night's bombing raid landed. We had boarded at 6:00 a.m. and both Eleanor Roosevelt and Tommy were asleep, but I stood in the cockpit. There were emergency vehicles, fire engines, ambulances lining the brightly lit runway.

"Look at that one," Denis said as a plane bumped down not far from us. I could see that a section of one wing was gone and that there were holes in the tail.

"How did he ever make it back?" I said.

"Good flying," Jerry said.

"And luck," Denis said.

We could hear the exchange between the air tower and the pilot. "Did you have a visual on Billy?" the tower asked.

"He got hit near Cherbourg. I saw him going down, but I didn't see the crash," an approaching pilot answered.

"His 'chute open?" the tower said.

"Not sure."

"In the last war they didn't even equip planes with parachutes. Said the pilots would be more likely to jump. Insane," I said.

"But then we don't have parachutes on this flight and neither do you," Denis said.

"That's right," I said.

"Don't worry, Aunt Nonie, we won't be flying through ack-ack or facing Nazi fighters. Ireland was chosen as a good place for training because it's far enough from German bases in France and the weather's right. Plenty of rain."

"Well," I said, "Andy Finucane told me the Nazis did pull off three bombing raids on Belfast last year before we got into the war. Would have burned the whole city down except fire brigades from Ireland crossed the border and were on the scene in hours. He told me de Valera made a speech in which he said that the people of Belfast were our people. Then de Valera gave the Germans hell. Andy said it had made Hitler back off."

"Hitler was afraid of de Valera?" Mike said. "That doesn't sound right."

"According to Andy, Hitler thought Dev would convince Irish-America to push the US into the war."

"Hitler should have known we never would have sat this one out," Mike said.

Better not to remind him how many people, including Joseph Kennedy when he was ambassador here, wanted to keep the US neutral. Denis spoke up.

"If not for Pearl Harbor who knows if we'd be here right now."

If, I thought. If. And suddenly I was back in Miami that night. Move closer. Move closer. A few inches and Roosevelt would never have been our president. It didn't bear thinking about.

"Listen," Mike said. "Hear that?" The engine sounded much louder than those of the other planes. "It's a B-52, one of ours. We met the crews last night. There was a navigator from Chicago called Dick Garvey."

"What parish?" I asked.

"I don't know."

"You didn't ask him? Why, we probably know some of his people. He could be Garvey the lawyer's son . . ."

"Yanks, you're cleared for takeoff," the tower said.

"Get into your seat, Aunt Nonie," but as I turned I heard another voice with an American accent saying, "Apache 105 and Cherokee 6 were shot down."

"Damn," I heard Denis say, but Mike had the propellers turning and there was no time for any more talk.

He pulled us up above the clouds into a light blue sky, but after about ninety minutes we made our descent into Belfast through rain that blurred the landscape before us. We disembarked into a downpour.

Once again the British Army took Tommy Thompson and Eleanor Roosevelt away. "We have our own photographer thank you very much," I was told.

We would wait for them here at the airport, which was about thirty miles from the city. They would spend six hours in Belfast visiting another Red Cross Club and a hospital. This time I protested.

"I'm not just a photographer," I said. "I'm here as her guide," I told the British officer, another colonel who could have been a double to the London fellow. "I've traveled in Ireland before and I'm Irish myself."

"You're American, madam," he said. "You should thank God every day your ancestors left here on that boat. Winston Churchill was right about the dreary steeples of Fermanagh and Tyrone. The whole place is a kip." With that he got in a car and the official party drove away.

But this time we found an American canteen and a group of soldiers.

"The British don't seem too pleased with us being in Northern Ireland," I said to one.

"Oh, they're not," the fellow said. "They say we're overpaid, oversexed, and over here, but we tell them that *they're* underpaid, undersexed, and under Eisenhower."

Something miraculous about the way the sun suddenly took over the horizon as our plane followed the Foyle River to a small airport just west of the city of Derry. Then two rainbows appeared. No pale arcs either but wide swathes of vibrant colors. Still shining above us as we got off the plane.

"I suppose there's a leprechaun with a pot of gold at the end of those," Mike said. Jerry and Denis laughed.

"I wouldn't joke about leprechauns," I said.

"You don't really believe in fairies do you, Nora?" Jerry said.

"I don't, but they're here."

The welcome committee was an all-American team this time—a Naval officer and a Marine. For the first time I heard Eleanor Roosevelt's code name—Rover.

"I'm Commander James Logan," said the Navy man who was the older of the two, a stocky build with white hair. "And this is Major Jim Duggan of the US Marine Corps." This fellow was well over six feet, with red hair and a big smile. Irish through and through.

"Welcome, Rover. We all admire the sense of adventure embodied in that name. Excellent timing," Duggan said. "Our Marine Corps Birthday Ball is tomorrow and here you are, Mrs. Roosevelt, the mother of a Marine, so a perfect guest of honor delivered right to us with two other beautiful ladies along with you." He took Eleanor Roosevelt's hand, and while he didn't really click his heels, there was something gallant about him. "Wasn't that a swell rainbow," he said. "And just wait. We're about to have a spectacular sunset. No matter how bad the weather is here at the end of the day this place serves up a sunset." The rainbows seemed to color the clouds red and orange and purple streaked the sky. "Of course the Druids believed Paradise was out there in the west," he said pointing at the horizon.

Who is this fellow? I wondered as he escorted the First Lady, Tommy, and me toward one of the big Buicks waiting for us. He got in the front seat and the three of us in the back. Mike and Jerry and Denis rode with Commander Logan in the second car.

"There are five hundred of us Marines stationed here," Duggan said as the car drove out of the airport onto a country road. "Most bunk in Quonset huts on the grounds of an estate called Beech Hill. There's a wonderful old house on the property and that's where the officers live."

"About your ball. I didn't anticipate the need for evening clothes," Eleanor Roosevelt said. "Although the king and queen did dress for dinner and I suppose I could wear that garment. But I doubt if Miss Kelly or Lieutenant Thompson brought anything suitable."

Oh no, I thought, was Eleanor Roosevelt going to turn Tommy and me into Cinderellas and keep us away from the ball?

"You're fine just the way you are, ladies," he said. "The men will be so happy to meet anyone from home they won't worry about what you're wearing. We need some cheering up now. Three of our Marines died in the North African landings."

"Ah," Eleanor Roosevelt said, and Tommy and I just shook our heads. Nowhere to escape this war. Not even in this green place that seemed so far from violence and death.

Mike and the boys were staying at the bachelor officers' quarters in the Navy section of the base, Duggan told us.

"The pilot is my nephew," I said. "I hope we'll have some time together. I've been here before but it's his first time in Ireland."

"Of course technically we're in the United Kingdom," Eleanor Roosevelt said.

Duggan laughed. "Yes, ma'am. But Miss Kelly is right too." He turned in his seat and pointed to a patch sewn onto his uniform. Under the eagle, globe, and anchor—the symbol of the Marine Corps—was a shamrock.

"I had these made up for all of our men. Great for morale. The rest of the Corps calls us the 'Irish Marines.'"

"That's very unconventional," Eleanor Roosevelt said. He smiled.

"Corporal," Duggan said to the driver, "take a left here."

We left the main highway and turned onto a country road that twisted past low stone walls. The other car slowed. The driver honked his horn. Duggan leaned out of the window and waved him to follow. We reached a humpbacked bridge where there was a hut at the side of the road. A Marine stepped out. Our car stopped. He saluted Duggan and we drove on with Logan's car behind. At the bottom of the bridge we stopped.

"Do you want to stretch your legs, ladies?" Duggan asked.

"I don't feel it's necessary," Eleanor Roosevelt began, but Duggan was out of the car holding the back door open. I stepped out, followed by Tommy Thompson and a reluctant Eleanor Roosevelt. The Navy car had stopped behind us and now Commander Logan joined us.

"What's going on, Duggan?" he said, not pleased.

"A bit of sightseeing before we lose the light," he said. A lingering brightness was still in the sky. Mike and the boys came up beside us.

"May I escort you?" Duggan said to Eleanor Roosevelt and offered her his arm. She hesitated but did place her hand on his arm. Then Mike came over to me and did the same. And Jerry said "May I?" to Tommy.

So there we were, lined up as if going into a dinner party. Duggan took a few steps forward and we followed with Denis coming up behind.

"There," Duggan said, "you are in the county of Donegal, in the Irish Free State."

"Donegal," I said, "the pride of all."

"Peaceful," Denis said.

"Quiet," Mike agreed. The only sound came from the wind in the trees.

"Yes," Duggan said. "No war here."

"So close," Denis said.

"And you're allowed to just go here?" I asked.

"No," Duggan said, "we're bending the rules. We're all deserters right now, but we have a good relationship with the people here, especially the Gardaí—the police—and we turn a blind eye if some of our men cross the border now and then. The beer is cheaper over here and they have real butter. Nothing like a hot loaf of brown bread slathered with butter."

"That's not an official policy," Logan said. "I wouldn't like the commander-in-chief to get the wrong idea."

We all looked at Eleanor Roosevelt. Dear God, I thought, she'll turn the lot of them in. But she laughed.

"Sneaking across the border to get beer and butter is just the kind of adventure Franklin would enjoy," she said.

Duggan turned around and led Eleanor Roosevelt back toward the car with the rest of us coming up behind, but Denis didn't move. A place without war. I wondered if he was remembering those burning planes crashing into the deck of an aircraft carrier. For one second I thought he might just start running toward the Donegal hills but then I heard a bell ringing.

"The Angelus," Duggan said. And that big tall Marine with his movie-star looks made the sign of the cross and, standing right there next to the car, said, "The Angel of the Lord declared unto Mary."

I answered him. "And she was conceived of the Holy Ghost." We said the whole prayer with Mike and Jerry, and to my surprise, Tommy Thompson joining in. Just as we finished, Denis turned and walked toward us.

"Those are the monastery bells," Duggan said as we got back in the cars and began to drive back toward Derry. "The monks told me they dedicate their evening office to us as a prayer for our safety. I say the Angelus to kind of join them."

"You went to the monastery?" I said as we turned back onto the highway.

"I visit them often. A beautiful place built right next to the ruins of a two-thousand-year-old fort called the Grianán of Aileach. A spectacular view from up there."

Donegal—Father Kevin's home place. I wondered if I could go to the monastery, maybe arrange for a mass to be said for Peter's soul.

Full dark now as we turned in the drive toward Beech Hill House. There were lights in the windows of the house, which was Victorian, Duggan said, though there were bits dating back to the seventeenth century when the Skipton family drove out the O'Kanes, the chieftains of the area, and took their property. A stone arch that had to be centuries old stood on one side of the driveway as we approached the house.

"I always think the house looks like a mother hen and all these are her chicks," Duggan said. He pointed. "There are rows of quonset huts lined up across the property. You'll see them in the morning."

"I'm Mrs. Nicholson and you are most welcome." The woman who stood in the entrance hall looked to be at least eighty. Her white hair was in a bun. She said, "It's too cold to stand here. Come into the Morning Room. It's the warmest place in the house."

She took us into a small room. Easy chairs were arranged in front of a tall stone fireplace where three logs burned. Unusual that, turf was the standard fuel for the hearths in Irish houses, I'd learned when I traveled around the country with the Quakers. Only the big houses where the landlords owned the surrounding woods could burn logs. The flames jumped up cracking the wood, giving off a smell I recognized. I was back at Ed's Eagle River house where we warmed ourselves against the chilly Wisconsin nights around fires like this.

Mrs. Nicholson pointed us toward the chairs. "Sit," she said. We did. Eleanor Roosevelt and Tommy on one side, me on the other, while Duggan stood beside the fireplace. "Now that you're all nice and cozy," Mrs. Nicholson said, "I can welcome you, Mrs. Roosevelt. You do our house a great honor." She sat down next to me.

I felt the heat splash over my feet and I realized how cold I had been. So excited by our arrival I hadn't felt the chill but now . . . I pulled my chair just a bit closer to the fire. Mrs. Nicholson noticed.

"Bitter out there," she said. "We're very far north you know. Same latitude as Newfoundland, my husband the judge always said. I insisted on us having what he called robust fires, and beech wood burns so slowly. Logs like this will last through the whole evening. Won't they, James?" she said to Duggan.

"Yes indeed," Duggan said. "And may I tell you a few things about our hostess—" But Mrs. Nicholson cut him off.

She leaned past me and looked over at Eleanor Roosevelt. "I admire you very much, Mrs. Roosevelt. Not easy to be married to a powerful man, but you have refused to merely stand in his shadow. The judge was a good husband but his ideas about a woman's place were very traditional. I don't know what he would make of his wife becoming a kind of landlady to the American forces."

"You're much more than that, Mrs. Nicholson," Duggan said. He turned to us. "Mrs. Nicholson kindly turned over this estate to the US Marine Corps and those of us who live in the house are especially grateful. The evenings we spend here with her in this room are most delightful."

"Now, James," she said, "tell these women the truth." She turned to us. "He and his young fellows indulge me and share an after-dinner port in this room while we listen to the news on the wireless, which they very kindly brought to this house."

She pointed to a Philco radio that stood on a table in the corner. "Sometimes we play a rubber or two of bridge but then I retire and I know the men travel into the town. But I do insist that they return by eleven o'clock. Sleep is so important don't you think, Mrs. Roosevelt? Essential to health as the judge always said."

"Quite right, though I don't believe I've had a really good night's sleep in months," Eleanor Roosevelt said.

"I suppose you get up early like they do at the camp," Mrs. Nicholson said to her. "The bugle sounds well before dawn." Eleanor Roosevelt didn't respond. Her head rested against the back of the chair and her eyes were closed.

Tommy was nodding too. I looked at Mrs. Nicholson. She smiled. "Food and bed I think," she said.

Eleanor Roosevelt stirred. "I believe I am to visit the hospital tonight. Am I correct, Major?"

"Yes, ma'am."

"Reschedule," Mrs. Nicholson said. "How can Mrs. Roosevelt be expected to cheer up the patients if she's exhausted herself. Now," she stood up, "don't you move. Gunny Butler has made an excellent soup and I've taught him how to prepare wheaten bread. You'll have your supper on a tray right here. Your rooms are ready and there are hot water bottles in the beds."

That was our first evening in Derry. The soup was delicious. Potato and leek. Very thick and hot with chunks of ham. Then warm wheaten bread with plenty of smuggled butter. As we followed Mrs. Nicholson up the stairs, I said to Major Duggan, "Where are the other officers that are staying here?"

"I allowed them to go into town early tonight," he said.

Mrs. Nicholson showed Eleanor Roosevelt into what she called the star chamber, which had been the judge's room. From the landing I could see a four-poster bed.

"You'll have your own bath, Mrs. Roosevelt, and the heater has been on the whole day so the water should be nice and hot."

Eleanor Roosevelt took her hand. "Thank you, Mrs. Nicholson," she said, and I thought I heard tears in the First Lady's voice. "I'm not accustomed to being mothered," she said. "You are very kind."

Tommy and I had smaller rooms and our bathroom was out on the landing. While the bath water was hot, the house was cold, and I moved very quickly into the bed and searched with my feet for the hot water bottle. I thought of the Marines sleeping in the quonset huts as I listened to the wind hit the two windows. I think I was asleep by nine o'clock but then wide-awake a few hours later. I turned on the bedside lamp. Two a.m. and I had to get up. Mrs. Nicholson had pointed to the chamber pot next to the bed. "Women of our age," she said, and didn't finish the sentence. Our age, I thought. She's got a good twenty years on me. I can still walk to the toilet. Freezing on the landing now and I was glad for my flannel nightgown and wool knitted slippers. Just as I put my hand on the doorknob, a cold draft swept over me as if a window had been opened.

At the end of the hall the window frame was slowly going up. No one else was awake. The window was moving on its own. A ghost? Poltergeist? One of the vanquished O'Kane chiefs returning? Crazy thoughts I know, but here I was shivering and feeling a certain urgency—Get in the toilet, shut the door, my rational mind said, but I couldn't stop staring at the window. Then I saw one leg cross the windowsill, then another, and a whole man slid onto the landing. He saw me.

"Don't scream," he said. A Marine, and from the stripes on his uniform, an officer. I saw the shamrock patch. He wasn't as tall as Duggan but another handsome fellow, and now he was grinning at me. "I'm George Ludke. Captain George Ludke," he said. "You must be with Mrs. Roosevelt."

"Yes," I said. "My name is Nora Kelly." And we actually shook hands. He turned and put down the window.

"There's a very handy lattice that goes to this window," he said. "Mrs. Nicholson doesn't understand that an eleven p.m. curfew is too early for a Marine. She wants to make sure we're all on time for Mass."

"Mass?" I said. "Tomorrow's not Sunday."

"Mrs. Nicholson has a daily Mass said in her private chapel here in the house."

"What?"

"Oh yes, the Nicholsons are Catholics. The chapel's above the library. One of the monks bicycles over from the monastery every morning to say Mass at seven a.m."

"I'd never have thought . . . ," I said. "I mean landowners in this country are Protestant or English or both."

"Not the Nicholsons."

Like the Lynches, I thought, remembering Granny Honora's stories about their landlord in Galway who somehow had remained Catholic.

"But I thought a family called Skipton took this property."

"That was a long time ago. Get Mrs. Nicholson to tell you the story. They gambled it away and the estate passed through many owners before the Nicholsons bought it."

"Mr. Nicholson must have been a brilliant man to become a judge as a Catholic," I said.

"The military has advised us not to talk about religion in Northern Ireland. Funny thing is most Marines are Catholics. You should see the Sunday services at St. Mary's, the chapel up the road. Well good night," he said. "I won't delay you any longer."

"Right," I said and went into the toilet. Was ever anything predictable in Ireland?

I was already up and dressed when I heard the bugle sound for Reveille. It was still dark out but I followed the smell of coffee down the stairs to the dining room. I found Major Duggan and Captain Ludke having breakfast at a long table with two other men who stood up when I came in.

"This is Captain Donald Kennedy," he said, "and Sergeant Major Carlton Kent. I understand you've met Captain Ludke." He smiled.

"Good morning, ma'am," the other two said.

"Please sit down," I said.

"Help yourself," Duggan said and pointed to the sideboard where there was a coffeepot, a large chafing dish full of eggs, and a platter with bacon and sausages. The whole service was silver. And there were china plates piled up at the end of the buffet.

"Mrs. Nicholson insists that we use her dishes. She said that since she's our hostess, meals must be served properly."

I piled up eggs and bacon on my plate and sat down next to him.

"Mrs. Roosevelt?" Duggan said.

"Still asleep, I think," I said. "She could use a lie in. She's been going pretty hard."

"Oh there you are, Father," Ludke said to the man who had just walked in. "I was afraid you might have been arrested crossing the border."

"No, just got a late start. The guards know me," he said. He smiled at me. "Are you traveling with Mrs. Roosevelt?"

"Yes," I said.

"Mrs. Nicholson is chuffed about entertaining the First Lady," he said. "I'm Father Matthew by the way."

"Nora Kelly," I said.

He took off his heavy black cloak and I saw he was wearing a monk's robe. He reached into a slit in the habit and brought out a packet, which he set on the sideboard.

"You were running low on butter," he said to Major Duggan.

Father Matthew sat down but didn't take any breakfast. "You're fasting," I said, "and I've already eaten half my eggs. I guess I can't go to Communion."

"But you may. Bishop Farren has given a dispensation from fasting to all members of the American forces and those associated with them. So if you wish to receive, you can. The bishop is military chaplain for all of the North so his word goes."

"Too bad we couldn't get Mike and Jerry," I said to Duggan. "I think they'd like to participate."

"No problem," Duggan said. "Sergeant Major, would you put in a call to the BOQ and say we need the air crew with Mrs. Roosevelt here by zero seven hundred."

And that's how we ended up all together at Mass in the Beech Hill House private chapel. It was a jewel of a place with stained glass windows, a carved wooden altar, and four pews. I wasn't surprised that Tommy Thompson joined us but was astounded when Eleanor Roosevelt came in. And she knew when to stand and sit and kneel. Of course an Episcopal mass was pretty much the same as ours.

Father Matthew's Latin had an Irish lilt. He was a good celebrant. He didn't dawdle nor preach a long sermon. He simply welcomed us. "As today is the birthday of the Marine Corps, this Mass is being said for all Marines and I'm invoking both Columcille and the Druids. In Irish, Derry is Doire Columcille, 'the oak grove of St. Columcille.' He was the sixth century O'Neill prince who became a monk, bringing Christianity to Ireland and, through his followers, to most of Europe. But of course Druids had gathered in these oak groves for thousands of years.

Mike was next to me in the pew, and when it was time to go to Communion he stepped back and let me precede him. We knelt at the altar rail side by side. St. Columcille, I prayed, you're the patron of Derry, take a good look at Mike here, and protect him.

That was our last peaceful moment. Finally I was acting as Mrs. Roosevelt's official photographer, and every minute of her day was scheduled. Mike, Denis, and Jerry left in the car that was waiting for them. Mass was over at seven thirty and the sun was just rising as we left the house. Now I could see the rows of quonset huts that filled the grounds. Had to be at least one hundred. All the same. Corrugated steel shaped into a half circle; each one about twenty feet long.

"Since you'll be meeting the Marines at the ball tonight we decided not to interrupt their training to have them assemble now," Major Duggan said.

"Quite right," Eleanor Roosevelt said.

We could see that there was quite a bit of activity going on around the huts and in the fields beyond that. I would have liked to investigate, but a car had already pulled up for us.

"Well at least let me take a shot of you with the Marines who are staying here," I said, and lined up Duggan, Ludke, Kennedy, and Kent with the First Lady under the Beech Hill House portico.

"Wait a minute," Major Duggan said. He stepped inside and a minute later escorted Mrs. Nicholson out and placed her next to Eleanor Roosevelt. Two formidable women, I thought as I looked through my lens. I wonder do the Nazis understand what they're up against.

We spent the rest of the morning in the Naval hospital at a place called Creevagh. Our guide was a corpsman named Joseph Earhart Sardo, who told us he was a cousin of Amelia Earhart, who had landed in a field just beyond the hospital.

"So many coincidences seem to happen in Ireland," Sardo said. "We have fellows here whose ships were torpedoed," he went on. "They survived days in the water before they were rescued, and suffered from frostbite and hypothermia. The doctors here have devised new treatments that saved their feet and legs from amputation. Our medics have also made advances in taking care of shrapnel wounds. We get the flyers who've been shot down too."

Mrs. Roosevelt took time with each of the men in the wards, bending over listening as they told their stories. In my photographs I focused on her face, trying to show how intensely she took in every word. "I was on a destroyer escort," one sailor said. "Built in ninety days. Our decks were only a few inches thick. Don't protect much against a torpedo." Hard to hear from this sailor about how the torpedo ripped through the ship.

The hospital was preparing to handle many more battlefield causalities after the invasion of Europe began. "And to tell you the truth it can't come soon enough," Sardo said.

Next we toured the ship repair yard where Commander Logan guided us through acres and acres of activity. "This is a state-of-the-art facility," he said. "We employ civilians as well as Navy technicians. More than a thousand in the workforce, both men and women. We've got plenty of Rosie the Riveters here. When a ship arrives after crossing the North Atlantic it can be pretty beat up, even if it hasn't been attacked. The sea itself can cause a lot of damage."

He took us to an area where what must have been a five-hundred-foot-long ship was in dry dock. More than thirty welders with shields over their faces were repairing large holes in the hull of the ship. Sparks spit from their tools.

"A hailstorm caused those," Logan said. "They were lucky to have made it into port."

I got a great picture of Eleanor Roosevelt in the midst of all this activity. When I asked if any of the workers would like to have their picture taken with the First Lady, a number stepped forward. Two of them lifted their visors. Women.

"Fantastic," I said, and set the two up next to Eleanor Roosevelt. "Why don't you put on a visor and hold a welding torch," I said to Mrs. Roosevelt. Right away one of the women offered her visor to the First Lady. But she nodded no.

I remembered that Ed had once said funny hats have gotten many a politician in trouble. Especially Indian headdresses.

Commander Logan spoke to the group. "I'd like you to know that I had a letter from a ship's captain who said that you turned around his vessel in less time than any Stateside repair yard could have. Why don't you tell the First Lady where you're from."

The welders gathered around. Derry, said some, Tyrone, others chimed in, but there were a good few who answered Donegal, Cavan, Leitrim, and even Dublin. I photographed each of them with Mrs. Roosevelt and Logan. As we walked away, the commander said there was a lot of nonsense put out by the British suggesting that the IRA would try to put saboteurs in the repair yard.

"We've never had a bit of trouble," he said.

"Major Duggan told us the same thing," Eleanor Roosevelt said.

"He should know. He deals with the Irish Army all the time. You'll meet some of their officers at tonight's ball," he said as we walked back toward the car.

"But don't you think the Irish Free State is making a mistake by remaining neutral?" Eleanor Roosevelt asked.

"I'm afraid that's above my pay grade," Logan said.

5

"Our ballroom has been closed off for years and years," Mrs. Nicholson said. We were in her bedroom. Modest enough. Part of the old servants' quarters. She'd turned over the grander spaces to the Marines. I was doing up the at least two dozen pearl buttons along the back of her lavender crepe dress and not making a great job of it. The material was very thin and I was afraid I'd rip it. "No dances since before the Great War," she said, "when Ireland was one country and my son was still alive."

I'd been surprised that Mrs. Nicholson had asked for my help in dressing. "Arthritis," she'd said, showing me her hands, the fingers bent, the knuckles enlarged, "and I can't reach behind my back anymore, and of course I no longer have my maid." Now Mrs. Nicholson was a good soul and a Catholic, so not your typical lady of the manor, and yet I felt a little uneasy as I carefully pushed each button through the hand-sewn hole.

My aunt Máire had been a maid in a big house similar to this one and had been raped by the landlord. I should be staying in one of the tenants' cottages, I thought. Except Major James Duggan, one of us, an Irish-American in every inch of that six-foot-four frame was in charge here now. It was our house in a way. Still paying rent though, as I'd discovered.

"Couldn't just take over the estate," Duggan had told me. "Not the American way."

"We had three hundred people at that last ball," Mrs. Nicholson was telling me, "but Major Duggan said there'll be twice as many there tonight. He's gotten the boys to build an extension out the back through the French doors, a kind of marquee. A tent really but they'd figured some way to heat it."

"They're very handy these Marines," I said.

"At our last ball," Mrs. Nicholson said, "we had half of Donegal here. Hard to think of ourselves as separate from the rest of Ireland now."

"Maybe not forever," I said.

"We can hope," she said.

I'd buttoned her up now and she moved over to a small vanity and sat down in front of the mirror. I was surprised to see her take a box of powder and a puff from her drawer and begin to pat it on her face. "I used to add rouge and just a touch of lipstick, but at my age it can look like you're decorating a corpse. Thank you very much, Nora. Now you'd better go change yourself."

"This is it, Mrs. Nicholson. I'm wearing this suit." It was the same gray wool that had taken me through the entire trip, though I had rinsed out my white silk Chanel blouse, which, I thought, still looked good after twenty years.

"Oh, my dear, the men expect us to be festive. Of course the Wrens will be in uniform, but I think the rest of us must make an effort."

"I didn't bring any party clothes, Mrs. Nicholson, and you look good enough for both of us." And she did. The lavender crepe fell to the floor in soft folds, and now she asked me to fasten a diamond necklace around her neck which, if the stones weren't real, were very good imitations. She tried to brush her hair, but I took over and gave her a French roll instead of her usual bun. Still something of the girl who had danced in the days I'd heard Maud Gonne and Constance Markievicz describe. Ireland before the First War, before anyone could imagine civilized European nations slaughtering each other until they'd extinguished a whole generation. Home Rule seemed inevitable and Ireland would be a nation once again, though still safely tied to Mother England, and all would be well. Except—well not an evening to think about except.

"Don't worry about me, Mrs. Nicholson. I'm sixty-three years old and everyone's aunt and this suit will do."

"No, my dear, you are wrong. I was not enamored of Queen Victoria, but she maintained her style to the very end. The judge and I went down to Dublin for her visit in 1900. Rather embarrassing really. She had invited herself. Most of the city officials, including the mayor, were Nationalists with no love for the crown but what could they do? And she stayed for three whole weeks ensconced in the viceroy's lodge. They were desperate to keep her amused. I attended one of the many receptions. Funny enough we were there the day Maud Gonne stole the queen's thunder. The British had arranged a big do for the children, but attendance had not been good. Then Maud Gonne and her Daughters of Erin sponsored their own day out and thirty thousand children turned up. Plenty of sweets and games and music. The judge and I wished we'd brought the family down with us."

I wanted to tell her that Maud and I had been good friends in Paris and in Ireland, too, but she was off in her own memories.

"My point is Queen Victoria never referred to her age or allowed anyone else to mention it. She was the monarch full stop. And though she dressed all in black, it was very expensive black with lots of lace and plenty of diamonds. She never did stop mourning her German prince, but then she herself was German. All those Hanovers on her father's side, and her mother was a German princess, who, they say, never even learned English. There were some tales about how this Irish officer ran her mother's household and, well, I did examine at the queen's face to see if maybe she did look a bit Irish. Gossip can be cruel. The same kind of scandal attached to Victoria herself. There was a manservant called Brown on whom she became very dependent. My dear Nora, I'm going round and around to say that a woman's age does not define her. You are as young now as you ever will be and you're not going to the ball in that suit."

She got up and walked across the hallway and opened a door. A blast of camphor hit us and I could see shrouded garments hanging from a rod.

"I appreciate your concern," I said, "but . . ." Now how could I put this? "I'm not Cinderella. I worked with some of the greatest couturiers in Paris. If I wanted to dress up, I'd find a way and . . ." But she was holding a dress out toward me. Not the froufrou ball gown I'd feared, but a plain green sheath with full-length sleeves and a scooped neck. I had to reach out and touch it. The material caught the hall light.

"Irish poplin," she said. Though green, there were shimmers of blue, red even on the surface. "It will suit you," Mrs. Nicholson said. It did.

I realized I must have lost a few pounds on the trip because it fell down easily over my hips and I didn't have to suck my stomach in. I twisted my hair up on top of my head and accepted a pair of earrings from Mrs. Nicholson. Emeralds or some facsimile. We looked at each other in the mirror and smiled. I felt as if we were poking the war in the eye. I thought of Mariann walking down the aisle in her kelly green suit. We were lighting a candle against the gloom.

Eleanor Roosevelt and Tommy must have felt the same, because I could see both had made an effort with their hair, and was that rouge on Eleanor Roosevelt's cheeks? Her blue velvet gown was perfectly pleasant, and Tommy had added a long skirt to her jacket.

"Shall we go?" Mrs. Nicholson said. As we marched down the stairs, I heard the Notre Dame victory march in my head. Maybe we would win overall.

Major Duggan, Mike, Jerry, and Denis were waiting for us at the bottom of the stairs. "We usually don't invite the Navy to our Birthday Balls, especially flyboys, but we're making an exception tonight," Duggan said. "You all look very beautiful. May I escort you into the ball, Mrs. Nicholson?" he said.

"Mike," I said under my breath and looked over at Eleanor Roosevelt. He understood and offered her his arm.

"Come on, Denis," I said. So he and I, Jerry and Tommy walked behind the other two couples as if we were on our way to a grand cotillion. We passed through the dining room and down a long hallway where double doors opened out into the ballroom.

"Oh," Mrs. Nicholson said. "Oh. Oh." We stood in the entrance. "How did you transform this dusty wreck into a . . ."

"A movie set?" I said, because I did feel as if we were all about to step into a film. The Marines had strung colored lights along the walls and across the ceiling where mirrored balls hung to reflect the light, making patterns on the floor. And it was warm. How had they managed? And then I noticed the electric heaters. What a crowd. Were all five hundred Marines attending? A mass of khaki filled the ballroom and the tent beyond. Girls in party dresses were interspersed among the men.

"You ladies look so wonderful I wish we could have worn our dress blues in your honor, but in theater even at the ball, this is as formal as we get," Duggan said.

Captain Ludke and Captain Kennedy and Sergeant Major Kent had joined us. "Most enlisted Marines don't have money to spend on fancy dress," the sergeant major said.

"Well their dates are making up for it," I said, as we moved through the dancers toward a table set up for us at the side of the room.

"I've learned that Irish women have a lot of style," Kennedy said. "My fiancée is from Dublin. She's coming tonight."

"And of course our Derry girls are famous for their good looks and high spirits," Mrs. Nicholson said.

A band was set up at the other end of the room. About fifteen players, all Marines. I saw a lot of horns.

"The band leader was with Fred Waring," Major Duggan said as the men pulled out our chairs and we sat down at the long table. Red and gold chrysanthemums decorated the center of our table and the small tables along the edge of the dance floor celebrating the Marine Corps' colors and their unexpected flower arranging skills. Lots of couples were dancing and there was a crush of Marines around the many bars.

"A happy bunch," I said to George Ludke, who was across from me.

"Oh yes," he said. "We all know how lucky we are to be here instead of on some God-forsaken island in the Pacific crouched down in a trench hoping the next Jap bombardment won't wipe us out."

"Now, Captain," Major Duggan began, "not a night for such talk."

"But I can't help thinking of all those fellows in those jungles. Imagine how they're celebrating the Marine Corps' birthday."

"They'll find a way, Captain," the sergeant major said. "Believe me, they'll find a way."

"It's all so random," Ludke said. He looked at me. "When we got on that boat, the *Santa Rosa*, none of us knew where we were going, but we assumed it was somewhere in the Pacific. There were no Marines in the European theater. The Army didn't want us. They still hadn't gotten over the publicity we'd gotten in the last war. All those stories about how the Germans were afraid of us and called us Devil Dogs. In April, when we left, our fellows were being destroyed. Bataan, Corregidor, casualty rates of fifty percent. Not to mention getting jungle rot and . . ." He stopped and then went on. "Look, we knew what we'd signed up for. We chose to be Marines but then we landed here. It was as if we'd come to Camelot. Green fields, friendly people, great pubs, and nobody shooting at us. Luck."

"Our turn will come, George," Duggan said. "You can be sure of that, but for now why don't you take Mrs. Nicholson out on the floor? And you can tell her how much you appreciate the good night sleep you're getting." Ludke laughed and Mrs. Nicholson said thank you very much and stood up.

Now Major Duggan turned to Mrs. Roosevelt. "May I have the pleasure, ma'am?" And they joined the dancers.

"What about it, Aunt Nonie?" Mike said to me. When was the last time I'd danced? I wondered as we walked onto the floor. Somebody's wedding, I guess. Not Mike's though. No time for music there. A young woman was up at the bandstand.

"And now the US Marine Corps Band is proud to introduce Derry's own Maureen O'Reilly."

A beauty with long dark hair, big smile.

"We'll meet again," she began singing. *"Who knows where, who knows when."*

A kind of hush as the couples moved slowly together. Who does know, I thought.

Mike and I could only take small steps in the dense crowd, but we did well enough, I thought, until the band started a jitterbug.

"I can't, Mike," I said. "Though if it was a Charleston I'd give it a try."

A circle had formed around one of the couples. The fellow was short and compact and moved in a crouch across the floor toward his partner, then jumped up, took her hand and twirled her four or five times. She was wearing the uniform of a Wren. Wren, Women's Royal Naval Service. I could see she was having a hard time keeping up with him, especially when everyone in the circle started clapping, which made him move even faster, practically slinging her from one side to the other. She stopped and laughed.

"I can't," she said.

"I can," said another young woman who took her place. The Wren stood next to me taking in air, holding her chest.

"Ralph's a demon," she said. "He never stops."

"I'm Nora Kelly," I said.

"I'm Sally Jenkins," she replied.

"This is my nephew Mike," I said. "Lieutenant Kelly."

Mike nodded but he didn't smile. "Good evening, Lieutenant," she said.

"Is that private a friend of yours?"

"I hope so," she said, as we watched the young Marine and his new partner dancing with great energy. "As you can see I have competition. Ralph's not ready to settle down with one girl."

"Probably just as well," Mike said.

"Mike, please," I said.

"I think he's referring to the difference in rank between Ralph and me. Officers and enlisted men are not supposed to, what's your word? Fraternize." Mike didn't answer.

The music stopped and the young Marine came over to us. "You wore me out," Sally said.

I thought of what George Ludke had said. Half these boys would be dead now if that troop ship had gone in the other direction. No wonder Ralph jitterbugged with such ferocity.

"They all look like babies," I said to Major Duggan when we went back to the table.

"They are," he said. "Eighteen, nineteen."

And then I thought I was starting to hallucinate, because I heard bagpipes. Not one bagpipe, not some ceremonial call to attention, but a battalion of bagpipes, a swirl of high-pitched sound accompanied by pounding drums. Thunder and lightning marching into the ballroom.

"What is this?" I said to Duggan.

"The Marine Corps Pipes and Drums," he said to me and laughed. He leaned over and shouted into my ear. "I was with the Lord Mayor of Derry two months ago and I guess I was going on about my Marines because he interrupted me and said, 'You say your Marines can do anything, well they can't play the bagpipes.' I found an instructor, asked for volunteers, rounded up some pipes and drums which I paid for myself, and now we have the Marine Corps Pipes and Drums."

There must have been thirty men coming toward us. The pipe major carried a tall silver mace. As they got closer I saw it was Sergeant Major Kent who was leading them. I grabbed my camera. First I got a shot of Eleanor Roosevelt. The expression on her face. No matter where she's been, I thought, or what she's done, she's never seen anything quite like this. I recognized the tune, "The Minstrel Boy to the War Has Gone." I crouched down and photographed the sergeant major from below and then did quick portraits of the individual pipers.

Major Duggan escorted Eleanor Roosevelt as they followed the pipers to the bandstand. I put a new roll of film in my Seneca and headed after them.

There were rituals at the Marine Corps Birthday Ball, Major Duggan had explained to me. The youngest and the oldest Marines were called on to ceremoniously cut the cake with a sword. Ralph was the youngest and Major Duggan the oldest. He'd told me he'd been in the Marine Corps Reserve since 1925 and had had to use all his clout to be sent overseas at his age.

A giant birthday cake was carried out and set on a small table in front of us. No wonder so many Catholics serve in the Marine Corps. Something liturgical about the cutting of the cake with the crowd silent and the Marines standing at attention. Major Duggan raised his sword and very deliberately sliced into the cake. He pulled the sword out and handed it to Ralph. Very solemn. I noticed the blade of the sword was smeared with icing. Turn your swords into plowshares or pastry knives. If only, I thought as I photographed the proceedings.

Major Duggan introduced Eleanor Roosevelt. "I am beyond delighted to introduce our guest of honor, Eleanor Roosevelt, the First Lady of the United States, representing our commander-in-chief, at this one hundred and seventy-first Marine Corps Birthday Ball."

The solemnity lifted as the Marines applauded. A few of them whistled and then they all barked out "Oorah," which startled Eleanor Roosevelt but she recovered. Her high-pitched voice and that oh-so-cultured accent should have been off-putting, but she was so completely herself in that old-fashioned blue velvet dress with the ever-present fur piece nestled around her shoulders that they couldn't but embrace her. She was very familiar to them. She represented home. She began by talking about her son who was a Marine in the Pacific, and she assured them that every one of their mothers prayed for them every day as she did for her sons. I thought of the women at the Our Lady of Sorrows novena, wouldn't they like to see swords become cake cutters? She kept her remarks short and ended with a promise.

"Your commander-in-chief and the entire country stand with you. Together we will defeat the evil unleashed on our world. Good will always triumph and no matter how dark the times. Remember it is better to light a candle than curse the darkness, and you"—she gestured toward the revolving mirrored balls—"have created rainbows." That got a laugh, more applause. She smiled and waved at the crowd.

"Well said," I called up to her and snapped more photographs. She nodded. She was more like her husband than I'd thought, getting energy from the crowd. Not the shy woman I thought her to be. There was evil stalking the world. Thank God we have a strong commander-in-chief. Not much opposition to him these days. The Roosevelt-haters had gone quiet. I suddenly had a flash of memory. Miami. "Move closer." Oh dear God what might have been.

Major Duggan led Eleanor Roosevelt back to the table and turned to me. "We're supposed to have a closing prayer but Father Matthew hasn't appeared yet. I hope he didn't go off the road on his bicycle." Then the sergeant major nudged Duggan and pointed. Father Matthew was hurrying toward us. As he got closer I saw there was mud on the bottom of his cassock. An accident? Major Duggan took him right to the bandstand.

"I hope we can quiet them down one more time," Duggan said to him. He pointed at the bugler who sounded a call that brought the crowd to attention.

"I'm sorry to interrupt," Father Matthew said, "and I really regret missing your party."

"We're just getting started, Padre," someone shouted out.

"Alright then," he said. "Major Duggan has asked me to deliver a final benediction. I'm bringing you St. Patrick's prayer—a good one for warriors, because it really is based on an invocation the old Irish used before they went into battle. It's called the Lorica of St. Patrick, which means the breastplate or shield. It's a reference to the Irish god Lugh, a blacksmith who forged his own weapons. The prayer's also known as the Deer's Cry, Fáed Fíada, which refers to a mist of invisibility that can conceal a warrior from his or her enemies. The women of the Celts fought too! Patrick took this invocation and, as he did with the entire old Celtic religion, overlaid it with Christianity. Didn't destroy the so-called pagan beliefs, he adapted them. So now as I say this prayer for you, I'm asking all of Ireland's powerful spirits to surround you.

"May you bind to yourselves the power of Heaven, the light of the sun, the brightness of the moon, the splendor of fire, the flashing of lightning, and the depth of the sea." Father Matthew's voice had taken on an incantatory quality. And almost unconsciously the crowd was moving to the rhythm of his speech. Swaying slightly at each line, and then one of the Marines stamped his foot.

"God's power to guide you, God's might to uphold you, God's strength to shelter you, God's host to secure you." More of the fellows joined in the stomping, so a loud boom boom punctuated each line. Father Matthew raised his voice, harmonizing with the thumping.

"Against all those who seek to harm you, every merciless power, against poison, burning, drowning and a death wound."

Boom, boom, boom.

"Christ be with you, Christ before you, Christ behind you, Christ above you, Christ at your left, Christ at your right." The stamping had become continuous. The words were riding on top of the sound as if the Marines were accompanying the prayer. Father Matthew shouted out the last lines.

"I bind you today to the Eternal Trinity, I bind you to the Creator of the Universe, amen."

Has any prayer ever gotten that Marine "Oorah" salute before? It took another bugle call to calm the troops down. The band started the dance music again. But those warriors had been as well and truly blessed in Doire as the ancient Celts had been in the nearby oak groves for thousands of years.

The Druids had sent men—and women, too—into battle with similar words.

"Well done, Father," I said, as he sat down with us at the table. Eleanor Roosevelt leaned over Major Duggan, and Tommy to say to him, "Unusual, but effective." And the two began talking.

I noticed a second priest who must have accompanied Father Matthew, moving toward our table. He sat down in the empty chair next to me. "Welcome, Nora Kelly," he said.

"Oh, dear God," I said. "Seán MacBride." Maud Gonne's son.

I'd known him as a boy and had seen him again in 1920 when he'd come to the Irish Race Convention in Paris as de Valera's secretary. Thousands of delegates had attended from all over the world. Each one with roots in Ireland.

The star of the show was the Duke of Tetuan, whose O'Donnell ancestor had been awarded a title by the king of Spain. Seán had used my apartment for the meeting between the duke and de Valera, where the Spaniard had assured Dev that the de Valeras were nobles of Spain, too. The Duke had no concrete evidence, but both Seán and de Valera were delighted with the information. Though why two revolutionaries would celebrate an aristocratic connection, I'm not sure. De Valera had never known his father, so why not surround himself with a bit of romance?

Now, here was Seán, who must be about forty—and a priest?

He crouched down next to me.

"Seán," I said. "Have you become a monk?"

"Only for the evening. I thought it would be safer to cross the border on the back of Father Matthew's bicycle. The Marines on guard probably have a dossier on me. They're very nervous about the IRA. Though we've got enough on our plates without trying to blow up US Navy ships."

"But why are you here?"

"The chief wants to meet with Mrs. Roosevelt," he said.

"De Valera's coming to Derry?"

"Impossible. She'll have to be brought to him," he said.

"But, why?" I said.

"He wants to explain our neutrality," Seán said. "But don't tell her. We'll figure a way to get her across the border. If she knew in advance, she'd tell the American and British officials and that would be that."

"But I can't deceive the First Lady," I said. "Besides, she wants to meet Dev. She said . . ."

"Well, she won't if the Brits find out," Seán said. "Do it our way. You owe it to your country—both your countries. Major Duggan is friendly with a general in the Irish Army and has visited him at his home in Galway. The general has offered to host the meeting, and Duggan is on board. He understands that Ireland has no choice but to remain neutral."

"I don't know," I said. The Brits would be apoplectic if Mrs. Roosevelt met Dev secretly. I remembered those colonels.

"But, Seán," I said, "even if I wanted to help, how are we going to get her to Galway?"

"The best way is to go through Omagh and cross the border into Monaghan. It's not guarded the way the one between Derry and Donegal is. There's only one unit stationed there. A colored group. Not combat troops."

"Colored," I said.

"Yes," he said. "They just arrived a couple of weeks ago. The camp's outside a little place called Carrickmore. Five of our volunteers live there and I hear the colored fellows got quite a welcome. Boom times for the town. Sitting rooms turned into pubs and a big shed has become a dance hall. The one motorcar is a taxi. The people there are making money hand over fist and the kids are drowning in sweets."

That must be where the colored soldiers we met in London were going, I thought. "Mrs. Roosevelt just might change her schedule to visit with them," I said.

"Run across the border there, head west and Bob's your uncle," Seán said.

"And Major Duggan will go along with this?" I asked.

"He knows that the propaganda the Brits are putting out is ridiculous. They say the Irish are secretly supporting the Germans. That neutrality is cowardly. They claim that U-boats are being fueled along our west coast, as if we had those kinds of facilities or even petrol. Totally false. Roosevelt said the Irish were like a man who puts his head under the covers hoping the fight will be over. But that's not it at all. We have to be neutral. There's really no choice. How could we defend ourselves against the Nazis? The Brits would take over again. The chief thinks Eleanor Roosevelt will listen to him. She's an intelligent woman. Reminds me of my mother. Though very different in style," he said.

"Very different." Oh dear God, Maud and Eleanor Roosevelt. Now that would be an encounter. One so ebullient—actress, muse of Yeats, his unrequited love; and Eleanor Roosevelt—earnest, respectable, mother of six, helpmate, social crusader. And yet Seán was right. Both women came from privileged backgrounds, but they'd thrown their hats into the ring of the suffering and dispossessed. Very different hats, of course.

"Mrs. Roosevelt might take a detour to meet the Negro troops at Carrickmore. Maybe. But I want something too, Seán. Do you remember Peter Keeley, the professor at the Irish College in Paris?"

"I do. He was kind to me when I was a boy, and I knew him when he fought with the Galway Brigade during the War of Independence. But, I thought he . . ." Seán stopped.

"I know," I said. "He was killed by a student of his after Michael Collins was assassinated. The young man was from Cork, and his family was friendly with the Collinses. I understand that he came to find Peter at the IRA camp in the Connemara mountains and killed him."

"I remember hearing something about that. But, Nora, so many unfortunate incidents during those times. We don't speak of them anymore."

"Ná habair tada?" I said, trying to put a good dose of bitterness into the words.

But Seán only nodded. "You've got it in one," he said.

Seán looked down the table, then back at me. "Was the professor a special friend of yours?" he asked.

"Yes," I said.

"I'm sorry for your troubles, but we've more immediate concerns."

"I want to visit his grave. I'd say he was buried in Connemara, near Carna, his home place. I've been trying to find the place for twenty years. If I were to arrange for Eleanor Roosevelt to come to Galway, could you find a way for me to go to the graveyard? As I remember, Carna is not that far from Galway, and while she and de Valera are meeting, could you take me there?"

"Mmmm," Seán said. "It's far enough from the general's house over bad roads, but the chief will have his plane. I suppose a short hop would be possible, but we'd have to have better information."

"There's a man who would know. Cyril Peterson."

"Cyril? He's a part of this?"

"He was with Peter when it happened. He came to Paris to tell me Peter was dead, but he didn't seem to know where he'd been buried. I wrote to him and got one letter back but he basically told me to forget the past. Never heard from him again."

"Cyril's a hard man to keep track of."

"But he was a de Valera man. Surely, you could find him. And then I'll—"

"So you're bargaining with me, Nora Kelly? I've heard that you'd become part of the Chicago political machine. Learned a bit of horse trading, have you? Let me see what I can do."

"I'd have to convince the First Lady to change her schedule. We're due to fly out at first light."

"Not if there was a bit of mechanical trouble with your aircraft."

"For God's sake, Seán!"

"Oh, very minor, Nora. Easily fixed."

In the end, Seán didn't have to sabotage the plane. Ireland herself took a hand. The cloak of invisibility settled over Derry, just before dawn.

Father Matthew managed to get to Beech Hill, but said he'd hardly been able to see his hand in front of his face. As we went in to breakfast, he took me aside. Seán had a message for me. He'd found the information of my friend that I'd been looking for. Our trip was on.

6

"We're socked in," Mike told us the next morning. "The whole coast has such a low ceiling we can't take off. It's supposed to last for at least forty-eight hours."

Commander Logan had come with Mike to deliver the news. We were all dressed and ready in the entrance hall of Beech Hill House.

"Two days. But that's impossible," Eleanor Roosevelt said. "I must get back to Washington."

"I'm sorry, ma'am," Commander Logan said.

"Well," she said, "I suppose I can make myself useful here. I did have some ideas about how your hospital might be run more efficiently." I saw Logan look over at Major Duggan.

"That's very kind of you," Logan said, "but Major Duggan has mentioned that you didn't have a chance to meet any of the children here. Very bright kids. St. Columb's College is a fine boys' school and Thornhill School teaches the girls. Very high academic standards. The children of some of Derry's finest families attend them."

"Those that can pay," I said.

"Well, yes," he said. "Free education ends here at age twelve."

"So only the well-to-do go on to high school?" Mrs. Roosevelt asked. She was shaking her head. "I'd like to meet the children that don't have a chance for education."

"I'm not sure, Mrs. Roosevelt," Commander Logan began, but Major Duggan spoke up.

"George Ludke and Don Kennedy and some of the other Marines started a baseball team with kids from one of the elementary schools. Perhaps the First Lady could visit them."

Eleanor Roosevelt nodded.

I looked over at Major Duggan. He winked at me. An hour at the school, then visit the Negro troops and over the border by lunchtime.

"These look like the tenements on the Lower East Side of New York," Eleanor Roosevelt said to me as we drove past streets packed with terraced houses, one leaning against the other as if trying to hold each other up. Keeping their balance against the road's steep pitch. A knot of women stood in front of one stoop watching the cars go by. One woman waved.

"Could we stop?" Eleanor Roosevelt asked.

Major Duggan was driving us with Mike sitting next to him. George Ludke and Don Kennedy had gone ahead.

"The children are expecting us," Major Duggan said.

"I would like to get these women's point of view," Eleanor Roosevelt said. "They're the ones who know what a community needs." He stopped the car.

"Let me get out and talk to them first, Mrs. Roosevelt," I said.

These faces. We could have been in Bridgeport. Are there only so many varieties of Irish features scattered around the world? One woman looked exactly like Aunt Máire and another resembled Mame McCabe. Best to be very respectful, I thought, as I approached these women. Very easy to offend the neighbors. I introduced myself.

"I'm Nora Kelly," I said. "From Chicago. It's Mrs. Roosevelt here in the car."

"We knew it," one of the women said. "She's traveled round the whole town and it's about time she came to see the real people of Derry. I'm Annie Hume and you're very welcome. Bring Mrs. Roosevelt in for a cup of tea."

Impossible to say no to this group, and soon Eleanor Roosevelt, Tommy, Mike, the major, and I were sitting in front of a turf fire in Annie's kitchen drinking tea from white mugs. Four children stood in the doorway. And Annie was pregnant.

"What a lovely family," Eleanor Roosevelt said.

"Stair-steps," Annie said. She pointed. "Harry is five, Paddy and Sally, the twins, are four, and Agnes is two. Johnny's the oldest but he's at school, thank God. He's the one learned that baseball from your fellows."

"Johnny hit a home run," Harry said.

"Whatever that is," Annie said.

The children resembled each other and again could have belonged to any family in Bridgeport. The boys had dark hair and brown eyes, the two girls were fair. They all wore sweaters that I could see had been darned and probably passed one to the next. None wore shoes. Annie must have seen me looking at their feet because she said, "No point in wasting shoe leather inside."

"Every one of us has shoes," Harry said. "Da bought them for us."

"He works at the shipyard," Annie said. "First time he's had a job in his life. They don't employ Catholic men in this town, Mrs. Roosevelt. And when the Yanks came to Derry we thought it would be the same. Only Protestants need apply. But thank God you Yanks hired anybody who could do the work. Even fellows from across the Free State border. I've always had a job. Catholic women could always get work in the shirt factory and when you've a big family the bosses let you take the shirts home." She pointed to a pile. "I sew the collars by hand here. Get paid by the piece."

"When do you find time to do it?" I asked her.

"At night," she said, "after the children are in bed."

"I hope you get the proper rest, Mrs. Hume," Eleanor Roosevelt said as we got up to leave. "Very important in your condition. I enjoyed being in your home."

Two of the women laughed.

"Not our homes, Mrs. Roosevelt," one woman said. "These places belong to the landlord and he's not too fussed about providing much. There's one toilet out the back for all ten houses. A pump for water, and half the time that doesn't work. The electricity is off more than it is on. Families with eight or nine children shoved into four rooms. Two up and two down."

"Ah now, Bernie," Annie said, "we're doing alright. And, as they say, if you're raised in your bare feet you'll never get pneumonia in the snow."

But the woman was riled up. "Do you know, Mrs. Roosevelt, that our landlord gets forty votes—one for every property he owns and my grown son has no vote at all. Now if the tricolor flew over this city as it should," she said, "this would be a much different place."

"I don't know about that, Bernie," Annie Hume said. "I don't think they're doing much better in the South and as my husband, Sam, said, you can't eat a flag. It's decent jobs, a roof over our heads. That's what we need." Annie walked us to the door, the children trailing behind her. Five children under seven, I thought, another one on the way and she's sewing shirts at night and serving strangers tea.

"Mother Ireland," I said to Mike as we walked to the car. I wondered if he realized that this was how our people had lived. If only I could show him Galway.

George Ludke and Don Kennedy were outside the school when we pulled up. A one-story brick building attached to the church.

"The primary schools are funded by the government but administered by the clergy both Catholic and Protestant," I said. "So the children of each denomination attend separate schools."

"But that's wrong," Eleanor Roosevelt started, but I stopped her.

"Not now," I said, because the man approaching us had to be the headmaster.

"Mrs. Roosevelt," said George, "I'd like you to meet Master Sheerin." Not as old as I imagined a headmaster would be. Maybe thirty, thirty-five. He was tall, dark, smiling, a jolly primary school principal, I hoped. He looked a lot like Marguerite's husband, Tom McGuire. Does every Irish person have an American echo? I wondered.

"The children are very excited to meet you," Master Sheerin said. He took us into a classroom where the boys were on one side of the room and the girls on the other. Six students sat on each of the benches set behind long tables. There seemed to be about forty students. "In this class we have children aged six and seven. May I introduce their teacher, Miss O'Reilly."

The young woman who stepped forward was the same girl who'd sung with the band at the Marine Corps Birthday Ball. Now here was someone kids could relate to. She turned to the children.

"Please stand to welcome Mrs. Roosevelt. You know she is the First Lady of the United States of America." A shuffle of feet as the rows stood up. "We've been learning a song that I think would be very appropriate to greet you." She began singing, *"Oh beautiful for spacious skies,"* and the children joined in. Never had the song "America" been sung more beautifully. Their voices were very pure and they harmonized on the last verse:

> And crown thy good with brotherhood,
> From sea to shining sea.

Eleanor Roosevelt had to get out her handkerchief, and Tommy was sniffing back tears. "But that's extraordinary," Mrs. Roosevelt said.

"Derry people are great singers," Miss O'Reilly said. "And they start early."

In every country children like these had fathers who were fighting and dying in this war.

"This war," I said to Master Sheerin. "And to think there are children just like this in Germany also." He nodded.

"I tell my students that hating someone because they are different makes no sense. After all, difference is only an accident of birth. No one chooses where they are born. But the tribal instinct is strong in human beings."

Eleanor Roosevelt and Tommy were going up and down the rows speaking to the children. Miss O'Reilly was telling them each one's name.

George had one little boy stand up and led him up to Mrs. Roosevelt.

"This is Johnny Hume," he said to her. "The star of our team."

"The home run hitter?" I said. "We met your mother." The little boy reached into his pocket and took out an American penny. He held it on his palm.

"George gave me this," he said. "See those words. That's Latin."

Eleanor Roosevelt leaned down to the boy. "*E pluribus unum.* And do you know what those words mean?"

"George said it means 'one from many,' the motto of the United States. George said that in America people can be who they are and still get along. Doesn't always happen that way in Derry."

"Maybe that will change one day," Eleanor Roosevelt said.

"It will," he said. "Has to."

"Well said, young Mr. Hume," Eleanor Roosevelt said. She opened her pocketbook. Oh good, I thought, maybe she's going to give him a dollar bill. Explain the symbols on that. But it was her card that Eleanor Roosevelt handed him.

"When you grow up, young man, bring that to the White House and tell whoever is president that Mrs. Roosevelt sent you."

It was me who put a pound note into the boy's hand, after I'd taken photographs of Mrs. Roosevelt with the class. George and Don passed out Milky Way candy bars to each member of the class, and left a supply for Mr. Sheerin to give to the rest of the school.

The fog was still thick when we came out. Mike shook his head. "It's not lifting," he said.

"Now what?" Mrs. Roosevelt asked Major Duggan.

"Perhaps we can take a ride to the Army camp where the Negro soldiers are stationed," I said.

"Fine," Mrs. Roosevelt said. "Fine." She turned to Major Duggan. "I enjoyed meeting those children. They were brighter than I expected. You seem to be doing a good job connecting with them."

"Perhaps you would put in a good word for us at Marine headquarters. They're questioning the amount of money we're spending on candy. And with Christmas coming we're planning a big party for the children," he said.

"Make a note, Tommy," Eleanor Roosevelt said. She didn't seem to be as worried about a schedule. We headed east toward Omagh.

As we went further inland the fog broke up, and we saw actual sunshine on the hills, which Major Duggan told us were the Sperrin Mountains.

"Not very tall mountains," Eleanor Roosevelt said. "But picturesque."

"The good land is down here in the valley," Duggan said.

"Protestant farmers, I suppose," Tommy said.

"You're aware of the history?" I said. "I'm surprised."

"My mother's family is from around here, and she used to say that even after two hundred years her people still remembered being pushed off the good land into the mountains," Tommy said.

"The Duggans have similar stories," the major said.

"And so do the Kellys," I said.

"But all of you are Americans," Eleanor Roosevelt said. "I've never understood the Irish obsession with the past."

"Thus speaks the woman who can trace her ancestors back to the year *dot* and tell you the rank of every one of them who fought in the Revolutionary War," Tommy said. Eleanor Roosevelt laughed. She didn't seem to mind when Tommy teased her. Maybe she had a sense of humor after all.

"A lot of good my heritage did me when my fellow Daughters of the American Revolution refused to allow Marian Anderson to sing in their hall," Eleanor Roosevelt said.

"You showed them, boss," Tommy said.

"Yes I did," Eleanor Roosevelt said. "I put her right on the steps of the Lincoln Memorial and she sang to an audience of fifty thousand, and if these Negro soldiers are not being treated properly, well . . . ," she said, and pulled the fur close around her neck.

No quonset huts in this camp. These fellows only got green Army tents. About twenty in two rows. On the ride over Major Duggan had wanted to stop at a pub to call the commanding officer to let him know we were coming, but Eleanor Roosevelt insisted we arrive unannounced. A kind of surprise inspection.

"I understand Southern officers have mistreated Negro troops and I want to make sure I see the situation with no advance warning," Eleanor Roosevelt said.

When we pulled into the camp a Negro sentry stopped us. Major Duggan rolled down the window. "Good afternoon, soldier," he said. The man saluted.

"Major," he said, and then looked beyond at Mike and saluted again. "Lieutenant."

I put down my window and waved to the man. He stepped toward us, looked into the back seat, and saluted one more time. "Welcome, Mrs. Roosevelt," he said. Then he smiled. A tall, well-built young man. His skin a shade lighter than his brown uniform. "I didn't believe the fellows when they said you'd be coming, but here you are."

"What fellows?" Major Duggan asked.

"I bet it was the men we met in London. Right, soldier?" I said.

"Yes, ma'am," he said. "It's lunchtime. The men are in the mess tent and I'm sure the cooks would be very happy to make up plates for you."

He pointed us down the center thoroughfare toward the largest tent in the camp. When we arrived at the tent there were five soldiers lined up ready to meet us. Major Duggan got out of the car, followed by Mike.

"Good afternoon, Captain," he said to a Negro man. Bill Dawson had been a lieutenant when I'd met him in Paris in the last war. I was glad Negro soldiers were moving up in the ranks. Would there be colonels or even generals before this war is over? This fellow reminded me of Dawson. He had that same look of authority. Erect. Broad-shouldered. At ease in his body. The captain opened the car door and the three of us got out.

"We're honored to welcome you, Mrs. Roosevelt," he said, "I'm Captain Davis." He offered her his arm and escorted her into the tent. There was a wooden floor, though I couldn't feel much heat. About 150 men were seated at the tables. They immediately stood up and began applauding.

Eleanor Roosevelt raised one hand. "Please, please, I don't want to interrupt your lunch." But the men wouldn't stop cheering.

Finally Captain Davis hollered "Attention!" and gestured for the men to sit down.

"Such enthusiasm," Eleanor Roosevelt said to Captain Davis.

"The men are proud to serve, though most of the fellows would prefer if we were a combat unit. We're quartermaster troops. We handle supplies for the main camp."

"Very important work," Eleanor Roosevelt said, "after all an army travels on its stomach."

"Except these men signed up to fight. As Frederick Douglass said about the Negro troops in the Civil War—'Once a man carries a musket on his shoulder in the defense of his nation, he cannot be denied full citizenship'—though we're still waiting."

"But progress has been made, Captain," Eleanor Roosevelt said. "I've been working with the NAACP on the Double V campaign—victory abroad, victory at home." Captain Davis nodded.

I noticed that four men sitting near a back table were waving at us. "Look,"

I said to Eleanor Roosevelt, "the men from London. May we go and speak to them?" I asked the captain.

"Of course," he said, and escorted us to the back of the tent. Eleanor Roosevelt beamed, put out both her hands, and I think she would have hugged the men then and there except they took her hand and began shaking it.

"Did you get your hot dogs and mustard?" I asked.

"Oh yes," the tallest of them said. "Mac has them for us."

"That's a pub in the village," another one said. "Mac's the owner. As soon as he found out we liked hot dogs he got a bunch in. They're sausages really, but close enough and somewhere he found mustard and buns."

"That was considerate," I said. The men laughed and the captain smiled.

"Considerate is not the right word," the tall one said. "The people of Carrickmore treat us as if we're members of their own families. There used to be only one pub in town but now four houses have turned their parlors into shebeens—that's what they call the bars here."

"They even made a big shed into a dance hall and there's music there every night. They're the friendliest people I've ever met," another man said.

"So no . . . ," Eleanor Roosevelt began.

"Discrimination?" the captain asked. "Not a bit. Though we did have an incident."

"What happened, Captain?" Duggan asked.

"Well, as I said, as soon as we arrived the town put on a big welcome. There was even a sign across the main street saying 'Hello Yanks.' Nobody seemed to care what color we were. People would stop us on the street to thank us for coming. They said they were sure we'd end the war soon. One man told me he felt as if we'd stepped off a movie screen and marched in to save them. He also said that the people of the village had a hard enough time making ends meet and were glad to have a chance to bank some American dollars, which I told him we were happy to spend. They especially enjoyed learning our names. We've got a good few Murphys, O'Neills, and O'Briens among us. In fact I have some Irish roots myself."

"Very interesting, Captain, but what was the incident you were speaking of?" Major Duggan said.

"Well a few days ago a group of white soldiers came to town. They couldn't believe how well we were being treated. They came into the shed and when they saw my soldiers dancing with local girls they went crazy and started fighting with us. It turned into a real brawl. My men held their own and I called the MPs in. Headquarters wanted to make the whole town off-limits but a delegation of townspeople complained. They said it was the white soldiers had started all the trouble and that my troops were gentlemen. So headquarters relented. The next day the people put signs in the window of every pub and hung a big banner over the dance hall. All of them said 'No whites allowed.'"

Tommy laughed first. A sound that came from deep within her. Eleanor Roosevelt joined in and then we were all laughing.

"Wonderful," Eleanor Roosevelt said. "Just wonderful. Carrickmore. I must remember that name. Franklin will enjoy this story."

7

"Let us now add your name to *An Banshenchas,*" Seán MacBride said as he opened our car's back door.

"What's he saying? Who is he and where are we?" Eleanor Roosevelt asked me.

She and Tommy had fallen into a doze I can only attribute to some fairy intervention soon after we left the Army camp in Carrickmore.

Major Duggan had kept the big car moving along fast in spite of high hills, narrow roads, and sheep that trotted in front of us. We cut diagonally across to Galway and in less than three hours were at General McGrory's house, which was about twenty miles from Barna, where my granny Honora had been born, and sixty from Connemara and Peter's homeplace.

"*An Banshenchas* is the chronicle praising famous women listed in ancient Irish manuscripts—including the *Book of the O'Kellys.* And you're in Galway, home of the Kellys though it's a MacBride from Mayo greeting you," I said.

"What are you talking about, Nora?" Tommy said. "Galway. We can't be in Galway. That's in the Free State."

"It is," I said.

I stepped out of the car and let Seán reach in to take Eleanor Roosevelt's hand and help her out. Standing in the doorway of the general's house was Maud Gonne, well into her seventies, I thought, but as straight as ever.

Maud came down the walk, her long black veil blowing in the wind. I heard Tommy gasp. She was part Irish after all. Here was the crone from one of her mother's stories come to life.

"I'm Maud Gonne MacBride," she said as she stuck out her hand to Eleanor Roosevelt, who took it. "A great honor, Mrs. Roosevelt. I think of you as the First Lady of not just the United States but of the world," she said.

Always could turn a phrase, our Maud, and Eleanor Roosevelt smiled.

"Nora," Maud said turning to me. "Nora." And I got a full-on hug. "Twenty years since we last met. How can that be?"

"It can be," I said. "I'm more aware of that every year."

"True enough at our age," she said.

You're a good thirteen years older than I am, I thought but didn't say. Still traces of the woman who'd hurt Yeats into poetry and the Nobel Prize for Literature in 1923, the very year I'd left Europe for Chicago. Those verses! How prophetic the words I'd heard from his own lips had become. "The best lack all conviction while the worst are full of passionate intensity,"—the War, a most horrific second coming.

I'd been staying with Maud and Yeats at her villa in Normandy when he wrote the words, "Changed, changed utterly: a terrible beauty is born." In this poem, "Easter 1916," he evoked the men executed as rebels by the British, among them Maud's husband, John MacBride, Seán's father.

He'd recited the poem for us on that beach in Normandy in front of the villa, the rocky face of La Pointe du Hoc in the background. Yeats had been dead nearly four years now—resting in peace, I hoped, spared the need to find meter for horrors that were beyond thought.

Maud seemed to know what I was thinking because she said, "Willie came to visit me a few months before he died. 'Old and full of sleep' both of us, though he was wiser than me. He let go. Ah, Nora, shouldn't have to live through more than one world war."

Eleanor Roosevelt heard this last bit and said, "Although your country has chosen not to participate . . ."

"Our country," Maud said, "but not our young fellows. Thousands enlisted in the British Army and if you added all the Irish-American young men fighting with you, Mrs. Roosevelt, I'd say Ireland is punching well above our weight."

"Yes, well," Eleanor Roosevelt began but Seán was moving her up the path with Maud on the other side and Tommy coming up behind. I dropped back to Mike and Major Duggan.

"What is going on, Aunt Nonie?" Mike asked.

"We're on a secret mission," I said, and Major Duggan laughed.

There, standing in the doorway, was the Chieftain—*Taoiseach* in Irish, Éamon de Valera. The prime minister of Ireland. Leader since 1922. Seán brought Mrs. Roosevelt up to him. He was very courtly to her. But he hardly looked at Mike or Tommy or me when Seán MacBride presented us.

"This is providential," Eleanor Roosevelt said. "I've wanted to speak to you."

He pointed Eleanor Roosevelt to another room and left the rest of us standing there—Maud, Seán, Tommy, Major Duggan, Mike, and me. What now?

"Welcome. Welcome." The man was dressed in the uniform of the Irish Army—the youngest yet oldest force in the world, "A nation once again," with a crucial battle being fought in the next room.

"I'm General Michael McGrory," he said. "I have a meal waiting for you in the pub down the road. An Taoiseach doesn't mean to be rude but he's very aware of security."

"Neither he nor Eleanor Roosevelt would want the details or even the fact of their meeting leaked out—the British would not be pleased," Seán said to us as we walked the short distance to the village. "But if de Valera could convince Mrs. Roosevelt that we had no choice but to be officially neutral, and if her husband would make some statement acknowledging this new nation's right to abstain from the war, that would be helpful. Your president certainly knows that, unofficially, we're with you."

General McGrory said that the Irish government was already assisting the allies by allowing US planes to fly over Donegal, and quietly sending aircrews downed in Ireland back across the border to the North. "A whisper of this to the Germans, and the Nazis would invade and be goose-stepping down O'Connell Street," he said. "And there are factions in the British Army who wouldn't mind driving a fleet of Saracens down from Belfast to reclaim what some of them still think of as their colony."

Not sure what Tommy made of this. Maud had placed Tommy beside her in the Galleon Bar where a table had been set up for us.

"Eleanor Roosevelt would like this," Tommy said. "Rustic."

"Local pottery," Maud said, "and handcrafted furniture. You'll be eating fresh salmon caught in the Corrib that runs through Galway City."

Major Duggan and Mike went up to the bar. After a time they returned with pints of Guinness for all of us. Tommy took a sip and gave a thumbs-up. She was Irish, alright.

I'd been watching Seán, waiting for a signal. When are we going to Peter's grave? Finally, I leaned across the table and tugged on his sleeve. "Don't you think we should leave to visit that friend of mine? You did speak to Cyril, didn't you?"

"Oh, yes," Seán said. "But I'm afraid the news isn't good." He looked over at Maud.

She said, "We've sad news for you, Nora." Then she looked at the others. "A dear friend of Nora's and mine died a number of years ago, and . . ." She looked at me. "Shall we go outside, Nora?"

"No, Maud. I've been waiting twenty years to visit Peter Keeley's grave. Tell me where it is—"

"But, you can't visit him, Nora. Peter Keeley has no grave."

"What?"

All the others were waiting to hear what Maud was going to say.

"Come outside, Nora."

"No. I'm tired of all this Irish evasion. Tell me directly."

"Alright," Maud said. "When he was shot, his body fell into the sea—and it was never recovered."

Silence at the table.

"And that's all you can tell me?"

Maud shrugged. "Many others at rest in the Atlantic Ocean, Nora. 'Full fathom five,'" she started to quote.

I got up. Walked out. Stood in front of the pub, looking west.

Ah, Peter—no chance now that I'll find the place where you are lying and bend and tell you that I love you, as the song says. And wasn't it you yourself told me that since before history began the Irish have felt duty-bound to honor the graves of their dead? "Crucial to mark their passage to the other world," you'd told me, "a way of asserting our faith in life after life."

I remembered how excited Peter had been to show me photographs of the monumental tomb called Newgrange that had been uncovered in the Irish countryside. Built five thousand years ago, he'd said. Older than the pyramids, and Homer. Boulders weighing tons had somehow been transported twenty, thirty miles, then carved with intricate designs.

"Newgrange is called *Brú na Bóinne* in Irish, which means 'the mansion on the river Boyne.' The home of the Celtic gods in our mythology. But during the last century when aristocratic English antiquarians examined the site, they were sure the Egyptians or Phoenicians must have washed up on our shores and built the thing, because the mere Irish couldn't possibly have constructed such an extraordinary monument," Peter had said.

He'd shown me a slot above the doorway in the photograph. At the winter solstice the rising sun sent a spear of light through this opening into the tomb, he'd explained, "Illuminating the darkness."

Now I prayed that perpetual light was shining on Peter, his spirit somehow alive, even though his body was lost to the sea.

Only a few minutes until Mike joined me. "Is there anything I can do, Aunt Nonie?"

"There isn't, Mike. Nothing at all," I said.

"While I was waiting for our drinks I met this fellow at the bar. He's the prime minister's pilot," Mike said. "He'd be willing to take us up. Would it help if you could look down and . . . ?"

I nodded. Time to let go once and for all. To accept. Maybe now I'd stop recalling that Ojibwe ceremony, wouldn't hear Bridget say "He's not dead." He was. Confirmed now. Peter was dead.

De Valera's pilot wore the same kind of leather jacket Mike had on. A matched pair. If the Great Starvation hadn't forced Granny Honora to make a run for it so her children could live, maybe Mike would be an aviator in the Irish Air Force.

"His name is Michael J. Kelly, too," Mike said.

The man nodded to me. "This lad told me he's never seen his home place," he said.

"We're from Barna. Just west of the city on Galway Bay."

"I know it well," the pilot said. "Aren't I from just up the road in Salthill?"

"Not near the Silverstrand?" I asked.

"Played there as a boy. Walk it now."

"That's where your great-grandfather, the first Michael Kelly, came swimming out of Galway Bay and met Honora, who was a Keeley," I said to Mike. "A fisherman's daughter. They married and began their lives there."

"Would you fancy a flyover?" the pilot said.

"Could we also go along the coast toward Carna?"

"We can, of course," he said.

Cold and dark at the bottom of the sea, with so many lost to its depths. All those fishermen who had drowned, Aunt Máire's husband among them, along with those who died on those long terrible voyages to America. And now Peter had joined them. Some joy in showing Mike the homeplace of his ancestors. Sunshine and shadow.

I took a breath and followed Mike to Dev's plane.

"Look, Mike," I said. "Straight over that stretch of beach—the Silverstrand."

Mike was sitting in the copilot's seat. A good-sized aircraft—six seats in the back—but I was standing with them in the cockpit. Bright enough below with the last of the light turning the water beneath us red.

"Another name for that stretch," our pilot said, "Trána gCeann. Place of the Skulls because the O'Flahertys battled the O'Cadhlas there and left bones under the sand."

"O'Cadhlas—the Keeleys—Lords of Connemara until the O'Flahertys arrived," I said.

"You know your history," the pilot said.

"My grandmother, Honora Keeley, was born right there," I said, pointing below.

The pilot nosed us down through the clouds. Only a swathe of grass was visible where there had been thirty cottages—a whole community of fisher families.

The pilot circled and went down lower. "Look, Mike. Look. See just above the rocks? What's left of a road."

"Mag's Boreen," said the pilot. "My gran said that was a haunted place. No one has ever built there though it's right on the bay. She said that the landlord tried to sell the land to make a seaside resort during the Great Starvation when bodies were lying unburied in the roads. He evicted the fishermen in that village to make a playground for the rich. But he didn't succeed," the pilot said, "and now the people of Ireland own the land of Ireland for the first time in eight hundred years."

Mike hadn't said much, but now he put his hand up, spread his fingers, and I realized he was holding the setting sun against his palm.

"Oh my God," I said.

"What? What?" Mike asked.

"I just remembered Granny Honora told me that my da, your grandfather, would stand and salute the sun going down into the bay as a little boy just as you are doing now, Mike."

"Mmmm," Mike said. "I'll come back, Aunt Nonie. I promise you that—for my father, for Michael Joseph Kelly."

"You will," I said.

"Has Uncle Ed ever been here?" he asked.

"He hasn't," I said. "But he'll come too. Let's make a pledge to get the whole kit and caboodle here someday."

We followed the coast another thirty miles. Somewhere down there, under the sea he lay.

Rest in peace, Peter, I prayed. Aunt Máire had said that sometimes Galway Bay was lit from below. Phosphorescence. May that perpetual light shine upon you, my love.

"Someday," Mike repeated, as the other Michael J. Kelly turned us away from the red and purple clouds and headed east.

"You cut it close enough," Tommy said to us. She and Maud and Major Duggan were back in the general's house. The whole lot of them sipping whiskey by the fire. I'd never seen Eleanor Roosevelt drink hard liquor. Preferred sherry usually. All very at ease. The meeting must have gone well.

"I quite understand, Mr. de Valera," Eleanor Roosevelt was saying, "why you are trying to urge a continuation of the simple life. I, myself, facilitated the building of such a community in West Virginia."

As we left de Valera shook each of our hands.

"Thank you, Miss Kelly," he said to me. "I think we've reached a new understanding." Still not sure if he remembered me. Not one to let on was Dev.

"Quite a nice man, Mr. de Valera. Related to the Spanish royal family I understand. So, not just . . . ," Eleanor Roosevelt said as we drove away from the general's house.

I was between Eleanor Roosevelt and Tommy and so could stick my toe into Tommy's foot. *Not just plain Irish,* Eleanor Roosevelt had meant to say but didn't.

We'd left at first light but were flying into darkness. The sunrise and Ireland were behind us. I hadn't realized how much I'd wanted to find Peter's grave. He was gone so completely. I thought I had accepted his death. But now, with Eleanor and Tommy asleep, and the stars right there in the plane's window, I let myself weep. Raging inside. Killed because of politics! At least, to die fighting the Nazis had a certain nobility, but to lose your life in what was essentially a family feud seemed beyond sad.

I hadn't realized that Tommy Thompson was awake and was watching me. But now she said, "A very emotional visit all around. I wish I could have brought my mother here. Her name was Kathleen, and at family parties, her brother would sing 'I'll Take You Home Again, Kathleen.' But she never made it back. The saddest thing she ever said to me when she grew old was that so many of her friends had died, she didn't look forward to reading the obituaries in the Boston papers anymore. All her generation was gone."

"They were great women," I said.

"They were indeed. I tried to explain them to Eleanor but she's got this picture of an Irish washerwoman stuck in her mind and—"

"My granny was a washerwoman. She fed her children by scrubbing dirty laundry." And so did the mother of the elegant First Lady of Chicago, I thought but didn't say.

"Of course," Tommy said, "and I'm proud of every one of them. But I want Eleanor to appreciate the drive and determination of those women. Their intelligence. We stand on their shoulders."

"We do," I said and I remembered Atlas holding up the heavens framed by the doors of St. Patrick's Cathedral. The statue should have been a woman, I thought then and laughed out loud.

"What?" Tommy asked.

I told her that it should be a statue of a woman in the plaza of Rockefeller Center.

"Not a bad idea but fat chance."

"There is one statue of a woman-warrior in New York," I said. And I described St. Joan of Arc standing up in her stirrups looking over the Hudson River from that small park on Riverside Drive.

"Lots of Irish live up in that neighborhood," Tommy said.

"I wonder if they might not visit her and say a quick prayer for courage like I did at the statues of St. Joan during the war in Paris. The sculptor was a woman too."

"Have to tell Eleanor. Take her up there when things get tough," Tommy said.

I wondered how many times Eleanor Roosevelt had talked out her worries to this woman, with her serviceable face and the deep laugh that had surprised me so often on this trip. She was a decade younger than I was but there was something wise about Tommy. How valuable she was to the First Lady. Even now a portable typewriter rested in her lap. Eleanor dictated copy for her column "My Day" to Tommy, who took it down in shorthand, then typed it up and sent it out to the syndicate of newspapers. Unusual for any woman to reach such a big audience. "Maybe someday there'll be a statue of Eleanor Roosevelt in that park," I said.

"Sshh." Tommy touched my arm. Eleanor was stirring. "Funny, she has trouble sleeping at home but put her in a moving vehicle and she drops right off. But if she wakes up . . ."

"You know her needs," I said.

"Too well, my husband said."

"I didn't know you were married."

"I'm not now. Fred was a good man. A schoolteacher. I was working for Eleanor when I met him. So he knew my job was demanding. But I think it's hard for a husband not to expect that his wife will be, well, a wife. Dinner on the table, children. You know. . . ."

"And did you? Do you have kids?"

"No. Might have been different if we had. But when I hit forty-five and it was obvious to Fred that he'd never be a father, he began to really resent the time I spent with Eleanor. I'd wasted my life and his too, he said, serving a woman who doesn't really appreciate me. But, of course, he was wrong. Eleanor knows that she couldn't do what she does without me." Tommy laughed softly. "I'd say the efforts of Malvina Thompson Schneider may not be everything but they're something."

"Something indeed."

"And you, Nora, did you sacrifice a husband and children on the bonfire of Ed Kelly, mayor of Chicago?"

"No. When I went to work for Ed I was already a widow, I think."

"You think? How could you not be sure?"

"My husband was killed in Ireland during the Irish Civil War in 1922, but I've never seen his grave. I was hoping to visit it during this trip, but I was told his body had never been recovered from the sea."

"Have you ever thought of marrying again?"

"No. Not that there have been many opportunities, but I couldn't guarantee getting a dinner on the table. Although I would have liked to have had children."

"Me, too. I regret not having at least one. Eleanor doesn't understand how lucky she was. She had six no bother. Although she still mourns the baby who died. The first Franklin Junior and now the grown-up children are giving her fits."

"My friend Rose says the children we didn't have will never make us smile but they won't make us cry either," I said.

"Tommy." Eleanor was awake. "I wonder if there's coffee."

We'd had none at Beech Hill. Mrs. Nicholson didn't hold with coffee. She was a tea drinker. Plenty of tea in the North and she'd been trading it for butter with a farmer in Donegal who was suffering because British merchant ships weren't going into Irish ports. The tea ration in the Free State was down to half an ounce a week, she'd told me, quite a hardship for people who usually drank four or five cups a day.

"Maybe you should tell FDR if he promises to send a fleet of cargo ships stuffed with tea, Ireland will sign on with the allies," I'd said to Eleanor Roosevelt.

Tommy took out a thermos and some cups and poured Eleanor a coffee. "Got it from the kitchen of the camp mess." She'd even brought along a bottle of milk and added some to Eleanor's cup.

"No sugar," Tommy said. "I didn't like to ask for any. Even the servicemen have a restricted sugar allowance, which I am told they share with local families." She turned to me, "Coffee, Nora?" and handed me a cup.

"Thanks," I said. "What about Mike and the others in the cockpit?"

"I made sure they had their own thermos."

"Good woman, Tommy," I said.

"She is indeed," Eleanor said. "I couldn't live this life without her."

"Now, Eleanor," Tommy said.

"It's true. You keep me organized and are so good in a crisis. After that incident in Miami, I wanted to fly down to Florida immediately and ride back on the train with Franklin. Tommy had a cooler head. We talked it over. Franklin said that it would be wrong to give the attempt on his life too much importance. We'd always known the risk was there. After all, Theodore Roosevelt became president because that Pole shot McKinley, and then when Uncle Teddy was campaigning for the Bull Moose Party, that crazy German shot him. Franklin always admired how he carried on. The bullet hit the folded-up pages of his speech, which he showed the crowd. Then he went on to talk for an hour. It was only when he reached the hospital in Chicago that it was discovered the bullet had gone into his chest. The press never knew how serious the wound was, though the incident certainly took the wind out of Uncle Teddy's sails. And it might have contributed to his defeat. Edith Roosevelt kept her feelings to herself, and I knew Franklin would want me to do the same. After all, the Italian had missed."

"Of course, not all assassins are immigrants, Mrs. Roosevelt," I said. "Look at John Wilkes Booth."

She didn't respond. Caught up in her own memories. "At first, we thought everyone had survived the attack and that Mayor Cermak would recover," she said.

"Yes," I said. "We all did. I was there."

"You were?" Tommy asked. "Why?"

"Cermak hired me to photograph him with President Roosevelt. I was taking the picture when Zangara fired. I told them to move closer and sometimes I wonder . . . ," I said.

"Surely, you don't blame yourself," Tommy said.

"My goodness, Nora," Eleanor said. "The only one responsible was the assassin."

"But here's the strangest part, Walter Winchell took me with him when he interviewed the gunman, so I took Zangara's picture too. Winchell still believes the Outfit hired him to kill Cermak," I said.

"And what do you think, Nora?" Eleanor Roosevelt asked.

"That an ignorant little man with a bad stomach who was full of hate and resentment almost changed history," I said.

"Exactly," she said.

Period. The end.

Suddenly, the plane plunged.

"Seat belts. Seat belts," I heard Mike shout from the cockpit. I grabbed the arms of my seat. Held on tightly. Turbulence? A storm? Tommy was leaning over Eleanor, fastening her seat belt.

"My goodness," Eleanor Roosevelt said.

I eased my hands away, found the buckle of the belt and the tongue and jammed them together. Now it felt as if we were climbing. I looked out the window. Where was the dawn? Shouldn't there be more light by now? But a solid bank of dark clouds surrounded the plane and then suddenly lit up. Lightning flashed around us. Streaks of it. If one hits the plane, we're finished.

"Bad," I heard Tommy say. "Bad, bad, bad."

The plane shimmied, and now I could see sheets of water on the window. Rain slashing at us.

"Mike," I yelled. "Mike, what's happening?"

"Be quiet," Eleanor said to me. "Don't disturb him."

I remembered that Tommy had told me that the First Lady had taken flying lessons. Had wanted to get a pilot's license. She seemed to know what was going on in the cockpit.

Help Mike, I prayed. Please, God, help him. St. Michael the Archangel, defend us in battle.

I must have said the words aloud because Tommy looked over at me and put her finger to her lips. Eleanor had her forehead against the window, but pulled back when a rattatatat hit the plastic. Gunfire, I thought. Gunfire. A Nazi fighter plane was using the storm as a cover to attack us. There were no weapons on our plane. No defenses at all.

"We must hope the plane's wings don't ice over," Eleanor said. "The sudden drop in temperature caused by the storm is dangerous and now with this hail . . ."

"Hail? That was hail?" I said.

"Relatively harmless. It can't pierce the skin of the plane but if the winds don't shift soon . . ."

The plane shook, and the wind pushed us to one side and then the other.

"Oh my God," I said. "We'll break apart."

"Contain yourself, Nora," Eleanor said. "We don't want the pilot to hear you. Show some faith in your nephew. After all you were the one . . ." She didn't have to finish the sentence.

I'd recommended Mike to lead her personal air crew. Plotted to take this trip and now . . . I'd saved Franklin but would kill Eleanor Roosevelt. Not Mike's fault. He hadn't the experience. I'd let my love for him blind me to the obvious. Now our aircraft seemed to be spiraling down. I remembered those awful newsreel clips from the Battle of Midway. The planes on fire twisting down into the ocean. Had lightning struck us? Were the instruments out? Maybe the wind had loosened the nuts and bolts holding the wings on. These planes had been turned out one after the other from factories proud of the speed in which they'd been constructed. Maybe more time should have been taken. Had Rosie really riveted this craft well?

Stop it, I told myself. She's right. I do believe in Mike and women factory workers. Then I heard Mike shout.

"We're through the worst of it. I'll be able to find us some smooth air now," Mike said.

And he did. Not five minutes later, we were cruising along as if nothing had happened.

"Well done, Captain," Eleanor shouted toward the cockpit.

"Yes. Yes," I said. "Great, Mike. Thank you. Thank you."

We were safe but I was appalled. I'd been in worse situations. Had Tim McShane's hands around my neck, ready to squeeze the life out of me. Nursed Marines at Belleau Wood, and yet I hadn't lost the run of myself. But I had never been so frightened as I was during the storm. Bad enough for me to die, but losing the First Lady would have devastated the country. Especially if a Nazi fighter had shot us down. I'd been told since childhood that I had too much imagination and, as I sat back in my seat, I had to agree. But worse, had I become a coward? Me who had fought the Black and Tans. Acted as a messenger for the IRA. Me? Surprised yourself didn't you, Nonie, said that voice inside me. This will teach you some compassion.

I looked over at Eleanor Roosevelt. She was one brave woman.

"I feel as if I've made a friend," Tommy said, as she and Eleanor Roosevelt got into the car that would take them to New York from Floyd Bennett Field. The crew and I were having dinner at Mike and Mariann's Brooklyn apartment, where I'd stay the night and leave on the train the next morning.

"I do, too, Tommy," I said. "And it was an honor to travel with you, Mrs. Roosevelt."

"I think it's time for you to start calling me Eleanor, Nora," she said to me.

"Thank you, Eleanor," I said.

Mike asked me not to mention the "turbulence" to Mariann. I didn't.

8

LATE NOVEMBER 1942

"You're not yourself, Nora," Margaret Kelly said to me a week after I arrived back in Chicago after my trip. She and Ed and I were driving home from what had come to be called "the Kelly Bowl," the annual high school football championship game Ed had initiated in 1933, which was held at Soldier Field around Thanksgiving. The winner of the public league played the top Catholic school team in a hard fought contest that always attracted a huge crowd. In 1937 the west side Austin High School defeated Leo, the south side high school named for a pope. One hundred twenty thousand fans filled Soldier Field—the biggest attendance anywhere ever for a football game. This year Leo had faced Tilden High School and the Catholics had beaten the Publics. Margaret wasn't much of a sports fan but the proceeds of today's game were going to the centers for servicemen and women that she oversaw. So she'd come onto the field at halftime to receive the check for one hundred thousand dollars from Ed, and I'd photographed the presentation. Cold on the field, and I was glad for the green Donegal tweed coat with the fur collar that was an early Christmas present from Ed and Margaret. A bit funny, that gift, because usually the money raised at the game went to Chicago's own Christmas Benefit Fund to buy clothes for needy children. Ed had started the Fund in 1933, his first Christmas as mayor, and the Democratic Party organization in each ward delivered the packages to families. Even with all the New Deal programs, there was something to be said for the personal touch, and not bad to remind voters that the mayor cared. But this year the Armed Forces had priority, so I was the only one getting a coat from Ed Kelly.

And to be fair, with all the jobs in defense industries most kids in Chicago were fairly well dressed, as Ed told the newspapers. He was trying to explain why the second event in the annual fund-raising effort wasn't going to happen at all. For the last eight years Ed had spearheaded the "Night of Stars," an extravaganza at the stadium that lasted seven hours, with as many as forty acts mixing movie stars, big bands, opera singers, church choirs, tap dancers and vaudeville comics, in the come-one come-all spirit of our city. Where else but in Chicago would Gypsy Rose Lee introduce the surplice-wearing boys of the Paulist choir? Almost a half million dollars raised to clothe poor children, between the two events. But someone in the federal government had decided the "Night of Stars" was too frivolous for wartime, and besides, was charity really necessary when the economy was booming? Best not to draw attention to the pockets of poverty that still existed.

The word had come down last week, and I knew that both Ed and Margaret were disappointed at the cancelation. So was I. I'd enjoyed photographing everyone from Mary Pickford and Joan Crawford to Milton Berle and the radio pair Fibber McGee and Molly. But if I was "not myself," it was because I was mourning Peter Keeley, not the "Night of Stars," as Margaret assumed.

"I certainly understand how you feel. Ed and I were shocked, too, but what can you do?" Margaret said as we pulled up in front of the apartment building.

I followed them upstairs into their apartment and now Ed let loose a bit.

"So unfortunate. And Jules Stein had arranged for the entire cast of this movie that's coming out, *Du Barry Was a Lady,* to appear—Lucille Ball, Red Skelton, Gene Kelly. I had a little bit of patter all worked out about being Kellys together. I guess I'll have to call Stein Monday and let him know the whole thing is off," Ed said.

I knew Stein was the reason the "Night of Stars" had always been so, well, star-studded. I'd photographed Stein with Ed when Jake Arvey, the alderman from the Jewish Twenty-Fourth Ward, brought the young eye doctor and impresario to Ed's office.

A short, intense man, Stein was in his mid-thirties then and Ed had just taken over Cermak's term. Stein explained that he had left South Bend, where his father ran a dry goods store, for Chicago at eighteen to attend the University of Chicago. After graduation, he'd gone on to study ophthalmology at Rush Medical College. He supported himself during his student days by playing in a band for Jewish weddings and bar mitzvahs, later taking over management of the group. When Prohibition created hundreds of speakeasies that wanted entertainment, he began representing all kinds of musical acts. Of course, all these places were run by the Outfit. And while no one ever came right out and said that Jules Stein was in business with Al Capone, they obviously had an understanding or Stein's clients would not have been booked.

He became so powerful that even the legitimate ballrooms had to go through Stein. He started to represent famous bandleaders—Tommy Dorsey, Glenn Miller—and, if a nightclub owner wanted to hire one of those bands, they were expected to take some of Stein's lesser acts, too. It worked the same way with the groups. Stein would book them into the Palmer House alright, but in return, they might have to play a roadhouse in Cicero, too. No complaining or else . . .

Though Dr. Stein had been a practicing eye doctor, he wasn't fitting many pairs of eyeglasses anymore. He set up his Music Company of America and eventually left Chicago for the West Coast. Once in Hollywood, he expanded the company and it became a top agency for movie stars. But Stein had stayed in touch with Ed, and invited him out to California last year.

Ed had traveled out west with Jake Arvey. Jake acted as a kind of patron for Stein and for the Chicago Jewish businessmen who were rising to national prominence. They all came from the same neighborhood in the Twenty-Fourth. The Pritzkers, the Annenbergs, the Crowns, who'd changed their name from Krinsky, and the Korshaks were all wealthy and all rumored to have ties to the Outfit. Supposedly they'd gotten started by investing mob money in legitimate businesses. Not that Ed seemed worried about such connections. "We all came from the streets," he'd say. And he'd been happy to put on a white tie and tails and sit between Louis B. Mayer and Jules Stein at a fancy dinner in Los Angeles.

But the fellow he talked most about when he came home was Sidney Korshak, whose brother Marshall worked in the city treasurer's office. Sidney was a lawyer who divided his time between Chicago and Los Angeles. Ed said he seemed to know every single person at the dinner—actors, writers, directors, and all the executives. He had told Ed that if he ever needed a star for a bond rally or his Christmas benefit to give him a call. I asked Ed why he had so much clout out there. "He represents the unions," Ed had said. "He could shut down production on any movie set in the world." Clout.

We were drinking coffee and eating chocolate chip cookies in Ed and Margaret's living room now, looking down at the frozen lake. Ed was shaking his head.

"I keep thinking of all the great shows we had in the past," he said.

"Will you ever forget Frank Sinatra?" I asked.

In 1939, the Harry James Band was appearing in Chicago, and Ed had asked the bandleader to perform at the Christmas benefit. James hadn't wanted to commit the whole band, but instead sent a small combo, along with the band's young singer, named Frank Sinatra.

The reaction from the audience in the stadium had stunned Ed. Margaret and I had tried to explain to him what it was about this skinny young man that made teenage girls scream.

Ed had been fascinated. He'd made a point of talking to Sinatra at the party for performers after the concert in the Lake Shore Drive apartment. I'd heard all about how much Chicago reminded him of Hoboken. Sinatra had told Ed that he felt he was wasting his time with Harry James, and his dream was to sing with the Tommy Dorsey band. Ed was friendly with Bobby Burns, Dorsey's manager, who was at the party, and introduced him to Sinatra. A week later, two dozen roses arrived at the office, with a note from Sinatra. He was now the main singer of the Tommy Dorsey Orchestra, and would be happy to appear at Ed's benefits at any time. "And thank Nora for that sheet music," he'd written. I'd given him a copy of the song "Chicago." "Tell her I'll learn it and sing it for her one day."

"That was such a great night," Margaret said. "Awful not to have anything at all this year. All the service people in town would love to see Lucille Ball!"

"It had to be somebody high up that put the kibosh on the "Night of Stars," Ed said. "We better just go along. I can't be seen to be involved in anything."

"How about a scaled down show that has nothing to do with you?" I asked. "Let the movie cast perform somewhere. Not sponsored by the city. A free event for all your troops, Margaret."

"Easier said than done, Nonie," Ed said. "The cast expects to be here in two weeks. Who could put something like that together so quickly?"

"What about Mariann's brother Jim? He's a producer and seems like a doer. At least let me call him and set up a meeting in your office."

Mariann's brother was a real Chicago fellow, I thought, as he walked into the office the next morning. A tall, broad-shouldered, well dressed man in a camel hair coat, he held his fedora in one hand with the other outstretched across the desk for a handshake with Ed. Good-looking, dark hair and blue eyes. Early forties, I'd say. He already had a plan.

"The Chicago Theater," Jim Williams said to Ed and me. "It's the classiest place in town, right in the Loop—and the manager's a pal of mine. He's willing to substitute our event for the usual stage show that goes on before the movie. An audience of only three thousand, compared to the twenty-five thousand you've gotten at the stadium, but Nora told me you want something smaller, and they will all be in uniform."

"Sounds good," Ed said, "but I have to be hands off."

"Is it okay that we list Mrs. Kelly as the patroness? Part of her work for the troops," Jim suggested.

Ed nodded.

Jim went on, "So, as I understand it we'll be presenting a performance by the cast of *Du Barry Was a Lady* that's being released in a couple of months, right?"

"Yes," Ed said. "Jules Stein arranged for the whole group to come to Chicago before we knew the 'Night of Stars' was going to be canceled."

"We won't waste this opportunity," Jim said. "We can put on a great show. There is just one problem. *Du Barry* is an MGM picture, and Paramount bought the Chicago Theater from Balaban and Katz. The studio might balk at promoting the opposition."

Ed smiled. "Bessie," he called out. His secretary opened the door. "Could you please get Abe Balaban on the phone? Use the New York number."

The Balaban brothers and their sister's husband, Sam Katz, had built most of the fancy movie theaters in Chicago, then expanded throughout the Midwest. Now they were doing very well for themselves in Hollywood and New York. They were friends of Jake Arvey, so strong supporters of Ed Kelly.

In the end, Abe Balaban called his brother, the president of Paramount pictures, and by the time Jim left the office the Chicago Theater was ours. No charge at all.

"Before I go," Jim said, "there's something I want to tell you, Ed. My grandfather and your father were close friends."

I was surprised. "Mariann's father never mentioned that connection when we met him," I said.

"That's because I'm not Ralph Williams' son. He's always been Pa to me, and no distinctions were made in our family but my mother was a widow, and I was just two when they married. My dad was Jim Ryan. He was on the force, as was his father, another Jim Ryan. He and your father Stephen Kelly were cops together in Bridgeport," he said to Ed. "You and my dad were born about the same time, and I guess played together as little boys. Anyway my mother knew about the connection. She used to point out stories about you in the papers."

"Well how about that!" Ed smiled at him. "The Chicago Irish are all one big clan."

Both men had big grins in the photograph I took of them.

Problem solved.

A very different tenor to the next meeting in Ed's office. These were two University of Chicago fellows, both Nobel prize winners in physics. Arthur Compton looked like a small town midwestern businessman, and indeed he was from Ohio. I'd photographed him with his wife at the Hall of Science during the Century of Progress. She was a McCloskey, and we'd toured the Irish Village together. Enrico Fermi could only have been Italian, very courtly. A small man, balding, with a nice smile.

As soon as I'd taken the photograph Ed said to me, "Why don't you call Margaret and tell her about our meeting with Jim Williams." I knew he wanted me to leave—this was a private meeting.

I gave it an hour and then came back. The men were gone.

"What was all that about?" I asked Ed.

He was sitting at his desk, rubbing the holy medal. He didn't answer right away.

"They're conducting some experiment at the university next week," he finally said. "Compton says the lab they built under Stag Field is very secure. Perfectly safe. But they want me to have six fire engines on hand just in case."

"Oh," I said. What else had they discussed, I wondered.

After a while, Ed said to me, "The last time I was in Washington, the president asked me if I knew Compton and I said yes. Then he talked about letters that Einstein and other scientists had written to him, warning that the Germans were working on a superbomb. The scientists urged him to get the US working on a comparable weapon."

"Is the University of Chicago experiment part of that?" I asked.

Ed nodded. "We shouldn't even be talking about this, Nora. I think Franklin was sorry he said anything to me. We were alone, waiting for Grace to wheel in the drinks trolley so he could mix the cocktails. I was telling him how well the steel plants in Gary were doing. Three shifts per day, same as the Ford plant that's manufacturing airplanes now. He smiled and said, 'We Americans are good at getting things done when we put our minds to it. We'd better be. I just hope those scientists are as productive as our assembly line workers.' That's when he brought up Compton.

"He hinted that something big was going to be happening in Chicago. I said, 'No better place for it. After all, we gave the world the Century of Progress.' And then he got very serious, almost glum, and said that he only hoped it was progress."

"Jesus Christ, Ed."

"Then Grace arrived with the drinks cart and the rest of the gang came in. Franklin put on his big grin."

"And did he say any more to you later?"

"Not another word."

"I wonder if Eleanor knows about this project," I said.

"She wasn't there. Of course Mrs. Roosevelt usually doesn't come to the Children's Hour—that's what Franklin calls cocktail time. He's a remarkable man, Nonie. I've always said that Roosevelt was my religion but to see him now . . . if ever there was a man who carried the weight of the world on his shoulders, it's FDR. And yet, most of the time you'd never know it. In the same way he makes you forget that he's crippled, he keeps the worst possibilities at bay. I don't know how he does it."

"Women," I said. "It's the women he has around him."

Ed smiled. "He does have quite a harem. Grace Tully has taken over Missy LeHand's duties and is just as devoted, and now he's got the queen of Norway living at the White House. His two female cousins visit him in Washington, are on call at Hyde Park, and Grace told me a Mrs. Johnson comes to dinner when Eleanor is away. Though that's not her real name. She's an old friend of the president's. A very old friend."

"Who? Oh, no, not Lucy Mercer. That's mean, Ed. Eleanor would be devastated."

"She'll never find out. Anna Roosevelt told me her father needs to be admired unconditionally, especially now that his mother has died. And Eleanor is too honest to give him that kind of approval, so . . ."

"Lucy Mercer," I said again. And, once more, Ed shushed me.

"Nora, please."

A superbomb, Franklin Roosevelt's old flame, and the stars of *Du Barry*. Just another day in the mayor's office.

DECEMBER 18, 1942

Ed had gotten good at welcoming celebrities. He had me read up on where they were from and find some way to connect their hometown with Chicago. When Lucille Ball arrived with her husband, a good-looking dark-haired fellow from Cuba named Desi Arnaz, Ed began by talking about her hometown.

"I understand you're from Celoron, outside of Jamestown, New York. A friend of mine named Al Neary used to run the carousel on the boardwalk there. I hear it was quite a vacation spot. He was from the South Side. Started here during the World's Fair, the first one. Ran a kind of carnival on the midway and then headed out to New York."

Lucille Ball was nodding her head. "I remember him," she said, "from when I was a kid."

"Must have been fun growing up in a resort town," I said.

"It was," she said. "There was a ballroom there where big bands played. I even got to sing along with a few of them."

"Okay, Lucy," her husband said. "That's enough. The mayor isn't interested.

It was a real hick town. Lucy got out as soon as she could. My name is Desi Arnaz, Ed. I'm from Havana. Lots of men from Chicago in Havana." He smiled at Ed as if the two of them were sharing a secret.

"Yes there are," Ed said. "I've made quite a few trips to your city. A friend of mine raced his horses at the Havana track."

"Did he win?" Desi Arnaz asked.

"He did alright."

"Men from Chicago usually do," Desi Arnaz said.

The Outfit again, I thought. There was a silence. Lucy spoke up.

"I'm not saying I'm a great singer but I can always put across a song. I did two numbers in *Du Barry Was a Lady.* A Cole Porter score, but a silly story. The janitor in a nightclub falls in love with the hatcheck girl, that's me, May Daly. I had to dye my hair red for the part, but I think I'll keep it this color."

"You should," I said. "It looks great. And there is something about being a redhead, isn't there, Ed?"

Ed laughed.

Lucy went on, "May is in love with another guy. The janitor gets hit over the head and imagines that he's Louis XV and all the other characters are in his court. I'm Madame Du Barry. Nutty, I know, but my songs are great. This one's a duet with the king but I'll sing both parts." And she did.

If you're ever in a jam, here I am.
If you're ever in a mess, S.O.S.
If you're ever so happy you land in jail, I'm your bail.
It's friendship, friendship, just a perfect blendship,
When other friendships have been forgot, ours will still be hot.

Now when she'd started singing, Ed and Desi had stared at her as if she'd lost her mind. True, she didn't have a great voice, but what she could do with her face. Her eyebrows went up and down. She batted her eyes, puffed out her cheeks. This beautiful woman became a joyful clown before our eyes. I was laughing and clapping along from the beginning and by the time Lucy had reached the end of the chorus Ed and Desi were smiling too. *"La da la da la da dig dig dig,"* she sang and gestured for us to join. We did. You couldn't resist her. *"La da la da la da dig dig dig,"* we sang. The door to Ed's outer office opened. Bessie O'Neill, his secretary, stood looking at us with five or six of the men waiting for appointments behind her.

Lucy started a new verse.

If you're ever down a well, ring my bell.

I doubt if City Hall had ever known such a performance. Lucy finished by dancing down the main hallway, past open doors and applause.

A good half hour before I could get Ed and Lucy lined up for the photograph. By then Lucille Ball had reverted back to being a glamorous movie star and the picture was okay, but it was Lucy the clown who had the real talent.

"You know, Mr. Mayor," Desi said, "my wife needs a better agent. She's been trying to get in to see Jules Stein. No luck. I understand he's a friend of yours."

Ed smiled. "Bessie," he called out. "Could you please get Dr. Stein in Los Angeles?"

Desi Arnaz took the call in the private booth in the back of Ed's office. He came out smiling. "We have a meeting with Stein next week, Lucy," he said. "He wants to talk about setting up a production company with me. How about that?" He turned to Ed. "I remember when I played in Xavier Cugat's orchestra how scared Cugie was of all your crowd."

Desi pressed his finger against his nose and pushed it down. Not our crowd, I wanted to say. Ed, speak up. Don't let him think you're connected to the Outfit. You're the good guy, Ed. Tell him. Tell him.

But Ed said nothing. He ushered the couple from his office while inviting them to a party at his apartment after the show. I waited until the two were well away and we were alone. I shut the office door. "For God's sake, Ed, what's wrong with you? You let him think you were friendly with gangsters!"

"Stein isn't a gangster, Nora, and keep your voice down."

I hadn't realized I was almost shouting. "And what are all those Chicago people doing out in Hollywood, anyway? I've heard rumors about the Pritzgers and Annenbergs and Korshaks . . ."

Ed interrupted me. "Look, those families faced the same kind of oppression we did. The tsar and his Cossacks would have been happy to kill all the Jews in Russia, the same way the British wanted to get rid of us. They ran for their lives just as we did. Do you think Jake Arvey is going to tell fellows who saw their parents slaughtered to check the pedigree of every dollar? Do you think Rockefeller's money was so clean, or Carnegie's or Pullman's or any of the men who made fortunes exploiting their workers? Grow up, Nonie. I've never taken a dime from the Outfit. They know I can't be bought. Remember what Jesus said, 'Judge not and you shall not be judged.' Jake Arvey will be there tonight—Colonel Jake Arvey now, serving his country just like Captain Sidney Korshak. Grateful to the country that gave them incredible opportunities. Think of the influence they have in Hollywood. I got seven hundred fifty thousand votes in Chicago, the most of any mayor ever. But one movie is seen by fifty million people. That's clout, Nora, and it's no bad thing to stay in with the people who've got it."

Red Skelton, Virginia O'Brien, and Gene Kelly arrived the next day. The concert was scheduled for that evening, so Jim Williams set up an afternoon rehearsal. He'd booked a few local acts—the old St. Pat's Choir, the five dancing Murphys, and a magician to fill out the hour.

There were klieg lights in front of the Chicago Theater that night, as young people in uniform entered the ornate building. Ed and Margaret sat in a box to the right of the stage with Jake Arvey—every inch a colonel in his dress uniform, the gray-green wool so distinctively Army. Next to him, Marshall Korshak and a man who must have been his brother Sidney, both in uniform. Officers too, though fighting the war from Stateside bases.

I was in the prompter's box, ready to photograph everything on stage. Suddenly, there was Desi Arnaz next to me. "Nobody wanted me to play my bongo drums," he said. "I guess this will be an all-Micks show with the Jews as the go-betweens. Business as usual."

"James Petrillo has forty in his orchestra," I said. "I'm sure he'll find a place for you if you ask."

"I don't ask . . . I'm a bandleader myself. Had my own club in New York. I invented the conga line, you know." He grabbed my waist and twisted my hips, pushing me forward as he sang "la da la da la da dig dig dig."

"Hey," I said. "Hold on."

"Think you're too old to have some fun? Don't sell yourself short," he said.

"Desi. Desi." Lucille Ball caught sight of us from the wings and gestured to him.

"Babalou," he said as he left. Catch yourself on, fellow, I thought.

A minute later, I saw Desi put his arm around Lucy and whisper in her ear. Gene Kelly said something to Desi, and Red Skelton shook his head and shrugged. Kelly tapped Lucy on the shoulder. He sketched out a dance step and she imitated it. Kelly shook his head and did the step again.

In short order, the choir from old St. Pat's sang, the Murphys danced and the magician actually pulled a rabbit out of his hat. The audience was getting restless. Finally, the orchestra played the opening notes of "Friendship."

Before the cast of *Du Barry* took the stage, Kelly made Lucy do the step one more time, then led the four performers on. Kelly whirled Lucy around then passed her off to Red, who grabbed Virginia O'Brien's hand. The four belted out "Friendship, friendship, the perfect blendship." The audience responded to the energy onstage and stood, clapping in rhythm. I was so glad they were having a good time, and wondered how many of these young men might soon be headed for combat.

"Hoo-rah," somebody shouted.

Gene Kelly waved, then suddenly was upside down, walking on his hands and bouncing across the stage while the other three shuffled from side to side. Kelly flipped back up to his feet and held out his hands to Lucy, Red, and Virginia. They moved in for the big finish, slapping their knees, throwing their arms in the air, the audience with them hooting and shouting. The orchestra finished with a flourish, the performers took their bow and ran off, but the applause brought them back a second and then a third time.

The stage filled up as the local groups joined the stars. Lucille Ball took the hand of the choir director, and Gene Kelly brought the five Murphys forward, four young sisters with their brother. The orchestra played the song Kate Smith had made a hit. "God Bless America," we all sang.

Through the night, with a light from above.

Please God.

"Schmaltz always works," Gene Kelly said to me. I found myself standing next to him at the party after the concert in Ed and Margaret's apartment.

"I thought the concert was very moving," I said. You jerk, I thought.

"It was. It was," he said. "It's just I'm getting sick of all this safe patriotism when there are fellows out there risking their lives. I want to enlist."

"Well what's stopping you?"

"Louis B. Mayer. The bastard won't let me. He says I'll do more for my country by making pictures to boost morale."

"Mmm."

"I know. It's a lame excuse and I could just walk down to the recruiting office, and then MGM would sue me and I have a wife and a daughter to support."

"Well you're no kid, Mr. Kelly, I suppose . . ."

"I'm only thirty."

"But not eligible for the draft."

He nodded over to where Desi Arnaz was talking to Margaret and the wives of Jake Arvey and Sidney Korshak. "The Latin lover over there got his induction notice and then conveniently broke his leg right before his induction physical."

"Oh," I said.

"Yes," he said.

"You don't like him?" I asked him.

"I like him alright. Who wouldn't? He's fun. He'd show up on the set while we were shooting *Du Barry,* usually near the end of the day when everyone was exhausted, carrying those bongo drums. He'd start playing and pretty soon he'd have the whole place laughing. Even got me to dance with him, but the guy has a chip on his shoulder. He's an aristocrat in his own mind. I guess his family had money in Cuba. His father and grandfather were in politics and when Batista came in, they had to run for it. They arrived in Florida broke. Though Desi will tell you how he went to the finest Catholic schools and was on his way to becoming a lawyer." Kelly laughed.

"But then, so was I. In my first year of law school, when my father lost his job and the family needed money. My brother Fred and I worked up a dance routine. We'd perform at local talent shows. Won a hundred dollars one night and that was big money in 1932. Of course most of the time we danced in joints. Cloops, I call them—a combination of clubs and chicken coops. All of them run by the Pittsburgh version of the mob. What is it about show business that attracts gangsters?"

"Prohibition, cash, and chorus girls," I said.

"I guess so. I suppose Desi and I have a lot in common. He went to work to support his family too, except I'm in love with my wife and I'm not about to ruin my marriage by screwing around."

"And Desi will?"

"Mmmm," Kelly said. "None of my business. But Lucy's got so much talent. She's not really a glamour girl. She can make people laugh. Take them out of themselves. That's a rare gift."

"Is that what you want to do?"

"Yes," he said. "Dance is unique. You train like an athlete. Very physical. Learning the steps, making your muscles respond, forcing flat feet like mine to point and move. You know I have no instep."

He did a quick pirouette. "But then the music starts and it takes you over. The physical and the spiritual all connected and the audience knows it. Something very elemental in us all that wants to move. The crazy rhythm." He stopped. Shook his head. "Why the hell am I going on like this to you? I sound like some professor or something."

"Maybe I remind you of your mother," I said. He laughed.

"Harriet Curran Kelly. Quite a woman my mother. Got my middle name from her father. Wild Billy Curran came from Derry to New York with nothing. Ended up in the coalfields of West Virginia. Wouldn't go down into the mines. Opened up a general store instead. Married my grandmother who was from Alsace-Lorraine. My mother said she got her business sense from her. Old Billy did alright then lost everything. Yet my mother married another Irishman, Joseph Patrick Kelly, who also made a good living for a while. The biggest seller of phonographs in the Midwest but he lost his job when the Depression hit. She saved us. Got a job as a secretary/receptionist in a dance school. Ended up employing all of us kids. We made a bundle. I was good if I say so myself. I directed local shows and revues. The toast of Pittsburgh. Sometimes I think I should just go back there. Then I could enlist and not be controlled by Louis Bastard Mayer."

"You can't go back to Pittsburgh," I said. "It's like that song 'How Ya Gonna Keep 'Em Down on the Farm After They've Seen Paree.'"

"Never made it there," he said.

"It's an extraordinary place," I said. "Truly the City of Light. Awful to think of the Nazis covering it in darkness."

"And what am I doing to stop them? Running around a sound stage. Clowning in front of an audience in Chicago."

"We appreciate you taking the time," I started. He waved me silent.

"I suppose I do owe your city something. The first real training I ever got was here at the Chicago Association of Dance Masters. Spent two summers studying with some of the best teachers in the world. Crazy, though, mornings I'd study ballet with Diaghilev and afternoons Spanish dance with Angel Cansino. What a juxtaposition. His niece Rita was in the class. They changed her name to Hayworth in Hollywood."

"That's our town for you."

"It was during the Century of Progress. Plenty of work. My brother and I would appear in the clubs inside the Fair and then dance at the after-hour joints around the edges," he said.

"Too bad I didn't know you then. I could have taken your pictures."

"Are you a real photographer? I saw you shooting photographs backstage but I figured you were, well . . ."

"Somebody's elderly aunt with her Brownie?" He shrugged. "Ed Kelly is my cousin. I work for him. The official photographer."

"Well that figures. In the city that invented patronage," he said.

I wasn't going to let this fellow from Pittsburgh patronize me. "I've studied with some pretty good teachers myself. The camera I use was a gift from Eddie Steichen and it was Matisse taught me about light." I stopped. No reason a hoofer would even know these names.

"I bought a few Stieglitz prints when I lived in New York," he said. "But I would need a couple of box-office smashes before I could get near a Matisse. Funny thing though, Mayer brags about his Cézannes and Matisses and

Picassos all the time. As far as he's concerned, that's real art. But you know, Miss Kelly—"

"Nora."

"The movies can be as much an artistic expression as the greatest paintings or opera or ballet, and for the first time in history millions of ordinary people can experience what only the rich could."

"Spoken like a true Kelly. Did you know our ancestors were famous for the great parties they threw? Open to everybody. With poets and harpists and singers and dancers. The entertainment lasted for months. *Failte Uí Ceallaigh*—the welcome of the Kellys. Still a phrase used in Ireland to describe a really extravagant occasion."

"Sounds good. Though I have to tell you I'm not one of those 'shure and begorrah' Irishmen."

"Oh for God's sake, Gene, nobody is. The English created the stage Irishman. We saved our souls with music. Dancing when we had no instruments at all, lilting for rhythm. Nothing could stop us. And talk about warriors. The name Kelly means contention, and for that matter Eugene comes from Eoghan, Prince of the O'Neills, who ruled Derry and Tyrone where the Currans lived."

Gene Kelly held his hands up. "Okay. Okay," he said. "You win. I do know that when Irish step dancers met Negro shufflers that tap dancing was born."

While we were talking, the rest of the party had moved over to the piano. Jim Williams introduced Eddie Burke from the Sixteenth Ward. He was an unlikely musician, but he knew how to plunk out a tune that would get people to sing along. He sat down at the piano and started with a surefire favorite, "Happy Days Are Here Again." Lucky Davis began conducting the group while Ed, Margaret, and Lucky's husband, Loyal, stood to the side watching, smiling. Trust Lucky to outshine the stars with swooping gestures that sent the phrases up and down.

"Who's that?" Gene asked me.

"Our actress-in-residence. She was a professional once but now she plays her most demanding role—respectable wife with just a little whiff of the wicked stage."

The group finished with a great big *"Shout it now"* and applauded themselves.

Jim Williams said, "How about another song from the movie?"

"Why don't you do the ballad, Gene?" Red Skelton suggested.

"No, I'm not a real singer," Kelly said.

"So you just pretend to be one in the movies?" Skelton said. "Come on, Gene, it's a great song. One of Cole Porter's best."

"Alright, alright," Kelly said as he moved around to the piano bench. Eddie got up, bowed to Kelly. "This is one of the songs we kept from the Broadway show. I sing it to May Daly, Lucy's character. Come on over here, Lucy."

"She's fine where she is," Desi answered from the couch where the couple was seated.

Mmmm, it was a love song, and I suppose it's one thing to sing it on screen to her and another . . .

"Easy, Desi," Gene said. "Lucy and I are pals."

But Lucy didn't budge. "Well then, Aunt Nora," he said to me, "will you stand in for her?" So I did. Taking a place at a curve of the grand piano as Gene Kelly started playing and singing.

A pleasant voice. How a regular guy would sound singing to his girl. He delivered the words. No frills.

"Do I love you, do I?" he began. *"Doesn't one and one make two?"*

Do I love you, do I.
Does July need a sky of blue?

He was mugging a bit. Not being serious. Winking at me but then he turned his head to look out the window. The night sky had absorbed the lake. A hard-edged moon stuck in the center.

"Would I miss you, would I?" He was singing, more softly now, not fooling around.

If you ever would go away.
If the sun would desert the day.
What would life be?

I wondered if he was thinking of his wife and that baby daughter. Did he realize that if he did manage to enlist and get into combat he might never see his wife and child again?

"Will I leave you? Never. Could the ocean leave the shore?"

Except tens of thousands, millions of men were leaving.

"Will I worship you forever? Isn't Heaven forevermore?"

Do I love you, do I?
Oh, my dear, it's so easy to see,
Don't you know I do?
Don't I show you I do,
Just as you love me?

Quiet in the room now. Everyone here had someone on the frontlines. And heaven no consolation.

He almost whispered the last words and for a moment nobody spoke or applauded and then Lucky Davis shouted, "Terrific," and started everyone clapping.

I've had only one love in my life. Peter Keeley and, even if he were dead, he still had my heart. *"Could the ocean leave the shore?"* Somewhere right now a woman was writing a letter to her husband with his photograph propped up before her. A fellow in a sailor suit smiling back at her. She doesn't know that his ship has been torpedoed and that he is dead. Would she stop loving him when she found out?

Ed walked over to the piano. Shook Gene Kelly's hand.

"That was really beautiful," he said. "Thank you."

Gene Kelly struck a chord on the piano and began "Has Anybody Here Seen Kelly?" Ed joined in. *"K-E-double-L-Y. Has anybody here seen Kelly? Have you seen him smile?"*

"Come on, Nora," Ed said. "You're a Kelly, sing." So I did.

> Sure his hair is red and his eyes are blue,
> And he's Irish through and through.

Jim Williams was singing with me. Lucky moved in front of us and conducted the group in the last of the song. *"Has anybody here seen Kelly? Kelly from the Emerald Isle."*

Eddie Burke sat back down at the piano and pounded out "McNamara's Band." Then "My Wild Irish Rose" and "When Irish Eyes Are Smiling." Even Desi Arnaz was singing. Red Skelton and Virginia O'Brien danced in the middle of the group.

Gene Kelly leaned over to me. "Shure and begorrah," he said.

"Just sing," I said. Because no one could be sad while belting out these songs. I mean here we were only one generation away from starving to death and our Irish eyes were smiling. Now, Blessed Mother, the saints and the God who is love, hurry up and end this goddamn war.

9

JANUARY 1943

A quiet Christmas. I did all my shopping at Kroch's Bookstore where a clerk helped me find something suitable for each member of the family. I bought the new novel *Laura* for Margaret and a very serious book on economics by a fellow called Schumpter for Ed, and the latest C. S. Lewis for Rose. I chose a selection of Agatha Christie mysteries for Mariann and the Kelly girls, and a book by the French flyer Saint-Exupéry for Mike. We had no big gathering, with so many of the family away. Rose and I had dinner with Margaret and Ed at their apartment. Margaret and I often had our meals together, now that Ed was working so late. And most days I rode with Ed to city hall in order to be able to take the photographs that had become a kind of historical record.

No hint of dawn at seven o'clock on this January morning, when the lights of Ed's limousine arrived out of the darkness and pulled into the driveway. I'd been watching from my window and saw the two detectives step out of the car. One stood guard in the driveway, while the other went up to the apartment to escort Ed down. Security for Ed had been increased. He was the highest-ranking civilian in the Midwest, responsible for the civil defense in five states.

I was down in the lobby by the time the elevator opened and Ed stepped out. One detective opened the car door, and we got into the back seat. Not much conversation. Too early.

We stopped for seven thirty Mass at Holy Name Cathedral—his daily ritual. I had time to pray for Peter Keeley. *Requiem aeternam*—eternal rest—was surely his if I didn't get on with it and do my job. Live. The feast of the Epiphany and I thought of the T. S. Eliot poem, "A cold coming we had of it, Just the worst time of the year." But the Magi had persevered, and so would I.

Then we drove down to the LaSalle Hotel across from City Hall. There was a table set up in the dining room for Ed. Four mugs of coffee and cinnamon rolls in place. Half the city council had breakfast in this room every day and our eggs over easy came quickly. No dillydallying here.

The business of the day began. Alderman Paddy Bauler was German. His real name was Mathias, but he'd picked up his nickname as a boxer. He was the first one over, with a story about a friend whose liquor license had been suspended. "A good guy," he told Ed, "but bad with details." Would Ed make a call? After all, it was wartime, and Chicago was a Liberty Town. Only patriotic to keep the bars open. Ed had laid a small notebook on the table. He passed it and a pencil over to Paddy, who scribbled in a name and phone number.

Ed poked a piece of white toast into the yolk of his egg and took a bite, as the next fellow approached. I knew that Ed had a meeting scheduled with the chief engineer on the subway project—worth millions of dollars and thousands of jobs to the City. But it wouldn't do to rush the alderman. A revolt in the city council could shut down the most innovative project. Ed had become Boss Kelly and he told me that it was important to maintain that position.

The war had silenced Wilcox, and even the Hearst papers were supporting Ed. Wouldn't do to tear down the man overseeing the most productive defense industry in the country.

This morning Ed had made time for John Sengstacke, who had taken over the *Chicago Defender* from his uncle, Robert Abbott, upon his death. John was the grandson of the German sea captain and Abbott's mother. The paper had printed my photographs of Mrs. Roosevelt with the Negro soldiers in County Tyrone on the front page, along with a feature story by Marjorie Stewart Joyner, a wealthy Chicago businesswoman who also wrote for his paper.

Ed was being made an honorary member of the Bud Billiken Club, named for the fictitious character Robert Abbott had created as a protector of children. The *Defender* sponsored a giant Bud Billiken parade every year, and Ed was delighted when Sengstacke invited him to march. I photographed the two of them together.

As he was leaving the office, Sengstacke said to me, "How would you feel about taking on a special assignment for the paper?"

"Are you hiring me?" I asked, following him into the hall, where we stood and talked.

"I'll pay you ten dollars for this job and then we'll see. My main photographer just shipped out to the Pacific with a Navy construction battalion. So far, the Navy has only allowed Negro sailors to be cooks or stewards or laborers. Put us in a whole separate branch with a different uniform, but I understand something new is happening at Great Lakes. About time. Negro sailors were on John Paul Jones's ship and served during the Civil War. But then they kicked us all out and have only let us back as servants. Anyway, this war is forcing even the Navy to change. Tomorrow, the first Negroes to graduate as seamen with rates are participating in the ceremony at Great Lakes. Think you can cover it? I'll throw in train fare."

"Yes! Thank you. Yes."

I took a taxi from the Lake Forest train station. The driver got me through the front gates of the base and we were directed to the auditorium where graduation was taking place.

The ceremony had already started. I eased into the back of the huge hangar-like building, and stood looking at row after row of shaved heads. Must have been over four hundred sailors. One of these ceremonies every week. The Boot Camp consisted of six weeks of basic training followed by six weeks of special schools. It took ninety days to build a ship and a sailor.

"Are you a family member?" The fellow asking me the question was an older man in a dress uniform with a lot of gold braid.

"I'm a news photographer," I said.

"Did you make an appointment with the public affairs officer?" he asked me.

"No, I didn't. See, I usually work in the mayor's office. I'm Nora Kelly."

"Okay, then. Mayor Kelly is very popular around here. Chicago's the only city that offers everything free to servicemen—transportation, lodging, food, entertainment. Welcome, Nora Kelly. I'm Admiral Abernathy. Why don't you come and stand in the front so you can get a good shot of each sailor when he receives his diploma."

"Thank you, Admiral. I'm taking pictures on assignment for the *Chicago Defender*, the Negro paper, and I understand this is the first class in which colored men are graduating with special accomplishments."

"Well, yes, that's true," he said. "A bunch of those colored boys passed the tests required to get rates. First ones of their race to qualify as seamen for specialty schools where they can become signalmen, engineers, radar operators. Kind of a surprise."

Now I had time to look at the crowd. "Where are they?"

"What do you mean?"

"Where are the Negro men who are graduating?"

"Oh, Miss Kelly, please. You're not one of those crusaders are you? The fellows are in a separate camp. Hey, Chief Potts," he called out. A man sitting in the last row turned around. The admiral waved him over.

"Take this lady over to Smalls," the Admiral said to him.

"I'll tell Ed I met you," I said, but he didn't answer. I followed Potts outside of the auditorium. A jeep was coming toward us. He flagged it down.

"Too far to walk," he said to me. "Especially in this wind. I'm from Alabama and I hate this Yankee weather. The niggers shiver worse than me all through the winter."

Right out! That word.

"Are you referring to your fellow sailors," I said, "who enlisted to serve their country?"

"You Yankees have a lot to learn about—" he paused "—the colored. Best never put them on a ship. As soon as the first shots are fired they'll jump overboard."

He climbed into the back seat of the jeep and waited while I pulled myself up onto the step and got in beside him. No helping hand for me from Chief Potts. The driver drove forward.

The jeep crossed the railroad tracks and we were at the main gate of another post. "Camp Robert Smalls," the sign said.

I photographed the name plaque on the gates. "Who was Robert Smalls?" I asked Potts.

"I don't know, and I don't care," he said.

We pulled up in front of a corrugated iron shed. Nothing like the auditorium in the main camp. We went inside. Here were the same rows of chairs and heads facing forward. As I walked up the side aisle I saw there were many more family members. The women wore fancy hats and the children seemed to be dressed in their Sunday best.

I knew the man standing at the microphone, Congressman William Dawson, newly elected to represent Illinois.

"Ladies and gentlemen," he was saying. "You all know the story of the twenty-two year old messman who became the hero of Pearl Harbor. He was serving on the USS *West Virginia* when it was bombed. He carried his wounded captain to safety, then took over a gun firing back at the Japanese, though he had no real training in operating the weapon. Later he said, 'I aimed it and shot.' At first the Navy only referred to heroic action by an unnamed Negro. But as you know, Robert Abbott began a campaign to find him. We did. He was from Waco, Texas. He was called after the midwife that delivered him. So this six foot three boxing champion is named Doris

Miller. He's been nicknamed Dorie. He's the first one of our race to be awarded the Navy Cross. May I present the hero of Pearl Harbor."

As the tall, broad-shouldered young sailor stepped forward, the audience and the graduates stood and applauded.

Dawson motioned for silence, and Dorie Miller began to speak.

"I'm wearing this," he said, holding up the Navy Cross that was pinned to his blue uniform jacket, "for all of you and all of our ancestors. You know we've been serving on US Navy ships since the very beginning of America. Now Robert Smalls—there was a real hero. I was just doing my job. But fellows like you are the ones who will give us a chance to show the white boys what we can do. Rated seamen, now that's something to be proud of. I wish you all fair winds and following seas. I only hope the Navy lets us have our own ship. The fellows in Tuskegee got to fly. Why shouldn't we take a US Navy ship into combat?"

Well that set the crowd off. From among the family members there were shouts of "Amen," and "Yes, Lord."

"Disgusting," said Potts.

"Run along," I said to him, walked up to the front, and found a spot where I could photograph both the sailors and the families.

I took a shot of each sailor as he accepted his diploma from Dorie Miller to huge applause from family and friends and then shook hands with Congressman Dawson.

"I'll introduce you to the men if you'd like," Dawson said to me after the ceremony. Dapper as always. He and Ed always eyed each other's suits, and Dawson had even sent his tailor up to the mayor's office to refit the Brooks Brothers specials Ed bought, saying that a suit can't just hang on you. Something touching about two such powerful men caring about how they dressed. I thought of Pat Nash and Jake Arvey. Doubt if they ever thought twice about their suits.

Today, Dawson wore a navy blue suit, white shirt, and gold tie.

"I'm very proud of these kids," he said, pointing at the class. "Many of them have never even graduated from high school, and yet they got higher scores on the qualifying tests than the white sailors across the road. Are you wondering why, Nora?"

Dawson always told you what question to ask and then answered it.

"Because all Negroes were put together. The college-educated fellows, who by rights should be in Officers' Candidate School, were thrown in with the youngsters. The older men set up classes and taught math and English and drilled the younger fellows on the material that was covered in the official Navy classes. Those young kids scored so well Admiral Abernathy thought there had been some cheating and made them take another battery of tests again with monitors walking the aisles, and guess what? They scored even better. The admiral wanted to submit the lower scores but one of the college men reached out to me and I spoke to the admiral. You have to remember, Nora, that the Navy is a Southern service—Annapolis and all that—with officers coming from the old Confederacy. But they can't argue with excellence and that's what today is about. Excellence."

Dawson had paid for the punch and cookie reception in the mess hall that followed the graduation ceremony. He took me from family group to family group, introducing me to young sailors as I took pictures and scribbled down names.

"I'm from Harlem, USA," Gordon Buchanan told me. Lorenzo Dufau was from New Orleans. He was sitting with a woman and a little boy. All three of them speaking French. Next to them James Graham told me he was from Lake City, South Carolina, the vowels coming out long and slow.

As we were walking out Dawson said to me, "I have a car, Nora. I'd be glad to give you a ride back to town."

"Thanks," I said.

As we walked through the crowd, Dawson said, "These men better get a chance to prove themselves in combat or Jim Crow will have won another victory. The Navy is tough. Men in close quarters on a small ship. Eating together, sleeping nearby, lots of white boys wouldn't stand for that. And these men"—he pointed at the sailors—"are going to move up the ranks. They'll be chief petty officers themselves, able to give orders to white sailors and that could cause trouble."

"Yes," I said. "I heard some of that today. But the military can order obedience, can't they? I'd say the president would be sympathetic."

"You would think so, but remember he was assistant secretary of the Navy when his cousin Theodore sent the great white fleet sailing around the world. TR fired the black sailors. Replaced even the cooks with Filipinos. The Navy will never change until they see what Negroes can do in combat. I understand you traveled with Mrs. Roosevelt."

"Yes. To the Navy base in Derry."

"A lot of destroyer escorts there," he said.

"That's right," I said.

"The little ships that could," he said. "That's what the sailors called the DEs. Dozens being turned out every month. Something noble about their mission, protecting the convoys of troop ships," he said.

"My nephew protected them from above," I said.

"Important to bring the men and materials across to Europe who are going to defeat Hitler."

"With France the battlefield again," I said.

"The poor French," he said. "You saw the dead bodies sinking into that mud. The French Army defeated, and now the children of the men killed in that war are dying in this one. Believe you me I can give you chapter and verse on the faults of the American military beginning here with these young men, segregated even in the classroom, every obstacle put in front of them. Yet look at what they've achieved. I want to see them in the fight, Nora. Double V–victory over there will lead to victory at home. When you brought Ed to meet me, I didn't want to make too much of the fact that I'd spent time with his wife and cousin in a bistro in Paris. Some men wouldn't like that."

"Ed's not 'some men.'"

"You're right. He's not the typical fellow from his background. He's a decent man, your cousin."

"I'm not sure you understand just how poor we Kellys were when my grandmother and great-aunt hauled their children off that boat. Ed's not white in the way that Big Bill Thompson is. No privileges for us. No family money. And you know, Mr. Dawson, there were plenty of 'No Irish Need Apply' signs in Chicago. Now I'm not saying our people faced what your people did."

"I'm glad you know nothing compares to being enslaved for three hundred years, but I understand the case you're making."

"And I think you can push Ed a little bit. I'm sure he could arrange for you to meet with the person who can get you your ship. Eleanor Roosevelt has asked a lot of favors from Ed and I'm certain she'd do one for him in return."

"Thank you very much, Miss Kelly."

"This is what you wanted all along, isn't it? This is why John Sengstacke sent me out here today. Why didn't you just call Ed?"

"You have more influence than you realize, Nora. We politicians may seem crass but we don't forget those who believed in us in the beginning. Harder to trust as time goes on, they are fewer and fewer. Ed has you."

We'd been standing to the side of the reception and I hadn't noticed that most of the families were leaving. "Say, say," I heard. One of the sailors was calling out to us.

"I think someone is trying to get your attention, congressman," I said, but the young man was waving to me. He came over.

"I met you on the president's train," he said. "I'm Melvin Grant Junior. My father was the porter and now look at me."

"Look at you indeed," I said.

I turned to Dawson. "We can get the whole crew for the new ship right here and now."

"We could," he said.

I rode back into the city with William Dawson. "Strange to name a segregated camp after a hero of the Union," he said and told me the story of Robert Smalls.

"He was born into slavery. Down in Beaufort, South Carolina. That's Gullah country where the ties to Africa are very strong. Those people down there found ways to resist and Smalls managed to convince his owner to hire him out to work in Charleston. He had a lot of mother wit and became a pilot on a ship in Charleston Harbor. He was only twenty-one years old when the Civil War started but he convinced the Confederates that he was a loyal darkie and was put in charge of the crew of a ship called the *Planter*. One night when the officers went ashore, he and the crew smuggled their families aboard. Smalls dressed up in the captain's uniform and put on a hat that the captain was known to wear. He'd copied his mannerisms and was a good enough actor to fool the guards in the battery above the harbor. Sailed right past them. Went up the river. Ran up a white sheet and surrendered to the Union Navy. He brought all the Confederate codebooks plus a number of big guns and a load of ammunition that were supposed to be delivered to the troops the next day. He was a celebrated man in his time. They say he was the one who convinced Abraham Lincoln to let Negroes enlist in the Union Army. After the war he was a congressman and did a lot for Beaufort and South Carolina during reconstruction until Jim Crow came to town and shut everything down and now a segregated Navy slaps his name on the colored-only training camp.

"But give these young sailors a ship and they will change all that," Dawson said.

And they did. The USS *Mason* was commissioned in Boston on March 20, 1944. It was a destroyer escort that had been built for a regular Navy crew but turned over to 160 Negro sailors who would perform all the duties required to take a ship into combat.

Ed and William Dawson and the National Association for the Advancement of Colored People had worked with Eleanor Roosevelt to persuade the Navy to commission the ship. Their first foreign port was Derry, and the *Chicago Defender* carried the front page story headlined "Irish First to Treat USS Mason Crew as Americans."

The story described the warm welcome the Irish people gave the USS *Mason* crew. "They called us Yanks," one man said. "I felt like a real American for the first time in my life."

William Dawson had the story framed for Ed, who hung it in his office.

Ed held no campaign events during the run up to the 1943 mayoral election. "It's war time and I have important duties to perform," he said to me after he won the nomination in February.

"The people know who I am and what I've done."

"And McKibben is the weakest candidate you have ever faced," I said. The Republicans hadn't been able to find anyone substantial who was willing to take Ed on. "I'll keep to my daily schedule," Ed had said. "Visit the defense plants, broadcast my radio addresses, confer with the president and you'll—"

"Photograph you as you don't campaign and get the pictures in the papers," I said. Ed had smiled.

"Right. And you might take a few shots of me and the kids helping Margaret to pour coffee and hand out donuts to the servicemen at the USO," he said.

Ed's noncampaign ended with his ceremonial ride on the new State Street Subway two days before the polls opened. The subway, paid for with New Deal money, had taken five years to construct. I don't think Ed ever enjoyed anything more than collaborating with the teams of engineers that came to work on the project. At first, he'd been told it would be impossible. Chicago's soil was too porous to support a subway, especially one that was five miles long and went under the Chicago River. But Ed found some younger men and a very bright woman who figured out that if they went down forty-eight feet they'd reach solid ground. It took a lot of skill and guts to dig a trench in the Chicago River and sink huge steel tubes so far below the surface. "Make no small plans," Ed kept saying to them. "No small plans." Now the subway was ready to go and I planned a very special photograph. One of the construction crew tied me to a pillar on the platform in the Michigan–Chicago Avenue station. I leaned over the tracks and just as the lead car came whooshing through the tunnel, I snapped a photograph of Ed sitting next to the driver front and center. His face was bright in the shadows.

The citizens of Chicago went to their polling places the next morning, carrying newspapers with Mayor Ed Kelly on the front page under the headline

"We Did It!" Ed won with an overwhelming majority with especially high totals in the Negro wards.

But the sweetest moment for my cousin came when a Western Union messenger marched with great ceremony into the mayor's office on April 7, 1943.

"From the White House, Washington, DC," the kid said.

Ed read the telegram. He reached into his pocket, handed the kid a five-dollar bill.

"Jeepers creepers," the kid said. "Thank you, Mayor Kelly."

Then Ed gave me the yellow paper with its tape of words. It read YOUR REELECTION MAKES YOUR OLD FRIEND VERY HAPPY. FDR.

"Some tribute, Ed," I said.

"All I'll ever need," he answered. He folded up the telegram, took out the leather case that held his holy medal, and put the telegram inside.

A week later, a gigantic box arrived. Pat Nash was there when Ed opened it. It was a gift from Mayor Fiorello LaGuardia of New York. A life-size representation of Chief Tammany, with his faithful dog that looked very much like a wolf.

Ed laughed. "We'll ship it up to Eagle River," he said. "There will be an Indian on Indian Point at last."

It was June 5, 1944. Mariann and Mike's second wedding anniversary. I'd called her that morning. Mike had been transferred to Cherry Point, North Carolina, where he was learning to fly off carriers. No way of dodging the dangerous assignment. A very chancy undertaking, and I could tell she was nervous. Some good news, though—she was expecting a baby in November, and planned to move to North Carolina so she could be close to Mike.

I told her I was attending one of the concerts in the Grant Park Music Festival that Ed had started. As president of the South Park Board, even before he was elected mayor, Ed had built a band shell in the park, and all during the Depression years, and now throughout the war, James Petrillo, as head of the musicians' union, had assembled an orchestra to play free concerts. Ed had agreed to pay each musician ten dollars for two hours of playing, which was very good since they were only earning twenty-five cents an hour in the clubs.

Big stars came to Chicago regularly. I'd tried to photograph the crowd who turned out to hear Lily Pons sing in the summer of 1939. Never had so many people been together. Three hundred and thirty thousand. I'd stood on the stage aiming the camera but all I got were heads and hats. James

Petrillo had hired a photographer in a plane and got a good shot of the park—people shoulder to shoulder stretching all the way to the lake.

Tonight's audience wouldn't be as big as that. Lily Pons had been a movie star as well as an opera singer. Besides, thousands of the young fellows who'd come to hear her were off fighting in North Africa, Italy, and the Pacific.

Ed's driver parked right on Michigan Avenue in a special place guarded by four policemen. Margaret and the kids were in Eagle River so I would sit with him in the section reserved for the mayor and his family. Ed seemed preoccupied.

"Everything alright?" I asked.

"Don't say anything, Nora, but Grace Tully is very worried about the president's health. He can't shake this bronchitis."

"He needs a vacation," I said. "A real rest."

"Not a chance," Ed said. "Grace told me something important is about to happen. We'll know very soon."

"The invasion?" I said.

"Sshh," Ed said, though nobody was near to us as we waited in the car for the police to clear a path for us through the crowd into the park. It was common knowledge that the Allies were going to move into Europe. The only question was when and where. A big secret and I doubted Grace would give Ed any details over the telephone.

We followed the two policemen to the special area to the left of the band shell. Ed wanted me to photograph him with the people who came up to shake his hand, then take their address and send them a print. First the aldermen lined up to say hello, then regular people. A word to his bodyguard and they were passed through. An older couple told Ed they had three sons serving. One in the Army, one in the Navy, and one in the Marine Corps.

"Thought there'd be more safety in spreading them around. We're from Bridgeport," the woman said. "My mother was friendly with your grandmother when she worked in the parish office. Anyone in need got some help."

"And what was your mother's name?" I asked after I snapped the picture.

"Ann McIntyre," the woman said. "She married my father, George McKenzie."

"I think I knew them. Did they live on Archer?"

The woman looked at me. "I thought I knew all the Kellys. I don't remember." She stopped. "Oh, are you that Kelly woman who—" She looked at her husband. "Sorry," she said. "I'm sorry."

Dear God, I thought, I'm sixty-five years old and still the black sheep of the family.

Ed didn't seem too interested in the Beethoven or the bit from Bach or even Schubert's "Ave Maria" sung by a young woman I thought was as good as Lily Pons. He hardly looked at the stage at all but kept turning around, looking out of the park as if expecting someone. Which, of course, he was. Because just when the orchestra began its second encore right about eleven o'clock, a detective walked up fast and whispered something to Ed.

"Come on," Ed said to me.

"What?"

Ed was very quiet as our car pulled up to City Hall. We went down to the basement radio studio. What's he going to do? Broadcast? But the big radio set was tuned to receive.

"It's the BBC," the technician said. "They've just announced that there would be important news soon."

Static. Then a voice came through.

"The greatest armada in human history is moving toward the coast of France." He sounded like an American, and said he was aboard one of the hundreds of ships now off the coast of France. We could hear the sounds of guns, wind, and waves and then screams.

"Dear God, Ed," I said.

The technician fiddled with the dial trying to bring in the broadcast more clearly.

"Achtung, achtung," we heard, and then reams of German.

"We've picked up the German report," the technician said.

"They're denying there is an invasion," Ed said, "but at the same time saying their guns are destroying the advancing fleet."

I'd forgotten Ed had learned some German from his grandfather Lang. After midnight now, 7:00 a.m. in France, on what would be called "The Longest Day." Strange it was Rommel who came up with the phrase when he said that the first twenty-four hours of the invasion would be decisive.

"This is it," Ed said. "Pray."

"I am." We spent the whole night listening to the radio transmission.

But a week would pass before reports came from Normandy. One story described the terrifying assault of a cliff face by a company of Army Rangers. They disabled a Nazi gun emplacement that had been firing down on the fellows trying to run across the beach to find some shelter. The place was called "Pointe du Hoc," a rocky outcrop fifty feet about the beach.

Pointe du Hoc. That was Maud Gonne's beach, I thought as I read the report and remembered Willie Yeats standing on that same stretch of sand declaiming his poem.

"We know their dreams only to know they dreamed and are dead."

"Easter, 1916." His verses were about how the execution of ten Irish revolutionaries "changed, changed utterly, a terrible beauty is born." And was "a terrible beauty" being born on that same beach on D-Day? Were the boys who were crawling across the sand propelled by a dream, or were they only scrabbling to stay alive, terrified, praying for five more minutes of life? Changed, changed utterly? Beauty? Certainly these boys had died to end a great evil. Hitler and the Nazis, but would that console their families?

Margaret, Ed and I listened together to the Philco radio in their living room, as Roosevelt addressed the nation on the end of the "Longest Day." He told us "the road would be long and hard" and that "the enemy was strong and would try to hurl back our forces." He warned that our boys would be "sore tried by night and by day without rest but they would not stop until victory is won."

Much later we would see newsreel footage in which lines of "our boys," bent down under their packs, marched up through France. The survivors of that horrendous landing were going off to take on the enemy and risk death again. But they would bring us peace, the president had promised.

I prayed for all them and for Franklin Roosevelt too.

"Not well," Ed had said to me, at the end of the broadcast. "He's just not well. Only sixty-two, younger than we are. But . . . but . . ."

10

JULY 15, 1944

Most Americans didn't know the name Harry Truman, the man who would become the vice presidential nominee, when the Democrats started arriving in Chicago for their convention that summer. No massive demonstration would be needed this time to ensure FDR's nomination, even though he would be serving a fourth term. But how could we replace the commander-in-chief with victory a real possibility? "The challenge," Ed said, "was to nominate the right vice president."

Ed and the other Big City Bosses mistrusted Henry Wallace. It wasn't that the present vice president was too progressive. Nobody was more of a New Dealer than Ed. How many hundreds of times had I heard him say, "Roosevelt is my religion." It was Wallace's strange beliefs that made the bosses nervous. Wallace was connected to esoteric societies. Wallace believed that the Great Soul of Russia was being expressed through the Soviets, and that he understood how to contain the shadow side of Josef Stalin. Now, Roosevelt himself had been taken with Uncle Joe—but the bosses recognized a power-hungry tyrant when they saw one. "Power corrupts, and absolute power corrupts absolutely," was one of Ed's favorite sayings. Grace Tully had told Ed that Wallace participated in séances where a Sioux Indian spirit guide gave him information that he shared with the president.

"Can him," Ed Flynn of the Bronx had said.

The president had agreed to consider replacing Wallace, but wasn't being clear about whom he preferred. Ed and Flynn of New York wanted Truman.

He had been elected to the Senate with the help of the Kansas City boss, Tom Pendergast—which was held against him by some, but Ed thought Pendergast was a good judge of men. And after all, Margaret knew Truman and his family, and had introduced me to Truman in Paris at the end of the last war.

The convention was to begin on Wednesday, July 19. On the Saturday before, Ed received a call from Grace Tully. He was to go down to Union Station that afternoon. The president was on his way to the Philippines via California and had arranged to have his private railcar stop on a siding so he could meet secretly with Ed and a few of the party leaders.

"Roosevelt gave me a letter that I'm supposed to release at the convention that names Harry Truman and William Douglas as acceptable running mates," Ed said when he came back from the meeting. "Both of them?" I asked Ed. We were in his apartment. Very hot in Chicago, Margaret was with the children in Eagle River, but would come back to see Ed, as mayor, open the convention.

"Our president always leaves himself room to maneuver. In fact, Roosevelt wants me to call Jimmy Byrnes in Washington and tell him to come to Chicago," Ed said. "He is encouraging him to go for the VP spot, too." I knew about Byrnes. He'd been an Irish Catholic until he'd converted to his rich wife's Episcopal religion to run for governor of South Carolina. Now he was a congressman. He'd voted against the anti-lynching bill.

"William Dawson will have a fit," I said.

"I know," Ed said. "It should be Harry Truman, but he's giving interviews to Missouri reporters telling them he absolutely will not be a candidate for vice president. It seems he's terrified at the thought of stepping into Roosevelt's shoes. He is hiding out at the Stevens Hotel."

"Well, that's refreshing," I said. "I wonder if I should talk to him. I think he'd remember me." But Ed was out the door, off to the Blackstone Hotel where the deals were being done.

I thought of Miami. "Move closer." How easily Garner would have been president and now . . . Please God, not Byrnes.

Truman was a good man. A point for him that he doesn't want the job! Why shouldn't I talk to him?

"If you're looking for Ed, he's across the street at the Blackstone. That's where the action is but my idiot editor sent me here." Manny Mandel had seated himself in a big armchair just inside the lobby of the Stevens Hotel. I'd walked the two miles along Michigan Avenue from my apartment to this cluster of hotels, glad for the breezes that stirred the humid air. Always cooler by the lake.

"Where's your popgun, Nora?" Manny said. "Or doesn't the mayor want proof of his shenanigans?"

"Are you afraid of a little competition, Manny?"

"From you?" He laughed. "You had some good instincts but you were never able to go for the jugular. I guess that's because you're a woman, Nora. That's your problem. No dame really has the stomach to—"

"Put a sock in it, Manny," I said.

I started toward the desk. Manny followed, camera in hand. What was I to do? Ask the clerk to put me through to Harry Truman's room with Manny listening to every word. He'd take my picture. Label it "Kelly emissary in secret meeting with Truman." I turned around.

"So long, Manny," I said. "Happy hunting."

I stepped into the revolving door and pushed the panel. As I came around to the street a man was waiting to step into my place. "It's you," I said. "Did I conjure you up?"

"Excuse me?" Harry Truman took off his hat. I knew he wanted to go into the revolving door but I didn't move.

"Good evening," I said. "I'm Nora Kelly."

"Do I know you?"

"Margaret Noll's friend. Paris. You and your unit came to my apartment. We had lunch at Maxim's."

"Oh. A long time ago but nice to see you," he said, trying to edge by me.

"Please," I said. "Could I speak to you for a minute?" I stepped closer to him, away from the door. "I'm Ed Kelly's cousin and Margaret is his wife. Quite a coincidence, isn't it?"

"I suppose, but . . ." He was trying to get inside.

"Do you want to go for a walk?" I said, desperate.

"I just finished my second constitutional. Good night."

"Give me fifteen minutes. I bet you haven't seen Buckingham Fountain yet. And it's not far away."

"Well . . . ," Truman said. He was a polite little guy. What could he do when I took his elbow and directed him across Michigan Avenue but walk along with me?

"One of the largest fountains in the world," I said, as we climbed the steps and stood on the plaza. "And it was Ed convinced Kate Buckingham to donate the money to build it and then pushed through a hundred different obstacles to make it a reality. He gets things done, Mr. Truman. He's a good man to have on your side."

"We've got fountains in Kansas City," Truman said.

"But do yours have eight hundred lights that turn the water into a dozen different colors?" Right on cue a jet of crimson shot into the sky, and then turned yellow, blue, purple, green. "Ed worked with the engineers to position the lights," I said. "Nothing like it in the world when it was opened in 1927."

"Impressive," Truman said. "Now I'll be heading back. My wife and daughter are arriving tomorrow morning and I'd like to get at least one night's rest before they come."

"Not sleeping well?" I asked.

"Please, Nora. Don't pretend you don't know what's going on. Go back and tell Ed and the others I'm not going to change my mind. No way will I be a candidate for vice president."

"But why not?"

"Well for one thing Roosevelt wants Byrnes."

"I don't believe that. The president's playing some kind of a game. Byrnes would be an awful choice."

"He's able enough. I like Jimmy. He asked me to make his nominating speech and I said yes."

"Ed and the others believe that you'd be the best vice president. Why are you resisting?"

Truman didn't say anything. Just stood looking up at the fountain. The light show was over. The water was clear again.

"Well, good night," Truman said and turned.

"Wait," I said. "Look at those sea horses. Each represents a state that borders the lake—Illinois, Michigan, Wisconsin, and Indiana. All of them voted solidly for Roosevelt and will again unless the convention picks a vice-presidential candidate that the unions and Negro voters hate. In other words, Byrnes. You have a duty. You—"

Truman cut me off.

"While I was home in Independence I talked the whole idea over with my wife Bess and daughter Margaret. They're both against me running. Wouldn't want the newspapers to go after Bess."

I knew there'd been criticism of Truman for employing his wife. "Oh, that old stuff about her getting paid as an assistant on your Senate staff? The voters wouldn't care. A man should be able to help his family."

Harry Truman laughed. "I suppose that's how you would look at it in

Chicago. To be honest I did it because we needed the money. Hard to run two households on my salary. And we've no other assets. I've been living in my mother-in-law's house from the day we got married, but we pay all the expenses. I had some business failures and . . ." He stopped. "Bess is the most important thing in my life. I've loved her since she was six years old. I couldn't bear to see her attacked and it's not just the job she held. Bess's father died when she was very young and she's never really recovered from the loss."

"We can get some friendly reporter to do a profile on her. A devoted daughter and wife who was just trying to help her husband out and . . . ," I said.

"You don't understand," Truman said. "Her father took his own life. Ran up all kinds of debts and couldn't face the consequences. Can you imagine what the Republican newspapers would do with that story? Strangely his name was Wallace. Bess's mother collapsed after the suicide. Raking it all up would kill her. No, Nora, I have found my place in the Senate. But as vice president I'd be this close to the presidency." He held up his index finger and his thumb. Just enough light to see the small distance between the two. "And we both know Roosevelt could go at any time. Bess couldn't survive life in the White House and my daughter Margaret is only twenty-one years old. She wants to be a singer. Can you imagine how hard it would be for her to perform as the president's daughter? The kind of reviews she'd get from the papers opposed to me?"

"Here," I said. While he was talking, I'd taken a penny out of my purse. I handed it to him. "Toss this into the fountain. Make a wish. But you have to ask for something you really want."

Truman hesitated. He shook his head at me. But he did take the coin and threw it into the water. He wants more, I thought. He *is* ambitious.

I didn't see Ed again until Monday afternoon at his apartment. "I had to get away from that place for a while. You wouldn't believe the horse-trading that's going on," Ed said as he poured himself a cup of coffee from the pot he'd made. "I've been with Bob Hannegan. You'd like him, Nora. Robert Emmet Hannegan, Jesuit-educated in St. Louis. He's always worked hard for the Democratic Party and supported Truman. But Truman told Hannegan that there was no way he'd make a run so we'd all agreed on Byrnes. Then the president released a statement this morning saying he wants to let the convention decide, but that if he were a delegate he'd vote for Wallace. None of us are sure what that means."

"Why doesn't Roosevelt just say I want Wallace?"

"Because he doesn't want Wallace. That's one thing I'm sure about."

"Please not Byrnes, Ed. He's a jerk. I like Harry Truman."

"So do I. But he's as stubborn as a Missouri mule. Bob showed him that letter from the president saying he'd accept Truman but Harry thinks Bob wrote it himself. Told him that no means no."

That's when I explained to Ed how I'd come to take Truman to Buckingham Fountain.

"Hells bells, Nora, can't you ever just mind your own business?"

"This is my business," I said. "He wants it, Ed. I saw his face when he made that wish but he's afraid that running for office would destroy his wife. But I think she might be tougher than he knows. Look at your Margaret. She hated the whole idea of politics. Was terrified of public speaking. But see how she's reached out to the servicemen at the USO. She gives interviews now, no problem."

"Chicago isn't Washington, Nora. The press there is even more vicious and the stakes are higher," Ed said.

"We've survived. And so can they. Somebody has to put steel in Bess Truman's spine. How will she feel if another man is president while her husband is thinking, that could have been him."

"And I suppose you want to be the someone who sets Bess Truman straight. I forbid it, Nora. I forbid it absolutely."

"Dear God, Ed. You never have spoken to me like that before. I understand if you think talking to Bess Truman isn't a good idea but as far as forbidding me . . ."

He didn't say anything and I thought, Is that it? Am I about to fall out with Ed after all these years? But he took a deep breath and slowly exhaled.

"Sorry, Nonie," he said. "Boy, I really miss Pat Nash." Pat had died in October an hour after his son had brought his newborn grandson into his hospital room. Another Patrick Nash born in the same hospital on the day Pat died. Dramatic.

"I'm supposed to set up a dinner," Ed was saying. "Ed Flynn and a few of the others want to talk to Byrnes privately. I can't do it here or the press would torture us. You'll laugh at this. I'm borrowing Colonel McCormick's apartment. The man whose paper attacks FDR and all Democrats. I figure no one would ever expect us to be there. Then tomorrow morning Truman's agreed to go over and have breakfast with Sidney Hillman, the labor leader, in order to convince him to support Byrnes. A pretty good indication, I'd say, that Harry will not accept a vice-presidential nomination whatever you say, Nonie, which is why I don't want you bothering poor Bess Truman."

I'd seen Truman's face tighten in the reflected light from the fountain. Saw him set his feet. Pull his arm back. Throw that penny. I'd heard the splash.

I didn't see Ed again until the next day, Tuesday. I'd watched his car arrive and had gone down to the apartment. His driver, Dave O'Toole, let me in but pointed at the closed study door.

"Don't disturb him, Nora. He's on the phone," he said. "The shit is hitting the fan and Mrs. Kelly is expected any minute."

"What's going on?" I said to Ed when he came out of the room.

"Wallace just gave a press conference. Said he has enough votes to be elected on the first ballot."

"No."

"We probably can stop him but I was just talking to Ed Flynn. He's put the kibosh on Byrnes. Said we'll lose the Negro vote in New York."

"And in Chicago too," I said.

"Sidney Hillman said the labor unions hate Byrnes. They see him as a strike breaker, so I guess we're stuck with Wallace."

"But what about Truman?" I asked.

"Bob talked to him again this morning. No dice. I have to go. Could you make sure this place looks respectable before Margaret comes home?"

"Margaret is home," a voice said.

We turned. Here she was. Just off the overnight train from Eagle River. Sitting up for fourteen hours in 90-degree heat and 90 percent humidity and not a bother on her. Cool and unwrinkled in her beige linen suit.

"I left the children with Rose and your mother, Ed," she said. "I couldn't bear to pull them away from the boat races. So you'll just have to make do with only me in the box seats when the convention opens tomorrow."

"The way things are going," Ed said, "we both should go up to the lake right now."

"What's the matter?" Margaret asked.

"Nora will explain. I've got to go."

As he passed Margaret he leaned over and kissed her on the cheek. "Thanks for coming back. It helps to have you here."

She touched Ed's shoulder. He does love her, I thought, and she, him. I envied them that bond. Marriage. Long years together. Common, and yet precious.

He and Dave O'Toole left.

"Come on, Nora. A cup of tea and then I need a bath and a long nap," Margaret said.

I followed her into the kitchen. Margaret filled the kettle and set it on the front burner of the mammoth stove and turned on the gas. No match needed. Very modern. She took out a tray and lifted two porcelain cups and saucers down from a shelf, along with matching sugar bowl and milk jug. I waited until she measured the tea into the pot, poured in the water, put a tea cozy over it, set it on the tray, carried the whole thing into the dining room, then sat down and poured tea into the cups.

"You take three sugars, don't you, and a lot of milk?"

"Yes," I said. She took hers black.

"Now," she said. "Tell me what's going on."

I took a sip of the sweet milky drink. "Ed and the others want Truman for vice president but he's refusing to run," I said.

"Mmmm," she said. "That's a strange way for a politician to act." She took a drink of tea. "It's Bess, isn't it," she said.

Never underestimate Margaret.

"I remember when her father, David Wallace, killed himself. One of the papers printed all the details. He died in his bathtub. I always wondered if he'd intended to slit his wrists and lost his nerve. Instead he shot himself in the head," she said.

"That's terrible. And I suppose it was Bess's mother who found him," I said.

"I think they both did. And he was such a handsome man. Bess's mother's family, the Gates, had the money. They owned Queen of the Pantry Flour. The only brand my mother would use. She said it made the best biscuits. Bess had three younger brothers. She must have been about eighteen when her father died. Her mother collapsed. Moved them all to Colorado. That's where Kansas City people go to get away from the heat in the summer. My mother heard it was Bess who convinced her mother to come back to Independence. They moved into the Gateses' house and Bess and Harry have lived there ever since," she said.

"Truman's afraid the press will go to town on the suicide and Bess and her mother will break down," I said.

"I wonder," Margaret said.

She took a sip of her tea. "You and I know something about holding our heads up, don't we, Nora?"

It had been years since Margaret had alluded to her life before Ed. I was the only one who knew of her two previous marriages, wiped away. Even Wilcox hadn't been able to dig them up. She was the most respectable of matrons with a life as well ordered as her kitchen.

"And Ed thinks Truman is the best choice?" she said.

"The only good choice," I said. She nodded.

"Well then," she said.

"Mrs. Truman, we don't mean to bother you," I started. Though of course that's what we actually intended to do. Margaret stood behind me in the hallway in front of Bess Truman's room at the Morrison Hotel late Tuesday afternoon. Hadn't been hard to find her. Manny Mandel was only too delighted to show off how much information he had.

"Truman's got his wife, his daughter, and his brother, who's called Vivian—imagine hanging a moniker like that on a kid—stashed in the Morrison Hotel. Guess he doesn't want them soiled by politics," Manny had told me.

The woman holding the wooden door open only a few inches did not look like someone who wanted to take on the hurly-burly of the convention. She wore a light blue dress belted where she'd once had a waist. A solid figure. She was the matron Margaret was pretending to be. I could imagine her presiding over teas at her church but not being the hostess of the president of the United States at the White House.

"I'm sorry," she said in a very soft voice. "My daughter is out, and I'm not receiving visitors." She started to close the door.

"Wait," I said. "We want to welcome you to Chicago and give you this packet that Mayor Kelly has put together for the families of those attending the convention."

I pushed the big manila envelope toward her. "Here are tickets for the Art Institute which has a wonderful collection of Impressionists, the Museum of Science and Industry, the planetarium, the aquarium. There are even passes here for Comiskey Park where the Chicago White Sox play and . . ." She didn't take the envelope but instead moved back into the room and closed the door.

"Thank you but I really have to go," she said.

Margaret moved in front of me and put both of her hands on the door. "Hello, Bess. I'm Maggie Noll from Kansas City. My mother is Lizzie Burke. She grew up in St. Joe with the Pendergasts. She used to sing at Tom's St. Patrick's Day parties. I bet you attended a few of those."

Bess smiled. "Harry did take me a time or two. My mother couldn't believe I'd actually go willingly into . . . But truthfully I enjoyed those evenings. Mr. Pendergast would have Harry play 'Danny Boy' on the piano and everyone would sing along. And after all they'd been very good to Harry, which Mother could never understand. But what are you doing here in Chicago, Maggie?"

"I am married to Ed Kelly, the mayor." Bess stepped back but now Margaret had pushed the door open.

"I know about him," Bess said. "He's the one putting pressure on Harry to run for vice president. Well you can tell your husband that my husband is not interested and neither am I."

"That's what we want to talk to you about," I said. Margaret gave me a look that was equivalent to a kick in the shins. I'd moved too fast. Bess Truman was like a frightened kitten we had to coax out from under a bed.

"Nora here is Ed's cousin. She works with him. I don't get much involved with the political side of his life."

"Neither do I," Bess said. She smiled at Margaret. Two women with much in common.

"I always tell Ed it's better for me to keep my distance. That way when he wants to talk something over with me, I can apply common sense rather than be lost in all the maneuvering," Margaret said.

"Yes," Bess said. "I've told Harry the same thing because he does seem to value my advice."

Proud of that, I thought. Maybe not such a mouse after all. Margaret took Bess's arm and leaned in close. "And sometimes I see things more clearly than he does."

I expected Bess to shake Margaret's hand off. But she didn't. She nodded.

"I have a room just down the hall," Margaret said. "I wonder if you could spare us a few minutes."

The Morrison had found space for us to use even though they were completely sold out. The suite was being held for some bigwig from California who was arriving the next day when the convention would formally start. The manager of the Morrison told Margaret we could use it for a few hours. I think he thought she was arranging some secret meeting for Ed and the boys. We led Bess Truman through the door into the living room of the suite. The manager had done us proud. On the sideboard was a platter of sandwiches. Next to that were two large urns. One marked "Tea" and the other "Coffee." A selection of soft drinks stood next to bottles of scotch, bourbon, and gin.

There was a big silver bucket of ice and rows of shiny glasses. Margaret hadn't let go of Bess's arm and guided her over to the couch while I headed for the sideboard.

"What can I get you, Mrs. Truman? Coffee? Tea? Ginger ale?" I asked.

Bess hesitated. Looked over at Margaret.

"How about a real drink, Bess. It's after five," Margaret said.

"Well Harry and I usually do have a cocktail at this time of day when he comes home from the office. I wonder if you could make me a Presbyterian?" she asked me.

"That's scotch and ginger ale, right?" I asked.

She nodded.

"I'll have the same," Margaret said.

"Okay," I said. "Me too."

Such a strange name for a drink, I thought, as I poured a jigger of scotch into a highball glass, added ginger ale and ice. I took a sip. Not bad. Made the scotch taste ladylike somehow. I mixed two more drinks and put them on the coffee table in front of the couch where Margaret and Bess sat and then went back for my drink and the plate of sandwiches. Ham and roast beef. As I sat down I raised my glass.

"What should we drink to?" I said.

"Missouri," Margaret said, putting an *a* at the end of the word, pronouncing it in a way I'd never heard her use before.

Bess took a sip. "Refreshing," she said.

"We need something in this heat," Margaret said.

The Morrison had put two large fans in the living room and the windows were open. So it was pleasant enough. All these hotels will have to get air conditioning, I thought. I knew how hot and oppressive the stadium was going to be with all those sweating delegates. Many of them smoking the cigars that seemed to be issued to the members of each delegation. I'm sure Bess Truman and Margaret Kelly would have preferred to never set foot in the place but instead spend the entire convention right here sipping Presbyterians and talking about gardens, which was what they were doing now.

"My garden is at our place in Wisconsin," Margaret said. "It's cold up there through May so my hydrangeas don't bloom until the end of July. But they are gorgeous in August."

"Mine come out in early June," Bess said. "My mother prefers all white but this year I planted the colored variety without telling her. They were gorgeous. Blue and pink and even a wonderful rusty red."

"Sounds beautiful, and of course you've got the right kind of soil in Independence," Margaret said.

"Yes. But my mother said the colored ones in our yard made her ill so I had to dig them up," Bess said.

"That's terrible," I said.

"The house does belong to her family. It's her yard," Bess said.

Margaret and I said nothing. Bess went on, "Mother's very good really. Set in her ways, but last year she let me redecorate our bedroom though she didn't approve of the double bed I bought."

Was that a giggle I heard from Mrs. Truman?

"Mother said twin beds were more appropriate and, after all, we had managed to have one child and it wasn't as if . . . Well it was my daughter, Margaret, told me to go ahead and buy the bed. After all it was Harry's money. Margaret hadn't even consulted Mother when she did up the spare room for herself, but then Margaret's her father's daughter."

Bess picked up a roast beef sandwich and took a bite. "Very good," she said.

"And how do you organize meals?" Margaret asked.

"We have a cook. Elise has been with the family since . . . Well since we came back from Colorado. She and Mother choose the menus but Elise knows what Harry likes and manages to slip in some of his favorite dishes."

The place sounded like a genteel prison camp and Bess Truman was a sixty-year-old woman! I wanted to lean over and shake her. Ask her how long she was going to take orders from her mother. But Margaret was smarter than I was.

"A blessing to still have her with you," Margaret said. "My mother passed away years ago and I miss her every day."

"I am lucky and Harry's mother is alive too. She's still healthy and sharp. Harry's sister lives with her near their old farm," Bess said.

"And what does she think about all this?" I asked.

"What?" Bess said.

"Harry's chance to be vice president. President even," I said.

"Oh well I suppose every mother would love to see her son in the White House, and Mrs. Truman is a true dyed-in-the-wool Democrat. I remember Harry's sister saying once that she'd never even met a Republican. His mother told her that she hadn't missed much."

We laughed.

"Of course," Bess said. "His mother has no idea of what politics demands, though . . ." She stopped. "You see," she said. "Harry's mother was never happy about his association with the Pendergasts. She remembers stories about the Irish farmers who came into Missouri in the forties just before the war. Desperate for land. Hiring out at first but then buying any scrap they could get."

At first I thought she was talking about some recent immigration of Irish farmers that I hadn't heard about. Then I realized the war Bess meant was the Civil War. It made sense. Truman's mother was probably in her nineties and born in the 1850s. The refugees from the Great Starvation would have still been alive and beginning to prosper.

"Harry was friendly with these two boys. O'Connor and Broderick. Each one of their families had nearly ten thousand acres and did very well. Much better than the Trumans, to tell the truth. I think that bothered his mother. These interlopers. Of course they had to marry each other because, well . . ."

She set down her drink. "You see Harry's family are Baptists. Very strict in their ideas."

I wasn't going to save her. Wasn't going to jump in to say something about how clannish we Irish were. Let her explain why the good citizens of Independence would never let their daughters marry one. But Margaret was kinder. She turned to me.

"People at home in Kansas City tend to stick with their own kind," she said.

Bess nodded. "Yes," she said. "It took my mother a long time to let me marry Harry. His family being Baptist, when we're all Episcopalians. Marry Harry," she repeated. "That rhymes doesn't it?" Bess Truman giggled. "Though I met Harry at a Presbyterian Sunday school." She held up her drink.

Was that Presbyterian going to her head? I wondered. I'd put the envelope with Ed's welcome-to-Chicago tickets on the coffee table in front of the couch. Bess pointed to it.

"And there are passes for a White Sox game in there?"

"Yes," I said. "They're playing the Red Sox tomorrow afternoon."

"The Red Sox," she said. "They've got a good team this year."

"You follow baseball?" I asked.

I guess I sounded surprised because Bess said, "Don't sound so surprised. I know Harry's always telling people how he fell in love with this dainty little girl with golden curls and big blue eyes."

Wait, was Bess imitating Harry, exaggerating his accent? It sure sounded like it.

"But I was a real tomboy. My brother Frank was two years younger than I was and when my father taught him to play baseball I insisted on taking part in the lessons. Well wouldn't you know I could hit the ball farther than Frank and could catch and throw too. It tickled my father and Frank got a great laugh from bringing me along to the sand lot down the block. At first the other boys didn't want me to play, but Frank acted like he'd been saddled with me. I remember the first time I got to bat. I knocked a homer all the way into Diggers' Woods. After that the fellows fought to have me on their team. My dad would bring my little brothers, George and Fred, down to watch us play. Fred was just a baby. Only three years old. He doesn't remember Daddy at all. I think a lot of his problems come because . . . Well of course my father's death was hard on all of us but at least I have great memories of him."

Here it was. The ticking time bomb. What to say now. Once again it was Margaret who stepped in.

"No way to really understand why someone takes their own life, I suppose," Margaret said.

Bess didn't respond. Her head was bent down over the drink. Oh Lord, I thought, Margaret has made a mistake. We should have stuck to the Irish principle of *ná habair tada*, say nothing. Margaret had gone too far. But then Bess looked up. Blinking.

"My mother still goes over and over his last days. Had she been too hard on my father? Had my grandfather said something to him? Yes, he owed money but my grandfather Gates was very wealthy. He could have settled his debts. I wondered if my father had asked him for the money and been turned down. Would a man leave four children behind because his pride had been hurt or was he so ashamed that he just couldn't go on?" She stopped.

"You're trying to be rational about the irrational," I said. "The Irish talk about someone being taken over by evil fairies, being driven mad. It's shame that opens the door to them. Keeps you from thinking straight. So worried about what you imagine people think that you can't see clearly anymore. When you were a little girl whipping that bat around did you give one snap of your fingers about what the boys you were beating said about you?" I asked her.

Bess laughed. "I did not. I'd run those bases with my arms in the air. My brother Frank wanted me to try out for the all-girls' team the Kansas City businessman Jim Wilkinson was starting. Mother would have fainted dead away."

"All girls? When was this?" I asked.

"Let's see, it must have been about 1909. I was twenty-three. Jim was a pal of Frank's. The team was barnstorming throughout the Midwest. I was tempted, believe me. Wilkinson started another team that he called All Nations with men, women, colored players, even American-Indians. The best of them became the Kansas City Monarchs, the Negro team. Frank took me to quite a few games. Those fellows could really play. I suppose baseball's my way of connecting with the past."

I sipped my drink. Chose my words carefully. "And your father," I said.

She nodded.

Which was why I spent the first afternoon of the Democratic convention not in the stadium but sitting in the box seats behind the White Sox dugout at Comiskey Park with Bess Truman and Harry's brother Vivian. Grace Comiskey, who'd taken over the team when her husband, Charles Comiskey's son, had died, pushed out the boat for us. Charles Comiskey, who'd founded the White Sox, had been friends with my great-uncle Patrick. Another Irish Rebel. A picnic basket waited for us with hot dogs, popcorn, and peanuts. A steady parade of beer sellers appeared and, miracle of miracles, the White Sox won. Beating Boston 5–4 after losing to them 11–0 just the week before. I didn't say another word to Bess about the vice-presidential nomination as I watched her drop her frightened-little-woman façade and cheer the Chicago team home. Yelling when Luke Appling homered to win the game.

I wondered if Harry Truman knew that there's a tomboy still inside his matronly wife? "Always good to win when you've been counted out," I said to Bess as we rode in the back of the car Ed had arranged for us.

"I told Harry I'd meet him in our hotel room at five," Bess said. "And, Nora, you can tell your cousin that if the president really wants Harry, he won't say no."

"Good," I said. Nothing more.

And indeed Ed told me later that very evening they'd brought Harry Truman into Bob Hannegan's room at the Blackstone where Franklin Delano Roosevelt was on the telephone speaking from San Diego.

"We could all hear Roosevelt," Ed said. "That booming voice of his. He asked Bob if he had Truman lined up. Bob said no. That Truman was a goddamn Missouri mule. Roosevelt was shouting. He told Bob to tell the senator that if he refused he'd be responsible for breaking up the Democratic Party in the midst of the war. Then the president hung up."

"And what did Truman say?" I asked him.

Ed laughed. "He said, 'Oh, shit.' But agreed."

So . . . Lots more maneuvering, and Ed later told me that he and Ed Flynn and the other city fellows spent most of the night promising jobs to any delegate that was wavering. But on Friday night, July 21, 1944, Harry Truman got one thousand plus votes and became the party's nominee for vice president. Margaret and I were sitting with Bess Truman; her daughter, Margaret; and Harry's brother, Vivian. As delegation after delegation declared for Truman, Margaret Truman jumped up and down with every announcement. When Truman's victory was announced, Bess did smile, but was a still point in the pandemonium.

Two nights before, the convention had listened in silence when Roosevelt accepted the nomination for president by radio hookup. That familiar voice had filled the hall. He'd wanted to retire, he said, to lead a quiet life but he would continue in the office because the stakes were so high. "We must win the war," he said. "Win it fast. Win it overwhelmingly." And then he said that we would work with all peace-loving nations to make sure there would never be another world war.

And now here was Harry Truman, the fellow who might very well have to fulfill those promises. He fought his way up to the platform through delegates that were still demonstrating, holding placards that said "Roosevelt, Roosevelt." Finally he made it to the stage. Truman spoke for about a minute. He said that he appreciated the honor his nomination meant for Missouri, and that he would continue the efforts he made in the Senate "to help shorten the war and win the peace under our great leader, Franklin D. Roosevelt," he concluded. "I accept this honor with all humility. I thank you."

I imagine that everyone in the hall was thinking exactly what I was. This man is not a politician. He's just an ordinary guy. He could be me. God help him.

I was stationed under the stage snapping away when Harry Truman turned to Ed, who was standing next to him. He took Ed's hand and held it in the air. I took the photograph. The *Life* magazine reporter said they'd pay me one hundred dollars for the picture. No credit. They said their photographers were all anonymous.

"Fine," I said. A way to have history show Ed's role in getting Truman the nomination. I also collected another twenty-five for a shot of Spencer Tracy, who was also celebrating with us that night. They had done it. Ed and the bosses had put in Harry Truman.

The Roosevelt–Truman ticket won, but only four months after the election, FDR was dead. Harry Truman was president.

"Shorten the war and win the peace," Truman had said. On May 8, the Nazis surrendered, but the Japanese vowed to fight on to protect their homeland. An invasion would have terrible casualties. When the two atomic bombs were dropped on Japan one after the other, the American people had no details on how many were killed. We only knew that the most terrible weapon ever invented had ended the war. But Ed remembered that experiment at the University of Chicago and Roosevelt's fear at what was being unleashed. Still, I was relieved.

Mike had been within days of being sent to the Pacific, assigned to an aircraft carrier at a time when over half of all fighter pilots were being shot down or killed in crash landings. Ed had tried to intervene, but Mike would have none of it. He'd gone through rigorous training at Cherry Point, North Carolina, and was ready. They were the elite and he was honored to have this chance to lose his life. I'd tried to dissuade him. Using the best of arguments. "Mike, you're a father now." Because Mary Patricia Kelly had been born on November 18, 1944. Mary Pat.

"Both of our mothers were Mary," Mariann told me. "I added Pat so when we have our son they can be Pat and Mike."

An innocent. Didn't even know that all those so-called jokes about Pat and Mike were meant to be insulting. Ah well, maybe that's progress. Celebrate what they think we should be ashamed of. Giving birth had exposed Mariann to what it means to being in Mayor Kelly's orbit. Ed was holding a big Bond rally in mid-November and Tyrone Power was scheduled to attend. I looked forward to photographing him and wondered if he'd remember how we'd met in Sally Rand's dressing room. Power was a Marine aviator now stationed at Cherry Point where Mike was training. So what could be more natural than that Mike would be assigned to fly Power to Chicago? I'd like to think that the Navy was sensitive to the needs of a father-to-be and decided Mike should be with his wife as she gave birth to their first child. But it was Ed who made the call to Mike's commanding officer and also to St. Anne's Hospital. "Give her the best," he'd said.

Except the press got mixed up and a *Sun-Times* headline said it was Tyrone Power's wife who was in St. Anne's Hospital giving birth.

"Are you Annabelle?" the nurses asked Mariann.

The spotlight can be a mixed blessing, but there was nothing mixed about the announcement on August 15, 1945, Feast of the Assumption. The war was over. There would be no invasion of Japan. Mike and millions more were safe.

A terrible price paid, as we learned later. But the day the war ended I could only be glad that Bess Truman had put aside her fears and told her husband that it was alright to seek what he secretly wished for. And if Margaret Kelly and I had influenced her decision, good. One definite contribution I made to Harry Truman was when I told Bess after the convention that Harry'd better find a decent secretary. I was only half joking when I told her that the ideal person would be an Irish Catholic woman who'd graduated from a college run by nuns. And guess what? His brother, Vivian, had just the woman working for him. Rose Conway. She went to Washington with them and was Truman's private secretary in the White House and then worked with him at his presidential library in Independence. Missy LeHand, Grace Tully, Rose Conway. Irish above all.

So the war had ended. The world was settling down. With my checks from *Life* magazine, my savings were up to four hundred dollars. I longed for Ireland. No grave to visit but maybe I could find Peter's home place. Meet his family. Then go on to Paris. Peace.

11

AUTUMN 1945

The returning veterans seemed determined to repopulate the world. Mike and Mariann would have a second child in early 1946. Not a boy to be Mike with their Pat, but a girl they called Rose Ann. Very appropriate because it was Rose who was the honorary grandmother. After all she was Mame's sister and the one who had raised the Kelly kids. Even now the youngest, Frances, lived with her in the same South Side apartment on Yates Avenue where they'd moved after the bank had taken Michael's house in Argo. Mike and Mariann would go on to have three more girls, Margaret, Susan, and Nancy. Then in 1957, Michael Joseph Kelly, who carried the name of his great-great grandfather, was born.

Granny Honora. "We wouldn't die."

Marguerite and her husband, Tom McGuire, had returned from the Army base in Texas where he'd been stationed. They came back to Chicago with their baby daughter, Kathleen, who soon had a brother named Thomas, then Carol, Sheila, Michael, and Jeanne. But that was to come. Still, a new generation had begun.

In 1945 the two families had bought a house together in a new development, built on a stretch of prairie just within the southernmost limits of the city, that was designed for burgeoning young families—rows and rows of duplexes with common backyards that seemed to stretch for miles. I was out there visiting the day when a dozen trucks pulled up, full of black dirt. One crew of men spread the soil over what had been prairie while the other followed tossing out handfuls of grass seed.

Merrionette Manor, the neighborhood was called. The developer, Joseph Merrion, named it for himself. He promised that there'd be a shopping street but so far the only thing besides the houses that had been built was a Catholic school. The archdiocese had slapped something together fast to contain the expected explosion of children. No church. Mass was held in a storefront while the parishioners began to raise funds. Their flesh and blood was the future. Stone and mortar could wait. The Depression was over. The war was won. Time for a victory lap, I said to Ed when I described this booming new development.

"And all bought with mortgages financed by the GI Bill," he said. "Now the Republicans want to destroy all these programs just because Roosevelt put them through. My God, Nonie, these fellows know how to hold a grudge."

A nasty campaign was shaping up already against Harry Truman, who had decided to run for his own term as president against the party's wishes. Even Democrats didn't think he had a chance against Thomas Dewey. But Ed was sticking with Truman. After all hadn't he done the same thing? Run for the office he'd been appointed to. "You'll win," he'd told the president when Margaret and Ed had been invited to a White House dinner in September of 1945. Bess Truman had surprised everyone by restoring the presidential social calendar and insisting that the White House be renovated.

"Bess told me that Eleanor never really noticed her surroundings," Margaret said to me after they returned from Washington. "But I think Bess feels, now that she has a home of her own, she's going to put her own stamp on it. Spiff the place up a bit. Let it reflect her taste. The Midwestern aristocracy. Wall to wall carpeting and sofas stuffed with down feathers."

In October I went to Washington with Ed. He was meeting with the head of the new housing authority that was meant to deal with the terrible shortage of homes for returning veterans. And in Chicago's case, for the tens of thousands of Negroes who were moving up to the city from the South. Ed had already gotten a chunk of federal money in 1937 and appointed the Chicago Housing Authority to spend it. William Dawson had recommended a Negro businessman named Robert Taylor to be head of the board. And somewhere Ed had met a social worker called Elizabeth Wood, whom he'd appointed to run the CHA along with a clutch of patronage workers who mostly just stayed out of her way.

The first housing project, Altgeld Gardens, was on the South Side. Now

I'd met and admired Elizabeth Wood, but her parents had been missionaries in Japan. In fact she had been born there. She'd reminded me a lot of Jane Addams and the women who'd worked at Hull House. Full of good intentions but sure they knew what was best for "the people." Elizabeth insisted on interviewing every family before they were allowed to move into their apartment. She wanted to make sure that the mother had the requisite housekeeping skills, and she was emphatic about the ethnic mix. So many Irish, so many Italians, so many Germans, so many Jews, so many Negroes. And she'd done a good job, I'd have to admit. Altgeld Gardens was a lovely place with big sunny apartments and gardens that the tenants cultivated themselves. The second development, Bridgeport Homes, a group of row houses in our old neighborhood, was even nicer. It really looked as if the government was going to do something right. That the citizens of Chicago would have decent places to live.

But I knew when Ed invited my camera and me along on the trip to Washington it was because he needed to flatter somebody. "Here," he'd say, "do you mind if we took a photograph together that I could hang on the wall in my office in city hall?" And of course the fellow would smile and whatever Ed was asking for he'd usually get.

On this trip Ed's target was the fellow in charge of the entire federal housing project with a budget in the billions. A good man according to Elizabeth Wood, but Ed was finding him too rigid in the requirements he imposed on the contractors Ed was hiring. Herman Strauss had made headlines by promising that public housing would be built at half the cost expended in the private sector. No frills in these government dwellings, he'd vowed. Not a penny of taxpayers' money would be wasted.

"Why not?" Ed had said to me on the train down to Washington. "Why is he being such a tightwad? It's not his money and the Congress will just take back what isn't spent. Why not make these apartments nice? Believe me there's not much real difference in the cost. Better to do a good job even if it takes a little longer."

"And hire bigger crews of construction workers," I said.

"Well, there is that," he said.

"That" was always in the front of Ed's mind. Jobs. During the war the Defense plants had employed hundreds of thousands. But now those positions were gone. The city was lurching back into a peacetime economy, but government contracts were still the surest way toward employment. The number of houses being built in Chicago had dipped down into almost nothing during the Depression, and though developers like Merrion were ratcheting up construction, nothing beat a check from Uncle Sam.

And it wasn't just wages these projects represented, but tons of cement, miles of pipes, truckloads of bricks. A bonanza.

"This guy Strauss is such a typical bureaucrat," Ed had said. "Only cares about making himself look good. Big on cutting the budget. Doesn't really give a damn about what that means to people. It's all numbers with these fellows."

Which was proving to be the case as we sat in his office. "Now let's talk about location," Strauss said. A bureaucrat no question. This small man wore a suit I'd already passed four or five times in the halls of this federal office building. Ed had introduced me as his aide but Strauss had taken no notice of me. He had a map of Chicago pinned up on the wall.

"Now"—he pointed to a swath of land along Madison on the West Side—"all this is substandard housing. Landlords have been dividing what were three-bedroom apartments into four so-called studios, with a hot plate for a kitchen and a bathroom in the hallway. Unfortunately, Negroes coming from the South are so desperate they take anything on offer. We've put out feelers to these landlords and they are more than willing to sell. And we can move ahead with demolition fairly soon but . . ." He pointed a bit east of the area. "We're meeting resistance here. People are refusing to sell."

"That's an Italian neighborhood," Ed said. "Those people own their own homes."

"Which are substandard," he said.

"Couldn't they be fixed up? Repaired?" Ed asked.

"That's not the model we're working from. This office has been tasked with slum clearance. That's our mandate."

"But there's plenty of vacant land throughout the city and some really depressed areas. Why not let me make a survey and tell you where to put the housing?" he asked Strauss.

"May I remind you, sir, that I have studied housing projects in Europe and New York? I have a team of experts that are working with me and input from amateurs such as you would not be helpful."

Geeze Louise, I thought. I'd noticed a model of six high-rise buildings on a cabinet behind his desk and now had to ask, "Are these what you're proposing to build in the city?"

"Yes," Strauss said.

"It looks like a prison complex. Why not build low-rise town houses the way the Chicago Housing Authority did in Bridgeport and Altgeld? Or at least keep the buildings under six stories," I said.

"I'll have you know, madam, that Mies van der Rohe himself approved these plans."

Ed shook his head. "Don't you think it would be better to have buildings that would fit in with the old neighborhood?"

"You're missing the point. There will be no old neighborhood. We're creating new neighborhoods. New communities. Cities within cities where the poor will finally be housed."

"But without frills?" I said. "In these grain storage elevators?" The way he said "the poor" made me squirm. No one poorer than the Kellys when Granny and Aunt Máire stepped off the canal boat into Hardscrabble, Bridgeport's original name, with eight children and no money. Run out of their own country by bureaucrats like this man who wanted to manage the poor. I know, I thought. He is a New Dealer and building affordable housing is an important and worthy project. But why not make the homes appealing, as Ed said, and put them throughout the city? Strauss was not listening to us.

"If you don't want these multi-million-dollar projects all funded by the federal government built in your city, I'm sure Detroit, or Cleveland, or Indianapolis would be happy to accept our plans," he said.

"Please, Mr. Strauss, I'm just asking that you be open to some local input," Ed said.

Now Ed didn't realize it but his career in politics was ending right there in this fellow's office. In a few months, the clearances began. Families were turned out. Houses demolished. There were no places to put these people while waiting for the "urban renewal" to begin. Veterans were especially vulnerable. Ed twisted a few arms until emergency housing was put up near Midway Airport. A Negro veteran and his family moved into one of the units. He had been in the Battle of the Bulge. The white people in the neighborhood went nuts. Shocking. I mean this fellow had defended our country. Didn't matter to the crowds that gathered to throw stones at the house. Let "the niggers" in and the value of all their brick bungalows would go down. Ed sent the cops in to stop the riot and protect the family. He went down there himself. Made a statement that was carried on the radio. "All law-abiding citizens may be assured of their right to live peacefully anywhere in Chicago," he said. The right thing to say no question, but the alderman from that district got on the radio himself. The mayor was naive. The mayor was out of touch. Let the Negroes live in Bronzeville or on the West Side. Put up housing for them there.

The city council voted to take over the Chicago Housing Authority. Ed tried to fight back. He'd battled them before and won but this was different. He was stepping outside of the tribe. William Dawson backed him, and maybe if Pat Nash had been alive to defend Ed . . . But "open housing" became a slur aimed at the mayor. The party would drop him in two years. His time as mayor would end in 1947.

Of course Ed didn't know any of this when we left Washington. He'd gotten so many projects up and running. Look at the subway. A miracle! He could outmaneuver this fellow Strauss too. "The important thing is that we don't create ghettos," he said. Other big plans in the works, too.

"We've taken over the site of the Orchard Place Ford plant. We'll be able to have direct service to Europe as well," Ed said to me as we rode home on the train. "You'll see ORD listed as the destination for flights from all over the country, all over the world."

"You should name it Edward J. Kelly International Airport," I said.

Ed laughed.

"That would be a sure way to get the project killed all together," he said. "No, I was thinking of calling it O'Hare Airport after the young Navy pilot killed in the Battle of Midway. His father was Al Capone's lawyer. Word is that the father traded his testimony against Capone for his son's appointment to Annapolis. For all kinds of reasons no one in the council will oppose that name," Ed said.

Chicago, I thought. His second big idea was to propose Chicago as the headquarters of the international association of all the countries in the world that was being called the United Nations. It made sense. No victory over the Nazis and Japanese without the manufacturing might of the Midwest. Plus we were America while New York, the other contender, was New York, a separate entity. Ed thought the site of the Century of Progress would be perfect for the new institution. Ed said, "Imagine the jobs the place would generate, first in construction but the whole world would come to us. Diplomats, translators, bureaucrats buying homes, shopping, eating in our restaurants, hiring maintenance people, secretaries. A chance to know Chicago the beautiful."

Ed was planning to lead a delegation of politicians and business people to London to present our case to an executive committee that was to decide where the headquarters would be located. American Airlines offered to inaugurate a nonstop flight from Chicago to London for the group over Thanksgiving. And I'm going to be on that flight, I thought as we got off the train. I had my own plans.

NOVEMBER 18, 1945

"I want to go to London with you, Ed," I said. "And then take you to Ireland. You can't imagine what it feels like to stand on the piece of Irish soil that belonged to the Kellys. Step into the waters of Galway Bay at the very spot where Granny Honora was born."

We were celebrating Mary Pat's first birthday at Mike and Mariann's small house in Merrionette Manor. I hadn't realized how loud I was talking until all activity in the dining room stopped. "Sorry," I said. "Sorry." I looked over at the one-year-old sitting up in a highchair. If the development of little humans wasn't so common, the front pages of newspapers would be full of headlines. She walks! She talks! I'd watched Mike's child take her first steps holding on to the old coffee table, one of the few pieces Rose had saved from the house in Argo. Both Rose and I had used Ed's car and driver to visit the two families who shared this attached house. Neither of them had a car.

Every day Mike took a long bus ride to the advertising agency in the Loop, where he worked. Not the career he'd planned. Mike had told me that he had intended to go back to DePaul University for a law degree and then follow Ed into politics. I was there in the office two months before in mid-September when he'd come in to discuss his plans. Just out of the Navy. Back in Chicago. Ed had arranged for Mike to come in to him at the same time Joseph Kennedy and his son Jack were visiting. He and Ed were friendly enough now that Ed had helped Kennedy buy the Merchandise Mart and had arranged that the huge complex, the biggest office building in the world, would remain nonunion. How Ed, who was the champion of unions, managed that I never knew. Lots of secret meetings and no photographer required.

Both Jack Kennedy and Mike had still been in uniform. The war was over but no one had been demobilized. Such a funny word, especially in the way it was shortened to "demobbed." Removed from the group? Leaving the crowd? All these fellows who'd been part of this tremendous movement, marching in step with millions of others, had been cut loose now. I'd heard from Colonel Duggan, who'd commanded the Marines in Derry. He'd gone to the South Pacific, as had many of his men. Iwo Jima, Saipan, Okinawa—names none of us had heard before that now were part of the national vocabulary. Still we civilians had no real sense of what they had faced. The living and the dead. All the boys coming home from somewhere we could never travel. Here were two of these returning heroes in the flesh, though of course they would never let me call them heroes to their faces. When I'd told Mike he was a hero he'd bitten my head off. The real heroes were the ones who didn't make it home, he'd said.

Jesus, Mary, and Joseph, I'd thought, what a good-looking pair. Hard to believe only one generation before their grandparents had been starved out of Ireland. Running for their lives. Jack hadn't changed much from the skinny sixteen-year-old I'd met on the train in Florida. Didn't look like he weighed much more, but then Ed had told me Jack was still recovering from the—now I have to say "heroic"—rescue of the crewmen he commanded on the PT boat the Japanese had sunk. He'd led the survivors on a brutal four hour swim through the shark-infested waters to a tiny island. Jack had towed one badly burned sailor, clenching the strap of the man's life jacket in his teeth. For six days Joe and Rose thought they'd lost another son to the war.

I'd put the two young naval officers next to each other with Ed on one side of them and Joseph Kennedy on the other.

"Don't know if I want to stand this close to a flyboy," Jack had said.

"Well at least my uniform doesn't still smell of salt water," Mike had replied, and the two boys laughed.

Joseph Kennedy hadn't even smiled but then his oldest son had been a pilot. Dead.

Jack had looked at me. "Wait," he'd said. "You were the photographer on the president's train. Weren't you somehow involved in saving Roosevelt—"

His father had cut him off. "I sometimes wish that Zangara had been a better shot. John Nance Garner might have been a decent-enough president and then some Republican would have been elected in 1940 who would have figured out a way to outmaneuver Hitler," he'd said.

"My dad has a strange sense of humor," Jack had said to us.

Ed had a kind of bar in a closet in the corner of the office. Nothing fancy. A table with a collection of bottles and glasses. He'd walked over there, opened the door and looked at the other men. "Irish?" Ed had said.

"I prefer scotch," Joe had said. You would, I thought. But Jack had said he was glad to see Ed had Jameson and he'd like his neat, and Mike ordered the same. I'd been a little nervous when I saw Ed pour himself a shot. He handed each of us a glass.

"Sláinte," Ed said.

Jack had smiled at me. "The Irish word for health, right?" He really had remembered me. Ed had directed the men to the corner of the office where Margaret had set up as a kind of sitting area. The two young men sat together on the leather couch while Joe and Ed took the high-backed wing chairs on each side of the coffee table.

"What now, fellows?" Ed had asked.

"I suppose I'll finish law school first and then, well," Mike had said.

"Jack's running for Congress," Kennedy had said, interrupting Mike. "There's a seat opening up in '46. I'm putting together a team now."

"But," I'd started. I hadn't been invited to sit down with the men so I'd drunk my whiskey down and was near the door when I'd heard Kennedy's statement. "But," I'd said again, "what happened to giving each one of your kids a million dollars so they could become poets?"

"Jack can do some writing. His senior paper about England's lack of preparation for war is being published and now he's going to write an account of PT 109," Joe Kennedy had said.

"I'm not, Dad, I told you," Jack had said.

"Well somebody is and you'll collaborate," his father said.

"Dad has a team," Jack had said and looked at Mike, who'd shrugged. Is that what happens now? I'd wondered. Bad enough that old men send young men to war, but would they then take credit for their victories? Find ways to capitalize on their service?

"I think our generation does have a responsibility to make a difference," Mike had said. Their generation. Both these young men were not yet thirty but had already survived the Great Depression and world war. Surely they deserved the miracle of normal life. Mike was over the moon about his baby daughter. Why not embrace peace and the time to enjoy it? But both Mike and Jack had been fidgeting on the couch. Jack had tapped his toe on the Oriental rug Margaret had used to create this island in Ed's office, while Mike had shifted forward on the couch ready to make his argument. Joe and Ed had leaned back, resting their heads against the places where these leather chairs were already stained from hair tonic and sweat. Power. They both had it. Now they were inviting their own flesh and blood. To claim it so they could pass it on to their sons.

I'd thought of the Scoundrel Pykes, the landlord family in Ireland that had nearly destroyed the Kellys altogether. They'd rack-rented land, raped my aunt Máire, starved their tenants to death, and then employed the Black and Tans to keep Ireland enslaved. Did fathers and sons in those big houses meet and maneuver like this? Did they scheme to keep power and property in their own hands? We Irish weren't like that, were we? All the descendants of Granny Honora had made their own way. True, Ed's position had given us a boost. The city of Chicago had paid my salary for twenty years but I'd done my job. Earned my money. Had Kennedy taken that chance away from Jack? Denied him the satisfaction of making it on his own?

And Mike. What was he expecting from Ed and the Cook County Democratic Party? Mike had said to Jack, "Congress . . . I suppose serving there would be a way to have a real impact. Maybe I could run too. The two of us together, that would be something."

Joseph Kennedy had laughed and turned to Ed. "Better set this young man straight. Washington is not Chicago. Why, your pal Roosevelt wouldn't even let *you* run for the Senate, Ed."

I'd wondered what he was talking about. Ed had never said anything to me about wanting to be a senator.

"Just an idea, Joe. I didn't really pursue it. In fact, I'm surprised you even knew," he'd said. "I never meant—"

Kennedy had interrupted him. "Hey, I'm not saying you wouldn't have done a damn good job. All those old men in Congress are doddering fools but they look the part and face it, Ed, you just don't. I heard it was Eleanor put the kibosh on you. She said it was bad enough to have Truman, a senator representing a boss, but to actually have a senator who was a boss . . . She called you, what was it she called you? Oh yeah, an archetypal Irish pol. It's your mug, Ed, and the red hair. If I was casting a movie and needed a big city Mick mayor you'd get the part. But Senator Kelly, it just wouldn't work. Why do you think Jimmy Byrnes converted before he ran? So they couldn't call him a Papist."

I'd had to speak up. "I can't believe Eleanor—"

"You don't know New England WASPs the way I do," Kennedy had said.

"But you think there's a place for Congressman Kennedy, Senator Kennedy . . ."

"President Kennedy," Joe had finished. "Yes, I do. I did right by my boys. Prepared them." He had turned to Mike. "Where did you go to high school?"

"St. Rita," Mike said.

"And college?"

"DePaul."

"See what I mean," Kennedy had said. "You kept him within the tribe, Ed, and now it's too late. Joe and Jack went to top prep schools. Wiped the asses of those pansies both academically and athletically and then did the same at Harvard. Proved themselves in the big arena."

"And stayed Catholic?" I'd asked.

"Of course! Their mother would have killed me if I'd ever have suggested anything different. And I didn't want to. Didn't have to. I follow the faith, Miss Kelly. I give to the Church. I say my prayers every night and there's a Jesuit I go to for confession who's a man of the world. I don't think Rose could have survived Joe's death without attending daily Mass. She started going every day after Rosemary." He'd stopped and looked at me. No secret that their oldest daughter lived in a home run by nuns. Though exactly what was wrong with her I didn't know.

"I'm not here to give you our family history," Kennedy had said. "I'm sure Mike's pedigree will stand him in good stead in 'city politics.'"

He'd made the words so dismissive that Ed laughed. Jack had caught on.

"I'd say our family owes a lot to city politics," Jack had said. "After all, I'm John *Fitzgerald*. Don't leave mother's father out of our family history. As mayor he did a lot for Boston and for you too, Dad."

"He did. He did. But could you ever imagine Honey Fitz in Washington? They'd grind him up. No, lad," he'd said to Mike. "Stick to what you know. Maybe there'll be a second Mayor Kelly someday. Wouldn't that be grand, Ed?"

"Chicago's not keen on dynasties, Joe," he'd said.

"Another mistake we Irish make. Every WASP in the Senate is grooming his son to take over his seat. Bush was parading his Naval aviator boy around Washington last week. No hesitation there. We could learn from them."

I couldn't let that go past. "Come on, Mr. Kennedy, you want America to be ruled like England by rich families. You don't know much Irish history then." I'd tried to sound like I was joshing him but he wasn't buying it.

"I don't need any lectures, thank you. And I don't think we need any more photographs either." He'd waved at me, pointing his hand toward the door. Well that put the tin hat on it.

"Oh I'm sorry if I offended you, Mr. Kennedy. I forgot that your daughter is Lady Harrington now. Was that part of your plan? Get one of your girls to marry a marquis? Out-WASP the WASPS. Even the Bushes don't have a title," I'd said.

Joseph Kennedy stood up. "That's enough," he'd said.

"It's not," I'd said. "I let it go before, but how dare you make a joke of the Miami assassination. Only a fluke that Roosevelt survived. And Mayor Cermak did die. You're so proud that you're sending your son into the same arena. Senator Kennedy. President Kennedy. Anything could happen."

"That fellow in Miami was a nut," Joseph Kennedy had said. "A once-in-a-lifetime occurrence."

"Oh really? What about the guy in Milwaukee that almost killed Theodore Roosevelt? And remember Teddy only became president because an assassin had gotten McKinley and not long before that it was Garfield. My grandmother took her children down to the courthouse to see Lincoln's body brought by horse-drawn carriage. My own father was called up to sing 'The Lament for Owen Roe O'Neill' in honor of the dead president. But of course that's more mickology and you wouldn't be interested. You've probably never even heard of Owen Roe, the chieftain who took on Cromwell's army. They couldn't beat him in a fair fight so the English poisoned him. Probably relatives of your daughter."

Ed had stood up. Dear God, I'd thought, if he reprimands me, that's it. I'll walk out of this office and never come back. But to my amazement Ed had begun to sing.

Did they dare, did they dare to slay Owen Roe O'Neill?
Yes, they slew with poison him they feared to meet with steel.
May God wither up their hearts! May their blood cease to flow,
May they walk in lasting death who poisoned Owen Roe.

"Well done, Ed," I'd said.

"Excellent, Mr. Mayor," Jack had said, and he turned to his father. "There's something for you, Dad. You've always enjoyed revenge."

"Sing the rest, Ed," I'd said.

He took a breath and began.

Sagest in the council was he, kindest in the hall!
Sure we never won a battle, 'twas Owen won them all.
Your troubles are all over, you're at rest with God on high,
But we're slaves, and we're orphans, Owen! why did you die?
We're sheep without a shepherd when the snow shuts out the sky,
O why did you leave us, Owen. Why did you die?

Now Ed was a bit of an actor. Part of the reason Pat Nash chose him to be mayor, the front man, was because Pat knew Ed was a performer. Could give a speech and be master of ceremonies at Knights of Columbus dinners and party conventions. He did have a beautiful tenor voice and even Joseph Kennedy had joined Jack and Mike and me in applauding.

"Very nice, Ed," Joe had said. "But you make my point. No Irish songs are sung in the White House."

"Well not yet," Jack had said.

And dear God I saw it in his eyes. The same calculation I'd observed in Harry Truman. "I could do this," he was thinking. Jack had turned to Mike. "Let's stay in touch." I think my nephew would have enlisted in Team Kennedy right there on the spot.

So. The Kennedys had left. Ed and Mike and I were having a second glass of whiskey. Joseph Kennedy and Jack were lunching with Adlai Stevenson at the Century Club. Joe had assured us that Stevenson was going to be the next governor of Illinois. Ed had laughed. "Well his grandfather might have been vice president of the United States and his father secretary of state but the party isn't so sure about young Stevenson."

"You'll choose him. He's got the pedigree," Joseph Kennedy had said.

I had gotten in one parting shot. "His family is Irish too, Joe. They're from the North but then so was Owen Roe. Of course they weren't Catholic. So they were fit for higher office."

"So Mike, what did you think of the Kennedys?" Ed had asked him.

"I like Jack," Mike had said.

"And you want to get into this rat race, Mike?" Ed had asked him.

"I think I do," Mike had said.

"What did Kennedy mean about your wanting to run for the Senate?" I'd asked Ed.

"Just a notion I had. But what Joe said was true. I got no encouragement from the president."

"Geeze Louise. I thought you'd never give up being mayor."

"Well," he'd said, "a couple of fellows came to the office after the Midway Airport incident and told me that if I didn't stop blathering on about open housing I could forget about having another term. I told them to go to hell."

"Oh, Ed. They can't get rid of you. Can they?"

"Not now. But the dogs are yapping at my heels." He'd leaned forward. Looked Mike right in the eye. "Mike," he'd said, "you're young and strong. You've survived so much. You've got a great wife, a family. Forget politics. It's a dirty business, Mike, and we don't have to do it anymore."

Mike and I had looked at Ed. I had been surprised. The man who had lived and breathed politics for forty years and had just said that we don't have to do it anymore. "A dirty business?" But he had wanted to be a senator and they'd turned him down. And never said anything to me, or Margaret either. She would have told me. Too proud to have acknowledged the rejection, I had supposed. And was Kennedy right? Would we Irish only ever be allowed to go so far and no further unless we made ourselves over in their image? He'd scrubbed away Jack's past to give him a future. Would this Harvard-educated Navy hero be the one to breach the barricade? Nothing of the Irish pol about John Fitzgerald Kennedy.

Joseph Kennedy had essentially told Ed that for all his tailored suits and good grammar, he was still a Mick, a Papist, a mackerel-snapper. But had Joe been reacting to the Boston-Brahmin prejudice that had pressed down on him his whole life? I should have said that in Chicago we didn't have to erase who we were to succeed. We didn't apologize for being Irish. We'd built this town, I should have told him, and had never let meatpackers and tradesmen make us ashamed.

I had tried to put these scattered thoughts into words for Mike and Ed.

"Mr. Kennedy's been infected," I'd said. "He thinks the WASPs are better than he is. Probably saw them sneer at his father-in-law. I imagine he cringes at the very name Honey Fitz."

"Not easy to have a powerful father-in-law when you're a young man starting out," Ed had said. What had he meant? Margaret's father was long dead. And then I remembered. Mary Roche, his first wife, had been the daughter of a rich man. A power in the city when Ed had been cutting trees on the banks of the canal. He might have remained there if he hadn't punched the Republican boss on the job for discriminating against him and discovered that Colonel McCormick, the man in charge, liked a fighter. He promoted Ed. Which to a city job as an engineer. Only then had he courted Mary Roche.

Joseph Patrick Kennedy has no idea who the Irish were, I'd thought. He knew so little of his own heritage that he actually admired the English aristocracy. As the American ambassador to England, the Court of St. James for goodness' sake, he should have enjoyed forcing the English into accepting an Irishman as the representative of the most powerful country in the world at a time when they needed our help. But I think he'd fallen for the pomp and preening. All those titles—lord and lady this, dukes and barons, not to mention king and queen, were made up really—smoke and mirrors. Or maybe Joseph Kennedy was so competitive that he'd wanted to beat the Brits at their own game?

I'd wondered if Kennedy understood that Ed was Irish above all? And yet, neither he nor Ed had ever touched the vellum page of an Irish manuscript, marveled at the intricate script, the fabulous animals drawn in the margins. Never wondered at how the monks had copied and preserved classical manuscripts, illuminated the Gospels, recorded the history over thousands of years. They had never walked through the ruins of a thousand-year-old monastery and imagined monks and nuns and lay people living together cultivating farms, celebrating magnificent liturgies. Nor did they know the old stories of Maeve and Cuchulainn, the oldest epics in Europe. Never visited one of the holy wells or climbed a sacred mountain. Our ancestors had kept the faith alive through all the darkest days of oppression. Had remained Irish above all. And we had triumphed. A nation once again. Had outmaneuvered the British Empire and turned them out after eight hundred years.

"We wouldn't die and that annoyed them." Granny Honora's words. One million of our people murdered yet two million escaped. We'd saved ourselves, one helping the next. One of the great rescues in human history. Doing well all over the world while still rooted in that little island.

Eire. Named for a goddess, and Joseph Patrick Kennedy had the nerve to wince when Ed sang a song of one of our heroes. And he had made Ed feel just that bit ashamed. After that meeting with the Kennedys I had resolved that I was going back to Ireland and Ed was coming with me. I was not going to take no for an answer. And so I said again. "You owe me, Ed."

We'd sung happy birthday to little Mary Pat. Applauded as she pointed to each of us and said our names. Aunt Rose, Aunt Nonie, Uncle Ed. The next generation.

"Nonie," Ed said, as we walked from the house to his car. "It's too late. The flight is leaving the day after tomorrow. This is my chance. If I can make Chicago the headquarters of the United Nations, I'll have all the clout I need to run for mayor—whatever the party says. And I'd win. I can't risk the distraction."

"And that's what I am? After all these years? A distraction? And is Ireland a mere distraction, too?"

"I know you, Nonie. You couldn't help yourself. You'd be insulting the English, causing all kinds of problems."

Ed didn't say another word to me all the way back to the apartment, didn't even invite me in for a coffee. Margaret was off visiting Pat at her convent. Each generation of Kellys gave one girl to the nuns, and Pat was this generation's offering. Steve was away at college, but Joseph was home on leave from the Navy, waiting to be released. I wondered if he would be traveling with Ed.

"Good night, Ed," I said at the door. *"Slán."*

NOVEMBER 20, 1945

I hadn't argued with Ed or asked again, I just showed up at the airport with my camera, passport, and a suitcase, wearing the my green coat with the fur collar he and Margaret had given me. American Airlines had arranged a special lounge for the delegation. "I'm with the group," I said to the young woman at the desk.

"At last," she said, "a female," and guided me to the restricted area. Twenty of them. And not one woman. Ed and the lieutenant governor were the only politicians. I knew some of the others. Barnet Hodges, the corporation counsel, Jimmy Cleary, who worked for the advertising agency that had prepared Chicago's pitch to become the headquarters. The others looked like bankers. There were three reporters. One from the *Tribune*, one from the *Sun-Times* and the other from the *Chicago American*, and dear God, sitting next to the bar, was Manny Mandel. I should have known he'd get himself included. Now he called out to me. "Nora Kelly, traveling on the taxpayer's dime."

The look on Ed's face when Manny hollered his accusation. He's going to send me away. Humiliate me in front of everyone. The rest of the delegates had stopped talking and were staring at me. Ed stood up.

"Nora has paid her own fare," he said. "And she has very kindly agreed to act as my guide to Ireland, where we will visit my grandmother's birthplace in . . ." He paused.

"Galway," I said. "Barna. On the shores of Galway Bay."

And I walked over to Ed. "Thank you," I said. We stood smiling at each other as three reporters surrounded us and Manny photographed me with Ed and his son Joseph who I was glad to see.

"I'm so happy you're coming with us, Aunt Nonie," Joseph said to me. Here was another good-looking Irish-American Naval officer, I thought. He was waiting to be demobilized too. Younger than Jack and Mike but well turned out in his uniform.

"Thank you," I said to him. "I wouldn't miss it and you'll get to see the land of your ancestors." Manny heard me.

"Wait a minute," he said. "Aren't the mayor's children—" But I turned and walked away before he could say "adopted." Took Joe's arm and headed for the buffet American Airlines had provided.

Margaret and Ed knew the identity of their children's birth parents, but Margaret had decided that unless the kids asked for the information there was no reason to tell them.

"I'm their mother and Ed's their father," she'd told me, and none of the three had ever inquired. But over the years Margaret had talked to me about Steve's Irish temper, or how the twins had the map of Ireland on their faces, so I knew that Joe was probably returning to the land of his ancestors in every sense.

But first I had to settle Ed down. He came smiling over to the buffet. "Excuse us for a moment, Joe," he said, took my arm and walked into the hallway. "What do you think you're pulling, Nora Kelly? Blindsiding me like that."

"You rose to the occasion, Ed."

He shook his head.

"Look, I know you didn't want me along on this trip because you thought the press would criticize you. Well, they tried and you headed them off. Perfectly natural for your cousin to accompany you to the family home place," I said.

"I was only trying to shut Manny Mandel up but as I said the words I realized that I really do want to go to Ireland. Don't know why I've never gone before. It isn't as if Margaret and I never traveled in Europe . . ."

"Don't you think it's because that when we were growing up Ireland was always this magic mythic place?" I said. "Not somewhere you could actually go. Granny told me once that she would see Ireland again after she died. You sing that yourself, Ed. 'Galway Bay' is one of your party pieces."

And now I croaked out the last words:

> And if there's going to be a life hereafter,
> And somehow I am sure there's going to be,
> I will ask my God to let me make my Heaven
> In that dear land beyond the Irish Sea.

Ed couldn't keep himself from smiling as I finished.

"Alright. Alright," he said. "But I don't want you mouthing off about perfidious Albion, Nonie. No headlines about you attacking the English. This is our chance to show Chicago as the city it really is. Not gangsters machine-gunning each other, or even the City of the Big Shoulders, but the place I built against all the odds. The parks, the museum, the universities, the skyscrapers, the lakefront. Our Chicago, Nonie, opening its arms to the world. If I can pull this off, I'll still be mayor when we get the United Nations headquarters. But you have to keep quiet during the week while we're in London. Then we'll go to Ireland and I'll stand on the shores of Galway Bay and sing every rebel song I know. Is that a deal?"

"It is, Ed," I said.

I'd be polite to the Sassenach for the sake of Chicago and himself. But the English had a way of getting people to sell their souls and then not paying them. Still, I went along.

Not a peep out of me when the British rolled out the rituals they used to disguise reality on our arrival on Wednesday, November 21, 1945. We were met at the airport by troops from a Scottish regiment, complete with kilts and bagpipes. Manny went mad, posing Ed in the center of a cluster of pipers and all I could think of was the Battle of Culloden. The Scots had been betrayed and slaughtered and now they were happily serving in the army of the enemy. Did I say anything? I did not. But then British customs officers impounded Jimmy Cleary's film, which meant to show the city in such glory that all fifty-two members of the panel would choose Chicago. We'd just checked into the Savoy Hotel when Ed called me to come to his room. Jimmy and the film were being held at the airport. He was on the phone.

"I'll get on to the embassy," Ed told Jimmy.

The American ambassador, John Gilbert Winant—he insisted that all three names be used—had been at the hotel when we arrived. The fellow was a Republican and a former New Hampshire governor. Tall and thin with those sharp cutout features that seem to be issued to WASPs. Easy for him to fit in with the British. So now Ed called the embassy. Could he please speak to the ambassador? While very polite, very calm, the woman who'd answered was not helpful. I was standing next to Ed, and he was holding the phone out so I could hear.

"Mr. Gilbert Winant is unavailable," the woman said. An English accent.

Manny had already filled me in on the gossip. The American ambassador was having an affair with Winston Churchill's daughter Sarah. Even though both were married to other people. "The British upper classes don't consider a roll in the hay as anything serious," Manny had said. "Though my sources tell me poor Johnny Winant's head over heels. I doubt if Winston cares too much. They say he can't stand Sarah's husband, who's an Austrian Jew and a performer in music halls. How's that for sticking it to dear old Dad?"

Ed had no luck with the embassy receptionist even after he described our problem. It was impossible to get in touch with the ambassador. Besides, she said, the British Customs and Excise Authority was entitled to enforce their own laws and shouldn't we have made proper arrangements before our arrival, etc. etc. Ed held the phone out as the lecture continued. Goodbye, he said, and slammed it down.

"Goddamn," he said. "I hate bureaucrats."

"Let's call the Irish embassy," I said. But when I asked for the number, the clerk at the Savoy desk told me there was no Irish embassy.

"Ireland is part of the Commonwealth," the clerk told me. "I believe there is an Office of the High Commissioner."

"Well give me that number," I said. I dialed it and handed the phone to Ed.

"You talk to him, Nonie," Ed said to me. "You're the one claims to know all these Irish officials. Drop a few names."

Well, of course the best name was the prime minister himself. But what could I say? I'm a friend of Mr. de Valera?

"Mr. Dulanty's office," the woman on the other end of the line said.

"Please," I said. "I'm calling for Mayor Ed Kelly and—" She cut me off.

"What is the nature of his business?"

"Well," I said, and tried to hand the phone to Ed. But he shook his head. I'd been bragging about all my Irish connections. Now I had to prove myself. "It's something the mayor would like to talk to the commissioner himself about, and—"

"Impossible, madam." Not an Irish accent. Another English woman.

Now what? "You see we're here to make a presentation to the UN Committee on behalf of Chicago and—"

"Pardon me. You did say Chicago didn't you?" Was I going to have to listen to this woman make some remark about Al Capone?

But she said, "One moment please." A good three or four minutes before I heard another voice.

"So you're from Chicago." It was a man speaking now. Definitely Irish. "My father was with Dev in Chicago in 1919. And had great stories. Everybody in the office has heard me retelling them. I think they collected a hundred thousand dollars."

"He probably met Mayor Kelly. He's a member of the Irish Fellowship and they're the ones got you all that money."

"Put him on," the man said. He explained to Ed he wasn't the commissioner, which was just as well, as Mr. John Whelan Dulanty was very much a by-the-book kind of fellow who'd been born in England and had served in the British Civil Service until 1920 when he'd come over to the Irish side. We were talking to his aide. A fellow called Dáithí Ó Ceallaigh. "David Kelly in another life," he said. "And so your kinsman." He told us he wasn't concerned about "the book" at all. He seemed to know what buttons to push with the British and a few hours later Jimmy Cleary and the movie were in Ed's suite.

"Keep that Kelly fellow's number," Ed said to me. Jimmy told us he'd been within an inch of socking one of those fish-faced English bastards in the jaw.

I smiled and said, "No, Jimmy, they are our hosts. Turn the other cheek."

NOVEMBER 22, 1945

Thanksgiving. We assembled with thousands of American troops in Westminster Abbey to hear Ambassador Winant read President Truman's declaration. Harry wasn't soft-pedaling what our American boys had done to win the war. I couldn't resist a few glances at the Brits as President Truman's words echoed through the Abbey. We had won the blessing of Providence, he said. "With the courage and blood of our soldiers, sailors, Marines, and airmen."

I thought Winant mumbled just a bit, but he ended strongly enough, evoking those "high principles of citizenship for which so many Americans have given their all."

Remember that, you Brits. Our young men died for you.

Manny was everywhere snapping away. "Want a picture with the ambassador?" he asked me.

"No thanks," I said. I spent my time photographing the troops, getting their names and hometowns. I'd send their pictures to their local papers.

The next day they paraded Ed through the House of Commons making sure he bumped into Winston Churchill, which of course thrilled Manny Mandel, who must have taken twenty photographs. I took none. Back at the Savoy, I repeated to Ed what Churchill had said after World War I, that in the midst of the cataclysm that had swept the world, the dreary steeples of Tyrone and Fermanagh were still in place. "He's saying the quarrel between the North and the South in Ireland would never be solved, though he was the one responsible in many ways. Whatever he did during World War II, he was no friend to the Irish. He was against Home Rule and for the Black and Tans."

"Pipe down, Nonie," Ed said. "This is exactly why I didn't want to bring you along."

We were in Ed's room—his suite, rather—living room, dining room, and two bedrooms. Pushing out the boat for him but charging him full price. In fact a little extra. Dáithí had told Ed that there was an American tax added whenever a shopkeeper heard our accents.

But Ed wouldn't be drawn into criticizing our hosts.

"The British have a lot of influence on the committee. I had lunch with the lord mayor of London and he said the government supports Chicago's bid," he said.

"Lord mayor," I said. "And did he wear a red coat, ermine collar, three-cornered hat, and gold chain of office?"

"He did," Ed said.

"But don't you see that's all part of the con. The Beefeaters at the Tower of London, so picturesque, but they're guarding a place of execution where our people were imprisoned and beheaded. . . ."

"Easy, Nonie." I had refused to go on the tour, but Ed and Joseph had come back full of stories about the wonders of London, especially the Crown Jewels.

And now I said, "And as far as all their crowns and scepters, where do you think all those gems came from? Stolen. Taken from Africa and India and all those other colonies they left in pieces. Divide and conquer. Muslim against Hindu. Jew against Arab."

"Can it, Nonie," he said. "The presentation is tomorrow. Try to behave until then."

Then Jimmy Cleary stomped into the suite. "Goddamn it, Ed, they've screwed us again."

He'd left the written presentation that was to accompany the film at a British lab that had promised to have fifty-five photostats ready by today. He'd just come from there where he'd been told they were awfully sorry, and now Jimmy slipped into the accent. "'A bit of a cock-up and your job will not be ready until midweek.' Jesus. Midweek. And the fellow actually smiled at me. Something's going on here. First Customs try to keep the movie and now this. Do the Brits have any reason not to want Chicago to be the UN headquarters?"

"Any reason?" I started. "Every reason. They don't like us, boys. Forget the banquets and wood paneling. They were number one and now we are. They're furious."

Jimmy nodded.

"Wait a minute," I said. "What room is Manny Mandel in? The *Tribune* has a lab here. They can make the photostats for us. They'd have to work through the night but they could do it."

"We'll pay them double time," Ed said.

I brought the papers to Manny and went with him to the lab and waited there while the fifty-five copies were made. We sat through the night drinking bad coffee and making small talk. Finally at about 2:00 a.m. Manny said to me, "I have nothing against you, Nora, but you've always been too ambitious for a woman. I've got enough to do competing against the other guys, but a dame!" I let him go on. We needed those photostats.

NOVEMBER 23, 1945

Chicago put on quite a show the next day. We were the only city with a movie, and ten times better than the other American contestants—Miami, Denver, and Richmond, Virginia. New York was our only real competition, and Ed made a great case for our city, pointing out how much more livable Chicago was. New York was a snarl of traffic and craziness. With so much going on there the UN wouldn't be the focus it would be in Chicago. But that night Ed got a call from his new friend, Dáithí. He hung up the phone.

"Damn," he said. "That was Dáithí."

"What, Ed?"

"The fix is in. England made a deal with Russia for Vienna to be the headquarters. Anything to keep it away from us. Hell's bells," he said. "Is nothing ever on the square?"

"Time to go to Ireland," I said.

12

NOVEMBER 24, 1945

Ed figured we could get away for two days. Saturday and Sunday. The rest of the delegates had scattered. Some were on the bus tour arranged by the British government—Stratford-upon-Avon, etc. Poor Shakespeare. Always trotted out to impress the visitors.

"We need to fly to Galway," I told Dáithí Ó Ceallaigh.

"There's no regular service between London and Galway but we did pick up a Lockheed Hudson during the war and I think I might be able to commandeer it," he said.

"Picked up?" I asked.

"The American crew had to make a forced landing in Ireland. Remember we were neutral. Should have interned them but Dev made a deal. He returned the crew and kept the plane. Can you be ready to fly by first light?"

"Of course," I said.

"No press," Ed said, when I told him the arrangements. "We're not making this trip public. I want two days with you and my son Joseph. We'll tell the others I've come down with a terrible cold and I'll be working in my room."

Still dark when we left London for Croydon Airport the next morning. Dáithí picked us up at the hotel. He'd brought his wife, Antoinette, with him.

"Michael Collins kept a plane at this airport during the Treaty negotiations," Antoinette told us. "Ready to take him home if the talks fell apart."

I told her I had met Michael Collins.

"To think he was only thirty-two when he died," she said. "The same age Dáithí and I are now."

"Mmmm," I said, and didn't point out that Collins was probably assassinated on orders from their prime minister. *Ná habair tada.* Say nothing.

Just dawn when Ed, Joseph, and I boarded the small plane. A different pilot than the fellow who'd flown Mike and me. Dáithí had agreed to send a telegram to John and Maura O'Connor at Lough Inagh. John would meet us, though it would probably take him longer to drive the thirty miles from Connemara to Galway than for us to fly from London.

"There, Ed," I said pointing down. "There she is. Eire. Named for a goddess, Joseph. Ireland is a woman no question." And pleased with herself, shining in the morning light. The end of November and she was still green. We followed the fields west until they sloped down to a rocky shore where waves broke against ancient stones.

"There, Ed. See where the waters change colors, and the blue meets the gray, that's Galway Bay flowing into the Atlantic. That's where Granny Honora and Aunt Máire rowed out in a curragh to catch the ship that brought your father and mine to America."

Ed pushed his forehead against the window. "My God," he said. "I always took that for some kind of a tall tale. Not real. But now. It is real, isn't it?"

"As real as you and me," I said.

The pilot was from Cork and told us the airfield there was much superior to Galway Airport and it would take all his skill to land well on these inferior runways. But he set us down, no problem. John O'Connor was waiting for us in the same old car that John had used twenty-five years ago when I'd toured the west with the American Friends Service Committee, reporting on the atrocities of the Black and Tans. I had experienced their brutality firsthand.

Part of me wanted to launch into the whole story. Tell Ed and Joseph how close I'd come to being hanged as a spy. But I didn't. This was the new Ireland. Free. And John was smiling.

"We even have a clear day for you," John said. "And feel it, there's warmth left in that sun. Maura is at the Lodge preparing a welcome dinner."

John drove us through Galway City.

"Quite a nice city," Ed said, approving the gray stone buildings, the active port, the wrought iron gate that led to the college grounds. Ireland doing alright for herself.

"Where are the shops the Black and Tans burned out?" I asked John O'Connor.

"Rebuilt," was all he said. No tale for Ed of those brutal convict soldiers and the reign of terror they'd unleashed during the 1920s. The Irish had won against all the odds. Independent now and soon to be a republic. The last ties to England severed. Let the past bury the past.

"Here's the dream come true," I said to Ed as we drove along the ring road. "All those AOH picnics where we'd shouted out 'A nation once again.' Fulfilled. Galway is an Irish city now."

John parked the car. We followed him into the oldest part of the city to a stone gate that had once been part of the walls. He pointed out an inscription—"From the fury of the O'Flahertys, O Lord deliver us."

"The merchants inside the city were always loyal to the English Crown and were afraid the Irish clans would overrun them and reclaim the city," John said. "Funny enough it was the British who betrayed them, but by that time it was too late to ally themselves with the Irish."

Ed nodded. Politics.

"Wasn't Galway named for an ancient Irish princess?" I said to John.

"Gaillimh," he said, "and she's still here. Never left. Through all the centuries of oppression she held on. And now she's victorious and I'll show you why."

He led us through narrow streets down to an open space bordering the water. He pointed at a stone arch. "That's the Spanish Arch," he said. "Galway traded with Spain and Portugal."

"Oh I see," Ed said. "Those kind of alliances must have helped the Irish resist the English."

"Not as much as you think," John said. "It wasn't economics or politics or diplomacy that saved us. You'll see what made us strong."

The wind off the water had picked up. Cold now. Ed turned his collar up. Tied his cashmere scarf tightly. I was glad for the warmth of my green Donegal tweed.

"Put on your watch cap," I said to Joseph. He hadn't said much since we'd left the airport. Sitting between Ed and me in the back seat, taking it all in. Now he shook his head at me.

"Aunt Nonie," he said. He was twenty-three years old. A man. A US Navy veteran but I'd been part of his life since he was a little boy. So he pulled the cap out of his pocket and put it on. Appropriate, I thought. The sailor returned. Wearing the navy blue peacoat, those bellbottom trousers, with a bit of a roll in his stride. He'd managed to make it into the last few months of the war serving on a destroyer.

Now we heard voices, a chorus of shouts, high-pitched. We turned a corner into an open space filled with women.

"The fish market," John said. "These women are mostly from the Claddagh. They have the morning to sell the catch. Fierce competition among them. But cooperation too. They are Ireland's secret weapon. Our women saved us."

As we moved closer I could see that the women were dressed in traditional clothing. Long red skirts, black shawls tied at the waist. Each one had a basket of fish in front of her and was calling out the qualities of their wares.

"Herring, herring, herring," the woman closest to us shouted. "King of the sea." She was younger than the others with very black hair and those blue eyes I'd grown up with in Bridgeport. White skin. Her cheeks reddened by the wind. She waved us over to her. "You Yanks never tasted anything as fresh as Galway Bay herring. Restores your liver. Good medicine for you, young sailor."

"But we're not Yanks," I said to her. "At least not only Yanks. Our grandmother was one of you. Sold fish right here along with her mother and sister."

"And what was the name," the woman asked.

"Kelly," Ed said. "We're Kellys."

"Kelly? Half of Galway is called Kelly, but I don't mind any fisher folk with that name. Kellys were farmers mostly."

"She was a Keeley," I said. "Her father and grandmother came to Freeport from further west, Carna." This was the information I'd gathered when I had come to Ireland twenty years before when Maura O'Connor had introduced me to an old woman who remembered my Granny Honora. She was probably long dead.

"Keeleys. They were blow-ins," she said.

"No, no," I said. "They lived in Barna a hundred years ago."

"A hundred years ago?" She laughed and snapped her fingers. "No longer than that. My family, the Kings, have fished these waters since beyond memory. I'm Katie King."

A group of women had gathered, watching us and listening. Now Katie spoke to them.

"What's she saying," Joseph asked me. "Is that some other language?" Katie was speaking in Irish.

"That's our mother tongue, Joe," I said. "Lost to us."

"I remember," Ed said. "Something familiar in the rhythms. The throaty sounds. But I don't recognize any words."

"Granny tried to teach us but we wouldn't sit still long enough to learn," I said.

"Oh, I get it," Joe said. "That's Gaelic."

"Irish," I said. "Our own brand of Gaelic."

Now Katie turned back to us. "There are stories of Keeley women alright," she said. "One of them was, well, taken advantage of by the Scoundrel Pykes."

"Yes, yes," I said. "That's our family. My aunt Máire was a prisoner in the big house. Her sister Honora is our granny."

"So they did live," Katie said. "We never knew what happened to our people after they left." She pointed to a very old woman, though not the one I had met all those years ago. Small, a network of wrinkles on her face. "Bridie's nearly ninety. Born just after the Great Starvation. She has knowledge from her mother. Those who died. Those who escaped, and those of us who endured here."

The old woman stepped closer to Katie and spoke to her in Irish. Katie nodded and said to us, "There are not many fishermen left in Barna. All driven out years ago. But here you are come back."

"Yes," I said. "My granny Honora used to say we wouldn't die and that annoyed them."

Katie laughed and translated the words for the other women, who nodded and smiled. Survivors, I thought. We are the survivors. I understood why John O'Connor had said that these women were Ireland's secret weapon. Hundreds of thousands of them had been as determined as Granny Honora had been. Their children would live. And if they had to leave Ireland to save them, well they would always be Irish. Irish above all.

I looked at Ed. Did he understand that these women were heroes, as our grandmother had been? Joseph was looking down at the ground, pointing something out to Ed. No shoes. Many of the women had no shoes. Nobody in Chicago was so poor as to go barefoot. Weren't there always shoes in the mayor's Christmas boxes? I hoped that Katie hadn't seen that exchange between father and son. Why embarrass her? But she lifted her foot up and was wriggling her toes.

"If you grow up in your bare feet you'll never get pneumonia in the snow," she said. John O'Connor laughed.

"See," he said to us, "the poor English never really understood what they were up against."

"And was your grandmother really that poor?" Joseph asked me as we drove along the coast road toward Barna. He's picturing his mother in her ermine coat, I thought. Their fancy Lake Shore Drive apartment. The house in Eagle River. All of this from a barefoot fishmonger?

"It was much worse then," I said. "Our whole family almost starved to death. Our grandfather did die and so did a million more."

"Was that the Potato Famine?" Joe asked.

"Not a famine," I said. "Plenty of food in the country. But our people were like the sharecroppers in the US. The landlords owned everything. The people turned over their crops to pay outrageous rents on land that had belonged to them."

Joseph was looking out at the wide waters of the bay, touched by a winter sun that kept shining.

"Our people had no control over their lives then," Ed said. "They couldn't vote. Couldn't elect anyone to speak for them. They only had the potato which sustained them until the blight destroyed the crop."

"Dead bodies all along this road," John said. "People desperate to get to Galway City to beg for help but they were turned away. They just collapsed and died where they fell."

"And the government didn't . . . ," Joseph said.

"It wasn't their government," Ed said. I turned to Joseph.

"Think of how your father helped the people of Chicago during the Depression. Remember, he was working for them. Maybe politics isn't such a dirty business after all," I said to Ed. "This area could have used a few powerful aldermen."

We arrived at Barna. John parked next to a pub and led us down to the shore.

"Here, right here, Ed," I said. "Granny was born here at this spot."

"But there are no houses here," Ed said.

"There were," John O'Connor said. "Thirty cottages. A fishing village called Freeport—in Irish, *An Chélbh*."

We were standing on a jumble of rocks, some as big as boulders, others only round pebbles, but all packed together on the shore of Galway Bay.

"But there's nothing here," Ed said again.

"The landlord who owned their cottages sent in soldiers at midnight to drive the thirty families out and set fire to their homes," John said. "They didn't worry about the people inside. Thatch goes up very quickly. Some didn't escape, too sick and weakened by starvation to flee the flames."

"Horrible," Joseph said.

"Pyke the landlord didn't see the Irish as human beings," John said. "He wanted the land to build a seaside resort."

Ed turned and looked at the empty space. I could see that he was imagining the scene. Cottages jammed together in this small area all burning in the darkness. The terror, the confusion. Women carrying their children as Granny had held Ed's own father, Stephen, only a year old. My father, Patrick, seven, had tried to help his mother.

"And many of those who survived the fire died soon afterwards," said John. "No food, no shelter. No one had anything."

"And yet here we are," Ed said.

"She saved us, Ed," I said. "Granny, Aunt Máire and their children escaped in our great-grandfather Keeley's boat. They sailed out onto the dark waters of Galway Bay, with your father in her arms, pregnant with our uncle Michael. Eight children between them, escaping. We didn't die."

And Ed understood. He reached over and took my hand, and then put his arm around Joseph. "So many lives depended on her courage," Ed said. "All the Kellys."

"And millions more. All of us Irish-Americans are descendant from someone who got out against all the odds," I said.

John O'Connor had been standing a little apart. Ed and Joseph and I were wrapped in a cloak of emotion, like in the old Irish tales. We had somehow been transported back in time so that the young Honora, as well as the baby who would become Ed's father, Stephen, along with my father, Patrick, Uncle James, Aunt Bridget, all of them were somehow here. Aunt Máire's children. Johnny Óg who would die in the Civil War, the son of her young fisherman husband who had drowned. Her other two boys born of the landlord, as was my aunt Grace. All of them now married with families. Hundreds of us down through the generations. Overwhelming really.

Now John O'Connor spoke. "Against the odds certainly. Hard for us to imagine how difficult it was for the people to escape. Starvation brings a kind of passivity. Some families just lay down together in front of the hearth, barricaded the door against the packs of wild dogs that fed on corpses, and waited to die. Those who did survive usually had someone who'd gone over before and sent back money for the fare."

"For us it was our great-uncle Patrick, our grandfather's brother," Ed said. "Nora and I knew him as an old man. Full of stories about his work on the I & M Canal and the years he spent trapping furs up north with the Ojibwe. He sent the money."

"Don't forget Aunt Máire stole the landlord's jewels," I said.

This got Joseph's attention. "Stole?"

"And proud of it. She told me the Scoundrel Pykes owed her that and much more," I said.

John O'Connor nodded. "Even when people had money in their hands for the fare, the landlord could still stop them. He would send soldiers onto the ships confiscating money, claiming he was owed it for rent or as a reimbursement for handing out some sacks of Indian corn."

"But that's disgusting," Joseph said. "How could anyone defend against that?"

"The people were clever. They wouldn't assemble until a ship was in port.

A piper alerted them. You've heard the song 'Danny Boy,' 'the pipes, the pipes are calling'? That describes how a piper signaled them to sneak down to the ship.

"Some walked hundreds of miles. Whole families, children and old people staggering along, somehow made it to Cork or Dublin and piled onto ships that provided little food and brackish water. Others got to Liverpool. All had rough crossings."

"The coffin ships," I said. He nodded.

"The Atlantic Ocean is a graveyard," John said. "It's said one-fourth of those passengers perished. One ship sunk a few miles off the coast. Relatives waving farewell saw their loved ones drown."

"Our granny's two brothers died. One had got as far as Canada. French families took their children in. There's a story about our two French cousins arriving with Uncle Patrick. I wish I'd listened more closely," I said.

"Every family in Bridgeport who came from Ireland left behind death and despair," Ed said.

I turned to John O'Connor. "Ed left school at twelve," I said. "Had all kinds of jobs. More or less taught himself how to be an engineer and built Chicago into the city it is now. Saved it from bankruptcy. FDR himself depended on him and so does President Truman."

I'd never been struck so forcefully by the sheer unlikeliness of Ed's rise. Of all our successes. Joseph Kennedy had never spoken about how his family had escaped. But surely they hadn't had an easy passage either. Thirty million Irish Americans and most of us without a real notion of what our ancestors suffered or the kind of determination it took to make the journey. Ed began speaking but he sounded as if he were talking to himself.

"Half the Irish workers on the I & M Canal died," he said. "Froze to death in below zero temperatures sleeping in unheated tents. Dead bodies discovered in the morning. Others were crushed when inferior equipment failed. Similar statistics for those building the railroads. Did you know, Mr. O'Connor, the Irish were used on projects considered too dangerous to give to slaves? After all slaves had value. We didn't."

We. I'd never heard Ed talk about the defeats, the losses the Irish had suffered. He always spoke of our victories. All those men at the Irish Fellowship Club were proud of how they'd earned their fortunes. Patting each other on the back. And yet each one of them had come from some place like this.

The light was leaving the sky over the bay. The sunset turned the clouds a kind of purple-red. Long stripes on the horizon.

"Tír na nÓg," John O'Connor said. "In Irish mythology the land of the ever-young was just beyond the horizon in the west. Amerikay."

"Amerikay," I said.

Ed smiled. "I can hear Granny pronouncing America that way. She once told me she was afraid that this Amerikay would swallow us up and we would forget that we were Irish."

He looked over at Joseph who was skimming flat stones across the water. Three, four, five skips, not listening to us.

"For Joseph, being Irish is Notre Dame winning football games, the St. Patrick's Day parade, the Christmas party at the Irish Fellowship Club," Ed said.

"He's young," I said. "I was his age when the old women would gather in front of the fire at 2705 Hillock—Hickory Street then—full of stories about auld Ireland, I didn't pay much attention. I was modern. I was American. Not tied to some ancient place that seemed to only exist in sad songs."

John O'Connor had been listening and now he said, "Yet we are not a tragic people. We did survive the Great Starvation. Even it couldn't destroy the fun we make for each other. I think I'd better take you to a session. Get Paddy John the fiddler to come to the Lodge along with Larry Martin the *sean nós* singer, and round up some dancers."

We entered Connemara after full dark had fallen. John stopped. "To me this is the most Irish part of the country." Not that we could see anything. The car's headlights illuminated only a few feet of the road ahead of us. "You can't see them now but we're surrounded by mountains. The Twelve Pins," he said. "They were once taller than the Alps. So ancient they've been rubbed down to the core. And lakes. Dozens of lakes."

Joseph sat in the front seat trying to see beyond into the darkness. He rolled down the window. We could smell the sea.

"When they escaped the fire at Barna, our own fathers landed just west of here, Ed," I said. "Can you imagine how terrified those little boys were? Their home aflame, soldiers shouting and threatening, then the journey in their grandfather's boat. And finally safety at the Keeley place at Ard near Carna."

"And is that where we're going now?" Ed asked.

"Not tonight," John O'Connor said. "I'll take you there in the morning. My wife is a Carna woman and she'll show you the Keeley home place. Though none of that family is left there. There are other Keeleys in Kilternan a few miles away. Your in-laws, Nora, I believe."

"I didn't know you were married, Aunt Nonie," Joseph said.

"A long time ago, Joseph. And that's a tale for another time."

Ed leaned close to me in the back seat. "But you never really married that fellow did you, Nonie? I mean not properly."

"Please, Ed. Not now."

John turned off the coast road. "There's the Lodge," he said. Still miles away. But the only light in that whole dark landscape came from the Lodge windows. A kind of beacon in the blackness.

Maura O'Connor had dinner waiting for us. Thick potato soup and wholemeal wheaten bread. Still hot, so the butter melted right in. A taste uniquely Irish with a sweetness that comes from new grass and soft rain.

"So," Maura said to me. So. As if we'd met only days ago, not more than twenty years. "So. Tell me all your news."

"Nice place," Ed said, looking around what had been the front parlor when the Lodge belonged to the Berridges. Not a titled family like the Marquess of Sligo, who claimed most of the land north of here. Just wealthy English people who wanted to fish famous Lough Inagh. Maura explained to Ed that she and John had taken care of the property for the family who only came one month a year.

"The Berridges left during the Civil War," Maura said. "Let us buy it on good terms."

"They couldn't sell it to anybody else. And they knew that many another big house had been burned to the ground," John told him.

"Still, it was kind of them," Maura said. "We've just paid off the last of the mortgage. We had planned to open it as a hotel for Irish Americans such as yourselves. But then with the war . . ." She shrugged.

"People will be traveling soon enough," Ed said. "The US will start booming. Lots of money to be made and a place like this . . ." Ed laughed. "Something satisfying about lounging around the big house. Getting some of our own back."

John put turf on the fire. The five of us very comfortable in the Berridges' overstuffed armchairs as we stretched out in the warmth.

"All of Connemara belonged to the Keeleys once," I said to Joseph. "Our granny's family."

"And was that before the war?" he asked. The O'Connors laughed.

"Quite a few centuries before," John said. "When was it, Nora? About 1300 when the O'Flahertys took over?"

"About that. And they held it for about four hundred years until—"

"Let me guess. The English. It's hard to believe that all those people who were so nice to us in London are really our enemies," Joseph said.

"Please God, they'll be our paying guests," Maura said. "Ireland still has a great draw for English people. And our hotel will be open to all. But to-night is just for family. Come along."

Not easy to get up from those comfortable chairs. Only eight o'clock but I would have been very happy to go to my bed. Instead she'd led us down a long hall and then opened a door.

"Oh, Maura," I said. "How did you ever manage this?"

They had created a pub in what must have been some kind of a storage space behind the kitchen. But this was a dream pub. Polished wood walls. A stone floor. A floor-to-ceiling fireplace, cushioned benches along the wall, round tables with stools scattered across the floor and a carved bar that curved along the far side of the room. A wall of bright bottles behind it. With two shiny brass spigots. The whole thing would have seemed unreal, a stage set, if it wasn't for the crowd of people within it. No actors these. Locals. Farmers and sheepherders I'd say with their wives and children. Little kids too. All in their Sunday best. The men in suit coats. The women wearing woolen skirts and hand-knit jumpers. There was a circle of stools near the turf fire, and sitting in the middle was a fiddler.

"Now, Joseph," Maura said. "We're going to take you to the hidden Ireland. Beyond history and oppression. The deep-down real source."

The fiddler played us into another place outside of time. Maura pulled Ed and Joseph and me into the reels. I half remembered the steps from childhood celebrations in Granny Honora's parlor.

Maura and John's daughter claimed Joseph, grabbing his hands, crossing one over the other, his partner in reel after reel. Are we all possessed? I wondered. Had the fairies crept in from hollows in the dark mountains or from under the still, deep lakes? Invaded us. As good an explanation as any for Ed, who was leaping and ducking like a young boy. Laughing as I hadn't seen him do since before Ed Junior's death.

But at least the reels had borders. Set pieces, which the other dancers knew and through which they guided us. But all limits dissolved when Dominic O'Morian, Maura's brother, brought out his bodhrán. That round narrow drum covered in goatskin. Invented in time beyond memory. The dancers had been walking away from the reel toward the bar where John was pulling pints. Laughing, talking, glad for a break. Then the beat began. The rhythm was so intricate that we all stopped and turned. Two young men, fifteen or sixteen I'd say, and barefoot, moved to the center of the floor.

"Seán nós dancers," John said.

They didn't keep their bodies stiff in the style I associated with Irish dancing. They were completely supple and fluid. Swinging and dipping—shoulders and arms and hands moving together. And their feet! Slap, slap, slapping against the floor. Not exactly keeping time to the bodhrán's drumbeat but talking back, setting up a kind of counter beat, the dancers and the drummer communicating with each other. Expressing something beyond words. Beyond thought really. Some deep down reality every person in the room understood.

Ed said to me, "Like the Ojibwe." Here was something older even than language. I can't explain how but each one of us in that room was suddenly connected and almost compelled to form a circle around the dancers. Moving side to side, back and forth, imitating the dancers' steps. We went faster and faster and then joined arms, elbows pressed tight against the body on either side until we were a tight collar around the dancers. I don't know who started the chant. It was in Irish of course. One word repeated over and over. *"Saoirse. Saoirse. Saoirse."*

"It means free," I said to Ed. "Free. Free. Free."

Here we were in the very house that the Black and Tans had invaded, ransacked, where that sergeant's filthy hands had grabbed my shoulders, pulled down my dress. The oppressors had stood with their boots on our necks for eight hundred years. They were gone, gone, gone.

"Saoirse. Saoirse. Saoirse." Ed, Joseph, and I shouted along with the rest. If only Granny could be here, I thought, and I swear I heard a voice soft under the tumult "I am a *stór*, I am."

"Two women and a load of children in a currach? I heard that story as a boy told in the same breath as Finn McCool's building the Giant's Causeway," Dominic said. We were in Carna now and glad to have Maura's brother Dominic as our guide. Every person we passed in the street nodded at him. He was a O'Moran after all. A family well established in this village set on fingers of land that reached out into the bay. And Dominic was a handsome young man with a great smile.

He took us into the church that he said was dedicated to St. MacDara, where we lit candles at the altar. "I wonder did our granny come here," Ed said.

"This place is only recently built, but there was always some kind of a chapel here where she surely prayed."

He pointed out the coves and inlets carved into the coast.

"Your Keeleys lived across about three miles distant in Ard. No roads in those days. The only transport was by water. So a currach was life, not only for fishing but for any kind of contact with the neighbors. And so the story of two women who were such powerful rowers that they flew across the sea all the way to Amerikay was very appealing. Fanciful though it might be," Dominic told us.

"But the story is true," I said. "Our granny and Aunt Máire did escape with their children, our fathers among them."

"They flew across the sea?" Joseph said and laughed.

"My father told me that his mother had got them aboard a sailing ship," Ed said.

"They could have managed to get aboard," Dominic said. He pointed. "Just out near that small island named for St. MacDara, the sea meets the bay and sailing ships did slow down there. So it's possible they were taken on board."

"But, how could they even know a ship was coming?" Joseph asked.

"Well now," Dominic said, "in those days signal fires served the same purpose as telephones do today. Sometimes the coast would be lit up as far as Sligo when a vessel was coming. In the tale of the two women the ship had come from Derry. A winter passage to—"

"New Orleans," I said, really excited now. "Aunt Máire told me they landed there and that a Negro nun helped them. They were headed for Chicago and had to come up the Mississippi River to the I & M Canal." I looked at Ed. "Why didn't we listen more carefully to their stories?" I said.

"But what about when you came here twenty years ago. Why didn't you inquire?" Ed asked me.

It was Dominic who answered. "As I understand it Nora was running from the Black and Tans. Not much time for sightseeing or tracking down family legends."

"No," I said.

I'd spent my last night ever with Peter Keeley at Lough Inagh. My husband had died on a mountain that bordered the sea.

Dominic had arranged for us to meet Peter's brother in the pub that his family had owned for generations. It was called O'Morian's, of course—Moran's, in English.

"It was only a little shebeen where fishermen gathered for a nip on cold mornings," Dominic said. "But two years ago we built a proper structure. Kept it where it always had been, only yards from the church. Always have been great sessions here after Mass on Sunday. It was music kept us alive in the worst of times. Thank God a singer only needs a voice. Even the most rack-rent landlord never found a way to charge for the use of your own vocal cords."

I expected, hoped, I guess, that Peter's brother might resemble him, but this short squat man looked nothing at all like my tall wiry love. He had the same blue-gray eyes as Peter but the rest of his face had been scored by years of wind and rain. There were pouches under his eyes. Younger than Peter, he would be about sixty. There was a glass of whiskey in front of him on the bar but he was glad to accept Ed's offer of another drink.

"No bird ever flew on one wing," he said.

Dominic had told us that this man, James Keeley, had good English.

He waited until the bartender had poured him another whiskey then picked up both glasses and walked toward the corner of the bar where there was a small table and four stools. Joseph didn't follow.

"I'd like to take a look at one of those currachs," he said to Dominic. "After all I am a sailor."

"I'll be glad to show you," Dominic said.

So only Ed and I and James Keeley sat together. There was silence for a good few minutes then James drained his first drink and then the second.

"If you've come for the land, you'll have to show me some proof," he said.

"Pardon me," I said.

"Dominic tells me you claim to have been married to my oldest brother. A thing I find very hard to believe since he never spoke even a syllable to us about having a wife."

"He was protecting me," I said. "He was on the run. A wanted man. He was afraid if the English knew about our relationship they'd try to use me to get to him."

"Your relationship, is it?" James said. "Where are your documents? Don't think you're the first American who's come sniffing around here talking about family claims. It was your lot who deserted us and now that we finally have some little chance at making a go of it, you're back trying to take it away. My neighbor down the road was sued. Taken to the High Court by some distant cousin from Boston trying to get the land. You ran. You cannot come back and expect a big welcome and the keys of the kingdom turned over to you."

"Look, pal." Ed was mad. He never called anyone pal unless he planned to demolish them. "The last thing we'd do is trade Chicago for this place. My cousin came for a friendly visit and you insult her. Come on, Nora, let's go." He stood up.

"Wait. I only wanted to see Peter's hometown."

He nodded. Fair enough.

"And now you have," James Keeley said.

"For years I imagined visiting Peter's grave but . . ."

"His grave is out there." He pointed through the window out to the sea. "The fellow who shot him threw him over the cliff about five miles from here. The man who saw it happen came and told us."

"Was he called Cyril Peterson?" I asked.

Now James Keeley spoke directly to Ed. "I meant no offense. But while you were living the soft life in Amerikay we continued the struggle here. Ireland is still a poor country and none needier than Connemara. But we finally have a chance and so when so-called relatives appear, well, you understand why I have been a bit touchy." He turned to me. "Whatever you were to my brother I see you truly cared for him and you have my sympathy, but I suggest you go back to where you came from. I'll say goodbye. *Slán abhaile*. He stood up and left the pub."

Geeze Louise . . . families!

But Dominic had promised that he'd put the word out for information, and that night a man came to the hotel pub. Very late. Joseph and Ed were in bed. I half recognized him from the wild session of the night before. Younger than I was though. In his forties. So only a boy when Peter had been ambushed. But Dominic assured me that this man had been with the IRA in the mountains.

"I knew the professor surely," he said, lifting the Guinness Dominic set before him. "They pull a good pint here for all their airs and graces," he said to me. Dominic nodded and walked away from us to the far end of the bar. "And I saw him shot. Took us all by surprise. The gunman only a young student. He claimed to have a message for the professor from his wife that was also a shock because we didn't think the professor would have bothered with the women. A teacher through and through. And even in camp he held classes in Irish history and had us local lads try to teach the Dublin jackeens *an Gaeilge*. We had a spy in the Free State garrison to warn us if the army was on the move. Very suspicious we were. But this boy seemed harmless until he took out that pistol and fired at the professor." The man leaned forward. "Hit him square in the chest. As the man said, there are no bad shots at five yards' range. The professor had taken the student to the side and by the time the rest of us realized what had happened the fellow was dead and the professor was unconscious. Only Cyril Peterson was there. Said the professor got him."

"How could the gunman throw Peter's body into the sea if he'd been shot himself?"

"The sea? Our camp was right there on Derryclare Mountain. Nowhere near the sea."

"What? I was told Peter's body was lost in the ocean."

"You were told wrong," he said. But Maud and Peter's brother had both said the same thing. And then I realized they'd each gotten their information from Cyril Peterson.

"So what happened to Peter's body?"

"I don't know. I was sent out to see if the Free State army was coming. When I came back the professor's body was gone and so was the redheaded Dublin man, Cyril. I heard later he took the professor's body to Kylemore Abbey and they buried him in the graveyard there."

"Buried? A grave?"

"What I heard," he said.

Finally—Peter's resting place.

The next morning I told Ed that I was staying. He and Joseph were ready to leave at six a.m. so John O'Connor could get them to the airport by seven. Still more events in London and a dinner that night hosted by Adlai Stevenson, head of the US committee on the UN. I explained what the man last night had told me.

"And you believe him?" Ed said.

"I have to see," I said. "I've waited so long to kneel at Peter's grave, that if there's the slightest chance that he's in the Kylemore graveyard, I have to check. And I know some of those nuns. Today's Monday. The plane from London to Chicago doesn't leave until Tuesday night. I'll take the train to Dublin this afternoon, catch the night boat to London, and be there tomorrow morning."

"Alright, Nonie. I hope . . . I don't know what I hope." He reached into his pocket, took out some folded bills, and handed them to me. "Just be there Tuesday night by departure time."

13

KYLEMORE ABBEY

NOVEMBER 26, 1945

"Mother Abbess doesn't entertain random visitors," the nun said to me.

"But I know her," I said. "More than twenty years ago I came here and—"

"Twenty years!" she laughed. "Do you know how many Kylemore girls have passed through school in twenty years. Hundreds. Thousands. We are one of the top schools for young women in all the world. Our students come from Europe and America as well as every county in Ireland. I presume you are the mother of one of our alumna or the grandmother?"

"No, I'm not. But I must see Mother Columba."

"A spiritual crisis then? Father Brian is very understanding. He comes in for daily Mass so perhaps you'd like to attend the service tomorrow morning and then afterward—"

I interrupted her. "I have to see Mother Columba now." Why was this nun being so difficult? Maura had told me that she was a local girl who regarded her position as porteress as a license to control the abbey. The nuns were Benedictines and semi-cloistered, teaching the girls and supervising the dormitories where the boarders lived, but not seen out in the area.

The convent had quite a history. The Benedictines had been expelled from Ireland in the seventeenth century by Cromwell, as had all the Irish religious orders. The nuns had established themselves in Belgium, planning to come back to Ireland. It only took 250 years. In Belgium the school of Les Dames d'Irlandaise offered Irish women a chance for the education that was denied them in Ireland. For two centuries, no Catholic was allowed to attend school, and girls were especially deprived. The remnants of the old Gaelic aristocracy sent their daughters abroad to the sisters. Some of those girls had remained there as nuns.

A peaceful enough life until the Germans invaded Belgium during World War I and bombed the convent. These women, who had spent their lives in the cloister, found themselves walking thirty miles to safety. I'd heard the story when we'd escaped to the abbey after the Black and Tans attacked Lough Inagh Lodge. Brave women and good at business too. They'd raised enough money to buy this abandoned estate with its castle-like building and a miniature gothic church, built by the first owner as a tribute to his dead wife. The nuns had just opened the school when I'd been here. It seemed to have thrived. There was nothing ramshackle about the place now. The buildings had been restored and the lawns were green, even in November. The lake in the center reflected both the mountains and the castle.

"Sister," I said, lowering my voice and setting out each word. "I must see Mother now. It's a matter of life or death. Tell her Professor Keeley's wife is here and I'm not moving until she agrees to see me."

It didn't work. The nun only stared at me. "Good morning," she said and turned away.

"Please," I said. I couldn't keep my voice level, desperation breaking through. "At least speak to Mother. If she says no, I'll leave and never come back I promise."

"Are you in that much need?" she asked me.

"I am," I said.

"Alright. I thought you were another one of those Yanks who expects everyone to drop everything to accommodate them. But you do look a bit shattered."

"I am. You are my last hope. Please." She nodded. Gestured me toward a chair and left.

It was a good half hour before she returned. I found myself praying "please God" as I stared at a huge oil painting of the Sacred Heart. I'd never had any devotion to the Sacred Heart with its dripping blood and the vacant look on the face of Christ. But now I was imploring Him.

Finally, the nun stood before me. "Mother is in the church but she said I could bring you there. I'd say a bit of prayer would do you no harm."

Mother Columba seemed unchanged by the past twenty years. Not a wrinkle in the face framed by the white linen wimple and black veil. She turned to me and smiled. She has to be eighty, I thought. She was sitting in the first pew of the church, a miniature gothic cathedral with walls of green

Connemara marble and an altarpiece that showed Mary holding the Child Jesus. A more appealing picture than the Sacred Heart.

"Thank you, Sister," Mother said to the young nun, who seemed in no hurry to leave. But now she gave a quick bob of the head and walked out. Mother Columba gestured for me to join her in the pew and I sat down. A faint odor of rosewater from her habit.

"Good morning, Mother," I said. "I'm Nora Kelly."

"I know, my dear. How could I forget you? Maura O'Connor and I often reminisce about that great adventure. The two of you dressed in habits with that redheaded man in a cassock, marching right past the Black and Tans."

"It seems like a dream now or a scene from a movie," I said.

"Much quieter here now," she said. "Peace at last. To think the world went to war again. Horrifying. Many of our girls and past students suffered. I pray every day for those fathers and husbands, brothers and sons who served. Not all of them survived."

We both were silent for a moment.

"Mother," I said. "The redheaded man who was with us that night and dressed as a priest, Cyril Peterson, I was told he came here again."

"And who told you that?"

"A man who was at the IRA camp when the young man came there to avenge Michael Collins and . . ." I stopped because Mother Columba had turned her head away and closed her eyes.

"A terrible, terrible time. Brother fighting brother. Families torn apart. There was even division among the sisters. It was as if a kind of madness took over the entire country. It's best not to go back. Ireland has come to a kind of peace but the wounds are very close to the surface. I really can't tell you anything, my dear."

"But you have to. If Peter Keeley is buried here, at least tell me where. I'd given up the hope of finding his grave. I was told his body was never recovered from the sea. But I don't believe that's true . . ."

"Not in the sea," she said. Now Mother Columba opened her eyes and turned to me. "What are your intentions, my dear?"

"What do you mean? I just want to visit his grave. Perhaps have a Mass said here for him. Do something."

"But he is not buried in our graveyard."

"Where then?"

"I don't know. You see, he did not die here. He survived. We nursed him but as soon as he was able he left. He made us promise to tell no one that he was alive."

What? Alive! Peter had been alive?

"I don't understand."

"I don't think you know the true story of what happened. The professor told me and I think you should know, too. He was seriously wounded by that young man but he defended himself. He killed the fellow and was so full of guilt that he actually prayed to die. And when he didn't, when his strength returned, he said he would spend the rest of his life doing penance."

"Penance. Where did he go?"

"I don't know. Cyril Peterson drove him away but that was many years ago. The professor was not in good health, mind or body. I doubt if he is still alive."

"You're alive. I'm alive. Peter Keeley may be alive. I have to find him."

"Do you really think that's wise? Surely he would have written to you if he wanted you in his life. When we enter religion we sacrifice the past. Our families. The world. The only way to truly do God's will is to leave all distractions behind. That is the path I believe Professor Keeley chose. You must respect his choice. I suggest you return to America. That is where God has placed you. Acceptance is a great gift."

"I can't," I said. "I simply can't." Mother Columba shook her head.

"I fear you are opening yourself to a lot of suffering. Go home, Nora. There are things in Ireland that you will never understand. The Civil War almost destroyed us. We have finally begun to heal. Leave us to it, please."

I wanted to shout at her. Scream until my voice bounced against the green marble walls. I can't, I wanted to say. I can't. I'm going to find him dead or alive and God Himself can't stop me. Love is stronger than all your piety, Mother. I will not give up. I remembered Bridget, with her Ojibwe wisdom. Could Peter be alive?

"Peterson. A mother and son, and her husband was a docker. Died young. They lived in this building."

John O'Connor had driven me to the Galway train station that afternoon. One thing the British did leave Ireland was a decent railway system. I was in Dublin by 5:00 p.m. and walking up to this row of flats in the north side neighborhood that Cyril had taken me to all those years ago. There had been rubble in the street then left from the bombardment by British naval guns in response to the 1916 Rising.

The debris had been cleared away but the neighborhood still had that hardscrabble look I knew from areas of Chicago where the buildings seem to lean against each other. Sad and tired. The bricks darkened by soot. Cold out. The narrow street funneled the wind that battered me with a near-Chicago force as I stood in front of the door held half open by a woman with a black shawl draped over her head.

"And who are you to be asking?"

"A friend," I said. She laughed.

"Never heard of them having any Yank friends. Dublin people didn't go running to America like the culchies in the West did. Ma Peterson wouldn't have been shy about any connections. Would shatter your ear but she did have a good heart, God rest her soul."

"She's dead?"

"Of course she's dead! The woman lived until ninety. Isn't that enough to expect from anyone. Served her time did Ma Peterson."

"She went to prison?"

"What? She never—although the peelers did take her in a time or two. But that was when Cyril was on the run. They tried to get her to inform on her own son. Imagine. But then they tortured all of us. I remember as a young girl being turfed out by the soldiers. Said they were raiding the flats looking for fugitives. They knew right well that no fugitive would go home and hide with his own family. Just an excuse to make all of us stand outside, shivering in our nightclothes. Some of the children in nothing more than raggedy shirts. Wouldn't even let us get dressed but Ma Peterson would give out to them. After Independence, Cyril arranged to get a medal for her when he got his job in Government Buildings."

"So Cyril is an official?"

"Not sure official is the right word. What he does is give tours when folks come up from the country anxious to have a look at the Dáil. That's what we call the parliament. Renamed everything in Irish. Which is a bit difficult for the old ones who don't have a word of it. I studied the language in school so I have a few words. And I can spell 'Taoiseach,' but my mother still calls Dev the prime minister. So if you're looking for Cyril that's where you'll find him."

She started to close the door.

"You'll think I'm terribly rude not asking you in for a cup of tea but times are powerful hard. We thought if we got rid of the English we'd be away in a hack. But those British bastards are still acting the maggot. Not paying decent prices for Irish goods. Doing all kinds of underhanded things hoping the whole country will fall flat on its face. Read the *Irish Press*. You'll see."

I took out the wad of money Ed had given me and found a twenty-pound note and held it out to her. She stepped back.

"Christ on a crutch. Did you think I was begging?"

"Of course not. But please take this. Consider it an early Christmas gift." I put the note in her hand.

"Are you mad entirely?" she said. "This is twenty quid. A fortune. Do the Irish earn this kind of money in America? No wonder all the country people headed for the ships. What my brothers should have done. Too late now."

"Why? There's plenty of work, and soon there'll be visas available."

"Visas? They're both dead, love. One got shot fighting with Mick Collins and the other with Dev."

"Oh, I'm so sorry," I said, looking for more words.

"Doesn't bear thinking about. Between the wars and one thing and another most of the men were taken. Ah well, at least my mother and I will have a happy Christmas, thanks to you. Take care of yourself, love. And give our regards to Cyril if you meet him. Too much of a muckety-muck for his old neighbors. But sure, that's the way of the world. Always some people do well no matter what."

The desk clerk at the Gresham Hotel helped me send a telegram to Ed. "Remaining in Ireland. Please have American Airlines hold my ticket with an open date." But after I paid him, the clerk watched me recount the money I had left. "Best find a B and B, miss. Our rates wouldn't suit you," he said. I had five ten-shilling notes left. Two and one-half pounds, around $15.

Maud Gonne, I thought. She lived in a house on St. Stephen's Green. A long walk but possible though the cold had settled in now. Thank God for my coat. And even O'Connell Street was dark. Only a few dim streetlights. She'd lied to me but I'd decided she'd been a victim of Cyril's deception too. He was alive and in Dublin. In twelve hours I would be confronting him. Except when I knocked at the door of the house on St. Stephen's Green where Maud had lived, the maid who answered the door had never heard of Maud Gonne MacBride. She did allow me to step out of the night into the foyer. But that was as far as I got. The new owner made it clear he was not about to invite a strange woman into his house. No hard times here, I thought. Even though it was late in the evening he was dressed in a suit and a tie. Probably in his mid-fifties. Yes, he had purchased the house from Madam MacBride though he didn't know exactly where she lived. Somewhere out in the country he thought. And that was it. So much for Irish hospitality, I thought as I walked down the steps.

Ten o'clock now. No one on the street. The bulk of St. Stephen's Green looming across from me. I began walking. Wait. Here was the church Maud had taken me to. Administered by the Jesuits, I remembered, as a kind of chapel for the students at the university. I walked down the steps. Tried the door. Unlocked, thank God. I stepped in. Such a familiar space. The faint scent of incense. The rows of vigil lights, small dots of flame, and then the larger tabernacle light glowing behind red glass. I looked up. Another huge Sacred Heart. I went straight up to the stand of candles below the portrait. I'm giving you a chance, I said. Then stuck a ten-shilling note into the brass box attached to the stand and took the taper from the shelf under the candles, put it into a flame, and lit up a whole row of vigil lights. Alright, I prayed. If there's anybody up there at all you'd better get to work. I need some good news.

I sat down in a pew. Could I just sit here all night? Why not? Remind the Sacred Heart to get to work. I nodded off. Woke up stiff and uncomfortable. What the hell, I thought to myself and stretched out full length in the pew. At least I have my warm coat. I turned up the fur collar and fell asleep.

"Missus, please, wake up. Wake up." It was a young boy shaking my shoulder. I opened my eyes, sat up to see an altar boy and a priest. Both vested and ready for Mass.

"Good morning, Father," I said. "My name is Nora Kelly and I thank you for the use of your church."

"My dear woman, whatever possessed you to—"

"Money, Father. Or the lack of it. It's a long story," I began when I heard noise in the back of the church and realized his congregation was arriving. What is it about daily Mass? The same mix of about twenty women and older men here as at Mass at Holy Name every morning. Retired fellows starting the day at church rather than the office, and the women, well, women of all ages always had something to pray for.

The service was quick-paced just like in Chicago, and Father had the good manners to forego a sermon. No collection either. These people did not need any frills. They had their own lines to God and the saints, as the priest well knew. They were only asking him to provide a focus and to give them Communion.

I knelt on the cushion that padded the step under the altar rail.

"Corpus Christi," the priest said as he placed the host on my tongue.

"Amen," I said. Walked back to my pew. Knelt down and prayed. If there was anything at all in what I both believed and didn't believe, then surely somehow I'd find Cyril Person today. And he'd lead me to Peter Keeley. I'd pictured myself in a country churchyard laying a beautiful wreath of roses in front of a Celtic cross. I won't allow myself to imagine him alive and us together. False hope. False hope. But the Sacred Heart was staring at me. Why not believe in a miracle? What could I have to lose?

There Cyril stood in a uniform, no less. Dark green woolen jacket and trousers. Silver buttons up the front of him. He was at the bottom of a flight of marble steps that led from the lobby of this two-hundred-year-old mansion up to the parliamentary chambers. Twenty plus years since I'd seen Cyril. He must be seventy—more. His red hair was white now but he still reminded me of the early bird who catches the worm. His head moved in time with his words as he spoke to his tour group. Country people, as Peterson's neighbor had said. Most of them stared up at the vaulted ceiling, taking in the walls with their intricate molding, the tall windows and velvet draperies. This was a rich man's house that now belonged to them.

I stood out of sight in a kind of foyer across the lobby. I could hear every word. Cyril's lecture sounded like a vaudevillian's patter.

"Well now, I won't say welcome because this is your house now and you pay the salary of every single person who works in it. The TDs, the senators, the security people, the cleaners, and yours truly, Cyril Peterson present and accounted for, depend on you." He clicked his heels and threw back his shoulders. Before he'd become a revolutionary, Cyril had been a private in the British Army.

"Now you may wonder what a fellow with a name like mine is doing here in the Oireachtas. Well my father was an Englishman—I'll pause to let you nudge each other and roll your eyes—but remember Padraig Pearse's old dad served in the British Army so no one's perfect. Take for example where we're standing right now. Leinster House. The ducal palace of one of the grandest families in Ireland. Dripping with honors from the crown for centuries and yet who are they when they're at home? The Fitzgeralds. And stuffed to the gills with rebels. Anyone here ever hear of Silken Thomas?"

One man lifted his hand.

"Good on you, sir," Cyril said. "He led a revolt against that fat heretic Henry VIII and Thomas wasn't twenty years old. But even then he had a bit of a flair. His fighters wore fringe on their helmets and so they called him Silken Thomas. All of them young, but then our 1916 men were not much older. But here's the interesting part about Silken Thomas. The Fitzgeralds and the Tudors were cousins. Strange isn't it but as you know their name means son of Gerald. The great-great, well many greats, grandfather of Thomas came to England with William the Conqueror way back in the eleventh century. The Normans, who were really Vikings, had acquired a bit of polish in France. This Gerald took over Wales and married a Welsh princess, a Tudor. And had a lot of children. Sent one of his younger sons across the water to us and he proceeded to marry the daughter of an Irish chieftain. But she was a strong woman and made a proper Irishman of him. The sons followed the mother until the English complained that all the fellows they sent over to conquer Ireland were conquered themselves.

"More Irish than the Irish. After a few generations the Fitzgeralds didn't even speak the same language as the Sassenach. Wrote poetry *an Gaeilge* but they were clever and learned to stay in with the Brits after what happened to Thomas. He'd been lured into peace talks in London only to be hanged, drawn and quartered with five of his uncles. That'll teach him, the Brits thought, and if the rest of the clan wanted to keep their land and titles and money they had better take the soup. And as you can see from this place they got a hell of a lot more than soup. Ah well, the rich get richer. They were the lords of Kildare, the dukes of Leinster. But by the start of the eighteenth century there were Fitzgeralds scattered all over the country. Most of them without titles but true to their Catholic faith. Decent altogether."

The man who'd raised his hand spoke. "I'm from Limerick. Lots of Fitzgeralds in Brue, but most of them in the States now. They went to Boston and doing alright for themselves. Though they were far from rich when they left."

"All from the same clan though," Cyril said. "But the family fell on hard times. Had to sell off Leinster House more than a hundred years ago. The Royal Dublin Society bought the place and used to hold their big horse show right out on the lawns. All those ride-to-the-hounds Protestants jumping over hurdles on their horses outside and drinking Pimm's Cup No. 1 never imagined that one day we Fenians would own the whole shebang and culchies like you would be tripping across the marble floors and attending our very own parliament and senate renamed the Dáil and the Seanad. That would have given Silken Thomas a good laugh, thank you very much. I'll be turning you over to my colleague now who will take you into the chambers, but first I'd like you to raise your eyes and take in that portrait just above the staircase. A grand lady but nothing to do with the Fitzgeralds. That's Countess Constance Markievicz herself and I'm sure you know her."

The portrait was of Con alright but as a young woman in a full-length ball gown, a tiara on her piled-up hair. I'd met her a good ten years later when she wore the uniform of the Irish Citizen Army that she'd designed for herself, complete with a slouch hat and a holstered pistol at her waist.

"You wouldn't think to look at her that she commanded a combat unit in St. Stephen's Green during the Easter Rising," Cyril said. "But then the best of the toffs landed on our side. Look up Yeats's poem about the countess and her sister, the Booth-Gore girls, 'One beautiful, one a gazelle.' Now, on your way and be sure to have my colleague here point out the framed copy of the Proclamation at the top of the stairs. 'Irish men and Irish women.' The countess was only one of loads of women fighting to free Ireland as that American lady who's trying to hide herself across the way could tell you."

He pointed over at me. Of course the whole crowd looked over. I smiled and half waved but the other tour guide was not about to let them linger and he started the group up the marble steps as Cyril walked over to me.

"So did you enjoy my performance, Nora?" he asked. Bold as brass as if we'd met two days ago. Before I could say anything he went on. "A little heavy on the Fitzgeralds maybe, but it's important for people who still remember what it was like to be terrorized by some landlord to realize that they own the big house now."

"It is a beautiful place," I said.

"The Fitzgeralds had taste. A classy bunch." And I thought to myself that I must write a note to young John Fitzgerald Kennedy, remind him that the grandfather he was named for connected him to a heritage more profound than Honey Fitz singing "Sweet Adeline." Jack would like Silken Thomas.

"And now what do I do with you," Cyril said. "I suppose I always expected you to appear some time full of questions and queries since you never were able to let sleeping dogs lie."

"If you mean exposing the lies you told me and everyone else about Peter Keeley—" I began.

"Would you ever keep your voice down. These marble floors are whores for echoes." I noticed that two men in uniform had entered the lobby and were looking over at us.

"Come along," he said. "Nobody in the Members' Dining Room this early. I take my break at eleven o'clock anyway. How about a cup of tea and a scone to go with the story."

"Story? I'm not here for a story. I want answers. First of all is Peter Keeley alive?"

"As to that I couldn't say. And I ask you to please modulate your tone. Come on."

"I'd prefer coffee," I said after Cyril had settled us down in a corner of the wood-paneled room that had once been the scene of fancy dinner parties. Had the Royal Dublin Society met here to plan their horse show? A teapot and a plate of scones had been set in front of us by an older woman in a black skirt and white blouse who'd smiled but said nothing.

"Coffee? We haven't been infected that way yet. But I believe they serve the stuff at Bewley's on Grafton Street. For some reason Quakers like coffee. But here." He poured the tea into my cup. "Put plenty of sugar and milk in there. Helps with the shock."

"Tell me right now."

"Hold on, Nora. Hold on. Take a good drink and bite off a chunk of that scone. You look like you could use something."

All I'd eaten since yesterday were the sandwiches Maura made for me to take on the train. The scone did taste good. I tried to take dismissive bites but ended up chomping the whole thing down. Cyril picked up another scone and set it on my plate. I ate the second one more slowly. Drank half the tea, took a breath, and said, "First of all, you stood in my apartment in Paris and lied to me when you told me Peter Keeley was dead. You broke my heart, destroyed my soul, all for nothing."

"I saved you, Nora, and the professor too."

"Bullshit."

"Whisht, whisht," he said. "The ladies will be setting up for lunch soon and they're very proper altogether."

I leaned toward him. "You tell me what happened or I'll grab you by the lapels of that uniform of yours and shake it out of you."

"Dear God, Nora Kelly, you must be over sixty years of age and still giving in to the fiery temperament. Just listen to me. Obviously you know some of the—"

"Mother Columba told me you brought Peter to the abbey and he was alive."

"Barely. The bullet had gone right through him but it hit an artery and he was losing so much blood there seemed little hope. Still he was luckier than the young lad who shot him. He died on the spot."

"And Peter . . . Peter killed him?"

"Not deliberately, as I said to the professor more times than I can count. After the boy fired, the professor went to grab the gun. I don't think he even realized that he was wounded. Now I think there is a good chance the lad turned the gun on himself but the professor was convinced that he had forced the trigger down. The bullet went right to the boy's heart."

"But surely Peter acted in self-defense."

"As I told him, but remember he knew the gunman. Young McCarthy was one of his own students. A boy he liked."

"Yes, I knew him too. A good kid but passionate about politics."

"And devoted to Mick Collins. Though why he decided to take it out on the professor . . . Well I suppose he was an easy target."

"Because he could," I said. "He knew Peter would welcome him."

Getting closer to lunchtime because the woman who'd served us had been joined by three other waitresses who were setting the tables with silver and china. Maybe the mark of a successful revolution is a certain level of comfort. More of the members of the Dáil and Seanad were walking in, chatting, laughing. These fellows had taken up arms against the most powerful empire in the world and beaten it. I'd heard Michael Collins himself say that when the British offered a ceasefire in 1922, the IRA had run out of ammunition. Never more than a few thousand fighters on the Irish side, pitted against thirty thousand British soldiers in Ireland, plus the brutal Black and Tans.

I watched as the politicians, former fighters many of them, pulled out chairs, and settled down at the tables. A confident, well-fed bunch.

"Let the dead bury the dead, Nora," Cyril said.

"Except Peter Keeley may not be dead."

There, I'd said it.

"You're jumping to conclusions, Nora. I haven't said that. One thing is sure, young McCarthy is gone. I was one of the men drove his body down to Cork. Left it at the door of his family's house. But did the deed with respect. Put him on a board, covered him with a woven blanket, washed the blood from his face, left him looking just as he should for his poor mother. Pinned a note to his jacket saying he'd been a civilian casualty caught in a gun battle between the Free State Army and the IRA."

"And his family believed that?"

He shook his head no.

"The problem was that his father was an important man. Not a politician himself but one of those boys in the know, calling the shots, choosing candidates."

"Pat Nash," I said.

"That wasn't his name. I told you he was called McCarthy. Lots of McCarthys in Cork and I'm not about to tell you which one he was, but he was determined to avenge his son and it didn't take him long to track down the boy's movements. Came to Connemara and put out the word that there was money available to anyone with information. Well, Nora, I don't need to lay out chapter and verse. Ireland's curse is the informer. The father discovered that Professor Keeley had killed his son, and the informer didn't bother to mention self-defense. But he did have the good sense to tell him the professor was dead. Soon after that the Civil War was over. We all kissed and made up. But Mr. McCarthy went to Dev himself, who had his own gaggle of spies. We had to get the professor out of the country. Couldn't send him to England because the British would have arrested him. I'm not saying where he went."

"Was it Rome?" I asked him.

What had Father Leonard said about the Irish scholar at the Vatican Library? Suddenly I was sure Peter had landed in the library.

"What are you quizzing me for if you know? I'm not saying I agree with you."

"Goddamn it, Cyril."

"Language, Nora. You're in the seat of the Irish government. And as Dev has made it clear we are a very moral and Catholic country. But the good thing about the Church is there are always some priests who don't care to take orders from a man who couldn't take orders himself if you get my meaning." He laughed. "Your professor should have gone ahead and become a priest when he was young. Saved himself a lot of trouble."

"So that's what I was? A lot of trouble?"

"Women complicate things," Cyril said. "I had me ma and she was enough for me."

Now the dining room had filled up and our waitress came over. "Better skedaddle, Cyril, before somebody objects to the lower orders invading the place," she said and pointed. And there were a few heads turned in our direction. Still some upstairs downstairs divisions, I guessed.

"Back to work," Cyril said to me, standing up.

"What? But you haven't told me if Peter is alive."

"You weren't listening, Nora. I told you I didn't know."

"But surely you were in touch with him."

"Why? He got out of the country with a clean pair of heels. My part was done."

"But that was more than twenty years ago. At least tell me if he died in Rome."

But Cyril took my coat from the back of my chair and started walking out of the dining room with me following behind him.

"Dear God, is that Nora Kelly?" a voice said. I turned. Seán MacBride. "Lunching with Cyril Peterson are you?" MacBride said. "No better man."

"Just having a cup of tea, Seán," Cyril said.

"Don't apologize to me. I'm not a member either. At least not yet. You wouldn't know this, Nora, but I've started my own political party. In fact I could use some advice from your mayor. Ed Kelly seems quite a vote getter. Dev still talks fondly of Chicago. Collected more money there than any place else in America."

He looked over my shoulder. "So where's the rest of your delegation?"

"No delegation. Just me. Ed went back to London. They're all flying home tomorrow."

"So, are you catching the night boat?"

"I'm not leaving 'til I get some answers. You lied to me, Seán. Cyril told me that Peter wasn't killed."

Seán looked at Cyril.

"I tried to explain to her that those were bad times."

"I'm not talking about twenty years ago. I saw Seán three years ago in Derry."

"Derry?" Cyril said. "You were stirring up things in the North, Seán?"

"I was working for the Taoiseach. When I met Nora there she was escorting the First Lady of the United States. Was hardly the time to talk about old mysteries."

"Seán, I've known you since you were ten years old. Your mother told me that Peter Keeley was lying at the bottom of the sea. Now he may be alive. I have a right to know if my husband—"

"Husband? Isn't that a bit fanciful, Nora?" Seán said.

"We were married in the chapel of the Irish College in Paris. I admit we never had a chance to register our marriage civilly but . . . Why am I explaining all this to you? You're the ones owe me."

My voice was getting louder.

"Easy there," Cyril said and took my arm.

"Don't you dare tell me to calm down," I said. "You'd better come with us, Seán," I said, "or I'll start screaming. Don't think I won't."

Seán took my other arm and waved over his shoulder, as if assuring the other diners that this crazy woman would not disturb their lunch. The two men more or less marched me down the stairs to the lobby and then out to the courtyard.

"Here, you'd better put your coat on. Donegal tweed. Fur collar. Lovely," Cyril said, draping it over my shoulders. "There, now you look the part of a rich American lady. Why don't you just go back into your life and leave well enough alone?"

"Nora, none of us can afford to look back. When I saw you in Derry I assumed you'd had a husband in Chicago. Children even," Sean said.

"You assumed wrong, Seán," I said.

He went on not paying a bit of attention to me.

"I have a suggestion. I can arrange a flight for you to London now. Meet the rest of your delegation and fly back with them to Chicago this evening."

"Where is de Valera's office? I'll go and pound on his door and don't think I won't. Surely he knows something."

"Alright," Seán said. "I'll take you to my mother. I'd like you to meet my wife and children anyway. I've become respectable, Nora. A family man. A solicitor."

"Pull the other one, Seán," Cyril said.

"What the hell do you mean? If you're passing gossip on about me, you'll regret it," Seán said to Cyril.

"Jesus, Seán, I just meant you're still defending the rebels. Your private life is your own business and I can well see how it would be handy to have your secretary living in your house, if your wife doesn't mind. And why not add that French girl? After all you need a translator I suppose."

"That's enough from you, Cyril," Seán said.

Seán turned to me.

"I'll drive you out to Roebuck House. You can have lunch with Madam and I'll pick you up at two. Fly to London then onto Amerikay. For the best."

"Not until I get some answers," I said.

"My mother knows quite a bit. She always has," Seán said.

Maud's relationship with her son and daughter, Iseult, had never been easy and so I wasn't surprised when Seán dropped me off in front of the big red house outside of Dublin and drove away.

14

"When you are old and grey and full of sleep and nodding by the fire," Yeats had written about Maud Gonne, imagining her sitting alone, her face furrowed but still beautiful, finally able to appreciate the devotion of the man who'd loved her not, as so many others had, for her golden hair but for her pilgrim soul. She would be at rest longing for him. But now Yeats was dead and rather than being full of sleep, Maud seemed to be overseeing, well . . .

"A mad house," she said, as we walked through the entry hall of Roebuck House. Maud's household had always been full of people coming and going. But whether in Paris, the villa in Normandy, or the house in Stephen's Green she'd always managed to live in the best neighborhoods. And now here she was in Dublin's most expensive suburb with this mansion on an acre of land.

"Quite a house," I said.

"It belonged to John MacBride. Though I never did find out where he got the money to buy it. He left it to Seán and there's room for all of us. Dagda!" she shouted.

An Irish wolfhound came rushing at us. He was huge, barking his head off, with a gray shaggy coat and hair coming down over his eyes. He's going to knock me down, I thought. I'll hit my head on the slate floor and that will be that. Maud was still a tall woman but thin and frail. She reached for the dog's collar, but I knew there was no chance she could hold him. I turned.

"Don't show fear," she said. "Tiernan," she shouted. "Come and get the dog."

The boy who ran into the hall could only have been Seán MacBride's son. He had the same dark hair and eyes and Maud's high cheekbones. He tackled the dog, holding him around the neck.

"Sit," he said. "Sit." And the big wolfhound obeyed.

"Now take Dagda out to the garden, please, and come in and join us for lunch, so you can get to know Nora," Maud said and turned to me.

"Tiernan is fifteen and very interested in America. His school is on holidays now and he's using his time to do research on your country, he told me."

"I'm happy to meet you," Tiernan said, "but I can't stay for lunch, Madam. I'm going to the cinema this afternoon. Mother said I could."

"I hope it's something uplifting," she said.

"Well it does have the word 'tall' in the title."

"Isn't that one of John Wayne's? I saw it last year. It's very inspiring," I said to Maud. "All about tenants standing up to evil landlords."

Maud smiled. "That's fine. No reason why cinema can't be artistic and used as a tool to rally the people against injustice. When Alice Milligan, Eithne Carbery, and I toured Donegal during the centenary of 1798, we'd put on performances, entertain the people with patriotic songs. Much better than making political speeches."

"Well, this movie is rousing," I said.

"A gunfight?" Tiernan asked me.

"Many of them," I said.

"Good," he said and snapped his fingers.

The dog followed him out.

"A very commanding young man," I said. "He could make his own movies one day."

"I am blessed with my grandchildren. See that statue up there?"

She pointed to a carved wooden figure about three feet tall on the shelf above us.

"That's the Blessed Mother," Maud said. "Iseult's son, Ian Stuart, has been studying wood carving with the monks at Glenstal Abbey. He's only nineteen but he's going to be a great sculptor. He'll fill the churches of Ireland with the best of modern art. The girls are clever too. Seán's daughter, Anna, is like her mother, Catalina. Strange name that. She was born in Argentina of Irish parents. We call her Kid."

We had moved from the hallway into a room where a turf fire was burning and two chairs were drawn up on each side of the hearth. But Maud didn't sit down. She walked to the window and gestured for me to join her. She pointed to a cluster of outbuildings.

"I set up workshops," she said. "We made jam, knit sweaters. It gave work to the widows in Dublin. We had to stop during the war. I suppose I should start it up again but . . ." She turned to me and smiled. "Not sure I have the energy," she said. Crossed over to the chair and sat down. I took the other chair.

I knew she was more than ten years older than me. So what age was she? Seventy-five? Eighty? She still wore black as she had since John MacBride had been executed in 1916. Though I'd been in Paris during their bitter divorce.

"I'm sorry Seán didn't join us," Maud said. "But he and Kid, well, the curse continues. Difficult marriages all around."

I knew the story of the priest who'd cursed one of her ancestors who'd stolen church land. No Gonne would have a happy marriage.

"You remember Iseult's husband?"

"Oh yes," I said. I'd been in Dublin when Iseult had run away from Francis Stuart to Maud. "A self-important bully," I said.

"Did you know that he worked for the Nazis during the war?" Maud said.

"I didn't," I said.

"He wrote scripts that were broadcast to Ireland and then had the nerve to send a German spy to my house. A man named Hermann Goertz. Parachuted into the country. Knocked on my door claiming that Hitler was willing to send troops so that we could unite the North and the South. Didn't mention that the Nazis would then be running the whole country. Well, Iseult fell for him. Hid him in the country but then didn't she take him shopping at Brown Thomas. He had wads of counterfeit American dollars that had been issued to him. Well, the clerks took one look at the money and they were both arrested. Iseult spent a month in jail. After the war the Americans took custody of Goertz. Killed himself right on the spot standing in front of an American colonel. Iseult was shattered. That girl has never made a wise decision about men in her life."

"But then she did have a hard time when she was growing up," I said, remembering the young girl with the flower face who had to pretend she was Maud's cousin.

"I suppose I should have acknowledged her. But if I'd admitted that I had an illegitimate child it would have destroyed my reputation."

"And then Iseult's own baby daughter died," I said.

"As my poor little George did. I suppose that's one thing she and I have in common. But, Nora, my grandchildren are bringing me nothing but joy. I feel the best of me, of John MacBride, of Millevoy, is being passed down through the generations. And all of them thriving in a free Ireland. They have never lived under English oppression. Think of it. Where we are right now is no longer Kingstown. No longer carries the brand of imperialism. This is Dun Laoghaire. Named for our own Irish hero. And my grandchildren take liberty for granted."

"You're a lucky woman," I said. "I wish . . ." I stopped. Maud reached over and patted my hand.

"It is too bad you and Peter Keeley never had a child. All his intelligence lost to the world. Though there was some talk that he and an Italian woman . . ."

I stood up. "What?"

Maud looked up at me.

"When he was in Rome. Isn't that why you've come? To hear that part of the story?" She stood up. "Kid should have lunch ready now. Let's eat and then—"

"Stop," I said. "You lied to me. You all said Peter was dead and he was alive!"

"What's happening? Are you alright, Madam? Who is this woman?"

"I'm fine, Kid," Maud said. I hardly registered the woman who had come into the room. Short, sturdy. Seán's wife, I supposed. In her forties. Two younger women stood behind her, next to them a girl of about thirteen. Maud's granddaughter? Seán's wife came up to me and took me by the shoulders.

"You cannot upset Madam. She is not strong and she has eaten nothing today," she said.

She let go of me, crossed over to Maud, and took her arm. "Come," she said. "Your favorite dish, Boeuf Bourguignon, is ready." She looked back at me. "I think it's time for you to leave. I'll have no shouting in this house. Show her out, Hannah," she said.

Still another woman dressed in a black dress with a white apron came in. The cook, I supposed. Odd to ask a servant to do the actual throwing out in a house of revolutionaries. She stepped away from the group and said to me, "Better if you went quietly, Miss."

"I am not leaving," I said.

Not shouting but loud and firm. Women who should be my sisters-in-arms were pushing me away. Why? What secret were they hiding?

"Enough," Maud said. "I'll tell you everything you need to know about Peter Keeley but we must eat first."

I let myself be led into the dining room. The food did smell good and the scones I'd had were many hours away. I remembered Maud's cook Josie from my visits to the Paris apartment and Maud's villa in Normandy.

Look at them, I thought, as we sat ourselves around the table. Six women connected to each other by one man. Spokes of a wheel with him at the center. Hannah filled our plates. More like Irish stew than Boeuf Bourguignon, but delicious. I might as well listen to Maud's news on a full stomach.

"I don't know why you can't forget about the professor. After all you've escaped the usual fate of women. Your life doesn't depend upon a man. Look at us," Maud said, pointing around the circle. "Each one of us talented and intelligent and yet Seán . . ."

She stopped.

"I must say I was thinking the same thing," I said. "You're his mother, Kid is his wife, Anna is his daughter, and two secretaries? A lot of support for one man."

"But that's what men expect," Maud said. "Willie Yeats's love for me didn't stop him from marrying a woman who would take care of him. He continued to have other women in his life all the way up to the day of his death. His wife and mistress were at his bedside." Maud laughed. "I guess we just have to accept that the male essence is different than the female. No wonder it takes so many of us to nurture them."

But Kid was not smiling. Nor was her daughter Anna. Maud leaned forward, her forearms on the table, speaking in the same voice she used to lecture crowds.

"You have to understand, Nora. Dev betrayed us. After all we women did to win Ireland's independence, when the constitution was written we were ordered out of public life. We could vote alright. Even hold office but by law our life was to be in the home. We were wives and mothers full stop. Our identity depended upon the man we married, or the son we bore. Surely you heard about the infamous Article 41.2," she said. "The one that restricted women to the home."

"I didn't," I said. "I was always proud that the 1916 Declaration was addressed to Irishmen and Irishwomen and that universal suffrage was granted in Ireland years before America agreed that women could vote."

But Kid said, "Once a government was established they forgot all about us."

"Kid was a fierce warrior," Maud said. "She spent time in jail just as Seán and I did. But now . . ."

"It was the priests," Kid said. "Archbishop McQuaid and that Jesuit. They were obsessed with 'woman's role.' Always quoting the encyclical the pope wrote about women. They were terrified of us. What can you expect? They live in their own world where all authority is male. Not even a wife to make them catch themselves on, only nuns and housekeepers hanging on their every word." Kid shook her head.

"It was even worse than that," Maud said. "Do you remember in Paris there were two kinds of priests at the Irish College? Some were inspired by equality and fraternity but the others were reliving the reign of terror. Ultra conservative, wishing that France had a king again."

"I do. I know that Father Kevin got in trouble for working with the poor and befriending women like you and me," I said.

"He was a good friend. And there are still some priests like him in Ireland but something happens to men when they get power. The Church is no longer beleaguered. The bishops have become as arrogant as the landlords were. And our constitution is based in that kind of reactionary religion. It's against the law for a married woman to teach, work in the civil service, or do any job a man would fancy. Oh we can still be charwomen and cooks and nannies but if you graduate from university and get a well-paying job, when you marry you must give up your post."

"That's terrible," I said. "And that's the law?"

"It is," Maud said. "Which is why I'm telling you that you're lucky to be free of entanglements. Look at us. The money we live on comes from my mother's inheritance and yet I can't spend a penny without Seán's approval." She shrugged.

"And it's not as if the State helps women and children. They should make some kind of payment to the mothers if they value them so highly, but they don't," Kid said.

"Do you know," Maud said, "a bishop actually wrote a letter to the women in his diocese, forbidding them to wear mannish clothes. No trousers. When I think of Queen Maeve and Grace O'Malley and all the other women we celebrated in those early days. It was a way to hearten the Irish people and it worked. You saw it, Nora. My Dublin slum children doing Irish dancing, playing the bodhrán and telling the ancient stories of warrior queens and now . . ."

She leaned across the table and took my hand. "You live on your own, don't you?"

"I do."

"Earn your own living."

"Yes."

"Go where you want, when you want."

"Right."

"Then why would you want to tie yourself to an old man who wants nothing to do with you now?"

Tie myself? Now!

"So Peter Keeley is alive," I said. "And you know where he is."

"I didn't when I saw you with Dev. Cyril lied to me too. I found out Peter was in the Vatican only last year from an Irish diplomat. But he left Rome and has buried himself in a monastery in Donegal."

"He became a priest?"

"He never was ordained. Probably too old, but a member of a monastic community, Nora, living out the last days of his life. Go home. Leave him alone. Be glad you live in a country with someone like Eleanor Roosevelt where women don't have to quit their jobs when they get married."

"Ah well, Maud, now that the men have come back they're taking back their old jobs. Maybe there are no laws but, believe me, many in America would prefer that women stay in the kitchen too. I must see Peter. Even if he rejects me. I'll risk it."

Alive, I thought. Alive! We could go back to Paris. Begin again.

It took me all day to get from Dublin to this part of Donegal on a bus that followed the border between the North of Ireland and the South. Not taking a direct route but going all the way west to Sligo and then up through Donegal Town, Letterkenny, and out here on the Inishowen Peninsula only five miles from the city of Derry but isolated and rural. Córas Iompair Eireann (CIE), the government-run bus company, did not travel through occupied Ulster, I'd been told at the bus station in Dublin.

I'd wanted to start out as soon as Maud told me where Peter Keeley was living, but no buses left until the next morning. So I'd stayed the night at Roebuck House.

I'd given up being mad at Maud. The more I found out about the family the more I realized how chaotic her life had been. Both of her adult children had been jailed not only during the Civil War but also in the years after. Seán came to dinner and told me that Dev had ordered the execution of some of their old IRA comrades.

"And yet you want to serve in the Dáil," I'd said.

"I do," he'd answered me. "We have to stop killing each other."

We'd sat up until well after midnight.

"At least there'll be no raids tonight," Maud had said, as she led me up to what had been a maid's room on the top floor of the house. When I'd stayed the night with Maud at the St. Stephen's Green house twenty-five years before, the British Army had forced their way in and wrecked the place entirely. At least they weren't going to batter down the door again, I thought, as Maud tried to explain to me the twists and turns Irish politics had taken since 1923. I began to understand why Peter might have chosen to hide away in the monastery. But why not be honest? Why not write and tell me what life he had chosen? Why let me believe he was dead for all these years?

It wasn't quite four when I arrived at the monastery. Getting dark but the abbot received me. He was a youngish man, under fifty I'd say, sandy hair, slight, wearing the Benedictine monk's habit. The monk who'd answered the door and led me to the abbot had told me this foundation had connections with the nuns at Kylemore Abbey. Their order, too, had been driven out of Ireland, but the community had built their new home in modern style. No gothic arches. No vaulted ceilings. The building was round, built to echo the ruins of the ancient fort above, the Grianán Aileach. I remembered the Benedictine priest who had been chaplain to the Marines.

"Is Father Matthew here?" I'd asked the young monk.

"In America now," he'd said.

"I would like to see Peter Keeley. Now," I said to the abbot. We were seated in the reception room. Very spare, wooden floors and benches. No armchair or turf fire.

"I'm not sure if he should be disturbed," the abbot said. "He only arrived a few months ago. I don't know how the professor managed to get here from Italy but he was at our door one morning, unannounced, much like yourself. He had a letter from a Vatican official, an Irishman, and so—"

"I don't care how he got here or when he got here. I insist that you take me to him right now."

I walked past the abbot and stood at the door that I assumed led to the cloister. "Do you want me to go up and down the halls shouting Peter Keeley's name?"

"He doesn't live in this building. We have a small cottage on the hill next to the Grianán that we use as a kind of hermitage. Professor Keeley asked to live there and, well Miss Kelly, as he said himself he wouldn't be needing it for very long."

"What do you mean? Is he sick?"

"Well," Father Abbot started, and stopped.

"I don't care. He's alive now. I'm going to see him right this minute."

"But it's nearly dark and the climb up the hill can be dangerous."

"Give me a flashlight, Father, and get out of my way," I said.

He finally handed me a metal lantern with glass sides and a candle at the center. The abbot offered to come with me if I was willing to wait until after Vespers, which I was not. The sun had fallen into the sea at the western horizon but still lit the stone wall of the ancient fort above us. There was a light in the cottage window next to it. I forget sometimes that I'm sixty-five years old but my legs remember, and after ten minutes of walking up that steep hill I almost turned around.

There must have been a window open in the monastery chapel because I could hear the monks chanting. Go back, I thought to myself. Wait for the abbot. That would be the sensible thing to do. Peter's alive, I answered myself. He's alive and there's a light in his window. I persisted. Right foot, left foot, as the sun's light disappeared and the narrow path became more difficult to see.

By the time I reached the top, the fort itself was only a hulking shape in the dark. But as I approached the cottage, I saw that the door was open and a man was standing there.

"I've been watching you climb. You walk like a young woman, Nora." Peter Keeley. Dear God, it was Peter Keeley!

"Come in," he said, just like that. As if I were his neighbor stopping by for a cup of tea. "Come in," he said again.

I reached out, to what? Not embrace him but at least touch his arm. He was leaning on a gnarled stick—a blackthorn shillelagh. He gestured me into the small front room of the cottage. A turf fire burned in the hearth with chairs in front of it and a small table piled with papers.

"Would you like a cup of tea?" Peter said. Lines in his face. He'd aged, no question, but not coughing or obviously ill. Old, but then so was I. A spurt of anger went through me.

"A cup of tea? No, I don't want a cup of tea. I want an explanation."

He limped into the room. I followed him. I saw a sink with a pump and next to it a kind of camp stove with a kettle on one of the burners.

Peter leaned against the sink, picked up the kettle, and filled it with water from the pump. Still some strength in those arms.

"There's part of a loaf of brown bread wrapped up in that tin. I've got butter on the windowsill and a few bits of cheese. The knife is there," he said.

"You want me to slice the loaf? Butter the bread? Me?" I started to laugh. Maud was right. Even a hermit would cede housekeeping duties to the first woman to appear.

"That's better, Nora," he said. "You always had a great laugh and a sense of the absurd."

"Oh Peter, Peter, where have you been?"

"Lost, my dear, lost."

And suddenly, there he was, the Peter I had known all those years ago. The shy scholar I had . . . say it, Nora. Seduced. Surely there was a better word for what had happened between us. Maybe some Irish phrase that means "leading your partner into sensual pleasure to which he happily responds"? I opened my arms, stepped forward, embraced him. "You're found now, Peter," I said.

Peter stood very still, patted my shoulder, leaning on his shillelagh. He moved away from me.

Easy, Nonie, I thought. Give him time.

Peter gestured again toward the tin and the knife.

While he brewed the tea, I served up supper. We carried our plates over to the chairs by the fire. The wheaten bread was good. Moist and dense and the cheese was delicious.

"All made here by the monks," Peter said.

"And are you one too? A monk?" Maud had said he'd never been ordained but maybe he was some kind of a lay brother.

"I'm not. Father Abbot calls me a sojourner. Very kind of him to let me stay here. I wanted to come home. 'Better to die 'neath an Irish sky.'"

"What is it? Cancer? TB? Should you be in a hospital? You don't look like a dying man."

"But then we're all of us dying."

"No philosophy, Peter. I want answers. Straight-from-the-shoulder answers."

Now he laughed. "Always the American, Nora. I've had two heart attacks and the doctor tells me another one could happen at any time. And there's the gimpy leg."

"What's the prognosis?"

"Drink your tea, Nora. I've already lived longer than my father or any of my uncles."

"Your brother seemed healthy enough to me. And don't tell me he doesn't know you're up here."

"He doesn't, Nora. Simpler that way."

"Very selfish of you, Peter Keeley. To turn your back on those who love you."

"Oh Nora, how can I explain?"

"You'd better start."

"Where can I begin?"

"Alright . . . I know about McCarthy's attack on you and, well . . ."

"I killed him, Nora. Shot a nineteen-year-old boy. My own student."

"Because he . . . ?"

"It doesn't matter. I lived and he died. At the time I wished it was reversed but Mother Columba said God had spared me for a reason. At first I couldn't listen to her. But she kept telling me that such a miraculous survival meant that I had a purpose."

"How *did* you survive?" I asked.

"He aimed at my heart. Stood only a few feet away but the closeness saved me. The velocity of the bullet carried it right through my chest. It missed any vital organ. I didn't feel anything. I grabbed for the gun and then . . . I must have fainted because I came to in Kylemore Abbey. Mother Columba said I would have drowned in my own blood if someone, Cyril I suppose, hadn't plugged up the wound. I felt what had happened to me was happening to Ireland. We were drowning in our own blood. I wanted to somehow atone."

He stopped. I supposed he thought I'd be sympathetic. Poor Mother Ireland. Her children fighting each other, but I was back in my small Paris apartment listening as Cyril Peterson told me how Peter had died. Remembering those long days and nights I'd spent sitting and staring out at the Place de Vosges from my window. Nothing special about me. Paris was full of widows. The Great War had cut down an entire generation of young men. But I was so angry. For God's sake, it was one thing to be killed by an enemy, but to be murdered by a friend?

I was trying to find words to express this jumble of thoughts as Peter watched me. His eyes were still that same dark blue. And his gaze. Never did look away.

"Oh damn, damn, damn," I said. "Cyril shouldn't have lied. I would have come to Ireland. I could have nursed you."

"Just what he'd feared you'd do, Nora. Much better for you to go home. He told me that you had returned to Chicago for a family emergency. For the best, he'd said, and I'd agreed. You were a young woman who should marry and have a family which is what you did."

"What? What do you mean?"

"Cyril told me you married a Chicago politician and had children. I was glad for you. It was a life I couldn't give you."

"But I didn't marry anyone, Peter."

"But he said . . ."

"Cyril said a lot of things. I never found another man I could love as I loved you. And I wasn't willing to settle for less."

"But I thought women wanted children and a home, and . . . I'm sorry, Nora, so sorry."

"For God's sake, Peter, nothing to pity in my life. I've had a great career as a photographer. Helped raise my nieces and nephews and even played a role in the world. Without me my cousin Ed might not be mayor of Chicago, or FDR president, or Harry Truman wouldn't have been chosen."

Peter was shaking his head.

"I'm sorry, Nora. I've been so long out of the world I can't follow you. After I recovered enough to travel I was put on a fishing boat and landed in Italy. There had always been rumors among scholars that there were ancient Irish manuscripts in the Vatican Library and it was arranged for me to live in the Vatican and catalog the collection."

"And no one knew?"

"I didn't use my own name, Nora. I kept to myself. On the faculty of the Irish College there were divisions. I did make one friend. A young seminarian. He said he was from Kerry but his name was O'Flaherty. I told him his ancestors had to come from Galway. Surely you remember our lesson about the O'Flahertys, Nora? We Keeleys were the lords of Connemara until the O'Flahertys showed up in the fourteenth century. Don't you remember? We read Ruairdhrí Ó Flaithbheartaigh's *Ogygia*—his history of Ireland."

"Oh right," I said, but I wanted to shake Peter. How could he go on like this? With me sitting right in front of him? Peter kept talking about this seminarian whose father was from Galway, a member of the Royal Irish Constabulary until the War of Independence. He'd quit the police and got a job as the caretaker of a golf course in Kerry.

"So of course my friend Hugh learned the game," Peter said. "He was a natural. He used to take me with him to a golf club just outside of Rome. Got himself invited by some nobleman with relatives in the Vatican."

"Wait a minute. Are you telling me that in the midst of the nervous breakdown that made you hide yourself in the Vatican Library you played golf?" I said.

"I did not but I did walk along with him and carry his golf bag. Good exercise. Hugh said I had to get some sunshine. He was a fellow who saw no shadows. Hugh was supposed to go to South Africa. An Irish bishop assigned there had sponsored him in the seminary and he looked forward to the climate, but the Vatican officials saw he would be more valuable as one of their diplomats. Some priests just have a knack for getting along with people."

"Dial O for O'Flaherty," I said. "Like Bing Crosby in *Going My Way* and *The Bells of St. Mary's*."

Of course he had no idea what I was talking about. He'd probably never been to a movie. Hiding out in the Vatican, buried in books, joking with this Father O'Flaherty, safe and protected while the world went to hell. True, he'd been snatched out of his scholar's life before. Peter had only just escaped execution by the Germans during World War I when he tried to stop them from burning that library in Belgium, then he'd battled the Black and Tans.

I understood how devastating it was for Peter to kill that boy, but had he the right to step out of life as he had? Maybe Maud was right. What did he and I have in common anymore really? He was nearly seventy years old, not much older than I was in years, but I wasn't ready to stop living. Did I really want to sit myself down in a rocking chair where I'd pray for a happy death with Peter?

"And what about the war? Did Hitler and Mussolini let you go on studying and playing golf?"

"According to the Lateran Treaty, Vatican City was its own state and the pope had declared it neutral and so we were safe enough," he said.

Peter must have seen the Nazis occupy Rome. Watched them send Italian Jews to concentration camps and murder Italians who resisted them, and yet he'd been happy to meditate in a garden or translate some ancient manuscript or. . . . Peter went on talking about this priest O'Flaherty.

"I'm sorry, Peter, but I'm not interested," I said.

"But he was part of a group of Irish people who got together and—"

"And what? Had parties? I know about the Italian woman, Peter."

"You do?"

I stood up. I'd been seeking my lost love and instead found a man I didn't recognize. I wished I'd found his grave instead. I could pray for a brave warrior who died for Ireland. But this fellow sipping tea and rattling on about Rome, he was not the Peter I remembered.

I stood up. "I think you're a selfish bastard," I said. "Alright, you killed somebody. For God's sake there are millions of soldiers who did the same thing and they went home to wives and children and got on with life."

"Life is short and art is long. My work in the Vatican Library was important."

"You snuck away to the neutral Vatican while the world fell apart. I'll bet the pope never missed a meal and neither did you while millions starved."

I expected him to yell at me. To defend himself. Instead sipped his tea, looked up at me and said, "A lot of what you're saying, Nonie, is true."

He rarely called me Nonie. He said it was my little name reserved for our special moments when we . . . Peter looked so defeated watching the fire die away. The least he could do was stir the embers before they went cold completely. It was me who picked up the poker.

"Oh, Peter," I said, my back turned toward him, poking at the fire. "I actually thought that if I found you alive we could go back to Paris and make up for lost time."

"That's an American expression. Make up for lost time. Isn't it? I don't know if that's possible. Did you know the American Army made the Irish College its headquarters? All changed."

"Changed utterly?" I said.

He nodded and used the shillelagh to lever himself up. Turned me away from the fire, took my hand.

"The great thing about America is you're not burdened by the past. You start over. You do make up for lost time. While we Irish . . . All our stories begin *fadó* because a long time ago is never very far away. The world beyond this place is dark and dismal. The war was evil beyond reckoning, and yet somehow the Grianán endured and in this monastery the monks never stopped chanting the hours. The British tried to destroy us Irish, but it was places like this that saved our souls. I've been given refuge here. I'm not able for the outside world, Nora. The life we lived in Paris can only exist in our memories. Now I can only piece together bits of ancient manuscripts, watch the sunrise over the Grianán and see it go down again. I get a small pension that's paid to Father Abbot so I'm not a burden."

"Okay, if not Paris, then Chicago. I have an apartment and a job . . ."

"Chicago is no place for me, Nonie. I remember some lines from the poem you used to recite. 'Laughing like a fighter who's never lost a fight.' I've accepted my loss. There's a lot to be said for accepting what you can't change."

"Accepting . . . I've never accepted anything in my life! I want to change what's unacceptable."

"You'll have to accept this, Nora. The Lord gives and the Lord takes away. Blessed be the name of the Lord."

He'd been holding my hands but now he dropped them.

I couldn't believe it. He was rejecting me. He had reverted back to what he had probably always been meant to be: a hermit monk, living in a beehive hut in some beautiful place. One with nature and God. Dammit.

"Come," he said. "I have a lantern too. I'll walk you down to the monastery. They have guest rooms. Best if you stayed the night. I think it's going to snow."

"No thank you. I'll find some way to get to Derry and I have my own lantern. If you could just light the candle for me."

"But the path down is hard to find in the dark. There are stony places."

"So what else is new?"

"You must let me walk with you. I'm fine if we go slowly," he said as he stuck a taper in the fire and lit the candles in both lanterns.

So like a man, I thought. Giving orders until the very end. But what could I do? We were hardly Romeo and Juliet. An elderly man and woman who'd once loved each other and now were saying goodbye. Be sensible, Nora, I told myself. Some satisfaction in flouncing out but what profit if you broke your leg and died of exposure near a pagan monument? That would prove nothing to anyone.

15

When we stepped outside of the cottage, I could feel that the weather had changed. The wind was definitely not at my back but pushing against me, trying to knock me down. Both of us held on to Peter's shillelagh as we hobbled down the hill. I felt like it was two in the morning, but it was barely eight o'clock when we came to the door of the monastery. Very proper and polite was Father Abbot as Peter explained that I was a friend from America and asked could I spend the night.

I interrupted Peter. Surely Father Abbot knew someone in the town of Burt who ran a taxi service. I was willing to pay whatever to be taken to Derry. Father Abbot told me that in fact a fellow called Hugh O'Neill had a good car and was very accommodating, but no one in the whole area was going anywhere that night. There was to be a concert in the monks' church and the whole village would attend. He said that if I wanted to stay, he'd be more than happy to offer me a place in the pilgrims' wing.

"I'm not a pilgrim," I said, speaking loudly. They both stepped back. But I had no time to rise to the height of sensibility necessary to deal with these two. I wanted out before the concert started. I imagined lots of Gregorian pieces and a few hymns like "Oh Lord I Am Not Worthy." Nothing I wanted to stay around to hear. "I'm sure sacred music is very nice, but . . ."

The abbot held up his hand. He said to Peter, "Maybe you'd better explain about the singer. She's your friend, after all."

"You see, Nora," he said to me, "she's someone I met in Rome and . . ."

Had the Italian woman traveled all the way up here? No. I had my pride. I was leaving. I had a life in Chicago. My work. My family. I'd been living in the fantasy of Peter Keeley for too long. This was the reality. Time to get out. "No thank you," I said.

"But you'd really enjoy her singing," Peter said. "Delia Murphy has done more to resurrect Ireland's traditional ballads than all the scholars in the university."

"That's because the scholars at the university had no use for the old songs," the abbot said. He turned to me. "What we call the 'come-all-ye's' had fallen out of favor. Too culchie for the Dublin intellectuals. The country people became ashamed to sing them, especially since they weren't rebel songs or one of Moore's melodies. Our parish priest preached a whole sermon against the dangers of tinker doggerel and it's true there were some bawdy lines, but these songs were the party pieces for my mother's generation and now here was Delia singing them on the radio. Making records. The music was suddenly valuable."

"Delia was in Rome because her husband was the Irish ambassador to the Vatican. I think I mentioned that . . . ," Peter started.

"Yes, you did mention your friends who sat out the war with you," I said. Now, I didn't want to be rude. I only wanted to get away. But both men actually leaned away from me and turned toward the door.

"Is it me this Yankee woman is talking about?" A woman speaking.

How to describe that voice? Music critics would go on about the rugged simplicity, the directness of Delia Murphy. One even complained that he couldn't categorize her as a soprano, alto, or contralto. In fact her voice was beyond definition and it was loud. So was her speaking voice. She came in out of the night bringing a smell of the cold air on her fur coat. Younger than I was but not by a lot. Fifties maybe. Short dark hair and what my sister Henrietta used to call gypsy eyes. Intense. I'd find out that though she'd learned her songs sitting at the fire in a travelers' camp, she herself was the daughter of a prosperous Mayo farmer.

She was a sturdily built woman, though it was hard to tell much under that fur coat, with a full face. No trace of wartime starvation there. I could well imagine her on the stage as she crossed the room and went right over to Peter Keeley and kissed him on each cheek and then once again.

"Three times is the Italian way," she said as she went for Father Abbot, who stretched out his hand for her to shake.

"You're very welcome, Mrs. Kiernan."

"Now as you well know, Father, I'm not Mrs. Kiernan when I perform. I'm Delia Murphy. I kept my own name and Tom was more than happy to have a bit of distance from a wife such as me. Though Murphy's my father's name. My mother was a Fanning from Tipperary, but Delia Fanning-Murphy is a bit of a mouthful. And, after all, my mother's name was really her father's but at least I never succumbed to becoming Madam Kiernan, the ambassador's wife."

She turned to me. "And are you Mrs. Somebody?"

"No. I'm Nora Kelly and my mother was a Kelly too."

"Wait. Are you that American Professor Keeley told me about?"

"Now, Delia," Peter started.

"Ah now Peter, I know drink had been taken but you told me a very sweet love story and I had you down as something of an old stick but I was wrong there, wasn't I? I thought you were refusing her royal highness because you were too shy, but you told me that you'd only ever loved one woman."

What was she talking about? Plenty of questions for her if I could ever jump into that stream of talk.

She turned to the abbot.

"Now I hope one of your monks has some class of musical instrument around here because the fellow that was supposed to come with me deserted entirely," Delia said.

"Father Martin plays the fiddle."

"Oh dear God. Not the fiddle. Those screechy high notes do me in."

Peter spoke up. "One of the lay brothers here is a powerful man on the accordion."

"Mmmm," she said. "My father often said that the definition of a gentleman was one who could play the accordion and doesn't."

I laughed. She was funny and though I had decided not to like her, I found myself drawn in by her. This is what she must do to her audiences, I thought.

"They've got the church as full as if it was a fair day. You'd better get out there, Delia. They're Donegal people and they'll start stamping on the floor," a voice said.

Of course, it was Cyril Peterson. Why wouldn't he be here? No shame at all. Nodding first at me and then at Peter.

"Believe me if all those enduring young charms," he said and then went on to sing the words, *"That I gaze on so fondly today."*

Delia turned on him. "It's enough I had to listen to your blather all the way from Dublin, but please don't sing."

Cyril turned to us. "And that's the thanks I get for providing transport for the grand lady."

He'd ruined my life, Peter's too, with his lies. Our love was gone beyond repair. Peter was right. You don't make up for lost time in the real world. And here was Cyril acting as if nothing had happened at all. He took a tin whistle out of his pocket.

"Surely you've got somebody can blow into this thing, Father," Cyril said.

"Well, actually I played one in my younger days," the abbot said.

"Take it, Father. I just need a note or two," Delia said.

"Come along Nora Kelly-Keeley. I've got front row seats for you and the professor," Cyril said.

Now I wanted to say, "Go to hell, Cyril," but we were in a monastery and a procession of monks had just appeared.

"Some of your countrymen have come for the concert, Nora," Cyril said. "I arranged a Yank section in the first two rows on the left."

Cyril directed Peter and me to the last two places in the pew.

"You know the Marines, I believe," Cyril said. "Here's Colonel Duggan, promoted since you met him and his aide Major Berndt. And this is an Army pal of mine who arranged for us to get the fine car that brought us up from Dublin, Captain Jones." The soldier nodded at me. "And would you believe he and Major Berndt are both from Philadelphia. That's a place I'd like to see. Imagine a city built around a place called Independence Hall."

Berndt, could he be related to the Marine I'd known at Belleau Wood, I wondered.

Cyril pushed me into the pew. Now I wanted to take one of Cyril's bony little arms and push him out into the night so I could yell at him. Not possible when Irish people are gathered together for a good singsong in a church of all places. No scenes allowed. And here were my Marine friends alive and well.

"I thought the Marines had left Derry," I said to Duggan. "Didn't all of you end up in the Pacific?"

Not a good choice of words. Many of their comrades had died on those islands with odd names. Iwo Jima, Okinawa, and Tarawa. But Colonel Duggan didn't seem to take offence.

"Hard duty," he said. "Though there was a great moment when one of the pipers from the band we started in Derry piped us ashore on Iwo Jima."

Cyril's head turned at that. "Jesus Christ," he said. "That must have been something. I hope he played a rebel song."

"I believe it was 'Wearing of the Green,'" Duggan said.

"Must have confused the Japanese," I said.

But now Father Abbot stood in the space in front of the altar and called for silence, but the rustle of talk continued until, holding the whistle in one hand, he started the sign of the cross with the other.

"In the name of the Father, and of the Son, and of the Holy Ghost." The congregation instantly quieted and answered, "Amen."

"Now," Father Abbot said. "This is not a traditional religious concert but it's very suited for this sacred space. Our choir director, Brother Stephen, says that music is the coagulate of Irish culture. When we as a people were bleeding to death, our songs somehow staunched the flow and let us hold on to ourselves. You know that well and many of you are singers in *Gaeilge* as well as in English but the woman we have with us tonight—from Mayo, God help her—did our music a great service by taking the old songs and performing them in concert halls and on the radio. When my mother heard Delia Murphy sing 'The Spinning Wheel' on the radio, she wept. Her party piece was being sent out to the whole country. A kind of affirmation. We had no extra money in our house, but that radio always had new batteries and my father bought a phonograph so my mother could play Delia's records and tonight we have the woman herself with us. She and her husband represented Ireland at the Vatican and I'd like to imagine her leading a singsong with a gaggle of cardinals, and who knows, the pope himself."

Now I was getting impatient. I still resented Peter Keeley being cossetted while the world fought for survival. Singsongs at the Vatican while the Nazis strangled Europe? But Father Abbot had finally finished his introduction, and Delia was walking up from the back of the chapel. Father Abbot moved to the side of the altar, and Delia stepped right through the gate at the center of the Communion rail and onto the altar step.

"Now really," I heard from behind me. A man, I guessed, because he continued. "Women are not permitted into the sanctuary."

"Would you ever shut your gob, Reverend dear."

Cyril of course. Just behind us. Delia took off her fur coat and dropped it over the railings. *"Mo mhuintir, mo chroí."*

"My people, my heart," Cyril translated for me, leaning forward, though he had little enough Irish himself. "The way she starts every concert in Ireland."

"My friends, I am so happy to be home in Ireland, and particularly glad to be in Donegal to spend time with a friend from Rome, Professor Peter Keeley."

I looked over at Peter. He smiled but kept his head down.

"Now as you've probably heard me say before, I learned many of the songs I sing from the traveling people who camped at the edge of our farm in a road called the Featherbed because they'd often leave their old mattresses behind. I wish you could have been there with me sitting around the fire, the stars blazing out of a black sky, but perhaps you can imagine the scene.

All their songs told a story. I suppose I should start with the one Father Abbot's mother knew. It was my biggest hit." She nodded to Father Abbot. "Listen carefully to the words. It's not like so many Irish songs where the lovers are separated or die or the woman is deserted. No. Eileen knows her own mind so here goes."

> Mellow the moonlight to shine is beginning,
> Close by the window young Eileen is spinning,
> Bent o'er the fire her blind grandmother sitting,
> Is crooning and moaning and drowsily knitting.

Delia had a straightforward voice. Strong and dramatic. She created the scene, becoming Eileen spinning, then the crooning, moaning old grandmother and even the sound of the "autumn winds dying."

The audience was delighted. The scene she described could take place in their own kitchens. Then Delia became the wheel itself. *"Merrily, merrily, noiselessly whirring,"* they were with her, hearing the wheel spinning. Their own feet stirring. But I knew this song too. Granny Honora's friend Mrs. McKenna sang it. I had liked the story because when Eileen's true love appeared at the window and invited her to go roving in the moonlight she'd stood up, put one foot on the stool, and had been ready to climb out.

As Delia sang I remembered that Eileen had hesitated, looking at her grandmother, and Delia managed to make us feel both the young girl's ambivalence and her eagerness to leap into the arms of her lover. Back in Bridgeport I had been too young to understand why the song spoke to Granny and her friends. They had run, not from a cozy kitchen, but an Ireland where a million people—their own friends and relatives—had starved to death. But I had heard them speak too of "the before times" with spinning wheels and sweet voices singing. Though my aunt Máire had said to Granny that the song was really the gentry writing lies about old Ireland, the place they had destroyed. But Granny had said, "What harm and at least the lovers had some joy. But it was hard on the grandmother though maybe the girl only enjoyed a night of courting and didn't desert her altogether."

And of course I'd been too young to think about what it meant that Granny and Aunt Máire had left their parents behind, as had all the women in that room.

Delia's audience sang along with her. The spinning wheel went slower and slower until it stopped entirely as the lovers ran away to the grove. I'd never heard a congregation hoot in a church, but this one did. Stomped its feet too.

"Outrageous," the voice behind me said.

"Hold on there, Father," Cyril said to him. "You're not the parish priest tonight. You're only a guest. Maybe she'll sing 'Ave Maria.'"

No hymns in the concert. Delia Murphy was here to lift the spirits of the people. True, they had avoided the worst of the war—no bombs had fallen on Donegal—but many sons and husbands had enlisted in the British Army for the same reason Irishmen had always taken the king's shilling: for the shilling. Although I'm sure standing up against the evils of the Nazis added to their motivation. Some of them had surely been killed or wounded.

Delia started singing, *"I've been a moonshiner for many a year."*

Are we the only race that can make "It killed me old father and now it tries me" funny? *"Bless all moonshiners, And bless all moonshine,"* the congregation bellowed. No sound from behind me. The priest had probably fainted.

As she continued her program, Delia changed moods. Sometimes she was plaintive. *"If I were a blackbird,"* she sang, her voice shivering, but even then this blackbird was not going to lose her true love no matter what. That did seem to be Delia's theme. In her songs women asserted themselves, complaining sometimes as in "I Wish That I Never Was Wed," a song I didn't know but the audience did. Lots of female voices were raised in that chorus.

And they were with Delia in every note of the "Three Lovely Lassies of Bannion," and each woman asserting that she "was the best of them all." Happy to be getting her shoes mended, her petticoat dyed green, to dress like a queen for a marriage that would surely be happy.

Even when she sang her most political song, "Down By the Glenside," it was a woman who told the story. We women are alive. We survived.

"We wouldn't die," Granny Honora said, "and that annoyed them."

Brother Stephen was right. Music was the coagulant of Irish culture. We hadn't bled out yet.

"I have one final number I'd like to do for you," Delia said. "The air has had quite a high-class life. Thomas Moore had a go at putting words to it, as did Ludwig van Beethoven himself but I prefer the original lyrics to 'Nora Críonna.'"

"Right you are," someone shouted out.

"But it's a duet," Delia said. "I need a man. Surely there's one among you can help me."

And suddenly just like that the audience was taken with shyness. Feet shuffled. No one spoke. I was surprised but Delia wasn't.

"Not to worry," she said. "That was a bit of a setup really. I came here tonight to see an old friend who shared some dark days in Rome with me. We sang this song together on Christmas Day 1944, only last year, but it seems another lifetime. We'd gathered in a residence for priests within the Vatican. Heard Mass in a little chapel and now were in one of the priest's rooms talking about songs and this fellow asked me did I know 'Nora Críonna.' He said he knew a Nora who was wise and full of life like the woman in the song, and me being the forward body that I am, I said to him, it sounds like you were in love with her. Now he was a shy fellow and I expected him to duck his head and change the subject. But he said right back to me, 'I was, and I am.' And I thought, 'Something interesting here.' I had put him down as a man who, as the Mayo fellows would say, 'didn't bother with the women.' Though I knew this man had plenty of nerve because . . ."

Delia knew she was losing the audience. Get to the song, they were thinking.

"Well, sorry for losing the run of myself, but he taught me not only the song but what each of the allusions meant. So that's why I'm calling him up here tonight. Stand up and join me, Professor Peter Keeley," she said.

And he did. Left the pew and took a place next to Delia. So, I thought, Peter Keeley could sing. Never knew that before. And a song for Nora. He'd told Delia I was the woman he'd loved and yet he had never tried to get in touch with me. Even if he thought I had married, my husband could have died, or left me. Wait, I thought. I hadn't a husband.

Peter surely didn't look like an entertainer. Was this song to be the one failure in a brilliant evening? Delia Murphy had stared at me as she talked about Nora. Now, Nonie, I said to myself, why not be glad you did matter to Peter? That your relationship wasn't a total fantasy and be happy he'd had friends and a life instead of castigating him for being locked away in the Vatican?

Delia said, "Do you want to introduce the song, Peter?" He leaned forward. I knew that expression on his face from our sessions in the library of the Irish College. A teacher ready to deliver a lesson. Nothing made him happier.

"Now the heroine of this song is *Nora Críonna*, which means 'Nora the Wise,' though there are a lot of gradations of meaning in the word," Peter said. "For example, it also means clever, inventive, canny."

Delia interrupted him. "We don't have time for linguistics. Just give them the history."

"Because of the references," he said, "we can date the song to Napoleon's time, though the music of the jig is even older. Now the hedge schoolmasters at that time knew Latin and Greek and kept their students informed on current events, even though teaching Catholics was against the penal laws. All the references in this song are historically correct."

"That's fine, Professor. We believe you," Delia said.

"The very first line refers to the empress de Janina, and there was such a person. The wife of Ali Pasha. Shilna was a Hindu goddess, and Tilburnia a character in one of Sheridan's plays."

Delia put her hand on Peter's sleeve. "But the most important person in the song is Nora Críonna so let's introduce her." Peter smiled and started singing.

Who are you who walks this way
Like the Empress de Janina
Or is it true what people say
That you're the famous Shilna Greena,
Or are you the great Ramsey,
Our beloved queen the bold Tilburnia,
Or are you Dido or Dr. McGee?

How Peter enjoyed listing each of those names, and how well Delia acted Nora's amused dissent.

"Oh no," Delia sang.

I'm the girl that makes them stir from Cork to Skibbereenia,
All day long we drink strong tea and whiskey with Nora Críonna.

And then Delia threw out Nora's own list of classical figures.

Who are you that asks my name?
Othello, Wat Tyler, or Julius Caesar?
Or are you Venus of bright fame?
Or that old fogey Nebuchadnezzar?

She tossed a few more names at Peter before he answered.

There, my lass, your eye is out for I'm Napoleon Bonaparte.

That started the whole place laughing, and Delia rode the laugh before she sang the chorus one more time. She was the girl who made them stir. In the next verse Peter invited Nora to dinner and promised a guest list that included people who were celebrities in their time. Irish chieftains like McGillycuddy of the Reeks and O'Donoghue of the Glen as well as enemies such as the Duke of Gloucester and Oliver Cromwell. Delia sashayed across the space in front of the communion rail and then invited the audience to respond with her.

"I'm the girl that makes them stir," she sang. She finished the chorus and walked over to me and improvised a second chorus.

> You're the girl that makes them stir from Maine to Chicagoeena,
> All the day we'll drink strong tea and whiskey too, said Nora Críonna.

"Now stand up, Nora and come up here with us. Here's the woman," she said to the audience, "inspired us to sing this song. The professor's lost love. United at last."

What could I do? I stood up and moved next to Peter.

The audience went wild. Cyril put his finger and thumb between his lips and whistled. I took Peter's hand and I wasn't about to let go.

"Thank you, Delia," the abbot said. "You've brought joy to all of us. None more than the woman sitting right there in the front row."

He pointed at an old lady holding her shawl around her. "Give Delia a wave, Mother," he said.

Dear God, I thought. I am in Tír na nÓg with a touch of "Going My Way." Delia's singing had created an out-of-time moment. Peter had taught me that the ancient Celts believed you could enter the other world through a lake, a river, a spring, or a sudden insight. Add singsong to the list. And if Peter and I could just stay in this moment I would be Nora Críonna. We'd live in that cottage next to the Grianán of Aileach and watch the sun rise each morning and set each evening. Peter hadn't forgotten me.

I squeezed his hand. He turned and smiled at me. So what if he'd been just a little bit of a coward. Why not stay out of the war? But then the two Marines, Colonel Duggan and Major Berndt, and the Army officer stood up and came walking toward us. And there it was. The war. Unassailable, unavoidable.

Peter and Delia had performed their party piece, protected in the Vatican while men such as these risked everything . . . Easy, Nora. Weren't you the one left France after the Great War a convinced pacifist? To shoot bullets into healthy bodies was obscene. Don't blame Peter for what Hitler and the Nazis did. I had accepted Ireland's neutrality. Even argued the case to Eleanor Roosevelt. Dev couldn't risk invasion by Germany or Britain either. But Peter had been in Rome spending his days bent over old manuscripts with an occasional break for a singsong while Mussolini and Hitler took over Italy.

Who was I to judge, but I knew I couldn't join him in his hermitage. And isn't it just as well he hasn't asked you, a voice inside said to me. All this back and forth in my mind happened in the time it took for Colonel Duggan to begin speaking.

"I'm Jim Duggan, US Marine Corps, and this is my aide, Major Martin Berndt, and our Army guest, Captain Jones. We have all enjoyed this performance tremendously. Evenings like this are what all Marines who have had the good fortune to serve in Derry will always remember. Many of them are bringing more than memories home. There are over fifty girls from Derry and Donegal who married Marines and are waiting right now to board the ship that will take them to the United States. It's called appropriately enough the *Marine Haven* and will sail within the next week if the North Atlantic cooperates. Marty here is organizing the logistics. Probably the most pleasant task anyone has had during this war."

Leave it to the Marines, I thought. When I was in London, I'd heard there were fifty thousand war brides stranded in England and the wives of the Corps were getting door-to-door service.

"But now I'd like to introduce Captain Jones. He's here tonight on a secret mission so I'm going to ask you all to keep what happens in the next few minutes under your hats. Captain Jones."

"Good evening," the Army officer said. A deep voice coming from this rangy man. "I'm very glad to be back in Ireland again. I was one of the first GIs here, stationed up the coast near Castle Rock when an Army officer called Darby got the idea that the US should have a commando unit. He asked for volunteers from those of us who had come over with the first US expeditionary unit. He wanted three hundred volunteers but he got three thousand. He chose enough to create the US Rangers, the only US Army unit ever formed on foreign soil. He gathered us all in a town called Carrickfergus. He said he'd chosen the place because that's where the first US Navy battle took place when John Paul Jones's ship, the *Ranger*, captured the *Drake*."

"There were Marines in that battle," Berndt interposed. Jones only shook his head.

"We Rangers fought our way through North Africa, over to Sicily, and then up the boot of Italy, except the Nazis stopped us at Casino. They captured some of our fellows and made them walk in front of the German tanks. We would have had to shoot our brothers. Anyway the whole lot of us ended up as prisoners of war. The Nazis put us on a train going to Germany. This was early 1944. The Nazis knew they were losing but they were going to revenge themselves on us. The guards putting us on the train told us not to expect a nice POW camp. This was a death train. One of our guys was a football player from Minnesota. Bing, we called him, because he could croon a song as easily as lift three hundred pounds. Bing decided we had to escape. He used the buckle on his belt to start digging at the floor of the boxcar. We all helped. In the end we were scratching up pieces of wood with our fingernails. Then we had some luck. The train stopped for a few hours on a mountain pass in the north of Italy. We were able to pound out a hole in the floor of the boxcar. Five of us got out. The others were too tired and too sick to follow. We ran like hell down this mountain pass, sure the Nazis would be after us. We hid in a cave and the next day some villagers found us. Risky for them to help us but they did. Plenty of stories like mine. Italian peasants aiding POWs and downed pilots. We couldn't stay in that area. Too many Nazis. We had to get to Rome. The priest in the village gave us a note to give to the pope. Imagine."

Up to now the people had been silent, listening. What a story! But now they laughed.

"It took us ten days and we made it all the way to St. Peter's Square. Five pretty raggedy-looking fellows, but Rome was full of refugees from all over. Even the Nazis couldn't keep track of all of them. We'd been told by the priest in that village that if we could make it into Vatican City we'd be granted sanctuary, except the Swiss Guard were not about to let us in. Later we found out that anyone discovered aiding a POW would be executed on the spot. The Guards were taking no chances. But then I saw this tall man, well over six feet, wearing a cassock and one of those round hats. He was standing on the steps just behind the Swiss Guard. 'No worries, Captain,' he said to the guard. These are my guests. I've been waiting for them.' And that was Monsignor Hugh O'Flaherty."

O'Flaherty, I thought, wasn't that the priest Peter had been going on about?

"Now the story isn't well known," Captain Jones continued. "Father Hugh never bragged about what he had done, but he put together a network of Irish priests, Italian women, and a widow from Malta to form a kind of underground railroad that hid escaped prisoners and downed pilots as well as Jewish children and their families. He stashed them in seminaries, convents, and Vatican buildings. My boss, General Clark, thinks his group saved at least ten thousand lives. And of course Father Hugh and the rest knew that if they were caught it would mean their own deaths. Two of the people Father Hugh depended on are right up here with me. Probably horrified at what I am about to do. I have two Medals of Freedom, the highest civilian honor the United States awards civilians, to present to Delia Murphy and Peter Keeley."

Here came Cyril carrying two velvet boxes. I tugged on Peter's hand but he was looking down at his shoes.

"Delia and her husband," Captain Jones went on, "represented Ireland at the Vatican. Now as you know, both Ireland and the Vatican were neutral, so what Hugh and the others were doing not only endangered their own lives but put their country at risk. The Nazis were looking for any excuse to invade both Ireland and the Vatican. We know now Hitler planned to kidnap the pope and take over the treasures of the Vatican. Plus Operation Green was a German Army plan to land troops in Ireland."

He turned to Peter and Delia. "Quite a decision for you to make. Perhaps you can explain, Delia."

"I did wrestle with my conscience and prayed for guidance about what I could do to help Father Hugh. But a voice inside said that God intends that we extend charity to all humanity in war as well as peace. There were big posters all over Rome saying anyone who helped Allied prisoners of war would be shot. When Italy surrendered, the Italian prison camps had let their prisoners go, so there were lots of these fellows roaming around. I don't know if the Nazis would have shot an Irish minister's wife, but everyone in our group knew that helping even one Allied soldier meant the firing squad and some of us did die. But I had a car and we had food. I don't think my husband ever told the Irish government what I was up to. He turned a blind eye even when I stole thirty pairs of German army boots from the factory next door to us."

The audience laughed. Delia turned to Peter Keeley.

"You had to make the same decision, Peter. Didn't your boss at the Vatican Library forbid you to get involved with us?"

Now I was staring up at Peter. He'd been saving Allied soldiers, helping Jewish families?

"Like you, Delia, I thought we answered to a higher authority. After all, isn't the greatest of these charity and we had a splendid leader. I often thought of the words on Galway City's gates 'From the fury of the O'Flahertys, O Lord deliver us,'" Peter said.

Now the audience was leaning forward in their seats. A bonus. First the concert and then this drama unfolding right in front of them. Peter hadn't been locked in a room but defying the Nazis.

Delia went on, talking directly to Peter now.

"And of course you and that Italian princess were so good at forging papers, lucky the Nazis never questioned why Vatican employees went from two hundred to four thousand." She looked at Captain Jones. "But really our activities were supposed to be secret. I promised my husband."

"Well this is a very private moment," he said. "Delia Murphy, Peter Keeley, present yourselves to be decorated."

So . . . I did not get into Colonel Duggan's car with Marty Berndt, Captain Jones, and Cyril to drive to Beech Hill. Not because Peter Keeley had begged me not to leave. No. No one drove anywhere because while we were in church, snow fell all over Donegal, and the narrow lanes that led to Burt, difficult when clear, became impassable. Not a problem for most of the audience, who were well used to walking to their homes no matter what the weather but, as Father Abbot said, it was not a night for motorcars. Delia was stranded too. She had intended to stay in a hotel in Letterkenny. After the medal ceremony Father Abbot had called out, "All pilgrims to the refectory." And now here we were. Delia, the two Marines and Captain Jones, Cyril, Peter Keeley, and me, sitting on two long wooden benches pulled up to a rough-hewn table. Cold in that room and it was only natural that I would move close to Peter and put a corner of my coat over his knees.

Captain Jones had pinned the medal on the front of Peter's old tweed jacket. I had cried at that moment and I had to admit that one or two of those tears came from the shame I felt at underestimating Peter. Which I had tried to say to him as we followed Father Abbot through the passageway from the church to the refectory.

"You were a hero," I'd said to Peter. "You could have been executed."

"Don't make too much of what I did. Most of it was behind the scenes," Peter had said.

But Delia heard him and turned back from her place, leading the procession with Father Abbot.

"Make him tell you the truth, Nora Críonna. No one better at blarneying the Nazis than he was. Fearless. We had an RAF flyer who'd been hiding in a seminary who had acute appendicitis. His appendix had to be removed or he'd die. Peter got me to pick the fellow up in the embassy car and we drove through Rome, the Irish tricolor flying. At every German checkpoint Peter convinced the soldiers that we had a sick priest in the back seat. Did the same thing at the hospital. It was full of wounded Nazis, and Peter put the pilot on a gurney and wheeled him right up to the operating room, limping all the way. He'd arranged to have a sympathetic surgeon operate on him. Then it was back in the car and to the Vatican. The professor knew how to seem kind of doddery, which helped. Got the Nazis to feel sorry for us."

"You became a good actor then," I said to Peter as we walked into the refectory. "Nothing doddery about you. A Knight of the Red Branch, one of the Fianna."

"Whisht," he said to me as he sat on the bench and then slid along the smooth wood, leaving room for me.

Thank you, God, for not letting me shoot off my mouth about those who hid away from danger. And now I wanted details. Peter wouldn't tell me much. But Delia began to reminisce about the Jewish children they'd taken to Catholic orphanages while their parents hid in convent basements. Still she was worried about accepting the medal.

"At least you're not the Brits," she said to Captain Jones. "They wanted to make me a Dame of the Empire, which would not have sat well with my revolutionary husband or me either. Of course, the Americans called me a dame, too. One day in June the Germans started leaving Rome, running away. Nazi soldiers headed north where they did manage to hold out for a few months. Suddenly it was very quiet in the city. I went out with my children and this jeep pulled up. 'There's a dame looks like she knows something,' I heard. The jeep was full of American soldiers trying to find the Tiber River."

Both sides of the table laughed. "But my husband would be appalled if what he called 'my adventures' were too well known. There were other members of the Department of Foreign Affairs who were very angry at me for risking our neutrality."

"I wouldn't worry, Delia," Father Abbot said. "It's as a singer this audience will remember you. And a grand one, too."

"Thank you," Delia said. "I had a good partner in the professor. I never thought I'd meet his Nora and are you two really married?"

"Yes," I said.

"No," said Peter.

"Yes and no," Delia said. "My husband Tom might say that about our marriage, and all those brides you're transporting to America, Colonel, are they of the yes and no variety?"

"Our couples are all certified," Colonel Duggan said. "The men had to jump through plenty of hoops to get permission to marry and send their wives home."

"Do you remember Donald Kennedy, Nora?"

"I do."

"He married a lovely girl from a prominent family in Dublin," Colonel Duggan said.

"What about Ralph, the jitterbugging Romeo?" I asked.

"Interesting story about Ralph. He'd lied about his age to enlist. The most popular Marine in Derry was only sixteen."

We all laughed.

"We have visas for everyone, even have a few extras in case of a last-minute romance. You see, Professor, you're not the only one who can expedite paperwork," he said.

"Funny you should say that, Colonel," Delia said.

"I'm Jim, ma'am."

"And I'm Delia, though I did like the Italians calling me *Excellencia*. They made titles sound fantastic. Like the *principessa*, the one who was working with you, Peter," she said. "Remember we thought you'd have to wed that woman to properly protect her. Make her an Irish citizen as well as a Vatican resident."

Everyone at the table was listening now.

"Peter was the only non-clerical bachelor," Delia said. "You'd think he would have jumped to make a match with a young, beautiful, rich, and noble widow. But not our Peter. Dragged his feet. Faithful to Nora Críonna, I guess. Father Hugh figured out a way to make the princess a member of the Swiss Guard, and Switzerland was even more neutral than Ireland."

"We don't have any princesses among our brides," Duggan said.

"Spoken like a man who doesn't know Derry women," Father Abbot said, and it was while everyone was laughing at this remark that I felt Cyril's hand on my shoulder.

"Would you mind stepping out for a word?" he said to me. And then to Peter, "Shove down a bit, Professor, and give this Kelly woman room to swing her legs out. Knees creak a bit, do they, Nora?"

"Cyril, Cyril," I said, but I did manage to get up from the bench. What did he have up his sleeve now, I wondered as I let him pull me toward the alcove at the entrance to the refectory with two tall windows.

"Put it right out of your mind," he said to me.

"What?"

"I saw your face when that Marine was talking about visas and a ship leaving for the States. You're planning to kidnap the poor professor," he said.

"I am not," I started.

"You are," he said. "Already thinking of how you can parade him as a hero around Chicago. You'll do what the Nazis couldn't. Destroy him entirely."

"You're the one ruined his life and mine with your lies. Well, it's not too late. He's alive."

"I am," Peter said. He joined us now at the windows. We could see snow blowing across the landscape with the Grianán fort covered too.

"And as the rain and the snow come down from Heaven, and return no more," Peter said. "But soak the earth and water it, and make it to spring forth giving seed to the sower and bread to the hungry. Isaiah." Peter smiled at us as he finished the quotation.

"See. See," Cyril said to me. "How would that kind of nattering go over with the gangsters in Chicago? They'd put him down as mental."

"But maybe I can move here. Find a place for us," I said.

"Impossible, Nora. The people in the village wherever you settled would be polite enough to you at first and then what? Would you set yourself up in some big house as the lady of the manor? With the professor as a kind of pet? Or maybe you'd find a little cottage and keep house for him. Not the one he's living in now. That belongs to the monks, and he lives there on their charity. No room for you. You'd have to find your own place and get used to no central heating, no running water, no inside toilet, if you were going to prove that you were one of the people. And how much money do you have? I guess that you haven't been very *crionna* about finances. Sucking on the public tit haven't you been? Just like the mayor."

Peter was looking out the window. Cyril grabbed his arm.

"I think you would have too much self-respect to join her on the dole, Professor," Cyril said.

"I've earned my salary. I'm a photographer." But Cyril was shaking Peter's arm.

"Send her on her way, Professor. This Kelly woman will bring you nothing but trouble."

"Why did you turn on me, Cyril?" I said. "We were friends. Comrades-in-arms really. You were the one schooled me in Irish politics. Didn't we three stand together against the Black and Tans? Why is it so important to you that Peter and I be kept apart?"

"I told you. Peter Keeley is a wanted man. The family of the boy he killed would still prosecute him if they ever found him. He's fragile, Nora. For all that he rose to the occasion in Rome, he's a wreck really."

"So you've been telling me, Cyril." Peter turned away from the window, lifted Cyril's hand from his shoulder. "The first months when I was recovering from my wounds I saw that boy's eyes every time I closed mine. But, Cyril, I have recovered. Time and the war . . . and now I wonder why you still want to divide Nora and me. I can forgive you for your lies then. But now, why now?"

Peter turned to me and smiled. The way he said "now." Could he be actually considering spending the years we had left together? Did he want to be with me? If that was true I could overcome any obstacle. Live here, in Paris, in Chicago. We would find the money. If, if . . .

"Peter," I began, but he was looking at Cyril.

"Let Cyril answer," Peter said.

"Oh for God's sake. Do you want to be arrested for murder?" Cyril said.

"But it was self-defense," I said. "In the heat of battle. No court would convict. If you'd told me the truth, Cyril, I could have helped. Gotten a lawyer . . ."

"Which I'd say Cyril knew very well," Peter said. "And I wonder. So much of what happened that day I can't remember. Always relied on you, Cyril. I grabbed for his gun but . . . Wait a minute. Cyril, was it you killed Jimmy McCarthy?"

Cyril was shaking his head, but his face . . . red, his eyes squinched together.

"I saved your feckin' life, didn't I? And what do I get for it? Only accusations. So twenty years ago I acted as a soldier should. Took out the enemy. But the McCarthys would have raised an awful row, come after me. I had things to do. A position to fulfill. And all you wanted to do was lock yourself away with papers. It didn't matter about you."

"I didn't kill Jimmy McCarthy? It wasn't me? You did!"

"You botched it," Cyril said. "Soft. For all your revolutionary blather."

"My God, Cyril," I said. "Who are you?"

Because this man wasn't the quick-witted fixer, the cheerful bird hopping through danger and destruction yet somehow catching his worm that I thought I knew. He was furious. Puffed up beyond his height, his voice low, slashing out his words.

"You, you amateurs. We had a country to build. I grew up in a flat where the boy downstairs died of a rat bite. So I'm not going to waste my time listening to your whingeing. I performed a service. Don't expect me to pin a medal on you. You Yanks will make a dog's dinner of it, just as the Brits did and every other imperial power going back to the Romans. Hell, to the Persians. Your little love affair matters less than a fiddler's fart."

He turned and walked back to the refectory. I stood with Peter at the windows. The snow had stopped and a full moon rose above us.

"I need time to take this in. For all these years I thought I was a murderer," he said. "I have to get out of here. Let's go up there now."

"Where?" I said.

"To the Grianán. I have to think."

I thought I'd never see a brighter moon than the one that rose up above the shores of the lake in Wisconsin that night of the Ojibwe ceremony, but we now stepped out into a landscape saturated with light. Not one moon shadow but dozens. Every rock that marked the path was outlined in silver and cast its own image on the snow.

Peter placed his stick in the drifts and swung himself forward. Reminded me of FDR.

"And the moon on the breast of the new fallen snow gave a luster of mid-day to the objects below," Peter said.

"You remember that." I'd quoted "The Night Before Christmas" to him the first time we'd walked together on the streets of Paris during a similar snowstorm.

"You told me it was an Irish poet called Moore wrote it. I made a copy of the words."

"Oh, Peter," I said. "We can't lose each other again. It's terrible you had to live with guilt but . . ."

He started up the path toward the fort. Anchoring his shillelagh before every step. Not that much snow really. Nothing like a Chicago storm with a foot or two on the ground. Only a few inches blew across the path. Halfway up Peter stopped. He pointed down at the church. Pools of color were appearing on the snow. The stained glass windows were lit from within.

"The monks are assembling to chant Lauds."

"Do you want to join them?" I asked.

The monastery had been his refuge. Peter didn't answer but he reached back, took my hand, helped me walk through the snow. We were close to the fort now. I could see the rocks that made up the walls. The moon picked out bits of mica, a kind of glitter. We walked through the arched entrance. Inside, the snow had blown away, leaving an opening. We stepped into the center.

"Look up," Peter said. "See the moon is directly above us. Every culture has had a moon goddess but our ancestors never liked anything clear-cut so we have a few. Some say the moon belongs to Áine, the queen of the fairies but it's the *cailleach* I favor. Of course she has many dimensions. Do you remember our lessons, Nora?"

He certainly was a professor. Here we were surrounded by moonlight, two pilgrim souls finally united and he's going on about Irish mythology. But hadn't I always been a good student? Besides I understood the *cailleach* a lot better now at sixty-five than I had at thirty-five when he'd been teaching me at the Irish College.

"She's the wise woman," I said. "Though I know her name can be translated as the hag, but she's the old one who the Shannon was named for and the Seine and—"

"Very good," Peter said. "I thought she might be waiting for us out here because winter belongs to her. In some tales she grows younger as the months pass, emerging as a beautiful woman in the springtime."

"Is that when she met Niall at the well?"

"You remember," he said.

"Of course. Now don't tell me. I know the story. Niall was the youngest of all the king's sons." I tried to imitate the singsong cadence of Peter's voice as he'd presented me with the tales that were my heritage. "He and his brothers were out hunting and they came to a well in the forest. Always a fraught symbol," I threw in.

"Very good, Nora," he said.

"A *cailleach* old and ugly stood there holding a golden cup, also significant."

He nodded.

"She'd give them a drink if each one kissed her. Well, the older fellows turned her down flat, but Niall had a kind heart and he was thirsty, so he gave her a peck on the cheek and drank the water. As he did she whispered to him, 'I will give you the sovereignty of Éireann.'" I paused.

"Because . . . ," Peter said urging me on.

"Because all the Irish goddesses represent sovereignty. That's why Ireland is named for a woman," I said.

"That's right," Peter said. "But there was a catch. Remember?"

"Yes," I said. "When Niall was made king he'd have to marry her."

"Which he agreed to," Peter said. "Because he thought there was no chance for him to be king, not with all those older brothers."

"But they elected him," I said, remembering Pat Nash and the Gaelic origin of Chicago political structure. "The night before his coronation, who should show up only the *cailleach*."

Peter nodded.

"Now if I recall when a prince gives his word he can't renege or disaster will follow," I said.

Peter nodded again.

"Poor Niall," I said. "To be married to this shriveled-up crone, but he agreed to the wedding then put his head in his hands. When he looked up he saw a beautiful young woman. Probably shocked him."

"Probably did. Not expecting her to appear after all this time," he said. "Thought that she was living a much different life."

"And she thought he was dead."

"And did she explain?" he asked me.

"Oh she did," I said. "The woman explained that for twelve hours of every twenty-four she could be her gorgeous self. For the other twelve the *cailleach*. And she asked him which period he would prefer. Which was a dilemma for him. Did he want a wife who was beautiful at night for himself alone or was it better that she show her real self during the day so all the other men could see what a prize he'd married. And he couldn't decide," I said. "Some men are like that. They equivocate."

"And did he tell her how unsure he was?"

"I think he took her hand," I said and reached for Peter's, holding it in both of mine. "And told her, you choose. And just like that the spell was broken," I said. "Because he acknowledged her sovereignty."

"She was her own lovely self," Peter said.

"And still the *cailleach*," I said.

"No separation for the Celts," he said. "No past or future, natural or supernatural, all one in some mysterious way. Spring waits in winter, and a long time ago is never very far away."

I tugged on Peter's hand, stepped forward, and looked right into his eyes.

"Oh, Peter, I know why you never became a monk. It wasn't because of me. You're a pagan."

"Maybe I am," he said.

"Well, then Chicago will suit you down to the ground."

So. I'm not saying I didn't have a bit more convincing to do, but I kept talking as the moon slowly moved away and the darkness faded. A red sun pushed up from the horizon, illuminating the archway and turning the snow pink. I could hear the birds. Peter started to talk about the connections between Grianán and Newgrange. I stopped him.

"We'll be the folks who live on the hill," I finally said to Peter.

"What?"

And God forgive me, I sang him a bit of Bing Crosby's hit song.

Someday we'll build a home on a hill up high,
You and I shiny and new,
A cottage that two will fill
And we'll be pleased to be called
The folks who live on the hill.

I explained to him how when I'd first heard the song, I'd pictured us together in spite of him being dead. I realized I'd never really accepted the fact that he was gone and hadn't I been right? We had to take the chance being offered us. But still he resisted. Then I remembered another of Peter's lessons. The story of an Irish heroine, Grainne, who was said to have taken the man she fell in love with by the two ears as if he were a calf and told him they were in love and to get married. And I did the same to Peter, holding on to his two ears until he laughed and said.

"You are Nora Críonna. You are the girl that makes them stir. I've missed you."

And that was that.

Marty Berndt got us a visa and a place on the ship. Father Abbot solemnized our marriage with Delia and Major Jones as witnesses and the monks chanting the "Salve Regina" in our honor. We drove back to Derry. I thought Cyril would try to stop us, but he decided having Peter and me far away in Amerikay was better for him and got us a marriage certificate at the Guildhall. However, Peter's name on the certificate was Peter Caplis. Cyril produced a passport to match. "Better to be safe than sorry," he said.

DECEMBER 21, 1945

"Well, Nonie, you never disappoint," Ed said to me when we finally got back to Chicago, just before Christmas.

Peter and I were sitting in Ed's sitting room watching the snow fall on Lake Michigan. Margaret and the two boys were at their new winter place in Palm Springs, California. Pat was happy in her convent. I had told Peter about Agnella and promised we'd see her in the spring—he was delighted. He had translated a manuscript by Erigina in the Vatican library. But now I had to explain to Ed why I wouldn't be able to accompany him on the campaign trail this spring.

"Don't worry, Nonie. I'm not running."

"Probably smart, Ed," I said. "Go out on top. None of us are getting any younger. Peter and I lost so much time and you and Margaret need to be together."

"I'm not leaving by choice," Ed said. "They will drop me, Nonie. Lots of people are mad at me for insisting on open housing. And when we didn't get the UN headquarters, I lost any chance."

Peter looked questioningly at me.

"Ed wants Negro people to be able to live anywhere they want to in this city," I said.

"What's wrong with that?" he asked.

"Nothing. It's the right thing to do but some of our countrymen have forgotten where we came from," I said.

"Strange, isn't it, Nonie?" Ed said. "Nobody poorer than us Irish when we arrived in Chicago, Granny running from starvation, desperate for a better life for her children, just like the people coming up from the South, wanting the same things we Kellys did. All the Irish staggered off those coffin ships with nothing and now—well Joe Kennedy always said, 'Give an Irishman a quarter and he becomes a Republican.' Time to quit," he said. "Spend time with Margaret and the kids in Eagle River."

I took Peter to meet Mike and Mariann and Mary Pat. Nice to have them next door to Marge and Tom and their baby daughter Kathleen. Tom sang "I'll Take You Home Again, Kathleen" to her as a kind of lullaby.

16

NOVEMBER 1960

A happy ending to the Kelly story except Ed didn't have much time. Dead in five years. Only seventy-four.

Peter and I are well into our eighties now. We live up here in Wisconsin in the cottage bought with the money Ed left me. Plenty in his estate. Over a million dollars. Stocks and bonds, real estate and paintings. Though Margaret had said there was a safety deposit box with a million dollars that had somehow disappeared. She accused the executor of the estate of stealing. They made Margaret out to be a mad woman, and I'd say the stress of the case shortened her life. Dead at fifty-six.

But here on Medicine Lake we flourished. After Ed and Margaret died, the place on Eagle River was sold. Our cottage became the place my nieces and nephews, their children and Ed's kids gathered every summer. Mariann's two priest brothers became chaplains at the nearby camp set up by Ray Meyer, the De Paul University coach. So we saw a lot of both Father Williamses. The local doctor, Michael Byrne, said that if Peter walked three miles a day, ate fish, vegetables, and potatoes, his heart would be fine. And it is. We grow what Peter calls "pratties" and vegetables, and he catches walleye pike in the lake.

I have my city pension and Peter gets a bit from the Irish government. We don't need much. I've gone back to the kind of photography I practiced in Paris. Landscapes full of lights and shadows. I sell them at a gallery in Eagle River. The most popular are my seasonal pieces that show Medicine

Lake reflecting the trees on the shore—pines and maples, oaks and balsams. Sometimes touched with the new green of spring, or in summer's full leaf, or blazing red and gold in autumn. Though some prefer the *cailleach* scene where the branches are bare but still alive, holding on as we are.

Peter writes some lines for each photograph. Ancient Irish text with a bit of the Ogham alphabet, explaining how every tree corresponds to a letter. The gallery owner said those are the most popular with buyers since most of the visitors to the Northwoods are Chicago Irish and the added context helps.

A cozy place. When Ed's house was sold, I bought the handmade carpet and had it cut to fit each room. No big expenditures for us except the radio we bought to follow the presidential campaign. And we will find out tonight if the dreams of Ed and Pat Nash and all those Irish aldermen and precinct captains down through the generations will come true. Will John Fitzgerald Kennedy become president of the United States? The election was over. We were waiting up for the results.

I had to explain to Peter the ins and outs of the electoral college.

"It will all come down to Illinois. To Chicago really," I told him. "Now let's see if Ed Kelly and Pat Nash can shower the ballot boxes with grace."

Peter fell asleep at about five in the morning, and so I had to shake him awake with the news.

"He won, Peter," I said. "He won."

"God help him," Peter said.

"Christ before him, Christ behind him," I started. "Let's say St. Patrick's prayer."

"It's really a pre-Christian invocation that calls on the strengths of Heaven, the light of the sun, the radiance of the moon, the splendor of fire, the speed of lightning."

"Even better," I said.

See, I told you. Peter is a pagan. More so now than ever in this place where we live so close to lightning and wind, the moon and the stars. Our Ojibwe cousin, Patrick, reappeared and he and Peter have found all sorts of correspondences and connections between Irish and Ojibwe mythology. They are collaborating on a book about the similarities, with Erigina thrown in for good measure, which I told Agnella in one of our weekly letters.

"Now that's a book I'll be able to sell," the gallery owner said.

Peter and I have become something of a tourist attraction ourselves. Driving around in Ed's 1939 Packard, which is still perfectly good. Me dressed in trousers. A style that has become so common that the Town and Country shop in Eagle River carries a great variety.

"The professor and that Kelly woman" they call us. And when the roads are too icy our neighbor does the messages as Peter says, and keeps us in firewood.

A good life and as I say, we don't need much. Peter is writing a compressed history of Ireland to send to Jack Kennedy.

"I think he'd appreciate that, Peter," I said. "He is interested in his Irish heritage."

Peter and I had both gone to Chicago a few years before when the Irish Fellowship Club hosted the young Senator Kennedy. He'd compared the struggle of Iron Curtain countries with Ireland's long fight for independence. And quoted the lament for Owen Roe.

> Sheep without a shepherd, when the snow shuts out the sky,
> O why did you leave us, Owen.
> Why did you die.

But there were no laments that morning, November 9, 1960. Our youngest president, I told Peter. Forty-three.

"About the age I feel inside," he said.

"I'd say I'm still twenty-one."

"The *cailleach* growing younger," he said.

Except I'm happy enough for life to narrow. Deep rather than wide. So a few weeks later, when I found the impressive square white envelope in my post office box, I took my time opening it. Embossed on the corners the return address read "The Joint Congressional Committee on Inaugural Ceremonies, Washington DC."

And underneath, written in a kind of calligraphy, "Nora Kelly, Three Lakes, Wisconsin."

I waited to get home to open the envelope with Peter and read the invitation to attend the inauguration of John Fitzgerald Kennedy.

"Well," he said, "you're going of course."

"I'm not," I said. "I'll send my invitation on to Mike's oldest girl. Mary Pat's the type will figure out how to get herself there."

Peter and I listened to Jack's inaugural speech on the radio, sitting before the fire, sipping Jameson. Peter nodded his head as Kennedy called for peace and cooperation. Both of us struck by the phrase that would become famous. "Ask not what your country can do for you. Ask what you can do for your country."

And his conclusion. "Here on Earth, God's work must be our own."

Peter had never asked much for himself and I suppose neither had I. And yet we had everything. And now the election of John Fitzgerald Kennedy had healed our own people's suffering.

Peter was delighted with the intertwining of Irish history.

"Think of it, Nonie," he said to me. "On one hand, he's a Kennedy descended from Brian Boru, and on the other a Fitzgerald whose people were the Norman conquerors who defeated the High Kings. And now the two strands are joined together."

"Wonderful," I said, and looked up toward heaven and winked at Ed. I was thinking of more immediate battles. Of the "No Irish Need Apply" signs. Of Big Bill Thompson's ethnic slurs. Even FDR's comments about temperamental Irish boys. Here was healing, no question. A happy ending.

Kellys *Abú*. Thank you, God. We are Irish above All.

ACKNOWLEDGMENTS

I have drawn upon my own family history to tell the Irish-American story through *Galway Bay, Of Irish Blood,* and now, *Irish Above All.* Therefore I am grateful most of all to my mother, Mariann Williams Kelly, who lived these events, and to my late aunt Marguerite Kelly McGuire, who remembered so much. My sisters Randy, Mickey, Susie, and Nancy, my brother Michael, my brothers-in-law Ernie Strapazon, Ed Panian, and Bruce Jarchow, and my sister-in-law Martha Hall Kelly are great supporters. My nephews, nieces, and their spouses, along with my great-nephews and great-nieces, inspire me to preserve these stories. My cousins play an important role—those I've always known and those I met through these books—especially Tom Rauch and Nicole Temmi, our genealogists, Tom McGuire, whose kindness makes so much happen, and the late Kathleen McGuire Roche and her husband Mike. A very special thank you to cousin Lucy Kelly, who preserved Ed Kelly's papers, a legacy from her husband Stephen Kelly, and who, with the team at Edward V. Demmer Memorial Library in Three Lakes, Wisconsin—Erica Brewster, Nancy Brewster, Stacy Orr, and Maryann McCloskey—is preparing a wonderful exhibit on the Kelly legacy in the North Woods. Thanks also to Gerald Burkett, Rick Maney, Joanie Keefe, Susie and Larry McPartlin, all of Eagle River, and the welcoming Keeleys in Carna, County Galway—Padraig Keeley, Erin Gibbons, her husband, Ned Kelly, and their children Olwen, MacDarra, Rosa, and Fiona.

To all my readers, I am touched by those of you who tell me my books make you want to learn more about your own families, and so enjoy being part of your book clubs! I am grateful to Irish-American organizations that host events, particularly Nancy Wormington, Rosemary Stipe, Marilyn Stearns at the Kansas City Irish Center, and Maureen Kennedy and Kent Covey at the Irish Heritage Center of greater Cincinnati. I love speaking at universities, schools, libraries, and parish churches, and thank Catherine O'Connell and Mary Deady for lending their beautiful voices to many of these appearances. Kathy Hurley rolls out the red carpet at the Union League Club in Chicago. Appreciation to bookstores for all that you do, with special thanks to Elizabeth Merritt of Titcomb's Bookshop and John Barry at Paddy's On the Square.

In Chicago, I thank Mary Evers, Marilyn Antonik, Father Roger Caplis, John Fitzgerald, Darrell Windle, the always wonderful Dave Samber of Polo Inn Bridgeport, Rick Kogan, Katie O'Brien, Skinny and Houli, the parishioners of St. James, Roseann Finnegan LeFevour, Joan O'Leary, the Frank O'Connor family, and Cliff and Cathy Carlson with all at IBAM. I was pleased to participate in Siamsa na nGael—thank you Bill Fraher, staff and performers, especially Senator George Mitchell. Of course, I am always grateful to The Group.

In New York, Loretta Brennan Glucksman encouraged me, as did Dee Ito, Laura Jackson, Sheila Cox, Laura Aversano, and thanks to Colleen Ambrose, Pamela Craig Delaney, and all the book buddies. I am grateful to Lynn Garafola, Daria Rose Foner, and Eric Foner, and thank Mary Gordon, Mary Higgins Clark, Peter Quinn, Malachy McCourt, Michael Carty, Jr., Ellen McCourt, Julia Judge, Charlotte Moore, Ciaran O'Reilly, Kay Voss, Kathleen Walsh Darcy, the Irish American Writers and Artists, and the Kelly Gang. Salon d'Ange members Roberta Aria Sorvino, MaryAnne Kelly De Fuccio, Monique Dubois Inzinna, and Danielle Inzinna hearten me, as do Jim and Alice McQuade, Rosalind and Patrick McElroy, and the Harte family. Bill Ndini and Barbara Farrah gave me wonderful feedback during the writing process.

In Ireland, I'm grateful to Patsy O'Kane and all at Beech Hill House Hotel—an important location in the story—including Conor Donnelly, Mark Lusby, Ashley, Brenda, and Roisin. Thanks to Aine and Colm O'Keefe, Roisin Nevin, Pauline Ross and the staff of the Playhouse in Derry, Sharon Plunkett, Antoinette O'Ceallaigh, Geraldine Folan, Máire O'Connor, Dominic Moran at Lough Inagh Lodge, and Sister Máire MacNiallias. I value my connection to Kylemore Abbey, Mother Máire Hickey, Sister Magdalena FitzGibbon, John Feerick, and Robert Mulderig. Diana and Lt. Gen. Martin

Berndt and Sergeant Major Carleton Kent connect the U.S. Marine Corps story to Derry, while John and Pat Hume and family enlighten and bear me up as do Jackie Dearbhla and Mark Durkan.

I so appreciate those who helped me prepare the manuscript for *Irish Above All*. Thank you first to Liz Taafe, then Ellen Howard, Mary Gallagher, Mary Terese Kanak, and Karen Wilder. I am especially grateful to my closers Karen Daly—who contributed her publishing career expertise—and Deb Spohnheimer, an extraordinary musician who also can bring magic from the computer keyboard. I could not have finished without you.

All Irish Americans owe much to Patricia Harty, cofounder and editor-in-chief of *Irish America* magazine. So do I.

Though a work of fiction, much research went into *Irish Above All* as I tried to get the history right. For specific references and a discussion of what is fact and what is fiction, visit my website at marypatkelly.com. Special recognition to librarians in Chicago, New York, Dublin, Galway, and Paris, for your help, and Leslie Martin of the Chicago History Museum and Bonnie Rowan, ace researcher in Washington, D.C., as well as the staff at the presidential libraries of Franklin Delano Roosevelt, Harry S. Truman, and John Fitzgerald Kennedy.

I'm very happy to be published by Tom Doherty Associates/Forge and thank Linda Quinton; my one-of-a-kind editor, Robert Gleason; Elayne Becker; and copy editor Deborah Friedman. My agent, Susan Gleason, is a gift to me in every way. Thanks!

I appreciate the support of my longtime friend, actress, producer, and best-selling author Roma Downey, and writer Ann Peacock. Fingers crossed!

To my husband, Martin Sheerin—your love, patience, intelligence, and knowledge of all things Irish fill me with gratitude always.